STAR MAGE SAGA
BOOKS 1 - 3

J.J. GREEN

STAR MAGE QUEST

PREQUEL

Sign up to my reader group for your exclusive copy of the Star Mage Saga prequel, *Daughter of Discord*, and the rest of your free J.J. Green starter library at https://jjgreenauthor.com/free-books/.

Books of the Star Mage Saga

ONE

Carina slung her Jensen 31 across her back and crawled beneath the remains of a desk. She had to bend low to avoid snagging the weapon on broken wood. The door to the room was slightly ajar, and from outside came the whispers and hisses of pulse slugs and the stamp of running, booted feet.

She hated hiding in the middle of a firefight but if she didn't do something soon, it would all be over for her and her merc band, the Black Dogs.

Easing into a spot where she was hidden from view, she bit on the fingers of her silicon mesh glove, pulling it off. She dropped the glove and worked on the other until both her hands were free. Removing her protective gear was reckless, but she needed bare fingers to tell if the wood splinters from the desk were real. If they weren't, the Cast would not work.

Of course, casting brought its own risks. She faced slavery and torture if anyone found out what she was about to do. Not for the first time, she wondered whether being a mage was more of a curse than a blessing. On the other hand, saving her and her merc buddies' lives would be a definite benefit.

The door banged against the wall as it flew open and someone burst in. A pulse fizzed and a body hit the floor. She peeked from underneath the desk. A fellow merc was lying flat on his stomach and facing away from her, a smoking hole at the weak point where his helmet connected to his body armor. The man trembled once then was still.

Though she couldn't see his face, she recognized the dead man. It was the latest recruit, his new career cut short by the suicide mission they'd been sent on.

Another figure ran in. Carina saw the calves and boots of one of the attackers. She shrank backward and lifted her Jensen, resting her finger on the trigger. If the soldier looked under the desk, he would receive a pulse round in his face. But the legs turned and left, and she heard footsteps running up the stairs to the next level. It was a lucky escape, but her luck wouldn't last much longer.

She picked up a splinter of wood from the desk and rubbed it between her fingertips. After peering closely at the fibrous strands, she closed her eyes to concentrate on their texture. The wood fibers were fine but not fine enough, and they were too smooth. The wood was fake. She threw down the splinter in disgust.

Her canister of base elixir was missing only one essential element: wood. The real stuff had proven hard to find on this desert planet. Even if she found some natural wood to add to the elixir, it was no guarantee she would be successful. There had to be fifty or more enemy soldiers in the embassy. She'd never cast at so many, but she had to try.

Crawling out from under the desk, Carina scanned the room. Before it had been blown apart, the place had been luxurious. Some kind of animal skin buffed to a fine sheen had covered the walls, though now it hung in tatters. A delicate translucent mineral, intricately carved, had supplied the window lattices. Broken pieces of it were sprayed over the floor.

The room must have belonged to a high-up embassy official, maybe even the Matahman ambassador—the kind of official to own real wood artifacts.

The sounds of the struggle for possession of the embassy were growing louder. Fighting was going on in the stories above and below. Skirting the body of the fallen recruit, Carina closed the door and went over to a cabinet. The door was secured, but a single pulse from her Jensen melted the lock. She levered the door open with the muzzle.

Reaching inside, she riffled through bottles of the local liquor, beakers, hard copies of documents, expensive-looking jars of some kind of local food or ointment, and boxes of different sizes. She pulled out the boxes and tried to open them, but they were fastened shut in a way she couldn't figure out—possibly DNA or electronic locks.

She had no time for cracking fancy locks, neither through ingenuity nor casting. After a brief glance at the door, she stood and brought the butt of her Jensen down hard on one of the more fragile-looking cases, smashing it apart.

Her luck seemed to be holding. Inside the case was an oblong object. From the complex design carved at one end, she guessed it was some kind of seal or stamp. More importantly, the artifact displayed the finely grained effect of wood. She drove down the butt of her Jensen again, the blow jarring her arms.

She'd split the seal at one end. Squatting, she dug her fingers into the split and ripped the object apart. She extracted a thin splinter and rubbed it into fine strands.

From outside came the sound of footsteps running downstairs. No time remained to figure out if the seal was natural wood and not another clever synthetic. She took out her canister of elixir, unscrewed it and dropped in the strands. She swirled the mixture once, brought it to her lips and swallowed a mouthful.

The elixir was foul-tasting, as usual, but Carina barely registered the taste anymore. Her eyes were closed and she was already writing the ideogram in her mind, willing herself to ignore the steps drawing closer.

Creating the character required the utmost concentration. The Cast was useless unless the strokes were completed perfectly and in the correct order. One after another they appeared in her mind's eye.

Just as she drew the final stroke, someone ran in. Her eyes flew open and she grabbed for her weapon, which was slung over her shoulder, but the newcomer was merc officer Lieutenant Torres.

"Come with me, Lin," the lieutenant said. "Up to the—"

Torres fell forward, the back of her helmet a ruined, burning mess. She squirmed at Carina's feet. Behind her, framed by the door, was the enemy soldier who had shot the lieutenant at point blank range. His weapon was now aimed directly at Carina. She didn't stand a chance. The soldier grinned.

Then the Cast began to work.

As always, the effect wasn't immediate. If the soldier had ignored it and fired, Carina would have been dead, but he was distracted by its sensation. The man hesitated, his weapon still pointing at her, and looked down at his arms in disbelief as they began to disappear.

He lifted his head to meet Carina's gaze, his grin quickly giving way to a look of panic. The next moment, he was gone.

And so were most of the rest of the enemy in the embassy, Carina hoped. She estimated the Cast's radius to be around forty meters, which had to encompass most of the enemy within the building.

She dropped to her knees at Torres' side. The woman was no longer moving, and Carina's stomach turned at the sight of gray matter oozing from the split in her helmet. Gently, she turned the lieutenant over. Her eyes were fixed and still.

Mourning the lieutenant, the new recruit, and whoever else had died on the hopeless assignment would have to wait until later. It was time for the Black Dogs to retreat before enemy reinforcements arrived.

Carina listened hard for sounds of fighting, but the embassy was quiet. Her Cast had given the mercs a little breathing space. She went to find the rest of her platoon. Speeding downstairs, she leapt over the corpse of a fallen attacker and empty steps before running into the embassy lobby. She skidded to a halt. Three Jensens were aimed at her.

"What the hell do you think you're doing, Lin?" barked Captain Speidel, lowering his rifle, "I nearly shot you."

His rebuke stung, though Carina knew in his eyes she deserved it. She had a lot of respect for the captain and hated being the object of his disapproval.

"*Are* we under attack, sir?" asked Staff Sergeant Brown. "The ones who had me and Halliday pinned down vanished. And I don't hear any fighting. Did you see what happened to the enemy?"

"I'm not sure what I saw," Speidel replied.

"Sir, Lieutenant Torres bought it," Carina said. "And the new guy too."

"Shit." Speidel turned away to speak into his helmet mic. As she listened in to his conversation with the mercs on the upper stories, Carina heard their confusion about the sudden disappearance of the attackers. The mercs on the roof reported more enemy forces approaching from every side.

It didn't need to be said. If they didn't get out of here soon, they were screwed.

Two

The mercs crammed into the shuttle that would take them back to their starship, *Duchess*. They laid the bodies of the fallen in sections under the floor. *Sleeping in the locker,* it was called.

No one said a thing while the shuttle lifted into the air and away from the embassy, which was now ripe for the taking. The atmosphere was tense as the mercs waited for ground-to-air fire while they made their escape, but nothing came. The enemy seemed to have lost interest now they'd retreated. Carina guessed it would be some time before the reinforcements realized their associates had disappeared. It would be still longer until the soldiers she'd transported returned from the spot where she'd sent them.

She was mind-weary after such a large Cast. She was also worried about the questions that would inevitably be asked about the unusual events of the firefight. In the two years since she'd joined the Black Dogs, she'd kept her Casts small, personal, and easily concealed. It had been the first time she'd risked doing something so noticeable.

After the shuttle left the danger zone, there was none of the banter and jibes that usually went on among the mercs at the end of an mission; none of the black humor they employed to deal with the loss of friends and even enemies within their band. They'd failed. They'd retreated, and ingrained into the men and women, who were mostly ex-military, was the shame that came along with that.

The mysterious disappearance of their attackers hadn't yet been mentioned, as if no one wanted to risk being thought mad or stupid. Carina was certainly not going to be first to bring it up.

The merc sitting next to her, Smitz, reached into a pocket and pulled out a wad of the foul herb he was addicted to. He bit off a few centimeters of the brown substance and pushed it into his cheek with his tongue before beginning to chew. Carina immediately regretted her choice of seat. She shifted her boots sideways in case he targeted his spit near her feet.

"Bastard lied to us," Smitz finally said, breaking the silence.

The Black Dogs' assignment had been to act as back up for the government force that was supposed to be defending the embassy, only the government troops hadn't shown.

His comment was met with mutterings and grumbles. Captain Speidel, who was sitting next to the exit and gazing out of a small porthole, didn't seem to have heard Smitz's words.

"Can't fight a company with a platoon," Smitz continued, drawing further murmured agreement.

"Quieten down, soldier," Speidel said, finally noticing the man's complaints. The murmurs ceased, and the captain returned to his morose contemplation of the view.

Carina felt for Speidel. He would be the one to take the blame if the top brass decided after debriefing he'd made the wrong call, despite the hopeless situation they'd found themselves in.

He was a good man who didn't deserve the shit thrown at him as the meat in the sandwich between Tarsalan, the company's owner along with commanding officer Cadwallader, and grunts like Smitz. Carina was, and always would be, grateful to Speidel for saving her from persecution and squalor in the slums of a nowhere planet. Though she rarely admitted it to herself, the older man was the closest thing to a father she had. She hoped he wouldn't suffer Tarsalan's ire, though it was unlikely he would be so fortunate. The woman was notorious for her fixation on profits and disregard for the lives that were lost to achieve them.

Still no one was mentioning what was on everyone's mind—that all the attackers within the embassy building and compound had suddenly, inexplicably, vanished.

In the end, it was Halliday who spoke. "Hey, did...er...did anyone see anything weird happen down there?"

The uneasy shifting of bodies was the mercs' only reply. Even Smitz, who was never slow to tell everyone and anyone exactly what he thought, was silent on the issue. From the corner of her eye, Carina could see Speidel shaking his head, no doubt wondering how he was going to explain to his superiors that the only reason most of them had gotten out alive was due to an impossible event.

The micro-gravity of low orbit was taking hold, and Carina lifted from her seat and bobbed against the straps of her harness. They were nearly back at *Duchess*. Soon, she would be able to return to her cabin and safely stash her canister of elixir away from prying eyes.

"Hey, Lin," said Smitz. "You got any water? I'm all out."

Thinking that if he didn't chew his disgusting herb he wouldn't be so thirsty, Carina shook her head.

"Come on, Lin. Don't hold out on me. We're nearly back at the ship."

"Then you can wait," Carina replied.

"Come on, give me some. I know you always bring extra. I can see your bottle sticking out like a third tit." Smitz made a grab for the pouch that held the elixir canister. Carina deflected his arm with her elbow, following through and driving it into his gut. The blow had no effect other than pushing him away a little, due to the man's armor. Smitz reached out with his other hand and Carina knocked that away too. She shoved him into the bulkhead for good measure.

"Smitz. Lin," barked Brown. "Cut it out, or you're both on report."

Smitz relented. Carina's racing heart slowed, and she was glad her face was hidden behind her tinted visor. Her skin was hot and moist with sweat.

It was with relief she felt the shudder that rippled through the shuttle as it engaged with *Duchess'* access hatch. After another few moments she was pulling herself through the short tunnel that led to the ship. As she went along, *Duchess'* AG field took hold and Carina's feet drifted to the floor. She let go of the bars she'd been grasping and walked.

Now they were back at their ship, the chances of reprisals for the mission went down. *Duchess* didn't live up to her name in terms of classy looks, being rather dumpy and squat, but she more than made up for the deficit with armaments. State-of-the-art pulse cannons fore and aft and fusion-rocket long-range missiles were supplemented by turret-mounted rail guns. As well as deterring space pirates with cocky ideas, *Duchess'* artillery meant that retaliation from the opposing side after a mission was rare. When it came to Tarsalan's own safety, she didn't skimp.

The same could not be said for the mercs. Carina and the others removed their armor and hung it up in the armory. The protection was flexible, light and tough, but it was showing signs of wear. At the embassy, their attacker's weapons had been able to penetrate it at close range. One of the problems of working as a merc was that levels of technological advancement varied widely between worlds. New weapons were constantly being developed, and they were never quite sure what they would be up against next.

Carina transferred her canister from its pouch into her shirt and went straight to the cabin she shared with three other mercs. It was empty. She slid the canister into the hole she'd dug in her mattress. Then, finally relaxing for the first time since she'd cast, she lay down on her bunk and put her hands behind her head. After around half an hour a comm woke her.

"Corporal Lin," came the message. "Report for debriefing immediately."

Her earlier tension returned. Why did they want to talk to her? Had someone seen what she'd done? Carina wondered how that might be possible, and her stomach dropped as she remembered Lieutenant Torres had been wearing a body cam like they all did. What if it had recorded her casting?

She swung down from her bunk, wracking her brain for an explanation as to why she would have taken a drink and then stood still with her eyes closed in great concentration, just before a horde of enemy soldiers disappeared.

By the time she reached the debriefing room, she hadn't thought of a logical explanation for her behavior.

THREE

"We don't need to know everything," said Lieutenant Colonel Cadwallader. "Only describe exactly what you saw toward the end of the engagement, Corporal. Don't leave anything out."

Standing to attention in the mission room, Carina's gaze flicked to Captain Speidel, who sat on one side, stroking his stubble and watching. Cadwallader and Tarsalan sat behind a desk.

Cadwallader's pale blue eyes seemed intent on piercing right through her, and Tarsalan's full lips, coated in a purple sheen, were set in a line. Neither gave a hint of what they were expecting her to say. Carina didn't know if she had to explain herself regarding Torres's body cam footage or only report on the disappearance of the enemy.

She hesitated.

"We don't have all day, Lin," Tarsalan said, her heavy-lidded eyes drooping lower. The woman drummed fingers bearing thick, bejeweled rings on the desktop.

"Around ten minutes before Captain Speidel gave the order to withdraw," said Carina, "I was alone in a room. I think it might have been the ambassador's office."

"What were you doing there?" Cadwallader asked.

"Checking for insurgents, sir."

"Go on," said Cadwallader.

Carina explained how Lieutenant Torres died. "After the lieutenant fell, the enemy turned his weapon on me," she went on. "He would have shot me too, except..."

Her mouth was suddenly very dry. She swallowed.

"Spit it out, Lin," said Cadwallader, frowning.

"Whatever you saw, or thought you saw," said Speidel, "all you have to do is tell the truth."

Carina focused on the captain. "The soldier disappeared, sir. Right in front of me. One minute he was there and the next he was gone."

Tarsalan gave a huff of bitter frustration. "Just like the others. This is ridiculous."

"We have the body cam vids," said Cadwallader. "They don't lie."

"It was an optical illusion," said Tarsalan.

"All fourteen of them?" Cadwallader asked.

"It makes no sense otherwise," Tarsalan countered. "If someone's invented cloaking technology for individuals, why didn't they use it when they attacked? Why use it in order to retreat, especially when by all accounts they had the upper hand?"

"I don't think it was cloaking technology," said Cadwallader. "I think it was something else."

"Like what?"

The lieutenant colonel was about to reply but he noticed Carina was still there, standing to attention.

"You're dismissed, Corporal," he said.

Carina saluted and left. She guessed her story backed up the testimony given at earlier debriefings. She hadn't been singled out for scrutiny, but Cadwallader's comment that the soldiers' disappearance had been *something else* had her stomach in knots again.

The sound of fast-moving footsteps from behind made her stop and turn. It was Captain Speidel, striding quickly to catch up to her.

"We're going in the same direction," he said. "Let's walk together."

As a subordinate, Carina's compliance was a given. The two continued on their way.

"How are things going for you?" Speidel asked.

"Pretty good, sir."

"You can drop the *sir* for the moment, Carina."

"Okay." Speidel had talked with her in this friendly way fairly regularly since recruiting her to the merc company, and she enjoyed their amiable conversations.

"I wanted to give you a heads up," Speidel went on. He put a hand on her shoulder. "Stop a moment."

Carina turned to him.

The man's expression was serious and pained. "You can't tell anyone else what I'm about to say to you. I can trust you, right?"

She nodded.

"Why am I even asking?" Speidel smiled. "You're tighter than a drum." He checked up and down the empty corridor. "I wanted to let you know, things might be over soon for the Black Dogs. We might be disbanding. So if you come across an opportunity to do something else, you should probably take it."

"Disbanding, s...?" She stopped herself just in time. "Why?"

"Tarsalan's been complaining for a while now she's pouring creds into the company and making no profit. This last job we just did might be the final straw. The client's refusing to pay the balance of the fee because the embassy was taken."

"But they lied," Carina exclaimed. "We were on our own and totally outnumbered. We could never have defended the place. If we hadn't withdrawn, we would have been slaughtered."

"That's not what they're saying at their end. But it doesn't matter what they say. If they won't pay, they won't pay."

"Maybe Tarsalan should send us on a mission to persuade them," Carina said bitterly. Working with the Black Dogs was her life. She didn't know what else she could do. She was damned if she would join the military and get paid a pittance.

Speidel gave a wry smile. "That might be effective one time, but as soon as word got out we'd never work again. It isn't like merc bands are difficult to find these days."

"So you're saying I should sign up with another company?"

"I don't know. Soldiering's a tough life. Maybe you should try something different while you're still young and it isn't burned into your bones. The galaxy's a big place. There has to be some way for a young woman to make a living that doesn't put her life on the line. You aren't dyed-in-the-wool military like most of the rest of us."

Carina shook her head. "Fighting's all I know."

Speidel sighed and resumed walking. Carina went along with him.

"I sometimes wonder if I did the right thing," Speidel said, "breaking up that fight you were in and signing you up as a merc. You might have ended up doing something less dangerous and more worthwhile."

"No. I wasn't gonna win that fight. I took two of them out, but I was five minutes from being beaten to a pulp. If you hadn't stepped in..." Carina's memory of the event was vivid. Though she'd learned her fighting skills the hard way over the previous six years since Nai Nai died, even she was no match for the five boys who had set upon her. Their motive was only to have some fun, it seemed, as she had nothing to give them. It was a heavily bruised, bleeding Carina Captain Speidel had brought back to *Duchess* and patched up. "Well, I wouldn't be here now, that's for sure.

"If you take my advice," Speidel said, "you won't be here for much longer." The captain's comm button chirped. He checked the message. "Looks like my dinner will have to wait. Think over what I said, Carina. It might be time for a change."

As the captain turned to go back the way he'd come, Carina thought she saw a look in his eye that indicated he knew more than he was saying. She felt sick. Had the captain's friendly advice been a cover for a deeper warning? Had he guessed her secret, and did he think that others were also drawing closer to the truth about what had really happened in the embassy fight?

Perhaps it was indeed time for her to move on.

FOUR

None of Carina's bunk mates had returned to the shared cabin, so she took advantage of the rare moment of solitude to meditate. Nai Nai had taught her the habit, telling her it preserved and strengthened one's powers.

The old woman had said that though mage abilities were genetically inherited, it wasn't a fixed thing like hair or eye color. Casting was also a skill that had to be learned, refined, and maintained, and she'd explained that if Carina didn't regularly perform mental exercises, her ability would lessen and perhaps fail. What was more, if she did lose her ability, there was no guarantee it would ever return once she was an adult, no matter how hard she worked.

Sitting in her top bunk, Carina crossed her legs and faced the wall. The steps to achieve a trance state were always the same. She mentally recited and embraced the concepts of the five Elements: wood, fire, earth, metal, water. Following the Elements were the Seasons: spring, early summer, late summer, autumn, winter. This second part of the pre-trance task was not so familiar to Carina. Though she'd visited many worlds while working with the merc band, she'd never encountered a place where the climate followed the pattern laid out by Nai Nai with its types of weather, variations in temperature, and fluctuation of daylight hours.

Next, she mentally wrote the Strokes. Each line had to be written perfectly, each taper and flourish correct. She wrote them separately and then together in the character that meant *forever*. Finally, she conjured up the Map in her mind. Nai Nai had made her draw the 3D image over and over again on her holoscribe while she was growing up. There were more than a hundred stars, and her grandmother would measure the angle and distance between each star carefully when she finished. If anything was incorrect, she had to draw it again.

The Map showed the birthplace of their clan, Nai Nai had said. At the center of the Map was the star system their ancestors had been driven from, so long ago no one knew when.

Carina had once asked her grandmother why they didn't try to return to their original home.

"No one knows where to go anymore, Mei Mei. No one remembers where we came from."

"But we have the Map," Carina had persisted. "Why can't we find it using that?"

Nai Nai had laughed and dipped her hand into a jar of sand she used for polishing the beautiful stones she sold for a living. She scattered the sand across the floor where Carina sat.

"Tell me, Mei Mei, how many grains do you see?"

Carina frowned. Was it a test? "Ten thousand? No. Fifty thousand."

"Probably about five thousand. Look closely, child, and imagine these are stars. In our section of the galaxy alone there are ten times as many stars as there are grains of sand lying here. It would take several lifetimes to visit each and check if the surrounding pattern of stars matched the Map. One would need to look at the groupings from many orientations. And our galactic sector is only one of thousands."

The young Carina eyed her holoscribe drawing, which had taken her over two hours to create. "Then why bother remembering it at all? Why not give up on ever returning home?"

"That is something every mage must answer for herself. But let me ask *you*, little one, do you feel as though this place where we live now is your home?"

Carina considered their two-roomed house, which in truth was little more than a shack. She considered the dirty street outside with its open gutter that kept the local rats well fed. She considered how different she felt from the other children, who didn't know the Elements or the Seasons or the Strokes or the Map, and who could not cast. She shook her head. "I don't, Nai Nai."

The old woman sighed. "My great-grandparents told me once they'd heard it said our birthplace was the origin of humanity itself—the world where humans first evolved, invented space travel, and journeyed out to colonize new planets. If we could find that place again, it would truly be something very special.

"But more important even than that, the Map gives us hope," her grandmother continued. "we are exiles and our clan has been scattered to the stars.

Nowhere are we accepted for being who we are. We live in secrecy, always. The Map holds the promise that one day we may live openly and together again in our homeland. Holding onto that possibility helps us to go on."

Remembering Nai Nai's words calmed Carina's anxiety, and she slipped into a deep meditative state.

Some time later, the sound of the cabin door opening entered the edge of her consciousness. She brought herself out of her trance and turned to see Thyrna Atoi, her bunk mate, bend down to sit on the lower bunk. She began to take off her boots.

"You missed dinner," said Atoi. "Not that you missed much. Chef's on a marine plant kick. Yeuuuch! *It's high in nutrients and protein*, he said whenever anyone complained."

"I wasn't that hungry anyway," Carina said.

Atoi threw a boot at the corner of the room. "Got it!"

"What was it?" Carina asked. "A roach?"

"Yep," said Atoi as she went across the room to retrieve her boot. She picked up the squashed insect by a leg and carried it to the garbage disposal chute.

"That's not a roach," Carina said. "That's a scalobite."

"What difference does it make?"

"Scalobites are good. They eat roaches."

"Whatever. Now it's a dead scalobite."

Carina sighed and lay on her back. The bunk shuddered as Atoi shifted her position. She was a large, heavily muscled woman.

"You missed the announcement too," she said. "Got another mission. Hykara sector."

"Where's that?"

"Don't know. A long way from here. We're fast-burning through the quiet shift."

As Atoi mentioned the fast burn, Carina began to feel the vibration of *Duchess's* engines powering up. She lay down and fastened the safety webbing over her bunk. Soon, the ship would lurch as they switched to FTL drive.

"What's the mission?" Carina asked, studying the rust patch in the corner of the ceiling above her bunk.

"Search and rescue. Kidnap victim."

"Huh? Isn't that one for a planetside control force?"

"You'd think, wouldn't you?" Atoi replied. "Word is, no one local will touch it. *Other mercs* won't touch it. We're only doing it because it's that or disband. Tarsalan says she'll pull the plug otherwise."

Unfastening her webbing temporarily, Carina leaned over the edge of her bunk to look at Atoi. The woman had the satisfied expression of someone spinning out a juicy piece of gossip.

"What else does the word say?" Carina asked.

Atoi smirked. "The boy who was kidnapped is a Sherrerr, and the kidnappers are—"

"Dirksens," Carina finished for her. She threw herself onto her back. "We've bought it."

"Yeah. Everyone's trying to bail but Tarsalan won't let them. Says they have to work out their contracts. No negotiation. After the last mission, people were already pissed. Some chairs got thrown, tables broken. Tarsalan exited at the first sign of trouble and left Cadwallader and Speidel to calm things down."

Carina could imagine the scene. She was glad she'd skipped dinner. Merc bands were mostly made up of men and women who had left—or been discharged from—the military because they were unstable or lacked the discipline necessary for service in the forces. They could be aggressive, anti-social, impulsive, and belligerent.

Her soldier buddies' personality quirks had never bothered Carina much. Surviving alone on the streets from a young age had brought her into contact with many unsavory types. In fact, the mercs' unpleasant characteristics made things easier for her. Superficial friendships and casual hookups were all she could risk in terms of relationships. In her time with the Black Dogs, she'd only ever contemplated something more with one man: Stevenson, the pilot, who was relatively sane. She'd avoided him ever since coming to the realization.

No, mercs were not to be messed with, and Tarsalan, in her usual nonchalant, disinterested manner, had just told a room of them their next mission was to be even more suicidal than their last.

FIVE

As Carina went to the armory to suit up before leaving on the mission to rescue the little Sherrerr boy, she was reconsidering her decision to go along. Speidel had advised her to move on from the merc band, and she had recently come dangerously close to revealing her ability. What was more, the assignment was highly risky. Even if they succeeded—which wasn't likely—the chances were the Dirksens wouldn't rest until they found and punished the people responsible for thwarting their plan. And in the list of possible punishments the Dirksens meted out, the best and rarest option was a quick death.

Despite Tarsalan's threats, there wasn't much the company owner could do to the mercs who refused to take part in the assignment other than fire them. Being let go was a problem that paled in comparison to the potential consequences of defying the Dirksens.

The Sherrerr/Dirksen feud was notorious. It had gone on for so long, the inciting event was lost in time, but the reason for their mutual hatred and constant clashes didn't matter. The Sherrerrs and Dirksens were equally wealthy, powerful, and corrupt, which meant their rivalry to be the ruling clan in that sector of the galaxy was inevitable.

Anyone with any sense had nothing to do with either family if they could help it. It was true that when you were on the inside, you had access to all the luxury and privilege the connection provided, but there was a large drawback: you could never leave. Once you were in, you were in for life and that was that. If you left, you were an unacceptable liability, and you would spend the rest of your prematurely shortened life looking over your shoulder, wondering where and when the blow would fall.

Carina guessed the Sherrerrs had promised Tarsalan rich rewards and life-long protection for her and her loved ones to persuade her to take the deal. The same recompense and safeguarding wouldn't apply to the grunts who did the actual work.

The mercs who had refused the job were dumped on a remote planet, unpaid. The rumor was that Speidel had threatened to resign, though for some reason he was now coming along. Perhaps his motivation was similar to Carina's. She certainly had no interest in the clan feud or in incurring the vengeful spite of the Dirksens, but she had thought more than once about the little boy they had taken.

According to the information the Sherrerrs had given, he was only six. Carina had been but four years older when she had also found herself alone with no one to protect her, and she hated to think how the ruthless Dirksens might treat a Sherrerr they had in their clutches. No ransom note had been issued, and no other explanation had been given for the kidnapping, so what they were planning to do was unclear.

Someone had to get the boy out. Carina had done some morally question-able things during her time as a merc. If rescuing an innocent child was to be her last mission, it would be a fitting finale to her career.

The armory was already busy with the rest of the mission squad. She took down the legs of her armor and stepped into them, tightening the fit before slotting the torso into place and sealing it. The arms came next. She slipped the canister of elixir into its pouch and adjusted its position so that it wasn't in the way. From the edge of her vision she noticed Smitz watching. She gave him the stink eye and bent down to pick up her helmet.

"Hey, what are you doing, you bunch of useless grunts?" asked Captain Speidel as he appeared at the door. "Didn't you hear the directive? If we go in there dressed like soldiers, we'll be blown to bits before we get within five klicks of the target. You're in civvies for this. And no guns. We don't want to draw any attention when we disembark. We'll buy weapons planetside. Get changed and get to the shuttle. We're leaving at eleven hundred and fifteen."

Half an hour later, Speidel gave them a final briefing as they descended to the planet.

"Listen up," he said to the eight mercs seated on each side of the shuttle, looking uncomfortable in normal clothes. "Orrana's a young world, geologically speaking. Too young to be settled, in my opinion. It's highly volcanic, and while that makes for lucrative mining operations, the effects are pretty much what you would expect on a relatively new planet: regular eruptions, earthquakes, tsunamis, geysers, boiling volcanic springs, and so on.

"The biggest settlement is on one of the most stable landmasses, and it's a pretty lawless place from what I can gather, which suits our purposes perfectly. That sword cuts both ways, however. If anyone gets into trouble, they only have themselves or us to rely on to get them out of it. There is a local civil control force but it's probably either ineffective or crooked. It's unlikely to interfere in any fights and we might find ourselves on the wrong side of it if it becomes known why we're there. If they don't already know what the Dirksens are doing, they probably aren't going to do anything if they find out.

"You're likely wondering how we know where the Dirksens are holding the victim. The simple answer is the boy's been fitted with a transmitter. It's embedded in him, so we have his exact coordinates. We only have to break or sneak through the Dirksens' guard, rescue the lad, and escape with him. *Duchess* will be ready to run the moment we have him aboard."

Smitz said, "You left something out, Captain."

"What's that, Private?"

"What's our cut and when do we get it?"

"What?"

"The Sherrers must be paying a fortune to rescue their kid. What I want to know is, how much of that cred are we seeing? What's our bonus?"

"No one's mentioned a bonus, Smitz."

"We're taking all this risk so Tarsalan can buy another pretty ring?"

"You'll get what you're paid," said Speidel. "Now be quiet."

"Right," Smitz said. "I'll remember that when the Dirksens have me cornered in a dark alley. I'll be sure to give them her home address." He spat into the gully that ran down the center of the small ship.

Speidel grimaced in disgust. "What the hell are you chewing, man? Hand it over."

His face set in anger, Smitz pulled out his packet of herb and gave it to Speidel, who put it in his pocket.

"Take these," Speidel said, handing out breathing masks. "Wear them at all times and never breathe the local air. The atmosphere has enough oxygen, but the CO_2 level will kill you. I'm hoping we won't have to stay the night there, but if we do, change the filter every day. Everyone take one of these too." He opened a drawstring bag containing small electronic devices. "They're comms with high level encryption, as you won't be wearing your helmets."

Carina took one of the small gadgets and pushed it into her right ear. She pulled her hair forward to cover it. When Speidel spoke again, she heard his voice loud and clear.

"Now I know we don't do much plain clothes work," the captain continued, "so some of you might not feel comfortable with it. What you have to try to remember is that, until we're inside the place where they're keeping the kid, you're to try to forget you're soldiers. Whoever's guarding the child will be on the lookout for anyone who seems like they could be ex-military."

Pondering the captain's words, Carina's gaze roved over her fellow operatives. Smitz was the largest of the bunch. He was built like a heavyweight fist-fighter and wore a permanent scowl. Brown was as tall as Smitz but more supple and lithe. He moved like a predator. Next to Brown was Atoi, who loved to work on her upper body strength. Her bull neck and biceps were stretching the material of her shirt.

On Carina's left sat Carver. She had a scar that ran diagonally across her cheek and under her nose, permanently lifting her top lip. It wouldn't have been expensive to get the scar fixed, but Carver seemed to like the look. Halliday sat on Carina's right. He had the gaze of someone who had seen enough horror for several lifetimes. Further on from Halliday were Jackson with his prosthetic arm and Lee, who had a nervous tic that made him blink excessively.

They were gonna buy it for sure.

Six

They set up at a hostel for transient workers while Captain Speidel went out to procure some weapons. Firearms of any kind were prohibited on the planet according to the signs at the arrivals section of the spaceport, but it seemed as though no one paid much attention to the rule. Carina had seen guns and rifles carried openly as they rode the transport to the hostel.

Orrana was a dark place in climate and mood. Thick haze generated by frequent volcanic eruptions blocked much of the sunlight. As a result, vegetation was minimal. Deep gray-green, straggly stems covered the black soil to the horizon. Speidel had told them that animal life was at the microorganism stage, so they had nothing to fear from the indigenous species. Carina doubted the same could be said for the Dirksens or their employees.

The locals she'd seen at the spaceport wore sour or suspicious or desperate looks, judging by what she could see of their faces. Their breathing masks covered the nose and mouth and were fastened by a strap on each side of the face and one over the top of the head. The clothes the locals wore were basic and utilitarian and their hair was plainly cut. Fashion was not of any importance on Orrana. Survival was.

The mercs' story was that they were a team of smelting workers. It was a subterfuge intended to account for their rough, burly appearance. If asked, they were to say they were looking for work and were not interested in setting up their own operation. Conflicts over land, mining rights, and raw materials were rife, and the mercs were to expect scrutiny in that regard.

As she stood in the shared hostel room and pulled tight the wide belt she wore, she hoped no one would ask her any awkward questions. She didn't have a clue about smelting.

Atoi stepped into the room. "Come downstairs," she said. Her voice was muffled by her mask, but the comm Carina was wearing conveyed the woman's words. "Speidel's back. We're leaving soon."

Carina caught her reflection in a mirror as she left. She so rarely looked at herself in a mirror, let alone saw herself in civvies, that she paused a moment to take in the sight. She was wearing narrow pants that went down to her calves, boots that fastened with interlacing straps and a plain, open-necked hemp blouse. Speidel had told them to stick to dark colors.

Her figure was athletic but not bulky, and she didn't—yet—have that hard, intense expression that a life of killing had given so many of the others. Of all the squad members on the mission she thought she looked the least like a soldier. Perhaps she could find another way in life after rescuing the little boy.

Did she look anything like a smelting worker? She didn't think so, but her outfit would have to do.

She followed Atoi downstairs to the hostel bar, where the others were hanging out. Speidel wasn't there, and they were drinking the local brew. When Carina sat down at the table, someone pushed a beaker of frothy liquid in front of her. The smell of it told her the drink was some kind of alcohol. When she hesitated to try it, Jackson leaned over and said, "Speidel said it's okay. Just one drink."

For the benefit of eavesdroppers, they weren't to use the word 'captain' in public, nor any other terms that might identify them.

Carina sipped the deep green liquid. It tasted like someone had fermented the local vegetation, which was probably the case. "I think I'll pass," she said, pushing the beaker away.

Smitz laughed. He grabbed her cup and drained it.

Speidel came into the bar carrying a bulging bag. He set it down on the table and handed out weapons. Though the bar was full of the hostel's patrons, no one took any notice. It was as though on Orrana *not* carrying a weapon would be strange behavior.

Jackson held up his gun to examine it. "Where are these from? The last century?"

Smitz snickered and poured himself another drink from the pitcher.

"That's what's available at short notice on the street." Speidel held out his hand to take the gun back. "Unless you'd rather go without?"

"No, no. Not complaining," Jackson replied, pushing the weapon into the back of his pants under his shirt. "No way. Just asking."

After quickly checking it over, Carina tucked hers into her belt.

Speidel said quietly, "I picked up some explosives too. C8 with delay fuses. They weren't difficult to find and they'll probably prove useful. They have thirty-second and two-minute delays. Okay, let's pay a visit to a smelting plant. I've hired one of the local transports. We'll talk more about the job on the way."

He clearly didn't want to risk their conversation being overheard at the bar. The eight mercs rose and left with the captain, making their way outside. As they went to where the transport was parked, Carina got her first close-up look at the settlement. She wasn't impressed. The place reminded her of where she'd grown up.

Like HER birth planet, Orrana was far from the center of the action and way off trade routes, and it showed. No one was planning to settle here, so no one had made any effort to create a proper infrastructure, like good roads or basic public services. From the flimsy pre-fabricated buildings to the dim street lights hung on makeshift poles, everything was temporary.

She pondered the advisability of building a smelting plant on a planet that was prone to earthquakes, but the financial savings of refining the ore planet-side probably offset the costs of rebuilding after a shock. The risk to the workers was undoubtedly low on the list of priorities, as it always was in ass-end-of-the-galaxy places.

Carina climbed aboard the multi-person transport Speidel had rented. The heavy vibration when he started it up signaled that the vehicle ran on some kind of organic fuel. Orrana really was about the most backward place she'd ever been. She slid into a window seat and rubbed a clear patch in the grimy window with the edge of her sleeve. Speidel input the destination and the transport pulled into the road.

"The smelting plant where the Dirksens are holding the kid is at the edge of town," Speidel said once they were on their way down the potholed street. "We're going to pretend we're looking for work. Gangs of transients looking for labor are common. The guards shouldn't be too suspicious at first. Don't forget you're supposed to be contract laborers. Low-skilled, boneheaded grunts."

"Sounds about right," Carver said, her scarred top lip rising in a gruesome grin.

"That way, no one's going to expect us to answer any difficult questions," Speidel continued. "All we need is enough of a cover story to get inside the plant. Here are the plans."

He handed out thin, transparent sheets.

"The red dot is the kid."

Carina studied the blueprint of the plant. It felt weird to not see the image on a visor overlay and not to be able to interact with it. The smelting plant was large and complex, and the Dirksens had secreted the boy on a basement level at its heart. As she saw the scale of the complex, the desperate nature of their attempt began to hit home.

The Dirksens had chosen the place to hold their hostage well. Not only was the boy in the least accessible part of the complex, the place was full of people working for Dirksens: tough men and women who had led hard lives. They wouldn't be averse to using their fists or whatever weapon came to hand to do their boss's bidding, and there had to be hundreds of them.

"You've gotta be joking, sir," said Lee, staring at the blueprint. His nervous tic had started up. Normally quiet, the man's outburst signaled the dismay the rest of the troop was no doubt also feeling.

"Lee's right," said Smitz. "They aren't gonna let a bunch of strangers in even if they believe our story, and if we try to fight our way in, we're dead. With our regular armor and weapons, we might stand a chance, but with these antiques, we'll never make it. Stop the transport and let me out. I'm going back to the ship."

"You'll stay right where you are, soldier," Speidel said.

Smitz spat a brown, greasy ball of spittle at Speidel's feet and got up to leave. The captain rose and roughly pushed the man back down into his seat. The soldier scowled and was about to stand again when Carina said, "Wait. What if we try something different?"

Smitz hesitated then buckled under the captain's glare.

"Like what, Corporal?" Speidel asked.

Carina outlined her plan. It would spread the mercs thin, and they would have to sacrifice force of arms to diversionary tactics and speed, but she couldn't see how they could retrieve the boy otherwise.

Speidel listened, his face betraying neither approbation nor disapproval.

"I'll go in to do the rescue," Carina added. "The kid's only six, and I think I'm the least scary of all of us. We don't want to frighten him into trying to get away. I'll need just one other person to come with me."

Atoi said, "I'll do it."

"Okay," said Speidel after a moment's pause, "we'll do it your way, Lin. It sounds like it might work."

SEVEN

Speidel stopped the transport two klicks from their destination and spent some time studying the smelting plant from afar. One of his eyes was an implant that had around ten times the capabilities of its biological equivalent.

While the captain was studying the processes of the plant and the movements of its workers, Carina checked her weapon over again. It was fully powered, but that was about all it had going for it. Jackson's earlier estimation that their guns were from the previous century seemed optimistic.

Her firearm was single pulse only, and the gauge on its side indicated that it had to build power between each discharge. Great. She hoped it didn't take long. What wouldn't she give for her trusty Jensen 31. Consulting with Atoi, she was relieved to find that the woman had received a better model. Hers didn't require time to recharge unless after rapid fire.

"Okay." Speidel turned around in his seat to face them. "The heap of ore on the right side is fed by a conveyor belt into a press to crush the rocks. Another belt takes the crushed rock inside—I'm guessing to furnaces to smelt it. We need to get some explosives onto the belt that enters the plant. That should mess the place up pretty good. Our second target is a pile of smoking waste on the far side of the complex. Nothing like falling red-hot ashes to rain on someone's parade.

"Another possible target is one of the chimneys. They're wide and they aren't that tall. Seems like concern for the environment is a concept that hasn't arrived on Orrana just yet. Someone with a good aim might get lucky. Anyone want to try?"

"I'll do it, sir," said Jackson. Lee and Halliday slapped the man on the back. With his prosthetic arm, Jackson was the obvious candidate.

"Good," Speidel said. "They've just turned on the lights, but their coverage isn't good. Should be plenty of shadows for cover. Brown and Carver, you're on target one. Halliday and Lee, you're on target two. Smitz, you're with us."

Smitz gave Speidel a surly glance but said nothing.

It was nearing twilight as the transport drew close to the plant. The emissions of its chimneys were dark gray against the deepening sky, leading from a dim glow at their bases. The mercs were well beyond the edge of town, driving down an empty road.

At a dip where the transport was briefly out of sight of the complex, Speidel stopped the vehicle again, and the five mercs who were to provide the diversions got out. They immediately stooped to grab handfuls of dirt. After mixing the dirt with a little water from their canteens, they would rub the resulting mud on their faces and exposed skin, helping them to melt into the encroaching darkness.

Speidel held out his weapon to Carina. "Take this and give me yours."

Carina pulled her pulse gun from her belt. "Why, sir?"

"Never mind why, Corporal, just do as you're ordered."

She took the captain's gun and briefly studied it before slipping it into her belt. His weapon was a better model than hers. He was swapping with her relic so that she could protect herself better.

A few moments later, the transport was on its way again, leaving the five disembarked mercs behind and slowly heading toward the light that glared from the guards' office at the main gate.

The figure of a tall woman could be seen sitting at a desk behind translucent, scratched plexiglas as they drew up. Carina glanced at the gates to the facility, which were large, heavy, and well-secured. There was no way they would be getting through them. Their only way inside was via the guards' office. She could see a shadowy exit at the back, blurred by the degraded glass of the window.

The guard was alone in the small room, her head turned toward a bank of roving holos that showed the activity inside the plant. She looked over as Speidel leaned out and spoke into the intercom. "We're here to see the manager about some jobs."

The woman's brow furrowed. "What's your name? I don't have any record of an appointment."

"You wouldn't," Speidel said. "We're only here to ask."

"The manager's busy," the woman said. "Check the job updates in the town news or make an appointment." She returned her attention to the holos.

"It would only take a minute to comm, ma'am," said Speidel. "We've got plenty of experience between us. Been working—"

"Get out of here," exclaimed the woman.

While Speidel dragged out the conversation with the guard, Atoi, Carina, and Smitz slowly opened the door on the side of the transport facing away from the guards' office and slipped out. Bent low, they crept around the vehicle and took up positions on either side of the window, just below its sill. All three had their gazes fixed on Speidel, waiting for his signal.

The captain raised his pulse gun, and they stood as one and fired at the plexiglas, cracking and melting the panes. Smitz drove his booted foot through the remains of the window on his side and Atoi elbowed out the rest. Carina followed them as they leapt into the room. The tall woman backed into a corner, her face pasty. The weapon she held was shaking. Clearly, she was just an ordinary guard and not one of the Dirksens' hired goons.

Speidel had also jumped inside. He took pity on her and fired a stunning shot. The guard slid to the floor as more appeared through the doorway at the back of the room. These men and women were professionals. They came out firing aggressively, but they weren't suited up. Carina, Smitz, and Atoi picked them off with accuracy, showing none of Speidel's mercy.

The mercs' position was dangerous. They had to avoid being pinned down in the outer office, trading shots with the Dirksen thugs while the local security force made its way over. They had to force their way inside, but stepping through the door wearing no armor would be suicide.

Still, they probably only had to wait a few more moments...

A boom split the air and the floor shook. Klaxons sounded. Someone had succeeded in placing a diversionary explosive.

Smitz and Atoi ran into the rear room, spraying pulses as they went. Carina and Speidel were hard on their heels. Two Dirksen hands were on their backs in the further office, their chests smoking. Speidel hit the arm of another who reached out from behind a cabinet to take a shot and Smitz finished her off. A fourth ran down the corridor leading from the room. Atoi shot him in the back.

They sped out and into the interior of the complex. The klaxons were still blaring, the sound penetrating Carina's skull. Another boom shook the plant. The general employees would be well-occupied at least.

Speidel took the lead as they ran deeper into the building. They fired at anyone who approached. Most of them ran away. The mission seemed to be progressing well, but Carina began to feel a nagging doubt about what was happening.

The captain took them down a set of stairs, along a corridor, and then downstairs once more. The sound of the klaxons grew quieter as they moved away from the busier sections of the complex.

"Okay," said Speidel, drawing to a stop at the top of a third set of stairs and panting. "We're here. Lin, Atoi, don't take too long. We can't hold off a sustained attack."

Carina and Atoi were to retrieve the Sherrerr child while Speidel and Smitz protected their rear. The two women ran quietly down the stairs. Though the klaxons were fainter here, Carina guessed the noise was sufficient to cover the sound of their footsteps. They were heading for a small room—not much bigger than a closet—in the corner of a large basement at the bottom of the stairs.

What they might expect to find, she didn't know. She hoped the child didn't have a large, round-the-clock guard, but it seemed unlikely the Dirksens would station lots of thugs right outside the kid's door.

At the top of the final flight of stairs, Carina and Atoi stopped. They checked their weapons, looked each other in the eye, nodded once, and bounded down the final steps, firing into the basement as they went.

The wide, low room was full of old, dusty, broken bits and pieces of equipment, lit up by the pulse flashes from the women's weapons. Carina couldn't detect any returning fire. The two split up and ran for cover behind separate hulking pieces of machinery.

Carina sat with her back to a machine and waited, listening. The room was dark, but she could see Atoi's position from the glowing dial of her pulse gun. The faint light shining from the stairs to the next level was the only other source of illumination.

No movement nor sound of any guards could be heard. Carina reached out and took a wild shot. No response.

"Atoi," she whispered into her comm. "I think the place may be empty."

"I was thinking that too," came the woman's response.

"Let's head round to the room where they have the kid," Carina said.

"You got it."

Carina crawled cautiously around the edge of the dark room, making her way to the door in the corner. Atoi approached it from the other direction. Carina arrived first. She reached upward, feeling for the door handle. She found it and pulled it down.

The door was unlocked. It swung open easily. Something was very, very wrong.

The smaller room was also dark. Carina stood and brushed the wall next to the door until she found the light switch. As it activated, Atoi arrived.

"What the hell?" the woman said as she saw the room. Aside from a few pieces of furniture, it was empty.

"What is it?" Speidel said over her comm. "Report, Lin."

"The kid isn't here, sir," Carina replied. "I think we're in the wrong room."

"If you're in the small room off the basement," said Speidel, "that's definitely where the child should be. I'm receiving the signal from the transmitter. Are you sure you're in the right place?"

"Yes, sir," Carina said. "But the whole basement is empty. Not even any guards."

Atoi had moved into the room. A couple of overturned chairs and a small, low table were its only furnishings. "I guess it's possible the kid was here but they moved him when we burst into the plant."

"The captain's receiving the signal from here," said Carina. "The kid has to be around somewhere. But where?"

Atoi was crouching down, looking at something she'd spotted on a stained part of the floor. "Aw, fuck." She stood and backed away, the color draining from her face.

"What?" Carina asked.

Atoi raised a hand to her eyes and shook her head. She didn't answer.

Carina went over to see for herself. She picked up the object for a closer look. Her stomach lurched and her legs turned weak.

It was a tiny chip, around the size of a baby's fingernail. Like the floor where it was lying, the chip was stained brown. The stains were dried blood, and the chip was the Sherrerr child's transmitter.

Eight

Carina forced down the bile rising in her throat. She'd seen plenty of blood and death in her time, but she couldn't imagine how anyone could harm a small, innocent boy.

As she gazed at the tiny chip in her hand, other things started to add up until finally it all made sense. The whole mission has been too easy. They should never have made it that far with their shitty weapons and no armor. "Sir, we found the boy's transmitter. I think it was put here to lure us in. It's a trap. The Dirksens want to capture us."

She waited for Speidel's reply, but none came. Perhaps he was distracted.

"Captain?"

Nothing.

"Sir?"

A loud *crunch*.

Carina turned to Atoi, her eyes wide. "We have to get back to them."

They flew out of the room and across the large basement, steering around the shadowy shapes of discarded machinery. Atoi gave a cry as she ran into a piece of equipment low down on the floor. She tumbled over it and landed on her face. Carina ran back and helped the woman to her feet. Blood was flowing from her nose and dripping off her upper lip, dark in the dim room.

She drew her sleeve across her face and spat. "I'm okay."

They climbed the stairs together, slowly. Carina hadn't heard a sound from the captain since his most recent words to her, and there had been no sounds of fighting from the next level. But then, pulse fire wasn't noisy and she wouldn't have expected to hear it above the continuing noise of the emergency klaxons.

They crept around a corner in the stairwell and found themselves staring down the muzzles of guns.

The two guards who were waiting for them were kitted out more like Carina would have expected from employees of the Dirksens. They were dressed in full armor and bearing gleaming new weapons of a kind she'd never seen before.

Their order didn't need to be verbalized. Both Carina and Atoi put down their guns in one slow, measured movement. One guard led the way while the other went around behind them. The group climbed the stairs to the corridor, where Carina was relieved to see Speidel was still alive. She even felt a mild satisfaction that Smitz also wasn't dead.

He was facing the wall next to the captain. Two of the Dirksens' thugs were holding weapons to their heads. Carina and Atoi were pushed against the wall next to them.

"Which one of you was it?" Atoi asked between her teeth.

"Shut up," said a guard.

"Which one of you held the kid down?"

Speidel looked from Atoi to Carina, a curious expression on his face.

The guard raised his voice. "I said, shut up."

"Who was it that dug it out of him?" Atoi yelled.

The guard fired, and Atoi screamed as a thread of light shot from the weapon and made contact with her back. She fell to the ground, writhing and jerking in agony. The guard kept his finger on the trigger, seeming to enjoy the spectacle. When he finally stopped firing, Atoi lay motionless, barely conscious and covered in sweat. Next to her was the captain's comm, which had been ground to pieces.

"We have orders to try to deliver you all alive," the guard said to her, "but the Dirksens won't mind if we slip up once or twice along the way. I was just playing with you then. Don't make me use the lethal setting."

He nodded at another couple of guards, and they hauled Atoi to her feet and pushed her against the wall once more. She swayed and staggered as she struggled to stand upright, gripping the wall with both hands.

The Dirksen thugs seemed to be waiting for something. From the corner of her eye, Carina saw the one who had tortured Atoi murmuring into his helmet mic.

Tense seconds ticked past. Carina wondered what the new weapons were the Dirksens had. Pulse guns fired bolts of concentrated energy that burned the target or, at a lower setting, shocked him into temporary unconsciousness. The

Dirksen guns seemed to emit a continuous flow of power that kept the victim in constant pain. Perhaps the lethal setting would stop the heart. She wondered what range the weapons had.

The men and women guarding the mercs were growing agitated and throwing glances from side to side along the corridor. Something was up. One of the women jabbed Carina in the back, and she gasped as the hard metal muzzle drove into her spine, causing a sharp jab of pain.

"Move," the woman said, jerking her gun to the right.

The other mercs were being pushed in the same direction. It seemed a good time to stage an escape attempt. Once the Dirksen thugs had secured them somewhere, getting away would be a lot harder. But Carina couldn't see how any of them could make a move without being immediately shot with one of the torture weapons.

The klaxons had finally stopped, and the lower levels of the plant were quiet as they went along. Carina was at the end of the line. A muzzle was thrust into her again, hitting her kidney. She bit back a yell.

"Faster," said the guard.

Carina imagined what she would do to the woman if she got a chance.

A *whompf* of detonation came from the corridor up ahead, the explosion deafening her. Cracks appeared in the ceiling and walls. Carina swung her elbow upward into the guard's helmet, toppling the woman. She snatched her weapon from her and fired. The thread of intense light shot out, but the woman only jerked in pain. Her armor seemed to absorb some of the energy.

The guard snatched at the muzzle and tried to stand. Carina pushed the weapon against the woman's chest and fired again. That time, the guard's body spasmed and was still.

"Fire against their armor," Carina shouted, her ears still ringing from the explosion.

An agonizing flame shot through her, but was cut off abruptly. She turned to see Smitz grinning and pulling his weapon away from the helmet of a falling Dirksen guard.

Three of the mercs who had planted the diversionary explosives came running down the corridor, shooting. Carina ran at a Dirksen thug who was about to return fire. She thrust her weapon against his back and pressed the trigger.

Speidel and Atoi were struggling with their captors. The captain screamed. His guard had shot him in the eye. He fell, clutching his face. Brown ran up and body-slammed the guard, at the same time relieving him of his firearm.

"Press it up against his chest," shouted Carina.

The third Dirksen thug died.

Carina was wondering if they should try to take the fourth alive when Atoi killed him. It was the one who had tortured her.

Brown was helping Speidel to his feet. The captain's face was a ruined, blackened mess, but he was alive. The staff sergeant pointed down the corridor, in the opposite direction to the area of the explosion, and the mercs began to run.

Carina's hearing was gradually returning.

"There's a hole in the fence north-north-west, where the chimney exploded," Brown said. "If we get split up, make for it and head back to town. We'll meet at the back of the hostel. We leave for the shuttle at 0600."

He didn't say it, but the implication was clear. Anyone who didn't make it to the rendezvous point in time would be left behind.

NINE

Things were turning ugly aboard the *Duchess*. The five mercs who had set the explosives had encountered Dirksen guards roaming the complex, and neither Carver nor Lee had survived. Brown, Halliday, and Jackson had fared better and headed to find out what had happened to their captain after they heard the fateful *crunch* of his comm.

Setting a small explosion in one part of the corridor provided the distraction to give the mercs the edge they needed to turn the tables on the Dirksen thugs. After escaping over what remained of the fence, the surviving mercs had eventually made it to the shuttle and returned to their ship.

That was where the shitshow really started.

Carina had always known that Sasha Tarsalan was a nasty bitch, but she'd never witnessed the level of fury the woman unleashed on the mercs who had failed their second mission in a row.

The heavily bejeweled woman ranted and raged at the six mercs, spittle flying from her mouth. Speidel was in the sick bay, where the ship's doctor was removing what remained of his ocular implant. Carina and the others stood to attention, facing the full brunt of Tarsalan's fury in silence.

'Incompetent' and 'inept' were among the nicer words she used to describe them. According to her assessment, they were also 'moronic grunts,' who were a 'waste of oxygen' and had 'brought the company to ruin' with their 'pathetic efforts.'

After a while, as Tarsalan explained how 'real' soldiers would have behaved like professionals and done the 'simple job' they were asked to do, Carina tuned the woman out. She watched her gesticulations, red face, and bloodshot eyes but paid little attention to what she was saying. Tarsalan's hair was piled into a tower on her head, and as Carina watched, the tower began to slip and hang at an angle. She wondered if, and when, it would fall down entirely.

The patience and stoicism Nai Nai had taught her from a young age meant it wasn't difficult for her to bear Tarsalan's dishonest, unfair ferocity. The other mercs, however, were not so well-equipped. Though none moved nor spoke, their growing rage was almost palpable.

Predictably, Smitz was the first to snap. He didn't say anything. He strode over to the woman and stood glaring down at her, his hands in fists at his sides and his broad, heavily muscled back tense.

Tarsalan's words dried up, and she seemed to suddenly realize she'd spent the last ten minutes insulting and berating six professional killers, and she was alone with them. She swallowed and looked up at Smitz. Her previously puce face paled, but she said tersely, "What do you think you're—"

Perhaps if she'd apologized, Smitz might have mastered his rage. Even if she'd said nothing at all, there was a chance he would have calmed down and stopped himself from doing something stupid. Though he was undisciplined and often offensive, Smitz had spent so long skirting the line of report-worthy behavior that he knew exactly where it lay.

As it was, Tarsalan's continued arrogant attitude made the man snap. He grabbed her throat, lifted her with one arm, and slammed her against the bulkhead, where she hung, wriggling. The company owner's eyes protruded from their sockets and her mouth was forced open by the pressure of Smitz's hand on her neck. Her tongue waggled wildly but not a sound nor breath left her mouth.

She plucked uselessly at Smitz's fingers while her feet kicked and jerked, suspended several centimeters above the floor.

Carina and the other mercs enjoyed the spectacle for a few moments until, halfheartedly, they tried to make Smitz release his hold. Staff Sergeant Brown gave him an order to drop Tarsalan immediately, and the others tried to open his fingers and pull him away from her.

With apparently great reluctance, Brown finally fired at Smitz and stunned him. As he collapsed, Tarsalan fell to the floor too. She was unconscious but still alive. The marks of Smitz's fingers on her neck were already showing.

"Good one, Smitz," spat Halliday. "Now we're out of a job for sure."

"We were out of a job anyway," said Atoi. "If he hadn't done it, I would have soon enough. He only did what we all wanted to do."

Jackson agreed. "I would've punched her, though. Probably more than once."

"Quit it," said Brown. "Lin, help me get her to sick bay. This son-of-a-bitch goes to the brig. You understand, Atoi? Halliday? Jackson?"

The three nodded glumly. Transporting Smitz to the brig would be no mean feat, whether he was unconscious or awake.

After notifying the doctor they were on their way, Brown and Carina managed to carry Tarsalan to the sick bay between them. She had begun to regain consciousness by the time they arrived. The two of them lifted her by her shoulders and legs and put her on a bed.

Brown quickly left. He might have been avoiding Tarsalan's fury, redoubled after Smitz's attack, but the man's hand had damaged her neck to the extent she could barely croak. The doctor told her to be quiet while he examined her and motioned Carina away. She had hung around in case the doctor wanted to know what had happened, but the evidence apparently said everything.

Carina had passed a curtained bed on her way into the sick bay. She guessed the occupant had to be Speidel. She peeked in. The captain was awake and reading an interface with his remaining eye. A patch covered the place where the other had been.

She opened the curtain wider. "Hi, sir." She spoke quietly so the doctor wouldn't hear and maybe make her leave.

Speidel's smile when he saw her eased her concern for the older man somewhat. He put down the screen. "Come in, Carina. It's good of you to come and see me."

She stepped close to the bed and drew the curtains closed.

"Did doc get all your implant out?" she asked.

"All that was left of it," Speidel replied, pulling himself into a higher position before relaxing on his pillows. "Several thousand creds gone in a single shot. But I was lucky, really. If the beam had hit my real eye, it would probably have fried my brain. Better one-eyed than dead, huh?"

"I'd say so. Are you going to get another implant or a new bio eye?"

"I'm not sure. I guess it depends on whether I continue soldering or take the hint and retire. Have you heard what's happening with the company yet? Cadwallader isn't answering my comm and the doctor won't tell me anything, except to rest up and not worry myself for a while. Like it's easy not to worry when you don't know what's going on."

"Well..." Carina wasn't sure if she should tell Speidel about the incident with Tarsalan and Smitz, but she guessed he would find out soon enough, what with being right next to the company owner.

"Holy shit," Speidel said when she reached the part where Smitz had tried to strangle Tarsalan. "What an imbecile. If it wasn't over for the Black Dogs before, it certainly is now. Tarsalan's definitely going to cut her losses and split after this."

"No doubt about it. Which kinda makes your advice to me earlier moot, doesn't it?"

"Yeah. But it was good advice, Carina. Brown, Atoi, and the rest will find another merc band to join. Even Smitz might find someone who's on the lookout for an insubordinate, aggressive bastard. But... Listen to me, okay? I've gotten to know you over the years, and you aren't like them. I didn't realize it when I dragged you out of that fight. I never told you, but I watched it going on for a while before I stepped in. I watched you defend yourself against those older, bigger street rats, and I saw your skill and strength. But that was all I saw.

"I thought providing you with a safe place to live and a regular paycheck was fair exchange for what you could bring to the band. And you stepped up and did the job, after a little training. It wasn't until later I saw a different side to you. You can fight and kill if you need to, but you don't like it. You aren't immune to it like half of the others, and you don't relish it like the other half."

Speidel half shut his remaining eye, scrutinizing her. Carina began to feel uncomfortable.

"There's something else about you too. Something more than disliking the fight."

Carina felt that familiar wrenching she had whenever she was worried someone might discover what she was. Time to change the subject. She had another topic on her mind anyway.

"What's going to happen now, sir?" she asked. "About the Sherrerr kid, I mean."

Speidel sighed. "Who knows? Now he no longer has his transmitter, it's going to be a lot harder to find him. Whatever happens, we're out of that game."

"Are we? It doesn't seem right to abandon him like that. He's just a little kid."

"He's just a little *Sherrerr* kid. If anyone has the money and influence to track him down, it's them."

"That's something I don't get," said Carina. "They're so rich and powerful, why did the Sherrerrs hire us to do their dirty work? Why not send in their own goons?"

"I never got that either," Speidel replied, "and, for what it's worth, I feel the same as you. I'm not happy about leaving the search to someone else, assuming someone else *is* searching for him. But I don't know what else we can do. He could be anywhere, and the Dirksens sure as hell aren't telling."

"That's the other thing that bothers me," Carina said. "Why did they kidnap him in the first place if they don't want to ransom him? They just took him and disappeared. What's the point of that?"

"Maybe for revenge. Maybe they already murdered him. That room where you found his transmitter, was there...?"

"No," Carina replied. "There was only a small amount of blood. Not enough."

"Whatever the Dirksens did with the kid, we've reached the end of the road. Even if we wanted to continue after Tarsalan disbands the company, we have no way of finding him."

"I guess you're right," Carina said, but inside she was saying, *Yes, there is.* She had kept the child's transmitter. The trace of blood on it held his genetic code—his unique signature in the fabric of the universe—and that meant that she could find him, but she would have to cast.

TEN

The doctor bought the mercs some time when it came to the breaking up of the Black Dogs. He insisted that Tarsalan remain in the sick bay and leave the running of the ship to Cadwallader for at least forty-eight hours. If the company owner had had her way, Carina was sure she would have thrown them all off the ship at the earliest opportunity with no time to pack their stuff or make arrangements.

As it was, after Smitz's attack, no one was in any doubt the band's days were over, and they acted accordingly. The soldiers began to clear out their cabins and pack the items they wanted to take with them. Cadwallader transferred the monies owed to them to their credchips, and people decided where they would go next.

Mealtimes became almost convivial as stories of old missions were recounted, then the mood would turn melancholy as the dead were remembered. Silence would eventually fall as the mercs no doubt inwardly reflected that their fate would be similar.

Captain Speidel was up and about the day following Smitz's attack, looking more than ever the old soldier with his eye patch. The skin on his face glistened with burn-healing gel and only very pink, fresh color remained of the damage the Dirksen guard's weapon had done.

Carina was happy to see him looking not too the worse for wear, and not only for his own sake. The plight of the Sherrerr boy had lain heavy on her mind and heart ever since the failure of their mission. She had made the Cast and found the child, but the knowledge was useless if she had to attempt a rescue alone. The Dirksen force was formidable, and she doubted she could defeat them even using her special abilities.

She needed help, yet how could she convince anyone she knew the boy's location unless she explained *how* she knew it? She would have to reveal that she could cast. The thought of it alone made her break out into a sweat. Nai Nai had impressed nothing else upon her more than the fact that she must never divulge her secret. Even the idea of it felt like an act of betrayal to the woman's memory, but if she didn't do something, she would be leaving a young child to suffer—perhaps even to be murdered.

Carina was glad the captain's recovery was going well because she'd decided that, of all the people she knew, he was the one she trusted the most. He'd also expressed his concern about the missing child and he might be persuaded to help her mount a rescue.

When her cabin was empty, Carina removed the canister of base elixir from its hiding place in her mattress and went to Speidel's room. She found him alone.

"Come in, Carina. I'm glad to see you. Have you come to tell me what you're going to do next?"

She stepped into the man's single cabin and waited for him to close the door before she spoke. "I have, and I need your help to do it."

Speidel sat on his bunk while Carina took the chair. The captain rested his elbows on his knees and clasped his hands. "Would you like me to write you a reference? I'm happy to, but I'm not sure how relevant it will be if you're giving up the soldiering life as I hope you are."

"I've thought about it," Carina replied, "and maybe you're right that I'm not suited to life as a merc. Maybe I will give it up, but it isn't over for me yet. I have one last mission I have to do. I want to rescue the Sherrerr kid."

Speidel straightened up. "I understand how you feel, but as I said, we're hamstrung on that. We don't know where—"

"I *do* know where he is. He's in the smelting plant. He was probably there all along. We were just tricked into going to the wrong part of it."

Speidel's expression was a mixture of confusion and disbelief. "But surely you're speculating. You can't know for sure, and we can't return to the plant on a guess. It's far too dangerous."

"I'm not speculating. I know where he is." Carina took a deep breath, trying to quell her racing heart. "I know because I cast to find him."

"You...?"

"Sir..."

The captain was looking concerned. Carina became even more aware of her flushing face and anxiety. Was she making the worst mistake of her life?

Perhaps, but she was committed. "You must swear to me that you will never tell anyone what I'm about to tell you. If you can't make that promise, then we can't do anything about the Sherrerr boy. It's very important that what I tell you remains a secret between us. My life depends on it."

Speidel nodded. When Carina waited expectantly, he said, "I swear."

"Thank you," Carina said. "It's a little difficult to explain, sir, but I can do things that most people can't. Things that I can't rationalize and that don't make sense scientifically, as far as I understand. Yesterday, when I was with you in the sick bay, you said there was something different about me. That's because I *am* different, though I don't know how or why."

Speidel didn't speak. He was giving her the space to finish what she wanted to say.

Carina explained how her Nai Nai had brought her up after her father and mother disappeared, and how the old woman had taught her to harness and hone her casting power. She didn't tell him the details like the Elements, the Seasons, the Strokes, or the Map. Those weren't necessary for the captain to know. He only had to believe what she could do and that the Sherrerr boy was where she said he was.

"It isn't a simple or easy process," she went on. "The reason I was able to cast to find the child was because I had something of his. I had the transmitter Atoi found. I can't find people randomly, or at least I never learned how. Nai Nai died when I was ten, and I was alone after that. I couldn't fit in where I was. Maybe the people in my neighborhood could sense the same thing you can—that I wasn't like them. I used to get picked on a lot."

She stopped. She felt she had said enough for Speidel to take on board for the moment. Oddly, though all her life she'd feared someone finding out she was a mage, she now felt relieved, as if a burden had been lifted from her. It felt good to share her secret with someone else. She realized how alone she had felt before.

Speidel rubbed his stubble. "That's quite a story, Carina." His tone was non-committal.

Carina's heart sank. He didn't believe her.

"I take it you can prove what you say," he said.

"Yes," she replied, her hope rising. "Yes, I can. I thought of a simple Cast I can do to show you, but I don't want to unsettle you."

"I've been a merc for eleven years and in the military for thirteen," Speidel said, laughing. "I don't think there's anything you can do to unsettle me."

She took out her canister of elixir and sipped a mouthful. She scanned the cabin for a handy object and saw the captain's uniform hat on a table. She closed her eyes and drew the ideogram in her mind. The Cast was an easy one.

She opened her eyes to see the captain had an indulgent, disbelieving look on his face. He opened his mouth as if about to say something to mollify her, but then his hat appeared on his head. He reacted as if a poisonous spider had just fallen on him. He threw the hat to the floor and leapt up so fast his legs hit his bunk and he overbalanced, falling comically onto it.

Carina tried to suppress her laughter but was unsuccessful. In all the years she'd known him, Speidel had been the model of self-control. She'd never seen him so surprised or amazed.

Still lying on his bunk in an awkward pose, Speidel blinked his single eye several times. He sat up. "Well, I asked you to prove it, and you did." He straightened his pants and ran a hand through his graying hair. Reaching down to the floor, he picked up his hat and turned it over in his hands. "I guess I believe you."

"You do?"

Speidel nodded. "It's a lot to take in, but to tell you the truth, it isn't the first time I've heard about such abilities. Of course, I never believed the stories before. What else can you do?"

"Quite a lot of things, though some are easier than others. I can move things, as you just saw, and find things that are missing if I have a part of the object—something to link to it. I can heal, though it's difficult and not fast. I can't prevent someone who's been shot from dying, for instance. I can start fires and engines at a distance, open locks, change my appearance—"

"Can you hurt people...kill them?" Speidel asked softly.

Carina looked down and slowly nodded. "But it isn't straightforward. Shooting or knifing is much easier."

There was a moment's pause as Speidel considered her response. "Oh," he suddenly blurted, his eyes wide. "It was you! At the Matahman Embassy. It was you who made the enemy soldiers disappear."

She gave another quick nod.

"Did you kill them? All of them?"

"No. Like I said, that's hard to do. I just moved them about a kilometer away."

Speidel whistled in admiration. His brow furrowed. "I saw you drink from that," he said, indicating her canister. "Is that essential to what you do?"

"Yes. I must take a sip of elixir. And...do some other things."

"So if I drank that, would I be able to do magic too?"

A shadow settled over Carina's heart. Was this what Nai Nai had meant when she'd said that knowledge of her abilities would turn friends into enemies? A change of direction to the conversation was needed. "I don't think of it as magic. 'Magic' sounds like something out of children's stories, like three wishes and wizards disappearing in puffs of smoke. I think my ability is natural, only it's very rare and outside our current understanding of the universe."

She paused. "Even if you had the ability, you wouldn't be able to cast just by drinking the elixir. It takes training and practice and there's a lot more involved besides." She handed him the canister. "Take a sip and try if you don't believe me."

He took the offered canister and lifted it to his lips. His gaze upon her, he tipped back his head and poured a measure of elixir into his mouth. Immediately, the liquid erupted as he spat it out, splattering it across the floor. He coughed and retched for a minute or so. Wiping his eye, he said, "You didn't tell me it tastes like weeks-old piss."

The corners of Carina's mouth twitched. "You get used to it. Are you going to try some 'magic' now?"

Still wiping his eye and mouth, Speidel burst into laughter. "Okay, you got me good. If I have to drink that sewer effluent, I'd rather stay non-magical. What's in it?"

"Nothing that's important by itself. What do you say? Do you believe I'm right about the location of the Sherrerr boy? Will you help me rescue him?"

"I do believe you. How couldn't I after your little demonstration? And I will help you rescue the child. But I don't think we should try to do it alone. I'll speak to some of the others. I'll tell them I received additional intel from the Sherrerrs. Maybe we can rope in some of them to help us. But we'll have to start soon."

"Yeah. I hate to think about that kid all alone among those thugs, especially after what they already did to him."

"Not only that," Speidel said. "I plan on us going in fully armed this time, which means we need to leave before the doctor lets Tarsalan get up."

Eleven

Somehow, Smitz got wind of what they were doing, and he insisted he wanted to come along too.

"He's just saying that so he can get out of the brig before Tarsalan recovers," Carina said to Speidel when he told her. "The minute we arrive planetside he'll be gone."

"I don't think so," the captain replied. "There's more to Smitz than meets the eye. I would have kicked him out of the Black Dogs ages ago if I didn't think so. He talks a lot, but he always follows orders in the end. And he came on the previous mission when he didn't have to. He could have bailed like most of the rest did."

"He was expecting a bonus, though."

"And when he found out he wasn't getting one, he came along anyway. I think he wants to help."

"I don't know, sir. I don't like it."

"I've been commanding mercs for a long time. They're a difficult bunch and it's easy to underestimate their better motivations. I think you should trust me on this."

Carina sighed. "Okay, if you say so."

Atoi had also quickly volunteered when approached, and Stevenson was happy to fly the shuttle.

Scans of the smelting plant showed the explosions had put it out of operation. The damage the mercs had caused was extensive. There was little movement and the furnaces were cooling after being shut down.

According to the results of Carina's Cast, the Dirksens had the Sherrerr boy in what seemed to be a staff locker room on the first floor. The room was central, which meant another deep infiltration from the perimeter of the building. Approaching the front entrance was out of the question. They had no reason to be there as the place had closed down for repairs, and they would be recognized immediately.

Carina's idea was to approach at night from another direction and enter the site through a breach in its fence.

"They won't be expecting us," she said. "They won't think we'll return to the same place."

"They might if they find out the intel about the kid was leaked," said Atol.

A look passed between Carina and Speidel. "I'm confident that won't happen," the captain said. "But I have another proposal," he added. "I don't doubt that the Dirksens will have alerted the planet authorities about us. If we land at the spaceport, we'll likely be arrested on a trumped up charge. Instead, we'll catch them by surprise. We tell Stevenson to fly us right onto the plant roof. We fight our way down to the room where they have the kid, grab him, and fly right out again. They don't have any spacecraft on site to pursue us. If we're fast enough, it might work."

"What about ships orbiting the planet?" Smitz asked. He was chewing his disgusting herb again.

"If the Dirksens had a starship in the vicinity that stood a chance of defeating the *Duchess*," said Speidel, "we would have been under attack by now. I'm guessing they didn't want to draw the Sherrerr's attention to Orrana by stationing one of their better ships here for no obvious reason. But that isn't to say one isn't on its way to force us out of the area after our escapade."

"Will the roof withstand a shuttle landing on it?" Carina asked.

"Enough to not collapse," Speidel replied. "And that's all that matters for our purposes. We'll be suited up, so we'll have some protection from the heat."

No more questions were forthcoming, and time was of the essence. Within quarter of an hour, they were in the shuttle and descending to Orrana's surface.

The descent was rapid. Stevenson swept them in at maximum speed. Carina and the others gripped webbing above their heads for extra stability as the ship tilted at a forty-five degree angle. The speed lifted them out of their seats, then they were thrown forward as the pilot employed reverse thrusters hard. The shuttle dropped precipitously to the smelting plant roof.

Before the shuttle had fully touched down, Stevenson opened the ramp, and the mercs ran out onto the smoking hot roof. The door to the building was locked, but in a heartbeat Smitz burst through it and led the charge down the stairs.

The mercs' attack was so fast, the first Dirksen guards they met were taken completely by surprise. Concentrated pulse fire from the mercs' Jensen rifles was sufficient to penetrate their armor, and some weren't even suited up.

By the time they reached the second floor, the news of the attack had arrived, and they met stronger resistance. Turning a corner on the stairs, Smitz ran into a shot from one of the Dirksens' advanced weapons. He was thrown back and lay unmoving on the steps.

His chest plate bore a melted patch from the glancing hit. Carina lifted his visor. Above his mask, the man's eyes were open. "M'okay," he said. "Just gimme a minute."

While Atoi sprayed pulse fire down the stairs, Speidel started the twenty second delay on an explosive. Through her comm, Carina heard him counting down. As she helped Smitz up the steps, away from the blast zone, she mentally counted with him. *Six. Five. Four.*

Speidel set the explosive rolling down the steps and sprinted up them with Atoi.

Three. Two.

The explosion roared up toward the mercs, sending a cloud of smoke and debris with it. Having no choice but to abandon Smitz for the moment, Carina, Atoi, and Speidel hurtled down the stairs and into the blast area, which was thick with a smoky haze.

Unable to see where she was going, Carina collided with a Dirksen guard and found herself sprawling on the floor. A muzzle appeared in her vision and she grabbed it, hauling the guard on top of her where the close quarters would prevent him from firing. She tried to wrestle the gun from him.

Letting go of the weapon, she jumped up and kicked it from his grasp. The gun went skittering down the stairs, and the guard tried to go after it, but Carina jumped on his back and wrenched open his visor. She ripped off the man's breathing mask and tried to throw it, but he tackled her from behind, grabbing her around the knees. Carina's helmet hit the edge of a step. The cushioning absorbed most of the blow but she remained tightly held as the guard fought to free his mask from her hands.

She was lying face down, head downward on the steps and her blood was rushing to her brain. She held the mask and her Jensen under her and was kicking backward to force the guard away. Suddenly, she felt the man's full weight upon her. She wriggled out from underneath him. He was dead, his face a melted mess, and Smitz was standing over him.

They continued to the bottom of the steps, where Speidel and Atoi had their backs to a corner wall. They were at the corridor that led to the locker room and the Sherrerr child.

Speidel lifted his weapon. Carina, Atoi, and Smitz nodded, then all four ran simultaneously around the corner, laying down suppressive fire as they went. Two Dirksen guards were in the corridor. The mercs' pulses focused on the first, penetrating his armor. He fell. The second guard fired at Smitz and hit him, the shot sent the man spasming to the floor. Speidel, Carina, and Atoi turned their weapons on the remaining guard and killed him.

Speidel lifted Smitz's visor. He was dead.

His voice strained, Speidel said, indicating a door, "The kid's in there."

They burst through, expecting to meet more resistance, but the room was empty save for the Sherrerr child. A sound from the corridor drew Speidel and Atoi outside again, leaving Carina alone with the boy.

Twelve

The child was smaller than Carina had expected, or maybe it was only that he was hunched in the corner of the room, his head bowed and turned to the wall. He was visibly shaking, plainly terrified.

Carina realized she was still holding her weapon ready. She slung the Jensen over her shoulder and went over to the kid. He shrank against the wall and squealed at her approach.

"It's okay," she said. "I'm here to rescue you."

The boy didn't seem to hear. He pressed himself harder into the wall and moaned in terror. He was wearing a child-size CO_2 filter mask. She suddenly realized how scary she had to look to him, suited up in armor and with a tinted visor covering her face.

She put down her gun and unsnapped the locks on her helmet. Lifting it off, she squatted down a short distance from the boy and held out a hand. "Don't be scared. We're here to take you home."

This time her words seemed to penetrate. The boy peeked at her from underneath an arm, and for the first time Carina saw the child's large, deep brown-black eyes.

"Carina," Speidel said, bursting in again, "what are you doing?"

The captain's abrupt appearance undid all of Carina's work at calming the boy down. He flinched and turned away again, sobbing and moaning.

"Grab him," Speidel said. "We have to get out of here."

"Okay, I'm coming." She put on her helmet and picked up her gun. She also scooped up the child, who wriggled and fought and bit her armor. With horror, she saw the cause of his terror. The boy's fingernails and toenails had been ripped off. The Dirksens had been torturing him.

Holding the struggling child firmly over her shoulder, she ran down the corridor, following Speidel's echoing footsteps. In her other hand she held her Jensen, muzzle up. The hiss of pulse rounds came from up ahead. Speidel and Atoi were in a firefight.

She brought down the smelting plant's blueprint on her helmet overlay and searched for another escape route. She didn't want to abandon Speidel, but taking the unprotected child near weapons fire would be insane. The blueprint was complex and she had no time to figure it out. Spying what appeared to be a different route to the roof, she turned down a narrow corridor on her left. She followed the next turning too and the next, going deeper into the complex.

The boy seemed to have gotten the idea that she was trying to help him. He'd ceased struggling and hung like a limp rag over her shoulder. He was small for his age and Carina hardly felt his weight as she ran.

She turned another corner and abruptly stopped. She was at a dead end.

"What the...?" She checked her visor overlay. She was sure she'd seen another corridor leading from the one they were in. Her heart sank when she saw that what she'd mistaken for a corridor was an air duct. Spinning around, she saw the access point: a square wire grid in the wall, behind which a fan whirred.

The sounds of battle were drawing nearer.

"Carina," Speidel said through her helmet comm. "Where'd you go? We have to leave. Stevenson heard from the *Duchess* that Dirksen ships are on their way."

"I'm making my way to the shuttle," she said. "I didn't want to take the kid within range of fire. Give me two minutes."

"You've got it," Speidel said. "Don't keep us waiting."

"I won't," Carina replied, wondering desperately how she was going to make her way to the roof in time.

Her gaze returned to the wire grid. She could melt it and the fan behind it with a pulse from her Jensen, but that would leave the metal too hot to touch, and the kid had nothing to protect him.

She put the child down and pulled her knife from its sheath. At the sight of it, the boy took a breath as if to scream. She clamped her hand over his mouth. "For the last time, kid. I'm not gonna hurt you. I'm here to take you back to your family. Now can you be quiet?"

The boy swallowed and nodded. She removed her hand and went to the grid. She pushed the knife blade behind it and prized the cover away from the wall. The fan was only slotted in place. She lifted it out and peered into the dark tunnel. The boy could fit in, but it looked impossibly small for her. She had no choice. She had to try to squeeze inside.

Hastily, she began to unclip her armor. "Get in the tunnel," she said as she worked. The boy looked from the dark opening to her. He shook his head.

"Get in," she repeated. "It's the only way. If we can make it up to the roof, we have a ship waiting for us, but they're leaving soon."

The boy still didn't move.

"Come on," she said. "Please."

He hesitated but then finally padded on his wounded feet over to the square, black hole. With a final look at her, as if checking she wasn't tricking him, he climbed inside. She had nearly removed all her armor. She unclipped the legs and stepped out of them. Crouching down to enter the shaft, she rued the fact that she had no way of reattaching the wire grid once she was inside, nor of making her pile of discarded armor disappear. Where they had gone would be glaringly obvious to anyone trying to find them, but it couldn't be helped.

She picked up her helmet and put it on. The internal gel that molded around the back of her head would hold it in place, and she needed it for light in the tunnel and comm with Speidel.

The soles of the kid's bare, dirty feet were all she could see of him. He was moving fast. Was he trying to get away from her?

"Hey," she called. "Wait up."

The feet paused. She was relieved. The kid seemed to trust her after all. His resilience impressed her. He'd been taken from his family, kept hostage, and tortured—tortured! What kind of sick fuck would torture a six year old? And why? Did they think a little kid had secrets worth telling? Or had they done it for kicks?

She blinked the blueprint into view again, overlaid on the inside of her visor. "Helmet," she said, "shortest route to the roof." A red line threaded through the mass of green ones. An arrow pointed at the next turn. "Go left," she called.

A flashing clock on the helmet display made her heart sink. Estimated time to destination: 10m 23s.

"Shit," she breathed. She stopped crawling. "Hold up," she called to the kid. Going faster wasn't going to help. She needed to think.

Somehow, the boy had managed to turn around in the narrow tunnel. His dirty, tear-streaked face, topped with shaggy hair came toward her. He hadn't yet said a word to her, she realized. He was probably too traumatized.

She was on her front, facing him. She knew there was only one way out of the situation for both of them, but still she balked at it. If the kid blabbed, she would be at extreme risk. But if she didn't do what she had to, she would be captured and killed by the Dirksens, and the boy would have lost his only possible chance of escape.

She debated trying to explain away what was about to happen, but decided to just do it. Later, she would figure out how to deal with whatever interpretation the kid made of it.

She reached into her shirt and brought out the elixir canister, which had been painfully squeezed between her and the metal floor of the tunnel. The boy's eyes grew round.

"Just wait a minute," Carina said. "I need to take a sip of this."

She swallowed a mouthful of elixir. "Hold my hand," she said. "You're coming with me."

Thirteen

Carina appeared in a corner of the roof at just the point she'd aimed at according to the blueprint. She was relieved to find that the boy, his eyes wider than ever, was still holding her hand tightly. The shuttle was there, and Speidel was pacing impatiently in front of it.

"Quick," Carina whispered, "come on."

She ran out a little way onto the roof. "We're here, sir."

Speidel turned. "Where have you been? And where's your armor? Never mind. Get aboard the shuttle."

He cried out and collapsed to his knees before falling forward on his face. A guard had emerged from a doorway behind him as he was speaking and shot him in the back. Carina leveled her Jensen at the guard and fired off a round that hit the man's visor. The plexiglas darkened and sagged from the blast, and the guard dropped his weapon, yelling with pain.

"Go up the ramp," Carina told the boy, who was frozen, staring at the guard who was clawing at his melted visor. She gave the child a push, and his trance broke. He ran aboard the shuttle. Carina tried to haul Speidel up, but his body was heavy and entirely limp. Turning him on his back, she opened his visor. The captain's face was still and peaceful. Her heart stopped.

Sounds blurred and her vision swam. Time seemed to slow down. He couldn't be dead. Carina blinked away hot tears that were dropping onto her visor and scanned the older man's face for any sign of life, but there were none.

"Lin, get aboard." It was Stevenson, the shuttle pilot. His words pulled her out of her frozen state. In the corner of her vision, she saw movement. More Dirksen guards were arriving.

With a terrible wrench, she let go of Speidel's body and ran up the shuttle ramp. As she reached the top, agony exploded behind her knee. Her legs collapsed. She'd been shot.

The ramp closed, and pain tore through her. Without her armor's pain-suppressing injector system, she felt the full effects of her wound. She lay on her back, trying not to scream. All she could see were the ceiling lights and the concerned face of the Sherrerr boy hanging over her.

What seemed an age later, Atoi appeared, staggering in the shuttle's rocky flight. She pressed an anesthetic gun to the inside of Carina's wrist, and the cool feeling of relief flooded through her. The drug made her groggy and confused too. She said to Atoi, "Where's the captain? We forgot him. We left him behind. I have to go and get him."

Atoi placed a gentle hand on her stomach. "Stay right where you are, soldier. An auto-gurney's waiting for you."

Carina's head flopped to one side. "Where's the kid?"

"He's right here," Atoi replied.

The child was sitting on his haunches against the bulkhead, watching her. He had an inscrutable look on his face. She wondered vaguely what he was thinking. What had he made of their impossible transference from the cramped tunnel to the rooftop? He was only six. Hopefully, his young mind would find a way of explaining it away.

A low hum signaled the arrival of the auto-gurney. They seemed to have made it back to the *Duchess,* though to Carina only moments had passed. Atoi stepped out of the way as the device lowered to the ground and secured her neck and spine before lifting her onto its base. The hum started up again as the vehicle moved away.

She could see only the corridor ceiling as she was carried along.

"Hey, kid," she heard Atoi call. "Come back here."

"I want to go with her," the boy protested. They were the first words Carina had heard him speak. The pain relief was clouding her senses, and she didn't hear if Atoi relented and let the Sherrerr boy accompany her.

The next thing she knew, she lying on a soft medroom bed surrounded by curtains.

She tried to sit up, but her right leg was restrained somehow. Her memory of the mission came flooding back, along with the knowledge of Speidel's death.

She lay down and wept, her tears running down the sides of her face and into her hair. After a long while, she lifted her head and looked down her body.

A cylinder of transparent plastic encased the middle section of her leg. Restorative gel filled the plastic, working on the wound she'd received. Her nerves in that part of her body were numb.

On the edge of her vision, she noticed the Sherrerr boy sitting down nearby. He came closer when he saw her notice him, and a pair of large, brown-black eyes stared into hers. The kid had been cleaned up and his hair was a little less shaggy.

"I saw what you did," the boy said.

Carina's chest tightened. Through a gap in the curtains, she could see the doc on the other side of the room. He didn't seem to have heard the child.

She tried to signal the boy with her eyes and lifted a finger to her lips. To her great relief, he seemed to understand the need for secrecy. He nodded solemnly and moved his chair until it was right next to her bed. He watched her face.

"We should have you back with your family soon," Carina said.

The doctor heard this. "Carina, you're awake? How are you feeling?" he asked, parting the curtains. He bent over her leg to look at it closely through the transparent gel. "Should have you back to normal in ten hours or so, and no scarring. This latest gel we picked up is very good. Stimulates your own stem cells to replace the damaged tissue. Your new skin will be as soft as a baby's bottom."

"And your little friend is still here," he went on. "I thought I told you to stay in bed," he said to the boy. "Plenty of vidgames on the system to keep you occupied."

The child lifted his hand and placed it gently atop Carina's. The hand was encased in a glove of healing gel.

"I want to stay here," he said.

The doctor grimaced as Carina lifted her gaze from the kid's torture wounds toward him. He looked as though he wanted to say more but was refraining due to the child's presence.

"I don't suppose it will hurt for you to remain with your rescuer for a little while. But if you feel odd or dizzy, it's straight back to bed with you, and you must let me know. Do you understand?"

"Yes, sir."

The doctor smiled. "You can call me Harvey, son." He addressed Carina. "Keep an eye on him for me, will you? I need to report to Tarsalan on how you're all doing."

"Is she up and around now?" Carina asked. "Has she recovered?"

"She hasn't fully recovered, no, but that didn't stop her from getting up and telling the Sherrerrs of your success the moment she heard about it. We're on our way to one of the planets they control right now."

"What's happening with the Black Dogs?" Carina asked. "Did she say anything about that?"

"You've been through a lot, Lin. Just take it easy for now, okay? I'll be back in an hour or so." He left, pulling her bed curtains closed.

"What's your name, kid?" Carina asked, realizing he'd only ever been referred to as the victim, the target, or the Sherrerr child.

"Darius," the boy replied. He leaned forward. "I saw what you did," he repeated.

The familiar, horrible clenching in Carina's chest returned. The boy's words also reminded her of something else she needed to be concerned about. She craned her neck to scan around for her belongings. Her clothes had been folded in a pile on the shelf next to her bed, and the metal elixir canister was on the top of the pile. A little relieved, she sunk back into her pillows.

She had to divert the child's mind to another subject. "How are you feeling?" she asked.

"I'm okay now." Darius's gaze shifted to his injured hands, and the shadow of a painful memory crossed his features. "Thank you for rescuing me."

"You don't have to thank me. I was only doing my job. Your family paid us to bring you back."

The boy's expression turned sad, and Carina realized her words sounded harsher than she'd intended, as if she didn't care whether they'd succeeded in their mission. "But I'm glad we found you and got you out of there."

Darius's expression brightened. "When we were stuck in the tunnel, I was scared. I didn't know how we were going to get out. I thought we would die in there. But I didn't mind too much, just so long as I was away from the people who were hurting me."

"But we did get out, right?" said Carina. "And now you're safe. So don't think about that anymore."

There was no stopping the child, however. "You took out your bottle, and you had a drink, and I wanted some because I was so thirsty, but I was too shy to ask."

He seemed hell-bent on going over how they'd ended up at the shuttle. Carina resigned herself to the fact and was grateful nobody else was around to hear him.

"Then you told me to hold your hand, and you closed your eyes," Darius continued, "and the next thing I knew, we were on the roof next to the starship, and I didn't remember how we got there."

"It doesn't matter how we got there, does it?" Carina asked. "We got where we needed to go. All that matters is that you're safe now."

"I guess so." The boy looked doubtful.

"So let's not talk about it anymore," Carina suggested. "It's only going to confuse people. You probably fell asleep while I carried you up to the roof, only you don't remember."

Darius's brow furrowed. "No, I didn't fall asleep. I know how we got there. You cast."

Fourteen

Carina almost—but not quite—swallowed the gasp that rose from her throat. The shrewd look on the little boy's face as he watched her reaction told her she had severely underestimated him.

Though she felt guilty at lying to someone so young, she made another effort to maintain her subterfuge. "What do you mean? We went up to the roof together. Don't you remember going through the vent tunnels?"

The boy giggled. "It's okay. You don't have to pretend with me. I know it's a secret. I won't tell anyone. I promise."

Carina was so deeply conflicted that, for a moment, she was lost for words. Her grandmother's warnings sounded in her mind as strong as ever. She felt an almost physical revulsion at the idea that the boy knew her secret, not least because the only person she'd ever revealed herself to was now dead.

Yet the temptation to speak freely again to another human being about her mage ability was strong. Telling Speidel had been a sweet release after her years of isolation and loneliness.

Adding to her emotional turmoil was a burning curiosity. How did this kid know about casting? Nai Nai had told her that her family were scattered across the galaxy. Could it be possible this child knew one of her long-lost kin?

She was reclining on pillows, but now she pulled herself upright. "Would you please open the curtains?" she asked the child.

He dutifully hopped down from his seat but then realized he couldn't do as she directed. He held up his thick-gloved hands.

"I'm sorry," Carina said. "You sit down. I'll do it."

She got out of bed and, hopping on one leg, she pulled back her bed curtains to the wall, checking the room was entirely empty and the door was closed.

She returned to her bed, settled herself once more, and looked into the child's eyes.

"Darius, please tell me what you meant by what you said. How do you think we got to the roof?"

The little boy rolled his eyes. "I already told you. You cast. You drank some elixir, and you closed your eyes, and I guess you thought of the right picture, because after you told me to hold your hand, we went to the roof together. I know that's what happened because I've done it before. I wished so many times I could do that when the bad people were hurting me. Only I didn't have any elixir."

The boy's chin trembled and his eyes swam with tears. Carina reached out and laid her hand on his shoulder.

"You can cast too?" she asked.

Darius nodded, teardrops running down his cheeks. Then suddenly he stopped crying and turned pale. "You aren't going to hurt me, are you? Mother told me I mustn't ever tell anyone what we can do. But you rescued me, and you seem so nice. I thought it would be okay to tell you because you're a mage too, so you know the secret already. You *are* going to take me back to Mother, right? You aren't going to keep me and do bad things to me like the other people did, are you?"

"No one's going to hurt you, Darius," Carina said, "and yes, we are going to take you home. But you and I have to keep this secret between us. Do you understand? You can't tell anyone else what we can do or say anything about casting except when we're alone. Nothing at all. You were very strong and brave to not give any secrets away to the people who hurt you. Can you keep quiet for a little longer? It's very important."

"Sure I can." Darius smiled. "I get it. No one else here knows you're a mage. I can keep your secret as well as mine."

Smart kid. "Thank you." Carina squeezed the boy's shoulder.

Her head was swimming with the implications of what the child had said. She had many questions for him but she didn't know where to start.

"Darius, is everyone in your family a mage?"

"Mother can cast, and Parthenia, Oriana, and Ferne. Castiel and Nahla can't, though, and they hate it," he added, somewhat gleefully.

"Are these people your brothers and sisters?"

"Yep."

"You have five? That's quite a lot. And are you the youngest?"

Darius nodded. He didn't look too happy about his position in the family hierarchy.

"How about your father?" Carina asked. "Can he cast too?"

At the mention of his father, the little boy's face clouded over. "No, he can't." His lips thinned to a line and he looked angry. Since his father was clearly a sore subject, Carina decided not to continue on that line of questioning. Something else was puzzling her anyway.

"Do you remember how you were kidnapped?" She was wondering how it was that, if Darius had mages in his family, the Dirksens had succeeded in capturing him.

The little boy's face clouded further and his cheeks flushed. His eyes filled with tears again. "It was my fault. I was naughty. Mother told me I must *never leave the garden.*" His voice became singsong as he mimicked his mother and wagged a finger at an imaginary Darius. Carina bit back a smile at the adorable imitation.

"She told me that bad people would take me, and she wouldn't be able to get me back because she couldn't give away our secret. But I so wanted to know what was outside. I wanted to see the city and all the different people, and no one would let me go with them. I made a hole in the garden wall and I went out. I was stupid. Outside, everything was boring. There was hardly anyone around, and no trees or flowers or anything like that. I walked away from the house. I was trying to find the city. Not long after, bad people found me. They took me away just like Mother said they would." His head hung low.

"Darius, it's okay," said Carina. "It isn't your fault. Everyone does stupid things every once in a while. You're very little. What happened is the fault of the people who kidnapped you. Besides, we're taking you home now, and you'll see your mother and all your brothers and sisters again. Aren't you glad?"

The child's easy smile quickly returned. "I'm very glad! I can't wait to see them! Except Castiel. I'm not happy that I'll see him. He always teases me. Or...maybe I'm a little bit happy that I'll see him." He finished in a rush, his eyes shining.

Carina was deeply interested in finding out more about the mage members of the Sherrerr family. It sounded like the boy's mother had married a non-mage and had passed on her ability to only some of her children. She wanted to know if there were any more mages among the Sherrerrs, and if they were part of the ancient family or newcomers, but she also wanted to distract Darius from the whole subject.

Now he knew he was safe, the boy's resolve to keep the family secret had obviously weakened. He'd already brought it up with her, only afterward thinking of the possible consequences. She needed to divert his young mind to other things.

She asked Darius to tell her about his home, and a wellspring of information gushed forth from the child's lips. He told her about his bedroom—he had his own and so did all his brothers and sisters—from which he could see the city. He said he hadn't realized how far it was. He also told her about the garden that surrounded the house, which was full of trees as tall as the roof, and lawns where he and his siblings played, and fountains and pools where they cooled down when they were too hot.

The children all had pets they could ride and that would fetch things for them. He described the animals, but Carina didn't recognize any. The pets would climb trees to bring the children fruit when it was ripe. Each child also had his or her own private tutor, who would teach them mathematics, reading, family history, leadership, charm, oration, deportment, and other subjects they would need to run Sherrerr businesses when they grew up. Only Mother taught them to cast, the boy said.

Carina steered him away from the subject of mages again with more questions about his lessons, though the boy clearly thought that was the least interesting aspect of his home life. She noted the comment about casting tuition being left to his mother, however, and filed it away for later reflection.

Darius was in the middle of a delightful impression of his tutor lecturing him about dignity when the doctor returned. "You two aren't still talking? And why are your bed curtains open, Lin? Back to bed with you, young man. That's plenty of chatting for today. The more rest you get, the quicker that gel will work. Come on, off you go." He shooed the little boy back to his own bed.

The child went happily, and Carina also felt better for their conversation. It had lightened the dark shadow that Speidel's death had thrown over her heart.

Whether or not Tarsalan had changed her mind about disbanding the Black Dogs now they'd fulfilled the assignment, Carina's time with them was over. She knew she wouldn't be able to remain where her memories of the older man were so strong.

Before, she'd had no idea what she could do or where she would go, but Darius's revelation had opened possibilities she could never have imagined.

FIFTEEN

Carina's heart beat fast as, holding Darius's hand, she walked with him from the city toward the Sherrerr estate. Behind them, Tarsalan waited and watched in the shade of a tree at the city outskirts. The Sherrerrs had insisted on a simple handover, much to Tarsalan's apparent chagrin, judging from the bitter tone she used when she informed Carina. Perhaps she'd hoped for a chance to meet members of the powerful clan—an 'in' to the exclusive Sherrerr world.

If an introduction wasn't on the cards, the Black Dogs' owner wasn't going to put herself in any danger by performing the handover. She'd noted the boy's attachment to Carina, however, and had ordered her to accompany him.

Despite the risk that the Dirksens might launch another attempt to capture the child, Carina wouldn't have had it any other way. This was her chance of a glimpse of Darius's mother, who might be able to tell her much about their mage clan. Carina also clung to a sliver of hope that the woman would be interested in meeting her too, once she heard what Darius had to say.

The Sherrerrs had told Tarsalan they would be watching while Carina brought the boy to them. Did they fear a trick? Carina didn't know. She was only uncomfortably aware of distant eyes on them as they went along. She also felt vulnerable out of her armor and with her face uncovered, as the Sherrerrs had requested. But it couldn't be helped.

They were nearly halfway down the dusty, empty road that led to the vast Sherrerr mansion, having walked around eight hundred meters, when Carina glanced down at Darius and remembered the child's feet were bare. His toes had healed up, though his toenails hadn't yet regrown, but the *Duchess* carried no child-sized shoes and Tarsalan had clearly been so eager to return the child she'd been in too much of a rush to do anything about it.

"Don't your feet hurt?" she asked him.

"Only a little."

"Let me see."

She squatted down to look at the soles of Darius's feet. Sure enough, as she'd suspected they were red and blistering. He wasn't a child accustomed to going barefoot.

"Darius," she said, "why didn't you say you were in pain?"

"It doesn't hurt much, and we only have a little way to go now."

She tutted. "Hop onto my back." She turned away from the boy and as he climbed onto her, she tucked his legs under her arms. The strange, misshapen shadow of the two of them stretched out long. It was nearing sunset, and the insect life in that region had started up its twilight song. Razor-backed beetles the size of small cats crawled out of holes and rubbed their legs along their serrated backs. Carina watched them with interest. She'd always had a thing for bugs.

Feeling the boy's body tense at the sight of one of the beetles flying across their path, she reassured him. "Don't worry. They won't hurt you." At least, she was pretty sure they wouldn't. A local had told her they were harmless.

The tall, wide, metallic gates of the Sherrerr estate drew nearer. She adjusted the child's weight on her back. She felt no strain carrying him but the movement eased her nerves a little. She scanned the high, blank wall, which glowed yellow in the rays of the setting sun. It was smooth and solid, unmarked by windows or patrolling guards along the top.

Darius wriggled. "Can you go faster, Carina? We're nearly there. I bet Mother is waiting for me at the gatehouse."

"I'm sorry. They told us I had to walk slowly. But it won't be long now."

They had only another couple hundred meters or so to go. Carina turned and looked back to where Tarsalan waited under the tree. The woman was barely visible in its shadow, but she hadn't left. She would wait until she saw the handover take place, she'd said, before returning to the ship. She wouldn't hang around for Carina, who had left the *Duchess* for the last time, having said all her goodbyes.

Parting from Stevenson had been particularly hard, and she had the impression he felt the same, but it couldn't be helped. Her life lay in another direction now, no matter what happened when she returned the Sherrerrs' child.

A clanking sound came from the gate, piercing the insect drone that surrounded them. They were less than a hundred meters from their destination. A small door at the base of the gate opened, and an armed guard came out.

"Stop," he called. "Wait there."

Carina did as he asked. The guard's armor was entirely black, as was his visor. She couldn't make out the man's face at all as he approached. She felt Darius stiffen.

When the Sherrerr guard was twenty meters away he said, "Put the boy down."

She squatted down, expecting Darius to slide off her back, but he didn't. He clung tighter. "You have to get down, Darius. This man's going to take you home."

The boy buried his face in the back of her neck. Reaching awkwardly around, she gently extracted him from her back and set him on his feet. His head was down and he crossed his arms defiantly.

"What's wrong?" Carina asked. "Don't you want to see your family again?"

He nodded but didn't raise his head. The guard had reached them, and Darius turned away from him, presenting the man with his hunched over back.

"Come with me, Darius," the guard said, holding out a black-gloved hand.

The boy made a grunt of refusal.

The guard sighed with exasperation. "Give me your hand, Master. You must come with me."

Darius repeated his grunt, adding, "I want Carina to come too. She's a—"

"I can't come with you," Carina interrupted before the dreaded word could leave the boy's lips. "That wasn't in the instructions, remember?"

The guard's blank visor turned in her direction, and she could feel the man's curious gaze burning into her.

"Please?" Darius asked, lifting his head, his eyes pleading.

"I'm sorry, I can't. But do you remember what we talked about?"

"Oh yes! I forgot." The returned memory lit up the boy's eyes. "Okay, I'll come with you," he said to the guard. Still refusing to take the man's hand, Darius skipped off, heading for home. The guard quickly followed him.

Carina stood and watched Darius the whole way. When he reached the small door, he turned around and gave her a wave. She waved back, smiling at the young boy's happy face. Then the door closed and he was gone.

She looked toward the spot where Tarsalan was waiting and just made out the figure of the woman leaving.

Hugging herself, Carina began what she feared might be a long wait. She went to the side of the road and sat down next to a small boulder. She didn't know how long it would take for Darius to tell his mother about her. She'd made him promise to wait until they were alone together, and that could take a while. The Sherrerrs would probably want to have the boy medically assessed after the joyful reunion, and who knew what else.

She passed the time watching the large bugs sing their song and perform their mating dance. She'd been to many worlds in the two years she'd spent as a merc and seen many strange sights. The giant beetles were another to add to her list. She relaxed against the boulder and watched the night's first stars appear.

So many suns, so many planets, she mused. *Life in so many varieties, sapient and non-sapient, vicious and peaceful and everything in between.* In her eighteen years, she'd seen both so much and so little of the galaxy. *Was one of those stars the sun that shone on the home planet of her clan?* Maybe one day she would find it and mages could return from their exile and live together again without fear.

The temperature was dropping fast now the sun had set. She shivered and rubbed her upper arms. The wall to the Sherrerr estate was dark gray, unlit by any external lights. From within the compound arose a glow that had to come from lights within the gardens Darius had mentioned. She imagined the lush grounds, with their trees, shrubs, flowers, and fountains, and the little boy playing happily within them, safely home again.

Darius, have you spoken to your mother yet? Have you told her about me?

The night wore on, and Carina grew colder. The beetles retired to their underground burrows, and silence fell except for the occasional animal noises in the darkness. In the city, movement in the streets diminished. She began to think about where she might sleep that night. She had held a faint hope that it might be within the Sherrerr mansion, though that was looking increasingly unlikely.

The garden lights went out. She was tired and stiff with cold, and her dreams of companionship with other mages were rapidly fading. It was so dark, she could barely see the road. The Sherrerr estate walls had become black and forbidding.

It was time to leave.

She stood and stretched her aching muscles. Finding the road by feeling with her feet as much as by sight, she began her return to the city. She had her wages from Tarsalan—any bonus for rescuing Darius noticeably absent. She should be able to find a hostel that was still open, and a hot dinner. And then... she would think about that tomorrow.

It was at that moment she missed Speidel the most. What wouldn't she have given for a word of advice from the older man?

The clank of the Sherrerr gate door opening sounded behind her. She paused and turned, her defeated heart lifting in hope. Through the gloom, she spotted a guard walking over. Was it the same one who had escorted Darius inside? She couldn't tell.

"You," said the guard. "What's your name?"

"Carina Lin."

"Here, this is for you."

He held out a pouch about the size of a large man's fist. She took it and pulled it open, but in the darkness she couldn't see what was inside.

The guard had already turned to leave.

"Excuse me," Carina said. "Do you have a light I can borrow?"

The man hesitated.

"Please?"

His black visor remained enigmatic, but the guard pulled a small flashlight from his belt, turned it on, and handed it to her.

She shone the light into the pouch. A handful of glinting gems were the first items she recognized. They looked valuable. She drew in a breath. The objects that had made her gasp were less impressive than the gems: a tiny transparent box of metal filings, a vial of water, a small container of dust, a tiny firestone, and a bundle of wood splinters tied with a thread: the base ingredients of elixir. Meaningless to an outsider, they were a sign that whoever had sent the pouch knew what she was.

The guard was shifting impatiently. She went to hand his flashlight back when its beam caught another item. This one made her knees go weak. It was a simple, almost valueless object, meaningless to an outsider, but to Carina, it meant everything. It was a pebble, polished to a fine shine to bring out its beautiful colors. It was exactly the kind of pebble her grandmother used to sell for a living.

She drew the strings on the pouch to close it and returned the flashlight to the guard. "Was there any message?" she asked.

"No. No message. I'd get into town if I were you or you'll be sleeping on the street tonight."

He marched away, leaving her alone in the darkness.

She took a final look at the Sherrerr estate. Somewhere inside was a mage who wished her well. Perhaps it was even someone who had known Nai Nai and understood her connection with the woman, but for some reason would not or could not talk to her.

For now, the Sherrerr fortress was impregnable and she couldn't see a way to change that, but in a way she didn't care. She was no longer alone.

Sixteen

Carina was too young to be so drunk. She stared morosely at the rough tabletop, blinking it into focus, drew her dagger from its sheath under her arm, and drove the tip into the wooden surface.

"Hey," shouted the barkeeper. Carina turned. He was watching her, but he took his objection no further. The tavern was a downmarket place, and the cut her knife had made only added to the many others that scored the ancient table. Nevertheless, she pulled the dagger out and returned it to its home. Her glass was half full of the strong local liquor and she didn't want to get thrown out before she'd drunk it.

Stabbing the table hadn't eased her frustration anyway. A few coins were all that remained of her wages after quitting her merc job three months previously. She needed another source of income, quickly. She was at a crossroads and whichever way she turned the road looked either unsavory or obscure.

Across the tavern, in a corner the dim lighting hardly penetrated, a pair of eyes met hers. It must have been the fifth or sixth time that evening. She had lost count as she'd downed more alcohol. They were dark eyes, belonging to a dark, slim, coltish figure.

She took another sip of the numbing alcohol and looked away. She had enough problems. A casual hookup would probably add to them, not solve them. A burst of laughter came from behind. She grimaced and ignored it. She'd already checked out the mercs who were responsible for the loud merriment.

Their behavior was dissuading her from signing up as a professional soldier again. If time had dimmed her memory of working with mercs, the bunch in the tavern was a great refresher. Scarred, loud-mouthed, and fond of throwing their weight around, the soldiers were almost exactly like her previous band, the Black Dogs. Only her impression of these wasn't softened by familiarity.

Could she really become a merc again? She didn't think so, but there didn't seem to be any alternative. Bile rose in her throat, and she didn't know if it was due to the liquor or her train of thought.

Her mind strayed to the pouch in her pocket and the angular edges of the objects inside that pressed into her thigh. Among the objects were precious gemstones. If she sold one, the proceeds would buy her another two or three months in this town, but to what end? If she hadn't seen any results from her efforts in all the weeks she'd been here, what advantage would more time give?

Her thoughts moved on to the other items in the pouch, and the familiar ache that crushed her returned. A small vial of plain water, a tiny bundle of wood splinters, tied up with thread, a thumb-sized box of metal filings, a minuscule firestone, and a container that held nothing but dry dirt. All inconsequential and worthless, yet when combined they created the base elixir that allowed mages to Cast.

The moment she had received the pouch was burned into her memory forever. After rescuing a kidnapped boy and returning him to his wealthy family, someone had sent her the pouch as a gift. It had been a thank you or a reward, but to her, the elixir ingredients meant so much more than the gems. They were a sign that the giver knew what she was, and that perhaps that person was a mage too.

For three months, she had clung to that hope.

Yet everything she'd done to try to enter the family's mansion or meet the sender of her gifts had failed. They were Sherrerrs: members of the clan that controlled that region of the galactic sector, which meant they were powerful, aloof, and unapproachable. Yet somewhere behind the tall imposing walls enclosing the estate dwelt someone who either knew the closely guarded secret of mages or was a mage and a member of the long-lost, scattered clan to whom Carina also belonged.

What would she do if she were ever introduced to that person? What she would say? She'd never been able to decide. Just meeting someone like her would be enough. She had kept her ability secret most of her life to protect herself from harm, but keeping the secret had isolated her. Always being alone was hard.

The dark eyes flashed again. She blinked. How had she happened to be looking in that direction once more? In her drunken state, her gaze had roamed. Her glass had also somehow emptied another quarter.

She took another sip, though she was forcing the liquid down. Maybe she should quit while she could still hold onto the contents of her stomach. Finding her way back to her hostel would also be useful. She tried to stand but her legs wouldn't obey. Pushing the nearly empty glass away, she watched the marked tabletop as it shifted and swam in her vision.

The pockmarks and lines seemed to coalesce into a pattern. She squinted and tilted her head. The pattern was familiar. It was the Map. The one hundred stars surrounding the birthplace of mages and perhaps of humanity itself. If she could find that set of stars, she would be home. She shook her head. It was impossible.

Suddenly, she found she was resting her head on her arms. If she took a little nap, she might feel better in a while. Not more than a few moments after she closed her eyes, however, a hand grabbed her shoulder and shook her so roughly she almost fell off her stool.

The barkeeper's face loomed, close and ugly. "Where do you think you are? A hotel? If you're in no fit state to drink, you're not welcome here. Get out."

The man's words echoed around her skull. She didn't have the ability or the will to argue about it. He was right. She should go back to the hostel. If only her legs would do as they were told. She stood up, wobbling.

"Awww, don't be like that, chief," yelled a merc. "Let her stay. We'll look after her. She's with us. Isn't that right, sweetheart?"

She gave the noisy soldier a dirty look, causing his fellows to shout with laughter. She swallowed saliva that heralded an eruption from the grumbling volcano of her stomach and, concentrating on putting one foot in front of the other, made her way to the door. Her path took her past the mercs' table. One stood up to intercept her, his arms spread wide. "Let's have a cuddle, darling. You'll feel so much better." She side-stepped the man, but as she passed him, he leaned in and planted a sloppy kiss on her cheek. Though she was heavily inebriated, she reacted by reflex.

She punched the merc hard on the side of his head.

What happened next was hazy. She heard raucous guffaws. She was shoved to the floor and a heavy body landed on top of her. Then the body was gone and the barkeeper grabbed her upper arm. "Let me give you a hand," he said sarcastically and half-supported, half-dragged her to the front door of the establishment before pushing her out into the night. "Thanks for your custom. You're very welcome to return—when you're sober."

The door banged shut.

Much to her surprise, she found she was able to stand. Maybe it was the cool, dry night air reviving her. Outside the noisy tavern, her head spun less and her stomach quietened its protests. Perhaps she would be able to walk the short distance to her rented room.

She checked she still had her pouch and knife and that the barkeeper hadn't pick pocketed them when he threw her out. Their bulky shapes under her hands reassured her. She put one foot forward, and then another. Wobbling a little but keeping her balance well enough despite the motions of the ground and surrounding buildings, she went down the street. Tomorrow she would regret her over-indulgence, and she still had no idea what she should do next.

From behind her came the sound of the tavern door opening and an accompanying explosion of noise and laughter. The door closed and the sounds were muffled once more. Resting a hand on a wall to remain upright, she looked back. The long, lithe figure of the stranger who had sat in darkness was following her.

SEVENTEEN

Carina pushed herself away from the wall and continued on. Ordinarily, she had few problems defending herself but at that moment she wasn't feeling her best. She had no friends or family anywhere, let alone in that town, and there was no enforcement agency to call upon. If you weren't a friend of the Sherrerrs here, you were on your own. The only people who would give a damn about her if she died tonight would be the ones who had to remove her body tomorrow.

She put one hand on her dagger and rested the other above the pouch in her pocket. She would happily kill with the first item to protect the second. Hurrying her pace as well as she could, she walked on.

The footsteps of the stranger grew faster and nearer. "You," a voice called. "You with the black hair. Stop a moment."

You with the black hair? Considering the street was empty but for the two of them, the definition was overkill. Maybe her pursuer was as drunk as she was. That would be useful.

"Don't be afraid," the person continued. "I just want to talk to you."

Ha! That's what they call it on Ithiya, is it? She didn't slow her pace. Triggered by the threatening situation, a rush of adrenaline was running through her veins, sweeping away the numb alcoholic fog. She wasn't about to answer the stranger. Answering only gave encouragement.

"Hey, come on. Stop, won't you?" The footsteps were running, and before she could get away, the person had caught up to her. She gripped her dagger's handle in a fist and spun around as she drew it. Bringing up her other elbow under her pursuer's throat, she pushed him up against a wall and held the tip of her knife below his breastbone.

"Whoa," said the man, the quick pallor of his face noticeable even under the sparse streetlights. He held up his hands.

"What," she said between her teeth, "did you want to talk to me about?"

"I only..." He swallowed. "I only wanted to..."

They stood frozen in their positions, eyes locked.

"You aren't really going to kill me, are you?" the man asked.

She blinked and peered at his face. He was very young, probably her own age if not younger, and he looked genuinely frightened. Maybe he didn't have any ill intent.

"I didn't mean to startle you," he went on. "I called out to you. Didn't you hear me?"

"Of course I did. That doesn't mean I have to stop. Now, what do you want?"

"You know, I actually forgot. But if you put away the knife, I might remember."

She studied the youth's expression. Life had thrust her into many dangerous and harmful situations in her eighteen years, and she'd become a fairly good, quick judge of character. This person wasn't setting off any warning bells in her. She stepped back and sheathed her dagger. "Whatever it is, I'm not interested."

Released of her hold on his throat, the young man collapsed. She turned and left. The encounter had cleared her head even more. She was tired and despondent. All she wanted to do was go to her room and sleep.

Her pursuer, who she'd begun to think of as more like a hanger on, didn't give up. He ran to her side, his footsteps matching hers. "I remembered what it was I wanted to talk to you about."

She rolled her eyes and didn't deign to respond.

"But I need you to stop."

She marched on.

"Just for a second."

She sped up. She was nearly back at her hostel. She hoped this exasperating person would have the good manners to not follow her inside.

"Please."

She halted and spun around so they were nose to nose. "What the *hell* is it you want?"

"To be honest," the young man said, "I only wanted to check you were okay and to walk with you wherever you're going. I saw you had a little too much to drink, and after you punched that merc, I was worried he might come after you for revenge. But now I'm not sure you need any help."

Her anger dissolved. She broke her stare and stepped away. "No, I don't need your help. Now please leave me alone."

"And I wanted to ask you something," the man said quickly as she was walking away from him once more. "Could I stay with you tonight? I don't have anywhere to sleep."

As she was about to say no, he went on, "I did help you with that merc. I know it's a lot to ask, but I was hoping you might be willing to help me in return."

"What do you mean, you helped me?" In truth, she barely recalled anything of the encounter.

"After he shoved you, I punched him. He fell on top of you. Don't you remember?" The young man smiled ruefully. "I hurt my hand." He showed her his knuckles, which were grazed and reddened. "It turns out it hurts to punch people. Who knew?"

Guilty at her misreading of him and the entire situation, Carina said, "Look—"

"How old are you?" the man asked.

"Not that it's any of your business, but I'm eighteen."

"I didn't realize. You look older."

"Right. Er, thanks? Look, I'm really sorry, but..."

The youth nodded. "It's okay. I understand."

She continued walking. After hearing his story, she wanted to help him. She knew exactly what it was like to have nowhere to sleep, but she couldn't risk it. She couldn't risk sharing her life with others, even if only for a short time. No matter how desperate they were.

Carina sighed. She halted and turned around. The man was walking away slowly in the opposite direction. "Okay," she called out.

He didn't need any more of an invitation. Immediately, he came running up. "Thanks. I'll be gone in the morning, probably before you wake. I promise."

"Yeah," she said, "you will."

Unperturbed, he said, "I'm Bryce. What are you called?"

"No names."

"Whoa. Okay."

In a few minutes, they'd reached the hostel. It was dark and silent. She led him up the outside staircase to her door, unlocked it, and went inside. The room was as dismal and bare as it had been when she'd left it. Strangely, the man's presence made her feel her isolation more strongly. "This is it. You sleep on the floor."

"Sure," Bryce said, but he didn't move. He was watching her.

She also remained still, watching him.

He reached up and touched her upper arms. She raised an eyebrow, but she didn't protest. He leaned toward her, his face coming close. To her surprise, she found she did nothing to stop what was about to happen.

The kiss was soft and warm, and she didn't think she'd ever been kissed so well in all her life. When it stopped and Bryce drew back, a pregnant pause hung in the air.

"You sleep on the floor," she repeated.

"Sure."

She took a blanket off her bed and gave it to the young man, who spread it across the narrow space between the bed and the chest of drawers that sat below the room's only window. She pushed her pouch deep into her pocket and, tucking her dagger in its sheath under her pillow, she lay down.

"You really don't have anywhere else to sleep?" she asked as Bryce stretched out on the floor.

"No, I really don't."

"You can't get a job?"

"I've got a job. It doesn't pay enough for my needs."

"You can't get a better one?"

He sighed. "It's a long story, No Names. Maybe we should go to sleep."

Complicated, shrouded backgrounds were something she could understand. "Okay." She closed her eyes and tried to sleep, but her alcohol-induced languor had given way to alertness. The kiss had awakened something in her—a need for closeness. She felt a compulsion to share something with this stranger, even if it wasn't her bed. "I'll be going offplanet tomorrow, so this really is just one night."

"Where are you going?"

"I'm joining that merc band. I just decided."

"What?" He sat up on one elbow and gawped at her. "After what happened?"

"That guy was just fooling around. As soon as I put him in his place, he would have left me alone."

"What makes you so sure?"

"I was a merc myself for a couple of years. That's just what they're like. They'll push you, but if you fight back you'll earn their respect and they won't bother you."

"Mercs don't sound like the best people to have as workmates."

"They aren't, but, like you, I don't have a lot of choice."

"Well, it's your life. But if you want to join that band, you'll have to leave early in the morning. I heard them say they were shipping out tomorrow."

"Right. Thanks. Good night."

"Good night."

Now she'd made her decision, she felt calm. Putting it into words had strengthened her resolve. It was time to give up her efforts to connect with another mage and accept that of her few options in life, the best one open to her was returning to the military.

EIGHTEEN

It must have been around three in the morning when Bryce made his move. Carina wasn't sure how long he'd been awake. Perhaps he hadn't slept at all and had been searching her room for anything valuable, or waiting until she was deep in slumber. She only realized he was a thief when she felt his fingertips at her side.

Disappointment and frustration at her own stupidity were her first reactions. She wasn't afraid of what he might do. Her dagger was under her pillow and her fingers rested on its handle. It was how she'd slept for months. But she was bitter and disillusioned at his betrayal of her trust and she cursed herself for being so gullible.

Never again, she promised herself. She must learn to never trust others' better natures.

His fingers were slowly inching into her pocket, the one that held her pouch. He was taking his sweet time, understandably wary of waking her. The fact he'd chosen that pocket meant he knew something valuable was in there. He must have watched her push it in deep before she lay down. He'd been setting her up to steal from her right from the start. Maybe he'd even deliberately punched the merc who hassled her in the tavern, *if* he punched him at all.

She mentally cursed again. It served her right for drowning her sorrows.

She debated whether to kill him. It would be easy enough. She could yank out her knife and draw it across his throat in one move. It had to be only death or kick him out. If she wounded him he might fight back and things would get loud and messy. Then again, killing him would be messy too, and her landlady would charge her extra to clean up the blood.

Bryce's fingers worked their way steadily deeper.

Decisions, decisions.

The fingers hooked around the drawstring of the pouch and the bulky shape shifted. She also moved, as if she were about to wake up. Bryce froze.

He was stuck now, she realized with a modicum of pleasure. If he moved his fingers again, he might wake her up fully and be caught red-handed. But he had to move his fingers at some point because she would wake up eventually anyway.

After a minute or so, she tired of the game. She was still suffering the effects of her drinking and really wanted to sleep. "Yeah," she said, "I'm awake."

He snatched his hand away and jumped to his feet.

When she sat up and turned on the light, his face was a red beacon.

"How dumb are you?" she asked. "After I nearly killed you tonight, you pull a stunt like that? What's wrong with you?" She rubbed her eyes.

"I'm sorry," Bryce replied, hanging his head. "You were kind to let me stay. I guess I should leave."

"Yeah," she said, "I guess you should, and be happy you're leaving with your throat intact."

Avoiding her gaze, he opened the door and went out without another word. Though she regretted her poor decision-making, she couldn't help but feel a twinge of guilt as the door closed. It was the middle of the night, he apparently had nowhere to stay, and judging from the thrum of rain against the window, it was pouring outside.

She turned off the light, thumped her pillow into shape, and thrust her head into it as she lay down. She couldn't afford to care about others. Look where that had led just tonight. If she hadn't had her wits about her, she could be dead.

On the other hand, if Bryce had seen where she kept her valuables, he'd also known about the knife under her pillow. He could have gone for that first. If he'd been quick she wouldn't have stood a chance. He might have oh-so-gently slipped her knife from its sheath and inserted it in her back.

He hadn't, though.

She turned over and stared at the ceiling as the rain steadily pounded the window. She couldn't shake the young man from her mind. She wondered what was wrong with her. She hadn't done anything to feel guilty about, yet she did. Was it something to do with the fact that, despite what he'd done, Bryce seemed intrinsically good?

She sighed and sat up. It didn't look like sleep would be returning to her.

She would meditate, as her grandmother had taught her, to refresh and retain her powers. She crossed her legs and closed her eyes. First came the Elements: earth, air, fire, water, metal. Next came the Seasons....

Five minutes later, her eyes opened. She couldn't stop thinking about Bryce.

She climbed out of bed and walked to the window. A river of rain was running down the glass, obscuring her view, but she thought she could make out a figure standing in the scant shelter of a wall. Was it Bryce? She couldn't tell.

A small Cast was needed. She picked up her plain, battered metal canister from the table and swallowed a mouthful of the contents. She closed her eyes and wrote the character, Clear, in her mind. When she opened her eyes, a circle of glass was repelling the rain so it ran around the sides, leaving the center open and transparent.

She looked down into the street and confirmed the figure was Bryce, looking wet and forlorn. She debated telling him to come inside. She would have to remain awake but it seemed she wasn't going to sleep again tonight anyway. It wouldn't hurt to give the man shelter for a couple of hours.

Just as she was about to go down to tell him he could come back in, he pulled a metal box from his pocket and opened it. He pushed up his shirt sleeve, took a syringe from the box, and pressed the end of it against the inside of his elbow.

She changed her mind. Now everything made sense. There was no reason a fit, healthy young man couldn't find a job that would support him. He was an addict. *That* was why his job didn't pay enough to meet his "needs". It also explained why he'd been so desperate to steal from her that he'd risked his life.

She returned to her bed. She wouldn't invite an addict into her room. That would be madness. Who knew what lengths he might go to for a dose of whatever local drug was his habit?

This time, meditating came more easily to her. She mentally went through the steps. Elements, Seasons, Strokes, and finally the Map. The Map was the most complex item of all to remember, and she wondered if she sometimes got it wrong. Perhaps she always did. Since Nai Nai had died eight years ago, she had received no feedback on her efforts. She had nothing to check her memory against. Like all things to do with mages and Casting, no physical record of the Map existed.

Perhaps even Nai Nai's Map had been wrong. After all the millenia that mages had been lost, the Map could have changed as the memory was passed down the generations.

By the time she finished her meditation, the rain had stopped, and the sun was rising. Bryce had disappeared from his spot under the streetlight, probably wandering off in a drugged-up haze. She looked out over the town, thinking it was her final view of it.

Her gaze shifted to the side and alighted on the Sherrerr estate. Little Darius, the boy she had rescued, lived there and it was within those walls another mage also lived—the person who had sent her the pouch and its precious contents.

For three months, her attempts to enter the estate had been unsuccessful. The Sherrerrs never hired people without checkable backgrounds and the place had airtight security. No one from there except non-corruptible servants and guards ever came into town, though she had spotted shuttlecraft leaving from within the grounds.

She took out her pouch and spread its contents on the table. More tantalizing even than the elixir ingredients was a simple pebble, pretty and shiny but lacking the luster of the gemstones it lay beside. It was the most humble item of all, yet to her it meant the most.

Up until her death Carina's grandmother had made a meager living by polishing and selling beautiful stones they found in the wild lands around their slum settlement. Had the mage in the Sherrerr estate included the stone because that person had also known Nai Nai? And if that was so, why hadn't the mage come out to speak to her when she'd returned Darius, their child?

All the time she had been trying to meet the mage in the Sherrerr mansion, she'd nursed a secret hope that the person would seek her out. It wouldn't have been too difficult to track down a strange ex-merc in that town. The fact that the mage hadn't seemed to imply they didn't want to. Maybe they didn't think she was important.

Whatever the reason, it was time for her to move on. But after her broken night, tiredness was assaulting her. She needed more rest before she left the hostel. She went back to bed and fell asleep.

By the time she woke, queasy and her head aching, it was already midmorning.

NINETEEN

After handing her last few coins to the hostel owner, she swung her small bag of belongings over her shoulder and went out into the street. She squinted against the sun's eye-piercing, blue-white glare. The star's unusually intense light was something she had never quite gotten used to on Ithyia, and she looked forward to leaving it behind along with her hopeless quest.

Not too long ago, a dear friend and father figure had advised her to give up the soldiering life. He'd told her to get out before she developed the mercs' tough skin, which allowed them to kill impassively and then forget. Well, she'd tried to leave. She'd spent all her cash searching for another path in life, trying to connect with her own kind, and she hadn't gotten anywhere.

She set her jaw and turned in the direction of the spaceport. Bryce had said the merc band was shipping out this morning. With some luck, she would catch them before they left.

She began to jog, her bag bouncing on her back, annoyed at herself for going down to the very last of her currency before deciding to leave. If she had only a little cash or some local credit she could take an autocab, but all she had left were the gems. Exchanging them for money would take time she didn't have.

The route to the spaceport took her through the center of the backwater town. The street was already busy with shoppers. Eating establishments were putting tables out on the narrow sidewalks ready for lunch, forcing pedestrians to step into the street. The narrow electric autocars that were the most popular form of transportation swerved around the walkers and gave out their alarm jangles. Children ran recklessly between the vehicles, which went slowly and braked within a heartbeat. At each interruption to their journey, the cars' occupants would open their windows and rage at the kids.

She had become familiar with the businesses, shops, and services that crowded the main thoroughfare, and no doubt the owners had gotten used to seeing her. Small towns were like that, as she knew well from having grown up in one herself, though her home planet was an ass-end-of-the-galaxy place.

Ithyia, on the other hand, was at the center of a Sherrerr-controlled region of the galactic sector. A bustling capital city of millions was a two-hour shuttle flight away, though she had never been there.

Working as a merc, she'd visited many planets. Though climate, location, and population created differences, she found they held some things in common. Humans—and most non-humans, too—had essentially the same requirements: food, drink, clothes, gadgets, entertainment, items for decoration and ornament, and places where they could gather to socialize. Then came the specialisms of the area. In this town it was splicing. The place was apparently known for its splicers, and that was what drew most visitors.

The results of splicing treatments had given her some idle interest while she had tried to find a way to contact the mage on the Sherrerr estate. Splicing to fix a medical condition was heartening to see. Someone with a horrible disease could enter a splicing center one day and emerge the next week or month entirely cured.

Yet splicing for body modification was more interesting. The least adventurous went for changes in their skin, hair, and eye colors. Others let their imaginations run riot, resulting in what appeared almost impossible and possibly painful adaptations. In her time in the town, she had seen plenty of examples. Some customers emerged from a splicer's shop with scaly, hairless skin, slit pupils or bifurcated tongues of lizards. Others sprouted soft fur and had their fingernails modified to claws, while yet more had skins with the smooth, metallic sheen of star grubs.

Carina wondered if the splicers could also confer a star grub's ability to survive in deep space. The creatures were known to float for thousands of years on the mysterious dark matter streams from system to system. If the splicers really could engineer that ability, did the people with those modifications ever attempt an outsystem journey? She'd concluded that, yes, some people really were that crazy.

She was nearly at the spaceport. Passing one of the larger splicing establishments, she gave an involuntary shiver. As a mage, she had a visceral fear of the places. She could never risk having anyone analyze her genes. Whatever it was that gave her her abilities could be discovered, and no splicer would be able to resist the prospect of the riches that would follow if he or she could give others the same talent. Her cells would be priceless, and her freedom forfeit. Splicing presented risks she would never take. She would have to remain a plain human, which was in fact exactly how she liked to be.

A shuttle was taking off. She held up her hand to shield her eyes from the glow of its engines. It was late morning. She began to run faster. If Bryce had been correct about the merc band leaving today, she didn't want to miss them. There was no telling when another troop might arrive, and her other options for escaping the planet were few.

Five minutes later, she arrived. Only a handful of spacecraft stood in the bays and none of them looked like typical merc vessels. One was the domestic carrier that left twice a day for the capital city. Another was a luxury ship, sleek and spotless. There were also some single-seaters for system cruising. Then she spotted one shuttle that looked promising, but its hold doors were closing. It was about to take off.

She ran over to it. "Hey," she shouted to a figure inside. "Are you mercs?"

"What? No, we're on a cargo run. The mercs left this morning." The doors closed with a hiss of compressed gas and the thunk of metal bolts slotting into place.

She cursed and put down her bag. She was out of breath from running. As she panted, she also cursed Bryce. If she hadn't helped him out last night, she would have woken up early and probably caught the mercs' shuttle.

An alarm horn sounded. The cargo shuttle was about to take off. She walked from the field, wondering what she could do next. She rued the fact that she hadn't asked about work on the cargo ship while she had the chance. It might not have paid well, but she would have been offplanet, and maybe even outsystem. Now, she didn't know when her next opportunity might appear.

As she returned through the spaceport building, she took a detour to the booking offices, but inquiring there brought her no solution. Nothing was scheduled to arrive from outsystem for the next week. She would have to sell a gemstone to get the funds to eat and sleep while she waited for her passage.

On her way out of the booking office, she stopped. "When does the shuttle to the city leave?" Her chances of finding a working passage to deep space would greatly increase at the capital's spaceport.

"Fourteen fifty," the clerk replied.

"And how much is a ticket?" The clerk named a sum that made her wince, but she could raise it. She had time. "And are there seats available?"

The man smiled. "There are always seats available. The flight isn't cheap, and after the visitors spend their hard-earned creds on splicing, a lot of them opt to go home by road."

"Great. I'll be back soon." She went out and through the waiting area before returning to the street and the bright midday glare of the sun. A familiar figure was leaning against a wall. It was Bryce, apparently waiting for her. When he saw her, he came over, his expression hopeful. "Did you change your mind about leaving?"

"What are *you* doing here? Have you been following me?"

"I remembered you said you were going to join the mercs this morning. I was hoping—"

"Forget it." She pushed past him and marched away.

He trotted beside her. "Have the mercs already left?"

"Not that it's any of your business, but yes, they have. Thanks to you I overslept and missed them."

"Well your loss is my gain I guess. You need a job, right?"

"No, I don't. And even if I did, I wouldn't take one from you. Not after you tried to steal from me. Besides, I won't have anything to do with addicts."

"Addicts? What makes you think I'm an addict?"

She didn't bother to answer as she sped up her pace. She needed to find a jeweler who would give her cash for a gemstone. Then she would return to the spaceport to buy her passage out of town.

"I said," Bryce reiterated, "what makes you think I'm an addict? I've never been addicted to anything in my life."

Narrowing her eyes as she glanced at him half-walking, half-running beside her, she said, "You know, you have a really bad habit of not taking no as an answer."

He grinned. "Guilty. Now, why would you...?" His eyes widened. "Wait. Did you see me take a dose of medicine in the street last night and think it was drugs?" When she didn't answer, he went on, "I don't take drugs. I'm sick. I have to self-medicate to keep my condition under control. I would show you a syringe, only I don't have any left."

This last comment caused her to slow down. "What's wrong with you?"

"It's a blood disease. Don't worry, you can't catch it."

She paused, trying to decide if he was telling the truth. Her first impressions of Bryce had been that he wasn't a bad person. If he really was sick, it would confirm her instincts and go some way to explaining his behavior.

"You don't believe me, do you?" he asked.

She didn't reply. He went on, "I can show you." He turned and lifted up his shirt, exposing his bare back. It was covered in light purple bruises, yet they didn't look like the marks of a beating.

Suddenly, it all made sense. "You have Ithiyan Plague," she exclaimed.

Passersby, hearing her words and seeing Bryce's exposed back, hurried away with horrified backward glances.

He let his shirt fall and turned around once more, looking down. "That's what they call it, but it isn't a plague. Like I said, you can't catch it."

"My landlady would put a pill next to my breakfast every morning," she said, "and tell me to take it to ward off Ithiyan Plague. She said it was a disease endemic to the planet. Something to do with radiation. How come you caught it? Why didn't you take the preventative?"

His jaw muscle twitched and he still wouldn't meet her gaze. "Like I said last night, it's a long story."

"Can't the splicers fix it?"

"They can, only I can't afford to pay right now. I've been sick with it for a while, but the medicine to keep it under control is expensive. So expensive I haven't been able to save up the money for the permanent fix. I'm kind of caught in a trap. If I don't take the medicine, I'll die. But paying for the medicine means I can't save enough money to pay a splicer."

"So you turned to stealing," she said, "and hanging around in taverns, looking for likely victims."

He nodded. "I really wouldn't have hurt you—"

"You got that right."

"But I was getting desperate."

"Look, I'm sorry, but I don't have a lot of money myself. I'm just about to sell something so I can buy a ticket to the city."

"That's okay. I don't want your charity. But I could use your help, and you're looking for work, right? That's why you were going to the merc ship? I have a job offer that would pay for my treatment, but I need another person. You'll get half the payment of course. I need someone who's handy in a fight but doesn't look it. Someone like you."

She began walking again. She needed to cash in a gem if she was going to catch the afternoon shuttle. They crossed the street behind a multi-person autocar with tinted windows. It was a luxury vehicle bearing the Sherrerr insignia of three stylized blades. She looked back thoughtfully. The car must have come from the Sherrerr estate.

But she'd made her decision. She wasn't ever going to be able to approach any of the local Sherrerr clan.

Fifteen minutes ago, she had thought she was going offplanet. Five minutes ago, she'd been planning to travel to the capital. Now a third possibility had opened up. If Bryce's story were true, it wouldn't hurt to help him out. *If* his story were true. She guessed she could find out more. "What's the job?"

He grinned again. "It's simple. We just have to find out some information about a place way up in the mountains. It is a little risky, which is why I thought it would be good if you came along. The client especially wants two younger people so we won't look suspicious."

A recon job. She had done plenty of those. It shouldn't be hard, yet she wasn't particularly interested. If she didn't do it, Bryce could probably find someone else. It wasn't up to her to fix his problems. She was about to refuse when something made her ask, "What's the place?"

"A Sherrerr stronghold."

Twenty

aye Sherrerr delicately held her napkin to her nose and then waited until her husband momentarily glanced away before slipping it beneath the table. During another brief lapse in his attention on her, Faye risked a peek at the napkin. Two bright spots of blood were vivid in the snowy whiteness. She slid the napkin into her pocket.

She placed her eating utensils side by side on the plate. It was a signal to her husband she had finished eating and wanted to leave the table. She could never state her intention or even ask Stefan out loud. Requesting permission gave the impression he was in control of what she did, which was absolutely true. It was just that over the previous ten years or so, Stefan Sherrerr had liked to imagine otherwise.

Faye wondered what his warped inner view of their relationship was like. He seemed to nurse a vision of a loving, respectful, equal partnership. Yet that existed nowhere except in his head. Whenever she said or did something that contradicted his vision—like asking his permission to do something—it would anger him. Yet acting without his prior approval would send him into an absolute rage.

Finally, Stefan paused in his lecture to their children long enough to notice her plate. He gave a slight nod.

She said, "That was delicious, but I think I've had enough. I'll see you all in the garden later."

As soon as she'd left the room and was alone, she snatched the napkin from her pocket. She was just in time to catch the blood that threatened to drip from her nose again. She went quickly to a bathroom, locked the door, and held her head over the basin, removing the napkin. For around a minute, blood slowly dripped from her nose before it finally stopped.

She washed the red puddle away and cleaned up. Her reflection in the mirror was pale and tired, and she wondered how much longer it would be before Stefan noticed she was ill. A lot longer, she hoped. So long it would be too late for the local splicers to do anything about it and her husband would be forced to take her to a hospital in the capital, where it would be much easier for her and the children to escape.

Someone tried the handle and a knock sounded at the door. "Who is it?" she asked.

"It's me, mother," her six-year-old son, Darius, replied.

She unlocked the door. "I've finished. You can come in."

"I don't want to use the bathroom. I was looking for you. I want you to play with me in the garden."

Though the boy was getting a little big to be carried, she scooped him up. "I'm too old to play with you. What about Oriana or Ferne?"

Her son had been understandably clingy for the three months since he'd been kidnapped, but she wanted to encourage him to be less dependent on her. If her ruse didn't work, she might be leaving him sooner than she wanted.

Darius's little arms were wrapped around her neck and his face was buried in her shoulder. "I don't want to play with Oriana or Ferne or Nahla or Castiel or Parthenia. I want to play with *you*!"

"But I'm an old lady," Faye replied. "I can't play with you." She lowered her son to the floor. "My joints are stiff, my bones ache, and I can't see farther than the end of my nose."

Darius giggled. "Oh yes you can. You're looking at me right now."

"No, I can't. I'm only looking in the direction of your voice."

"Oh Mother, you're teasing. You can see me. I know you can. You can see me here." He ran a short distance down the hall. "And you can see me here." He ran to the end of the hall. "And you can see me here," he said, waving his arms.

"Darius," Faye exclaimed. "Where have you gone?" She lifted a hand over her eyes as if to look a great distance. "You've disappeared."

The little boy came running back, chuckling. "Here I am. If you really can't see farther than the end of your nose, I'll have to lead you to the garden." He grabbed her hand and pulled her.

Faye allowed her son to drag her down the hall to the stairs. On the way down, they met Stefan coming up. Instantly, Darius fell silent and looked downward. He dropped Faye's hand and held his own together in front of him.

Stefan tutted. "What's wrong with you, Darius? Don't let me stop your fun." When Darius didn't move, Stefan said to Faye, "This is your fault. You're poisoning the boy against me. Don't think I don't know it." He turned to his son. "Hold her hand as you were before." Darius didn't respond, and Stefan shouted, "Do it!"

Darius said, "Yes, Father," before softly taking Faye's fingertips in his own.

"Now," said Stefan. "Continue downstairs."

Both mother and son obeyed, and Stefan said, "That's it. Have fun." He stumped upstairs, muttering to himself.

As soon as Stefan was out of sight, Darius perked up. "Come on, Mother." He pulled harder on Faye's hand as he led her into the garden.

She marveled at the small child's ability to shrug off his father's domineering behavior. One of the few happinesses in her life was the fact that the children her monster of a husband had fathered upon her seemed relatively stable and healthy, despite one parent's harsh, cruel treatment of them.

The girls and boys had the afternoon free after completing all their lessons that morning. As always, most of them were playing in the garden. Only Parthenia, her eldest, seemed to be absent. Perhaps she was in her room. Faye hoped that Stefan was not forcing her to practice her Casting.

Over the years, she had tried to limit the skills she taught her children, knowing the more they could do, the closer Stefan would bind them to him. In the beginning, she had even tried to pretend that Parthenia didn't have the ability. Then one day Stefan had said he would slit his daughter's throat if she was of no use to him.

Thankfully, her husband had softened since then and when it turned out that the child who came next, Castiel, really could not Cast, he had spared his life. It was to Stefan's own benefit, it had turned out, for Castiel grew more like his father every day and was now his favorite child. Ferne's mage abilities didn't attract the same good opinion, and neither did Oriana's, Ferne's non-identical twin. The same pattern was now playing out with Darius. It seemed that Stefan saw his mage wife and children as little more than chattel and tools to further his business schemes. While he saw Castiel, and Nahla, who also could not Cast and was Darius's elder by two years, as like himself: true Sherrerrs.

"What are you thinking about, Mother?" Darius asked. Faye had sat on a bench that gave her a good view of the garden, and Darius had contented himself with looking for fish in the pond at their feet, but now his young gaze was upon her.

"I'm just thinking how fast you're all growing and how well you're doing."

Darius got up and climbed onto her lap. He barely fit anymore. The little boy looked into her eyes. "I messed up my oration this morning and Tutor Peverel scolded me."

"Well, oration is quite difficult when you're six. I wouldn't worry about it."

"And I can never remember my family history. I get the people confused."

"There are certainly a lot of people to remember." Faye wanted to add, *you have another family too, somewhere,* but she dared not.

Darius gave a heavy sigh and squirmed around until his back was lying against Faye and his legs were dangling on each side of hers. His soft hair tickled her neck. Faye wrapped her arms around him.

"Mother," Darius said, his tone remaining sad.

"Yes?"

"I know you told me never to talk about her again…"

Faye's heart froze and she quickly checked that no one was within hearing distance.

"…but I miss Carina."

Faye hugged her son tightly and bent down to whisper in his ear. "Darius, please. You don't want any harm to come to Carina, do you?"

"No, I don't."

"Then…I know it's hard, but you really can't mention her ever again. Not even to me. Do you understand?"

"Okay. I won't."

Faye exhaled. She hoped with all her heart that her son could keep the secret. Stefan had nearly everyone she loved within the grip of his unrelenting fist. Their children lived within a glorious, luxurious prison, their mage abilities chaining them to him. She could not risk him finding out about the one child she had who was free.

Twenty-One

The next day, at breakfast, Stefan seemed pleased with himself. The children had all turned up on time, looking clean and neat, and the cook had made his favorite dish of lightly poached fish roe, but Faye detected there was something more responsible for her husband's uncharacteristically good mood. As always, she couldn't question or remark upon anything to do with him, so she remained silent and waited for him to explain, if he chose.

Parthenia announced to the table, "Tutor Peverel complimented me on my deportment yesterday. He said my posture and bearing were fit for the Assembly."

"Well done," said Faye.

"Yes, that is good to hear, Parthenia," said Stefan, "though perhaps you need extra lessons on charm. You won't endear yourself in company if you go around boasting about your achievements."

Parthenia flushed. "Yes, Father."

Faye felt for the girl. In her fifteen years of life, she'd never once received a word of praise or compliment from her father that hadn't been followed by a rebuke or criticism. Yet despite his ill treatment of her—or perhaps due to it—Parthenia seemed to crave her father's approval. Hence her tactless declaration.

Faye said, "Nevertheless—" Stefan turned cold eyes on her. She left the sentence incomplete. The only noise in the room was the scrape of Darius' spoon as he ate.

Stefan finished his roe and signaled to a servant to take away his plate.

Immediately, everyone put down their utensils. Breakfast was over. Two more servants began to clear the table. Stefan removed his napkin from his lap and wiped his mouth. "It seems like a fine day today, don't you think?"

No one answered, unsure whether the question was rhetorical.

"Yes," Stefan continued, "there's no sign of rain or even a stiff breeze. I was thinking to myself, this might be a good day to take a trip into town. What do you think?"

The children gasped. Even Faye's heart skipped a beat. Ever since Darius had been kidnapped, no one in the family but Stefan had been allowed to leave the estate. The Sherrerrs had been purging Ithiya of Dirksen spies and associates. Stefan had declared that until the job was done, it wasn't safe for them to step outside the walls. Was he saying they could go out once more? Or was it one of his cruelties? Was he implying that meaning but then he would declare that *he* would be the one taking a trip outside?

"I think that would be a nice idea, Stefan," said Faye. If she kept her response neutral, it might encourage him to be kind. Or at least not sadistic.

"I'm glad you agree, darling," he replied. "Well then, go and get ready, children."

The children yelled with happiness and scraped their chairs on the floor as they jumped up.

"Quietly, please," Stefan said sternly. The noise immediately stopped.

"Yes, Father," said two or three of the children before leaving the room.

Her husband hadn't yet mentioned if Faye were to be included in the excursion. She handed her plate to a servant and waited for him to say something that would indicate his permission.

"Do you have anything to do in town?" Stefan asked, his light eyes twinkling in his enjoyment of her plight.

"I do, but nothing urgent. If you would rather I didn't go..."

"No, no. You and the children have been cooped up here long enough. Chief Sherrerr's report says they've swept the place clean. It's safe to leave, or I wouldn't allow it. I insist you go and enjoy yourself too."

"I will then," said Faye, avoiding *Thank you* out of habit. Thank you meant he had given permission, contradicting Stefan's self image as a benevolent, loving, indulgent head of the family. It was bitterly ironic. She knew first hand what he was capable of, and she would never—could never—forget. But she stood and went over to her husband as he wanted her to, bending to kiss his cheek like an affectionate wife.

He turned and pulled her head close to his, kissing her fully on the lips. She fought down her revulsion. She tried to act as if she didn't hate what he was doing, though through the long years she knew Stefan had never believed her. She wondered if that made it better for him. She suspected it did.

When he finally released her, a hunger was excited in his eyes she knew he would sate tonight. She forced a smile and went out. In the empty hall, out of sight of the breakfast room, she wiped his saliva from her lips. It was a futile gesture but it brought her some small relief.

The children were already bounding down the stairs dressed in their expensive jackets and hats. Sherrerrs only wore the very best money could buy, and Stefan was sensitive about his family's appearance in public, even if they were only seen by the local townsfolk. Faye hurried through them as she went upstairs. If she wasn't at the front door quick enough, Stefan might decide to leave without her.

She opened her closet and took out a richly embroidered coat. It fitted her perfectly and suited her coloring, but she had never enjoyed the wealth belonging to the Sherrerr clan conferred. She had been so much happier when all she had in the world was Kris and Carina. Her heart was heavy with remembering the little girl as she put on the coat and fastened it.

How in the world had it happened to be her daughter who had brought Darius home? Her secret, hopeless dream was that one day she would be able to tell Carina it was her half-brother she'd saved.

"Mother," a voice called from downstairs. They were waiting for her. She hurried out of her room, but as she left, she coughed. The warm, iron taste of blood flooded her mouth. She ran back to pick up a handkerchief. In another minute she was downstairs just as everyone was leaving to walk to the gate.

A glossy multi-person autocar was waiting for them outside the main gates. Faye climbed into the plush interior with the children. Stefan had taken his seat at the front next to the servant, Nate, who would input their destinations. The doors slid closed almost without a sound, sealing the family inside a cocoon with tinted windows. They would probably visit a store where the children could choose candy and toys, and other places where Faye could pick plants for the garden or ornaments. The shops would be empty of all other shoppers, of course. Nate would call ahead to make it so.

Stefan loved to pretend they were a normal family. Faye doubted he knew what normal was. He must have grown up in the same way as his children, almost entirely cut off from the people who labored to generate the Sherrerrs' massive wealth.

"Look at those bugs," Darius exclaimed, pointing at something on the side of the road that leading the estate to the town. Beetles the size of cats were rubbing serrated legs along their razor backs.

"Urgh," Oriana said, "they're horrible."

"Run them over," shouted Castiel. "Kill them."

"No, don't, Nate," said Darius. "They don't hurt anyone." He went to say something else but stopped himself just in time. He gave Faye a smile. She got the impression he was heeding her earlier request. Had Carina told him something about the bugs? She'd liked bugs, even as a toddler.

Nate didn't drive over the insects as Castiel had urged, and they soon arrived at the edge of town. Stefan did suggest a candy and toy store to the children, and they so vigorously demonstrated their assent, the vehicle bounced on its suspension. Faye relaxed a little. Darius seemed to be remembering her warning never to mention Carina, Stefan was happy in his fantasy that he was a good father and husband, and the children were finally spending some time outside their gilded cage.

After the children had taken what they wanted from the store—Sherrerrs never paid for anything—everyone returned to the autocar.

"Now it's your turn, Faye," said Stefan, leaning an arm over his seat to look back at her. "Where would you like to go?"

She named a plant nursery on the far edge of town. Though she loathed stealing from the town's proprietors, she could at least lengthen the trip by requesting they go somewhere a fair distance away.

"Hmmm." Stefan checked the time before nodding to Nate, who input the destination.

The route they had to travel took them along the busiest street in town. The fact didn't slow them down too much as all the other autocars automatically moved aside as they approached. The town's traffic control program overrode other vehicles' drive systems when Sherrerr transportation was on the road. Faye's children had plenty to gawk at, however, as they went along. They pressed their faces against the windows and stared at the stores and other establishments that were ordinary to less important folk.

A little hand gripped Faye's arm. Darius had grabbed her. He was staring, open-mouthed, at something in the road. Her gaze followed his.

Her heart stopped. It was Carina. Though it had been fifteen years since she'd last seen her, Faye knew her daughter immediately. All her faint doubts that another mage with the same name had rescued Darius were wiped away.

Carina was crossing the road with a thin young man, busy in conversation. Faye thanked the stars their vehicle windows were tinted and Carina couldn't see Darius. She might have approached the vehicle, and Stefan was as observant as he was evil. He would have noticed Carina's resemblance to herself in a split second.

"What's wrong with Darius?" asked Castiel. "What are you looking at?"

The little boy struggled for a moment. His gaze turned to Faye. "I didn't see anything."

"It was just a big bug in the street," Faye said. "It's gone now." She had torn her gaze from her daughter and was facing forward. What was Carina doing still in town? She regretted her decision to send her daughter things that would tell her someone knew she was a mage. She should never have included that polished pebble either. Carina had obviously stuck around hoping to find out more.

She should have only sent her a little money and a thank you note, but she had wanted so badly to show her daughter she wasn't alone. If what she had done had put Carina at risk, she would never forgive herself. She had to get word to her that she must leave Ithiya and never return.

Twenty-Two

That evening, when Faye was finally alone in her room, she let her mask fall. Maintaining the facade of something resembling normalcy for her children's sake had become her habit, but the strain was almost unbearable at times. In her mirror, she daily saw the ravaging effect on her features.

She mulled over how to communicate with Carina in a way that wouldn't put her daughter in extreme danger. The simplest method would be to Cast. She could Enthrall a servant to find Carina in town—a visitor who had hung around for three months for no apparent reason shouldn't be too hard to locate. The servant would pass on the message without knowing what they were doing and would retain no memory of their action afterward.

But Casting was impossible. Stefan had made it brutally clear she was never to Cast without his permission. The safeguards he had put in place to prevent her were extremely tight. She had rarely even thought of attempting it.

Stefan knew she needed earth, metal, wood, water, and fire to create the elixir. Entirely removing the first four Elements from her environment would have been difficult, but it had proven easy to control her access to fire or anything that could create it. The region's climate was warm, so indoor heating was not required. Stefan had ensured a fire was never lit and electricity was never used anywhere on the estate except the kitchen, which was always kept locked even when in use. For lighting, the household used lamps filled with bioluminescent algae that absorbed the sun's rays during the day and glowed at night.

Faye could have created sparks for fire with a firestone, but Stefan had thought even of this and had all of that type of stone removed from the garden's soil. Only once, in many years of surreptitious searching, had Faye discovered a firestone in the garden. It had been a tiny fragment, too small to use. She had placed it in the pouch she sent out to Carina. To Faye, it had been symbolic of the freedom withheld from her but still available to her daughter, though she knew Carina couldn't have guessed the meaning.

The sun was setting. Olivia, Faye's maid, brought in a lamp and set in on her dressing table before leaving without a word. Faye looked out of the window, which gave a view of the road that led into town. If only she could walk through the garden, out of the gate, and down the road to find her daughter. She wondered how far she would get before she was stopped. Probably not even as far as the front door. It had been so long since she'd had that kind of freedom, she'd almost forgotten how it felt.

If she could not Cast, what could she do to contact Carina? Dare she risk bribing a servant to carry a message? The bribe wouldn't be a problem. Stefan enjoyed decorating his captive bird with expensive jewelry. But she pushed the thought aside. The servants and guards were fully aware of the long, excruciatingly painful death they would suffer if they betrayed Stefan. Even if one had been willing, Faye couldn't ask them to take that chance.

The door to her room opened again, and in her dressing table mirror, she saw Stefan come in. He never knocked, of course.

"Good evening, darling," he said. "Did you have a nice time today?" He began untying his cravat. Her stomach twisted so violently she thought she might vomit, but her face had resumed its usual amiable expression.

"Yes," she replied. "Going on an excursion into town is always pleasant. The children had a wonderful time."

"Yes, they were happy with their new toys, weren't they? But what about you? Did you enjoy yourself?"

"Oh yes, dear. Very much."

Stefan put down his cravat on the nightstand and unfastened the top buttons of his shirt.

Faye felt imaginary spiders crawling up her back. She wanted to scream. She wanted to jump out of the window and fall the three stories to the flagstones below.

Her husband pulled off his boots and lay down on her bed with his hands behind his head, resting on a pillow.

Mechanically, Faye unpinned her hair and brushed it out. Night had fallen and, with the lamp's glow on the window, she saw nothing outside but pitch black.

"You look very beautiful tonight, darling." Stefan patted the bed beside him. Faye got up and began to change into her nightdress. Stefan watched. "You look young for your age. I find it hard to believe you can no longer bear children. Yet Darius is six years old now and no little brother or sister has come along." He sat up. "What's that on your side? Is it a bruise? How did you get it?"

"I don't know. Maybe I bumped into a table." The disease assaulting Faye's body was beginning to show clear outward signs. She needed to be more careful. Perhaps Stefan would allow her to undress in the dark if she told him she was ashamed of her aging body.

He pulled his shirt over his head as she turned out the light. She joined her husband in her bed.

"Perhaps we will be lucky tonight," He breathed in her ear. "Perhaps your body has one last fruit to bear. And if not, don't feel bad, my love. You're useful to me in other ways. I have big things planned for you and our children. Very big things."

Twenty-Three

"Are you hungry?" Bryce asked. "We could eat, and I can tell you more about the job."

"I am hungry," Carina replied, watching the Sherrerr vehicle as it drove away, the other autocars parting before it like retreating waves. "But I don't have any money. Do you?"

Bryce shook his head.

She sighed. "Okay. Wait here. I'll be back soon." She headed up the street toward the market where the gem dealers plied their trade. It looked like she would be financing Bryce's expedition. She would claim back the outlay from the fee, assuming they were successful. With the money she received for one of the gems, she could buy the supplies, equipment, and clothes they would need to survive in the mountains. Bryce clearly didn't have a clue. If he'd set off without her, he would have died along the way. She wondered if he was dumb or desperate and concluded it was a little bit of both.

She hadn't gone far before a crowd barred her way. People were gathering around some kind of spectacle and blocking road and foot traffic.

It was hard for her to make out what was causing the disturbance—not that she really cared. She only wanted to get around or through the throng and be on her way. She forced herself between a couple of the gawkers and began elbowing into the ranks of jammed bystanders, all craning for a better view.

From the center of the crowd came the sound of a man yelping and pleading. A few of the audience laughed, though awkwardly as if embarrassed.

"Please stop," cried a voice. "I'll give you your money."

"First correct thing you've said all day," said another. "You're right. You will. After we have our fun."

She could see an open space ahead holding two large men. She pushed farther in until she made it near the center and whatever it was attracting all the attention. Unwilling to attract attention herself by traversing the open area, she tried to go sideways, but the people were packed shoulder to shoulder and they were unwilling to give up their prime viewing spots to make room. The path she'd cut through them had also closed up behind her.

She forged ahead and burst into the first row of people, drawing many disgruntled objections. She'd been mistaken. There weren't two men in the center of the crowd, there were three. The third had been invisible because he was down on all fours, his pants around his ankles. One of the men had a foot on his hands, pressing them together on the ground. The other held out a splicer's pole—a double helix of thin strips of steel—ready to strike the man's bare behind.

"What's going on?" Carina asked the person next to her.

"He's new around here," replied the well-dressed older woman. "Set up a splicing center. When the Sherrerr men came for their protection money, he wouldn't pay."

Carina grimaced. The splicer was either very cocky or a fool. Probably the latter. No one could be so arrogant as to think they could avoid giving the most powerful clan in the region a cut of business profits. Judging from the state of the man's face, the beating he was about to receive wasn't the first of his punishments today.

Though she pitied the poor splicer, she didn't want to interfere. She doubted she could take down both the Sherrerr men, and even if she could, she would only transfer the wrath of the Sherrerrs onto her own head. She wasn't *that* dumb.

All she wanted to do was get past the disturbance and reach the market. She began to edge slowly sideways across the front row, annoying the onlookers. A crack sounded as the first blow landed, followed by the howling sob of the splicer. "Please. I'll give you double. I'll give you everything." The men laughed and another blow struck loudly against skin.

She felt sick. She'd done plenty of fighting in her time, both hand-to-hand and fire fights, and she was used to people getting hurt, but there was something especially nauseating about the strong and powerful ganging up on the weak and helpless.

Another blow landed. The man shrieked. The splicer's pole would be cutting his flesh. Suddenly she wasn't so sure she could bear to pass by the splicer's punishment without trying to do something. She'd made it halfway around the inner circle of the crowd before she looked toward the group of three.

She found she was gazing into the splicer's face. It was a bruised, sweaty, bloody mask of agony. The thug who was standing on his hands had also grasped his hair and was pulling his head roughly backward, arching the man's neck. His partner raised his arm, ready to strike again.

"Don't you think that's enough?" Carina asked, before she was even aware she was about to speak. Instead of sneaking past, she realized she was standing upright and looking the man holding the splicer's pole in the eye.

His eyebrows lifted. "No, I don't." He landed a blow so hard it caused him to stagger backward. The splicer screamed long and loud. Some of the people who had been watching with morbid interest looked shocked. Some covered their eyes or began to back away, pushing against those behind them, trying to leave.

She took a step forward. If the men had been average citizens, she would have tried to reason with them. But she knew this type well. They enjoyed what they did and hated whatever came between them and the fulfillment of their pleasure. She knew in their eyes she was already the enemy and nothing she could say or do would change that. Only a response of equal violence could make them deviate from their path.

She ran at the closest one, feinting left then driving her right shoulder into his stomach. He fell into the crowd, who hastily stumbled away so that he hit the ground. She heard the whoosh of the splicer's pole and dived to one side, hoping she had guessed right. The pole smashed into the ground beside her. Before the thug could lift it again, she grabbed it and twisted it out of his grasp.

She whirled the pole into the first man, who had gotten to his feet and was drawing a weapon. The blow knocked the gun from his grasp and sent it flying into the rapidly dispersing crowd. She continued to swing the pole around, connecting with the second thug who was coming up behind her. But the blow didn't topple him. He grabbed the pole and tried to wrest it from her grasp. She gripped tightly and resisted, but she was no match for the man's superior strength. The pole began to slip from her hands, tearing her skin.

She ran to one side, forcing the thug to pivot on the spot. Behind him, his friend had found his gun and was raising it to take aim. She ran forward, forcing the man holding the other end of the pole into his partner. He was knocked down again. She continued running until she had pushed the pole-holding man against a shop wall. The pole was digging into his chest. He let go momentarily to adjust his grasp. She ripped the pole away from him and struck it against his temple.

His head bounced onto the hard stone wall and his legs collapsed beneath him. She stepped back, colliding with someone behind her, who grabbed her hair. She elbowed her assailant in the stomach, causing a whoosh of expelled breath. He ripped out of some of her hair as he went down. When she turned to finish him off, she found the person she'd toppled was the splicer, who had probably been seeking her protection.

The first thug was rising again, his gun in his paw. She kicked the weapon out of his hand and punched him in the jaw. He dropped like a stone.

The stragglers of the crowd were giving her frightened glances as they hurried from the scene. No one wanted to be involved in an event where someone had stood up to the Sherrerrs. Even the splicer was shuffling away, holding his pants around his thighs.

"You're welcome," Carina said sarcastically. She cursed. What had she done? After that stunt, the Sherrerrs would be after her blood. She probably had only ten or fifteen minutes before the men she'd knocked out would come around and tell their friends a face-saving story about a nasty woman who'd defied the Sherrerrs.

In fact, they were already coming around. Carina ran. She headed for the market. At the first gem dealer she found, she stopped and pulled out her pouch. Slamming a gem down on the counter, she said, "How much?"

The dealer, sensing her haste, offered her less than half the jewel's worth. She slammed the counter again with her other hand and glared at the woman. Entirely unfazed, the dealer only repeated her offer.

Barely controlling her anger, Carina said, "Give it to me then."

After the dealer had counted out the cash painfully slowly, Carina snatched it from her and went in search of supplies suitable for a mountain trip. She picked up water bottles, thick coats and boots, a backpack and two blankets. Scant provisions for the expedition, but they would have to do.

She raced back to find Bryce waiting patiently where she'd left him.

"You were gone a long time. I was worried you were never coming back. Why did you buy all those things? We could have gotten them after lunch."

"We don't have time to eat. We're leaving now."

Twenty-Four

"Are you sure you know the way to this stronghold?" Carina asked Bryce when they'd been walking about an hour.

"Yeah, I know the route. I would have known it even if the client hadn't explained. I've lived around here all my life."

"You've been to the mountains before?"

"When I was a kid we'd go there to see the snow. By autocar. It was a little faster."

They were walking through farmland. Carina had judged it safer than going by road. Sherrerr goons would probably be looking for her. They would have to make an example of her to discourage others from standing up to them. The trip would give her the chance to lay low.

Giant plowers and seeders were working steadily across the fields. Unmanned, low intelligence machines, they presented no risks providing Carina and Bryce kept out of their way. The machines moved so slowly it was easy to do. What concerned her more was the water situation. She hadn't noticed any streams along the way, and she couldn't see the glint of water anywhere between them and the white-peaked mountains ahead.

"We would stay at a little resort," Bryce went on, "and go snow-gliding."

"Snow-gliding?"

"You never heard of it?"

"There wasn't any snow where I grew up."

"Snow-gliding boards melt a very thin layer of snow beneath them. Makes them almost friction-less and super slippery. You can go very fast downhill."

"Sounds like fun."

"It was. Was it hot where you grew up? What planet was it?"

"Nowhere you ever heard of. Yeah, it was hot. Hotter than here anyway, though I've been to hotter places since. It was a dump and I'm never going back." There was nothing for her to go back for. When Nai Nai had died, she used the tiny amount of savings her grandmother left behind to pay for a cremation. She had scattered Nai Nai's ashes in the wildlands outside town where the two had spent many happy hours searching for beautiful pebbles to polish and sell.

"I'd leave here too if I could," he said. "I want to get out of the Sherrer/Dirksen controlled area and see what the rest of the galaxy's like."

She laughed. "The rest of the galaxy's a pretty big place, you know. I traveled a lot of it when I was working as a merc, and we were never in any area where the Sherrerrs or Dirksens didn't have some influence. You'd have to go pretty far, and you'd have to be rich to do it."

He sighed. "Crush my dreams, why don't you? I didn't say it would be easy. I just said I'd like to do it."

"Sorry. I'd like to get out of this sector and see more of the galaxy too. It's just that I found out first hand how hard it is." If she could, she would love to find the birthplace of her clan, but that was an impossible fantasy.

"If we had our own ship, we might do it," he said. "We'd only have to find money for fuel."

Mildly alarmed about Bryce's casual insertion of "we" where he'd used "I" before, she replied, "Do you know how much even a single-seater deep-space cruiser costs? Those vessels aren't cheap. On my wages as a merc I couldn't have afforded to buy one with a lifetime's savings. There's a reason everyone isn't system hopping for fun."

"I bet the Sherrerrs and Dirksens have plenty of cruisers. One each, probably."

"Yeah, probably. Bryce, do you know anything about the Sherrerrs who live in the estate just outside town?"

"Not a lot. That place was built around fifteen years ago. Everyone thought it was odd at the time. It seemed strange that Sherrerrs would build a home in a back-of-beyond place. The only thing the town has going for it is the regional spaceport and the splicers. It isn't pretty or interesting. You would think Sherrerrs would want to live in a city, wouldn't you? Or at least some place where there was more to do than watch the crops grow."

"It does seem strange." She had thought the same when she'd brought Darius home after rescuing him. She hadn't thought of the Sherrerrs as small town people. "Have you ever seen anyone who lives on the estate? They don't seem to come into town often."

"No, I haven't," he replied, "but they used to come out more. Every few weeks the family would arrive in their chauffeured car. I heard they have six kids and they take what they want from the shops. The kids might not even know they're supposed to pay for things. That's the only time they leave home, from what I hear. Unless they fly out. They have their own shuttle."

His words chimed with what Darius had told her. This branch of the Sherrerr clan had to seem weird to the local population, but she could understand the reason for their isolation. Some of them were mages. It was natural they would keep to themselves.

"Are you sure you're okay with doing this job?" he asked, perhaps misinterpreting Carina's silence as second thoughts.

"We're on our way now," she replied. "It's a bit late to be asking me that. But anyway, I don't have much choice." She explained what had happened outside the splicer's shop.

"That was you? I heard a commotion but I didn't know you were responsible."

"I wasn't responsible," she objected. "Those Sherrerr thugs were. They were torturing that poor guy."

"Okay, but you didn't have to step in. It isn't like what you did is going to change anything. They'll probably come down harder on the splicer now."

"Well thanks a lot."

"It's true."

They stopped as a seeder trundled across the path ahead of them. When the machine had passed, they continued in silence. The going was easy over the rough, soft dirt of the fields, and the mountains drew steadily closer. By the time the sun was setting, she estimated they must have covered around fifteen kilometers and have roughly twice that to go before they would reach the mountains' foothills.

When they arrived at a ditch that was relatively dry, she suggested they stop for the night. Bryce seemed grateful for the opportunity to rest. They wrapped their blankets around their shoulders to keep out the evening chill, continuing the silence that had persisted between them for the previous three or four hours. She wasn't bothered by it. She was used to taciturn mercs who saw no reason to indulge in meaningless conversation.

After a few more moments, however, the absence of speech appeared to get to Bryce. He blurted, "All right. I'm sorry, okay? I'm sorry about what I said about the splicer. Now can we please go back to being friends? We've got a long way to go and I don't want you to spend the whole time not speaking to me."

Carina, who had been reaching into her backpack for her water bottle, paused and said, "Er...okay. Do you want some food? We should eat now before it gets dark."

"Yes. I'm starving. What did you bring?"

She retrieved the dried meat strips, dried slices of fruit, and grain crackers she'd purchased, which had worked their way to the bottom of her backpack. He chewed hungrily on a meat strip.

"So what exactly do we have to do when we get to this Sherrerr place?" she asked.

"We have to find out as much as we can about their security arrangements. How many guards, what routines they follow, when they change shifts, and what defense systems and weapons they have. The guy said he asked me because he wanted people who wouldn't look too suspicious if they were spotted hanging around. We can pretend we got lost in the mountains or something like that."

From what she'd seen of the Sherrerr thugs' treatment of the splicer, she didn't think they would balk at punishing whoever they caught near their stronghold, no matter how innocent they seemed. They would have to be extremely careful.

He drew his blanket tighter. "Should we light a fire?"

"We probably don't want to attract attention."

"I guess so," he said, "but it's colder than I thought it would be."

"Just be happy that it isn't raining." She hadn't thought to bring fire starters because she could Cast to start a fire. If she'd been alone, that's exactly what she would have done, but of course, creating a fire by Casting in front of Bryce would be madness.

TWENTY-FIVE

By the time they found the rivulet running down the mountain foothills, they were parched. They'd walked the entire day on only the last of the water they had drunk from their bottles that morning. Carina had been seriously concerned about the situation. The snow line lay a day's climb above them. She might have made it that far, but she wasn't sure about Bryce. He'd slowed down a lot over the last few kilometers.

They sat on the bank and took off their boots before cooling their feet in the water. Bryce filled his bottle on the upstream side and took another long drink.

"Take it easy," she said. "Or you'll vomit it up."

He let out a sigh of satisfaction and lay back, his arms over his head while his feet rested in the water. The tiny stream was icy. It was melt water from the snowy peaks that now towered over them, taking up half of the dusky sky.

She took her feet out of the water and inspected them. The boots she'd had to buy without trying on were too big, and she'd stuffed the gaps with dry grass. Her feet were sore in places and her soles were blistered. Bryce's feet also didn't look too good. If she got a moment alone to herself, she would Cast Heal on both their feet. She would Heal their heels. She chuckled to herself.

He sat up. "What's funny?"

"Nothing." She wiped most of the water from her feet with her hands and pulled on her socks.

"Tell me. I need a laugh after that brutal march you made me do today."

"*I* made you? This was your idea, remember?"

"I know. I didn't say how fast we had to do it, though, did I? We could take more time about it."

"Only if we can survive on grass. I don't know about you, but I find it kinda hard and chewy."

"Ah. Good point." He lay down again.

"Where do we go tomorrow?"

"There's a pass, away over there." He gestured vaguely without looking.

"Where?" She was looking in the direction he'd indicated. They were in the shadow of the mountains, and darkness was creeping down the slopes. The place he seemed to mean was already in deep shadow. She took the evening's rations out of her backpack and tossed Bryce's half onto his stomach.

"Is that it?" he asked as he sat up again. "I'm skinny enough as it is. I'll be a ghost by the time this job's done."

"If you don't end up a real ghost, count yourself lucky," she replied. "What we're doing is crazily dangerous, you know. I take it the person who gave you the work is linked to the Dirksens?"

"He didn't mention them, but I guess it's obvious."

"No one else I know would be interested in security at a Sherrerr stronghold." She was getting drawn into the Sherrerr/Dirksen conflict again. It was a deadly place to be. Yet, despite the peril, she was feeling more lighthearted than she had in a long time. Perhaps it was because she finally had some kind of purpose after months of inactivity.

She also enjoyed spending time in Bryce's company. For the last couple of years, all the people she'd known had been mercs. They didn't exactly make agreeable companions. She'd discovered that if they weren't out-and-out psychopaths, they had other personality problems or were deeply psychologically scarred.

"What are you thinking about?" he asked through a mouthful of dried fruit.

"Some people I used to know."

"Before you came here? Who were they? Were they friends?"

"Not exactly. The men and women I used to work with."

"How did you get to be a mercenary?"

"By invitation. It isn't a very interesting story. How about you? You said you used to come to the mountains to snow-glide when you were a kid. What happened? How did you end up on the street?"

He paused a moment and then looked up into the darkening sky as he replied, "A couple of years ago, my dad had an accident and my mom lost her job. Both in the same week. It was months before either of them could work again. We all had to stop taking the preventative medication. It was either that or starve. If you don't take the pills, you stand a one in five chance of developing the disease. Out of my parents and brothers and sisters, I was the unlucky one. My mom and dad didn't have the money to pay for the cure. They could only just afford the medicine that controlled the symptoms. Then they couldn't even afford that any longer.

"They abandoned me. I woke up one morning and the house was empty. They'd left during the night. While I was trying to figure out what had happened, the landlord came around and told me I had to get out—that the rent was overdue and my family had been seen boarding the city shuttle. I don't know where they are."

She sucked in air through her teeth. "Harsh."

"It's okay. I don't blame them anymore."

"You don't?" She stared at the young man, his face dim in the half-light. He seemed to mean what he said.

"I don't think I could forgive anyone who did that to me, especially not family."

"The way I see it," he said, sitting up to look at her, "they had an impossible choice. They didn't have the money to pay for my treatment, and the cost of my medicine was bleeding them dry. They had to choose between sticking around while all of us ended up destitute, and when we couldn't afford my medicine anymore, watching me slowly die; or saving themselves and my siblings and sparing themselves the sight of my death. The end would have been the same. It was only a question of who I brought down with me and how long it took. The way they left spared us all a painful parting."

His revelation raised him in her eyes. Nai Nai would never have abandoned her in the way Bryce's family had, but if she had, she wasn't sure she would ever have been able to understand or excuse it. Whether his take on what his family had done was compassionate or only an attempt to protect himself from a grim truth, she wasn't sure, but it told of a depth to his character she hadn't imagined. "I'm sorry."

"You don't have anything to be sorry for. You didn't give me this damned disease. Anyway, it's okay about my family. I was angry at first, but I got over it when I saw their point of view."

She wondered if her gems were worth enough to pay for Bryce's treatment. She was young and healthy and could find work if she needed to. Though she'd only known him a short time, she felt like he was a friend.

Fear gripped her. What was she thinking? She was a mage. She couldn't afford to have friends. Nai Nai had told her she must never trust anyone, that the knowledge of her powers would turn the nicest, kindest people into selfish, grabbing devils.

"What's wrong?" he asked.

"What do you mean?"

"Your expression suddenly changed. You looked okay, but now you look angry about something."

"You like studying people, don't you?"

"It's a useful habit when you depend on others' generosity for your survival."

She pulled her blanket out of her backpack. "Nothing's wrong. We should get some sleep. We have a long climb ahead of us tomorrow."

He also got out his blanket. They wrapped themselves and lay down, putting their backpacks under their heads as pillows.

"How about you?" he asked.

"What about me?"

"Does your family know you became a merc? Are they still living on your home planet? Do they know where you are?"

She paused before answering, "My family all died a long time ago." Her history was a story she could never and would never tell him. "Good night."

Twenty-Six

The Sherrerr stronghold looked impregnable. Carina and Bryce were lying on their stomachs, peeking over a ridge that looked down on the fortress.

"Here, suck on this," she said, passing him a handful of snow.

"Why?"

"Just do it."

When he'd stuffed his mouth with the snow she explained, "It'll stop our breath from fogging and giving us away." Then she did the same. The guards patrolling the stronghold's walls would have been trained to look for signs of watchers.

Her gaze inched across the building and its surroundings. The fortress stood in a high valley, and a single, narrow, winding road led up to it. The main access to the place seemed to be by air. Most of the roof space was taken up by a shuttle landing pad. She glanced at the sky. They would need to be careful they weren't spotted from overhead if a shuttle arrived or left.

One vessel stood on the pad already and it could hold another three. The craft was black and carried no identifying insignia. It had arrived that morning, judging from its clean, snow-free exterior. Snow had fallen during the night, and the shuttle had melted a neat circle when it landed. Tiny footsteps of three or four passengers led to a closed door that had to be the stairway entrance.

Guard boxes stood at two corners of the roof, and the guards would no doubt be watching the airspace as well as checking arrivals. Solid stone, windowless walls made up the rest of the fortress. The only above-ground entrance other than the roof was a double door that fronted the road, though Carina didn't discount the possibility of a drainage tunnel that opened into a stream somewhere farther down the mountain.

She touched Bryce's shoulder, gesturing that they move down from the ridge. They went to a group of boulders. On one side of the massive stones, snow had piled into a drift. On the other side, only a light dusting covered the ground. They crouched in the sheltered spot.

"My mouth's frozen," he complained, spitting out the remains of the snow.

"That's the idea," she replied. "So we need to stick around for a few days and watch what happens. We'll do it in shifts. We can't stay up here the whole time or we'll freeze to death. We'll make a camp a little farther down the mountain and take it in turns to watch for a few hours."

"I'd forgotten how cold it is up here," he said. "And snow seemed a lot more fun when I was a kid. I was thinking, maybe we should just, you know, make up something to tell them. We can hang around somewhere warmer for a while, then I'll go back to my contact and give him a story."

"Are you crazy? If the Dirksens figure out you gave them false intel, your life won't be worth living. Anyway, I would never do that. We're being paid to do a job, so let's do it, okay?" She had seen fellow mercs die due to bad intel. She wasn't going to be the source of it herself.

They climbed one hundred meters or so down the mountain until they reached a shallow cave they'd passed on their way up. It wouldn't provide much protection from wind or snow, but it was better than nothing. The best thing about it was that it wasn't visible from the track—Bryce had discovered it on a quick trip to answer a call of nature. She expected that Sherrerr guards would frequently patrol the area around the fortress, looking for people who were doing exactly what they were doing.

They had a cover story if they were picked up, but she didn't have much faith in it. They had to avoid detection while they scoped the place out. If they could only remain here for the next two or three days, they could return to Bryce's Dirksen contact and pick up the reward. Then she would have to find a way to get to the capital that didn't involve leaving via the spaceport. She had no doubt the town was still hot for her after her escapade with the Sherrerr men and the ungrateful splicer.

When they had secreted their bags at the back of the cave, she said, "I'll take the first shift. You stay here and rest. Use both blankets to keep warm, and eat your ration if you like. I'll be back in a few hours."

He protested that he should watch the fortress while she rested, but she argued successfully that she'd done recon many times before and knew what to look for. She left him wrapped in both their blankets.

Before returning to the ridge, she stopped at an unusually shaped boulder. It looked like the head of a plains beast, a long-snouted animal that had lived in the wild lands on her home planet. She took out the pouch that contained her remaining gems and the elixir ingredients. If she were captured, the jewels would contradict their cover story. She put the pouch down next to the boulder and covered it with stones.

Soon, she was near the ridge and taking great care to move quietly and look around corners before proceeding. The way was clear of Sherrerr guards, however, and soon she had stuffed her mouth with snow and was peering down at the fortress once more.

It felt a little strange to be doing recon without the benefit of the devices she used to have as a merc. Having no scanning, recording, or special vision instruments made her feel not very useful. She could see the advantage of carrying no technical equipment of course. It meant they wouldn't have any items to incriminate them. It wouldn't be immediately clear the Dirksens were planning an attack. The downside was the true reason for their presence in that place was held only within their minds, and the Sherrerrs might stop at nothing to retrieve the information.

She gave a shiver, partly at the thought of interrogation and partly due to the cold that had begun to encroach into her bones. The fortress looked the same as before, except the shuttle had departed, leaving a bare patch of melted snow.

She wondered what it was the Sherrerrs held within their fortress that warranted such efforts for its secrecy and protection. It had to be something of great importance. The place looked newly built of manufactured stone. They would have had to haul the massive blocks and everything else required to build the fortress all the way up the mountain.

Were the Sherrerrs building a new weapon? That might make sense. It was difficult to keep activities like that under wraps. If they built the weapons at this highly defended location the Dirksens would find it hard to blow up the construction site. If that was what the Sherrerrs were doing, it didn't bode well for the citizens of that galactic sector. Weapons development meant war was coming.

The crunch of a foot on loose stone sounded from somewhere behind. Had Bryce come up to speak to her? It seemed unlikely. Carina couldn't think of anything he might have to tell her that couldn't wait until she returned to him. She eased down from her position overlooking the fortress. If someone was coming up the path, she needed a place to hide, but the only possibility was a low protrusion of the mountainside.

But anything was safer than meeting a guard face to face out in the open. She slid down behind the protrusion, cursing the very obvious trail she'd made in the snow. She searched her mind for a Cast that would make the snow look untouched. Obscure would do it. Her canister of elixir was inside her shirt.

Another soft crunch of a boot on stones.

She sipped the elixir, which was warm from the heat of her body. As she screwed on the lid and returned the canister to the safety of her shirt, she closed her eyes to write the character. But she had only completed four strokes before another *crunch* sounded, very close by. She had no time left. She opened her eyes just as a man in armor appeared around a rock.

Though he was facing away there was no point in hiding now. The minute he turned around he would see her. She leapt up and flew at him from behind. His armor and helmet protected him, while she wore nothing but a heavy coat and hat. Her only hope lay in taking his weapon. Before he even hit the ground, her hand was around the grip and she was pulling the gun from the holster.

She was the first on her feet. She aimed at the guard and was about to shoot when she heard another sound. Her last thoughts were, *Damn. There are two of them.*

Twenty-Seven

Carina woke up inside an interrogation room. She was sitting down, her hands were tied behind the back of the chair and her ankles were tied to the chair legs. Two burly men stood over her and from the looks on their faces, she wasn't about to experience a warm welcome to the Sherrerr fortress.

Before she even had time to speak, one of the men slapped her, snapping her head to one side. Then the other struck—a full-on punch to her jaw. She saw stars. "Pleased to..." She spat blood. "Meet you too."

This drew a chuckle from the corner of the room. A figure who had been standing in shadow stepped forward. She wore a gray uniform and appeared to be a superior officer, judging by the blazes on her collar.

"They said you were the tough one," the woman said. "Your companion whimpered and gave himself up immediately."

Carina's heart sank. Bryce wasn't built for what was about to happen to them. She just hoped he would be able to stick to their story nevertheless.

The woman turned to the men. "Soften her up. I'll be back in a while."

They grinned and nodded, one rubbing his knuckles on the palm of his other hand.

Carina had been beaten up enough times during the years she'd spent alone after Nai Nai died that she didn't fear what the men were about to do. Though she couldn't Cast without taking a sip of elixir, she'd learned the mental discipline of shutting off signals from her nerve endings. Still, she also knew she wouldn't be able to shut out the pain forever. She just hoped they wouldn't break any bones.

What seemed like a long time later but was probably only half an hour or so, the female officer returned. Carina's eyes were nearly swollen shut and, with her hands tied, she could only try to blink the blood away. So the woman looked blurry, but from the sound of her voice Carina could tell she was the same person.

"Not too pretty now," she said. "Quite like your friend, I have to say. The boys are having a wonderful time with him."

Carina winced.

The officer drew up a chair and turned its back to her. She straddled and leaned her arms on it. "So, my dear, now that we have the pleasantries out of the way, I'm ready to hear your story."

Speaking through puffy, bloody lips wasn't easy, but Carina tried her best to sound genuine as she explained that she and Bryce were friends who had hiked into the mountains with the intention of working for the Sherrerrs. Lies were most effective when they were nearly the truth, so that was the only deceit Carina uttered. Everything else she told the officer was true: that she was an ex-merc whose band had dissolved and she'd left the ship. She'd met Bryce, who'd told her he'd heard of the Sherrerr stronghold and suggested that they went there to sign up. He needed the money because of his disease. She needed the money to live, and she was already a handy fighter. They'd been trying to find the stronghold but Carina had gone ahead while Bryce rested off the track.

The officer studied Carina's face in silence as she listened to her story. When Carina reached the end she said, "It all makes sense, except for one fact. If you were so intent on joining us, why did you attack the guard who found you? Why not give yourself up?"

Carina swallowed. It was a good point. "I wanted to show you how well I could fight. I wouldn't have shot him. I planned on making him show me the way here. I thought, if I defeated one of your guards, you'd be impressed."

"Ha," the officer exclaimed. "If they didn't patrol in pairs, you might have succeeded too."

Carina managed a half smile. "I might have."

The woman stood up. "You're certainly a resilient young thing, and you know how to take down a man. Maybe you are an ex-merc looking for a job as you claim. If you can make it through Basic in your current state, you can have one. We're in need of new recruits so I'll take a chance. Don't doubt that you'll be watched closely. One suspicious move and you're dead. Even if the story you just told me isn't quite the truth, things are happening that'll soon show you the benefit of working for the Sherrerrs."

She went to the door. "Put her in a cell overnight. No food or water. We'll see what she's made of tomorrow."

Though the officer hadn't given them permission, the men allowed their fists and boots to become more acquainted with Carina before they finally untied her and dragged her to a cell. When they closed and locked the door, she lay on the bare, cold stone floor. The first thing she did was to feel for her elixir canister, but of course it had been taken.

She curled on her side, resting her battered head on her arm. The officer hadn't said what they would do if she didn't make it through Basic, but Carina guessed she hadn't needed to. The fortress was in an empty, lonely area of the mountains. No one would notice the body of a young woman thrown from a high place.

Now her beating was over, the resulting pain was overcoming her mental barrier. She wasn't sure which place hurt the most, but she didn't think the men had done her any lasting damage. If she had her elixir, she could heal herself overnight, though that would make her captors suspicious. Without her elixir, she would probably heal in a couple of weeks. Only she didn't have a couple of weeks.

Carina closed her eyes and tried to shut out her pain, hunger, and thirst. She needed to sleep if she was to survive the following day.

TWENTY-EIGHT

All she needed was a firestone, Faye reasoned as she wandered the garden. That was all. One insignificant rock, useless for anything except striking sparks. Then she could Cast Locate to find Carina, and Send to her to warn her to leave Ithiya. She wasn't sure that Locate would work. She'd been separated from her daughter so long, it would be hard to make the connection. If she had something of Carina's it wouldn't be a problem, but she had nothing. It couldn't be helped. She would have to try.

Faye had already scraped minute filings from an iron banister, gathered splinters of wood, and a pinch of dirt. She'd hidden each of the ingredients in a separate place—if Stefan came across them together he would know exactly what she was up to and would punish her severely. As time had gone on, she'd been persuaded that her efforts to create elixir were hopeless.

Until now. The sight of Carina still hanging around after returning Darius to her had sparked an inner rebellion that wouldn't rest. Faye had to get a message to her by some method. Any method. Stefan had six of her children under his control. He would not have a seventh.

Her husband was locked in his study, probably speaking with his Sherrerr relations via comm. The children were at their lessons. Faye had an hour or more to herself. She'd told her maid, Olivia, that she was tired and would take a nap. After the woman had left, she'd sneaked out and down the back staircase, hopefully unobserved. The servants all spied on her and reported to Stefan.

In a section of the garden that was obscured from the house by tall shrubs, Faye bent down and turned over the stones in the soil, examining them. Next she looked at the low wall that held the flower bed. It was made from larger stones, cleverly stacked so they stayed put without mortar. Small gaps had been filled by pebbles, wedged into place. Nothing. Faye sighed and stood up. She went farther from the house, her pulse quickening. She wondered if her maid had checked on her and found she was missing.

There were no rules that said she couldn't do exactly as she pleased within her home. No rules except the unspoken ones.

Water was so easy to procure she could leave it to last. But she had to have fire or all her efforts were worthless. Faye fought down the rising tide of hopelessness that threatened to overwhelm her. In the early days, she had searched endlessly for something with which she could make fire. The times Stefan had caught her and guessed what she was doing, he had beaten her so badly she was in pain for weeks.

It was around the time he'd threatened to beat the children instead of her that she'd finally been persuaded to entirely cease her efforts. She couldn't bear to be the cause of her children's suffering. The cage was sealed shut and in all the following years, she had never dared to try to prise it open. It was also around then that Stefan had begun to cultivate a veneer of decency and respectability, an ironic counterpoint to the reality of his nature and evil exploitation of his family.

Over the years, Stefan had used Parthenia, Oriana, and Ferne to give Sherrers the edge in business deals. He had taken them to the capital and made them Enthrall competitors in meetings so they agreed to unfavorable terms, or the children had performed other Casts that confused or wrong-footed adversaries.

Perhaps Faye couldn't prevent Stefan from treating their children as tools but she could save Carina, with a firestone. When the flame she would create was applied to the other elixir ingredients for the correct duration, it would prime the mixture.

Though she'd never made a fire in that way before, she knew it could be done. Before she and poor Kris had been captured by the Sherrerrs, they'd lived with Kris' mother, who used to be a geologist. She knew every stone in the wildlands that surrounded their town, and she'd spent many evenings showing them examples and explaining their origins and properties. At the time, Faye had found the explanations boring, but she did vividly remember the night the old woman had demonstrated making fire with a firestone. She'd said it was a skill every mage should have.

Little had she known how right the old woman had been. Faye hoped she was still alive, but she doubted it. She'd already been old when Kris and she had been captured. Also, Carina had gone outsystem. She'd loved her Nai Nai so much, she would never have willingly left her.

Carina. She had to Send to Carina.

Faye squatted down next to another flower bed and began to examine the stones. Again, she found nothing. She clenched her hands into fists. Firestones were commonplace, though few knew their special property. The gardeners had been digging the beds recently. Perhaps she could find a stone they'd unearthed. Then she saw it. An edge of the stone so precious to her protruded from the dirt.

"Faye," Stefan said quietly.

She shot to her feet. He was only meters away. How had he crept up so close without her noticing? Caught unawares, Faye was too flustered to put on her mask. She felt her face flushing crimson.

Her husband's features were hard, yet somewhere behind his eyes, Faye could also see the glee of an evil child who has been given an opportunity to freely act out their deepest desires.

"I'm so disappointed in you, my dear."

"But—"

He held up a hand to stop her. "Please don't insult me with lies. I know exactly why you're here, but I must say that it comes as somewhat of a surprise. After all our years of marriage, after our love-making last night, I'd thought that I'd come to mean something to you. That *we* had come to mean something to you."

He approached her, waves of evil intent emanating from him and washing over Faye like a tsunami of horror. What would he do? When and how would the punishment fall? She hoped desperately he would take it out on her and not the children.

He stood so close, their noses were almost touching. "Look into my eyes, my dear."

She unglued her gaze from his neck with its silken cravat and fixed it on his pale blue irises.

"Have I not been good, kind, and generous to you? You want for nothing. You have the very best of everything. Think back to the state you were in when I found you. Skinny, poor, and wearing clothes that wouldn't be fit for rags in this home. I've given you more than you could have even imagined. And this is how you repay me."

Thwarted in her efforts to warn her remaining non-enslaved child, Faye's frustration and rage overflowed. She worked her saliva into a gob and spat in her husband's face. "You bastard," she yelled. "You captured me and the only man I ever loved. A man whose shoes you weren't fit to lick. You raped me. You made me give up my secrets on the promise that you would spare my husband's life. Then you murdered him in front of me. I don't care how many jewels you throw at me. I don't care how many dresses you buy me. I don't care what fine foods you give me to eat. One day I'll make you pay for everything you've done. One day I'll have my revenge on you, Stefan Sherrer, you evil, perverted freak."

The color drained from Stefan's face. He grabbed her hair and marched through the garden, dragging her along. She screamed and fought, but his fury leant him extra strength. When she scratched and bit him, he dropped her, hauled her to her feet, then slapped her so hard she fell down. He pummeled her face, gripped her wrist so tightly it cut off the sensation from her hand, and pulled her toward the house.

As they got closer, Faye glimpsed the heads of the children appearing at windows then swiftly disappearing as their tutors or a sense of self-preservation told them it was wiser not to look. Despite her earlier bravery, Faye's courage was deserting her. The sight of her children reminded her of the punishment that lay ahead.

Please, please don't hurt my children. She couldn't speak the thought aloud. It would only fuel his sick satisfaction at meting out whatever it was he had in store.

No servants appeared when they got to the house. When Stefan was in a rage, they were wise enough not to show their faces unless called. He hauled her upstairs and threw her into her room, then closed and locked the door.

———

When he returned, hours later, she was in the same position she'd fallen when he'd thrown her to the floor. She had sobbed out her ages-old grief for poor, dead Kris and her despair at her predicament. She was lying motionless, only hoping that somehow it could all end.

"Get up," Stefan said.

Like an automaton, Faye rose to her feet.

"Come with me."

She followed him downstairs to the breakfast room, which was odd because it was late afternoon. When she went inside, her heart stopped. Darius was sitting at the table.

"Mother," he exclaimed, happy to see her. He went to get down from his chair to run over and give her a hug, but his father said:

"Stay where you are."

The little boy looked down and remained in his seat.

"Sit down, Faye."

Trembling, she did as he told her. She hardly dared to think what Stefan had in mind, but if he harmed one hair on her little boy's head, she would throttle him where he sat.

A dish of shaved ice and sweet pudding sat in the center of the table, just enough for one person. It took Faye a moment to understand what this might mean. When she did, the hairs stood up on the back of her neck.

"Darius," Stefan said, "you've been such a good boy recently, I've arranged a small surprise for you. I know how much you love Cook's desserts, so I had her whip one up especially as a reward. I invited Mother along so that we can both watch you enjoy it. Here you are."

He lifted the bowl and placed it in front of the boy. Faye gasped. It was poisoned. The dessert was poisoned. As her punishment, Stefan was going to murder their child.

Darius wasn't stupid. It was clear from his expression that he knew there was something very wrong with the situation.

"What's the matter?" Stefan barked. "Don't be an ungrateful child. Eat up."

Darius' gaze was locked with Faye's, reading the terror on her face. His lower lip quivered.

Stefan shouted, "Darius!" The child started and snatched up his spoon.

"Don't," exclaimed Faye. She turned tear-filled eyes to her husband. "Please." She swallowed. "Please. I'm sorry. I'll do anything."

Stefan folded his arms. He rubbed his chin. "Really? That's very interesting. Anything?" He said to his son, "Darius, you don't seem to want the nice pudding I had made especially for you. Is that correct?"

The little boy nodded.

"I see. Well, it would be a pity to allow it to go to waste. Shall we ask Mother if she would like to eat it?"

Darius turned questioning eyes to Faye. Before he could speak, and forever remember that he was the cause of his mother's death, she blurted, "Yes, I would like to eat it. I want to eat it. Do you mind Darius?"

"No, I don't mind. You're welcome, Mother. I hope you like it."

Faye took the bowl and spoon quickly, before she had time to think about what she was doing. She ate the dessert in large mouthfuls, forcing the sickly sweet substance down between gasping sobs. When the bowl was empty she sat with fat tears rolling down her cheeks, waiting for the poison to take effect. She kept her gaze on her sweet child so he would be the last thing she saw.

Darius had begun to cry too, though he couldn't have understood what was going on. For several minutes they sat, looking at each other. Just as Faye was thinking she should have left the room so Darius wouldn't see her final moments, Stefan burst into laughter.

"Aren't you two a pair of sad turtles? Look at you both. Crying over a silly dessert. How funny you are." He chuckled and shook his head, then got up from the table.

Faye nearly collapsed with relief. The dessert hadn't been poisoned. He'd only wanted to scare her.

"Darius," Stefan said, suddenly serious again, "go and play."

The little boy jumped down from his seat and ran out of the room.

"Faye, you really are a fool if you think I would hurt Darius. He's a mage and from what I can tell a very good one. With Parthenia, Oriana, and Ferne, I have four mages under my control, which makes *you* rather surplus to requirements, don't you think? I know exactly what you were doing this afternoon, Faye. If you ever attempt anything like that again, what I'll do to you will have you begging for a quick death from poison."

TWENTY-NINE

Stefan's sick punishment was turning out to be a watershed in their relationship, Faye realized a few days later. He had ceased to focus on her and instead began to show Parthenia much more attention than he had previously, usually within Faye's presence. When their eldest daughter wasn't looking, he would throw Faye a malevolent smirk, making clear his statement that now that Parthenia was growing into womanhood and her full mage power, Faye was indeed 'surplus to requirements.'

The idea that her husband was grooming Parthenia into his willing servant sickened Faye to the depths of her stomach, but she didn't know what to do about it. The poor child, who had craved her father's affection for so long, blossomed in happiness whenever Stefan spoke to her kindly, praising her efforts in her classes or her appearance. She began to decorate her hair every day with a ribbon or ornamental combs and pins, and every evening at dinner she would speak at length about what she'd learned, encouraged by Stefan's enthusiastic nods and smiles.

At such times, Faye could only listen and watch, wishing she could have given her daughter a better father, someone who truly loved her for who she was and would never have manipulated her young mind and heart—a man, not a monster.

One afternoon, in the garden, Stefan stooped lower than even Faye had thought he could go. He'd been away since the previous day—flying off to a clan meeting—and the usual sense of relief and calm had settled over the estate as it always did while he was gone. Faye was in an elevated spot that gave her a clear view of most of the expanse of manicured greenery and flowers, and so also of her children as they played.

Parthenia was teaching her pet tricks. She had a tarsul, a long-limbed, tree-climbing animal dappled pale green and brown—a camouflage that worked effectively when it was up among the leaves and branches. Tarsuls lived only three or four years, and Parthenia's had died a few months previously. One of Stefan's recent kindnesses to his eldest daughter had been to surprise her with a replacement. The animal arrived already house-trained, but Parthenia was teaching it to pick and bring her ripe fruit from the garden's trees. There was always something fruiting, and all the children loved to eat the freshly picked produce.

Oriana and Ferne were playing hide-and-go-seek, Castiel was bouncing a ball against a house wall. Nahla stood at her brother's side, begging him to play with her, but he was acting as though she didn't exist.

The children had, as usual, quickly and instinctively diverged into their two groups. The ones who had inherited her mage abilities and the two who hadn't—Castiel and Nahla—stayed subtly but distinctly apart. Oriana and Ferne would gladly have allowed Nahla to join in their game, but she preferred the company of Castiel, even though he was cool and dismissive toward her. At thirteen years of age, he was also five years older than her, while the twins, at twelve years old, were closer in age to Nahla. Yet still Faye's youngest daughter never gave up on her unrequited affection for Castiel. And though he rarely gave her the time of day, he was more often than not neutral in his attitude, whereas he clearly despised the others.

Of all her children, Castiel was the most like Stefan, Faye was forced to admit. In that regard, it was just as well he hadn't inherited mage power. She suspected that if he had, he would have been a dark mage, drawing energy from the unseen matter of the universe and using his ability to cause pain and create havoc.

Though she didn't know how to perform the test that would confirm her intuition, she guessed that Parthenia, Oriana, and Ferne were star mages like herself. Darius, however, she suspected was a spirit mage who relied on the power generated by living things.

Spirit mages were sensitive to emotions and the waxing and waning of the life force. On more than one occasion, Darius had shown himself to be highly receptive and responsive to the feelings of those around him, most recently during the horrifying episode in the breakfast room. He had picked up on both her terror and his father's fury.

Spirit mages were delicate beings who were happiest when protected from highly emotional states. Pushed to an extreme, they could lose their abilities, yet Faye could not explain that to Stefan. He would only be interested in what Darius meant in terms of how he could use him. Affecting the emotions of others at will, sometimes even being able to read their minds and speak to them without words would, to Stefan, only be an extremely useful weapon.

As if by thinking of him Faye had summoned him, Stefan appeared at the open double doors into the garden, back from his trip. She felt a chill like the sun had gone behind a cloud, though the sky was its usual clear, rosy blue. None of the children had noticed their father. They continued to play, and Parthenia continued to praise and stroke her tarsul to reward it for bringing her a fruit.

Stefan saw Faye watching him. He gave her a sarcastic nod and moved from his position of leaning against the door frame to walk toward his eldest child. She had crouched down to pat the tarsul. Stefan stood over her, his hands on his hips.

"How is he doing?" he asked her. "You seem to be doing an excellent job of training him. What did you name him?"

Parthenia said a name Faye didn't catch and stood up, brushing dust from her pants.

"It isn't as pretty as your name, my dear," Stefan said, "but I like it. What does it mean?"

Parthenia smiled in response to her father's compliment. "It doesn't mean anything. I made it up."

"Oh, well, it suits him. What have you taught him to do?"

Parthenia instructed the animal to perform various tricks, including standing on its head, playing dead, and walking only on its hind legs. Finally, she made it go and pick a fruit for her father, which it presented on open palms with a bow.

"Wonderful," Stefan said, laughing as he took the offered fruit. "What a clever animal, and what a clever mistress to train it so well."

"Thank you, Father,' Parthenia said.

Faye grimaced at the grateful tone in her daughter's voice.

"What's wrong, Mother?" Darius asked. He was lying on his stomach with his arm in the pond, trying to catch a fish. His dark brown hair had flopped over his face and his cheeks were flushed.

"It isn't anything important," she replied. "Have you caught a fish yet? Remember to be gentle if you do."

"Oh, I'm always gentle. I don't want to make them feel bad, because then I feel bad too."

Faye looked down on her youngest child. His ability was growing stronger by the day. She would have to prevent Stefan from finding out the truth about his six-year-old son.

Though she'd discovered a firestone in the garden, she hadn't been able to collect it. Stefan had ordered the servants to watch her around the clock. Her maid even stayed with her when she bathed. If only she could make her own elixir. She could warn Carina and perhaps she could even Cast to effect an escape for her children and herself. She wasn't sure how they would survive outside the estate's walls and avoid detection by the Sherrerrs, but perhaps they could do it.

If she couldn't Cast, her only hope lay in the other ruse she'd planned. The symptoms of her disease were growing more pronounced. Perhaps in another few weeks she would be so sick she would have to travel to the capital for emergency treatment. There, surely the greater freedom would give her more opportunities to escape. In the capital they would stand a better chance of getting off the planet.

She would have to allow herself to become seriously ill to do it, but it was a risk she was willing to take.

Faye had been watching Parthenia and Stefan as she weighed her options, then her husband did something that snapped her to attention. He put his hands on the waist of his adolescent daughter and regarded her figure.

"You're filling out most pleasantly, Parthenia. Becoming a young woman. We must see about getting you some new clothes more suitable for you. Some dresses and things not quite so childish. Would you like that?"

Parthenia was blushing. She looked uncomfortable and a little afraid. "Yes, Father, I would."

"There's my good girl. Perhaps you and your mother can go on a little shopping trip, as mothers and daughters do. Pick out some cloth and have a dressmaker sew you the latest fashions. But you must promise me you won't go flirting with anyone while you're in town. That wouldn't be at all becoming, would it? You mustn't forget that you'll always be my little girl."

He pulled her close and planted a kiss on her cheek. It wasn't the fond peck of a father to his child. Stefan pressed his lips closely against her soft skin and took his time.

Faye stared in disbelief. Stefan's eyes were closed, but then he opened them and, turning, gazed directly into hers, giving her a broad wink.

"Mother," Darius said, "what's wrong?"

Thirty

As Faye prepared to go into town with Parthenia, her mood was low. She couldn't shake the image of her horror of a husband giving her daughter that intimate, inappropriate kiss. His shameless wink had seemed to convey only one message, and it was one Faye could hardly bear to contemplate.

Stefan had commented recently that her childbearing days seemed to be over. She knew how little he truly loved the mage children she had provided him, while at the same time he wanted more due to the power they gave him and his clan. Now she'd borne him all the offspring she could, was it possible he planned on committing incest with his daughter? Faye's stomach turned at the thought. She hadn't been able to eat since the previous day.

Parthenia came down the stairs in the hall of the grand mansion, buttoning her coat. What Stefan had said was true, she was growing into a young woman. She was a head taller than Faye and she'd lost her child's figure over the recent few months.

She seemed calm and collected, as if she had forgotten or gotten over the embarrassment and confusion her father's embrace had caused. She gave Faye a quick smile as she reached the bottom of the stairs.

Faye couldn't remember when it had occurred, but at some point in her adolescence, Parthenia's attitude toward her had changed. She'd become distant and reserved. Faye had never figured out if it was because she saw her as competition for her father's affection, or if it was only a natural consequence of her growing up.

Some days, when the ache for the loss of Carina was particularly bad, she would imagine her first daughter wouldn't have been the same way. Then she would feel guilty and resolve to never again compare her children's displays of affection.

They went out together and climbed into the smaller, four-seater Sherrerr autocar. Two servants sat in the front. Nate was their chauffeur as usual, and another servant called William had come along. Both servants were Faye and Parthenia's guards and captors.

Nate input the destination and the car set off. He had been with the family for many years, and Faye had sometimes suspected he didn't approve of what went on in the household, but of course he couldn't say or do anything about it. The only people who worked for the Sherrerrs were either foolish or had little left to lose. Faye suspected Nate belonged to the latter category. Everyone knew that though the working conditions were good, employment with the Sherrerrs was a life sentence. Only idiots or those who didn't have another way of feeding themselves or their family asked for a job.

Faye and Parthenia sat together in silence as the car drove smoothly toward the town. Faye wished there was a way she could speak to her daughter out of earshot of the servants, but she might as well have wished for the moon. She wanted to reassure Parthenia she would do everything in her power to protect her from her predatory father, weak though her power was. Perhaps it was best she could say nothing.

Nate turned around and asked for confirmation of the textile merchant's shop he had input into the autocar.

"Yes, that's the one," Faye replied. "Do you remember it, Parthenia? I think we went there last year."

"Yes, I remember, Mother. Will you be taking some fabric too?"

"No, I won't. This trip is for you."

"That's right. Father didn't say you could, did he?"

Parthenia's face was half-turned away as she spoke, and Faye thought she saw an odd expression flit across it. An intense emotion had affected her daughter. If Darius had been there he would have picked up on it immediately, but Faye didn't possess his powers. She only knew her daughter was feeling something deeply.

"That's right," Faye replied. "This day is all yours."

Parthenia nodded, not removing her gaze from the wide, dusty plain outside. She didn't seem particularly happy about the trip. Faye guessed that perhaps the meaning of her father's actions was weighing heavily on the child after all. She reached over and took her daughter's hand, and the two sat hand in hand all the way into town until the autocar stopped outside the textile store.

The general shoppers were in the process of leaving. The owner was shooing them out the door, concern in his eyes as the Sherrerr car drew up and parked. A few pedestrians gazed curiously into the tinted windows, unable to see the occupants. Faye waited until the textile merchant had chased the people off before leaving the car and going into the store.

She always felt bad about taking things from the town's shopkeepers, but she had to. What was more, she had to take the best of what they had to offer. Stefan would be angry if they returned with anything second best.

Parthenia had gone over to look at a bolt of thick, rich purple fabric. Faye joined her and ran her hand down the material. It had a faint sheen.

"A very good choice, mistress," said the textile merchant. "That's a rare one. Comes from offplanet. Made from a plant that won't grow here. That's its natural color. Can you tell?"

Faye looked closely at the material. Its color was indeed a little uneven and not a single block of one shade, indicating the material hadn't been dyed in a factory. "It's very beautiful," she said to the store owner and then to her daughter, "It would suit you, Parthenia." She was speaking the truth. Parthenia had inherited her olive skin and dark hair and the deep purple complemented her coloring.

"Okay," Parthenia said. "I'll take this one. What else would you recommend?" she asked the merchant.

Nate, who had entered the shop with them while the other servant remained with the car, lifted up the entire bolt of material and took it out. Faye saw him placing it inside the roof box, ready to take to the dressmaker. It was a seemingly innocuous act, yet it was odd. The textile merchant would normally send over the fabric himself. That was how they'd always done it before. Was it possible Nate intended to give her and Parthenia a small break from their constant surveillance?

The merchant was busily showing her daughter a crimson fabric that would also look good on her. Faye went to the shop window and looked out into the street. Two small crowds had gathered on each side, a respectful distance away.

"I have a new previewer, if mistress would like to try it," the textile merchant was saying to Parthenia.

"I guess so," she replied without enthusiasm.

The man escorted her into a back room. Faye could hear him explaining the instructions. The machine would allow her daughter to see herself in any of the fabrics and styles she selected. For a moment, Faye was alone in the shop.

Then the owner returned. "Can I interest you in anything today, ma'am?"

"No, thanks. We're only picking up things for my daughter." Her heart began to race. Did she dare ask him what was on her mind? She had to take the chance. It would be the only one she would get. "I guess you must have heard about my son's kidnapping."

"Oh yes, of course. It was terrible, terrible news. Everyone was so relieved when he was returned home. I trust the young master is well?"

"Yes, he's very well, thanks. But..." Faye took a deep breath. "The person who brought him back... I didn't have the opportunity to thank her. I wanted to give her a reward. Is she still in town?"

"Do you mean the owner of the merc company, mistress? No. She left immediately after the young master was returned."

"No, not her. I meant the young soldier who brought him back to our estate."

"Oh, the merc," said the merchant. "Yes, she stuck around for quite a while. No one seemed to know why. But she's gone now. Got into a fight with..." He blanched and swallowed. "She was highly disrespectful toward some employees of Mr Sherrerr, ma'am. After they beat her thoroughly for it, she left town."

Relief and sadness intermingled in Faye. Though she was pleased her eldest daughter was out of immediate danger, she was also sad to hear she'd suffered at the hands of her husband's men.

"Though oddly enough, she left a part of herself behind," the merchant went on. He had the look of someone with a juicy piece of gossip.

Faye gave him the prompt he was seeking. "What do you mean?"

"Well..." The man edged closer. Outside, Nate was leaning one elbow on the roof of the autocar and chatting with William, who was sitting inside. "The altercation the soldier interfered with involved a splicer, ma'am," said the merchant. "Although your husband's men beat her in the end, of course, she put up a very good fight. The splicer grabbed some of her hair, and he's planning on selling her code for conception treatment."

"He's what?" Faye exclaimed. "He's going to use her code to engineer embryos? Surely that isn't legal."

The man made a dismissive gesture. "We don't tend to pay a lot of attention to what is and isn't legal around here, ma'am." He made a face that said, *As you know too well.*

It was a good point. Faye was, after all, stealing from the man's shop. "What splicer was it?" she asked.

"He's just over the way, ma'am, but I hope you won't tell him it was me who informed you. I was only chatting. I didn't know you would take it further."

"Don't worry," Faye replied. "I'm not going to have him prosecuted, but I would like to talk to him."

Parthenia came out of the back room. "I'll take those three." She pointed at the red fabric she'd been looking at earlier and two others, a green and a velvety black. "Do you think that's enough, Mother?"

"Yes, I think so. We have to go to the dressmaker next. But I have another errand to run first. Would you mind waiting here for me for a few minutes?"

Parthenia looked shocked. Doing anything other than exactly what they were supposed to do while in town was strictly forbidden. In front of the textile merchant, however, she could say nothing. "Okay, Mother. I'll wait."

Faye had no choice. If the splicer had Carina's code, whatever child he helped create would be a mage. The child's ability would be traced back to her daughter, and Carina's freedom and possibly her life would be forfeit. Stefan would make Faye pay dearly for an impromptu visit to the splicer, but it would be worth it.

THIRTY-ONE

The news of what Faye had done arrived at the estate before she did. Stefan was waiting for them on the steps.

"What's Father doing?" Parthenia asked as soon as she saw him. "Why is he standing there?"

"I'm not sure," Faye replied, though she knew exactly why.

The autocar drew up and they got out. Faye stared unflinchingly into her husband's eyes, not disguising her hatred. She'd already defied him. Whatever punishment he had in store, she would suffer it whatever she did.

"Go inside, Parthenia," Stefan said quietly. "Dinner will be served in a moment. Your mother and I will be eating alone."

Her daughter's gaze flicked between them before she obediently did as her father instructed. As soon as she'd gone into the dining room, Stefan gripped Faye painfully around her upper arm and pushed her ahead of him. He took her to the rear of the house to an open door that, despite her earlier bravery, made her quail. It had been years since she'd passed through that door and gone down those steps.

The cellar was where she'd spent her first few months in the Sherrerr mansion, tethered to the walls, beaten and raped day in and day out. For months, she'd remained defiant, refusing to give up her secrets, until Stefan had finally broken her by preying on her love for Kris. She'd told him everything in the foolish hope it would save Kris' life. Even then, she hadn't understood how truly depraved and evil Stefan was. Even then, she'd imagined he would keep his word. Right up until that final moment...

Faye gasped and shook her head, holding onto the door frame. Tears welled in her eyes.

"Not so courageous now, are you, my darling?" Stefan thrust his shoulder against her back, forcing her through.

She stumbled and fell down the steps, hitting her head at the bottom. The next thing she knew, Stefan was hauling her to her feet and pushing her into a cell. Restraints were fixed to the walls, and he slammed her wrists and ankles into them before marching back to the door and closing it.

"Think you can defy me and get away with it, you bitch?" he yelled. He grabbed her face and pushed her head against the wall. He ground his lips into hers, pressing the weight of his body against her. When he pulled away, Faye felt a trickle of blood run down her chin.

"Why did you go to the splicer? What did you want from him?"

Faye turned away her head.

"Never mind. I'll find out soon enough. The man may have packed up his business and left town, but my men are on his tail. They'll soon catch him and he'll tell me whatever I need to know." Stefan began pacing up and down the cell, his rage working higher. "I tried, Faye. I tried so hard with you. Those things I had to do in the beginning were unfortunate, but they were necessary. Afterward, if you had only allowed yourself to move on, everything could have been perfect between us. I wanted it to be perfect. But you were too stubborn and unforgiving. I hate it that you bring out this side of me. I hate it that you make me do this to you. But it's the only way. It's the only way to make you understand you must obey!"

"It isn't me who does this to you, Stefan," Faye said. "You like to think you're wonderful, don't you? You think giving me and our children this luxurious lifestyle means something. That all you ask, all I do for you when I Cast, is just payment for all you give me. But this life doesn't mean a thing because I didn't choose it. You treat us like your slaves and playthings. But we're people, with feelings and opinions of our own, though they might as well not exist for all the notice you take of them. You use us and control us, and when we don't do as we're told, you throw a tantrum like a five year old. Only you're a grown man. A grown man who's evil and out of control. *I* don't do this to you, Stefan. This is who you are."

He ran at her and punched her in the stomach. Pain radiated up, and Faye slumped against the restraints. Her mouth flooded with saliva. She vomited, and the vomit ran down her dress.

Stefan curled his lip in disgust. "You're revolting. Do you know that? Look at yourself." He grabbed the neckline of her dress and ripped it from her. Then he tore away her underclothes until she was naked. If he noticed the bruises her disease had created on her body, he didn't seem to think anything of them.

He kissed her roughly again and undid his belt.

———

When Stefan had finally exhausted himself by taking out his anger on her, he undid the restraints. Faye collapsed to the floor of the cell. She lay still, waiting for him to leave. But he hadn't quite finished. He squatted down, grabbed her hair, and lifted up her head so he could look her in the eyes.

"I haven't decided what I'll do with you yet. I may tell the children you've taken ill and are being treated at a clinic for a couple of days. Perhaps I'll allow you to resume your role within the household. I'm sure you still have some skills to impart to our offspring. I hope tonight's lesson will encourage you to give up those final secrets. On the other hand, I may just leave you here. The room is soundproofed. No one will hear you, and none of the servants will dare to interfere with your slow, agonizing demise."

He abruptly let go of her head and her skull hit the cold flagstones. Stefan stood and straightened his clothes. "In a way, this is so unfortunate. I sometimes wonder how different things might have been if only you had listened to reason in the very beginning. Imagine the life you could have led if you had consented willingly to join my clan. You would have been adored—no— worshipped for your powers. A far greater Sherrerr than myself would have claimed you as his own and there would have been nothing I could have done about it. And, floating high on the success afforded by your abilities, the Sherrerrs would have risen above all our competitors.

"But you chose a different path. Everything you've given me has been in tiny, niggardly doses, won at great effort. You made me work so hard for it all, Faye. Why? What was the point? So that you could end up back here again, where we began our time together? Such a shame. What a wasted opportunity." He went to the door. "But, never mind. I got what I wanted in the end. And you know what, my dear? When you say this is who I really am, I think you may have a point."

He smirked and left.

After several minutes, when she was sure he wouldn't be back for a while, Faye slowly moved into a sitting position. She probed inside her mouth with her tongue, working it up between her swollen gums and her teeth. The hairs she'd demanded from the splicer were still there. She pulled them out. Three long, black strands. All she needed was elixir. If she could only get that, she could Cast. She would Cast Locate to find out where Carina was. If she was still on the planet, she would Cast Send and tell her to leave.

Then, if she had enough elixir, she would Transport all her children far, far away. Perhaps she could Transport them to a remote place where they could escape recapture by the Sherrerrs.

And then she would kill Stefan.

Thirty-Two

From where she was standing, Carina could see the ridge she and Bryce had peeked over when they were watching the Sherrer stronghold. It was white with snow against a cloudy white sky and obscured further by grayish snowflakes swirling down. She would have given a lot to be up there again and not freezing her toes off working for the Sherrerrs.

She'd only just made it through Basic, receiving the dubious reward of recruitment into the Sherrerr forces. Still bearing the marks of her beating, Carina had been put to work at the lowest tier of the clan's military wing.

It was a bizarre conclusion to her and Bryce's effort to reconn the Sherrerr stronghold. As she stood on sentry duty on the fortress shuttle pad, Carina struggled to wrap her head around it. If the clan hadn't been undertaking their massive recruitment drive, she doubted the two of them would have been so lucky. As it was, she guessed their youth and lack of any military equipment had counted in their favor. Raynott, the officer who had overseen Carina's interrogation, might not really have believed their story, but she probably thought they were young and poor enough to quickly switch allegiance on the promise of a job, shelter, and a steady supply of food.

Which wasn't so far from the truth. Carina had no loyalty to the Dirksens. They had mercilessly tortured the little boy she had rescued. However, neither did she bear any love for the Sherrerrs. As far as she was concerned, both clans were as bad as the other. The sooner she could escape her accidental employment and go offplanet—preferably outsystem—the better.

She had only one problem: Bryce. She couldn't bring herself to escape and leave him behind. She wasn't sure how long he could survive without the medication that kept his disease under control but it certainly wasn't forever. The Sherrerrs would probably work him until he was too sick to go on and then put him outside the gates. If she left without him she would always have his fate on her conscience. She had to find him and Cast Transport to get them both out of there.

The only information about Bryce she'd managed to glean was that he'd been put to work dealing with slops and garbage somewhere in the bowels of the fortress. There could be no sneaking off during her long work hours to visit that area—she was certain that Raynott had given the order that she was to be closely watched—and when she wasn't working, she wasn't allowed to visit the men's quarters. Male and female soldiers were kept strictly segregated during their brief hours of downtime. She could only hope to find him while he was working and she wasn't.

New recruits were arriving at the fortress every day. Her guess that the Sherrerrs were developing a new weapon had been incorrect. The stronghold was for military training. No one said so, but there could only be one conclusion drawn from the fast, large increase in numbers of troops: the Sherrerrs were preparing for a conflict of some kind. Perhaps they were expecting an attack, but it seemed from the training they were planning an assault.

She stamped her feet. The sentry box on the fortress' roof provided only a little protection from the falling snow. Her boots had created a puddle of icy slush that had penetrated the leather. Her Sherrerr uniform was warmer than her civvies, but standing still for hours meant a chill had inevitably set in. She guessed she had only ten or fifteen minutes of guard duty remaining, but the seconds were dragging past.

When the comm in her helmet chirped, Carina's mood brightened, thinking her replacement had arrived. But the message was only to tell her and her fellow sentry to step below for five minutes. A shuttle was coming in.

They waited in the stairwell until the roar and vibration of the shuttle's landing ceased, then went out onto the roof once more. The air was noticeably warmer from the burst of energy from the shuttle's engine as it landed. A sleek, expensive vessel had arrived, a domestic model, bearing the Sherrerr insignia on each side.

The portal slid smartly open and the ramp extended. A tall, handsome, elegant man cloaked in furs and wearing a cravat and a haughty expression appeared, followed by a man and woman who looked like servants. Without a glance at Carina or the other sentry, the man paused a moment to allow the security scanner to confirm his identity, then he disappeared inside the fortress.

He was probably a high-ranking member of the Sherrerr clan, Carina mused, though not of the military arm. Still, his arrival added weight to her earlier assessment of the situation—the Sherrerrs were planning a big event of some kind. Their extensive extended family was involved.

She received the notification she was waiting for. Her replacement took over and she went down into the stronghold, making her way to the mess room. There, she grabbed a hot drink to help her warm up before setting out to find Bryce. If she could only touch him, it would be enough to anchor the Transport and she could whisk them both far away. Not off the planet, but hopefully somewhere they would be safe from detection.

The garbage processing area was in the basement of the fortress. Free passage through the building, even to such unsavory areas, wasn't allowed for lowly grunts like her. But though Carina didn't have the authority to go to Bryce's work site, she thought she would try. She went down the curving stone stairwell, sipping her drink and appreciating the feeling that was returning to her fingers and toes.

She patted the bottle of elixir at her side to reassure herself she hadn't forgotten it in her sleep-deprived haze when she suited up that morning. She'd made the liquid in the early hours. If she could only see Bryce for a few moments she was sure she could Transport him. The Cast might work with only her mental image of the young man, of course, but it wasn't worth the risk.

The last time she'd used Transport was to rescue the boy the Dirksens had kidnapped. She'd moved enemy soldiers a kilometer away from the scene of engagement. With one of the soldiers in front of her, it had been easy to fix on the others through the common factor of their uniform. Transporting an individual who was out of sight was much more difficult.

She turned the final bend in the stairwell. Her heart sank. There was no human guard at the waste processing zone for her to persuade to let her in for five minutes. The door was locked and unmarked except for a window the size of a human face. She looked through it but she could only see darkness. On the wall next to the door was an ID scanner. She guessed it was worth a try.

"Private Lin," she said into the mic while the device scanned her face and retinas.

A warm female voice said, "Entry denied."

Carina cursed. She was all ready to get them both out of there. She only needed a couple of minutes. Should she wait around? Maybe someone else would arrive and allow her to sneak inside with them, though she doubted anyone would risk being disciplined for her. She looked through the window again. This time she could see a light. A door was open, illuminating a dark hall. Someone was coming out, and as the figure entered the hall, motion-activated lights flickered on.

A burly soldier was walking toward her. It was one of the men who had beaten her up.

She hesitated. He was one of the last people she wanted to meet, but he was also the only person who could help her right now. The man's lip curled when he recognized Carina's face in the window. Pulling open the door he said, "Hello there. I heard you made it through Basic. I was surprised. I should have roughed you up better."

"You roughed me up well enough, thanks," Carina said as she tried to sidestep the man and slip past him.

"Wait a minute," the soldier said. He raised his arm, blocking the gap. "Where do you think you're going? Off to see your boyfriend? You don't have authority to go in there. But I don't want you to go away unsatisfied. Why don't we forget what happened and be friends? Maybe I could scratch your itch for you."

"No thanks," said Carina. "Your version of foreplay doesn't do a thing for me."

The soldier laughed. "And here I was thinking you were the type to like it rough. We can try a different style if you want. Come on, you must be desperate for it to try to sneak in here. The smell's bad enough to knock you out better than I did. I'm not so off-putting, am I?"

The conversation was taking a turn Carina had no interest in or time for. She was about to tell the man where to go and give up on her attempt to see Bryce when another of the doors in the hall opened. Carina glimpsed a familiar face. "Bryce," she called.

"Carina," Bryce said, coming through the door with a large sack on his back. "It's great to see you. Are you okay? I was worried about you."

"Yeah, I'm fine," she replied. She'd finally found him, but she couldn't Transport them both with the obnoxious bully looking on.

"What a touching reunion," said the burly soldier, "but if you don't want *me*, I'm not going to let you have *him*." He pushed her roughly out of the way and slammed the door.

At the same time, Carina's comm chirped. "Private Lin, report to the shuttle pad in fifteen minutes with full equipment, ready to ship out."

She looked through the window at Bryce. It was hopeless. She couldn't Cast in front of the Sherrerr soldier. She had no choice but to leave, not knowing when or if she could return to rescue her friend.

Thirty-Three

When Carina arrived at the shuttle pad, the domestic vessel that had arrived earlier had left and in its place was a craft occupying the entire rooftop. Along with the other soldiers who had been ordered to board it, she went up the ramp and inside the vessel. She stowed her equipment and took a seat. The craft was military style and reminded her of her merc band's shuttle—bare bones inside but solid and tough.

As she fastened her harness, the soldier in the seat next to her held out his hand. "Mandeville."

Carina shook it. "Lin."

"I haven't seen you around. You new?"

"That's right. I started a few days ago. You?"

"Six months in. First time I've gone into space, though. What's up with your face? Did you fall down the mountain on your way over?"

"Ha, no. I accidentally walked into some fists. Do you know what this mission's about?"

"I haven't heard anything. I'm guessing they'll tell us when we're aboard ship."

The shuttle was quickly filling up, and the vibration through the floor signaled that the pilot was warming the engines. A female soldier took the seat on the other side of Carina. She was a well-muscled woman who reminded her of a former fellow merc and bunk mate, Atoi.

Raynott, the officer who had ordered Carina's beating, entered the cabin. "Helmets sealed everyone," she said. "Taking off in two minutes."

Carina put on her helmet and sealed it. Now anything she said would broadcast to everyone, so she stayed quiet for the trip up to the Sherrerr ship.

When they arrived and the soldiers filed out of the shuttle bay, Raynott ordered them into formation. She addressed the group. "In four days we'll arrive at our engagement site. Until then, you'll do exercises aboard ship. You'll also be issued with new firearms and receive training on them so you know which is the mean end. Wait here until a crew member arrives to assign quarters."

As Raynott left, the soldiers broke ranks and removed their helmets. Carina guessed there were about a hundred and fifty of them, but as she looked around, the Sherrerr ship seemed large for such a number. The shuttle bay they had just left had been massive. Going by its size, she guessed the ship had a capacity of two thousand or more. She hadn't known the Sherrerrs possessed such large warships.

Over the next couple of days, Carina slotted easily into the ship's routine. Even more so than at the fortress on Ithiya, the lifestyle took her back to her merc days. She knew the ropes, but she wasn't happy about re-familiarizing herself with them. Though she didn't have a problem with fighting if she had to, she didn't feel like a soldier anymore. Her short time working for the Sherrerrs had really brought home to her the fact that she'd moved on.

Yet even as she was adjusting to her new view on life, she had an idea that would involve behaving like a good soldier for just a little longer. If she could distinguish herself in whatever conflict they had coming up, perhaps she could exploit the favor she might receive from Sherrer higher-ups for special permission to visit Bryce.

When the troops performed military exercises in the emptied shuttle bay aboard ship, Carina kept her head down and worked hard. Experience had taught her that among the average group of soldiers, even such simple behavior helped you stand out. Or at least it helped you avoid the ire of the commanding officer, which was just as beneficial.

On the day they were to go into battle, Raynott assembled the soldiers in a briefing room. She brought up a holo of a moonscape. It was a large ice moon with a thin, unbreathable atmosphere. The holo zoomed in, and an installation became visible. The place had looked like it was just another part of the rocky, icy surface until the camera got in close.

"This is Banner's Moon," said Raynott. "We stumbled across the place during part of a general surveillance exercise in Dirksen territory. The building you see is invisible to scanners and only visible to the naked eye at close range. The Dirksens clearly have something to hide here, though what exactly, we aren't sure yet. Not that that's going to stop us from storming the place and fucking their shit up." She smirked.

"Seriously," Raynott continued, "we're guessing they might be developing a new weapon or something similar. Whatever it is, we want it. So don't go blowing up anything unless it's absolutely necessary. Feel free to kill as many of the enemy as you like."

Raynott went on to explain what their company's role would be in the assault. They were to attack the facility from the spinward side. Theirs would be the first assault wave—in some ways the most dangerous, but they also had the element of surprise on their side.

When she'd finished laying out the finer details of the assault, she said, "Questions?"

Mandeville raised his hand. Raynott nodded at him.

"Do we have any clues about what we might be looking for?" he asked.

"If it is a weapon, even if it's only at the prototype stage," Raynott replied, "you can bet they'll be using it on you. That's probably the biggest flag you'll see. Other than that, follow the path of most resistance. Whatever they seem keenest to protect, whatever area has the strongest defense, go for it."

A small amount of chatter started up, which Raynott silenced with, "There's something I forgot to mention. We're blowing the place from orbit forty-five minutes after the first assault. We think we have about that long before the nearest Dirksen ship arrives. You'll see the countdown on your visor overlays. Get in, get what you can, and get out. You better be back here on time or you're not going home."

Some of the soldiers shifted uncomfortably. Even Carina with her experience of the callous attitude of her merc band's owner was a little shocked. The Sherrerrs weren't messing around. They would try to take whatever the Dirksens had on their moon, but if they couldn't have it, they were going to make sure the Dirksens wouldn't either. For many of the soldiers, it was their first live engagement. She hoped it wouldn't also be their last.

The briefing was over. The soldiers were told to go to the shuttle bay and into a waiting shuttle. Carina strapped herself in, secured her helmet, and checked her weapon. The firearm she'd been given was a new type of pulse rifle. It produced concentrated fire designed to penetrate the latest designs of armor, though they'd been warned it would only penetrate in one shot at close range.

Always the military tech race continued. Armor was developed to resist the current level of firepower, so more effective guns were designed, resulting in better-designed armor, and so on. Carina wondered whether the Dirksens were developing a weapon that pierced the armor she was wearing.

The shuttle lifted and carried them out of the Sherrerr ship. Mandeville gave her a thumbs up and she nodded. They'd become better acquainted over the previous days of training. He was a nice guy. In fact, most of the soldiers were just regular people. None were seasoned veterans like the mercs she'd previously worked with. She wasn't used to her fellow troops being normal. Some of them looked scared, reminding her of herself at her first engagement when she was sixteen. Her mentor and commanding officer, Captain Speidel, had gotten her through it safe and sound. She no longer needed the poor, dead captain, but that didn't stop her from missing him.

Suddenly, they were dropping out of the sky so fast the shuttle's artificial gravity drive couldn't compensate, and Carina found herself lifting out of her seat. From somewhere to the right came the whine of a soldier's armor sucking up vomit that had erupted into his helmet. She wasn't so far from upchucking herself. She'd spent so long planetside she'd lost her space legs.

Only moments later the shuttle hit the ground. The doors snapped open. Carina undid her harness and ran out with the rest of the company into a barren, icy moonscape. They were a minute from a low mountain—no, that was the Dirksens' facility, and those dark spaces that looked like cave entrances were windows.

She was running. Get in, get what she could, get out. Weapon fire burst from the installation. The defenders had realized they were under attack. She zigzagged randomly. Soldiers began to fall. One hit the ground right in front of her. She jumped over the squirming figure. Was it Mandeville? With tinted visors obscuring their faces, it was hard to tell and her visor didn't bring up a name. She hoped it wasn't Mandeville.

She was at the window. Others who had reached there before her had broken through and the site was depressurizing fast. She jumped inside, vaulting with one hand on the window frame, her hybrid silicon armor impervious to jagged shards at the edge. She was inside. The Dirksens had killed the lights, but her helmet beamed out its own. Sweeping it around she saw hand-to-hand fighting, a jumble of bodies. Her visor overlay tagged the figures as friends and foe.

Someone lunged at her. She swept her rifle around and cracked the butt against her attacker's helmet. As he fell, she fired point blank into his chest, breaking the atmosphere seal. Gas poured out, condensing in the frigid air. Blood also sprayed from the opening and instantly froze.

A pulse round hit her from behind. Her suit's sensors flared, the repair mechanism triggered as she spun around, firing. The shot had come from a now-empty doorway. She ran through it, showering the hallway with fire. She hit two enemy soldiers but didn't cause them much damage. They fired back.

More of her company poured through the opening. The two Dirksen soldiers turned to run but were quickly mowed down.

The corridor was clear, and she ran down it with other soldiers from her company. Her helmet was scanning and mapping the place, sending a real time positioning readout to her as she ran. The installation was vast. Much bigger than it had looked from the outside. It had to go underground too. They were heading into the heart of the building, but it was so far from the entrance, she doubted they could make it out in time before the Sherrerrs blew the place.

Then things went crazy. Everyone around her dropped to the ground. Screaming from her helmet comm was piercing her ears. It was the screaming of her fellow soldiers. Yet when she looked around, none of them seemed hurt. Their suits were intact and their bodies seemed undamaged, even if they were writhing around.

She turned down her helmet comm to its lowest setting so she could only just hear her fellow soldiers' shrieks. There was nothing for it but to continue the mission alone.

THIRTY-FOUR

Carina jogged along the corridors, following the route the enemy soldiers had attempted to escape along. It led to a large space that looked like some kind of production facility. She figured this was her best bet for finding the reason for the installation.

Enemy units were ahead according to her visor overlay. She stopped dead. Approaching the next corner slowly, she peeked around it. Three enemy soldiers were in the corridor, but they were squirming on the ground as her own company's troops had. Their hands were over their heads as if something unbearable were happening to them.

She imagined if she could hear them, she would hear their screams. They were clearly too incapacitated to cause her any harm. She ran around the corner and right past the prone figures. After several similar encounters, she arrived at a grim sight. Scientists who hadn't been able to reach environment suits in time when the site depressurized had died. Their bodies, pop-eyed and frozen, were lying near a rectangular object the size of a large piece of luggage.

The device was resting in a steel cradle but it was half lifted out, as if someone had been trying to move it. Whether the instrument was important, Carina wasn't sure, but it could be and that was good enough for her. She grabbed its handle and tried to lift it, but the object was surprisingly heavy.

As she dropped it to adjust her hold, she noticed three small lights pulsing at the top corner. Out of curiosity, she touched the lights and found she could push them in. She pushed one home and the light went out. She pushed the other two until they clicked into position and became dark too. Unsure what she'd done, if anything, she grabbed the handle with both hands and lifted out the device.

Even in the moon's low gravity, she struggled to carry it. If she'd attempted to do the same on an average planet, she would never have been able. Stepping carefully past the splayed bodies of the scientists, Carina went out and began the journey back to the shuttle.

She'd lost track of time, she realized, and checked her visor overlay. Fifteen minutes until the countdown to blow the moon was due to begin. She was already sweating with the effort of carrying the device. Should she leave it behind? If the device was important, delivering it to the Sherrerrs could be just the kind of act that would win her a lot of favor. Carina struggled on.

What wouldn't she have given for an a-grav trolley? She'd heard such things existed but were insanely expensive. Or a powered exoskeleton. Her armor doubled her physical strength, but it was barely enough. She wasn't sure she would make it.

Her visor flashed. Three enemy units ahead. She dropped the device and walked forward. Hoping the enemy soldiers were in the same state they'd been when she'd passed them, she quickly stuck her head around a corner to assess the situation. The soldiers were up and walking, and they were heading her way. One of them had seen her.

A pulse round flew by so close to Carina's face it hurt her eyes, despite the deep tint of her visor. She turned and ran, but the corridor was straight with no cover. It was also so long she would be shot in the back before she reached the end of it. The only protection she had was the device.

She threw herself to the floor behind the block and rested the muzzle of her weapon on top of it. Not a moment too soon, for the barrel of a gun appeared and a barrage of rounds sprayed out. Carina ducked behind her cover. A second later, she raised her head just in time to see all three soldiers racing toward her.

She fired, hitting one in his thighs, which slowed him down a little but didn't seem to do much other damage. She hit the second square in his chest, but the round dispersed harmlessly. The soldiers ran on. She didn't stand a chance, but she continued firing.

Soon, she wondered why she was still alive. She should have been dead, if the soldiers had been firing at her, but they weren't—they were firing too high. Their pulse rounds passed over the device, as if they were trying to avoid hitting it.

She shot again, this time piercing one of the enemy unit's armor. The woman was down. Two more to go, but they were nearly upon her and she wouldn't have the protection of the device. Her heart in her mouth, she fired again. Her last shot. This was it.

Then one of the soldiers slumped forward, a hole in the back of his suit. His fellow turned, confused, and was met with concentrated weapon fire. Soldiers from her company came running up.

"What's that, Lin?" a voice said over her comm. She recognized it. Mandeville. He was still alive.

"I don't know," she replied. "It seemed important, so…"

"Move it, soldiers," came another voice. Raynott. "Shuttle's leaving in two minutes."

Two minutes?

"Can you help me with this?" Carina asked her rescuers. "It's very heavy."

With the help of the three soldiers from her company, Carina carried the device down the corridors while the seconds on her visor ticked down.

"Captain Raynott," Carina said into her mic. "We've found something. I don't know what it is but I've a feeling it's important. We're bringing it out, but we might not make the shuttle. Can you give us an extra minute or two?"

"Negative," came the reply.

"Let's leave it," said Mandeville.

Carina was torn. She wanted to bring the device to the Sherrerrs so she could save Bryce, but she didn't want to endanger her fellow soldiers. "You go. Leave me. I can make it."

But the three men didn't reply, and they didn't leave. The room where they'd broken into the facility was in sight. It was empty except for the bodies of those who hadn't made it. The shuttle was visible through the destroyed window.

The distance to the shuttle was around a minute's run, Carina remembered. She checked her visor. They had forty-five seconds.

With a supreme effort, they got the device out the window. Each soldier holding one part of the long handle that straddled the top of the device, they set off across the icy stone moonscape. Carina's lungs burned and her visor fogged as her suit struggled to clear the condensation of her hot breath on the frigid plastiglas.

At the top of the shuttle ramp a figure stood, beckoning them. Raynott.

Five seconds to go. It was too far. They weren't going to make it. Yet not one of the soldiers let go of their hold on that device. They wouldn't abandon the others to save themselves. The shuttle ramp began to rise and the air around the exhaust ports shimmered as the engines began to fire. Raynott stepped back.

They were at the ramp.

With a grunt of effort, the four soldiers lifted the instrument onto the rising ramp and leapt up. Carina didn't make it. She fell back and hit the ground. With horror, she watched the ramp rising out of reach. Just then, a head and shoulders appeared over the side, reaching down to her, telling her to jump.

She had only one chance. Carina jumped for her life. The soldier's hands caught her wrists. She found herself being hauled onto the closing ramp, rolling down to the access hatch. The ramp snapped closed. The shuttle took off.

There was no getting up while the shuttle pulled away at top speed, escaping the moon's gravity. Even Raynott was forced to the floor.

Carina lay still, listening to the sound of her ragged breathing, looking at the strange instrument that had nearly cost her and her fellow soldiers their lives. She hoped it would prove worth it.

THIRTY-FIVE

Carina's palms were sweaty as she knocked on the door to the commander's office. It had been highly presumptuous of her to even request an audience with him, but the fact that he had granted it lent her courage. The door clicked and swung open a little. She pushed it the rest of the way and went inside.

The commander was speaking with a holo of the head and shoulders of a woman. He held up a finger to her to signal her to wait. The holo woman's hair was tightly groomed into a thick spiral rising from the top of her head. Her shoulders were bare, and she wore a sapphire-blue top that looked like the upper half of a dress.

Was this woman the Sherrerr mage who had sent Carina the pouch? She ached with frustration that there was no way she could find out. She had to give up on her dream and move on.

On the journey back from Banner's Moon, Raynott and the other officers aboard the ship had examined the device Carina had taken from the Dirksen installation, but as far as she knew they hadn't come to any conclusions. She explained that she'd pressed buttons and the lights had gone out. No one wanted to find out what happened if they turned the lights on again.

From what Carina could tell, turning off the lights had coincided with the lifting of the effect that had incapacitated the other soldiers. They hadn't been writhing in pain, she'd discovered, but terror. Everyone but her had been overcome with fear so intense they could do nothing but scream. Carina hadn't suffered any effects at all, but she hadn't told anyone that. They just assumed she'd managed to fight through the emotion, and she didn't correct them. Her natural immunity was odd. She wondered whether it had something to do with the genetics that gave her mage powers.

The fact that Carina, Mandeville, and the other two soldiers had managed to bring out the device, and at such a risk to their own lives, earned all of them plenty of credit among their peers and the higher ranks. Carina was hoping to exploit this.

The commander said goodbye to the woman. The holo faded.

"Private," said the commander, finally turning his gaze to her. His name was Calvaley and he was in his late middle years, but that was all Carina knew about him. She guessed as he wasn't a Sherrerr himself, he had some other close alliance with the clan.

"Sir," Carina replied, saluting.

"Well, what is it?" Calvaley said. "My time is precious."

"I was wondering, sir, if I might ask permission to visit the men's quarters. In daylight hours, just to talk to a friend of mine."

"And what makes you think you deserve that special privilege?" Calvaley's eyes were coal black and as hard as stone.

"I believe the device I helped remove from the Dirksens' moon will prove extremely useful to us, sir."

"Maybe it will." He stood and placed his hands on his desk as he leaned forward. "That doesn't mean you deserve any special recognition. You only did as you were commanded. Don't you think that's rather presumptuous of you, soldier?!" As he spoke, his tone grew louder, until by the time he got to the end of his sentence he was yelling, his face turning pink from the effort.

"Perhaps, sir," Carina replied coolly. "However, it doesn't hurt to ask."

The commander's anger fell away in a moment. He laughed. "Not easily intimidated are you? What's your name again?"

"Lin, sir. Private Lin."

He nodded as if filing the information away for later use. He sat down and drew his chair closer to his desk. "Yes. Permission granted." He flicked his hand at her, shooing her away. "Have fun talking to your friend, Private Lin."

Carina quickly left before Calvaley could change his mind. Finally, she could see Bryce. All their troubles would be over, or most of them at least. She bounded down the stairwell leading to the men's quarters. Mandeville had recognized Bryce from her description and told her where to find him when he wasn't working.

This time when she spoke her name into the scanner, the door lock clicked open. She went through. The hallway lights flicked on and she could read the signs next to the doors. She quickly found Bryce's dorm.

Before going in, she double checked she had her elixir with her. It would take only a moment to Transport them both away. She hoped her dumb luck would hold out and Bryce would be alone.

The door to the dorm opened and someone came out. It was the burly soldier who had beaten her again, of all people. She seemed fated to constantly run into the unpleasant man.

"Come to see your friend?" The man leered. "He's all yours."

He held open the door so she was forced to go under his arm to enter the room. When the nasty soldier didn't leave but stood in the doorway, his sick smile still decorating his face, she shoved his arm out of the way and closed the door.

"Urgh," she said, seeing Bryce sitting on a bottom bunk. "Does this thing have a lock?"

"Carina," he exclaimed. He came over and hugged her. "Thanks for coming to see me. I'm going crazy in here. It's nice to see a friendly face."

"How are you?" she asked. "Are you okay?" She thanked the stars the rest of the dorm was empty. He was alone.

He shrugged. "I've been better. How about you?" He reached up and touched the fading bruises on her face. "Looks like they roughed you up a bit too."

She grimaced. "Yeah, a bit. But I've had worse. What about you? How are your symptoms?"

"As good as I can expect. I need another dose of my medication, but the doctor says they don't supply it, only the preventative. Anyway, I'm glad you've come because I wanted to say I'm sorry I dragged you into this. It was all my idea. It was lucky they didn't kill us."

"Don't worry about it. I could have refused if I wanted. You didn't force me to come along. That's all behind us now. What we have to do next is get out of here."

"That's not possible," Bryce replied. "Believe me, I thought about it. The only way out that isn't via shuttle is through the main door, and that's guarded around the clock. Besides, I don't think I could make the journey back in my current state."

"Bryce," Carina said in a serious tone. "What if I told you I could get us out of here, but it would mean we could never meet again?"

"I'd say, that's great. And then I'd say, wait, why can't we meet again?"

"I can't even tell you that. Believe me, the less you know, the better for both of us."

"Now I'm really intrigued, and a little bit scared. Is what you're proposing dangerous?"

"Only for me. And it'll only be dangerous for you if the Sherrerrs catch you again. Then it'll also be dangerous for me."

"Huh?"

"I know it sounds crazy. If you don't want to take the risk, that's fine. I'll go now. This is the only chance I'm giving you. Take it or leave it."

"What'll happen if I say yes?"

"You'll end up somewhere near where we left the town."

"*What?*"

"Bryce," Carina exclaimed in frustration. "I can't explain. You have to decide now, quickly, before someone comes in. Whatever you choose, whether you say no and I go by myself, or you say yes and I get you out too, it's goodbye."

It was only as the words left her lips she felt the significance of what she was saying. Once Bryce knew what she could do, she couldn't risk being in his company again. She couldn't trust that he wouldn't betray her secret. She'd known that when she'd decided to help him. What she hadn't expected was just how sad it made her feel.

"I don't understand," Bryce said, "but you're saying this is it? I'll miss you."

"I'll miss you too. So you'll leave?"

"Why would I stay? Can I bring anything with me?"

"Yes, whatever you can hold."

He scanned the room. "Actually, I don't have anything."

"Me neither." Carina hadn't wanted to risk attracting suspicion by bringing a bag to the dorm. She took a breath. "Okay. Turn around." The less he saw of what she was about to do, the better.

Bryce gave her a quizzical look, then faced away from her, sitting sideways on the bed. Carina took out the bottle of elixir and sipped a mouthful. She placed her hand on Bryce's back. She didn't need to touch him to Transport him, but she wanted to say a final goodbye. The young man had been the closest thing to a friend she'd had in a long time. Forever, in fact.

She recalled an area between the mountains and the town they'd traveled from, where the countryside was empty of people. Next, she wrote the Transport character in her mind. The next moment, her hand was empty. Bryce had disappeared.

Carina looked sadly at the indent on the mattress where he'd sat a moment before. She sighed. It was her turn.

THIRTY-SIX

As Faye sat in the garden after breakfast, she pondered a paradox. Mages could create fire, but only when they had elixir to make the Cast, but to create the elixir, they needed fire. Thinking of such things focused her mind on the task that lay ahead. The mental activity also helped to distract her from the pain of seeing the shocked looks of her children when Stefan had let her out of the basement that morning.

The everlasting tension in the household had tightened to screaming pitch. No one spoke a word when she arrived at breakfast. Oriana had gasped and clutched her hand to her mouth. Ferne began to exclaim something but was cut short when Oriana elbowed him. Nahla said, "Father...?" but failed to finish her sentence when Stefan glared at her. Parthenia had studied her mother gravely before returning to her meal. Even little Darius seemed to understand the importance of not remarking on what had happened. When Faye had appeared, after taking one look at her he'd only stared down at his plate as he ate. Castiel had smirked.

After breakfast was over, the children virtually tiptoed away.

From Faye's viewpoint, the only good thing to have come from Stefan's most recent behavior was her new understanding of his feelings. She knew now that she was all-but valueless to her husband. He only hoped to glean what little she might have left to teach, then she would probably 'disappear' as a warning to their mage children of what would happen to them if they disobeyed.

What Stefan probably didn't guess was that this revelation gave her new power. His usual method of controlling her was through threatening the children's lives. Now she knew he wouldn't harm them. Only her own life was at risk—which hung by a thread anyway—and she had lost all fear.

Rather than making her give up her attempts to defy him, Stefan's actions gave Faye new strength and determination. She was going to Transport her children away from him if it was the last thing she did. Of course, they would all remain in danger of recapture. Stefan and the rest of his clan would leave no stone unturned in their search for them, but when they were all free to use their mage powers, they would have a chance of escape. It was a much better alternative to living in that miserable hole with their jailer father.

As she watched the garden, Faye became aware that she herself was being watched. Olivia hovered just out of sight through the open doors behind her. Stefan had departed early that morning by shuttle on one of his ever-increasing business trips, taking part in whatever big thing was happening with the Sherrerrs. If Olivia wanted to sneak to him to betray her, he wouldn't be back until the evening at the earliest.

"Olivia," she called. When her maid didn't immediately reply, she said, "For goodness sake, woman. I know where you are. Come here."

Olivia stepped out, not looking particularly shamefaced about being called out on her spying. Faye wondered if Stefan was dallying with her. If he was, she pitied the woman. "I want to have a bath. Please prepare one for me."

"A bath?" It was an odd time of day for the request, and puzzlement showed on the maid's face, underlain with suspicion.

"Yes, a bath. Have you suddenly turned deaf, or stupid? After what your master did to me, I want to try to ease my aches. Does that make sense to you?"

Olivia finally looked abashed. "Yes, ma'am."

"And ask Cook about herbs that help with healing. She may have some in the kitchen." It would buy her a little more time.

As soon as Olivia left, Faye went out into the garden. She walked directly to the spot where she'd seen the firestone, right before Stefan caught her. It was still there, in the exact same place, half-buried in the soft soil of a flower bed. She thanked the stars that her husband hadn't spotted it.

Her hands trembling with haste, Faye took out the bag she'd secreted under her skirt. It contained everything she needed, each item gathered from its individual hiding place. She set down the bottle of ingredients that needed only the final addition of fire to their mix to be transformed into elixir. She made a pile of thin, dry twigs on the stone path, then picked up the stone.

Faye didn't waste time checking she wasn't being watched. She didn't care anymore. She had this one opportunity to get her children out of that terrible place and she was going to take it. She took out the knife she'd slipped into the bag at breakfast and the fluffy tinder she'd hoarded for so long. After putting down the ball of fluff, she struck the stone against the steel knife blade.

It took her several tries, but eventually sparks flew onto the tinder. Three or four strikes later, the surface of the tinder glowed and blackened in a few spots. Faye picked up the precious stuff and blew gently on it until it smoked. A slender tongue of flame rose, and she put the ball into the center of the kindling. Crouching close to the ground, her head on one side, she blew steadily into the piled sticks. They caught fire.

Faye place the metal bottle on the little fire. She cursed as she realized she didn't have any tongs to lift the hot bottle out again. She pulled down the sleeve of her dress to cover her hand. It would have to do.

After brewing elixir all her life and often in front of Stefan when teaching the children how to Cast, Faye knew within a heartbeat how long the mixture needed to warm. When the time was up, she reached into the flames with her covered hand and lifted it out. The thin material of her dress was poor protection from the heat, but Faye mentally blocked the burning pain of her fingers.

Gripping the bottle, she glanced around. She'd been lucky. The garden appeared to be empty.

She would normally allow the elixir to cool. It would be too hot to drink yet, but she couldn't waste any time. The process had taken so long, Olivia would have filled her bath and already be looking for her. She had only a few minutes at most.

Faye took a sip of the scalding liquid that sent fire down her throat as she swallowed it. First, she would Locate Carina and Send to her. Of all of them, she had the greatest chance of getting away and surviving. She took out the three hairs she'd taken from the splicer and gripped them.

Faye closed her eyes, steadied her breathing and her mind, and Cast Locate.

If she was in the planetary system, Faye's Cast would mentally take her to her daughter. And when she knew exactly where she was, she could Send. It had been many years since Faye had used Locate. The business dealings of the Sherrerrs rarely required that Cast. Her mind lifted up into the sky and ballooned out over the landscape. She could see/feel the positions of her children directly below her. They were in separate rooms of the mansion, having their lessons.

Faye wrenched her mind from them. The Cast wasn't working well. It was confusing Carina with her other offspring. It had been so long since she'd seen her eldest child, aside from that glimpse of her from the autocar.

Had she already left the planet? Or maybe she'd gone to another region? It would explain why Faye was having problems finding her. Maybe she should make the Cast wider, though it would need more time and energy than she had. If she couldn't find Carina within the next few moments, she would have to give up and simply Transport the other children out.

Then she detected a tiny glow in the gray, shady landscape. It was deep within a mountain range. Faye's mind flew to the spot. The glow strengthened in brightness. It was her. She'd found Carina. She'd found her first born.

Now to Send. Without opening her eyes and losing her daughter's position, Faye took another sip of the burning liquid, which seared her tongue and throat once more. She wrote the character in her mind and formulated her message.

"Mother," a voice exclaimed.

Someone grabbed the bottle from her hand. Faye's eyes flew open. Parthenia's tarsul had the elixir in its paw. Parthenia was running down the path toward her, a look of terror on her face.

"You mustn't," Parthenia hissed. She took the bottle from her pet and tipped the contents into the soil. Faye knelt before her child, utterly dumbfounded.

"Ma'am," called Olivia. She appeared. "Ma'am, your bath is ready."

Olivia didn't give voice to the suspicion dancing in her eyes. Faye was in a ridiculous position, kneeling on the stone garden path for no reason whatsoever. Parthenia was rigid as she stared at her. Faye got up. "Thank you, Olivia. I'll be along shortly. I want to speak to Parthenia for a few moments."

"As you wish, ma'am," the maid said and left.

"What the hell did you think you were doing?" Faye asked her daughter as soon as Olivia was out of earshot. "Do you want to live under the control of that monster for the rest of your life? You've spoiled the only chance I had of getting us out of here."

"You mustn't defy Father," said Parthenia, a tremble in her voice. "You mustn't. He'll be very angry." She spun around and left without another word. Her pet loped along in her wake.

Had Faye not been beyond weeping, she would have wept. But she'd cried a lifetime of tears for her children and herself. She had none left. She could hardly believe she'd come so close to their escape only to be thwarted by her own daughter. Stefan had starved the girl of attention and affection so effectively, he'd turned Parthenia against her. The child would do anything to make her father like her.

But Faye hadn't given up. The firestone remained where she'd left it, undiscovered. Only Parthenia had seen the remains of the little fire she'd made. Olivia's view of it had been blocked by her daughter. Faye quickly buried the charred sticks under soil. Although Parthenia had taken her metal canister with her, she could find another somewhere and gather more elixir ingredients.

The next time she had the opportunity, she would Cast again. Eventually, she would succeed.

Olivia was approaching again. *Damn the woman.*

"Sorry, ma'am, but your bath is getting cold."

THIRTY-SEVEN

Stefan had sent a message they were all to wait for him before dinner was served as he would be late getting home that night. The dining room was silent as they waited. It was like the wake after a funeral, Faye mused. Only less convivial.

Parthenia was refusing to meet Faye's gaze. Whether it was out of anger, shame, fear, or another emotion, she couldn't tell. Her second eldest child had always been difficult to read in that way.

Time passed. The sky through the glass double doors darkened to starry blackness, and still Stefan didn't arrive.

Darius finally broke the silence. "Mother," he said, "I'm hungry."

"I know," Faye replied. "Father will be home soon, I'm sure. Then dinner will be served. Just be patient a little longer."

The small child kicked his legs and tapped his knife on his plate.

"Here he comes," exclaimed Nahla.

Out in the night sky, the glowing lights of the family shuttle approached. An almost-inaudible sigh of relief sounded in the room. Though she hated the very sight of her husband, Faye's stomach was empty and aching. She wished he would hurry up.

The family waited another quarter of an hour for the shuttle to land and for Stefan to arrive in the dining room. When he did, he seemed in unusually high spirits. He told Nate, who was attending, to be quick. "It's been a long day and I'm starving. Tell Cook to get that food in here fast, and it better be hot."

The servants also brought glowing lamps along with that night's dishes. The room had become gloomy, but to Faye the artificial lights didn't seem to push back much of the darkness. She wondered what had so invigorated her husband. She feared it was something involving them too, or else why had he wanted to gather them all around him?

The food arrived, and the children pounced on it until a sharp rebuke from Stefan made them behave more politely. They helped each other to portions and, when everyone's plate was full, ate in silence.

The cook had prepared a thick meat stew heady with spices and served in the upturned shell of the animal the meat had come from. It was an exotic species from the polar region, where the sun only rose for an hour or so per day. Along with the stew, there was a basket of leaves and herbs from the vegetable garden, picked that day. Homegrown, tiny nuts had been stirred into the leaves, and the oil they exuded had lent the foliage a soft sheen and savory flavor. The starch of the meal was supplied by the boiled, dried, and ground roots of a locally grown biennial plant that produced delicate, lilac flowers. Side dishes included pickled crustaceans and flower buds.

Over the years, Faye had gotten used to the food eaten by the locals, and whatever the family ate, it was always cooked to a rare perfection—the cook had worked at the most expensive restaurants in the capital city of the region. Yet often the meals tasted like cardboard, when she could bring herself to eat more than a few mouthfuls. Despite her hunger, that evening was one of those occasions. The chance to free her children and herself from bondage to her monstrous husband had come within her grasp, only to be snatched away. And by one of the very people she had been trying to help, the second child she had brought to life through pain and blood and deep sorrow.

She found herself chewing mechanically, the food moving around and around her mouth. She forced the mouthful down and took another.

Faye's thoughts on Stefan were also distracting her. Clearly something important had happened and he planned to make some sort of announcement at the end of the meal, or he wouldn't have made them all wait for him to return. Usually on such nights when he didn't make it back in time for the evening meal, Faye would be able to slip away to her room and avoid him while he ate alone.

She waited and watched as the family ate. It was almost comical watching them. Stefan was hungry after his long day, which made him eat faster than usual. The children knew they couldn't take another mouthful after he was finished, so they were trying to shove the food down their throats as quickly as they could, while at the same time trying to avoid attracting Stefan's attention and accompanying wrath.

Finally, her husband put down his cutlery and signaled to Nate. Castiel risked another forkful of stew, but the rest of the children's cutlery clattered to their plates. Darius looked sorrowfully at a lump of ground root he hadn't managed to eat in time.

The servant who had been waiting just outside the door with the pudding immediately entered. It was Olivia, doubling up on her duties. The strain of holding the heavy dish while she waited for the main meal to be over showed in her sweaty, creased forehead, and Faye was glad. It was a small revenge for the years of spying and betrayal, but she would take it.

Olivia lifted the lid from the dish, drawing a barely audible collective groan from the children. The cook had prepared a mousse made from the sweet flesh of a river fish, tree sap, and tiny black seeds that fizzed on the tongue. The pudding was a favorite of Stefan's. The children hated it, yet none dared to express their opinion. Like most of the food that evening, Faye took no pleasure in it and didn't register the taste strongly. She was waiting to hear what Stefan had to tell them and wondering what it would mean for her and the rest of the family.

After slowly eating small portions of their dessert, the children's torture was over and Nate removed all the dishes while Olivia cleaned the table.

It was late evening. Darius looked as though he might fall asleep at any moment, and the other children were tired and impatient. Even Parthenia, who had watched her father with affection throughout the meal and eaten all of her pudding, was looking as though she'd had enough. But no one could leave until Stefan gave permission.

"Nate," he said, "please bring wine, and also something special for the children to drink."

"Yes, sir."

Olivia took the hint and got out the rock crystal glasses kept for special occasions.

"Have you got some exciting news for us?" Castiel ventured.

"Yes," said Nahla, "are we going to have a toast?"

Nahla rarely spoke around her father, but she clearly felt confident that Stefan's mood was so good she could risk it. The child was right, for Stefan replied, "A toast is indeed in order, my dear."

"Ooooh," exclaimed the little girl. "What's it about?"

"Have patience, Nahla. Wait until everything is ready."

Nate entered carrying a tray bearing a bottle of wine from the cellar and a silver jug covered with a soft white cloth. Condensation was forming on the outside of the jug.

A tense excitement filled the room as Nate and Olivia filled the family's glasses. Faye felt dread enveloping her heart. Whatever it was that Stefan had to announce, she was sure it would not bode well for her children or herself.

Nate and Olivia completed their task and stood to one side, their hands folded in front of them.

"As Castiel and Nahla so astutely observed, I have something important to tell you. The most important members of the clan met today. Naturally, I was invited. We discussed many things, including the ongoing success in our campaign to wrest control of certain areas from the Dirksens and claim this entire galactic sector. Our family has been part of this increase in our strength, and I was delighted to receive personal praise and thanks from Raith Sherrerr himself.

"We decided today the time has come to step up our bid for control. Business and small-time power struggles are useful, but results come slowly and with plenty of backward steps. Now's the time to press forward with our advantage. So, Faye, children, raise your glasses. The Sherrerrs are going to war!"

Thirty-Eight

The next morning, Stefan announced over breakfast that they had two hours to pack whatever they wanted to take with them, and then they were leaving. He didn't know when they would be returning to the estate, he said, if ever. The children were in a frenzy as they tried to find treasured items they'd misplaced and fill their bags with their favorite toys and clothes. The choices they were making weren't particularly well thought out or practical—Oriana was packing for a hot climate, while Ferne was taking his jackets, cardigans and boots—but Faye didn't bother to say anything. Whatever they lacked, someone would arrange to supply at their destination.

Faye told Olivia to pack a range of clothes and left the maid to it. She went out into the garden and passed the time walking the paths. Despite her terrible situation and the years she'd spent confined and abused there, she could remember happy times in the garden with the children. There had been times when she'd momentarily forgotten her desperate plight and had taken simple pleasure in the company of her girls and boys, before the shadow of the existence of Stefan and his proud, cruel family had covered her heart again.

Parthenia's tarsul loped by, crossing Faye's path. Stefan had told the children they couldn't bring their pets with them, which had caused many trembling lips and silent tears as they absorbed the news while struggling not to anger their father with their reaction. Faye had wondered at the meaning of the information. It wouldn't have been much trouble to bring the animals along in a separate autocar or shuttle. Maybe Stefan's decision had only been a whim, heedless of the effect on his offspring, or a manifestation of his cruelty.

A ripe fruit was hanging down from a vine looping overhead. Faye reached up and plucked it. The sweet, slightly bitter juice dripped down her chin as she bit through the fuzzy skin.

An arm pressed close around her waist, making her start and drop the fruit. She coughed as the juice went down the wrong way. It was Stefan. He'd snuck up on her from behind while she was lost in reverie. He leaned so close to her ear his lips brushed it as he said, "I thought I might find you here, Faye. You always did like our garden, didn't you?"

She pulled away from him. "What do you want?"

"Always the cold-hearted bitch, aren't you?"

"You expect me to be warm toward my rapist?"

"Details, details. You should learn to enjoy it. I certainly do. In fact, I think I prefer it."

Faye smiled.

"That's what I like to see," Stefan said. "I'm glad I could persuade you to come around to my way of thinking. Though, I must say, please continue to scream and fight as you did before. It adds a special frisson."

"Oh, I wasn't smiling at the thought of you forcing yourself on me, dear husband. No, I was imaging the pleasure I'll experience when I see you pay for everything you've done to me and all the other evil acts of your life."

"Enjoy the thought, because a thought is all it will ever be," Stefan replied. "We Sherrerrs are more powerful than we've ever been. It won't be long before we've stamped the Dirksens into the ground. Then, no one will dare stand up to us and we'll have the richest pickings from every business and trade deal that goes on. And when we've secured our hold, we'll begin our move into the neighboring galactic sectors. What do you think about that?"

"Your megalomaniac family's ambitions are of no interest to me nor any other decent-minded person. What was it that went wrong with the Sherrerrs, Stefan? Did a splicer make an absent-minded slip a few generations ago that set your clan on its mad path toward galactic domination?"

Ignoring her question, Stefan replied, "Oh, but you should be interested, Faye. Our declaration of war on the Dirksens has important implications for the mages in the family."

They had been walking along a path as Stefan guided her back to the house. At his words, she halted. "Why is that?"

"I thought that might capture your attention," Stefan replied smugly. "I didn't want to tell the children last night. At their tender ages, it doesn't do to worry or alarm them too much."

She marveled at how he thought that beating their mother didn't worry or alarm the children.

"But the reason that we're moving to another location is due to the fact that they're going to play a major role in the conflict. I talked up their abilities to Raith Sherrerr. He's expecting high things of them."

Her heart racing, Faye said, "But I told you long ago, we can't kill. Mages can't kill. Or else how do you think it was possible to capture Kris and me?"

Stefan turned pale and glowered. "And I told *you* never to mention that man's name."

Her body was rigid and her fists clenched. "We can't kill. You won't make my children into murderers."

"You may not be able to actually kill—and I'm still not sure I quite believe that—but I'm sure there are other ways of causing harm to our enemies. What if you were to move a company of soldiers to the deep ocean, for example? Or make a starship's engine explode? I'm sure you could do it, with a little persuasion." He ran a finger down her neck to the top of her cleavage, making her shudder with disgust.

"No," Faye said. "It doesn't work like that. If Casting might cause harm to someone...it...it doesn't work. We can't do it." Her words sounded unconvincing, and Stefan wasn't slow to pick up on her hesitation.

"I'll soon find out the truth. You were always forthcoming when I threatened the children."

"That won't work. You'll never make me believe you would kill one of our children. Castiel and Nahla are too precious to you and the others are too useful. You've said so yourself."

"You're right," Stefan replied. "I wouldn't kill them. But that doesn't mean I wouldn't hurt them."

Rage exploded in Faye. She lifted her hand to strike him, but he caught her wrist and forced it downward, bending her arm so painfully she thought it would break. She cried out and grabbed at his face with her other hand. This time, she was too fast for him, and her nails gouged furrows in his cheeks before he managed to wrench them away.

He had both her wrists in his powerful grip. He forced her to her knees, his face a mask of glowering hate hanging over her. Her ability to control her reaction to her husband's maltreatment had all but disappeared. She lunged at his stomach and fastened her teeth on it, biting down with all the force she possessed. Through the material of his vest and shirt, she felt his flesh between her teeth.

"Arghhhhh," Stefan exclaimed. He let go of her wrists and wrestled her head away from him. He kicked her so hard she fell to the ground, her head hitting the stone path. Sparks flickered in her vision and blackness encroached.

She sat up and put a hand to her head. Her vision cleared, and she saw Stefan striding away.

THIRTY-NINE

Carina was up to her knees in mud. Trees surrounded her, their canopies blocking out the sky. The trees' roots rose as high as her head and the place reeked of odorous brine. She guessed that meant she was in some kind of estuary forest and the tide could come in at any moment. The planet had one close moon and the tides were high, the tidal zones stretching for kilometers.

Her Cast had gone a little awry, unsurprisingly. She wasn't well acquainted with the topography of the planet. Still, she shouldn't be too far from her intended destination—the capital city. At its spaceport she could expect to find some sort of passage on a ship heading offplanet.

She had some elixir left. Should she just Cast again? She was alone as far as she could tell and not in immediate danger. She decided it would be wise to conserve the precious liquid in case she encountered a situation in which she needed it more.

She tried to pull first one leg and then the other out of the mud, but she could only move them a little, and then she seemed to sink lower. As she struggled, she consoled herself that she hadn't Transported into a tree or into the ocean. There did seem to be some kind of safeguard with the Cast so that it wasn't possible to move a solid object inside another solid object, so arriving in the tree would have been unlikely, but she wasn't sure if the same rule applied to liquid.

Something in the mud slithered past her calf. Gulping down a squeal, she jerked her leg upward. It shifted a little and she strained to hold it where it was and retain the little movement she'd managed. She looked around. She needed something to grip. If she could hold onto something solid on the surface, she should be able to gradually ease herself out.

The only thing that looked as though it was within reach was a tree root. Carina put her hands on the mud and walked them forward until she was lying as horizontal as possible. Her knees were bent painfully backward, but she reached the root and grasped it firmly with both hands. As she did so, she noticed a layer of water on the mud grow deeper as she watched it.

She cursed. She gently moved her legs while at the same time pulling as hard as she could on the root. Her right leg lifted a little more, and then her left. The rapidly encroaching water was filling the gaps she was making around her legs, dissolving the mud and making her task easier. At last, one leg was free. She knelt with it gently on the watery mud while she worked on the other leg.

The mud released her left leg with a satisfying *plop*. Relying mostly on the pull of her arms on the root, she slid across the mud to the tree. Its cold, wet, sliminess penetrated her Sherrerr uniform and soaked her to the skin. She quickly climbed the limb-like tree roots until she was balancing on top of them. From the brightest patch of light in the canopy, she guessed the rough direction of the sun and so also the direction of the city, and set off toward it.

She used the roots as stepping stones to prevent her from needing to walk on the muddy floor, which was quickly becoming aquatic. But they were damp from their previous submersion and a black algae clung to them. Her chances of slipping and falling in were high. It was time to quit being so cautious, and Transport herself again to a hopefully more favorable location.

She took out her canister of elixir and unscrewed it, but as she lifted the container to her lips, she spotted a green bank through the tree trunks. She was only a short distance from higher ground, if she could make it without falling in.

Leaning on the rough bark of the tree trunks for balance and for purchase, she continued to tread carefully on the roots until she reached the foot of the bank. Her previous view of it had deceived her. The greenery began at a level higher than she'd thought. Across from the last stand of trees, over a narrow dip, was a swathe of black and brown, muddy foliage. The high tide mark, where the green, drier-looking stuff began, was two or three meters above her head.

Still, she thought she could scramble up it, and she was already covered in mud. She couldn't get any wetter or dirtier. She made the leap across the dip and clung to the slippery stems. At the same time, she dug the toes of her boots into the soft surface. Crawling upward spider-like, she reached the green ground in a few minutes.

After that, the going was easier. The bank sloped at an angle that meant she had to continue on all fours rather than two legs, but the air was fresher after the stench among the trees and she was no longer in danger of being swamped by the incoming ocean.

When she reached the top, she turned and sat down to catch her breath. She was looking down on the tree tops and out across a glimmering ocean. The sun hung low and the large, crater-strewn moon was high in the sky. She had visited many planets in her short time as a merc, and this was one of the prettier ones. It wasn't a surprise the Sherrerrs had chosen it as the base of their operations.

All she had were her skills, her wits, and a three-quarters-full bottle of elixir. The latter meant that she wouldn't go hungry, but she couldn't Transport herself to another planet, more was the pity.

Her breathing had returned to normal, and the wind was drying her sweat, leaving her cold and uncomfortable. A hungry ache had started up in her belly too. It was time to move on if she wanted to reach the capital by nightfall.

She stood and scrambled over the top of the bank. Farmland lay on the other side. Smooth, green, cropped vegetation sloped down from her feet, and animals were lazily grazing it. Hundreds of the knee-high bipedal creatures the locals grew for meat dotted the slope down to the bottom, where a large farmhouse stood. The capital city lay on the horizon.

The animals were entirely uninterested in her as she went across the field in long strides. However, the herders watching them were very interested in her.

"Hey," a voice yelled. "Where do you think *you're* going? You're not allowed here. This is private property."

She turned and spotted the owner of the voice: a youthful man in old clothes and a floppy hat, appearing above a fold in the land.

"I got lost," she called back. "I'm leaving now."

"Oh, are you?" another voice shouted. This person was approaching from below. She was older and her skin was reddened by the sun. "We'll see about that. Stop where you are. I want to make sure you haven't stolen any of our stock."

She supposed it was vaguely possible that she'd broken the neck of one of their livestock and pushed it inside her shirt, but it seemed an unlikely conjecture. "I don't have anything of yours," she snapped, and altered her direction to avoid crossing paths with either of the herders. The woman and youth changed direction too.

Carina was annoyed. She had enough to contend with. She didn't need suspicious farmers added to the mix. She adjusted her path again and began to jog.

"Catch her, Piffer," the woman shouted to the young man. "Show her she can't just wander over our land without permission."

Piffer started to run.

Carina sped up. The situation was ridiculous. She could fight off the man and the woman she presumed was his mother, but why should she? Why couldn't they just let her go on her way? "I told you, I don't have any of your stupid animals," she yelled. "Now leave me alone."

It wasn't until the man had nearly caught up to her that Carina understood what she needed to do. She'd been worried about her Sherrerr uniform being a liability. Any member of the clan or employee who saw her would wonder what she was doing, and perhaps demand to know. Yet everywhere on the planet and for most of the sector, the Sherrerr insignia was known and feared.

She slid to a halt on the moist vegetation and spun to face her pursuer. The stylized blade on her collar was covered in mud, so she roughly rubbed it with the edge of her sleeve. Her chin up, she stared the man in the eye as he drew closer. When he saw the emblem, he also skidded to a stop.

Carina glared.

"Mother..."

"What's wrong?" the woman shouted. "Grab her."

"Er, I don't think that would be a very good idea."

"Why not?" The woman arrived, sweaty and red-faced. "Oh."

FORTY

As far back as she could remember, Carina had known of the Sherrerrs and the aura of intimidation and disquiet they radiated. Like most people, she'd tried to avoid coming into direct contact with any of them or their dealings. Everyone knew the best place to be when Sherrerr—or Dirksen—business was afoot was as far away as possible.

Yet she wasn't prepared for the deference and plain fear the mother-and-son pair of farmers, Bunter and Piffer, displayed when they thought she was working for the clan. She'd only wanted them to let her go on her way in peace, but they insisted on her going back with them to the farmhouse so she could clean up and eat something before she left.

No doubt they were frightened of retaliation for their behavior and were anxious to put things right. She was cold, wet, and hungry enough to not take too much persuasion to agree to their offer. Bunter looked relieved when she said she would go with them, and told Piffer to run ahead and draw a hot bath.

"I'll make a roast," Bunter said, smiling deferentially, her already-rosy cheeks afire. As they went the rest of the way to the farmhouse, following Piffer's disappearing heels, Bunter twice stooped and grabbed one of the grazing beasts. She swiftly twisted the necks then slung the bodies over her back, holding onto their heads. The newly dead animals bounced in time with her steps. "Nice and fresh," Bunter said.

The bath was ready by the time Bunter showed her into the bathroom of the old house. She waited for Carina's uniform as she undressed and promised to get as much dirt out of it as she could while dinner was cooking. Carina retrieved her elixir bottle before handing the farmer the wet clothes.

She sank into the hot water gratefully after Bunter left. Perhaps it was all a trap, but she doubted it. The horror on the farmers' faces when they realized her allegiance hadn't been faked. She felt a little guilty about taking advantage of them, but quickly forgot about it when she remembered they'd chased her and had wanted to beat her.

There was a knock at the door. "I've put a bathrobe just outside," Piffer called, "to wear while your clothes are drying."

She began to soap herself and wash off the grit and grime of the marsh. The soap stung the cuts and grazes she'd gathered along the way. Next, she lathered her hair and used a jug to rinse it with clean water from the faucet. By the time Bunter called to say dinner was ready, she was feeling better than she had in a long time.

She dried herself and put on the bathrobe, slipping her elixir bottle into the pocket. The gown covered her legs to the floor and her arms to the wrists, giving her an idea. On tiptoe, she went across the landing and opened a door. The room held a single bed and a wardrobe. On the nightstand was a picture of a pretty young girl who bore no resemblance to Bunter or Piffer. She guessed it was the latter's room and the girl in the photograph was someone he liked romantically.

Piffer was about Carina's size. She went to his wardrobe and took out a pair of pants and a shirt. They were old and worn but clean. She put them on then covered them with the bathrobe before going downstairs. Her Sherrerr uniform had proven useful but she needed to ditch it before it invited too many questions she couldn't answer.

Bunter and Piffer were waiting for her in the kitchen. Only one place at the table was set. They weren't going to eat with her, only watch her eat. Awkward. She didn't think she would have gotten used to being a Sherrerr guard.

The meal was delicious and she enjoyed it despite the over-zealous attentions of the farmers. Her uniform steamed on a chair in front of the hot stove. Breaking the painful silence, Bunter said, "I got most of the mud out of it. Should be good as new in a few hours."

"I can't wait that long," Carina replied. "I'll have to wear it wet."

The news that she would be leaving soon caused a visible slackening in the tension on the farmers' faces. Then Piffer's positively brightened and he blurted, "I could try putting it in the seed airer."

"Yes, that might help," Bunter said.

The young man grabbed Carina's uniform and sped from the room.

"We have a machine to dry the seeds we keep for next year," Bunter explained. "It stops them from going moldy in storage."

"Oh," Carina said. "Good idea." She was distracted with filling her belly with as much of the roasted meat and other dishes she could. She had a long walk ahead of her tonight.

"It's funny," said Bunter, "we haven't seen Sherrerr troops around here for a while. And you're by yourself."

She nodded and swallowed a mouthful of food. "Surveillance. I can't say any more than that. Do you have anything to drink?"

"Yes, of course," Bunter replied. "Of course. What was I thinking?" She went into a pantry and returned with a jug. "Is beer okay? We don't have anything stronger." She leaned forward and said in a lowered tone, "Piffer can't hold it. Then he's no good for work the next day. I won't have it in the house."

"Beer is fine."

She was trying to think of a way to plumb the woman's mind for useful information, but every subtle inquiry she could think up was guaranteed to raise suspicion. She had no good reason to be asking about starships scheduled to arrive or depart from the capital's spaceport, assuming Bunter would even know, which seemed doubtful. And anything she might ask about the movements of Sherrerr guards or soldiers was definitely a bad idea.

When her stomach really couldn't hold any more, she pushed back her seat and said, "Thanks. I'm done. Can you ask your son if I can have my uniform? I'll be on my way."

"Are you sure you've had enough?" Bunter asked. "There's plenty left."

"Yes, I'm sure. It was very good."

"I'm glad you liked it. What about some dessert? I have some fruit compote in the pantry."

Carina had been in the process of standing up. She stopped and looked the woman in the eye. Bunter looked away. Something wasn't right. The farmer should have been glad to see her go, not trying to delay her.

She ran for the door, but when she flung it open, Piffer was there waiting. He moved to punch her, but Carina swerved. She caught him with an upper cut under his chin, snapping his head back and sending him unconscious to the floor.

When the two farmers had begun to suspect her, Carina didn't know. Probably while she was in the bath, when they had time to think over her presence, which made no real sense. Why would a lone Sherrerr soldier wander the area unless he or she lived nearby? Carina was a stranger with a weak excuse for being in those parts. The farmers must have contacted the Sherrerrs and been told to keep her here as long as possible while they made their way over.

They hadn't yet arrived or it would have been someone in a Sherrerr uniform waiting for her on the other side of the kitchen door. However, she probably didn't have much time.

Carina headed for the rear of the house, leaving behind the cursing and wailing of Bunter, who was tending to her son. The Sherrerrs would approach the house from the road. If she was quick enough, she could slip out the back before they surrounded the place.

With a gasp of frustration, she realized she was barefoot. Her boots were by the front door. She doubled back, ran past the still-prone Piffer and his lamenting mother, snatched up her wet, muddy boots, and scooted back the way she'd come. A thud resounded from the front door. Her heart leapt into her mouth. The Sherrerrs had arrived.

She didn't have time to put on her boots. She didn't have time to take any precautions. She had reached the back door. She threw open the bolts and raced outside.

"There she is," a voice shouted. A hiss of pulse round flew past her ear. Not far from the back door stood a hedge next to the fields behind. She ducked down and forced her way under it.

"Get her," someone shouted.

The bathrobe was snagging on the branches, and it was a pale color, easily spotted in the darkness. She undid the tie and struggled out of it, seizing her elixir bottle before she abandoned the garment.

Her boots in her other hand, she raced along the hedge, using it as cover. It split two ways, and she took the direction that led her out into the farmland, praying the Sherrerrs wouldn't bother to pursue her too far. She was a long way from the mountains. She doubted the local clan would have connected the report of someone masquerading as a Sherrerr soldier with the disappearance of another soldier many kilometers away.

Keeping close to the hedge, she ran on until a stitch in her side forced her to slow down. She risked a glance over her shoulder. The fields were dark. The only lights visible were from the distant farmhouse and a few vehicles clustered outside.

She slowed to a stop and sank to the ground, her breathing ragged. Her feet felt like they were cut to pieces from her run, but she could Cast Heal and in a few moments they would be okay. She was still far from the capital and the spaceport that was her route offplanet, but she'd swapped the uniform that would identify her for civilian clothes and she had a full belly.

She put on her boots. Things seemed to be taking a turn for the better.

FORTY-ONE

When Carina had been a little girl, she'd often wished she could create something out of nothing through Casting. Sadly, she'd found her Nai Nai never taught her that Cast, and eventually, when she'd gotten up the courage to ask about it, her grandmother had explained that though it was possible to create matter from energy, that was a job for top scientists, not mages, and that to create something from nothing was what she would call magic.

Carina could have simply Transported someone else's cash into her pocket. All she had to do was to see it. But that would have been stealing, and, as well as being intrinsically wrong, Nai Nai had told her that you never knew for sure if that person needed the money more than you.

She had Transported herself close to the city's outskirts but she couldn't risk suddenly appearing in busy areas. So, without credits for an autocar, she was forced to walk all the way from the outskirts of the capital to the spaceport. Her belly, which had been full the previous night, was soon empty again. By the time she arrived at her destination, she was footsore and ravenous.

The spaceport was one of the biggest she had ever seen. The field was divided into three sections: shuttles that ferried passengers to deep-space vessels traveling outsystem; shuttles that belonged to interplanetary spacecraft that journeyed to insystem planets or to go asteroid mining; and local shuttles that only went into orbit for fast journeys to distant countries.

She was on one side of the security fence and the vessels were on the other, with an access road running across the center of the field. Multi-person autocars ran up and down the road, ferrying the crew to the buildings at the far end of the spaceport, where their IDs would be processed if they wanted to spend time planetside.

The cargo loading bays and fuel stations were in another part of the spaceport, so once the crews had left, the shuttles stood still and silent. Somewhere above in high orbit, long range deep-space vessels awaited some of them. She hoped she would soon be aboard just such a spacecraft—a ship to take her far from the Sherrerr-controlled system and all the sad memories it held.

It was a pity she hadn't gotten to see the little Sherrerr boy, Darius, again. He'd been a sweet, smart kid, and the only mage she'd ever really known apart from Nai Nai. Her parents had been mages too, but she couldn't remember them very well. But it couldn't be helped that she hadn't been able to meet Darius or his family. Her time on Ithiya had been a wild goose chase.

She walked slowly along the fence, scrutinizing the shuttles. The local vessels bore the name of their company. Others were named according to the spacecraft to which they belonged: *Matador, Sandra, Ambition, Colossus, Marchana, Shooting Star, The Falcon, Whirlwind, Nightfall.* Most of the shuttles looked well cared for, even the older models. Failing to keep your vessel shipshape on space flights rarely ended well, and that didn't only apply to the interiors. A clean exterior where scratches were buffed out and holes and scrapes repaired made for a better attitude from the crew. Captain Speidel had told her that.

However, a shuttle that was well cared for was not what Carina needed. Such a craft would have strict protocols for hiring staff, and the crew would follow them or find themselves dismissed at the next planet. But she had nothing to prove who she was. She'd never carried proper papers. Sometime during her homeless period she'd lost them. Either that or she'd never had any. She wasn't sure. It hadn't mattered too much up until now. Merc bands were less interested in that kind of thing than they were in whether you could fire straight and had the guts to kill someone in hand-to-hand combat.

What she was looking for was a seedier kind of craft. A vessel that probably did a little contraband smuggling, like weapons, drugs, or people. If she'd had the gems, she could have sold them to pay for passage on such a ship, but they were halfway up a mountain, and now she had the harder task of persuading the captain to allow her to work her passage.

She saw exactly what she was looking for. It was a squat shuttle, a little small. Too small to be in the deep spacecraft section, yet here it was. A small craft had a small hold. Yet only the large starships could carry sufficient cargo to make the weeks, months, and even years-long trips between systems economically viable. If the shuttle was small, its spacecraft was also small, which meant it had to be carrying rare, expensive cargo, or, as was more likely, it was a smuggler.

What was more, it was scratched, scraped, pockmarked, and filthy. No one cared about this ship. They were only interested in making some fast money and moving on.

Someone in overalls was sitting on the ramp cleaning his fingernails with the point of a small knife. He looked like a seasoned space traveler—pale, greasy, and with dark circles under his eyes. His gut pulled his clothes tight as it hung out over his lap. She guessed he was a cargo hand or something similar. Not the person to talk to about being hired, but he would have to do.

"Hey," she called through the fence.

The man looked up at her and looked away again. He started cleaning the nails on his other hand.

"Hey," she shouted again. "What are you shipping?"

The man got up, ignoring her again and went inside the ship.

She cursed. But he reappeared and came over to where she was standing.

She began, "I was wondering—"

He was pointing a gun at her. He held it close to his side so it wasn't obvious.

"I don't mean any harm," she said, backing away. "I'm just looking for a ship to work passage on. I can work security."

"No you can't. If you could work security you would know not to ask stupid questions. Now fuck off." The man turned to walk away.

"I'm an ex-merc. That gun you're holding is a Deacon X5 and if I had to fight you I'd go for your left knee."

He stopped and faced her. "How'd you know about my knee?"

"The way you walked over. You favor your right leg. And knees are weak points anyway."

He rubbed his stubble as he scanned her from head to toe and back again. "You don't look like a merc."

"I started young."

He paused, considering. "I can't deny we could do with another hand aboard ship. The first mate's been arrested and won't be leaving the planet anytime soon. But we're a small operation. You wouldn't only be working security. You'd have to pitch in with everything. Cargo handling, maintenance, cleaning up in the mess."

"I don't mind. I'll do whatever you want. When are you shipping out?"

"Hold on. No one said you were hired. And what's your hurry? Is someone looking for you? Done something you shouldn't?"

"No," she lied. "I'm just sick of this planet. Can't wait to get off it."

"I don't want anyone coming after you. Like I said, we're a small operation. Can't afford to have the authorities breathing down our necks. You get what I mean?"

She got it. He didn't want to attract any attention that might result in a thorough search of the ship. She wondered what it was they were smuggling. "Sure."

"Okay, meet me at the crew entrance in a couple of hours."

"Is it a sure thing? Do I have a job? Or do you have to speak to the captain?"

"I am the captain."

FORTY-TWO

Two hours was a long time for Carina to waste. She had no money, nothing to do, and nowhere to go. She decided to hang around the departures area of the spaceport. Her work aboard the smugglers' ship was by no means guaranteed and she thought she might spot another opportunity that was possibly more legal. She found a quiet corner and sat on the floor while she people-watched.

It was the usual crowd that passed through such places. Ultra-rich travelers arriving for luxury cruises or to depart on their private vessels. These were easy to identify from their clothes, their bearing, and their retinue of servants, porters, and bodyguards. Carina considered approaching one of these groups to find out if they needed extra security help but quickly put aside the idea. Most of the wealthy in that area were either Sherrerrs or closely affiliated with the family. Coming into contact with the Sherrerrs again was the last thing she needed.

Much more common than the wealthy crowd were the local vacationers off on trips to far-distant countries or even tourist resorts on other planets or the system's moons. These were far less stately, less well-dressed, and louder. They let their children run riot around the place while they waited in line to go through to their gate.

In that galactic region there weren't many aliens, but they were naturally more likely to be seen at a major spaceport, and this one was no exception. She saw quadrupeds with prehensile noses, multi-limbed arthropods, and bipedal aliens in environment suits that protected them from the local atmosphere and possibly air pressure too. Most of the human passengers were polite enough not to stare, but many younger children would stop their play to watch the aliens pass, and sometimes they even went up and prodded them before being hauled away by an embarrassed parent.

Carina had encountered more aliens than most and usually without any problems. Sentient species tended to understand that even when clear communication was possible, the gulf between cultures and thought processes was too vast to be easily crossed, and so each left the other well alone.

The first time she had fought aliens was an event in her life she rarely thought about and would rather have forgotten. She'd been ten years old, and it was the first time she'd killed. The aliens in question were regians, who possessed the odd ability to shift in time. They didn't move far, only a few moments into the future and the past. Yet their ability made them a formidable enemy because they were so difficult to kill. The pulse round, knife or whatever had to hit them at the exact moment that they passed through the present in order to make contact. Otherwise the offensive weapon hit empty air.

She had managed to kill the aliens with a Cast called Split. The name said it all. The Cast tore the aliens apart, and because Casts worked over several moments, the effect was slow enough to hit the regians on target.

She shuddered. She hated using her mage abilities to kill. A shot to the head or a knife to the heart was fast and clean and would be her preferred method to go out with if she ever lost a fight. Casting to kill wasn't only more difficult than regular killing, it was long, drawn-out, and agonizing to the victim. She'd met some bad characters over the years, but she hadn't met anyone who she felt deserved that kind of death.

"Carina," a familiar voice said. "I thought I'd find you here."

Startled from her reverie, she looked up to see Bryce standing over her. "What the hell?" She stood up. "What are you doing here? I sent you back to that town, not here. And I thought I told you we couldn't meet again. Leave me alone." She began to walk away.

Bryce clutched her arm. "Don't go. Please. I came in on the morning shuttle and it's taken me hours to find you. I thought you would be trying to go offplanet. I only want to talk to you."

"Well I *don't* want to talk to you. I saved you, remember? If you're grateful for that, you can pay me back by doing what I ask."

"I understand why you don't want to have anything to do with me after what you did, but you can trust me, Carina. I wouldn't do anything to hurt you."

"Bryce," she said, her tone softening. "I don't think you would do anything to hurt me—at first. But things would change over time. You would see me differently. Eventually, I wouldn't be Carina to you, I would be a mage with all that entails. Understand me when I say I can't afford to have friends who know what I can do. It just isn't safe, especially for me, but also for you."

"Okay, okay. I think I understand. I won't force you. But let me get you something to eat at least. Let me return the favor, just a little?"

Was he being genuine, or was it a trap? Had Bryce divulged what she'd done, and had someone put him up to finding her and capturing her? Her friend's expression seemed open and honest. And she was very hungry. "All right, but I want to go somewhere I can see anyone who approaches us."

"Yeah, of course," Bryce replied, looking wounded.

Cafes and eateries sat at the edges of the departure area, and Carina chose one that had an empty table out front. The site gave her a wide view. Bryce went inside to order some food, then returned to the table with two glasses of the local brew. He put one in front of her and sipped the other as he sat down.

When he was seated, she swapped the glasses. He looked puzzled for a moment then said, "You don't really think I would drug you?"

"I don't know what you'd do, and if my caution upsets you, I don't care. I can't afford to take chances. You don't understand what could happen to me. You haven't thought it through. If you had, you wouldn't be surprised that I swapped our drinks."

He took a sip. "I guess you're right. I don't get it. If I could do what you can, I wouldn't be hiding it, I'd be using my powers to make myself rich."

"You might try, until someone figures out what you're doing and decides to make you make them rich instead. And what do you think they would do to you if you refused?"

"But I would just—"

"What?" she asked angrily. "What would you just do? It isn't easy or simple, you know."

"Okay, calm down. I was only trying to figure it out. If you say the best thing you can do is keep things under wraps, I accept that. You would know better than me."

"Damn right I would."

Their food arrived. Neither Carina nor Bryce said anything until the waiter had returned into the cafe. Then Bryce picked up his fork, dug it into Carina's food, and ate a mouthful. "Satisfied?"

She began to eat fast, glancing at the clock that overhung the departure area. She had an hour until it was time to meet the smuggler captain in the crew section, but she wanted to be done with this meal with Bryce.

"So you're going offplanet?" he asked.

"That's the idea."

"Deep space?"

"If I can. I want to put as much of the black between me and this place as possible."

"Because of the danger that someone will guess what you did at the Sherrerr place, and come after you?"

"That, and other things. I've had enough of Ithiya. It's time to move on. How about you? Have you found a way to afford your treatment?"

"I have, actually. That was why I was looking for you."

"Huh?"

"When I got back to my home town, I found out my parents had returned and they'd been looking for me. After they went away, they opened a business that turned out to be really successful. They came back to find out what happened to me. The first thing we did after meeting up was go to a splicer. I had the treatment overnight and it seems to be working. Another month or so and I should be cured."

"That's great, Bryce. I'm really happy for you."

"Thanks, but there's more. My parents are opening a branch of their business. They want me to run it. That was why I came straight here to try to find you. I guessed you'd be trying to get offplanet. I can help you. You can come with me and help me run the business."

"I appreciate the offer," she said, "but I really can't. Thanks for the meal. I have to go now."

What she'd said wasn't strictly true—she had a while to wait before she was due in the crew section—but she wanted to cut the conversation short. She knew Bryce meant well, but simply by saving him she'd irrevocably cut ties between them forever. It was kinder not to drag it out.

She stood.

"But Carina..."

"Bye, Bryce. It was good knowing you."

FORTY-THREE

Stefan argued with the spaceport official, but it didn't do any good.

"I am very sorry, sir, but there really is no other way. It isn't far, sir. Just a minute's walk across the public area."

"You *do* understand who I am?" Stefan asked the woman through his teeth, throwing sharp glances at passengers entering the departure area who were lingering, curious to see what the problem was.

Faye pitied the poor spaceport clerk who had been called upon to explain there was no private entrance for exclusive passengers—even Sherrerrs—and they would have to walk across the public departure area like everyone else.

"Yes, sir," the woman replied, looking plain terrified. "As I said, I am very sorry, but it's unavoidable if you wish to board a shuttle at this spaceport."

The autocar had left after depositing them at the departure area entrance. The children stood waiting quietly. Nate had placed their bags onto a trolley. He wouldn't be coming with them aboard the Sherrerr starship, *Nightfall,* and neither would Olivia, Faye had been delighted to discover. Her personal maid wouldn't be spying on her any longer.

The three Sherrerr guards from the estate coming with them shuffled and adjusted their grips on their weapons as they scanned the bystanders. Though the dangers of an attack were slight, they did increase the longer they stood around in public.

"Perhaps we should just go through, Father," Castiel suggested. "I don't like standing here with all these people watching."

Stefan's head snapped around at his son's words, but the storm that threatened didn't arrive. "Oh, very well. But this won't be the last you'll hear of this," he said to the clerk. The relief that had begun to flood her face upon hearing Stefan give up his objection was replaced with tension.

They set off through one of the doorways into the departure area, drawing more attention to their retinue. The clerk hadn't been exaggerating—the entrance for private passengers was less than a minute's walk across the busy space. Stefan had had his temper tantrum over nothing.

They were about halfway to the other door when Faye saw her.

Carina.

She was walking directly across their path.

Faye stopped dead in her tracks.

"Ow," Darius cried.

Faye was holding her son's hand, and she must have gripped it too tightly. She quickly let go and tried to compose herself and walk on before anyone spotted her reaction. But it was too late. Darius had picked up on her heightened emotions and he was looking up at her curiously. Then he turned his attention to the crowd to see what had caused her reaction.

"Carina!" shouted the little boy.

"Darius, no!"

She tried to grab his hand but he was too quick. He sped around Stefan and between the two bodyguards who were walking in front.

"Carina!" Darius shouted again.

This time, Carina heard him.

Faye watched in horror as her eldest daughter turned to see little Darius running toward her, his arms outstretched. Joy filled Carina's face as she too spread her arms. When the little boy reached her, she lifted him into the air and grabbed him into a hug.

All the Sherrerrs and their staff had drawn to a halt to watch the strange spectacle. Carina put Darius down and squatted so she could talk to him face to face.

Faye couldn't hear what they were saying over the general hubbub of the departure area. She only hoped Darius would remember in time that the subject of Carina was prohibited. There was still a chance her daughter would escape her husband's clutches.

Stefan was white-faced and rigid. "Darius," he barked. When his son didn't hear him, he instructed a guard to retrieve the boy.

Faye held her breath. Her heart raced. She thought she was going to faint. Perhaps she should pretend to faint and cause a distraction, but that might excite Stefan's suspicions. She could only hope her husband's rage at being an object of public scrutiny would distract him enough to fail to make the connection.

No!

Darius was dragging Carina over toward them by the hand. Faye let out an involuntary gasp. Her son probably wanted to show everyone the person who had saved him from the Dirksens. Her poor, sweet, kind, thoughtless boy. Parthenia turned to eye her curiously.

The guard met the pair and took Darius' other hand. He was telling him he had to come back to his father.

Please, Darius. Please do as you're told. Carina, leave now. Go!

Stefan had his hands on his hips as he watched and waited for his son to return. Then his stiff posture slackened. His hands fell to his sides. He'd noticed something. He took a step forward to peer at Carina.

Faye willed her daughter to look away so Stefan wouldn't see her face, but it was hopeless. Carina was clearly deeply interested in their group. Her eyes were scanning them. Though the effort nearly killed her, Faye avoided her daughter's gaze like she was avoiding death itself.

In her peripheral vision, she saw Stefan's head turn toward her, then back to her daughter.

"Guards," Stefan said, "seize that woman."

"Carina," Faye screamed. "Run!"

A moment's confusion flitted over her daughter's features, then she got the message. She turned to speed away, but she only made it a few steps. The guard who had gone to retrieve Darius caught up to her. As he grabbed her arm she swung at him with the other and punched him in the side of the head. Dazed, he let go, but the other guard had reached her and kicked her in the back. She fell forward. The third guard fired from a distance, stunning her before she hit the ground.

Faye's legs went weak. She found herself on her knees. Stefan had Carina. He had all her children, even the one he hadn't fathered.

Darius was by her side, sobbing. "I'm sorry, Mother. I'm so sorry. I forgot."

FORTY-FOUR

Carina was aboard a starship. She could tell that much from the slight vibration of the ship's engine through the floor. Slowly the memory of what had happened filtered through to her. She'd been shot and stunned, heavily. Her stomach cramped with nausea and fingers seemed to be digging agonizingly through her skull. She felt like she'd been out a long time.

Swallowing the saliva that was flooding her mouth, she risked opening one eye a slit. All she could see were two pairs of feet in expensive shoes. One was a man's feet and one was a woman's. The woman's feet were tied to chair legs. Carina moved her own feet and hands slightly, just enough to discover she was also bound.

"The resemblance is quite remarkable," the man said. "Even at this angle. I don't know what took me so long to see it. I must have been too preoccupied with our son's disobedience. I should beat him for it, but I can't bring myself to at the moment. I'm too pleased with the stupid brat for bringing me this prize. Hmm. She's taking a long time to come around. Maybe she isn't made of such stern stuff as it seemed when she tackled the guard."

He stood. Carina watched his legs as he walked over. One foot lifted as he prepared to kick her. She swung her feet forward and swept his other leg from under him. He crashed to the floor. In a heartbeat she was on her knees. She scooted over and drew back her head to strike his. If she hit him hard enough in the right spot she could knock him out. But someone grasped her hair and pulled her upright. The hand then threw her down onto her knees.

"Should I stun her again, sir?" a voice asked.

The man was getting to his feet. "No, that won't be necessary." He straightened his pants. "But some kind of reprimand is in order." He went behind Carina and kicked her in her kidneys. The pain that erupted left her unable to breathe. She drew in a great whooping gasp. Her vision swam.

The waves of pain eventually began to subside, and she could look about her. The man had returned to his chair and was watching her, his hands on his knees. The woman, who appeared to be restrained by her hands as well as her feet, was pale and scared.

"Sit her up, guard," the man said. "Looking at her face while she's lying down is making my neck ache."

Hands grabbed her shoulders and hauled her over to the wall, propping her into a sitting position. Carina gazed at the man and the woman. She realized she'd seen the man before. He was the haughty one who had arrived by shuttle at the Sherrerr stronghold. Yet he hadn't been anything more than a visitor. He didn't belong to the military arm of the Sherrerrs. Was it possible he knew she'd absconded from there? Carina was unsure of why she'd been captured by this family that she'd helped.

The man had to be Darius' father. The little boy had seemed troubled when he spoke of him, and now Carina could see why. Behind his handsome features deep arrogance and cruelty seethed.

The woman was drawing more of her attention. She seemed even more familiar than Darius' father, though Carina couldn't remember where she'd seen her before. Was she ever so slightly shaking her head? The woman had known her name—Darius must have told her, and she'd remembered. She'd told her to run, wanting to protect her from capture. Why?

"I have to say," the man said, "I'm more than a little disappointed. I was expecting a heart-warming family reunion. Yet you two are acting as though you don't even know each other."

"We don't know each other," said the woman. "I've no idea who this person is. She's entirely innocent, and she rescued your son when he was kidnapped. Yet this is how you repay her."

Something was going on that Carina didn't understand. Saying nothing seemed the wisest course of action. The man didn't appear to know about her mage powers, which was her greatest fear. The way Darius had acted, the woman had to be his mother. She was a mage, according to what the boy had said. So it was also probably her who had sent Carina the elixir ingredients, gems, and the polished pebble. But her husband was clearly evil. He'd trussed her up like an animal ready to be slaughtered. Why had she married him?

The realization dawned that Darius' father was holding his mother captive.

It was just as Nai Nai had warned. The father was using the mother for her powers and treating her like a slave.

"Oh, Faye…" the man said regretfully, as if a thought saddened him.

Carina's heart froze. She fought to keep her features still. She mustn't show any reaction.

The man went on, "Do you really believe after all this time I can't tell when you're lying?"

Carina's throat was tight. She wanted to scream, to shout, to do anything, but she couldn't. She mustn't. The pieces of the puzzle had all slotted into place at once but she could do nothing. Faye was her mother's name. The resemblance to herself was there, yet she could hardly believe it. Was it possible this woman with the haunted eyes, the gaunt face ravaged with pain and sorrow, this broken shadow of a woman, was really her mother? What had she been through that had done this to her?

This woman had given birth to her. Darius was her half-brother, and that retinue of children in the party were probably her half-siblings too.

The enormity of her realization threatened to overwhelm Carina. Nai Nai had said her father had died and her mother had disappeared. Carina had assumed that, after all the time that had passed, her mother was dead too. But she was still alive. She'd been kept captive all those years and forced to bear children for her vile husband.

Carina wanted to vomit. She wanted to run to her mother and hug her, tell her she would be okay, tell her that she would rescue her. She had to get her away from this evil monster.

Trying to keep her face expressionless, she gazed at her mother. Tears welled up in the woman's eyes. Carina looked away lest her emotions betrayed her. Her mother was right. They had to do everything they could to prevent her husband from confirming their relationship and knowing she was also a mage.

Then she could work on getting her mother out of here.

The man steepled his fingers and brought them to his lips. "Tell them to bring me the wand," he said to the guard.

A message spoken into the guard's comm button resulted in a long, slim, metal instrument being brought to the door a few minutes later. The husband took it and looked up its length before going over to Carina's mother and laying the instrument against her arm. She screamed.

"Good, good," the man said. "Just wanted to make sure it was working."

"I don't care how much you hurt me," her mother said, "you aren't going to make me implicate a stranger."

"But I'm not going to hurt you, my dear. I'm going to hurt *her*."

The man approached Carina. She struggled and lashed out at him with her legs as she had before. He tutted and stepped away. "Hold her still," he told the guard.

The guard pinned her into the corner with a heavy boot to her stomach. Her mother's husband approached again and laid the instrument against her head. White-hot pain blinded her. She tried to go inside herself as Nai Nai had taught her and ignore the signals of her nerves, but she couldn't. The torment was too strong. It beat through all her defenses and she became aware she was screaming. Then the pain eased a fraction. She was on her side, curled up, lying in her own vomit.

The husband tutted again. "Disgusting. I prefer to use the wand because it creates less mess. No blood, you see. And then you go and do that."

"Please, Stefan," Faye said. "Don't do this. She's a stranger."

"Maybe she is," he replied. "Maybe she isn't your daughter and a mage. So what? Then she's a nobody. If I torture her to death, it won't matter."

Carina caught a glimpse of the thin metal bar before the pain descended again and she was lost to it. There was nothing in the universe but her and the agony. When the pain lifted once more, she was in another part of the room. She must have been trying to get away from the torture instrument, though she had no recollection of it.

How often the man touched her with the bar, how long the pain went on, Carina didn't know. She lost track of time. She forgot why it was happening. She screamed herself hoarse. She begged for death. Anything to stop the dreadful agony descending once more.

The man said nothing as he carried out the torture. At least, if he did, it was during the moments when Carina lost all sense of what was happening. It seemed as though he was in no hurry to stop. He was only enjoying himself as the session drew to an inevitable conclusion.

Finally, dimly, she heard her mother's soft, trembling words. "Stefan, stop. You win. You're right. She is my daughter and a mage. Carina, please forgive me."

Laughter erupted from her husband. The man laughed so hard he dropped the torture instrument. "I already knew, you fool. I already knew."

FORTY-FIVE

Carina didn't know how long she drifted in and out of consciousness. Whenever she woke, her surroundings were the same: a bare room, harsh lighting, and the steady, subtle thrum of the starship's engine vibrating the floor. When she could finally stay awake she found she was no longer bound tightly. Restraints around her wrists and ankles were fastened by a line to the wall.

She sat up and was amazed to see no evidence on her skin of the torture her mother's husband, Stefan, had put her through. Her nerves remembered, however. They jangled painfully with every movement she made. Carina recalled her torturer's laughter after he had wrested the admission from her mother through forcing her to watch her daughter's agony. He said he'd known all along she was a mage. But how?

Her hand flew to her side and she felt for her canister of elixir. It was gone. Of course. The guards must have searched her after she'd been captured. They'd given the canister to Stefan and he'd known what it was.

Carina gingerly shifted herself to the edge of the room, where her restraints were attached to the wall. She could rest against it for support, though the pressure on her back made her wince at first. The door to the room was smooth on the inside, with no security panel or other means of opening it. She was in a cell of some kind with no hope of escape. She could only wait until someone decided to check on her.

She had no fear she would be left to die. Stefan would want to make her use her mage powers for his benefit. He would be back soon.

She tried to process everything she'd learned. Darius must have told her mother her name, and her mother would have guessed she might be the daughter she'd been forced to abandon. Nai Nai had told her that her mother had disappeared, but the old woman died when Carina was too young to press her for more information.

Nai Nai had also told her that her father was dead. If her mother had ended up married to that evil Sherrerr, it meant Stefan had probably killed him. Carina shivered then sobbed. She wept for her dead father and in pity for her mother. What had her life been like in the years she'd been gone?

It was no wonder she hadn't recognized her mother at first. She bore little resemblance to Carina's dim memories of the happy, gentle person from her toddlerhood. The poor, poor woman. Nai Nai had warned her so seriously and so often for good reasons. Her mother was living proof of the old woman's words.

And of course, little Darius hadn't told her of his mother's dreadful plight. At six years old, he would have no idea of the true situation of his family. Carina tried to remember what he'd said about his brothers and sisters. She seemed to remember he had four or five. Some of them were mages and some weren't. That made sense. If only one parent was a mage, some offspring would inherit powers and some wouldn't. Stefan had bred at least two or three more mages on her mother. Now he would want to add her to his collection.

Carina recalled her joy at seeing little Darius again. Now she understood the connection she'd felt with him. He was more than another mage to her. They shared the same blood.

The door opened. Carina stiffened. Stefan entered the cell. "Wait here," he said to someone behind him before closing the door. He leaned his back against it, regarding her as he folded his arms across his chest. Amusement crinkled the corners of his eyes.

Stefan's manner was the most disarming thing about him. If he hadn't tortured her within an inch of her life, Carina could have mistaken her mother's husband at first glance for a normal, not-unlikable man. He was very good-looking, and though he was middle-aged he wore the years well. When he wasn't inflicting pain and cruelty on others, his expression was intelligent. The monster inside him was obviously only visible when the occasion merited it.

Years of surviving alone on the streets and then fighting as a merc had given Carina nerves of steel, yet this man scared her. She couldn't imagine what he might be capable of, and neither did she want to find out.

"Ah, Carina," said Stefan. "You have no idea of the joy it gives me to find you at last. I knew your mother had borne a child before she came to me. Though she always denied it, I can tell these things, you know. I knew there was at least one more mage brat running around in this part of the galaxy. But it isn't only your powers that make me so pleased to meet you."

He squatted on his heels so he was at eye level with her.

"As I look at you now," he went on, "I'm reminded so strongly of the first time I met your mother. She was a little older than you then, but just as beautiful. Time has worn her features—strongly as it turns out now that I have the opportunity to compare the two of you, but she was breath-taking then. There's a special beauty to women who are hurt and despairing. I love their vulnerability. It excites me no end."

"I'm glad to meet you too, Stefan," Carina said. "I always promised myself that if I ever found out who had taken my parents from me, I would make them pay. And now I've finally found you."

"Ha! I'm sorry to have to disappoint you on that score, my dear. Your mother has threatened me with her revenge too many times to count, yet here I am. And here you two are, under my control. You won't be harming me in any way. On the contrary, you'll be helping me."

"I'll kill you first." Carina stood up, though her restraints pulled at her wrists and her legs could barely take her weight. The after-effects of the nerve torture screamed at her, telling her to be still.

If only he would come closer.

Stefan laughed. "I believe your mother said the very same words. Yet look where her defiance got her." He also rose to his feet. "Your arrival is as fortuitous as hers was. Through the careful deployment of her powers, my status in my family has risen considerably. I'm looking forward to adding you to my stable of mages now that we Sherrerrs are embarking on our push to destroy our competition and rise to supremacy. I imagine you have abilities that exceed even your own poor, dear mother's."

"I wouldn't fight the Sherrerrs' war for them even if I could," Carina replied. "Not after what you've done to my family."

"Hmmm...so you're also holding to the lie that mages cannot kill. I never believed your mother, and I don't believe you. You will fight for me, Carina, and willingly. Do you think I can't make you? You're mistaken. I have many years' experience of dealing with your mother. I know exactly how to force her to bend to my will, as you found out earlier. I have no doubt the same methods will work on you."

Carina didn't reply. She was willing him to move closer.

And then he did.

His confident swagger as he sauntered across the small space told her what he had in mind. She reasoned that a few moments' disgust was well worth the result.

"I have another reason to be thankful you turned up just now, Carina," Stefan said softly. His pupils were wide in spite of the strong light in the room. "Your mother won't be giving me any more children, but you're young and healthy. I'm sure you could bring seven or eight little ones into the world with my help. Another brood of mages would cement the domination of the Sherrerr clan, and in time, it would be natural for me to lead it. How does that sound? Wouldn't it be wonderful to be the Lady Sherrerr? First woman of this galactic sector."

He was so close she could feel his breath on her skin, hot and humid. But she couldn't act. She had to wait for the right moment. To hide her expression of loathing, she turned her face away. Stefan took her movement for acquiescence. He pressed his body against her, grasped her jaw, and pulled her face around to his. As he kissed her, he squeezed her breast hard while his other hand snaked down between her legs.

Carina twisted her head violently downward and fastened her teeth on Stefan's neck. She bit him with all her strength, grinding her teeth to reach his jugular vein. At Stefan's scream, the door flew open. A moment later, something struck her head, breaking her bite on Stefan's neck and nearly knocking her out.

She sank to the floor, his blood dripping from her chin. Stefan also fell. His hand clutched his neck, and blood ran from between his fingers, but it didn't run fast enough. She hadn't managed to reach his vein.

"Should I stun her, sir?" the guard asked.

Grimacing in pain, Stefan replied, "No." He gasped, "No, leave her be." The blood from his neck dribbled slowly down to his shirt. Though he continued to wince at the pain Carina had caused him, she was amazed and sickened to see a smile form on his lips. "Thank you for that, my dear. I'd almost forgotten what it's like to be with a woman who truly fights. I will enjoy our first encounter very much indeed."

FORTY-SIX

Several hours after Stefan departed, the door to Carina's cell opened once again. This time, two guards entered. While one kept his weapon trained on her, the other unfastened her restraints and hauled her to her feet. After tying her hands behind her back, the first guard pushed her out of the cell.

"Where are you taking me?"

Neither of the guards answered. They only guided her through the starship's corridors.

It was a large, military vessel similar to the one the Sherrerrs had used to blow up Banner's Moon, no doubt intended to take part in the effort to "destroy the competition" that Stefan had mentioned. She wondered if Stefan had commanded her to be brought to him so that she could Cast in an upcoming battle.

To her surprise, when the guards finally opened another door and pushed her through, she found herself in the entrance to a living compartment. The ties around her wrists were removed and the guards left and closed the door. The low murmur of quiet voices came from the lounge area. Carina followed the sound and found herself looking at a group of children, presumably her new family. A boy and girl of about the same age were playing a 3D game, a teenage girl was drawing on a holoscribe, a younger boy was wrestling with his sister on the floor, and Darius was lying across a sofa, his feet up on its arm as he read from an interface.

He was the first to notice her. "Carina," the little boy exclaimed. He threw down his screen and ran over to her, then stopped. "What's that on your face?"

Her mother appeared in a doorway. She turned pale as she met Carina's gaze. She swept across the room to grab her in her arms. "You're hurt," she said. "Come and sit down. I'll call a medic."

Carina finally understood what Darius had meant. "It's okay. It isn't my blood. It's Stefan's." She rubbed away the dry, crusty flakes.

The relief that swept across her mother's features was quickly followed by horror. "What did he do to you? What has he done?" Her voice rose to an almost hysterical pitch.

"He hasn't done anything," Carina replied. "I'm okay. Really."

Her mother covered her face with her hands. "Oh, Carina. I'm so sorry. I'm so sorry. I tried so hard to protect you."

"It isn't your fault. None of this is. It's that Sherrerr bastard who's to blame. I'm not going to let him get away with it."

"What's a bastard?" Darius asked.

"Oh, nothing," said Carina's mother. "A bad man."

"Are you talking about Father? Is he a bastard? He *is* a bad man. He ordered the guards to catch Carina. I hate him."

Carina's mother shushed the child and glanced fearfully into the living room. The teenage boy and his younger sister had stopped wrestling and were watching and listening to everything that was going on. All the children were. The boy and girl had stopped playing their game and the teenage girl was looking at them over her holoscribe. Carina's mother took a deep breath. She took her by the hand and led her fully into the room. "Children, I would like you to meet your sister, Carina."

After a moment's pause, the boy and girl who had been playing the 3D game came over and hugged her around her waist. The girl introduced herself as Oriana, and the boy said his name was Ferne. The teenage girl said gravely, "I'm very pleased to meet you, Carina. I'm Parthenia." She remained where she was. The teenage boy and younger girl ignored Carina and resumed their wrestling.

"That's Castiel," her mother said, gesturing to the boy, "and Nahla."

Now that she heard the names again, bits and pieces of what Darius had told Carina about his family came back to her. She remembered he hadn't particularly liked Castiel, and the boy had no mage powers. She imagined it would be hard growing up among siblings who could do things you couldn't.

Her mother announced, "Carina has had a difficult time and needs to rest. She'll be able to talk to you all and get to know you later." She took her hand to lead her away.

"Awww, Mother," said Darius. "I want Carina to play with me *now*."

"You'll just have to be patient," her mother replied. She took her into a bedroom.

After closing the door, her mother clasped her close and held her so tightly she could hardly breathe. Carina hugged her mother back as sobs wracked the woman's thin body. She felt like if she pressed too hard on the frail back, her bones would break.

Her mother was repeating the same words over and over through her tears. *I'm sorry. I'm so sorry.* Eventually, Carina gently loosened her mother's hold on her and held her at arms' length. The poor woman looked even worse than she had the last time she'd seen her. Carina didn't know how she was still standing. She guided her across to a bed and sat her down, wrapping her arms around her.

"I missed you, Ma," she said.

"I missed you too, darling," her mother replied, her voice thick with bitter sorrow. "When Darius told me a mage had rescued him and her name was Carina, I could hardly believe it. How could it possibly be you? And yet after he described your appearance I knew it *was* you—that by some strange, amazing coincidence it was my daughter who had returned my son to me.

"I knew how lonely you must be. Such is the life of a mage. I wanted to send you a sign that you weren't alone, that someone knew who and what you are. I hoped it would give you some comfort, even if I could do nothing else to help you. But I wish I'd never sent you those the elixir ingredients or one of your grandmother's stones. That was so stupid of me. I would rather have never seen you again than have you end up here with me and the other children."

Carina put her hand atop her mother's. "Don't worry about me. I'm not a child any longer. I can get us all out of this, and I will. I won't let Stefan or any other Sherrerr hurt you or any of my brothers or sisters ever again."

Her mother smiled sadly. "I wish that were possible. I've tried so many times. I've come so close but each time I failed. Stefan is too clever and his control is too strong. Why else do you think you're here? Why hasn't he kept you locked up in a cell?"

Carina had wondered about that. It seemed strange her mother's husband would allow them to be together and give them the opportunity to plot their escape.

"It's because he knows the closer we are emotionally to each other, the greater the hold he has over us," her mother explained. "He wants you and I to renew our relationship and for you to bond with your sisters and brothers. Then, to force us to Cast as he wishes, all he has to do is threaten to hurt someone we love. For a man with a heart that's never known anything but avarice and lust for power, he has a remarkable understanding of love. Like when he was torturing you. I couldn't bear it. I couldn't allow you to suffer that pain, even though I knew you would suffer worse things and for longer, if I confessed what you are." She began to weep again.

Carina hugged her. "You didn't make him do that, and your confession didn't change anything. He knew what I was. He was only enjoying torturing both of us, just in different ways."

"I know," her mother said, "but still, I gave in, again."

"Mother, please don't blame yourself. None of this is your fault."

Carina also felt like crying. Her mother's wretchedness was unbearable. But she wanted to remain strong. Perhaps her mother could draw strength from her own.

"Carina." Her mother swallowed. "I have to tell you, your father... he's gone. Stefan swore that he would let him go free if I would only tell him what mages can do. He lied. When I'd given him the information he wanted, he brought Kris in, and..."

"Please..." Carina sat and gripped her mother's hands until she finally mastered her emotions. "I knew. I already knew about Dad."

"You knew? How did you know?"

"Nai Nai told me he was dead. She said she didn't know what had happened to you, but that Daddy had died. I don't know how she knew. Maybe as she was his mother, she felt it somehow. But that man Stefan isn't going to hurt any of us anymore. It stops here."

"I've wanted it to stop for so long, Carina. I wished for it so hard. I tried everything I could, but he's too smart and too evil. All I hope for these days is for everything to finally end, one way or another."

"Don't give up. I've been in some hard places and I always found a way out. I'll find a way out of this too, for all of us."

"That's the problem. It has to be all of us or none of us. Anyone who's left behind will be made to pay for the escape of the others. That's one of the things that makes it so hard to leave."

Carina suddenly regretted her reckless attempt to kill Stefan. She hadn't thought about what his family might do to her mother if she'd succeeded.

"Besides," her mother went on. "I'm not sure if all the children want to be free of him. Parthenia seems to want to please him. And he isn't mean to Castiel or Nahla. They love him like any child loves its father."

Carina recalled the non-mage children in the family, who hadn't said a word when she was introduced. She hadn't felt the natural emotional closeness she'd immediately felt for Darius, the twins, and even the reserved Parthenia.

Yet Castiel and Nahla were her mother's children too. Of course she had to love them just as much as the ones who had inherited her mage powers.

"Castiel and Nahla don't know what their father is capable of," Carina said. "If they did, they wouldn't want to stay with him."

Her mother's wan, grief-stricken face sank further. "I don't know if that's true."

FORTY-SEVEN

Stefan's first move was to try to involve Carina in the upcoming attack on one of the Dirksens' military bases, a planet called Cestrarth. He brought her to the battle planning meeting.

Stefan was taking no chances with her physical freedom. He had her tied painfully tightly to a chair set back a little from the table. Castiel sat next to her. No one had said why. Carina wondered if Stefan was training up his son and her half-brother in his role as a torturer of the mages in the family.

Carina noticed with satisfaction that Stefan's neck still bore the wound of her attack. The ship's medic had applied a healing gel, but her bite mark was easy to see, each tooth distinct. *Ha, Ma managed to keep the Heal Cast a secret,* she thought. She smiled grimly to herself. The next time he gave her an opening, Stefan wouldn't survive.

She considered it oddly over-confident that he was making her attend the battle planning. She would of course become privy to the Sherrerrs' strategies and tactics. Either Stefan's need to show off his new mage to the other Sherrerrs was blinding him to the danger, or she was attending a mock meeting where she was only being fed facts it was safe for her to know.

The attendees filed in. Unlike Stefan, they wore the Sherrerr uniform. The family insignia was reiterated on their collars at a frequency that accorded with their rank. The officers were all older than Stefan. A gray-haired woman called Tremoille took the seat nearest Carina, giving her only a cursory glance. One of the woman's arms was prosthetic. A portly man with a long face arrived next and sat opposite Carina. He proceeded to stare at her unblinkingly. A short, younger woman sat next to him. When the next officer arrived, Carina stiffened.

It was Commander Calvaley of the Sherrerrs' mountain stronghold on Ithiya. After her special request to visit the men's quarters, there was no chance he wouldn't recognize her.

"Well, I never," Calvaley said as he dropped casually into his seat and got a clear look at her face. "If it isn't Private Lin, who disappeared right from under our noses. This makes a lot of sense."

"What's that?" Stefan asked.

"Your mage is no stranger to me," Calvaley replied. "She served in the attack on Banner's Moon. Served bravely and well. She appropriated a new Dirksen weapon that's designed to incapacitate the enemy with terror. It emits an ultrasonic frequency that resonates with the amygdala in the brain, triggering an uncontrollable emotional reaction. Your mage stole what we believe to be the prototype before we blew up their moon. Or perhaps you spirited it out of there?" He raised an eyebrow.

If only, Carina thought, though she said nothing. Casting Transport on that thing would have saved a lot of effort and stress. Too bad she couldn't sip elixir while wearing a helmet.

"Carina," Stefan said. "I'm impressed. You were helping in the Sherrerr cause even before I met you."

"I was just a soldier doing my job, before I knew the Sherrerrs were rapists and torturers. I won't be helping you again."

"Stefan," the portly man at the head of the table said. "Keep her in check, would you? We don't have much time. I'd rather proceed without interruption."

"Of course, General," said Stefan. "I apologize." He went over to Carina and bent down to speak into her ear. "If you think that my raping and beating your mother was bad," he said softly, "just wait and see what I'll do to her if you speak again."

Carina clenched her teeth. She was already feeling the effect of the power Stefan held that her mother had warned her about. She would give anything to save the poor woman from more suffering. A sense of desperation began to gnaw at her.

At her side, Castiel smiled.

———

Carina had no choice but to listen as the Sherrerr heads of command discussed their tactics to defeat the Dirksens' forces on Cestrarth. They were expecting to meet a vigorous defense and were working on the assumption that their attack was unlikely to be a surprise to their rival clan. As a result, they were bringing a large portion of their firepower to bear with the intention of striking hard and fast. The Sherrerrs wanted to utterly crush the opposing forces on the planet and take it over. Cestrarth's position lent it strategic importance, and losing the military forces would strike a major blow to the Dirksens.

One way or another, it would be a decisive first battle in the war, in space, in the air, on the ground, and at sea on Cestrarth. As the officers talked, Stefan would glance at Carina every so often, as if hoping she was thinking up Casts she could use to aid the Sherrerr cause. She was not.

She was trying to figure out how to get her mother and siblings out of reach of their psychopathic husband and father. It wouldn't be easy. Even if she could get the ingredients and create an elixir—a process she'd discovered Stefan guarded against effectively—she couldn't Transport the family off the ship. They were probably light years from any civilized regions, let alone habitable planets. The Sherrerrs would have gone somewhere remote in order to gather their ships in secret. Though she might have attempted a Transport Cast from a ship in orbit to a planet's surface, trying to move a human being planetside from deep space was highly likely to end in a nasty, painful death.

Even if she had elixir in her hand right now, escape of any kind was out of the question. Her only other option was to take command of the ship—a ship that was carrying tens of thousands of armed troops. It was no good. Escape wouldn't be possible until the ship traveled to an inhabited region. Carina would have to think of a plan that might work when they were near a habitable planet.

As soon as they were free, they could survive and avoid recapture with the help of their mage powers. At least, the mage children could. Carina wasn't sure what to do with the children who hadn't inherited her mother's abilities. Would they want to leave too? She wasn't sure. It seemed that Stefan had never behaved excessively badly toward them. Maybe they would prefer to remain living the rich, highly privileged lifestyle of the Sherrerr clan.

Castiel was watching her too. He was still smiling. He looked extremely like his father. Carina wondered what her mother thought of her eldest son.

The meeting was drawing to a close. The holo of Cestrarth floating above the central table disappeared and the officers began to push back their chairs and leave. The parts of the battle plan that had filtered through to Carina had given her no ideas on how she could Cast to influence the outcome, even if she'd been willing to try. The only time she'd Cast during a battle, all she'd done was Transport troops to another place. Killing took a lot of concentration and power, and it was grisly. She had no desire to do that to Dirksen soldiers, who, like the Sherrerr troops, were only pawns in the game the two great clans played.

Calvaley was walking around the table, heading over to her. "I haven't given up on you, Lin," he said when he arrived at her chair. "You're an excellent soldier, and with your abilities you could rise high in the ranks very quickly. You could occupy an influential, lucrative position where you would not be subject to coercion. What do you say?"

"Now wait a minute," said Stefan, rising to his feet.

"Sit down," Calvaley told him. "I shouldn't have to remind you that you are not an officer in the Sherrerr armed forces, and until you are, your surname counts for little. You are tolerated, Stefan Sherrerr, for what you can offer, and no more."

The rage emanating from the object of Calvaley's scorn was almost palpable.

"I would sooner cut my own throat than work for the Sherrerrs," Carina said. "When you tolerate the actions of scum, you sink to the same level. One of my deepest regrets is that I ever helped you. I won't make the same mistake again."

"Hmmm...shame," said Calvaley. "Not everyone thinks the same as you, you know. Control is the foundation of civilization. Without it, there is nothing but anarchy and barbarism. If you think our behavior is bad, you wouldn't want to see what happens in a society that lives without fear of retribution. A society that lacks a controlling force isn't a society, it's a collection of individuals fighting, maiming, and killing to get what they want. When we have ultimate control over this galactic sector, we will see peace and prosperity on an unprecedented scale."

"Keep telling yourself that, Calvaley, while you consort with rapists, torturers, and murderers. What you think you're fighting is what you are. I despise you."

Stefan drew back his hand to strike her across the face, but Calvaley stopped him with an impatient gesture.

"You're young and confused," he said to Carina, "and I have no doubt that Stefan has put your poor mother through a lot, so I'll forgive you that. In time, when we've won this war, you'll see I was right. Like I said, many see the sense of our actions. That other soldier who disappeared with you saw fit to return to our ranks after his little sojourn."

Calvaley could only mean Bryce. Bryce had rejoined the Sherrerr army? Carina said nothing, but her shock must have shown on her face.

"That surprised you, didn't it?" Calvaley said. "Yes. I spotted him aboard ship this morning. He enlisted under an assumed name of course, but I knew his face. You see? He left with you, but he's seen the error of his ways and come back to fight for a noble cause. What do you think of that?"

Carina's mind was whirring as she tried to think of why Bryce would have re-enlisted with the Sherrerrs when he had a new business to run.

"Consider my proposal, Lin. It stands—for a little while."

Forty-Eight

Ensconced deep within the Sherrerr ship, Carina was shielded from all the effects of the space battle going on with the Dirksen fleets. She had learned they were aboard the Sherrerr flagship, *Nightfall*. While the destroyers, dreadnoughts, and fighter ships of both sides fought for control of the planetary system, all she saw was the interface feed from drones at Cestrarth. The flying spies transmitted vids and data from the planet surface to the room where Stefan had put her along with her two guards.

A jug and a glass sat on the table in front of her. The jug was filled with elixir. Parthenia had made it, and she'd done it perfectly. She had wondered why, when Stefan clearly had a mage who was willing to help him, he bothered forcing her to do his bidding. Perhaps it was because he thought she was better at Casting, or he wanted to assert his power over her.

After guards had taken her to the room, Stefan had told her he would be back soon, and left. She knew that he'd gone to fetch someone he could threaten to hurt if she didn't do exactly as he asked. When he'd reappeared with little, sweet Darius in tow, her horror was almost equaled by her rage.

Stefan had his method of coercion honed to its most efficient and effective. It wasn't surprising he'd controlled her mother so well over the years. First, he picked his victim well. Carina had been expecting him to use her mother, but of course he'd realized they would try to collude and defy him, even at the cost of extreme pain. He'd passed over his wife in favor of another person he knew Carina cared about.

She'd loved the little boy even before she knew he was her half-brother. If she'd even guessed at what went on within Stefan's household, she would never have returned him. But at his young age, the little boy didn't know or understand half of it. Her mother had done a good job of protecting him. When Carina had asked him about his home life after rescuing him from the Dirksens, he had only told her the facts from his six-year-old perspective—his brothers and sisters, tutors, pets, and daily life. It seemed that up until recently, things had been fairly normal on the surface within the walls of the Sherrerr estate.

"Normal" was the last word Carina would use to describe what was happening now. She could hardly conceive of someone so depraved they would hurt a little boy, let alone their own son, in order to get what they wanted.

Darius was holding his father's hand trustingly and looking all about him as the pair entered the room. As soon as the little boy's gaze alighted on Carina he gave a beaming smile and tried to break away from his father to run to her. Stefan held tightly to his son's hand, however, saying, "There will be time to speak to Carina later, Darius. Please sit down here."

Looking a little confused, Darius climbed into the seat his father had indicated.

"We have an important job to do today," said Stefan, "and you're going to help us do it."

"Do you want me to Cast?" Darius asked. He'd spotted the jug and glass on the table.

"No. Carina will be doing the Casting today. She is older than you and her abilities are much stronger."

"Oh, am I here to watch?" asked Darius. "Like I have to watch Parthenia sometimes?"

"You are here to watch, to learn, and to provide encouragement."

"I can do that," Darius said, though without enthusiasm. He was watching Carina sadly.

She was nauseated with disgust and overcome with fury. At the word "encouragement," Stefan had drawn out the torture instrument he'd used on her from inside his jacket. He was holding it behind Darius, and the little boy couldn't see it. The implication was clear: if she didn't do as Stefan asked, he would use the device on the child.

Her nerves hadn't entirely recovered from the ministrations of the slim metal rod. They still tingled painfully at intervals when she was awake and asleep. Her whole being rebelled at the idea of Darius suffering the same agony she'd endured.

The little boy asked, "What's the matter, Carina?"

She'd been trying to keep her expression neutral. She was clearly failing at the attempt. "Stefan Sherrerr, you're a monster."

"No, my dear," he replied. "I'm very much a man, as I intend to demonstrate to you, to my great delight and pleasure, when I have a spare moment. Now, the situation is very clear, but as this is your first time, I think it wise to make it even clearer. I am well aware of the capabilities of mages, and also the limitations of their Casts. I know the effect is not immediate, that there is a lag, which is fortunate for me and very unfortunate for you. Both of the guards are under strict instructions to immediately retaliate with deadly force if anything should begin to happen to themselves or myself.

"You may wish to take a chance, but will your Cast work before you or your brother are under any threat? I can assure you from experience it will not. Your mother found that out the hard way, if only her poor feeble mind could recall it. Be assured, a pulse rifle fires faster than any Cast can work. If you do try, you will fail. You and your brother will be gone, and I will have four mages remaining at my disposal.

"But I would ask you not to attempt it, nevertheless, Carina, as step-father to step-daughter. Though you and I have yet to become better acquainted, I have grown quite fond of the boy, and I would be sorry to hurt him."

"Father?" Darius asked, looking up at Stefan with wide brown eyes.

His father ruffled his hair. "Never mind. Just sit there and be a good boy."

Stefan's words had been beyond his understanding, but Darius must have picked up on some of what was going on because he suddenly began to cry.

Carina couldn't stand it. "Take him out of here. I'll do what you want."

Stefan raised his eyebrows. "Capitulating so soon? I was expecting more of a fight from you. What was it you were saying? You'd rather cut your own throat? How dramatic. Yet here we are and you cave like a virgin on her first night."

"Done with your gloating?" Carina asked. "Take him away."

"No, I don't think I'll do that. I'd much prefer little Darius to remain present. His presence will keep my threat fresh in your mind, and he might learn something from watching you in action."

Carina herself didn't know what she could do to fulfill Stefan's command that she help the Sherrerrs win their battle. She only wanted to protect Darius. The child had already been tortured by the Dirksens to try to make him reveal his mage status. He'd been through enough without his father torturing him too.

She closed her eyes and gave a heavy sigh. "Has the battle on the ground started? You know I can't do anything in space, right? I can't affect the Dirksen ships." Starships traveling at even slow speeds were impossible for a mage to target, as far as Carina knew. In the handful of times she'd tried, she'd failed.

"Your mother did manage to convince me of that limitation on mage powers, under considerable duress. I remain convinced, for the moment."

"Then what's happening on the ground? And how the hell do you expect me to do anything about it from up here?"

"The battle has begun," Stefan replied. "See the drone feed." Four holograms flickered to life above the table. Each showed a different view of a planet. There appeared to be four separate military encounters about to take place. One was at a vast concrete complex that bordered a stormy ocean, a second was at a plain that lay within a circle of extinct volcanoes, the third was at sea—Carina guessed that the military installation was on the sea bottom—and the fourth was in a polar region. At all four locations, Sherrerr tanks, armored guns, military drones, and soldiers in exosuits were approaching and defensive fire had begun.

Carina thought of Bryce. Was he taking part in any of the battles? Calvaley had said he'd seen him aboard the ship. She hoped that was where he'd stayed. She also remembered Mandeville and the other soldiers who had helped her bring the Dirksen weapon to the Sherrerr shuttle.

For the first time in her life, her distaste for the bloodshed and violence of military combat turned to hatred. Before, when she'd been a merc, she'd seen armed conflict as a necessary evil of human society. It was going to happen anyway, she'd reasoned. She couldn't stop it so she might as well profit from it. Her feelings were different now. Her disgust for Stefan turned on herself when she realized what she had to do.

"Well?" Stefan asked impatiently. "Have you thought of something? Or do you need some persuasion?" He lifted the slim metal rod.

"I can't Cast across the galaxy," Carina said. "You'll have to take me closer."

FORTY-NINE

Carina asked Stefan over and over to leave Darius aboard the ship and not bring him with them on the shuttle to Cestrarth. She promised him she would Cast to help the Sherrerr side even without Darius present, but he refused to even listen to her. He took his son from the room, telling her they would all go to the surface together once a shuttle was prepared.

Powerlessness and hopelessness engulfed her as he left with his son. Stefan was right. Despite all her brave words, she was caught in the same trap her mother had been for all those years. She couldn't see any way out of it. And what had Stefan meant when he said her mother had found out 'the hard way' what would happen if she refused? Her mother hadn't mentioned any events along those lines. Carina wondered if the recollection was too painful.

A short time later, her guards took her to the shuttle bay. The place was nearly empty. Most of the shuttles were ferrying soldiers to the surface and the fighter ships had left to take part in the battle. Stefan and Darius were waiting for her, standing outside a shuttle at the far end of the bay.

When she arrived at the vessel, she repeated her request. "Please, Stefan. This is incredibly dangerous. We'll be flying right inside the battle zone. Anything could hit us and take us down. Drones, ground-to-air missiles, defense rockets, even well-aimed sniper fire. This isn't a military craft."

"We won't be as defenseless as you suppose," he replied. "We will have a support team. Let's go."

They went up the ramp and into the cabin. Stefan had brought the elixir along, only this time it was in a canister rather than a jug to prevent it from spilling during what promised to be a rocky flight. The shuttle's cabin windows were wide, providing an unusually good view. As well, a holo feed from the surface had been set up. She had all she needed to wreak death and destruction on the Dirksen troops with her powers.

Carina said, "What if I can't do this? I've never tried this before. This isn't how mages use their abilities."

"If you can't sway the course of the battle with your efforts," Stefan replied, "you'd better do a damned good job of convincing me you tried." He directed his son to a seat. "Fasten your safety belt, Darius."

The little boy did as he was told, giving Carina a look filled with fear. He hadn't spoken a word since his fit of crying. Her heart ached at the harsh introduction he was experiencing to his father's truly evil nature.

The pilot boarded, and the shuttle took off. "Which battle site do you wish to go to?" Stefan asked after an hour or so. "We're approaching the planet." He wore a headset enabling him to comm the pilot.

Carina still had no idea. She'd only decided she had to try to do something to sway the fight. Now they were on their way down, her mind remained a blank. Oceanside, a plain encircled by volcanoes, a sea bed, or the subzero, icy environment of a polar cap? The Dirksens had chosen the locations of their military installations well. All presented challenges to the attackers that their own troops would be trained to turn to their advantage. She was wracking her brains for a Cast that would dispose of Dirksen troops. She had to think of something.

"Which is it to be Carina?" Stefan asked again, a hard edge to his tone.

She had to pick. Which one? "The sea bed."

Stefan relayed her choice to the pilot.

"No, wait," Carina said. "The one by the ocean. Or..."

"Which one? Make a decision," Stefan snapped. "You're wasting time."

"The ocean, I guess. Yes, the ocean." She had the germ of an idea.

"Where are we going?" Darius finally piped up.

"Never mind," Stefan replied. "Be quiet."

"We're going to a place where soldiers are fighting," Carina answered.

Stefan frowned but said nothing. He gazed out of the shuttle window as if he had a lot on his mind. They were entering the upper atmosphere. A large, copper-yellow landmass spread out beneath them, stretching to the curved horizon, surrounded by blue ocean. They were sunside, and the border of the atmosphere was clear to see, shimmering as it faded into the blackness of space.

"Why are the soldiers fighting?" Darius asked.

Carina wished she could have gotten to know her little brother in better circumstances. "It's hard to explain. But, Darius, can you do something for me?"

"Yes, of course, Carina. What do you want me to do?"

"Soldiers fighting is a horrible thing to see. You're too young to be watching something like that. Can you promise me that when we arrive there, you'll close your eyes and keep them closed the whole time until I tell you it's okay to open them?"

Stefan rolled his eyes but again he chose not to interfere. Carina imagined he thought his son's welfare wasn't worth bothering about.

The landmass was drawing closer. The pilot was flying them to an area of coastline. As they got nearer, Carina could see the battle was well underway. Specks that were fighter pinnaces were circling the site, jinking to avoid missiles. Puffs of smoke and fire from bombs and other air strikes rose from the military complex they were rapidly approaching. Carina doubted the Sherrerrs were doing much real damage. The structure she'd seen close-up before had been wide but only one story high. Most of the installation had to be underground.

Three fighter planes were zooming up toward them.

"We're being attacked," Carina said.

"No," replied Stefan. "They're Sherrerr planes. They're for our protection."

"What's the state of the battle? Is there a chance this place will be nuked from above?"

"Didn't you listen to anything at all at the planning meeting? We want to *use* the planet, not destroy it. There's not much point in having control of an uninhabitable disaster zone, is there? We just need to gain control of their military sites and put down their defenses. So you need to help us overthrow this site. I have given my assurance you can do it, so my reputation in my family is riding on your success. You'd better deliver, or you, your mother, and all your new brothers and sisters will regret it."

No pressure then.

"You can do it, Carina," Darius said. "I know you can."

"Darius, this isn't what mages are supposed to do. We aren't about hurting people. I want you to understand that."

"Shut up and concentrate on your task," Stefan spat.

The military installation was clear to see now. It reached for two or three kilometers along the coast. The Sherrerrs certainly had their work cut out for them. The Dirksens' guns were firing back at their ground and air attackers, and though the Sherrerr rockets and missiles were hitting their targets, the damage seemed minimal. It was a battle that would take days and massive amounts of firepower to win, if it were winnable at all.

She needed a way to destroy the installation without also causing thousands of Sherrerr casualties. Carina's germ of an idea had grown as they were flying down. It could work. It really could.

FIFTY

"Tell the pilot to fly up and down the coastline," Carina told Stefan. She didn't really need to survey the area. She'd made her request just to buy some time as she marshaled her thoughts and feelings. What she was planning wouldn't hinge on the lie of the land, but on whether she could actually manage it. She rarely had occasion to Cast Rise, and she'd never done it on such a large scale before.

A Cast of that magnitude would require very deep concentration. If she allowed the things most prominent in her mind right now—concern for Darius, fears for her mother and the rest of her new family, worries about what Stefan would want her to do next—to dominate her thoughts, she would never succeed.

And she had to succeed. She simply had to. Stefan had been correct when he'd said that all her brave words had flown out the window the minute he threatened to harm her little brother. Darius had already been through so much when he was kidnapped. He'd had his tracker chip cut out of him by the Dirksens and they'd tortured him to try to discover if he had mage powers. He also had a monster for a father. She couldn't bear to see the little boy hurt again, even if it meant taking part in a war that was none of her business.

One day, hopefully soon, she would help Darius, her mother, and her other sisters and brothers escape from Stefan's clutches. Until that moment she had to do as Stefan asked. Her heart sank as she realized her mother must have told herself exactly the same thing many years ago. She wondered when Ma had finally given up hope.

She would never give up hope. She *would* find a way out.

They were flying at an incredible speed and jerking erratically as the pilot fought to avoid the fire targeted at them. A brilliant flash of light shone through the windows, an ear-splitting *boom* rent the air, and the shuttle rocked and spun upside down. They'd been hit!

Then the pilot righted the vessel.

"Lost one of our fighters," Stefan remarked, almost casually. "You must begin soon. Are you ready?"

Their remaining two guard pinnaces were shooting down the missiles, but they were in great danger of being hit at any moment.

"You'll have to tell the Sherrerr troops to evacuate. Now."

"What? I have no authority to do that."

"If you don't want them to be destroyed, you have to make them stop attacking and withdraw. It's the only way."

"I'm telling you—"

"Then take us back to the ship. I'm a mage, Stefan, not a miracle worker. I can't wave my hands and make the installation disappear or kill all the Dirksens with a nod of my head. You should know this. You've lived with mages for fifteen years and seen what they can and can't do. We aren't murderers. I hardly ever Cast when I was a merc. This isn't easy for me. So do as I ask or forget it, because no matter what you threaten, I can't help you." Despite what it might mean, she had to try to save some troops from what she was about to do. Bryce and Mandeville could be down there. Also, she knew how much this meant to Stefan. She wanted to exploit what leverage she had.

Stefan's brow furrowed in anger. He seemed about to give a retort, but thought better of it. He asked the pilot to patch him through to the Sherrerr command. A moment later he stated Carina's request. He was speaking with Calvaley. After some back and forth, he received the man's agreement.

The shuttle retreated to the upper atmosphere while the Sherrerr troops withdrew from the shoreline. Carina hoped they were moving sufficiently far away to be out of the danger zone.

As the shuttle hung in the upper atmosphere, she saw the fight for control of the planetary system space. Though the starships themselves were too far away to see, flashes and shooting stars signaled the space battle. She hoped that *Nightfall* and her family would remain safe.

After a while, Stefan said, "The troops have retreated. Are you ready?"

No. She would never be ready.

She nodded. Stefan told the pilot to return to the oceanside military base. He reached across the aisle and gave her the bottle of elixir. When they were in sight of the shoreline, she took a large gulp, swallowed the disgusting mixture, then took another gulp. She drank the whole bottle. Would it be enough? She had no idea.

Closing her eyes, she took mental steps down into her mind, disappearing into herself. She shut out the outside noise entering through her ears, the feel of the shuttle seat beneath her, and, with the greatest difficulty, her fear about what she was about to do. She both did and didn't want the Cast to work. Her pulse and breathing slowed. She was alone in the darkness.

In slow strokes, she wrote the character. Each stroke perfect, each in the correct order. *Rise.* When the character was complete, she sent it out. Now she could harness the power of her emotions. She let out her rage at her mother's long captivity and rape, her father's murder, her brothers' and sisters' confinement and abuse, and her own capture and exploitation. She gathered the raw feelings and flung them along the path of the character, speeding in its wake, propelling it to its destination.

Everything was gone. Her mind was blank. Her feelings spent. A terrible weakness overwhelmed her. She could barely open her eyes.

When she did and the shuttle interior swam into view, the first thing she saw was Stefan peering closely out the window. Darius was at his side, also looking downward with great curiosity.

"Darius," Carina said weakly, "get back in your seat. I don't want you to see this."

The little boy did as he was told. "Are you okay?" he asked as he fastened his safety belt.

She was not okay. She was definitely not okay. "I'm fine."

She didn't want to look out the window, but if the Cast had worked, she could guess what was happening. The ocean would be retreating. The waves that had lashed the rocks and concrete buffers of the Dirksens' installation would be gone, and the ocean bed would be laid bare for a kilometer or more from the shore.

If the Dirksens understood what was happening, and if they were quick, they could save a lot of their troops, though their installation would be ruined.

She hoped the Dirksens were quick.

Stefan was nodding. "I see. Very impressive." His back straightened. "Here it comes."

Once, when she was a little girl, before Nai Nai had died and she'd become a street brat, Carina had seen a vid at her friend's house of a natural disaster. Though humans had the technology to avoid many forms of death, they hadn't found a way to prevent eruptions, landslides, earthquakes, hurricanes, or tsunamis.

She had watched her friend's vid in horrified fascination as the water at a beach had disappeared then returned with terrible force, inundating everything in its path. She had watched the terrible weight of water destroying whatever it touched, swamping, crushing, drowning. As a little girl, she'd never imagined she could ever or would ever want to use the power of a tsunami herself.

The enormity of what she'd done settled over her like a suffocating gauntlet. She'd become a weapon of mass destruction.

She closed her eyes.

"Very good, Carina," Stefan said. "Well done."

Fifty-One

When Carina and Darius returned after the battle, the atmosphere in the family living quarters was subdued. Carina's mother greeted her sadly and the children looked up from their occupations momentarily, one or two of them murmuring greetings.

"Carina defeated the Dirksens," Darius said as he went into the living area. "She made a huge wave..." He mimed it with his arms. "And then she sent it crashing down on the Dirksen building. It was amazing." He threw his arms down. He hadn't seen the tsunami but Stefan, in a jubilant mood, had told his son what had happened.

"Shut up you little creep," Castiel said. "Carina only did what Father told her to do. It was Father's victory."

"No..." Darius said, confused. "It was Carina who did it."

Castiel got up from the sofa where he'd been lounging and stalked across to his young brother. "Who brought us here?"

"Father."

"Who took you out in the shuttle?"

"Father."

"Who told Carina to Cast to defeat the Dirksens?"

"Father did, but—"

"Then it was Father's victory. Carina was just Father's weapon."

"But—"

"But nothing," Castiel shouted, and he pushed Darius to the floor.

"Castiel," Carina's mother admonished. "Don't do that. Apologize to your brother and help him up."

Castiel snorted derisively and went back to the sofa. He threw himself onto it and lay down, his hands behind his head.

Ferne had run over to his brother and was helping him to his feet.

"You're a very bad boy," Darius shouted at Castiel, who only smirked and made a rude gesture.

"Stop it, please," Carina's mother said.

She looked worse than ever, Carina thought. She was pale and skeletal, as if something was eating her from the inside out.

"Well done, Carina," Parthenia said.

"Thanks," Carina replied bitterly. "Like Castiel said, it wasn't my idea." She went to her room, closed the door, and sat down on her bed. She couldn't bear the terrible tension that existed constantly between the family members. In her years of solitude after Nai Nai died, when in her darkest moments Carina had wished with all her heart she had her parents and a family, she'd never imagined it would be anything like this. Stefan's abuse had worn down her mother so much she looked like she was at death's door, and the children were split into deeply divided factions.

On one side were the non-mages Castiel and Nahla. The girl wasn't unfriendly while she was away from her brother, but in his company she mimicked his bitter, scornful attitude toward the others. In the other camp were Oriana, Ferne, and little Darius. They played together in quiet games where they pretended to Cast. Carina could remember playing such games herself when she was younger.

Parthenia kept herself apart from the two groups and was quite solitary. In some ways, she reminded Carina of herself, minus the growing-up-on-the street influences on her character. In other ways, Carina found her difficult to read. She'd noticed her looking at their mother with great sadness, yet at the same time she seemed to love Stefan very much and want his attention. Carina hadn't figured out Parthenia yet.

A knock sounded at her door. Carina's mother came in and sat down next to her. She took Carina's hand.

"It's hard when he forces you to Cast, isn't it?" she asked. "I'm sorry you had to go through that."

"I'm okay," Carina replied, a catch in her voice. "It isn't like I've never killed before." Her words were little more than lies intended to protect her mother from guilt and anguish. Nothing Carina said could have been further from the truth. She was constantly fighting to ignore mental images of thousands or even tens of thousands of Dirksen soldiers drowning in their underground bunkers.

She also wanted to spare her mother the details of how Stefan had threatened to hurt Darius. The woman could probably guess well enough, though, and didn't need her husband's methods spelled out to her.

Carina looked into Ma's sad, thin face. She sat up. "Is there something wrong with you? Are you sick?"

The woman took in a deep breath and let out a long sigh.

Her mother's face was filled with such despair, Carina saw her question had struck a nerve. She grabbed her hands. "You are sick! What's wrong?"

Ma swallowed before replying, "I guess I should tell you. I have Ithiyan Plague. I stopped taking the preventative some time ago."

"What? Why did you do that? Have you been to see a doctor?"

"No. I haven't told anyone. I wanted to become so sick that Stefan would have to take me to the capital, to a medical specialist. He would have brought the children with us. I was hoping that once we were outside the estate, I would have a better chance of escaping him." She smiled wryly. "Things didn't quite work out as I planned."

"You need to see a doctor right away. There has to be an army medic aboard the ship."

"I guess I should do that, now that my plan fell through. I just can't seem to get up the motivation. I've lived with this illness so long, I feel like it's part of me and my destiny."

"Don't talk like that," Carina said, filled with alarm. She'd learned from Bryce how quickly the disease became serious once it took hold. She clutched her mother's hands. "I only just found you." Her throat constricted and she couldn't speak. It was no surprise her mother looked so bad. She suddenly jumped up. "Come with me." She pulled on Ma's hands to try to encourage her to stand, but she remained sitting.

"Where? We can't leave these quarters."

"You have to see a doctor. You're seriously ill."

"Oh Carina, I don't know that I want to."

"You have to, Mother. If not for yourself, then for the rest of us. For me." Carina sank to her knees and laid her head in her mother's lap. "Please. As bad as things are, I can stand it. I finally found you. It was so hard being alone for all that time, always hiding what I was. I hate Stefan and I hate the Sherrerrs and everything they're doing, but I can bear it. We'll work out a way to escape together. But if I lose you, I don't know what I'll do."

Her mother stroked her hair. "I missed you so much, Carina, but it comforted me that you were safe with your Nai Nai. I knew she would take good care of you. I didn't think she would die so soon and leave you all alone. I'm sorry for that, but better a life spent alone on the streets than growing up in Stefan's luxurious slave camp."

"Maybe that's so," Carina replied. "But that's the past. I'm here now, and I'm strong. That evil monster hasn't worn me down. And I can fight. I'm determined to get us out of here, more so than ever now that I know how sick you are. I want to give you a reason to live, Ma. I never had you for so long. I want us to be together for many more years."

"I want that too, Carina. I just don't think it's possible. I tried to keep you safe from Stefan, but he caught you in the end. I guess I've given up hope." She sighed. "But if you want me to see a doctor, I will."

Carina jumped up and ran to the main door of the living quarters. She told the guards her mother was very ill and needed to see a medic immediately.

Fifty-Two

The ship's doctor spent only five minutes with Faye in her bedroom before contacting Stefan to ask permission to take her to sick bay. With her husband's say so, she went with the doctor to the medical center. No one was allowed to go with her. Carina argued for permission but Stefan wouldn't grant it.

After spending another hour examining her and running tests, the doctor left the room, saying she would return soon. Faye waited alone on the narrow examination table, naked under her medical gown. She hadn't looked at her body properly in weeks, and even she had been shocked at how thin she'd grown and the extent of the bruises that covered her skin.

The doctor returned. She sat on a tall stool next to the bed and folded her hands in her lap. "I'm sorry to leave you like that. I had to speak to your husband first. I'm sure you're well aware of how things are run around here."

"I understand. So, what did you tell him? What's the news?"

"Faye," the doctor said, "why did you stop taking your preventative? You must have been aware of the risks."

"I was fully aware, but my reasons for my actions aren't your concern. Are you going to tell me what you found out or not?"

"I also wanted to speak to your husband to ask permission to have you evacuated to the nearest friendly planet so you could begin medical treatment immediately." She paused and looked down. "That permission was refused."

"I see."

"If I had the equipment and the drugs, there might be a chance I could..." The doctor paused again. "The disease has progressed so far, it's now in its final stages. You have maybe one or two weeks left. I'm very sorry."

Faye nodded. It would be hard on Carina. Very hard. She regretted that. And little Darius. He loved her so much. But despite her regrets, she couldn't help but feel a tiny bit relieved that her long suffering would soon be over. If there were an afterlife, she would see Kris again. "I think I'll go back to my family now." She climbed down from the table and picked up her clothes.

"I'll prepare some medication for you to take with you," said the doctor. "It'll help ease your symptoms and make you more comfortable. I imagine you've been feeling some bone pain and tenderness and are having night fevers?"

"Yes, that's right."

"I thought so. I wish I knew why you didn't seek help earlier. What you have is entirely curable with the appropriate treatment even in its late stages. Maybe if I could get you to a hospital within the next week or so you might have a chance, but that seems unlikely in the circumstances."

Faye locked eyes with the woman. "You examined me, didn't you? You saw the scars. That's what he's done to me. For years. In my position, would you want to carry on?" When the doctor looked away and didn't answer, she said, "Please leave. I want to get dressed."

In the empty examining room, as she slowly put on her clothes, Faye wondered why she'd waited and done nothing while the disease ravaged her body almost as badly as Stefan had. She'd told herself it was for the same plan that she'd related to Carina, but the words she'd just blurted out to the doctor seemed to ring truer. She could have told Stefan how sick she was weeks before, but she hadn't. Perhaps, deep down, she'd never intended to go through with her plan. Perhaps she had only been trying to find a way out.

The guards escorted her back to the living quarters. It was late. All the children had gone to bed. Only Carina remained awake, waiting for her in the lounge. When she went inside, her daughter stood up. "What did the doctor say? Have you started treatment?"

She went over to the beautiful, strong, courageous young woman and took her in her arms. She could hardly believe the little girl she'd left behind had turned into such a wonderful, good human being. It hurt so badly to know the time she had left with her was painfully short.

She kissed her daughter on her cheek. How could she tell her? She couldn't find the words. Not now. Not yet. "Yes," she replied. "She's given me some medication."

Carina hugged her tightly. It hurt, but Faye didn't say anything.

"You're going to be okay?" Carina asked, her face buried in her mother's shoulder.

"Yes, I'm going to be okay."

FIFTY-THREE

Carina was sleeping soundly, relieved that her mother's illness could be cured, when guards woke her. They'd come directly into her bedroom. The two women watched impassively as Carina dressed, then they escorted her through the dark living area. The rest of the family were asleep. Carina didn't know what time it was but she felt as though she'd slept only one or two hours.

Tiredness tugged at her eyelids as the guards took her through the ship, one in front of her and one behind. Neither would answer her questions about where they were taking her or why. She could only hope she wasn't being permanently separated from her mother and siblings.

"Carina," Stefan said expansively when she arrived at her destination. "Glad you could join us." The guards had led her to a wide auditorium. Tiered rows of seating against one wall faced a window that took up the entire opposite wall and looked out on the local starscape.

"You mean you're glad your guards woke me up and forced me to come here," she retorted. Senior Sherrerr officers who had been at the pre-battle strategy meeting were also present, but she didn't care about embarrassing Stefan in front of his family. She would take every opportunity to demonstrate to them exactly what he was.

Stefan frowned in anger. "Come and sit here." He gestured to the seat beside him.

Other officers were here too. Twenty to thirty men and women in uniforms bearing the Sherrerr insignia were taking up most of the seats that faced the view of the galactic expanse. Carina recognized Raynott, who had orchestrated the assault on Banner's Moon. Calvaley was absent for some reason. A pair of guards stood at each entrance, though whether they were there for her she wasn't sure. She started. One of them was Bryce.

He didn't react when their eyes met, and Carina was thankful that no one seemed to have noticed her shocked reaction. She didn't think Stefan would want her to have friends among the guards. Once more, she wondered how Bryce had ended up aboard the Sherrerr flagship.

She sat next to Stefan. A guard stood on her other side. Stefan immediately leaned closer to whisper something in her ear. Certain he was going to communicate some nasty remark or an even nastier threat, she stood up and briefly pretended to straighten her clothes. When she sat down again, she propped her elbow on the armrest farthest from Stefan and rested her chin on her hand, so her mother's husband would have been forced to lean comically far across her seat to speak in her ear.

It was a petty gesture but Carina was taking whatever she could get. Stefan tutted under his breath. She wished she could reach over and break his neck. Only the knowledge that her mother and siblings would suffer the consequences prevented her.

Tremoille, the senior female officer Carina had seen at the strategy meeting, began. "Now that we're all here, finally, I'll play the vid data sent back by our drones. As you'll see, the intel we gathered on Cestrarth has proven to be correct and not planted information."

The window on the stars went black as it became a screen. A different starscape appeared.

"We sent out around three hundred drones," the older woman said. "This vid is has been compiled from all the recordings we received."

The starscape shifted, the lights in the room dimmed, and the area between the audience and the window became a room-wide holo of a field of stars. The stars were subtly moving, or rather, the drones had been traveling into them at high speed, faster than the fastest starship.

"So, where exactly is this?" a voice asked.

"Sacrasi Region," Tremoille replied.

"What?" someone exclaimed. "Right on our doorstep. The arrogant bastards."

"Last place we'd think to look," another audience member remarked.

"Exactly," said Tremoille. "If it weren't for the intel we got from invading their planet, we would never have thought to look here."

The stars in the holo continued to shift. The drones seemed to be heading toward a dark area of space at the center of the scene. Carina's curiosity had been piqued, but she was damned if she was going to ask Stefan to explain what they were watching.

A few moments later, she saw it. Or rather, them. The drones had sent back telemetry on heat signatures their scanners picked up. The specks of red were artificial structures in the depths of space.

"At this point," said Tremoille, "we began to lose drones." Tiny flashes of light peppered the holo. The red specks grew quickly larger and began to assume the rough outline of starships. "The Dirksens had spotted them and were picking them off. The volume and quality of data decreases until the last drone is taken out. Around..." The officer paused. "Here."

The hologram blinked out, and the window reverted to being a plain window again.

"Are we sure that was what we think it is?" someone asked.

"It would be a difficult fake to construct," Tremoille replied.

"Nevertheless, it could be a decoy," the questioner persisted. "The information we found on Cestrarth could be false after all. The whole thing could be an elaborate trap. If we send the strength of our fleet there, we would be leaving our own planets inadequately defended."

"On the other hand," said Raynott, "if it is the Dirksen shipyard and we destroy it, we will have struck a decisive blow. They would find it hard to recover and fight back after that."

"Agreed," the first officer said, "but the same applies to us. Even if it is the shipyard and not a trap, it will be very heavily defended. More so now they detected our drones and they know we know where it is. The battle to destroy it could cause us great losses we'll find difficult to recover from."

"What if we could take out the shipyard without expending vast amounts of firepower?" Stefan asked. "What if we only needed to get one heavily defended ship close enough for my mages to take out the entire place?"

Carina turned and stared at him. So this was why he'd had her woken up in the middle of the quiet shift.

"You're suggesting your mages could destroy the entire Dirksen shipyard?" Tremoille asked incredulously.

"I'm certain of it," Stefan said. "It's stationary, unlike starships, which they find difficult to target. Starships move too fast. We have the schematics of the place. I'm sure my mages could cause significant damage with a Cast."

Carina noted he didn't ask her for confirmation. She had no idea how to do what he was promising his clan.

"Aren't you being a little over-confident?" Tremoille asked. "I mean, the destruction of the military installation on Cestrarth was impressive, but attacking the Dirksen shipyard will be an order of magnitude more difficult.

And it isn't as though there's an ocean handily nearby. What do you imagine they would do?"

"I suggest you give them a chance," Stefan said. "It won't only be Carina here. The others are ready to take part in a battle. Even my youngest son." Someone in the room made a sound signaling disgust. Stefan ignored it and went on, "Working together, I'm sure they could destroy the place."

"We don't plan battles according to vague notions and possibilities," Tremoille remarked acidly. "I ask you again, what do you imagine they would actually *do*?"

"I've seen my wife move things with the power of her mind many times," said Stefan. "I'm sure that by combining their powers they could move a strategic ship or piece of equipment that would create a great deal of damage."

"Not in any shipyard I've ever seen," a voice murmured.

"Then if we could get something to connect them with a member of personnel," said Stefan, "they could control their actions and force them to activate a self-destruct."

"Why in all the galaxy would a shipyard have a self-destruct capability?" Raynott asked.

Stefan was beginning to look flustered. Carina was sorely tempted to leave him to flounder in embarrassment in front of the Sherrerr officers, but she had an idea. If she and her family really could destroy the Dirksens' shipyard, it might work to their advantage.

"I think we could do it," she announced. "I'm not guaranteeing anything, but I think we could. If you give us a chance."

"Hmmm..." Tremoille looked suspicious. She clearly didn't trust Carina, and she was quite right. Carina wasn't remotely interested in helping the Sherrerrs, but she would do anything to free her mother and siblings from captivity.

"Tell us then," Tremoille said. "What would you do?"

"If you can get us in close enough, and if you do have the correct schematics, we could Cast Fire into their fuel stores."

Fifty-Four

After a long debate among the Sherrerr officers, they agreed that Carina and her family would be given the opportunity to try to destroy the Dirksen shipyard. They decided to commit their largest and most powerful ship, *Nightfall*, to the attack. Defended by most of the rest of the Sherrerrs' fleet, *Nightfall* would bring the mages within Casting distance of the shipyard. The flagship could sustain a lot of damage before she was put out of action.

The practical and strategic aspects of the attack were out of Carina's control. She would have to trust the Sherrerrs' military arm to do their job. Destroying the Dirksen shipyard with the Fire Cast was up to her and her family. That part worried her. She didn't know how effectively her mother had trained her siblings in their Casting, but she suspected it was not very well—deliberately so. In her mother's position, Carina would have taken every opportunity to downplay her abilities and limit those of her children. She doubted her sisters and brothers were at anywhere near the proficiency she needed them to be. Yet if they were to escape, their Casts had to be successful.

"I confess I'm surprised at your congeniality," Stefan remarked to her as the meeting broke up and his voice wouldn't be heard over the hubbub. They were getting up from their seats. "What's brought about your change of attitude?" He turned and fixed his gaze on her, as if he were trying to bore into her mind.

Carina shrugged. "It doesn't benefit us if the Sherrerrs lose. You would only make our lives harder, wouldn't you? I'm not so stupid as to refuse to do something that would help my family."

Stefan looked unconvinced, but he said, "I'm glad to hear you're coming to your senses at last. It's a shame your mother has never been so sensible. Her life could have been much more pleasant if only she had been equally compliant. I only hope your new approach is genuine. If it isn't, the punishment I will inflict on all of you will be swift and merciless. You're aware what I'm capable of. Do you understand me?"

"I understand. But I think you'll be surprised at what we can do when we really make an effort."

"I hope I will be." Stefan paused, his gaze searching her face. He stepped closer.

Carina fought the urge to push him away from her, violently.

"Perhaps I misjudged you," he said. "I'd thought you were going to be as difficult and uncooperative as your mother, and I would be forced to exert the same level of control as I had to with her. Not without enjoying a certain amount of pleasure, I have to confess. But if you're of a different mind, I see no reason why we couldn't work together to rise to a preeminent, if not primary, position within the clan. *Together.* You couldn't do it alone as that idiot Calvaley suggested, but if we joined forces we could be a formidable couple, you and I."

"You seem to be forgetting something," Carina said. "You're already married. To my mother."

"Yes, but not for much longer. Didn't she tell you?"

"Tell me what?" An icy steel vice fastened around Carina's heart. What did Stefan mean? He must have heard about her mother's illness, but she was going to get better. "I know she's sick but..."

"Yes, she's very ill. The stupid woman. What possessed her to stop taking her preventative, I'll never know. The doctor informed me it was too late for her to receive treatment. She only has a week or two left."

"What?" Carina's legs gave way. She collapsed into her seat.

"So she didn't tell you."

"She told me she was going to start treatment and she would be okay," Carina replied, shock entirely disarming her.

"No, that isn't the case." Stefan was looking down at her impassively. "I don't know why your mother would want to mislead you on something so important, yet she has. Odd. Anyway, after a respectable period of mourning, we will marry. Think on it, Carina. You could repeat your mother's unhappy experience or you could be more agreeable and enjoy your life. Though I would, of course, expect to father another brood on you. Our marriage will give our children legitimacy. Those mage powers are too useful to waste."

Stefan's words barely registered with Carina, disgusting though they were.

Why had her mother lied to her? Why had she given her false hope? She was adrift. She held her head as if it might halt the spinning of her mind. Her mother was going to die after all, and there was nothing she could do to prevent it.

"Stand," a voice said.

Carina looked up into the expressionless face of a guard. Stefan had gone. The briefing room was almost empty. Minutes must have passed without her noticing.

Numbly, she rose to her feet. She'd been assigned two guards to return her to her quarters. This time, both of them were male. As she glanced at the other guard, she froze. It was Bryce. His eyebrows flicked up as an almost-unnoticeable acknowledgment.

"Move," the other guard said, motioning her toward the door. When she reached it, he went in front of her as they walked down the corridor. Bryce was behind her. Carina glanced over her shoulder a few times as they went along, but she didn't dare risk speaking to him while the other guard could overhear.

They took her back to her family's living quarters. The place remained quiet and dark, her mother and siblings still sleeping. The two guards escorted her inside the door, then left.

Carina stood motionless in the entrance area, still reeling from the news that her mother was going to die. Moments later, the door opened again and Bryce slipped inside. He closed the door.

"I told the other guard I had a message I'd forgotten to give you," he said. "I can only stay a few seconds."

"What the hell are you even doing here?"

"I saw what happened at the departure area at the spaceport. No one did a thing as the Sherrerr guards dragged you away, and neither could I. Not then. But I found out where you'd been taken. When I heard it was the flagship, I joined up."

"Yes, but why? What about your parents? They must be waiting for you. You said you were going to run a branch of their business."

"Why? I'm here to rescue you of course."

"What?!"

"You rescued me from the Sherrerrs' mountain stronghold. Now it's my turn to help you out."

"I've never heard anything so ridiculous. How do you propose to do that? You're going to get yourself killed, and probably me too. Stay away, Bryce. I've got a handle on this."

"Hmmm, yeah, looks like it. Let me help you."

"No. Don't you see? I can't trust you. Mages can't afford to trust non-mages, or *this* is how they end up. I helped you because I felt sorry for you, but that's it. My connection to you is over. Please do me the courtesy of leaving me and my family alone. I have to do this by myself. It's the only way."

"You think I can't be trusted?" Bryce exclaimed, trying to keep his voice low. "Carina, everyone on the ship knows what's going on in your step family. You think I'm like Stefan Sherrerr and I'm going to rape and torture you to make you do what I want?"

"No, but..." Yes. That's exactly what she thought. It didn't matter how nice her friend was. Knowing her would turn him into her mother's husband one day. "The knowledge of what I can do would change you. You think it wouldn't, but it would. It's natural. That's why mages always have to live in secret and keep their powers hidden. You might not understand but that's the way it is."

For the first time since Carina had known him, anger flashed in Bryce's eyes. "You know what your problem is? You want to help others, but you won't let anyone help you. You've got so used to living in fear it's damaged your judgment of people. Not everyone is your enemy. We aren't all like Stefan Sherrerr."

"I'm sorry, Bryce. I can't take the risk of trusting anyone else. I have to do this myself."

"You think that's the answer? How has that worked out for you so far? How did it work out for your mother?"

At the mention of her mother, the memory of the recent news flashed into Carina's mind. Sobs welled up in her chest and her eyes filled with tears.

Bryce's expression softened. "I'm sorry," he said, mistaking the cause of her distress. "I have to go. But I'll be around. I'm here to help you, Carina. Don't forget that. I'm not out to hurt you."

He left. Carina sank to the floor, grief washing over her.

Fifty-Five

The Sherrerr flagship was a hive of activity as the crew prepared for the attack. After successfully invading Cestrarth, destroying the Dirksens' main shipyard would be a hammer blow that would resound across the entire galactic sector. The Sherrerrs' enemies would struggle long and hard to regain their military strength after such a defeat.

Carina was also busy preparing her brothers and sisters. She avoided her mother, which wasn't difficult as her illness confined the woman to her room. The morning following the briefing meeting on the Dirksens' shipyard attack, she had coldly told her mother she knew she had lied to her about her illness.

Her mother had touched her arm and gone to speak, but Carina had walked away. She couldn't bear to listen to the woman's explanation of her deceit. She didn't want to hear any more lies. Her feelings were beyond anger and hurt. As far as their relationship was concerned, she was in a place she didn't think she would ever be able to leave. Unable to understand why her mother would treat her so badly after their many years of separation, she tried to avoid even thinking about the subject. The tension in their relationship was intolerable and a distraction from her work.

When they made their escape, she would take her mother with them so that she could die in peace, free at last. She deserved that. But she wasn't the person Carina had imagined her to be, and she didn't think her mother had really loved her as much as she thought she did. The whole thing was so confusing and hurtful, she simply had no idea how to deal with it.

Since her mother had proven herself untrustworthy, Carina didn't tell her about the escape plan. Neither could she trust her siblings with the secret. Darius was too young and not in control of himself, and she didn't know Parthenia or the others well enough to feel confident confiding in them. As for Castiel and Nahla, she wasn't even sure they wanted to escape or whether she should bring them along. As Sherrerrs who weren't also mages, they would probably fare best if they remained with the family, providing they weren't suspected of conniving in the escape. Carina was particularly averse to bringing along Castiel, who gave off the same nasty vibe as his father.

The first Casting lesson was hard. Carina and the four children with mage abilities sat on the floor in a circle. Four guards had rifles constantly trained on them. The children were accustomed to the set up, but Carina was not. She wished that the effects of Casting were instantaneous. If that had been the case, she could have taken out the guards within seconds and maybe even taken control of the entire ship.

The first thing Carina discovered about her siblings' Casting ability was that she was correct in her guess that her mother had taught the children badly. Only Parthenia had any real proficiency in simple Casts like Transport, Locate, and Split, and Carina had a feeling that it was in spite of, not due to, her mother's teaching. When she realized the children had noticed her disappointment in their skills, she had them practice Enthralling each other, which lightened the mood.

As the lesson progressed, Castiel and Nahla stopped their playing and watched. Carina guessed that Castiel was probably bitter and jealous that most of his brothers and sisters had a very special ability, but she didn't know what to do to make him feel better. She couldn't confer mage powers upon him. You were either born with it or you weren't. Nahla sat with him, mimicking his sour looks.

Darius was joyful about being taught by her, though his age made him like a puppy, willing but excitable. Oriana and Ferne were steady and industrious. Parthenia had an almost pathological need to do things perfectly the first time.

Carina taught the children for two hours before stopping for the day. Casting, even small Casts, was mentally tiring. She felt she'd done as much as she could to sharpen her sisters' and brothers' skills, and she'd gotten to know them all a little better as mages. Parthenia's Casts were steady, exact, and reliable. Darius's Casts were the most powerful, but he was unpredictable. One moment he would Cast quickly and effectively, another moment he wouldn't be able to Cast at all. Oriana's and Ferne's Casts were weaker than the others' but they didn't display Darius's momentary lapses in ability.

At the end of the session, when the children left the circle and Carina began to tidy up, Darius crawled over on all fours. Carina sat down to speak to him, and he climbed into her lap and rested his head on her shoulder. "Why are you sad, Carina?"

"Am I sad? What makes you say that?"

"I can feel it."

Carina had been expecting her brother to say she had a sad face or something similar. It seemed a strange remark from the little boy, and one that reminded her of something Nai Nai had once told her. "You can?"

"I know how everyone is feeling."

Wow. "That must be uncomfortable for you sometimes."

His little brown-haired head nodded like the most ancient and wise sage. "It is."

Carina recalled her grandmother had told her about mages who felt others' emotions, but she couldn't remember exactly what the old woman had said.

"I'm sorry you're sad about things," Darius went on. "Mother is always sad too."

"I guess she must be. She's very sick."

"I know."

Did Darius know how close their mother was to death? Was it Carina's responsibility to tell him? She hugged the child. "I am sad, but having you around makes me feel better."

"I know that too," he said as he hugged her back.

———

The next day, Carina moved on to her siblings' preparation sessions. *Nightfall* was fast-burning her way to the Dirksens' shipyard. Other Sherrerr ships were also on their way there, ready to defend their flagship as she maneuvered the Sherrerrs' secret weapons close enough to Cast. Stefan had told Carina they would be within range to make the final approach within seventy-six hours.

Her plan on what exactly she would do after they'd accomplished their mission wasn't clear. She was hoping for a lapse in concentration from their guards in the excited aftermath of victory. They would have elixir on hand. All they would need was a few moments. She hoped she could cause enough disruption to get her mother and the children off the ship.

But first they had to destroy the shipyard.

"You can all Cast Fire, right?" Carina asked. When her brothers and sisters nodded, she said, "That's great." Fire was one of the first Casts she'd learned. All the essential survival Casts were taught first. She'd hoped her mother had stuck to that custom. "So if you can already Cast Fire, what we're going to concentrate on now is distance. What's the farthest you've ever Cast?"

"I've Cast from our estate to the capital on Ithiya," Parthenia replied. "Mother said it wasn't possible to Cast any farther than that."

Castiel was present again. He lay on his stomach, resting his head on his hands, watching with hooded eyes. Acutely conscious that he would probably report whatever she told them to his father, Carina to tried frame her words to avoid directly contradicting her mother. "Actually, I might be able to teach you to Cast even farther. What do you think about that?"

"That would be wonderful, Carina," Darius replied, his gaze adoring.

Parthenia and the other two nodded.

"Okay," said Carina. "We're going to start practicing Casting really far today. You know how to use coordinates, right? I arranged for small tanks of fuel to be sent to these locations." She showed them the figures on an interface. "In a few days, we'll be helping in the war against the Dirksens by Casting Fire into their fuel stores at their shipyard."

Ferne's eyes grew wide. "Whoa," he breathed.

"Yeah," Carina said. "Boom. My point is, the Dirksens' tanks are going to be a lot bigger than the canisters we have to practice on. They'll be easier to hit. Our challenge with the canisters is going to be hitting them at a distance. I don't expect you to succeed at first. I want you to know that because I don't want you to feel discouraged if you miss. What I'm asking you to do is hard, but we have plenty of time to practice, and on the day it should be easier."

"How do we know if we hit?" Oriana asked.

"The ship's scanners will pick up the explosion. The bridge will comm us."

"Bet I hit it first," Ferne said, his face alive with excitement.

"That would be cool, but this isn't a competition," said Carina.

Under the watchful gaze of their four guards, the children began to practice. The task wasn't easy even for her. She'd seldom had a reason to Cast at great distances. Without being able to see the effect of the Cast, the practice was either ineffective or highly dangerous.

She took a sip of elixir, closed her eyes, and made the Cast. Just as she was beginning to wonder if she was going to embarrass herself in front of her siblings, and be forced to inform Stefan that her plan wasn't going to work, she hit the fuel tank. She felt the Cast strike home, then a few seconds later the confirmation came through the ship's comm.

After an internal *Phew!*, Carina said to her sisters and brothers, "Now it's your turn. Who's first?"

Ferne's hand flew into the air.

FIFTY-SIX

Stefan had sent guards to bring Carina to him. She was disappointed to see that Bryce wasn't one of them. In spite of their argument the last time they'd met, his familiar face would have been a welcome sight. On top of all her other problems, Carina was feeling anxious. After two days of trying, she hadn't been able to teach any of the children how to Cast the distances required to blow up the Dirksen shipyard.

That had to be why Stefan wanted to speak to her. Castiel must have reported their lack of progress. She didn't particularly care about Stefan's anger—she'd agreed to help in the attack on the Dirksen shipyard for her own benefit, not his—but she hated the idea of being alone with him. She gave an involuntary shudder as she went along. He'd made his sexual intentions clear and she couldn't stomach the idea. Externally, the man wasn't unpleasant. Internally, he was barely human.

The guards took her into a small office. When neither of them left, Carina relaxed a little. She doubted he would want to try anything serious in front of two onlookers, even loyal Sherrerr guards. Her earlier attack must have made him frightened to be alone with her. *Good.*

Her mother's husband was sitting at a desk, looking unusually haggard. The strain of worrying about fulfilling his promise seemed to be getting to him. That was also good.

"Sit down," he said as she went in.

She sat opposite him and the guards took positions on each side of the doorway. Carina estimated she could get over the desk to Stefan before they had time to react. She might even be able to kill him before they killed her. She fought her desire to avenge her father's death and her mother's torture. It would be a pointless victory while her siblings remained held in captivity.

She gazed at the man levelly, waiting for him to speak.

"I hear you haven't been successful in teaching the children how to Cast at great distances."

"That isn't true."

"Really?"

"I haven't been successful *yet*."

"Don't play with me, Carina. You know how important it is that the children and yourself make the Cast successfully. Are you going to be able to do it or not?"

"Make the Cast or teach the children?"

"Both, you idiot!" Stefan half-rose to his feet and leaned over the desk, pressing his fists into the surface.

His inner self showed most strongly when he was angry, Carina noted. His face had contorted with such fury he looked like a demon. She looked up at him coolly. "I will make the Cast. As to my sisters and brothers, I think they can do it."

"*Thinking* isn't good enough. It's vital we blow all the fuel storage tanks at once. We'll only get one chance. There are hundreds of Dirksen ships there. If we only cripple the station, we'll have a cloud of bees on our tail."

"Wasps."

"What?"

"You mean wasps. Bees only sting once and die. What's really scary is wasps. They'll sting you over and over again. Or you could say hornets. They're twice the size and ten times as mean."

Stefan thumped the desk and yelled, "Stop trying to be clever. Do you think you can make a fool of me by failing to destroy the shipyard? Is that your plan?"

"There wouldn't be a lot of sense in that, would there? Like you said, we'll be in a much more dangerous position if we don't make the Cast."

"I'm warning you, Carina. If you have some trick you're planning to pull, I'll make you regret it for the rest of your long, agonizingly painful life."

"I'll bear it in mind." She regretted not including the murder of Stefan in her escape plan. Maybe she could make an adjustment.

He sat down. "Is there anything you need to assist you in teaching the children?"

Carina's eyebrows lifted at his uncharacteristically civil question. "Well it's hard to teach when you have a gun aimed at your head. If we could lose the threat of imminent death that might help."

"Out of the question. The guards stay."

"Why? What do you think we would do? Like you said, it's in our interests that we perform the Cast. And do you really think one woman and a bunch of kids could take over the entire Sherrerr flagship?"

Stefan's flinty expression broke into a sly smile. "Not as stupid as you like to make out, are you? Neither am I, sadly for you. I repeat, the guards stay. Anything else?"

"The crew has been good at placing fuel canisters at the right distance from the ship. I don't think there's much else I can ask from them."

"And you have plenty of elixir?"

"Yes. Where's it from? I thought I would have to ask one of the children to make it for the lessons."

"We have a plentiful supply aboard the ship. Your mother made it. And, no, I'm not going to tell you where it is."

"Then, no. I can't think of anything."

"You know you only have thirty-five hours before the attack?"

"I'm aware of that, yes."

"You need results, and soon. Or things won't turn out well, especially for you."

"Is that it?" Carina asked. He was right. She had little time left. Too little time to sit around while he threatened her.

"You can go."

She rose and went to the door. A guard opened it. Before she went out, however, she turned to Stefan. "Mother's sinking fast, you know. I don't think she has long now."

Stefan had already turned his attention to his interface screen. He didn't look up. He only flicked his hand at her, gesturing that she leave. The guards escorted her away.

It had been too much to expect the brute to give a second thought to the woman he had held captive and tortured for fifteen years. And it wasn't like her mother wanted to see him, but Carina couldn't help feel a deep despair over the situation. Her own feelings regarding Ma were too powerful to face right now, though she knew one day she wouldn't have a choice about it.

A line of troops were also in the corridor, heading toward them. Carina didn't take a lot of notice. It seemed like the corridor was always full of soldiers on their way to exercises. *Nightfall* was packed with them to defend it from boarders and to board enemy ships.

Then she thought she heard someone say her name. She looked up and caught a glimpse of a familiar face. The next moment, the person she'd seen was past her but looking back, smiling, as she turned to stare.

It was Mandeville. The next second, he faced front and the troops marched away.

The sight of her former fellow soldier momentarily lifted her mood. She wondered what he thought she was doing aboard the ship and being escorted by two guards. He hadn't seemed surprised to see her, as if he already knew she was being held captive. Did the Sherrerr' troops know about the mage powers of her family? Was it common knowledge? Or did only the officers know?

She realized that if the entire ship knew what they could do, they weren't only at risk from Stefan and the other high-ranking Sherrerrs—everyone else aboard might be interested in capturing them too.

FIFTY-SEVEN

The officers wanted a dummy run. They wanted a demonstration that Carina and her sisters and brothers really could do what she'd promised. It made sense. The mage strike was a prominent step in their battle plan. It was probably the most important step. They needed an assurance, if not a guarantee, that the plan stood a reasonable chance of success. Carina wasn't sure herself if they could do it.

A test site had been set up and drones sent out to record visuals of the result. The officers were back in the briefing room, and this time the children were here too. The room was filled with quiet conversations as everyone waited for the tanks to be maneuvered into position. Carina spotted Calvaley, sitting at the top of the ranked seats, speaking with Tremoille.

The children still hadn't succeeded in hitting the tanks with their Casts. Their problem was, the only feedback received during practice was a no-hit. All they knew was that the fuel tank they'd been aiming at hadn't exploded. They didn't know where their Cast had appeared, whether it had fallen short or gone too far or veered too far up, down, left, or right. So they didn't know what corrections they had to make. Essentially, the mage children were shooting blind.

Carina couldn't bother her mother about the problem. The poor woman was so ill she hardly seemed to notice anything anymore. Carina also couldn't tell Stefan about it even if she could bring herself to voluntarily speak to the snake. He would only become furious and suspect that her failure was deliberate. And apart from the guards, her mother and Stefan were the only people she saw.

She began to regret her argument with Bryce. He'd meant well, and he couldn't be expected to understand her position. Perhaps he'd even been correct when he'd said that not everyone would want to exploit her as soon as they found out about her abilities. Perhaps Nai Nai had been wrong after all and there were people she could trust with her secret. It wasn't like she had a whole lot of friends.

Calvaley stood and addressed the room. "The test tanks are in position. Private Lin, you may proceed."

"Do we have the coordinates?" she asked. A guard appeared, carrying an interface. He handed over the screen, which displayed six sets of figures.

"Six sites?" Carina exclaimed. "We can only make five Casts."

"No," Stefan said, "six. We received additional intel and we need you to do six. That shouldn't be too much of a problem, should it?"

The children looked at her nervously.

"There are only five of us, Stefan. Five mages, five Casts. What do you expect me to do?"

"I'm sure you can handle it," Stefan replied smugly. "I have complete faith in you."

She would have to Cast Fire twice, simultaneously, at two different locations. Did Stefan know that was possible? It would make her job even harder, but she could probably do it. She had to do it if she wanted the other steps of her plan to fall into place.

Turning from Stefan, Carina asked Calvaley, "Can I say something, sir?"

"Go ahead, but don't make a long introduction. We all have plenty else to do."

"I didn't want to give an introduction. I just wanted to say, these are very difficult conditions for my brothers and sisters. Being observed like this puts them under a lot of pressure, and that makes it hard for them to Cast."

"We're at war," Stefan retorted. "What kind of conditions would you like? A tea party? A soiree?"

His response drew some muted giggles from the audience.

"They're children," Carina said. "*Your* children, and they're attempting something that's extremely hard for them."

"They're mages, and they're here to do a job."

"Stop it," Calvaley interrupted. "Get started, Lin. Your words have been noted."

Carina took a breath and turned to her sisters and brothers, who were seated on the floor in a square, facing each other. A jug of elixir and five beakers sat at their center. She showed them the interface and assigned a different set of coordinates to each child.

"There's no need to hurry," she told them. "It doesn't matter whether we hit them all at once. We only need to try to hit them, okay?"

"Carina," Oriana said quietly, "I don't think I can do it."

Oriana knew she was the weakest at Casting of all of them. Her ordinary Casts were often feeble, let alone the difficult Cast she was now required to do.

"Just try your best," Carina said. If Stefan hadn't suddenly sprung a sixth site on her, she could have tried to cover for one of the children's failures with a second Cast of her own. But now there was no chance of that.

The starscape view out the window turned black, and a holo of the test site appeared. It was a merged image, showing the six barrel-shaped fuel tanks in close proximity, though in reality they were kilometers apart.

"Which one's mine?" Darius asked.

"It doesn't matter," Carina replied. "Don't worry about it. Only concentrate on the coordinates." At six years old, Darius was in danger of becoming confused and Casting at the visual, not the tank itself. The Fire he Cast would quickly go out as there was nothing but the air in the room to sustain it. It would be an interesting display for the onlookers but a failure nonetheless.

The audience were shifting in their seats and murmuring as they grew impatient.

"Are you ready?" Carina asked the children.

They nodded with an attitude that showed they weren't feeling remotely ready.

"Okay. Let's do it." She poured each child a measure of elixir and handed out the beakers. Then she poured some of the mixture for herself. "Remember, shut out everything. It's you, the character, and the destination. That's all there is."

After waiting for the children to drink their elixir and shut their eyes, she downed her own, the bitterness of the liquid barely registering in her worry about what might happen if the children failed the test.

Would the Sherrerrs abandon the plan of using them as weapons in the attack on the shipyard? Would they call off the entire attack? She thought that was unlikely. Destroying the Dirksens' main starship manufacturing yard was essential to crushing their strength. But if the Sherrerrs were unsuccessful, she and the others were at risk of capture or death. And she needed the vast debris field the explosions would create. If they weren't allowed or able to blow the shipyard to smithereens, she had no plan B.

Silence had fallen as the spectators waited and watched for the mages' Casts to take effect. Carina closed her eyes. She could provide them with somewhat of a spectacle at least. Maybe that would be enough.

She sank down into the darkness of her mind. The sounds of breathing, shuffling feet, and shifting bodies disappeared. The red tint behind her eyelids retreated to blackness. She was alone in the dark. The first stroke cut across her inner vision, silver-light and glimmering. The second followed, sweeping down from the first. A third appeared to one side, short and tapering. Its mate appeared on the opposite side. The character was complete. *Fire.*

Now came the difficult part. She had to Cast Split into Fire, severing the character longitudinally, creating a perfect mirror. This took great concentration. Dimly, she became aware of a trickle of sweat running down the side of her face. She forced her mind back to the character, Fire. A touch of mental effort, and it slid into two images.

It was time to Cast the characters to their destinations. The fuel tanks were large. She didn't have to hit the exact coordinates. Pinpoint accuracy wasn't the problem, it was the distance involved. She gathered up all of her mental and emotional strength into one powerful bundle, and flung the Casts far from her, out into space, across the distance to the fuel tanks.

She opened her eyes and held her breath. The tanks hung above her, spinning lazily under residual momentum. Her sisters' and brothers' eyes remained closed, their faces strained with concentration.

A tank exploded, quickly followed by another. The silent spectacle filled the room with dazzling light. After the flash had departed, however, four tanks remained untouched. The audience watched them. Carina watched them too. Might Parthenia manage it finally, in her slow, steady style? Or might Darius hit lucky with an unpredictable burst of mage power?

No. There was no change in the tanks. Carina might have drunk more elixir and destroyed them herself, but what she was doing would have been obvious. The officers wanted to know that all the children could perform the Cast. In the heat of the battle, they might not have time for her to destroy the tanks one by one.

Oriana opened her eyes and looked up at the holo. "I'm sorry," she said. "I missed."

"I missed too," said Darius, also opening his eyes. Parthenia was shaking her head. Ferne looked glum.

"Idiots," Stefan hissed. "Carina, can't you teach them any better than this?"

"Be quiet, Stefan," said Calvaley. "That was you who destroyed the two tanks, Lin?"

"Yes, sir."

"Then it seems to me that we should only rely on you in the upcoming attack. We can leave out your brothers and sisters, for now anyway."

"No," said Carina. If she was the only one to take part in the battle, the chances were she would be separated from her family. It was vital they were all together when the shipyard blew. "I mean, no *sir*. I think they can do it. I really do. I just need to give them some more practice. If I might say so, it's the pressure of all these people watching that's the problem. Casting is much easier in private. If we were alone, I'm sure they could be successful. We can blow that place to pieces if you give us the chance."

Tremoille spoke in Calvaley's ear. He listened, nodded to her, then said, "You've got your chance, Carina. We've seen what you can do. Anything else your brothers or sisters can manage will be a bonus. We'll arrange a private room when the time comes."

"And guards," Stefan said. "The children must be watched at all times."

"Yes, of course," Calvaley replied. "Guards will be assigned."

Fifty-Eight

Faye heard the soft snick of her bedroom door opening. Beyond her closed eyelids, her room brightened. She opened her eyes. Light from the living area was spilling through the open doorway, silhouetting Carina in its frame.

"Come in," said Faye, pulling herself painfully to a sitting position. "I wasn't asleep. Just resting."

Carina stepped inside and closed the door. Faye activated the light, telling it to dim to fifty percent when the brightness hurt her eyes. Carina came over to the bed and perched on its edge, not meeting her gaze.

Faye drank in the sight her daughter. Though they looked alike, she could also see Kris's face in Carina's. The fact that a part of him lived on gave her some small comfort.

Without speaking, Carina took her hand. She looked both sad and angry. It wasn't hard to guess why. She knew she'd betrayed her daughter's trust when she'd lied to her about the state of her health. She'd only wanted more time to try to find the right words and the right moment, but neither had come until it was too late. It was only that she'd been unable to bear the thought of telling her daughter that, fifteen years after abandoning her, she was about to abandon her again, and it was her own fault.

"Carina," Faye said gently, "I'm—"

"Sorry," Carina interrupted. "I know." She sighed. "Ma, I need your help. I need to teach the children to Cast at a great distance. They can't seem to do it, no matter how much I try to teach them or how often they practice. They just can't hit what they're aiming at."

"I'm not surprised. I didn't teach them well. I wanted to limit Stefan's exploitation of them as much as I could."

"I get that. But now I really need them to do it. Can you help? Nai Nai taught me what she could until she died, but after that I was on my own. Everything I learned from then on was guesswork."

"There is a way," Faye said, "but why is it so important that they do this task you've for set them? You know the more they demonstrate what they can do, the more Stefan and the rest of the Sherrerrs will ask of them. Aren't their lives going to be miserable enough as it is?"

"No," Carina replied. "Not if I can help it. I have a plan, Ma. We can all escape. I only need them to do this thing, and it should give us our opening."

"Oh, Carina," Faye said. "I used to make a plan every week. I used to dream of the time when I would finally manage to escape. But look what happened. Here I am and here are your sisters and brothers. And whenever Stefan caught me, his punishment was severe. Do you want to go through that? What if he decides to punish the children too, in your place? Could you bear it? What about Parthenia? You know he has his eye on her?"

"I've noticed," said Carina. "His perversions are disgusting."

"Like everything else about him. I admire your fighting spirit. I wish with all my heart you and the children could escape the dreadful monster, but it isn't possible. I realize that now."

"It *is* possible. You're ill and tired and Stefan has broken you. You've given up. But it is possible for us to escape. And, Ma, if you come with us, we might reach a planet in time to save you. You might still respond to treatment."

Carina's expression belied the hope in her words. Faye saw the reflection of her own death in her daughter's eyes, and she accepted it. But maybe there was one last gift she could give her. Maybe she could summon a vestige of hope that there could be a different life for her children than the one she'd been forced to lead.

"I don't think that's likely," Faye said. "When I go to sleep I don't even know if I'll wake up again. But you know, Carina, I don't mind. Stefan pushed me so far, I don't think I can ever find my way back. And who knows? Perhaps I'll see your father again."

Carina's hand gripped hers and her eyes shone.

"I'm sorry," Faye said. "I don't want to make you unhappy. You said you don't know how to teach the children to Cast at a great distance? That isn't so hard to answer. If you can do it, then Nai Nai must have taught you. Don't you remember how?"

Understanding dawned in Carina's eyes. "Of course! It's so simple. How could I have forgotten?"

Faye smiled. "The children will pick it up quickly enough, I'm sure. Especially Darius. His ability is very strong when he puts his mind to it."

"Yes. Ma, is there something different about him? He says he can feel others' feelings."

"I think he's a spirit mage. Your Nai Nai would have been able to explain it better, but as I understand it, he draws his power from other people. It doesn't come from the stars like yours and mine. And as he draws in others' energy, he also draws in their emotions. He doesn't know what he is yet, but one day you can tell him."

"I will. I wish I could tell him more, but I know so little. Nai Nai tried to help me memorize information about mages, but I was so young when she died. I think I forgot most of it."

"The prohibition on recording anything to do with mages makes it hard to retain information. Perhaps I should try to tell you everything I know, while we still have time."

"I'd like that," Carina said. "Then I can pass it on to my sisters and brothers as they grow up."

"Okay," said Faye, "make yourself comfortable."

Carina moved over so she was sitting fully on the bed. She crossed her legs.

Faye began with the Elements, the Seasons, and the Map, but Carina already knew these. Nai Nai had taught her well. She also told her all the Casts she knew. There were a few Carina had never heard of—difficult Casts that Nai Nai might have been waiting to teach her when she grew older.

She also told Carina her understanding of the history of mages. She said that when she was young, her mother had explained that mages had first appeared thousands of years ago in a country on a planet called Earth. The first mage was a scientist. How she stumbled upon the correct ingredients in the correct proportions to make elixir, and performed the first Cast, no one knew. However, it was generally accepted that not long after, the first mage told her secret to friends, but when they tried to do the same thing they failed. The first mage wasn't believed until she performed a Cast to prove what she could do.

The word of her ability spread. Many attempted to repeat her performance. Most could not, but a very few could. Scientists speculated the ability was due to a random mutation in the first mage's genetic code, though at the time they couldn't discover what it was. They said the mutation might have appeared at intervals throughout human evolutionary history, but it was only the first mage finding the key to unlocking the skill that had brought it to light.

The self-discovered true mages banded together to share their experiences and knowledge, and to hone their craft. They retreated to a remote mountaintop where they would not be disturbed or scrutinized. Others who identified they were mages sought out the isolated place and were welcomed. The curious and avaricious, who nursed ambitions of profiting from the mages' ability also sought them out but, after their long, hard journeys, they were turned back.

"My mother told me the mages gave a test at the door to the compound," Faye said. "Any visitor would be offered elixir and an object they had to move from one side of the entranceway to the other. If the visitors couldn't perform the Cast, they would be refused entry. It didn't matter how low on supplies they were, or how cold and desperate, only mages were allowed inside."

"I bet that didn't make them many friends," Carina said.

"It didn't, but what choice did they have? If they didn't have that policy, they would be forced to house and feed every wanderer who appeared at their door. They only wanted to be left alone to work on their abilities. But their rule was their downfall. A few of the people they rejected died or were never found again. The public, who already feared them, grew to hate them, calling them murderers. General opinion also said they should be using their powers to cure everything that was wrong with the world, not hiding themselves away and selfishly hoarding the profits of their ability."

Faye told Carina how humankind had invented deep space travel at around the same time, allowing journeys far beyond the narrow confines of one planetary system. Realizing that if they didn't escape soon, they would be forced to do the bidding of governments or powerful corporations, the mages gathered all their folk together, stole one of the new starships, and traveled as far from Earth as they could.

In time, however, the rest of humanity caught up with them. As the memory of what had happened to them on Earth was still fresh in the mages' minds, they decided to hide their ability and remain anonymous but secure within the societies that were springing up all around.

Faye paused. As she'd been speaking, her little remaining strength had drained from her, and her voice had grown quieter and quieter.

Carina reached over and touched her mother's knee under the coverlet. "That's enough for now, Ma. You can tell me the rest another time."

Faye smiled, the effort hurting her face. "That's about as much as I know anyway. But I have another story I need to tell you, and soon." It was the most important story of her life, and she'd never told it to anyone. It would give her peace to tell it, and Carina needed to know.

"I'll hear it later," said Carina. "You should sleep now."

Faye's eyelids were already closing.

FIFTY-NINE

The two guards who had appeared to escort Carina once more to Stefan's office were grinning. She stood in the entrance to the living quarters and stared. It was Bryce and Mandeville. How in hell they had *both* finagled their way into pulling guard duty for her?

She had just left her mother asleep, or more likely passed out, after listening to her story of the history of mages. The woman's skin was so thin and pale her veins showed through, and each breath she took seemed an effort. Carina didn't know how anyone could look as she did and still be alive. It was like she was clinging on for a reason. Carina had hoped the reason was because she wanted to escape with them, but though it hurt her deeply to admit it, she was sure that wasn't the case.

Her mother was going to die and she wasn't sad about it. Maybe she was only hoping to see her children free at last before she went.

The corridors were busy. Carina, Bryce, and Mandeville couldn't risk speaking openly or delaying the journey to Stefan. The man was like a bird of prey in his exact, watchful habits. He would notice if they were late and would want to know why. But they could talk quietly as they went along.

"What's going on?" Carina murmured. "How did you manage this?"

"You've got more friends than you think," said Mandeville. "Not everyone aboard ship thinks what the Sherrerrs are doing is right. Not even all the officers. When I found out your family were being held captive, I couldn't believe it. Certainly changed my opinion of them."

"You mean you had a good opinion before?" Bryce asked.

"Kinda neutral."

"Mandeville here told me what you did on Banner's Moon, Carina," Bryce said. "What did you think you were doing, helping the Sherrerrs?"

"I was trying to help you, you idiot," Carina replied defensively. "How do you think I got permission to visit the men's quarters? Besides, that was before I knew they were holding my mother and half-sisters and brothers hostage."

"I guess that put a different spin on things," Mandeville remarked.

"Just a bit."

"So, Carina," Bryce said, "we don't have a lot of time. I wanted to tell you we're gonna help you escape."

"Really? How?" Though she appreciated the sentiment, Carina was skeptical.

"You need to drink that stuff to do what you do, right?" Bryce asked.

"Er, yeah."

"Mandeville found out where it's stored. They keep a pretty tight watch over it, but I think I can sneak some out for you."

"You can?" Her own supply of elixir could make a huge difference to her chances of success, but then she realized the implications. "Wait. I don't know if that's such a good idea." If Bryce was caught trying to steal elixir, it could throw all her plans into disarray. The Sherrerrs would conclude she had something to do with the attempt and they would cancel all plans to use her and the children. They wouldn't take a risk of things going wrong at such an important moment in the battle. It would be safer to keep them all confined until it was all over.

"What are you talking about?" Bryce asked. "Don't you want to get out? If I get you that stuff, you can just move yourself out of here like you did at the Sherrerr stronghold."

"There's a limit to how far I can Transport. I can't just fly across the galaxy, especially not with all my siblings in tow. If I tried that out here in deep space, I'd be moving us all to a freezing, airless vacuum."

"All right," Bryce said. "But you could use the stuff for something else."

She *could* use it. If she had free access to elixir, there were all kinds of things she could do to smooth the path of their escape. Only she still wasn't sure if she wanted Bryce's or Mandeville's involvement. It would complicate things.

When she didn't answer, Mandeville seemed to guess what was on her mind. "You're wondering if involving us is going to make things harder for you, right? I can see why you might think that, but you're wrong. Remember when we were on Banner's Moon? Would you have gotten that weapon out without the help of me and the others?"

She did remember. She recalled how she nearly got left behind, and it was only because Mandeville hauled her aboard the ramp of the departing shuttle that she got away before the moon was destroyed. Besides, was she in a position to turn down any offer of help? Though she'd tried to pretend to herself that she really could pull off the escape, deep down, she had her doubts.

"Okay," she relented, "I accept your offer."

They had arrived at Stefan's office. Before Bryce pressed the comm button, he gave her a wink. "Glad to hear it. It's about time you understood who your friends are. You won't regret it."

They went in. It was the same format as previously. Carina sat opposite Stefan and her guards stood on each side of the door. She felt a little better about spending time in Stefan's company knowing that Bryce and Mandeville were here, watching everything that went on. She hadn't forgotten Stefan's various threats, including the one he'd made that he would demonstrate to her he was a man. Knowing that neither Bryce nor Mandeville would stop her, the urge to put a final end to her mother's tormentor was strong. She gripped the chair's arms.

"That performance you put on at the test session was pathetic," Stefan said. "You embarrassed me, and I won't forget it."

"I told you the children weren't ready. What did you expect would happen? If you want to avoid embarrassment, pay attention to what I tell you."

Stefan glowered. "How are the children coming along with their practice? Will they be ready in time?"

"Yes, I think so. They don't have any problems with Casting Fire, only with hitting the target. I was reminded of something I'd forgotten. I think I can teach the children how to aim better now. When that obstacle's out of the way, I don't see any reason they shouldn't succeed."

"Good. I wanted to talk to you about something else."

She sat back and raised her eyebrows, wondering what Stefan's latest depravity could be.

"I don't want you getting any ideas about trying to escape during the battle," Stefan said. "If you're anything like your mother, you'll try to take advantage of the distraction. I'm not stupid, Carina. You haven't deceived me in the way I've noticed you deceiving Calvaley and the others. I know exactly what you want and what you can do, and I'll make sure you're watched like a hawk every moment during and after the battle. Any attempt to get away will be met with a severe response. Do you understand me?"

"I understand." Her hopes about the success of her scheme wavered. Stefan, as always, presented the largest barrier. But she wouldn't let his threat stop her from trying. Whatever punishment he had planned, she had to try. She couldn't live the life her mother had lived, and she couldn't allow her brothers and sisters to spend their lives in captivity, work animals to fulfill their father's desires.

"I'm not sure that you do," said Stefan. "You remember what I did to you when you were first captured, to force your mother to admit you were her child? That's nothing compared to what I'll do to you if you attempt to escape and take my children from me. But it isn't only you who'll suffer. You realize that?"

"I do, but—"

"Don't insult me with your assurances, Carina. I see through you. I read your mind as clearly as if I too had mage powers. I haven't brought you here to listen to your lies. I've brought you here to let you in on a secret that only I and your mother know, except she's managed to blank the fact from her memory. I'm telling you now so you understand what I do to the people who defy me.

"When I held your mother and father in captivity, it was the first time I had ever encountered mages. I suspected they existed, of course. Everyone knows the old tales. But I was the only person smart enough to set a trap to catch them. I played upon their compassion, and created a situation where only someone with supernatural powers could help. That was how I caught them.

"But when it came to forcing them to use their powers for my benefit, I was a novice. They refused. They denied their abilities, in spite of the evidence I had of what they had done. I had to think of a way of bending them to my will. Something that would be effective and leave a lasting impression. They were impervious to torture. It was then I hit upon the idea of using their love for each other against them. I threatened to kill one if the other refused to do my bidding.

"I threatened to kill the male—your father, because the female was more useful to me. Even as early as then I had conceived the idea, if you'll excuse the pun, of breeding a brood of mages all of my own. Parthenia had already rounded out your mother's body. To cut a long story short—and believe me, it's a very long story full of weeping and pleading and bargaining—your mother did not do as I asked, and so I killed her husband in front of her. It was a large sacrifice. I had only one mage instead of two, but I think it was worth it." Stefan paused, his eyes twinkling, as he watched the effect of his story.

She was struggling to breathe. Her mother had told her something entirely different. She'd said that Stefan had killed her father after she'd given away their mage secrets. She'd said Stefan had promised to set her father free in return, and he'd broken that promise. Who was telling the truth? Was it possible her mother's tortured mind had invented another story?

"So you see what I am capable of," Stefan said, a smile playing about his lips. "When the time comes to perform your task and destroy the Dirksens' shipyard, I want you to bear my tale in mind. You may go."

Numbly, she stood. Bryce opened the door and she went out. Mandeville followed. In silence, the three returned to her living quarters. Just before they reached the sentry guards, Bryce whispered, "Carina, don't worry. If you don't manage to take that fucker out, I will."

SIXTY

At the beginning of the next teaching session, and the penultimate one they would have time for before the flagship arrived and the battle began, Darius ran up to Carina and flung his arms around her neck.

"I'm sorry you feel so bad," he said. "Why do you feel so bad?" His big brown eyes stared into hers, their noses nearly touching.

Where to start? Carina wasn't sure if her mother would last out the remaining time before their escape attempt. The threat of Stefan's appalling retribution hung over her. Would he murder one of her siblings to punish her? She'd unfortunately clearly demonstrated to him that she had the strongest, most reliable mage powers of them all. Would Bryce or Mandeville get themselves killed trying to help her? And if she succeeded and did manage to get them all to a shuttle, could they escape the ship and get to a habitable planet without being recaptured?

Her resolve was wavering. She knew she would rather die than live the life her mother had, but the alternative put many more people than herself at risk. She hadn't asked her sisters or brothers if they wanted to be rescued—she still hadn't decided whether she should take Castiel and Nahla with her—and she didn't dare mention her plans to them in case word got back to Stefan. Was it really fair to take them out of the situation, considering all the dangers involved?

"Are we going to start?" Parthenia asked impatiently.

Carina jolted out of her ruminations. "Yes. I thought of a way to teach you to aim better. That's what we're going to practice today."

"What's that?" Oriana asked. "My aim is terrible."

"Well today it's going to get a lot better," Carina replied. "Trust me. When I was a little girl, my Nai Nai—"

"What's a Nai Nai?" Ferne asked. "Was it your pet?"

Carina laughed. It was the first laugh she'd had for a long time. "No, Nai Nai means your father's mother."

"Oh," Darius said. "Is she nice? I never met my father's mother."

"She was very nice," Carina replied, "but she died. My Nai Nai taught me to Cast long distances by using Transport and Locate. You take something and Transport it—"

"I get it," Parthenia exclaimed. "Then you Locate it, and see if it went where you sent it."

"Exactly," said Carina. "You can find out how far off target you are and adjust your aim accordingly the next time."

Ferne said, "Yes! I want to practice. I know I can do it now."

Carina had brought along some squares of cloth. The children would only have to hold them a moment to make the necessary connection, then Transport them to a set of coordinates. After the piece of cloth arrived, they would then be able to seek it out using Locate and match the coordinates with its actual position.

The session was informative. They discovered that Darius was Casting roughly twice as far as he should have been, and that Parthenia had only been missing the coordinates by a short distance. If the tanks had been as big as the ones they would be aiming for at the Dirksen shipyard, she would have hit them without any problems. Oriana and Ferne were erratic in the distance and direction by which their Casts missed, but by the end of the session their accuracy had improved enormously.

Throughout the two hours she taught her sisters and brothers, Carina felt herself growing closer to them. She'd begun to acquire the same ability to forget about the guards aiming rifles at them while they practiced as her siblings had. In turn, the girls and boys seemed to feel a closer bond to her as their Casting ability improved and the mood of the session lifted. There was a sense of shared achievement. It made Carina reflect on what her life might have been like if Stefan hadn't taken her mother and father from her. It would have been fun to be a big sister to the children who came after her.

There was still a chance she could have that, she reminded herself. She could put right the wrong Stefan had committed, and give the girls and boys the life they should have had, free of coercion and the constant threat of violence.

By the time Carina ended the session, Castiel had finally stumped off to another room, Nahla trotting in his wake, and slammed the door, probably sick of the constant attention on the other children. She was satisfied that the mage children would be able to send Fire accurately at the final practice before they arrived at the shipyard and the battle started.

The guards collected the unused elixir and beakers and left. For the first time, Carina was alone with her mage siblings without Castiel to spy on them. Dared she mention something of her plans? If they knew what was happening, it could make things a lot easier.

"You all did really well today," she said. "You worked hard and you never gave up. I'm proud of all of you."

"Thanks, Carina," Darius exclaimed, his eyes shining.

"Thanks," said Ferne. "You taught us well too. It's easy to understand when you teach us."

Carina guessed his subtext: better than when Mother taught us. But of course the boy had little idea of the reason behind the difference. "When we reach the target, I'm sure you'll be able to blow it up."

"I hope so," Parthenia said.

Carina checked the door to the room where Castiel and Nahla had gone was completely closed. She leaned closer to the circle of children. "What do you think will happen after the battle?"

"The Sherrerrs will win the war and then we'll control the whole galaxy," Darius said, and threw his arms in the air.

"Maybe not the *whole* galaxy," Carina said. "What I mean is, what do you think will happen to us?"

"I thought we would go back to our estate," said Parthenia. "Aren't we going home after this?" She looked confused and troubled.

"Yes," said Oriana. "Aren't we going home?"

"Is that where you want to go?" Carina asked.

Parthenia replied, "I do. I miss my tarsul. I don't think the servants are looking after him very well."

"How about if you went someplace else?" Carina asked. "How would you feel about that?" It was as much as she dared to say. If word of the conversation got back to Stefan, it could easily be passed off as idle speculation and not introducing the children to the idea of escape to a new life.

"I'd love to go somewhere else," Ferne said. "It's so boring living on the estate. We hardly ever go anywhere or do anything. I want to live in a city and do exciting things. I want to have my own friends and not have to play with my brothers and sisters all the time."

"Hey!" Oriana objected.

"I love you, sis," said Ferne, "but I'm tired of playing girls' games. I want to play with boys my own age, like I see other kids do in the vids. I want to go to school."

"I don't think Father would like to hear you say that," Parthenia said gravely.

Not for the first time, Carina had a weird sense about the girl. She didn't know how to take her. She seemed to always hide her true opinions.

Then again, Carina thought wryly to herself, *so do I.*

"You are coming back home with us, aren't you?" Darius asked. "Then when Mother gets better, you can sit with her and watch us play in the garden."

A shadow fell across Carina's heart, and the other children also looked sad and downcast. The little boy didn't know their mother was barely clinging to life. For the second time, Carina wondered if it was her responsibility to tell him. If she didn't, who would? To Stefan, Darius was only an instrument.

Parthenia was watching her. Then she turned to her brother and said, "Mother is very sick. She might not get better."

"Don't be silly," said Darius. "Of course she'd going to get better. That's right, isn't it Carina?"

She couldn't answer him.

Sixty-One

The doctor bent down and pressed a cold metal pressure syringe to Faye's neck. A brief sensation of uncomfortable tightness was replaced by a pleasant numbing sensation as her blood carried the medication around her body, alleviating its aches and pains. Her breathing grew easier and her head began to clear. Her vision also sharpened, bringing the doctor's concerned expression into focus.

Faye wet her dry lips with her tongue. "How long?" Her low, cracked, whispery voice sounded unfamiliar to her ears.

"I think another twelve to twenty-four hours. Your organs have begun to shut down, which is what's causing your discomfort. I'm giving you as much pain relief as I can without knocking you out, as you said you didn't want that. What's your pain level like? If you've changed your mind, I can ease the path for you, reduce the wait if you see what I mean."

"No," Faye replied. "I want to hang on as long as I can."

"Then the treatment I'm giving you will help. I'm sorry there's nothing else I can do to prolong the time you have left. If we'd been able to get you to a medical facility, it might have been a different story. But at times of war such things aren't always possible, even with the best intentions."

Faye could almost hear Stefan's voice as the doctor parroted his words. Explaining, justifying, and rationalizing his abhorrent, disgusting behavior. What tales was her husband spinning to the officers and members of the Sherrerr clan aboard the ship? Yet despite his facade, she was sure they all knew what he was like. They knew what he'd done to her and was doing to his own offspring, yet they chose to do nothing. As long as it didn't affect them and they profited from his actions, they would let him do whatever he wanted. She wondered who was worse—psychopathic Stefan or the people around him who winked at what he did.

"Is there anything else I can do for you?" the doctor asked. "For instance, would you like me to explain to your children what's happening? I don't relish the task, but I believe that sometimes it helps to hear the news from someone outside the family. And it is a large burden to place on, say, Carina's shoulders."

"I think most of them already understand, except maybe Darius. I'll tell him myself. I'd prefer it that way I think."

"Whatever you say." The doctor paused. "I'm sorry, but I have to ask you this. What would you like to happen after?"

It took Faye a moment to understand the doctor's subtle meaning. "After I die? I haven't thought about it, oddly enough. I'll let you know."

"The usual thing when someone dies aboard a starship is to hold the funeral ceremony and then eject the body into space. But I'm sure, given your standing as Stefan's wife, that the ship's company would make every effort to fulfill your wishes, whatever they may be."

Faye was sure the Sherrerrs would happily shower with every pomp and ceremony the woman they'd refused to help while she was alive. "I'll give it some thought."

"Right. Well, if you're feeling more comfortable now, I'd better go. I have lots to do. I have to prepare the sick bay for the upcoming battle."

"Are you anticipating lots of casualties?"

"On a ship this size, no. We're all pretty well protected behind the shielding. If the Dirksens manage to penetrate that, a few casualties will be the last of our problems. I doubt they'll show any mercy after what happened on Cestrarth. They'll probably do their best to destroy the ship." She smiled sadly. "You never know, you may even outlive me."

"You seem very calm about the idea of your life being in danger."

The doctor shrugged. "Life is strange. On the one hand, it seems so vital and indestructible. On the other, it can be snuffed out by the simplest thing. An awkward fall, a weak artery suddenly bursting, an overindulgence in the drug of one's choice." She snapped her fingers. "Gone. And there's nothing I can do about it. Seeing such things happen time and time again has given me a fatalistic outlook, perhaps. Everyone dies in the end. Perhaps it's insensitive of me to say so, but you have been given time to make your peace and say goodbye. Not everyone gets that."

"It isn't insensitive. I appreciate what you've done for me." Though the doctor was loyal to the Sherrerrs, Faye had found her compassionate and diligent.

"I wish I could have done more, but it wasn't to be." The doctor stood up. "If you need any additional medication, just let me know. At this stage, there's no point in worrying about long term effects."

After the doctor left, Faye thought over her words. She'd long accepted that her life was coming to a end, but she'd only thought about what to do with the time she had left. She hadn't considered what should happen to her body afterward.

Mages had certain funeral rites. The details were hazy, but she could remember the central idea. The five Elements were supposed to be used to send off the body. It was believed then that the mage's soul would immediately join the universe and blend with the souls of all the other mages who had ever lived. Ejecting her body into space wouldn't fulfill the requirements. She needed wood, metal, water, earth, and fire to ensure her spirit would find Kris's out in the deepness of space. She had had to beg Stefan to allow her to perform the necessary rites for her dead husband. If the Sherrerrs ejected her from the ship, her body would float frozen among the stars forever, never degrading. Her spirit would never escape and she would never see Kris again. She couldn't bear the thought.

Yet how could she arrange the correct funeral? Asking Stefan would be pointless. He had already almost forgotten she ever existed. The only person she could ask was Carina, but her daughter had enough on her plate.

The minute Faye thought of Carina, the door opened a crack and her daughter peeked in. "The doctor said it would be okay to come and sit with you for a while."

"Yes. It's fine. Come in. She's given me something potent and I'm feeling much better."

Carina stepped into the room, closing the door behind her. She sat at the end of the bed. "Ma, I wanted to tell you something. I know you don't have long, and I wanted to let you know what's going to happen. I hope it will make you feel happier."

"I'm listening."

"I wanted to tell you my escape plan."

Her daughter went on to explain how she planned to take advantage of the turmoil after the upcoming battle to steal a shuttle and get away.

When she'd finished, Faye said, "Oh, Carina."

"What's wrong?"

"I'm just so worried about you all. I don't have long left. It would be wonderful to see you all free, but I find it hard to believe it could ever happen. What will Stefan do if you fail?"

"What could be worse than living like this?"

At Carina's words, Faye saw herself through her daughter's eyes. She'd gotten used to seeing herself, empty of everything except despair, but to her daughter she must look shocking. She realized that when Carina saw her, she was seeing herself after a similar period of time with Stefan, and that she would rather die than turn into the shadow of a person her mother had become.

"But the children," Faye protested. "Little Darius…"

"Ma, I understand it'll be dangerous, but I'm doing my best to protect them. Can't you see that?"

"I don't know, Carina. I don't know." They seemed to be steering toward another falling out. She didn't want to start an argument, especially not now she had so little time left. Was this how it would have been if she and Kris hadn't fallen into Stefan's trap? If they'd remained a family, and Carina had grown up with them would the two of them have been at loggerheads? In the years she'd so deeply missed her first-born, she'd imagined an entirely different scenario. A too-sentimental one, perhaps.

"Why are you smiling?" Carina asked. "You don't think this is funny, do you? Are you feeling okay?"

"Don't worry. I'm not suffering the effects of my medication. I was only thinking that life rarely turns out as you expect it. If that's what you want to do, that's what you must do. I understand. It's just that the thought of my children being hurt is unbearable to me."

"There's more than one way of hurting people," Carina said, "and your husband knows it only too well. Maybe I can do it—I mean, maybe I can take the risk—because they aren't my children. I didn't give birth to them. Maybe it's easier for me. But I have a question. What about Castiel and Nahla? Should I take them too? Do you think they'll want to come?"

"Nahla will want to go wherever Castiel goes. As for him, I don't know. Maybe you should ask him when the time comes."

"I don't know that I'll be able to. I might not have time, or…"

"Or?"

"Ma, I'm worried he'll betray us. He might alert the guards, or even try to stop us himself."

"I don't think he'll do that. I don't think he would hurt his sisters and brothers. I know how he acts, but I think he feels a connection to them, deep down."

Carina looked doubtful, but she dropped the subject.

Faye said, "Carina, I have to talk to you about something. I only have hours left, according to the doctor. I need to talk to you about what I want to happen when I'm gone."

SIXTY-TWO

Although *Nightfall* was hours from her destination, the ship was at battle status. At any moment, Dirksen surveillance probes could detect their approach, along with the approach of most of the Sherrerr fleet that was accompanying them. As soon as the Dirksens saw what was coming, it was inevitable that they wouldn't waste time in parley. The number of ships the Sherrerrs were committing to the battle made clear their intent. The only rational response the Dirksens could offer was an immediate, aggressive defense.

The mages were on round-the-clock lockdown. No one was allowed out of the living quarters for any reason whatsoever. Someone—probably Stefan—was taking no chances that they wouldn't be exactly where they were needed at the crucial moment. Even the doctor had had to argue with the guards for admittance. Carina heard the raised voices outside the main door. When the guards finally allowed the doctor inside around half an hour later, she appeared harassed and angry.

I only have two minutes, she'd said to Carina as she pushed pre-prepared syringes into her hands. *These are for your mother, to ease her symptoms. I'm not allowed in to see her until after the battle, so you'll have to give her the shots.* She hastily explained the procedure, continuing in spite of the guard poking his head around the door and telling her that her time was up.

Take care, Carina, the doctor had said as the guard pulled her out of the entranceway by her arm.

Now, all Carina and the children had to do was wait. The minutes dragged into hours as the moment of their deployment edged nearer. The children played simple games like hide-and-go-seek for a while. Then they began to tease each other and fight until Carina, mindful of their sick mother in the next room, told them to play quietly or not at all.

The tension was getting to them, she knew, as if their feelings about losing their mother weren't enough. But arguing with each other only made the situation worse. The children then lay morosely on their beds or the sofa, reading, drawing, playing screen games or staring vacantly at nothing.

Carina hadn't seen Bryce or Mandeville since the last time she'd been to Stefan's office. She'd begun to have her doubts that they would provide her with elixir as they'd promised. Looking back on their most recent conversation, Bryce's confidence and optimism seemed ill-founded. She didn't even know if he or Mandeville were still aboard the ship. Troops might be moving between vessels as the fleet approached the Dirksens' shipyard.

After her initial reluctance, Carina had warmed to the idea that they would be around to help. Allies were a new phenomenon to her, but she'd been prepared to make an exception. Had she been too optimistic? Perhaps things were the same as they'd been for a long time—her alone against the universe.

She still hadn't decided what to do about Castiel and Nahla. She didn't trust Castiel at all and thought that her mother's love for the boy had blinded her to his true nature. When their mother had gently explained to Darius that she wasn't going to get better and that she would be leaving them soon and forever, Carina was sure she'd seen Castiel smirk while his brother sobbed his heart out.

She was hoping that Castiel would elect to stay and then Nahla would want to stay with him. Could she force him to remain if he wanted to come along? She was sure he would contact the Sherrerrs the first opportunity he got. She could just imagine his little evil smile when Stefan arrived to collect them from whatever hiding place they reached.

The door to the living quarters opened. Carina's heart leaped. The guard delivering their meal was Bryce. She struggled to maintain her composure. She couldn't let her joy be observed by the guards outside or Castiel or Nahla.

"Your meals, ma'am," Bryce said, maintaining the subterfuge. Smart guy. He guessed that the children might not be aware of her escape plan.

"Thank you," Carina replied, taking the packaged meals and drinks from him and putting them on the table. "Have you heard any news about the attack?"

"Only another hour or two at most," Bryce replied. "That's what we've been told. I was released from duty to bring you these."

"We appreciate it. Thanks."

Bryce looked like he wanted to say something but he hesitated. Finally, he said, "I hope you enjoy your meal, ma'am. The cook's given you a new kind of cordial to try. I've heard it's an acquired taste."

An acquired taste? Carina had never heard Bryce use such formal language. Then his meaning hit her. The elixir! He'd managed to sneak them some elixir. But if Castiel or Nahla tasted the drink, they would know immediately that something was going on.

"Oh. Maybe it isn't suitable for the children," she said.

"I would say not."

"I want some," Darius exclaimed, jumping up. "I want to try it."

Darius, no!

"Don't be stupid," Castiel said. "You won't like it. I bet it's like that wine that Mother and Father drink."

"That's what I heard, sir," said Bryce.

"See," Castiel sneered at Darius. "You're such an idiot."

"Don't be rude to your brother," Carina admonished.

"Can I have some?" Darius pleaded. "I promise I won't spit it out."

"No, you can't," Carina replied.

Castiel pulled an I-told-you-so face at Darius, who pushed his face into his folded arms and began to cry again.

"You," one of the door guards barked at Bryce, "out."

He nodded at Carina.

"Thanks again," she said as he left.

"Dinner's here," Castiel shouted, ignoring Carina's order to be quiet so as not to disturb their mother.

The children who were in their bedrooms emerged while Carina was hastily sorting through the drinks to find the elixir. They all seemed identical. How was she supposed to tell them apart without tasting each one? Bryce must not have had the opportunity to mark the one that contained elixir.

"I want a drink," said Nahla, holding out her hand.

"Wait," Carina replied. "One of them is different."

"Actually," said Castiel. "I'll have that one. Father says I'm nearly grown up. I'll probably like it."

"No," Carina replied. "You can have the same as the others."

"But I want the special one," Castiel said through his teeth. "Give it to me now."

"No. You can have this one." Carina had been quickly opening and sniffing the drinks. She held out one she knew didn't contain elixir.

Castiel dashed it from her hand. The liquid splashed across the floor and the container rolled to a stop. The other children, who had been opening their food packages, stopped what they were doing and stared. They'd seemed used to Castiel's behavior, but they were watching Carina to see what she would do.

"Well it looks like you're going without a drink, Castiel."

The teenage boy stamped his foot like a toddler. "No I'm not. *You* are. Give me yours."

Carina ignored him, continuing to sniff and then pass out the drinks to the other children.

"If you don't give me yours," said Castiel, "I'll tell Father, and you know what he'll do to you." His eyes narrowed and his expression grew vicious.

Carina got the impression he knew exactly what he meant. Castiel stepped up to strike her face, but she caught his arm in midair. The boy was strong but he wasn't as strong as her, and he had no idea how to fight.

"Parthenia," Carina said, "take these." The girl stepped forward and took the remaining two containers while Carina held onto Castiel's arm, their gazes locked. When she had a hand free, she slapped the boy full across his face twice, not as hard as she could have, but hard enough to teach him a lesson.

Castiel was clearly unused to corporal punishment. His defiant expression dissolved into one of shame and defeat, and the arm Carina was holding relaxed. She let go of it and was about to say something to mollify the boy when his vicious look returned. He ran at her. She stepped to one side and punched his jaw as he sped past. Castiel staggered and fell. Before he had time to regain his senses, She grabbed him and dragged him over to his bedroom before pushing him inside. She closed and locked the door.

Nahla was wide-eyed with shock and outrage. "You can't do that! Father's going to be so angry with you, Carina."

"Father can do what he likes," Carina muttered as she retrieved the drink containers from Parthenia. She sniffed one and returned it to the girl. She sniffed the final one. Bryce had done it. He'd brought her elixir, and his small favor could make all the difference.

Sixty-Three

Faye was slipping away. She could feel it. Her feet were mired and a shadow was creeping over her. The struggle to hang on was hard. If she could remain alive a little while longer, she might see her children free, finally. If she could only witness that, she would be content to leave and seek Kris again among the stars.

But it was so hard. The medication the doctor had given her didn't seem to work as well as it had. The pain and dreadful lethargy didn't go away when Carina gave her the injection. She no longer had the strength to even lift her head from her pillow. All she could do was lie still. All she could concentrate on was the sound of her own breathing.

She thought she'd heard shouting from the living area, but she couldn't be sure. Perhaps it was a dream. Her dreams and her waking life were melded. One moment she would be young again and in Kris's arms. The rest of her life was an un-imagined nightmare that would never come to pass. Then she would be back in her dimly lit room aboard the Sherrerr starship, waiting for the minutes to tick down and release her. She drifted away again, lost in avenues of time.

She was home. It was late afternoon, and she'd just come in from the garden. She'd harvested the roots that Po Po liked so much. Kris's mother spent all day caring for little Carina while she and Kris worked in the fields. The old woman was kind and gentle with her granddaughter and spent hours entertaining her and teaching her the beginnings of Casting. Faye was happy to cook for her in the evenings, tired though she was. She couldn't have wished for a better babysitter.

When she went into the kitchen, Kris was there stirring the soup she had set to simmer. Faye put the gathered vegetables down and her husband turned at the sound.

"You're back early," Faye said. Kris usually stayed at work on their farm until the sun went down.

"Did you hear the news?" Kris asked. "There's been a landslide."

Faye picked up her ear comm, which she'd left in the kitchen. She liked to cut herself off from the outside world sometimes. She pushed the comm into her ear at the same time as saying, "Where did it happen? I hope no one's been hurt."

"East Mountain Province. A whole village disappeared, they say."

The news report Faye heard through the comm was relaying the same information. One hundred and eighty-seven estimated missing, feared dead. "That's terrible," she said. "Those poor people."

"Faye," Kris said, "East Mountain isn't far from here. I want to go and help."

"What? Now?"

"Yes. If I leave immediately, I can arrive by late evening. I might be able to save some lives. There must be people still alive under the mud, trapped in their houses."

"But..."

"I only need to be gone a few days, just until there's no hope of reaching anyone alive. Will you come with me?"

Faye pulled out a chair and sat down. "I want to help too. But what do you mean exactly? Do you think we should go and help dig people out?"

Kris came over to her. "I mean that we can Cast. We can Transport things out of the way. We can Locate people if we have something that belongs to them. You know how I feel, Faye. How I've felt for a long time. There's so much good we could do in the world with our abilities. But we do nothing. We sit at home, practicing our powers, keeping the skills alive, but for what? What's the point of possessing the talent we have if we never use it? Meanwhile, people die in terrible circumstances, suffering pain and anguish, and we don't do anything about it."

"People die all the time, in their billions, across the galaxy," said Faye. "We can't help them all."

"No, but we can help some."

It was an old argument they'd had many times. Kris was bright and talented as well as being an excellent mage. Yet his mother's caution had confined them both to eking out a living as farmers, where she hoped their isolation from most other people would keep them safe. It was the way of mages, the older woman had told them. It was the only way they managed to survive.

To Kris, it felt like a prison sentence. Not only because there was so much more he could do with his life, but because he was so kind and compassionate. He yearned to do good and to help people. He didn't suspect others' selfish, cruel motivations like his mother did. Faye had been caught between the two, trying to appease both. She'd always known that one day their lifestyle would become too much for her husband. She only wished the moment hadn't come so soon. She'd hoped for a few more years of contentment and safety.

"What do you say?" Kris urged her. "I'm going there, Faye. I have to. It's like the opportunity was created for me to finally do some good with my powers. I only came back to see if you would come with me. I want you to, but I'll understand if you'd prefer to stay with Carina."

"Oh, Kris," Faye said. She was torn. She didn't want to leave her toddler daughter, but Po Po would take good care of her. She also didn't want Kris to leave, but his mind was made up. If she went with him, she could prevent him from being reckless or too trusting. He would have to Cast in absolute secrecy if he was going to help the landslide victims.

Her husband was watching her. "Three days," she said. "Only three days, then we come straight back."

He grinned. "Three days it is. I've packed our things and told my mother what we're doing."

"I bet she wasn't happy about it."

"No, and you probably don't want to hear what she said, but I brought her around to the idea in the end. It'll be good to help people. It's what we should be doing."

"Not if it means sacrificing ourselves."

"That isn't going to happen," Kris assured her. "You'll see."

"Wait. What did you say?" Faye asked. "You packed *our* things? You mean mine too?"

He winked. "I knew you'd agree."

The light in the kitchen was quickly turning darker, as if the sun were speeding to the horizon. Kris was still, frozen. He began to fade.

"Kris," said Faye. "Where are you going? What's happening?" It was like her husband had Cast Transport on himself. "Kris, don't leave me." But he'd faded almost to nothing. The kitchen was dark and hazy. "Kris, please, don't go. I'll come with you. I said I'll come with you."

Suddenly Faye was lying down in a bed. Someone was bending over her. It was a woman, a young woman who looked similar to herself. It was Carina, but she'd grown up. What had happened? How had the time passed so quickly? Faye couldn't remember anything after that conversation with Kris.

"It's okay, Ma," Carina said. "Don't worry. I'm here. I'll look after you."

"Carina? Where's your father? He's gone. I was going to go with him, but he left without me."

"You're sick. You've been dreaming. But I have some elixir. I can make you better for a little while."

"You're going to Cast Heal? Don't do that. Cast Locate. Find your father for me. I miss him so much."

But her daughter was already sipping the liquid. Her eyes closed. Her hand lifted and Faye felt its soft warmth on her forehead. The effects of the Cast began to wash through her, clearing her mind of its fog, easing the ache of her muscles and bones, lifting the veil on reality.

Faye exhaled, a catch in her throat, as her memory returned. Her daughter's face came into vivid focus, lines of care and worry etched on it that made her look older than she was. Faye struggled with the tormenting facts of her life as they returned to her. All she could muster to say was, "You have some elixir? Did Stefan give it to you?"

"No," said Carina. "A friend got it for me. I'm going to use it to set up our escape."

"You're going ahead with it then?"

"What choice do I have?"

"You're right. I hope with all my heart that you manage it."

"You changed your mind?"

"Nothing is too much of a risk to free yourself and the others. You have my blessing, and if anything goes wrong, I want you to promise me that you'll never blame yourself. Not ever. Understand?"

Carina nodded. "Thank you. That means a lot to me."

"And don't waste any more elixir on Healing me. You know the effects won't last more than a few hours. I'm ready to leave now. It's what I want."

"I know, but I need some more time if I'm to do what you asked. I need my plan to succeed."

"I'll try to hold on a little longer." Faye hadn't told Carina the story of how she and Kris were captured. She wanted to tell her. It was important that she knew, but Faye was too weak and the past seemed far distant.

"We're nearly at the battle site," Carina said. "It shouldn't be long now."

Sixty-Four

It had taken all the elixir she had remaining after helping her mother, but Carina had put in place the Casts she guessed she would need to get her and the children to the shuttle bay. Casting into the future was extremely difficult and she was long out of practice. She'd also used a considerable amount of guesswork to decide when and where she needed the Casts to begin, based on her understanding of the timing of the attack and her knowledge of the layout of the ship. She could only hope the Casts would work when the time came.

She wished she could have saved even a mouthful of elixir to Cast Heal on her mother one more time, but there was nothing left. To effect their escape, she would have to rely on the elixir that would be provided when they attempted to blow up the shipyard. There had always been a plentiful supply, so she didn't worry too much in that regard. Carina was more worried about her mother.

With luck, she would cling onto life just a little longer. Carina desperately wanted give her at least a few moments of freedom before she passed on, and she wanted to get her away from the Sherrerrs' ship. That would be the only way she could perform the rites her mother believed would commit her spirit to the universe, where she would be reunited with Carina's father.

Carina's bitterness over her mother's imminent death threatened to swallow her up at times. Stefan Sherrerr had torn them apart so long ago, she could barely remember her as she'd been when Carina was young. Now they were finally reunited, death was set to sunder them once more. Her memories would be of a tortured, broken ghost of a woman, not the happy, loving person Carina dimly remembered. It seemed so unfair.

Stefan Sherrerr's crimes against her mother, her siblings, and herself were abhorrent. Carina was determined he would meet justice one day, but she knew she couldn't allow her desire for revenge to get in the way of her escape plan.

While they waited for the moment they would be called to join in the battle, Carina remained with her mother, performing what small tasks she could to help keep her comfortable. She seemed to barely exist in the living world. Her gaze was distant, as if she were looking out into the stars, and her voice sounded as if she were speaking from another world.

From time to time, when her strength temporarily rose, she would tell Carina anecdotes from the time when they'd lived as a family. Short, inconsequential stories that held no significance to anyone outside of the two of them, tales that warmed Carina's heart with the realization of how much she had been loved by both her parents. Knowing she was hearing the stories for the final time was upsetting, but she was also grateful for the opportunity to hear them at all.

It was in the middle of such a reminiscence that the moment Carina had craved and feared arrived. The guard didn't knock. He came straight into her mother's room. "Bring the mage children and come with us."

Carina let go of her mother's hand and got up from her bed. She kissed her before motioning the guard out of the room and following him. "Only the mage children? What about Castiel and Nahla?"

"They are to remain here. The rest of you are to come with me at once." He laid a hand on his weapon, as if anticipating her resistance. Stefan must have warned him she might cause trouble. He was right, only not about the kind of trouble she would cause.

"We're coming," she said. "There's no need to threaten us."

Parthenia, Ferne, Oriana, and Darius were already waiting. Castiel and Nahla watched on.

"Let's go," she said to her mage sisters and brothers. Three more guards awaited them in the corridor, along with the two who would remain outside the living quarters. Already, Carina was calculating how she would tackle them and the many other obstacles that would soon stand in her way. Neither Bryce nor Mandeville had reappeared. Even one guard on her side would have been extremely useful, but it looked like she would have to do without.

One guard leading them, another following, and one on each side, the party was guided to the bridge. When Carina realized where they were going, she grew troubled. For her purposes, the bridge was the last place she wanted to be. Too much scrutiny. Too many people. Too many possibilities for something to go wrong.

When she stepped inside, a whirl of light and movement greeted her. The battle was underway, playing out in streaks of color on the holo that occupied the center of the room. Tucked away in the heart of the massive ship, Carina hadn't even been aware of it. The shipyard hung in the middle, Dirksen ships surrounding it, dwarfed by its massive size. Sherrerr ships were advancing upon them. Pulse cannon flashed out from both sides as the starships drew closer.

The activity was reflected in the behavior of the crew. They were intent at their consoles, hastily swiping and pressing their screens or holding one hand to their ear comms, concentrating on the information being fed to them.

Tremoille occupied the central console just in front of the holo, gazing into its depths, following the progress of the battle. She barely glanced at Carina and the children, only flicking her hand to one side to indicate where they should sit.

A low table and five stools had been set up on one side of the space.

"That's no good," she said.

"What?" exclaimed Tremoille, whirling around to glare at her.

"We can't possibly Cast in here. It's too noisy, too distracting. I said we needed somewhere private. You have to put us somewhere quiet or we won't be able to help you."

"What's that?" a familiar voice barked from behind her. Stefan had arrived.

"We have to go someplace else," said Carina. "Somewhere peaceful, or we won't be able to Cast. You know that."

"Is that right, Stefan?" Tremoille asked.

"Of course it's right," Carina said. "Why would I lie about it? You all agreed to it at the dummy run. Did you forget?"

"Stefan?" Tremoille repeated.

The admiral's question to Stefan remained hanging in the air. Carina stared at him, boldly daring him to contradict her over the issue. He needed this victory, this example of what he had to offer the Sherrerr clan, and she knew it.

"It would be better for the children to be somewhere quiet, Admiral."

"Why didn't you tell me that before?" the woman said testily. "Find them somewhere. Fast. We'll be within range in five minutes."

Stefan ordered Carina and the children to pick up the tables, chairs, and elixir and follow him. They went through the corridors quickly as he urged them on.

Carina's feet lifted from the floor momentarily before sinking down again. The children let out gasps and cries of shock. Parthenia snapped down the lid of the jug of elixir she was carrying.

"What was that?" Oriana asked.

"The a-grav went out for a second," Carina replied. "We must have taken a hit. If it happens again, use the bars to pull yourself along." On each side of the corridor, narrow bars were set into the walls, as was standard for military vessels, but the children couldn't have been expected to know.

"Are we going to be blown up?" Darius asked nervously.

"No, we're the ones who are going to be doing the blowing up, right?"

"Right," he replied, a determined expression settling on his young face.

"Will we be in trouble if we can't do it?" Ferne asked.

Carina was about to answer, when Stefan interrupted. "Yes. If you don't do as you're supposed to, you will all be severely punished. Do you understand?"

The children immediately looked down and murmured, "Yes, Father."

Carina didn't reply. *Just a little while longer. Just another ten or fifteen minutes, Stefan Sherrerr, before you say goodbye to us forever.*

He thumped a door access button. They were at the briefing auditorium where they'd been tested before. As they went inside, Stefan started up the holo display. The image of the battle blinked into life above their heads. The shipyard was larger, and the Dirksen ships nearer. It seemed to Carina that the number of starships on both sides had decreased, thousands of lives sacrificed to the battle between the warring clans.

Stefan ordered them to set up the tables and stools, elixir and beakers, ready for Casting. He was listening to information arriving via his ear comm. "Sit down and get ready," he ordered. "You have two minutes. You'd better make this happen, all of you. Believe me, if you fail, you'll regret it." He glared at Carina.

Just a little while longer.

SIXTY-FIVE

The Dirksen shipyard had drawn so close it nearly filled the entire holo image, though in reality it was still distant and beyond Carina's range for Casting. She guessed that Darius might have been able to reach it. But the distance was closing rapidly. Carina estimated they had another thirty seconds or so.

The plan was that the Sherrerr flagship would halt when they were just within range. Remaining stationary would make it vulnerable to attack, but Carina had emphasized that to Cast while the distance was constantly decreasing might be too hard for the children.

They were all sitting in position, full beakers of elixir on the table in front of them. The four guards stood close by, their rifles trained on them as always. Stefan was too smart to take any chances, but Carina clung to the hope that their success in destroying the shipyard would provide that little bit of distraction she needed. Taking out four guards and Stefan was a tall order, but she didn't think it was impossible. Stefan wasn't armed, so that was a bonus, and the guards seemed young and poorly trained. No doubt the best troops had been reserved for ship invasions.

As the final few seconds counted down, Carina's heart threatened to burst from her chest. She might never have a better chance than this to escape her stepfather's dreadful yoke. She had to make it work. She had to succeed. If she didn't, she would be condemning her sisters and brothers to slavery and herself to a life like the one her mother had endured for so many years.

"Nearly there," Stefan said. "Get ready."

"You've got this, kids," Carina said. "You can do it." She went to pour out the elixir, but the a-grav failed again. Her stomach lurched and she floated from her seat before sinking down with a bump.

The ship jerked, sloshing the elixir in its lidded jug. They must have taken another big hit. The shielding had to be failing. Darius was watching her, a worried expression on his face. She smiled confidently and poured out a couple of mouthfuls of the precious liquid each before carefully replacing the lid on the jug. It was all they needed for the Fire Cast. She wanted to use as little as possible. They would need all the elixir they could get later.

"Now," Stefan barked.

"Right," she said to the children. "Go ahead." She took a sip of elixir and closed her eyes, shutting out the kaleidoscope of colors playing out over her head. She steadied her breathing and her heart rate, shutting out her fears and worries, and sank deep into the inner darkness of her mind. The pre-prepared coordinates were carved into her memory. She quickly but carefully wrote the Fire Cast, Split it, and sent the two Casts speeding away from her, across the abyss of space. They would hit. She was confident of it. It was what was supposed to happen next that worried her.

Carina opened her eyes and focused on the shipyard. Her targets were out of sight, hidden somewhere within the colossal structure. Long seconds passed. One by one the children also opened their eyes and gazed at the heart of the holo where the shipyard hung, defiantly intact. What if the intel had been wrong? What if it had been deliberately planted to mislead them?

Nightfall was now at the center of the battle and being mercilessly pummeled by the Dirksen forces. What if it had all been a trick to lure them in? Stefan's expression was shifting to fury, his hands balled into fists.

Then the first fuel tank blew.

The flash was blinding. It filled the image with an impossibly bright glare, searing Carina's retinas for a split second before it was gone. Through the after image, she caught a glimpse of the shipyard, now distorted as it began to break apart. A second blaze of light erupted. "Close your eyes," Carina shouted.

She looked away from the scene, seeing the reflection of the brilliant flashes on the briefing room's walls. She couldn't afford to close her own eyes. The moment the explosions were over, she had to act, fast. The sixth and final fuel tank blew. She returned her attention to the guards, who had kept their focus downward on her and the children. *Damn. Stefan must have warned them.*

Like snow in a heavy blizzard, the holo showed the debris of the shipyard spinning around them. The flagship was in full reverse in the aftermath of the explosion.

"We did it," Darius exclaimed, leaping up.

"Yay," cried Ferne, waving his arms in the air.

The guards' holds on their weapons began to relax, and they smiled, also enjoying the Sherrerr victory. Now Carina had her chance. A split second before she made her move, however, Stefan barked, "Guards. Watch your charges."

The men and women resumed their focus, training their muzzles on Carina and the children once more. *Damn. Damn. Damn. Damn you, Stefan Sherrerr.*

He had robbed her of that small moment of distraction she needed. Her stepfather seemed to read her mind. The corner of his lip lifted in a triumphant half smile. "Good. You all did as you were—" The door chime sounded, drowning out his words. Irritated, he went to the door. When he opened it, Carina's heart leaped. It was Bryce. She couldn't hear what her friend was saying, only Stefan's side of the conversation.

"Calvaley? Why didn't he comm me himself? Hmpf. I see. Where?" He stepped out into the corridor and turned to say, "You're all to remain here until I return. Guards, keep them covered at all times, do you understand?" He went out and the door slid shut.

Carina didn't waste a second. One of the guards was watching the shipyard debris expanding across the holo and speeding toward them. Immediately, Carina was on her, driving her elbow upward into the woman's chin. She knocked her out cold. Before the guard hit the floor Carina had torn her weapon from her hands and shot another guard in the face. There was no point in aiming at any armored part of their bodies. A single shot probably wouldn't penetrate, but luckily they had their visors up inside the ship. She spun to aim at a third guard, betting on the moment of confusion caused by her actions. But her luck had run out. Before she could take aim, the other guard fired.

Something exploded in her chest. She was out.

———

When Carina came to, she was still in the auditorium. Only a few short moments seemed to have passed. She thanked the stars that the guard's weapon had only been set on a light stun. Stefan clearly valued them more highly than he made out.

She was looking at the wrong end of a pulse rifle. The guard she'd knocked out remained sprawled, unmoving, on the floor. The guard she'd shot was sitting up and rubbing his face. The one who wasn't aiming at her was speaking into her mic.

The situation looked hopeless. Stefan and the rest of the ship would soon hear what had happened. Within minutes, they would be hurried back to their quarters and locked inside for who knew how long while Stefan meted out his punishments.

But Carina was determined not to give up. Her mind whirred as she tried to figure out how to turn the tables on the three remaining guards. Search as she might, however, she couldn't come up with an answer. Desperation began to take hold.

Then Parthenia made her move.

None of the guards were watching the children. The one Carina had shot was distracted by the stinging, burning after-effects of being stunned, which Carina could also feel. One was focused with a laser-like intensity on her. The other was looking down as she murmured in her mic, half-turned away from Carina's brothers and sisters.

From the corner of her eye, she saw Parthenia take a sip of elixir. She could hardly believe it. What was her sister doing? She struggled to show no evidence on her face of her sister's behavior. Whatever it was she was planning, Carina had to take the opening her sister was giving her. They were all out of second chances.

She saw it. The unconscious guard's gun had fallen to one side of her body. It lifted, hovered, and began to slowly float toward Carina. Parthenia had Cast Transport and was sending her the weapon. Yet it would be of little use to her if she was looking down a muzzle.

The guard who she'd shot in the face uttered an expletive. He'd seen the floating rifle. The one who was watching Carina shifted his gaze for a split second to see what was happening. It was enough. Carina grabbed the muzzle of his gun and leapt up, wresting it from his grip. At the same moment, the weapon Parthenia had Transported arrived. Carina let it slide under her lifted arm and quickly fired off two pulse rounds. The previously stunned guard fell, unconscious once more. The one who had been speaking into her mic also hit the ground, face first.

As the remaining guard made a grab for his weapon, Carina squeezed the trigger a third time and sent a round into his stomach. He staggered backward. She lifted her weapon and aimed better. The fourth round hit him in his forehead. His eyes rolled upward as he toppled.

"Thanks," Carina said to Parthenia. "Grab the elixir. Come on, everyone."

"Where are we going?" Darius asked.

"I think we're going to escape," said Ferne.

"Not just yet," Carina said. "We have to collect Ma."

SIXTY-SIX

In the corridor outside the briefing room the lighting slowly flashed and an acrid stink hung in the air. *Nightfall* was on high alert. Somewhere on the ship, a fire was raging and the air filters were struggling to clear the smoke. The place was in chaos. Crew rushed through the corridors, only taking enough notice of Carina and the children to avoid colliding with them.

They ran.

Each time Carina had moved through the ship, she'd taken mental notes on its layout. On such a large vessel, signs were necessary, and she'd taken care to read those too. She knew exactly how to return to their living quarters and how to get from there to the shuttle bay. The only question was, could they do it without being recaptured? She didn't know who the guard in the briefing room had been speaking to over her mic or what she'd said, but they had only minutes of freedom at the very most.

The running children drew plenty of curious glances, but everyone appeared too busy or distracted to challenge them, even though Carina carried two weapons loosely hanging down by her sides. She guessed that the crew identified them as Sherrerrs, and the aura of the family was their protection. It would be a very temporary reprieve, she was sure.

They reached the corridor that led to their living quarters. The short dead-end was empty save for the two sentry guards. Carina had turned her weapons up to full stun. She quickly dispatched both the guards. They would be out for around half an hour.

She burst into the living quarters. Castiel and Nahla were in the living area, and they looked up, their eyes wide and their mouths gaping. Ignoring them, Carina ran into her mother's bedroom and over to her bed. The woman's heavy eyelids lifted.

"Are the children free?" she whispered. "Did you do it?"

"Not yet," Carina replied, "but I'm going to."

She threw her weapons' straps over her shoulders in order to lift up her mother, but then she had a better idea. "Ferne, Oriana," she called. The twins, along with the rest of the children, were already peering through the doorway. Carina said, "Do you think you can handle these?" She held out the two pulse rifles.

"You bet," Oriana said excitedly as she came over and grabbed them. She handed one to Ferne, who gazed wonderingly at the weapon.

"Just don't point it at anyone you don't want to kill," Carina said.

Castiel marched over too. "What are you doing?" he asked angrily.

"We're leaving," Carina replied. She pulled back her mother's blanket. The woman's body was wasted to little more than skin and bones. Gently, she lifted her into her arms. She was pitifully light to carry.

"You can't leave," Castiel said, outraged. "I'm going to tell Father."

"You do, and I'll shoot you," said Ferne. He aimed at Castiel.

"Are Castiel and Nahla coming too?" Darius asked.

Carina hesitated. *No* hung on the edge of her lips.

Her mother spoke. "Yes. You must all go with Carina."

Castiel's eyes hooded over. "Yes," he echoed. "We're coming too."

Foreboding tingling, Carina said, "Okay. Let's move then."

They flew through the ship. The twins ran in front, their weapons at the ready. Darius, Castiel, and Nahla came next, followed by Carina, carrying their mother. Parthenia brought up the rear, clutching the jug of elixir to her chest.

Carina expected Castiel to try something at any moment. He had some plan in mind, it was obvious. What it was and when he would make his move wasn't clear, but he seemed to be biding his time.

If Carina had Cast correctly with the elixir Bryce had stolen for her, each of the doors on their route that could be locked to bar their way should have quietly opened, and without alerting the security system. *If* her Casts had worked. If any of them hadn't, they would be sitting ducks.

They arrived at the first door. It was shut. The group halted. Perhaps the door had been locked as an emergency measure due to the fires and risk of depressurization, or perhaps the bridge knew they were attempting to escape. The effect was the same. Ferne turned to Carina. "What do we do now?"

"We'll have to Cast Open," Parthenia said.

"There's no time," said Carina, inwardly cursing.

The door slid to the side.

"Go," yelled Carina. The Cast she'd sent into the future had finally worked.

They sped through. The second door they encountered was already open. Carina had set a delay between each one. After her first miscalculation, her timing was perfect.

The sound of running, booted feet came from behind, constricting her chest. They were being pursued by guards. "Faster," she shouted, but the children were already running at top speed and they were beginning to flag. A life of luxury had left them physically unfit and quickly tired.

The running feet drew nearer, and the group had nowhere to hide. "You have to run faster," Carina urged. She looked over her shoulder. The guards had entered the corridor. Only Oriana and Ferne were armed and they were running in front. She considered telling them to fire at the guards, but it would be hopeless. They were kids against trained adult men and women.

They were going to be shot and there was nothing she could do about it. She only hoped the guards' weapons were set to stun. What was she thinking? Of course they were set to stun. Stefan wouldn't allow his precious commodities to come to serious harm. Carina looked down at her mother, who was clinging to life by a thread. Tears filled her eyes.

The guards began to shoot.

"I'm sorry, Ma," Carina whispered. "I tried."

She waited for the rounds to hit. She could see that the third and final door —the entrance to the shuttle bay—stood open as a result of her Cast, as if waiting for them. They'd been so close.

Pulse rounds were hitting the walls, searing and scoring the surfaces. So far, no one had been hit. More rounds flew past, above and around them. Carina became confused. The guards should have brought them all down. They had to be terrible shots, or very badly trained, or...

Holy shit!

The guards were deliberately missing them. They were allowing them to escape.

They ran into the bay. "Lock the door," Carina called. "Parthenia, Cast Lock." The guards might have given them a chance by being the worst shots in the galaxy, but she doubted their commanding officer would let them get away with not trying to enter the shuttle bay.

Four shuttles were inside the bay. Carina scanned them. She would have to fly one, but she thought she could manage it. When she'd been a merc, a pilot who she'd had a brief fling with had shown her the basics. She picked the shuttle that looked the most familiar.

"Come on, kids," she said. "This way." She had a short time to figure out the controls and fly it out of the bay before the Lock Cast would wear out. Carrying her mother in her arms, she set out toward the small vessel.

Then she noticed no one was following her. Carina looked back.

"Carina," piped Darius, "is Father coming too?"

Chilled with disbelief, Carina saw why all the children had stopped. Stefan was in the corner of the bay, next to the door. He had Bryce. His arm was around Bryce's neck and he was pointing a gun at her friend's head.

Stefan's smile was ghastly. "The minute I heard that you and the children had gone missing, I guessed where you were headed. Guards will be here any minute."

As if on cue, a helmeted head appeared in the small window of the shuttle bay door.

"Nice try, Carina," Stefan said, "but you lost. I'm going to have such fun teaching you the error of your ways."

"I did what you asked, Carina," Parthenia said quietly. "I Cast Lock."

Carina gave a slight nod, acknowledging her sister's words without taking her eyes off Stefan.

"Parthenia," she said. "Please help Ma."

She gently lowered her mother's feet to the floor. Parthenia helped the woman weakly stagger to one side of the bay. Carina was watching Bryce.

Her friend was sweating, but he didn't plead for his life. "Go," he said. "Just go."

Dull thuds came from the door as the guards tried to open it, but nothing would work against Lock. Nothing electronic or mechanical. Ten minutes. The Cast would work for around ten minutes. She had time to get everyone away before the guards would break through the door—everyone except Bryce.

It was an impossible choice. Should she save her friend's life and consign her sisters and brothers to a lifetime of slavery? Or take the children to freedom but allow her friend to die?

Blood was rushing through her ears. The hammering from the door seemed to be pounding through her head. From the corner of her eye Carina saw Castiel standing with his hands on his hips. Nahla clung to his side, appearing confused about what was going on. The weapons the twins were holding hung loosely in their hands. Even if they stood the remotest chance of shooting Stefan before he killed Bryce, Carina could never ask them to fire at their father.

Darius had sunk to the floor, his arms wrapped over his head, as if the turmoil of emotions in the room was too much for him to bear.

She'd nearly saved them all but, as always, Stefan's ploy was working. All he had to do was threaten to hurt a person his victim cared about. Carina couldn't see a way around it. She couldn't let Bryce die, not even to save her brothers and sisters. How could she spend the rest of her life living with her decision?

"Thinking it over, Carina?" Stefan asked. "The question is about to become moot. I know that Lock doesn't last forever. Soon you won't have time to get away. That door will open and the guards will round you up. I might as well blow your friend's head off whatever you decide. Usually, I'd rather not. I don't relish the idea of his blood and brains all over me. But I'm prepared to make an exception."

Carina's jaw clenched. She couldn't bring herself to say the words. She couldn't allow her siblings to return to this monster, but what choice did she have?

"What's it to be?" Stefan asked. "Your idiot friend or my children? I'm not waiting any longer."

Carina went to speak, but a movement off to the side of the bay caught her attention. From his position, Stefan couldn't see Ma. She had collapsed by a wall with Parthenia by her side. Her daughter was removing the jug of elixir from her lips. Ma's eyes were closed, and she was Casting.

"You're right, Stefan," Carina said coolly. "You won't have to wait any longer."

He frowned. "So you're giving up? Of course you are. But I changed my mind. I'm going to kill him anyway."

He dragged Bryce around and pushed the end of the muzzle to his forehead. But as he went to press the trigger, Stefan cried out. The gun fell and clattered on the floor. Stefan shuddered, and Bryce moved quickly away. Stefan shrieked and gripped frantically at his back, his face a white, rigid mask of agony. His legs buckled, and he dropped down onto his side. Blood began to spread from his back, creating a widening pool.

The children were fixated on the spectacle of Stefan's ordeal.

"Children," Carina shouted, "go to the shuttle at the end of the bay and get inside." When they didn't move, she said, "Bryce, please, take them to the shuttle." Her friend obliged, ushering the twins, Nahla, and Darius away and across the bay. Parthenia wouldn't leave her mother, but she faced the wall, her forehead pressed against it, her hands gripping her ears. Castiel refused to go. He was mesmerized, appearing fascinated as he watched his father die.

Carina recognized the Cast. She'd used it herself, long ago. Out of horror of its effect, she'd never used it again on a living being. As Stefan had been gloating and threatening to kill Bryce, Ma had Cast Split. Her husband was now slowly tearing in two.

While Stefan writhed and screamed, begging for mercy, Carina's gaze turned to her mother. She was moving, crawling bit by bit, grimacing with pain, toward him.

It was a horrible scene to witness. Though Carina had seen many fellow soldiers injured and killed in battle, she'd never heard the almost inhuman howls that issued from Stefan Sherrerr's throat. The pool of blood around his body spread wider, but still he didn't die.

In spite of everything he'd done to her father, her mother, and her sisters and brothers, Carina pitied the man. She hoped the end would come soon. His body was grossly distorted. His clothes seemed to be the only things holding him together.

As his cries became weaker, her mother reached him. Her hands slid through the pool of blood. Her nightdress soaked it up. When she looked down on what remained of Stefan's face, he was still breathing. She said, so weakly Carina could barely hear, "I told you I would have my revenge, Stefan Sherrerr. I lied. Mages *can* kill."

Then he was gone.

Sixty-Seven

They had no time left.

"Parthenia," Carina shouted. "Get to the shuttle." She ran over to her mother and scooped the blood-soaked, fragile woman into her arms and raced with her to the other side of the bay. Parthenia arrived at the shuttle right behind her, carrying the jug of elixir.

The door opened. Bryce had seen them coming. As soon as they were inside, he thumped the button to close it again. "I hope you know how to fly this thing."

"So do I."

Carina went into the passenger area and gently placed her mother in a seat before going into the pilot's cabin. As she strapped herself in, she ran her gaze over the console. She guessed she knew what most of the controls did, but as she glanced up, a bigger obstacle confronted her. The shuttle bay doors were shut. They could only be opened from the bridge.

Except that wasn't the only way. "Parthenia," Carina called back into the passenger cabin. "Cast Open on the shuttle bay doors."

While she waited for the Cast to take effect, Carina checked the other end of the bay. The door there was already opening. The Lock Cast had worn off and the guards were pouring through. They began firing at the shuttle. This time, their commanding officer was at their heels. The shots they fired hit their target. Their weapons weren't powerful enough to disable the shuttle right away, but neither could Carina afford to wait any longer. If only there were a Cast to fly a shuttle.

She activated the screen. It lit up. *Yes!* A pulse round hit the window, scoring a hazy gash across the outer shell. Carina started up the engine, giving the approaching guards a quick glance. If they didn't take the hint and get out of the bay, they were about to be fried.

The bay doors were opening, revealing a black expanse littered with stars, vapor, and flying debris from the shipyard explosion. They still had a chance of escaping into the confused mess of heat signatures.

Carina silently thanked her sister. She scanned the console, trying to find the take off mode. Another opaque gash appeared on the window. She thumbed the console, and the shuttle lifted up, wavering in midair. The bay doors had nearly opened wide enough.

Hesitantly, she attempted to maneuver the shuttle out of the bay. As she flew the vessel through the gap, she hit the edge of the upper door and winced as the screech of metal echoed through the ship. Then they were outside, but that was only the beginning of their flight from *Nightfall*. She had to fly the shuttle into the debris cloud and then hope the flagship's scanners would lose them.

Of course, they would be shot at all the way. The only thing they had in their favor was the fact that it was a military craft. She quickly found the jinking command and activated it as they cleared the ship.

"Carina."

Bryce was standing at the pilot cabin entrance.

"Kinda busy right now."

"I know. I'm sorry, but..."

When Bryce didn't complete his sentence, Carina guessed what he'd come to tell her. "No," she exclaimed. She stood halfway up before sitting down again. Sorrow and despair overcoming her, she said, "I can't leave the controls."

The shuttle window was filled with flashes of light—the remains of the shipyard speeding past. She had the shielding on full, hoping nothing large hit them. The shuttle's speed had to match the velocity of the debris if her plan stood a chance of succeeding. Some of those flashes were pulse cannon fire from *Nightfall*.

She had to focus. She checked the shuttle's scanner readings on the debris. Desperation was gnawing at her. Her mother was dying. That was what Bryce had come to tell her. But she couldn't go to her. She was the only one who could get everyone to safety. If she didn't do this right, the Sherrerr flagship would vaporize them.

She steered the shuttle out of the shadow of the Sherrerr ship and toward the debris cloud, setting a matching speed. The craft juddered and the scent of frizzled electronics invaded the cabin. They'd been hit. The control screen winked out.

"Carina." It was Darius this time.

"I can't speak to you right now," Carina said. The poor kid. He'd witnessed his father's horrible death and now his mother was dying. But she couldn't help him. She had to save their lives.

"Do you want me to Cast Cloak?"

Carina's gaze was still fixed to the pilot's screen. It had reappeared but it was flickering. The shuttle was nearly at the debris cloud's velocity. *Nightfall's* scanner would have a tag on them. It could read the heat signature of their engine, but the debris was also hot. It was time to deactivate the jinking function.

Darius's words finally sunk in. "Do I want you to Cast what?" Carina had never heard of Cloak.

"I can hide the shuttle if you want. Just for a little while."

She stared at her little brother. "What the hell? How?" But it wasn't the best time for explanations. "Yes. Yes. Whatever it is, do it, Darius. Do it."

The ship shook again. The pilot's screen went black. Carina glanced at the pilot cabin entrance but Darius had gone. She tried to reactivate the controls. After a few seconds, the screen returned to life, listing the damage to the ship. Their primary power was offline. The shot must have hit their main fuel tank or severed the lines to the engines. They were lucky the tank hadn't exploded. The shuttle was running on auxiliary power. Would it be enough to get them to the nearest planet?

Try as she might, Carina couldn't work the controls. But they were running at the speed of the explosion remnants. She'd done all she could do. For the moment, it seemed to be working.

She unfastened her harness and went into the passenger cabin. A strange scene confronted her. Castiel was tied to his seat and so was little Nahla, sitting one seat away from him. The other children were crowded together around the spot where she'd put their mother. Ma's bare, blood-stained foot poked out into the aisle.

When she went over to her, the children stepped away a little, making room.

Parthenia was utterly distraught. "I tried Casting Heal but it didn't work."

Carina said sadly, "It won't work at the very end. There's nothing we can do."

But for the slight rising and falling of her chest, Carina would have thought her mother had already left them. Her face was still and calm, a peacefulness resting on her features that Carina had never seen before, except maybe when she was very young. She stroked her mother's hair. It was fine and soft. One of the few early memories she had of her mother sprung into her mind. She remembered being carried in her arms and burying her face in her mother's hair.

At Carina's touch, the dying woman's eyes opened. They were dark and warm and sad as she fixed them on Carina. "Look after your sisters and brothers for me, will you, Carina? Especially Darius. And Castiel. They need you."

Carina looked up at Bryce, who was watching over the back of her mother's seat. He shook his head slightly as if to signal that her mother didn't know about the altercation that had resulted in Castiel's being restrained.

She swallowed. "I will."

"I love you all," Ma whispered. "I'm sorry. I have to go to Kris now." Her mother exhaled deeply, then her gaze was still.

Sixty-Eight

For a while, no one spoke. Though Carina had long known her mother's death was inevitable, now that it had actually happened, she almost couldn't believe it. A gulf had opened inside her.

For a painfully short time, she had felt whole. Now she didn't think she would ever feel the same way again. Rage and anguish battled within her. The injustice of it all was overwhelming. Ma had done nothing to deserve what she had suffered. Her children had been born into slavery through no fault of their own. Nothing could justify what had happened to Carina herself. And now they were finally free, nothing would bring Ma back.

Carina became aware of the sound of weeping. She looked up from her mother's unmoving face to see that it was the twins and little Darius. The three children were standing in a huddle, quietly crying. Parthenia stood apart, pale and still, as if frozen with shock.

She took a deep breath. She had to be strong. She had to get them all to safety. She was about to return to the pilot's cabin when Bryce put a hand on her shoulder.

"I'm so sorry, Carina."

She nodded numbly. "Could you try to find something to cover her up? I have to set a course for the nearest planet. Then I have to arrange some things for the funeral. Why are Castiel and Nahla tied up?"

"The boy made a grab for the jug of that liquid you guys use, but the big girl— Parthenia?—she was too quick for him. They started fighting and I dragged him off her. He started saying some stuff… I didn't really understand but maybe he'll tell you himself. Parthenia seemed to think it was very bad news. Tying him up was all I could think to do in the circumstances. And the other one—the little girl—she's like his puppet. I don't trust her either."

Dealing with Castiel would have to wait. Carina returned to the pilot's cabin to find the ship's autorepair had kicked in. The controls were slowly flickering back to life, but they were still running on auxiliary power.

Whatever Darius had done appeared to have worked. The Sherrerr flagship had ceased firing and wasn't on their tail. Its scanners couldn't locate them, though she didn't know how long the situation would last. Either her tactic of escaping into the debris cloud had worked or Darius had hidden the shuttle with his mysterious Cast. If the latter were the case, she hoped they would be far away and undetectable when it wore off.

Auxiliary fuel tanks wouldn't take them a great distance. They had to land somewhere before the fuel ran out. Carina located the nearest planetary systems. Only one was within range, and then only just. She selected the destination, and the shuttle maneuvered to the new heading. Then she turned down life support systems to the minimum for survival. Even so, they would barely have enough power for the rest of the trip.

She hadn't heard of their destination, which was good. An insignificant, quiet, backwater system was exactly what they needed.

Now she had to face the unpleasant task of speaking to Castiel. Carina didn't relish the prospect. She was barely holding it together as it was. She didn't think she had the strength to deal with the evil little worm right now. She wished she'd gone against her mother's wishes and left him on the Sherrerr flagship. Perhaps she could have taken Nahla away from him, but she doubted the little girl would have allowed herself to be separated from her brother. She was already heavily under his influence.

As he gazed up at Carina, Castiel looked more than ever like his father. His eyes were deep but they were soulless. There was nothing inside.

"Release me," he spat. "I demand that you untie me at once. I am a Sherrerr."

"You certainly are from the sound of it. Why were you trying to take the elixir?"

"Because I'm a mage too. I can Cast. I insist on my right to Cast like the rest of you."

"No, you're wrong. If you could Cast, you would have been able to do it from a young age. Mother would have taught you like she taught the others."

"She didn't teach me because she didn't want me to be a mage. She hated me."

"No, Castiel. She loved you." *Too much.*

The adolescent boy struggled against his bonds. "I *can* Cast. I know I can. I could feel it in me when I watched the lessons. I can write those characters in my mind. The only reason they don't work is because I don't drink the elixir."

Carina watched Castiel as he grew red-faced from futilely fighting his restraints. Could what he was saying be true? She didn't think so, but he seemed so certain. She didn't think it was possible to develop the ability to Cast later on childhood, but her main source of knowledge about magehood had been Nai Nai. Her mother might have known about the phenomenon, but now she had also passed on.

Castiel rested from his struggles and looked up at her from beneath hooded eyes. The color of the boy's hair was a mixture of her mother's black and his father's light brown. Faint, fine hairs grew on his upper lip. Had his mage powers been triggered late, as he entered puberty?

The thought that Castiel might be a mage was horrifying. All his father's cruelty and malice plus the ability to Cast would make for a truly terrible, extremely dangerous human being. She hoped he was wrong. On the other hand, if he was right, it was probably a good thing that she had taken him away from the Sherrerrs. What might they do with a mage of Castiel's personality working for them? Though perhaps he would find his way back to them soon enough.

One thing was certain—she would have to watch Castiel and his little sidekick very carefully.

"Carina."

Parthenia was behind her. Carina hadn't had a chance to speak to her sister since she had helped her escape the briefing room on *Nightfall*. The girl looked exhausted.

Carina took her sister's arm and moved her away from Castiel before enveloping her in a hug. "Thank you so much for helping. We wouldn't be here if it weren't for everything you did."

Parthenia's eyes were dazed and her lips trembled. "I gave Mother the elixir. I didn't know what she was going to do. I helped her kill Father. I helped my mother kill my father." Her voice had an edge of hysteria to it.

"Oh Parthenia, you didn't know. You couldn't know. It wasn't your fault. Ma had many reasons..." But Carina didn't go on. The life of rape and torture her mother had endured at the hands of her father would be something Parthenia would struggle with for the rest of her days. "None of it was your fault. You mustn't ever think that. And you did nothing wrong. Please don't blame yourself."

"And I never had a chance to say sorry," Parthenia choked. "I didn't have time to explain that I was always on her side. As I got older and I understood what Father was doing to her, I wanted to help her. I wanted Father to turn his focus onto me and leave her alone. I thought maybe then she would have some peace and freedom. I even protected her from him one time in the garden. She'd made some elixir, but I saw that her maid was looking for her and she was about to find her. I ran out and got rid of the elixir before her maid saw it. I didn't want her to be beaten again, Carina. I wanted to tell her I'd been trying to protect her, but there wasn't enough time. You can't imagine what he would do to her."

Carina could imagine, too well. She hugged her sister, not knowing what to say. What could she say? There were no words that would take away her pain. She hoped that with time and the love of her brothers and sisters—with at least one notable exception—Parthenia might come to terms with the events of the last few hours and in fact her entire childhood.

Bryce appeared. "I wrapped your mother in emergency blankets. It was all I could find."

"Thank you," said Carina. "Can you help me with some other things?"

"Of course. What do you need?"

She was about to answer when a little hand tugged at hers. She looked down at Darius. His face was blanched and grimy streaks ran from his eyes to his jawline. When he spoke, it was so quietly Carina couldn't hear his words. She squatted down to his level. "What did you say?"

"I said, I did it, didn't I?"

"You..." Carina had almost forgotten his offer to Cast something called Cloak. "You did, I think. Did you Cast to hide the ship?"

The little boy gave two brief nods, tremulous confidence hovering in his eyes.

"I've never heard of that Cast," Carina said. "Is it hard?"

"No. It's my own Cast. I made it up."

She had never heard of Casts being invented. They either existed or they didn't. Nai Nai had tried to teach her them all before she died, but maybe she'd run out of time or forgotten one or two. Ma must have taught Cloak to Darius and he'd forgotten that he learned it.

"It was really hard to think it up, though," Darius went on.

"To think it up? Darius, are you sure you don't mean it was hard to remember?"

"No. I had to imagine it, and that's really hard. I only tried Cloak once or twice before, when I was wishing I could hide better when we played hide-and-go-seek. We were trying to get away, weren't we? And I thought it would be best if we could hide. I tried it, and it worked, right? I hid us."

Carina could hardly believe it, but it seemed that what her little brother was saying was true. If it was, he was truly a special mage. "I think you might be right, Darius. You hid us. You saved us."

He smiled shyly, but then his mouth turned down. "I wish Mother hadn't died."

"Me too, Darius. Me too."

SIXTY-NINE

Ma's funeral was short and simple and bittersweet. Though Carina ached with the loss of the mother she had barely gotten to know as an adult, she couldn't help but feel relief at the knowledge that she was finally, utterly, free.

She had asked Parthenia if she wanted to help her wash their mother's body. She wasn't prepared to send Ma out to the stars besmirched with the blood of the man who had tormented her most of her adult life. When her sister agreed, Carina was glad. She would have felt lonely performing the task by herself, and she thought it might help Parthenia overcome her sense of guilt if she gave her mother this final demonstration of her love and care.

When Ma was clean, they poured elixir into her mouth. Traditionally, four of the five Elements would be placed with the body of a mage before it was consumed by the fifth, Fire, but Carina hadn't been able to find all four aboard the shuttle. She'd expected wood to be difficult to find, until Oriana remembered that her brooch was carved from a hard, black wood called ebony. There was plenty of Water and Metal aboard, but in the end it was Earth that stumped them. Where could they expect to find soil aboard a space vessel?

So Carina had chosen to sacrifice some of the precious elixir, which contained all the Elements, in the hope the stories were true and Ma's spirit really would live on and find her first husband somewhere out there in the universe.

As she was about to wrap her mother in fresh blankets, the sight of the disease-ravaged, scarred body seemed to remind Carina of something. It was something to do with mages and scars. When she remembered, her hand flew to her mouth.

"What's wrong?" Parthenia asked.

"Tracers," Carina replied. "Have you all been fitted with tracers?"

Her eyes widening in alarm, Parthenia nodded.

When Darius had been kidnapped by the Dirksens, his captors had misled the rescuers by cutting his tracer chip out of his body and using it as bait. Stefan Sherrerr hadn't had the opportunity to fit Carina with a tracer, but it looked like all the other children had them. As long as they carried the chips, the Sherrerrs would eventually hunt them down and recapture them.

"I'll have to Transport it out of you," Carina told her sister.

"Are you sure you can do that?"

"I think so. I haven't tried anything like it before, but I don't think it should be too hard if I know where the chip is." The Cast wasn't the problem. Carina was worried about using up more of the elixir. Until they landed on a planet, they wouldn't be able to make any more. They had to save it for essential Casts, but removing the tracer chips was vital.

Parthenia didn't know where her chip was. She only knew that one had been inserted into her when she was very young. Carina was forced to ask Darius about the chip's location. She went into the passenger cabin.

"Darius."

"Yes?" Darius replied through a mouthful of food. Bryce had found the emergency rations and was handing them out.

Carina went over to him. "I'm sorry to have to ask you this, but when the bad men took you and cut out your chip, do you remember where it was?"

The little boy put down his cookie, his contented expression turning glum. "It was here." He pointed to the top of his right buttock.

"Thank you," said Carina. "Just one more question. Did someone put another one in the same place after you returned home?"

"Uh huh." Darius took a bite of his cookie.

"Right. I'm going to take it out again." Carina's little brother looked alarmed. She added, "I'm going to Transport the chip out. It won't hurt. I promise."

"Okay."

Carina removed the chips from all the children including Castiel and Nahla, though the older boy objected and warned Carina to not come near him or she would regret it. She placed the tracers with Ma's body.

After each of the children had an opportunity to say goodbye to their mother for the final time—Castiel laughed when Carina offered him the chance, and Nahla echoed her brother's scorn—they placed Ma in the airlock.

Carina watched the still, wrapped figure for a long time through the airlock window. She tried to put from her mind the dreadful torture her mother had suffered and to remember the sweet, loving woman of her youth. Somewhere within her mother, that woman had still existed, and she had borne her love for Carina through the long years of pain. It gave Carina some comfort to know that, and it also comforted her to know they had been reunited for a short time, no matter how hard and painful that time had been.

Finally, when she was ready, Carina opened the outer airlock door and watched the small, slim bundle lift and float out into space. She went into the passenger cabin, where the atmosphere was quiet and pensive. The shuttle was growing colder by the minute on the bare life support the vessel was running.

"Are you going to Cast Fire now?" Darius asked.

"No," Carina replied. "Fire won't work by itself in space, and we don't have any fuel to spare. But don't worry, I'm going to send Ma off in the right way."

She went into the pilot's cabin. The scanners told her where Ma's body was floating, a short distance away. Carina adjusted the shuttle's course to the necessary position. As it came around, the flare from the engines caught her mother's body, instantly disintegrating it. Carina then returned the shuttle's course to its previous setting.

Relief washed over her. She lay back in her seat. Though her gaze was on the starscape through the shuttle's window, Carina didn't really see it. Her focus was turned inward. Her mother was free, and providing she could get her brothers and sisters to the backwater planetary system, they would be free too, though she still had no idea what to do about Castiel and Nahla. She would have to put them somewhere they wouldn't be in danger and then separate the rest of the family from them. Castiel would probably try to return to the Sherrerrs, but there wasn't a lot she could do about that.

Life would be hard for the children now. They'd been brought up in luxury and had no concept of how to survive day to day when you were nobody and had nothing. But Carina could teach them. That was certainly a life she was familiar with.

"Everything okay?" Bryce was looking into the cabin.

Carina had almost forgotten about him. "Yeah. We don't have anything to do now but wait. We should be at the place we're heading for in about eight days."

"What's the planet called?"

"Err..." Carina couldn't remember. She checked. "Ostillon, in the Floria system."

"Never heard of it."

"Me neither. But it's inhabited, so that's where we're going. It's more than we could have hoped for. In a crippled shuttle, we're lucky to be within reach of anywhere that supports human life."

"Are we still in Sherrerr territory?"

"I don't think so. I think this is a disputed district. One of the areas they want to take over when they beat the Dirksens into submission."

"Hmm. Okay. I guess we'll have to settle in for the wait." He paused. "Do you remember when I told you I wanted to leave Ithiya and travel the stars?"

"I do."

"This wasn't exactly what I had in mind."

Carina laughed, and it felt like it was for the first time in a long time. The mirth helped to ease her anxiety and grief. Then she remembered what Bryce had left behind in order to try to rescue her. "I'm so sorry, Bryce. Your parents and your brothers and sisters must be worried about you. Did you get a chance to tell them where you were going before you signed up aboard *Nightfall*?"

"I sent them a quick message. It's all right. They know I took the treatment for Ithiyan Plague and I'm not going to die. That must be a big weight off their minds. As soon as I have the opportunity, I'll let them know I'm safe."

When her friend turned to leave, Carina said, "I wanted to say something."

"What's that?"

"I wanted to apologize for mistrusting you. Without you helping us, we could never have escaped. I'm glad I accepted your help in the end."

He smiled. "No problem."

"And it wasn't just you, was it? Did Mandeville help you steal the elixir?"

"He did."

"When we were running to the shuttle bay, the guards who came after us were firing over our heads."

"It's like I told you, Carina. There were plenty of people on that ship who didn't agree with what the Sherrerrs were doing to you and your family. It's one thing to pick a side and sign up to fight for them, but it's another to be forced into service, especially using the methods that bastard used. I'm glad he died, and I couldn't think of a better way for him to go."

Bryce's expression had turned uncharacteristically angry. Carina decided she wouldn't like to be on the wrong side of him in a fight.

"I'm glad he's gone too," she said, though she didn't think she could ever use Split to kill someone unless she had no choice.

The cabin had grown so cold, her teeth were beginning to chatter. "Are there any more of those emergency blankets?" she asked. "It's going to get colder than this."

"I handed most of them out to the kids, but there are a few left."

Carina returned to the passenger cabin with Bryce. The shuttle would take them to their destination with no more help from her. In the cabin, Castiel and Nahla were asleep. Bryce had put blankets over them. The twins were also nodding off, wrapped in each other's arms under their blanket. Parthenia had Darius on her lap and she was whispering in his ear. No doubt she was telling him a story to help calm his fears.

Bryce handed Carina a blanket. "You know, two bodies are warmer than one."

She lifted a corner of her lip, but he was right. She searched for and found the weapons. She wanted to keep them close in case Castiel managed to escape his bonds. Carina and Bryce sat together and tucked the blankets around themselves. The cold was biting deeply. Carina's head was so cold, she laid it on Bryce's shoulder and lifted the blanket right over herself. After another adjustment of the blankets, they were both ensconced in darkness, the warmth of their bodies contained within the space.

She couldn't remember the last time she'd been close to another person in this way, not as a casual hookup. Though the warnings of her grandmother would probably haunt her forever, she thought she could get used to it.

Bryce's breathing was steady and regular. He'd fallen asleep. She felt herself drifting off too. The terrifying, harrowing events of the day were slipping away from her. Her mind was shifting to the future. It was uncertain, but at least they were free.

———

The days that followed as the shuttle crawled toward its destination were both boring and tense. Military craft were not fitted out to entertain children, and even if the vessel had contained toys and other distractions, the atmosphere wasn't conducive to play. Castiel's seething hatred of them all seemed to grow stronger every hour, and Nahla was morose and withdrawn. Carina would have loved to entice the little girl away from her brother but she wasn't interested, preferring to dwell in his overbearing shadow.

Even eating didn't provide any momentary interest. The rations stowed aboard the shuttle were enough for a much larger group of adult men and women, but they were bland, nothing more than calorie input.

The death of their mother and the excruciatingly painful murder of their father had thrown a pall over the children that Carina worried might never lift. She also felt especially ill-equipped to help them. She had lost her mother too, and she didn't think she had ever gotten over the death of Nai Nai or the loss of her father many years ago. She hadn't recovered, only moved on. She didn't know when or if the children would ever move on from the tragic events of their early years.

As the days wore on, she was grateful for Bryce's warm, friendly, calm presence. He would make sure the children were well covered in blankets during the sleep periods. The shuttle was so cold, an exposed foot or hand would soon chill and wake the sleeper. Carina and Bryce slept together as they had that first night aboard, sharing the warmth of their bodies.

On the final night before they expected to arrive at Ostillon, Carina was awoken by someone shaking her shoulder. She opened her eyes to darkness, then remembered she'd put the blanket over her head. When she pulled it down, Darius was standing in the aisle, looking cold and scared.

"What's wrong?" Carina asked. The rest of the children were sleeping. Bryce woke and sat up.

"The shuttle wants to tell you something," Darius said.

"What?"

"The shuttle was talking, but no one was listening to it, and it stopped."

Carina stared at her little brother for a moment as she came to her senses and tried to figure out what he was talking about. "The shuttle...? Oh, you mean there was a message broadcasting in the pilot's cabin?"

When Darius nodded, she leapt out of her seat and ran into the cabin. A message could mean many things, most of them bad. The shuttle might have been reporting a critical failure, or that someone had fired on them, or... The vessel juddered. Carina cursed. Then she saw where they were and her heart rose a little. Perhaps they weren't screwed after all.

"What is it?" Bryce asked, coming into the cabin.

"We're about to be boarded."

"Shit."

"I know. But the good news is, we're at Ostillon."

She ran out into the passenger area and found the jug of elixir. Metallic scrapings sounded along the hull. The children were waking up. She only had a minute or two at most. Carina ran back to the pilot's cabin and looked at the image of Ostillion on the screen. They were over a large landmass, thank goodness. She had no idea what the conditions were like down there. She just had to hope they weren't too harsh to survive.

"Carina," said Bryce. "What are you doing?"

"I'm going to Transport everyone down to the surface." She pushed past him. The distance to the surface was great, but she could manage it, providing she had enough elixir. She took a swallow, closed her eyes and focused. She couldn't send everyone together, but she could send them in pairs so they wouldn't be alone.

"Where are we?" Castiel said. "Unfasten these straps!"

Carina wrote the character and sent it out. When she opened her eyes, empty straps hung where Castiel and Nahla had been sitting. They were gone.

"Oriana and Ferne," Carina said, "get ready. You're next."

The twins held each other and nodded.

"Wait," Carina said. "Take something of Parthenia's. When you're on the planet, make some elixir and Cast Locate to find her."

Parthenia removed a bracelet and pushed it into Oriana's hands. Carina took another large swallow of elixir. She wrote the character, and the twins were gone. Wrenching sounds were coming from the airlock.

"You take one too," Parthenia said, giving Carina her other bracelet.

She put it in her pocket and gulped down some more elixir. She was feeling faint with the non-stop Casting. "Darius, go to Parthenia."

"But I want to—"

"Now!"

A jolt rocked the ship. The boarders had to have the outer airlock open.

Darius threw Carina a sulky look and stomped over to Parthenia, who held out her hand for him. Carina closed her eyes. When she opened them, her oldest and youngest siblings had disappeared.

Brilliant lights shone from the direction of the airlock.

"Get ready, Bryce," Carina said. She looked down into the jug of elixir. There was only a little left. Not enough to Transport two people safely.

Bryce registered her expression. "What's wrong?"

"Nothing," she replied, upending the jug to tip the remaining drops into her mouth.

"Carina, wait," said Bryce. "Don't you dare—"

He was gone. The cabin was empty. She put down the jug and picked up the weapons.

DARK MAGE RISES

ONE

As Carina Lin returned to consciousness, she struggled. Her wrists and ankles were tied and a gag was wrapped tightly around her face.

The hard floor she lay upon was vibrating ever so slightly, indicating she was aboard a starship. Wriggling around and pushing with her elbows and knees, she maneuvered herself to a sitting position. The room she found herself in wasn't much larger than a clothes closet and it was entirely bare. The door was smooth and featureless with no way to open it from the inside. She'd clearly been put in some kind of holding cell for prisoners, so the vessel was a military craft. Was that preferable to a criminal outfit, like human traffickers? She didn't think so.

Though she hadn't been able to get a good look at the attackers who had boarded the shuttle she'd stolen, she had a strong feeling they were the very last people she wanted to meet.

The last people she ever wanted to see again were the Sherrerrs. After her mother's experiences at the hands of those arrogant, aggressive meatheads, Carina was certain that if she encountered another Sherrerr before she died it would be far too soon. She doubted they would say the same about her. The clan would be very happy to have their shuttle back and a family of mages returned to their control. Yet there was another faction in that galactic sector that posed an even greater threat.

She had no idea how much time had passed since she'd been stunned. Perhaps an hour or longer, judging by how stiff and sore she was from lying on the hard floor. She recalled a brief battle, during which she'd managed to wound three of the shuttle's boarders. It was the last thing she remembered before waking up.

She waited, leaning against the wall with her knees drawn up, reflecting that her captors' decision to gag her seemed a particularly stupid move. What did they think she was going to do, shout her way to freedom? Then she recalled that time she'd bitten Stefan Sherrerr's neck. If she'd only managed to sink her teeth a little deeper, she might have killed her mother's rapist and torturer. She smiled grimly. Perhaps a gag was a good idea after all.

She twisted her hands and feet, attempting to improve the blood flow to her extremities. When would her kidnappers come for her and what would they do? Her thoughts turned to her half-siblings. She'd managed to Transport them all to the planet surface, using up the last of the elixir. Little Darius would be safe with Parthenia, her oldest half-sister. The twins, Ferne and Oriana, were together too. And nasty Castiel, who was a couple of years younger than Parthenia, was with his sister-acolyte Nahla.

She recalled Castiel's claims that he possessed mage powers, and shuddered. Parthenia, Ferne, Oriana, and Darius could be trusted to uphold the mage philosophy of never intentionally hurting anyone, but Castiel could not. If he was telling the truth, she dreaded what he might do. He was as evil as his father had been.

She'd been forced to Transport her friend, Bryce, alone to the surface, but he would be okay. He would find a way to return to his family on Ithiya. She was more worried about her mage brothers and sisters. They'd been brought up in sheltered luxury and hadn't developed the skills required to survive in a harsh environment. Even more dangerous to them was the fact that they didn't have any practice at concealing their mage skills. Ma had known all about the dangers of revealing her abilities to strangers, yet she'd still been captured and subjected to a life of enslavement and misery. What chance did the woman's naive offspring have?

If Carina escaped she had to protect them, but it would be hard to find them. Parthenia had given Carina one of her bracelets to help Locate her, but the kidnappers had taken it. Everything had been taken from her except her clothes. Parthenia had also given one of her bracelets to the twins, so at least they would be able to reunite with her. Maybe with the four of them working together they might remain safe.

As well as worrying about them, Carina already missed her brothers and sisters. In the few weeks she'd spent with Parthenia and her other mage siblings, she'd grown to love them. Only a few months ago, she hadn't even known she had a family.

If they ever got the chance to be together again, she would take them on a journey to find Earth, the planet where mages were rumored to have originated. In that remote place they might create a sanctuary where all mages could live openly without fear of capture. For the moment, however, that was all a dream.

Carina sighed and tried to clear her mind of gloomy thoughts. Escape was what she needed to focus on. There was a slim chance she was wrong about whose ship she was on. If she wasn't wrong, there was an even slimmer chance her captors wouldn't discover she'd crossed them in the past. She was in need of a lot of luck.

A metallic click sounded, and the door slid open. A man in uniform entered. His head was shaved, making it difficult to tell his age, though from his bearing he appeared to be a high-ranking officer. As he stepped closer, she saw the starburst insignia on his collar. Her luck was all out. He was working for the Dirksens.

The guard who entered behind him was carrying a chair. After she set the chair down, the officer waved her away. The door closed and the man sat, crossing his legs. As far as Carina could see, he wasn't armed. He was alone with a prisoner but carried nothing to defend himself. That didn't seem very smart, but before making a move, she waited to hear what he had to say.

The officer leaned forward, resting his elbows on his knees. He said nothing, only gazed at her. She returned his gaze. She wasn't cowed, if that was his intention. She had endured plenty of intimidation and beatings in her eighteen years. She could endure some more, and she would take her revenge if she got the chance.

The officer held eye contact for a while, not blinking.

"Eeeeennnnnoooor-e?" she asked through her gag.

He got to his feet, took two steps over to her and pulled it off. He then returned to his seat. "What did you say?"

"I said, is this a new torture method?" She worked her mouth to ease its dryness. "Because it isn't very effective."

A corner of the man's mouth lifted but then his eyes turned serious again. "I know your kind. We could go through the usual steps: I could ask you what you were doing aboard a Sherrerr shuttle, days from the site of a recent battle, yet not wearing a Sherrerr uniform. You'll stoically refuse to answer me. I'll tell the guard to rough you up a bit. You'll still refuse to respond. I'll threaten more pain and humiliation but after the guard does her job again, your lips will remain sealed. And so on and on. All very messy and distasteful and ultimately unlikely to bring either of us any satisfaction."

He tilted his head before continuing, "I know *you*. Where do I know you from?"

Carina's stomach clenched. This was it. She was going to be identified, and then everything would be over. It was a shame she wouldn't see her family again.

The officer leaned forward and peered at her. "I'm right, aren't I? I do know you."

Damn. He'd read her reaction to his words in her face. Carina fought to calm herself and clear her mind as Nai Nai had taught her. This interrogation was turning out to be harder than she'd expected. Pain, she could withstand. This officer's methods were subtler.

"Hmm... Shut down your emotional response, have you?" he asked. "So you've been trained to do that. Perhaps you rank highly in the Sherrerr forces. Maybe you're a spy. That might explain some anomalies." His gaze roamed her features closely. "Yet you're too young to be a high-ranking officer. You're even younger than you look, I think."

Carina watched him defiantly yet didn't trust herself to respond, not knowing what he might interpret from her words. She wasn't going to hand answers to him on a plate.

His dark eyes were thoughtful. "Don't have anything to say? You were quite talkative a moment ago, trying to speak even though you were gagged. Do you find my observations unsettling? I've caught you unprepared, haven't I? You were expecting something quite different, and I've shocked you into silence. Not so cocky now, huh?"

The officer stood and straightened his pants. "You're quite the enigma, but that's fine. I enjoy a puzzle. I'll figure you out." He rapped the door with a knuckle and was let out.

As the door closed she cursed. It was childish, she knew, but she wished she'd thought up a smart comeback to the smug bastard's assertions. He'd been right about nearly everything. Though he hadn't raised a hand to her, she felt defeated somehow. Even his lack of a weapon had been an attack, she realized, and he'd won. He'd been demonstrating that she posed no threat to him. He'd been right. His words had disarmed her.

Had he seen a vid of the attack at Orrana? Was that how he knew her? It had to be. The Dirksens never forgave anyone who opposed them. Carina had known that when she'd agreed to take on the job with her merc band. Though she would never for a second regret what she'd done, her past was catching up to her.

The Dirksen officer was clever. He would discover what she'd done sooner or later, though what would happen then depended on what else piqued his curiosity. He reminded her a little of Calvaley, a Sherrerr commander who had deluded himself into believing he was fighting an ethical war for the betterment of human civilization.

The smart ones were the worst enemies, not those who were naturally aggressive, belligerent, and evil. People like Calvaley and the Dirksen officer were intelligent enough to weigh up the pros and cons of what they were doing, yet do it anyway.

She shivered. She was sunk.

———

Hours of boredom took the edge off her tension, and eventually she dozed. Some time later—she didn't know exactly how much time had passed—the door opened again. The shaven-headed, dark-eyed Dirksen officer came in carrying an interface and looking pleased with himself.

She eyed the screen with dread. She knew exactly what he was about to show her. How should she respond? She had no idea how to react to make things go better for her. She didn't think there was a reaction that might have that effect.

"I knew I'd seen you before," the officer said. "I have a good memory for faces, but even so, I wouldn't have recognized you if you hadn't taken off your helmet."

Taken off your helmet?

"No need to fake looking puzzled," said the officer. "Or maybe you aren't faking. It doesn't matter. The resemblance is unmistakable."

Her stomach dropped as she remembered the moment she'd removed her helmet. This was looking worse than she'd hoped.

The officer dragged his chair over and sat down before holding the screen in front of her face. "Does this look familiar?"

The scene was indeed familiar. The interface showed the interior of the smelting plant on Orrana. Her merc band had been tasked with rescuing a kidnapping victim from there—the Dirksens had abducted a Sherrerr child.

She had thought the Dirksens might have vids of the first attack on the plant, when her band had gone in through the reception, but this scene was from the second attack after the first had failed. She was looking at the room where the Dirksens had held the child, the boy she'd later come to know was her half-brother, Darius.

A soldier burst in. It was herself, wearing merc armor.

She watched calmly, trying not to betray any emotion. In the vid, the soldier squatted down, and as the camera tracked her movement the kidnapping victim came into view. Little Darius looked even more terrified than she remembered, and it was no wonder. The Dirksen thugs had tortured him to try to make him confess his mage powers—unsuccessfully. Her brother was a tough young man.

But at that moment, he'd been frozen with fear. So to show him she wasn't as scary as she looked, she'd... There it was. The soldier took off her helmet.

The Dirksen officer paused the vid. He was smiling. "Those helmet visors make it impossible to identify faces. Thanks for making it easier for me. So you aren't a Sherrerr. You're a merc, though why you were aboard a Sherrerr shuttle remains to be revealed."

She didn't reply. She couldn't stand the man's gloating, and she shrank from what was probably coming next along with all its repercussions.

"But that isn't all, is it?" said the officer. "You aren't just a merc who took on a bad job. You know, that's what I like about you. You're so interesting. Right. I'll show you what I mean. I won't bore you with the slow bits." He forwarded the vid, skipping over the part where Carina persuaded Darius to come with her and they left the room. "Here it is." He slowed the vid to normal speed. "You carry the boy to a vent. Smart move. He would have been hurt if you'd tried to take him through the fire fight going on at the stairs. Your band's shuttle was up on the roof, and you figured you could climb through the network to reach it, didn't you? Only things were getting heated. You had a limited amount of time to reach the roof or your companions might have died waiting for you. One of them did die, in fact, I think."

Her heart ached. Poor Captain Speidel.

"Sorry," said the officer, "I didn't mean to bring back bad memories."

"Get to the point," she said between her teeth.

"I'm getting there, my young conundrum. No need to rush me. So, let's see. This is the time stamp for when you took the kid into the vent. Then here you are on the roof, only seconds later. You didn't have time to climb through the vent tunnels, especially with a kid encumbering you. So how did you manage it?"

She didn't reply. She'd Cast Transport in order to get Darius and herself up to the roof before the shuttle left.

"What a pity we didn't have surveillance cameras inside the vent system, huh?" the officer asked. "I would have loved to see exactly what you did. We had the boy because we guessed the Sherrerrs were pulling some weird shit. It looks like we were right, and that whatever it is, you can do it too. Is that why you were running from the Sherrerrs? Did you get tired of meeting their demands?"

When she remained silent, he went on, "Thanks for not insulting my intelligence by claiming ignorance. I appreciate it. I wish I could extend you some mercy in gratitude. Unfortunately, that isn't going to be possible. We lost the Sherrerr boy, but now we have you instead. And after that attack on our shipyard, my superiors are keener than ever to find out what this strange ability is. I can assure you they'll be expecting you to use it in their favor."

Two

The vibrations coming through the floor ceased. It had been several long hours since the Dirksen officer had left Carina's holding cell, but it looked like something was about to happen, and probably to her.

She wasn't certain where the ship was. So much time had elapsed since she'd been captured that it might not be at Ostillon, where she'd Transported her siblings and Bryce. The Dirksen vessel could have traveled to another planet or even to another system. Or it might only have been in orbit all the time.

What were the Dirksens even doing on Ostillon, if that was where the ship had stopped? According to the scant information she had managed to discover, the planet was one of two inhabited worlds in the Floria System, which was way off the main routes. As far as she'd been able to tell the system wasn't under Dirksen or Sherrerr control. Neither clan had taken an interest in the place, so it was officially 'disputed territory.'

Whatever the reason was for Dirksens to be lurking there, she guessed she might soon find out. Once more, her powers had placed her in a dangerous position. After witnessing what had happened to her mother after her abilities were discovered, she was prepared to fight to the death to avoid the same fate.

She waited tensely for what seemed an age before the door to her holding cell finally opened. This time, she didn't see the dark-eyed Dirksen officer. Two guards had arrived. One of them unfastened her ankle restraints and pulled her roughly to her feet. He grabbed her upper arm and pushed her forward. A hard metal edge was pushed into her head from behind. It was the muzzle of the other guard's gun.

"I understand, you know, language," she said as they forced her through the cell doorway. Her remark earned her a knock on her skull from the muzzle. It wasn't hard enough to daze her but she felt a trickle of blood run down her neck. Before another smart remark could slip out, Carina bit her tongue. Bravado wasn't going to help her escape and it wouldn't ease her tension either.

As the guard's hand fastened tightly around her bicep, he urged her along a corridor so fast she was almost running. The vessel was, as she'd guessed, a modestly sized military craft. The interior was bare, featureless metal, and she could hear the tramp of booted feet. She was probably inside a patrol ship. The Dirksens had been surveying the system for unscheduled arrivals of suspicious spacecraft. The stolen Sherrerr shuttle had been an obvious target.

A bright light shone ahead, and as they rounded a corner she saw it was daylight. They'd arrived at an exit ramp that led out onto the planet surface. The patrol ship was even smaller than she'd thought. Few space worthy ships could land and take off through a planet's atmosphere. She must have paused in surprise because the guard grunted, "Move," and pushed her down the ramp.

She caught a glimpse of a spaceport and a city before she was forced into the back of a ground transport. The door slammed, leaving her in total darkness on the floor of the vehicle. It lifted off the ground and then accelerated fast. She had been half-crouching. The sudden movement made her stumble. Her wrists remained tied, preventing her from saving herself. She hit the floor.

She was about to sit up when an idea occurred to her. It was a long shot but worth trying. Though she couldn't see a thing, she remembered where the door was. Lying on her back, she lifted both her legs and drove them hard against it. The door held firm, however.

Having nothing better to do as the journey progressed, she kicked the door again and again until a voice from the front of the vehicle growled, "Cut it out or I'll come back there and stun you."

She gave the door a final, defiant kick but then lay still, panting with exertion. She was uncomfortable lying on her tied arms so she turned onto her front. Where was she being taken? What Dirksen figure of importance was she about to meet? Would he be like Stefan Sherrerr, more monster than human being? What would the Dirksens do to her when they attempted to force her to reveal her mage powers?

She knew only one thing for sure: she would never admit to her ability to Cast. The minute she did that, her life would be over. The Dirksens would never rest until they compelled her to do what they wanted, by whatever means necessary. She recalled the time Stefan Sherrerr had forced her to raise a tidal wave against Dirksen troops, killing who knew how many of them. A clean fight was different. Mage powers were not supposed to be destructive.

She refused to live a life of shame and dishonor.

While waiting for the journey to end, she tried to recall what she'd seen of the city outside the spaceport before she'd been pushed into the transport. The metropolis had looked surprisingly high tech for a backwater place. Her home planet had also been in the middle of nowhere and life there had barely been above subsistence level. Other out-of-the-way locations she'd visited when working as a merc had been similar. Even the Sherrerr stronghold, Ithiya, had been provincial. She'd heard of highly developed places toward the center of the galactic sector, but she hadn't ever visited one.

Her glimpse of the cityscape had revealed tall blocks in many complex designs. Some had been decorated with vegetation and walkways linked the sections. She'd also seen small private transports flying between the blocks.

The vehicle turned a corner quickly, throwing her across the floor, and then a short while later it halted. A door at the front opened and slammed. The one she'd been kicking also opened. She looked past her feet, squinting in the sudden light. A burly man stood outside. She guessed he was the owner of the growly voice. Beyond him hovered an expensively dressed woman. Her expression reminded Carina of a type of bug she used to keep as a child. The beady-eyed insects had always been ready to pounce on whatever prey happened by, and the woman looked the same. Carina didn't relish the idea of being her prey.

The burly man reached in and grabbed her tied wrists before pulling her out of the vehicle in one smooth motion. She landed on her knees on the dusty ground and blinked in the piercing sunlight.

"Now then, Harmon," the woman said. "Not so rough, please. Help the girl up."

Harmon gripped her elbow and yanked her to her feet. They were under a wide awning outside a large residence. The city she'd seen at the spaceport had gone. The house seemed to be in the middle of nowhere, in fact. She was disheartened. If she managed to escape, she would have plenty of country to cross to reach an urban area.

"Come inside, dear," the woman said. "I do hope the guards haven't treated you too badly. They can be overzealous at times." She turned toward the entrance but then glanced back and said, "Remove her restraints, Harmon. How ridiculous."

Carina blinked again, though this time it wasn't due to the bright sunlight. The reception she was receiving wasn't at all what she'd expected. Harmon unfastened her wrist ties and, now that his mistress's back was turned, shoved Carina toward the door.

After another glance around—noting she wouldn't get five meters before Harmon could stun her—Carina followed the bug-like woman into the mansion. Harmon remained one step behind all the way to a lounge, where the woman invited Carina to sit. He hovered at her side until he was ordered, rather shrilly, to step back and "give the poor girl room to breathe."

"You must be exhausted," the woman continued. "I'll order some refreshments then Harmon will show you up to your apartment. I insist that you rest a while, for as long as you need. We can talk business later."

Carina was beginning to wonder if she was unconscious and dreaming. Perhaps she hadn't come around yet from being stunned on the Sherrerr shuttle. Perhaps the dark-eyed officer didn't exist. Or maybe she was still asleep on the Dirksen patrol ship.

"You seem confused," said the woman. "That's entirely understandable. Let me introduce myself. I am Langley Dirksen."

Perhaps Carina wasn't going mad after all.

"And it's my intention to make your life as comfortable as possible."

On the other hand...

Langley Dirksen lifted a comm to her lips and spoke softly, ordering food and drinks. When she finished she looked up at Carina and said, "And you are...?"

Carina was so taken aback at the situation, she almost gave her name as a reflex. But instead she clamped her lips shut.

"Of course," Langley Dirksen said, "I understand." Her tone carried a hint of iciness that betrayed the politeness of her words. She folded her hands in her lap, resting them on the fine, pale-green, silky fabric of her dress. After a moment, she said, "Well, this is awkward, isn't it? I hope that we can be friendlier over the coming days. I'm sure we will be. Oh, here we are."

A maid trolley had arrived carrying snacks and glasses of drink. It trundled to Carina first. While she was tempted to kick the thing over and make a run for it, she knew that was pointless. Besides, she was famished and thirsty. She seized several plates, piling them on her lap before grabbing two full glasses. After downing one glass of a syrupy but refreshing juice, she bit into a pink confection and swallowed it in two mouthfuls.

Carina was dimly aware of Langley's gaze upon her. The Dirksen woman probably disapproved of her lack of manners, but then from the look of her Langley hadn't ever starved. Carina wasted little time with concerns about what impression she was giving. After quickly finishing the snacks on her lap, she retrieved the remaining ones from the trolley. Carina wasn't waiting for Langley to help herself. She'd had her chance.

The snacks were light and not intended to supply much energy, Carina guessed. Then she abruptly stopped eating. What if the food was drugged?

"Aren't you going to eat anything?" she asked Langley.

"I'm not hungry," Langley replied, looking gratified that Carina had finally spoken.

"Eat something," said Carina. "Or make him." She looked at Harmon, who still hung around like a bad smell.

Langley sighed. "Harmon, have a snack."

Harmon reached into the trolley and picked out a pale yellow cake in the shape of a flower. He popped the entire thing into his mouth and chewed solemnly. After observing him, Carina proceeded to eat the rest of the snacks. When she'd finished, she burped.

"Well, you certainly were hungry, weren't you?" said Langley.

Carina drank her second drink and returned the empty glass to the trolley. "I don't know why you've brought me here, but I take it if I try to leave, Harmon might have something to say about it."

"He might indeed, and so may the many other Harmons who patrol my estate. But we're starting off on the wrong foot. As I see it, there's no need for us to be on opposite sides. We can have a mutually beneficial relationship."

"If that's the case," Carina replied, "I suggest that, as a gesture of good faith, you allow me the freedom to leave."

"Hmm... Not just yet. You're tired and you've been treated badly no doubt by those military types who picked you up. Please, rest for a while. When you've recovered, we can talk business. Harmon, show our friend to her apartment."

Carina didn't have much choice except to do as Langley Dirksen directed, though she distrusted the woman's fine words. Even if Langley's intentions were currently noble and she really did want to strike up a fair deal in exchange for Carina using her mage powers—which Carina doubted—the woman's attitude would soon change. That was what knowledge of a mage's abilities did to people. It turned them into envious, exploitative, evil monsters like Stefan Sherrerr.

Whatever good treatment she received, Carina would never admit she was a mage. And when Langley Dirksen finally realized she wasn't going to get anything, her reaction would show just how well-intentioned she really was.

Meanwhile, Carina worried what would happen to Parthenia and the others. How were they going to survive? She hoped they would have the sense to never let anyone know they could Cast.

THREE

"Can we Cast Transport to bring us some food?" Darius asked.

He'd asked the same question twice already, but Parthenia guessed her little brother didn't remember. She couldn't expect a six year old to have a good memory. And he was probably as hungry as she was, if not hungrier, and very tired. "Well, we don't have any elixir, and we would need to see the food, or at least know exactly where it was. You know that. And it would be stealing."

She pushed aside a low branch of a tree that stood in their way and let Darius go ahead of her. They were following some kind of track through the forest. She wasn't sure what had made the track, but she hoped it was human.

"Would it be stealing?"

"Yes, it would because it would be taking something that doesn't belong to us. I know that when we went into town the store owners would let us take whatever we wanted, but that was because Father made them. Most people can't do that. Most people have to pay for food with money. We don't have any money."

"Oh. How do we get money?"

"I don't know yet. Maybe we can work. That's how most people get money." The truth was, Parthenia didn't know what they were going to do. Somehow, they would have to make a new life and it would very different from the one they'd been used to. She didn't even know how to begin. All she knew was that the first step was to reunite with their mage siblings since Carina had been forced to Transport them all separately from the shuttle to the planet surface. They had to find each other again.

She'd been waiting for hours to hear from Carina or perhaps Ferne or Oriana. She'd given one of her bracelets to her older sister and another to her twin siblings. They should be able to use a bracelet of hers to Locate her and then Send a message. Then they could all meet up and together they could decide what to do. She guessed Oriana and Ferne were having the same difficulty as her with creating elixir in the middle of nowhere, but Carina was resourceful and smart. She would have made contact sooner.

Darius hadn't spoken for a while, which was unusual. He was looking worried. She gripped her youngest brother's hand tighter. "Don't fret. Carina will Cast Send soon. I'm sure she will. Until then, we'll keep on walking and trying to find our way out of this place, okay? Carina wouldn't want us to just sit around waiting to be rescued, would she?"

Darius said, "No, I don't think so. But what if she doesn't Cast Send? What do we do then?"

"Carina would never abandon us, Darius. I mean, she wouldn't forget about us if she knew we needed her."

The little boy nodded. "When the bad men took me, she came and found me."

"That's right. She'll find us too, but it might take a while. So let's see how brave we can be and find out all the things we can do without her help." Her skirt caught on a thorn and ripped. "Oh, wait a minute." As she carefully pulled the cloth away the back of her hand brushed another thorn, receiving a scratch. "Ow!" Parthenia sucked on the drops of blood oozing from the wound.

"Does it hurt?" Darius asked, standing on his tiptoes to try to see her hand. "I could Cast Heal. Oh no, I can't. Are you sure you don't know how to make elixir?"

"I do know. I just don't know how to make it out here. I don't know how to start a fire, for one thing."

Darius came down from his tiptoes and hung his head. "I miss Carina."

"I do too." Parthenia took her brother's hand again and they continued walking. The barely visible thread of worn ground wound through the undergrowth. Sunlight slanted through the tree branches. Parthenia guessed it would be several hours before the sun set. She hoped Carina would find them before then. She didn't want to spend the night alone in the forest. They hadn't seen or heard anything except bugs and some kind of arboreal creature that had swung away as they approached, and then climbed high and flew. Maybe animals that preyed on humans lived here.

It had been hours since they'd arrived on the planet, and they'd been walking ever since. Parthenia's legs were aching. Darius was probably even more tired, though he hadn't mentioned anything except his empty stomach. Deciding it was time to call a halt and let her brother rest, she said, "Hey, let's stop for a while. Let's find somewhere to sit down." She led Darius off the track and over to a gap between two tall trees where nothing else grew. She sat him down on a root that protruded from the ground.

"I'm thirsty, Parthenia." Darius squashed his little body into the scant remaining space on the root.

She sighed. "Me too." If only Carina would Send soon. Perhaps she might even Transport herself here and then take them both to a safe place. Her talk about showing her sister how brave they could be had been just that—talk. She didn't feel at all brave. She'd begun to realize how ill-prepared they were to live an ordinary life in the real world.

As she'd been growing up, Parthenia had gradually come to understand she led an unusual life. It was only through reading books and during brief visits to the local town and even briefer visits to the capital she'd realized other people didn't live in large estates and have everything they needed given to them. Although her father had been very controlling and had treated her mother worse than an animal, Parthenia had never been hungry or deprived of material things. She'd slept in a comfortable bed every night and the only work she'd had to do was schoolwork, making elixir, and Casting.

If she was ever sick a splicer would come to the house to treat her, and she'd always worn expensive dresses and had all the toys, paints, interfaces, and other playthings she wanted. She'd even had her own pet. Thinking back to the tarsul she'd left behind on Ithiya, Parthenia suddenly felt so sad she wanted to cry. But she didn't want to upset Darius with her tears so she swallowed and bit her lip.

"What's wrong?" her brother asked. He climbed into her lap, though he barely fit there anymore.

"Nothing. I'm all right," Parthenia replied.

Darius wrapped his arms around her neck and rested his head on her shoulder. "No, you aren't."

There had never been much point in trying to hide emotions from Darius, Parthenia reflected. He always knew what you were feeling, whether you admitted it or not.

Now they'd stopped walking for a while, she was growing cold. They were wearing the thin clothes they'd worn aboard the battleship, and they'd left the shuttle so quickly Parthenia hadn't even thought to grab the emergency blankets they'd been using to stay warm on the chilly ship.

"It's time we started walking again," Parthenia said. "Have you rested enough?"

"I guess so," Darius replied, getting up, though Parthenia heard the tiredness in his voice. "But where are we going? Are we nearly there?" They set off again.

"I was hoping we might find a way out of these woods," said Parthenia. "If we can find a house or a small town, maybe someone will give us some money for my bracelet." She hadn't thought of the idea until she said it. She'd only been intending to make something up to distract Darius from his hunger and thirst for a while. But it was actually a good plan.

Carina might take a long time to find them. They might even have to wait until tomorrow. Parthenia had one bracelet left. She wasn't sure how much it was worth, but she guessed it might be a lot of money. Father had always insisted his family had the finest of everything.

If they found other people, maybe she could sell them her bracelet for enough money to last them for days. But then the idea of encountering other people got her worrying. "Darius, if we do see anybody, we must remember what Mother told us."

"I know," her brother replied. "I won't tell them about Casting. I won't tell them we're—oh!" His foot had caught on a vine lying across the path. He fell hard into a patch of thorny plants and squealed as he tried to get up.

"Don't move," Parthenia exclaimed, fearing he was going to scratch himself some more.

Darius obediently stopped wriggling and lay still, looking up at his sister with tears running down his face.

"Keep still and I'll untangle you."

It took Parthenia several minutes to detach the thorns from Darius's clothes and skin, and she received plenty of scratches during the process. Eventually, however, she could finally stand the boy on his feet. His mouth was turned down and his chin trembled, though he'd finally stopped crying. He looked like he was at the end of his strength, yet he'd walked for hours with Parthenia without complaint.

"Would you like me to carry you?" she asked him.

Darius gave two firm nods and a small smile.

"Okay." Parthenia turned around and squatted down. "Climb aboard."

With her brother's legs tucked under her arms she continued down the track. She could feel him resting his head on her back and guessed he might soon fall asleep. She was tempted to stop so they could both lie down, but fear of what might happen while they were sleeping would probably keep her awake.

Parthenia pushed on through the undergrowth. She was beginning to think the track must have been made by animals. What would be the point of people walking so far in the forest? With her gaze focused on the vegetation ahead, she desperately hoped to see some sign of an end to it, but there was nothing visible except leaves, branches, and vines.

In fact, that part of the forest looked familiar. Had they come this way before? It was so hard to tell. Surely the track led somewhere, or had they been going in circles?

"Parthenia," said Darius, "what if Carina didn't Transport out of the shuttle? What if the people who were coming aboard caught her?"

"Don't be silly," Parthenia replied. "Of course that didn't happen. Carina wouldn't let them capture her." It was a possibility Parthenia wasn't willing to entertain. The idea they might have to survive without their oldest sister's help on a world where they knew no one was horrifying. Even if Ferne and Oriana managed to find them, the four of them wouldn't be much better off together than apart.

How would they get money? After she sold her bracelet, Parthenia didn't know what else she could do. She didn't know how to work at a job. Everything she'd learned in her classes had been academic or oratorical. She didn't have any simple skills like cooking or cleaning or fixing broken tech. All she could do was Cast, and doing that would extremely risky. From what she could understand, that was why Father had treated Mother so badly. He'd used her because she was a mage. She hadn't wanted to marry him. Mother must have been married before because Carina had a different father. Parthenia had never found out what had happened to him.

"Are you sure Carina Transported off the shuttle?" Darius asked. "She wasn't caught?"

"I'm sure. I don't know how long it'll take her to find us, but she will. So don't worry about it, okay?"

"Okay. I won't."

Parthenia pushed the prospect of trying to survive without Carina's help far from her mind. Her sister would come. She had to. Parthenia couldn't look after Darius all by herself. She couldn't keep them both safe on her own.

Darius said, "I wish we could Cast Transport to bring some food."

Four

Carina waited five minutes before trying to open the door from the suite in the Dirksen mansion. Predictably, it was locked. Harmon was probably outside too, she guessed. She was standing in the lounge of the suite, which also contained a bedroom and a bathroom. The first thing she'd done was to quickly search the rooms for ingredients to make elixir, but she was out of luck. Though there was plenty of wood and metal and she could get water by pretending she wanted a drink, there was no earth in the rooms or any way for her to make a fire.

She went to the lounge window. It was also locked and the square frames that held the panes were too small for her to squeeze through, assuming she could break the glass without someone hearing it. Outside, the grounds of the estate stretched to the horizon. No fences or walls broke the wide, flat parkland landscape. If she tried to cross it in daylight she would be spotted easily, and at night infrared sensors would pick up her body heat.

Carina wasn't about to let those facts stop her from trying to escape. The estate probably had a shuttle pad and a few private shuttles, or perhaps she could steal one of the hover vehicles used for transportation on this world. Turning from the window, she skimmed the room with her gaze.

She walked over to an internal wall and touched it, running her hands over the surface to find out how it was constructed. If the wall was only made of board, she might be able to break through it, though then she would have the problem of getting out of the house. On the other hand, she was only on the second floor. Perhaps she could make a hole in the external wall? Or maybe she could remove the entire window frame?

She peeled back the fabric wall covering and found plaster underneath. Using the metal base of an ornament to dig through plaster, she discovered the internal walls were made of bricks. She could chip away the mortar and remove the bricks, but it would take time. And she would have to choose a wall that didn't adjoin the main corridor or her efforts might be noticed. Perhaps she could make a hole into the room next to her bedroom. That room's window might be unlocked.

Carina continued through the suite, trying to figure out how she could slip away. But after half an hour's investigation she hadn't managed to find a quick escape route, though she'd thought up several plans. All of them would take time to execute, however. After her long confinement on the patrol ship and the journey to the Dirksen estate, she was exhausted. Carina lay down on the sumptuous bed. Worrying about her mage sisters and brothers, she fell asleep.

———

She woke to the sensation of someone gripping her shoulder. Reflexively, she punched where she guessed the person's head might be. Her fist connected with a skull. As she opened her eyes, she rose up and grabbed for the person's throat. It was muscly and thick—too thick for a proper grip with one hand. She grabbed it with her other hand too, though it ached from the punch.

Harmon's very surprised face swam into focus. He brought up his arms between hers and broke her grip before shoving her onto the bed. "Calm down, huh? I just wanted to wake you for dinner. You didn't answer when I knocked." As he turned away, he rubbed his head where she'd punched him. "I'll wait for you outside." He walked out of the bedroom, still rubbing his head.

Carina nursed her sore knuckles. She'd been deeply asleep and dreaming when Harmon had woken her. The threads of the dream were already slipping from her mind, but she recalled a large monster leaning over Darius. Somehow, she'd known the monster was her brother's father, Stefan Sherrerr, and he was taking him to whatever dark place he'd gone after he died.

She rubbed her upper arms, chilled even though the room was warm. Stefan Sherrerr had died a terrible death, and though he would never hurt Darius again she was concerned about how the little boy was faring. Parthenia would do her best to look after him but Carina still worried. None of her mage brothers and sisters would adapt easily to their new lives.

When she went into the lounge, Carina saw that night had fallen. She'd slept for hours. Clothes had been spread across the sofa: fine dresses, pants, and shirts, all her size. They were intended for her, no doubt. Was she supposed to change her clothes before going down to dinner? Carina sighed. She wasn't a doll for Langley Dirksen to dress up.

When she tried the door, it opened. Harmon was waiting in the corridor, his hands clasped in front of him. He looked her up and down. "You have to—"

"I go down like this or not at all," said Carina.

Harmon sneered and wordlessly gestured for her to go first. As he followed her, she said, "Is this your usual job around here, Harmon? Locking up young women? Your family must be proud." She smirked at him over her shoulder.

The burly man pushed her, forcing her to face forward. "You better shut up or I'll hurt you where it won't show."

When they reached the first floor, he guided her to a room for dining. Langley Dirksen was sitting at one end of a table and a man was sitting at the other. Carina thought this had to be Mr. Dirksen but then the man stood and turned to face her and she saw he was much younger than Langley. Though he was tall, he was an adolescent.

Langley's gaze drifted briefly down Carina's clothes and back up again before she forced a smile. "Thank you for joining us. I hope you slept well."

"No need to thank me," Carina replied. "I didn't have any choice about it. Harmon here woke me up with a slap and dragged me downstairs."

"Harmon!"

"Not true, ma'am. I believe our guest is trying to cause trouble."

Langley looked concerned. The young man stifled a small grin. He was her son, judging by the resemblance between the two.

"Please, join us," said Langley.

Carina pulled out a chair and sat down. She began piling food on her plate. "Tell me, is it normal around here to lock your guests in their rooms? I've never encountered that before and I was wondering if it's a local custom." She dug a fork into a pile of some kind of starchy vegetable and filled her mouth.

At this, Langley's son gave a brief snort of laughter before putting a hand over his grin. His mother glared at him before turning to Carina and saying, "Please believe me, I would not be doing this unless I felt it was necessary and beneficial to both of us in the long run."

Carina raised her eyebrows, chewed, and swallowed before lifting up another forkful of food. She wasn't going to allow this woman the satisfaction of thinking she was doing her a favor by locking her up. But Carina was hungry again. There was no point in passing up the opportunity to fill her belly while her future was so uncertain.

"Let me introduce you to my son," Langley said brightly. "This is Reyes."

Reyes nodded at Carina. His gaze briefly slipped back to his mother before turning down to his plate.

"Reyes is an inventor," said Langley. "Isn't that right, dear?" Reyes didn't look up but he gave a small nod. "He's so smart. I don't know where he gets it from."

Carina wondered what had happened to Reyes' father. No fourth place was set at the table. She didn't ask. Indulging in small talk would send the wrong signal. It would give Langley the impression that her behavior was acceptable.

A serving dish piled with meaty ribs sat in front of Carina. She picked one up and began to gnaw it.

Langley took a drink, appearing to attempt to quell anger or anxiety or perhaps both. "Shall we get down to business?" When Carina continued to ignore her she put down her glass and went on, "I will be entirely frank with you and I hope that in return you will show me the same respect.

"Firstly, I know something of what you can do, so there's no point in hiding it. I'm sure you're aware of the rivalry between the Dirksens and the Sherrerrs. In recent years, my clan has lost considerable ground to our competitors—business dealings, allegiances, military technology development, and so on. In many areas, the Sherrerrs have overwhelmed our interests. Some movement back and forth is to be expected, of course. We can't expect to win all the time. But certain events have been very odd. Businesses that had been loyal to us for generations suddenly made deals with the Sherrerrs—deals that were to their disadvantage. Secret military installations have been attacked and weapon prototypes stolen. These events were so remarkable, we paid one arms trader a lot of money to allow us to send a spy as his representative in a business deal.

"Obviously we couldn't implant any kind of bug on our spy. The Sherrerrs would have detected any tech immediately. All we had to go on was his report on the meeting after it took place on the Sherrerr stronghold on Ithiya. Interestingly, during the meeting he agreed to a deal that would eventually put the actual arms supplier out of business. Something odd had happened. The spy reported that the only abnormal thing he remembered was that a young woman had sat in on the meeting for no apparent reason. It was almost too preposterous to countenance, but we were forced to conclude that this young lady had done something to influence our spy's decision-making, causing him to sign up to an agreement no one in their right minds would accept."

Carina continued to eat, not allowing her expression to betray the thoughts whirring through her mind. She had a good idea of what had gone on in that meeting.

"Further reconnaissance efforts revealed the young woman lived on a country estate with her family," Langley said. "We watched the estate, curious about what it was the girl had done to influence our spy. When another child in the family left the estate's grounds, we took him for questioning."

You took him and tortured him. Carina fought to keep her features neutral. It was possible that Langley wasn't aware of what Dirksen thugs had done to Darius. Not that it was an excuse.

"Reyes, be quiet," Langley snapped.

The young man, who hadn't been making very much noise at all, put down his knife and fork.

"My dear," Langley said to her, "I know you rescued the boy. I've seen the vid. I also know that you have some kind of special ability too, and you became caught up with the Sherrerrs somehow. None of that matters to us. I don't want to be unreasonable about this, but we need your help. We're prepared to reward you handsomely if you will perform similar services to those the Sherrerr girl provided for her clan. That's all we're asking. And what you see around you is only a taste of the benefits you could enjoy if you agree."

All the while Langley Dirksen had been speaking, Carina had been eating. She was now full. She finally lifted her gaze to the older woman. "*If* I knew what the hell you were talking about, which I don't, do you really think it's reasonable to lock me up? Do you actually think someone you *kidnapped* is going to help you? That's got to be the craziest thing I ever heard. You Dirksens hauled me off my ship, locked me up, pushed me around, and forced me somewhere I didn't want to go.

"If you're as nice and reasonable as you make out, prove it. Let me go. You might as well, because it won't matter how long you keep me here, how much nice food you feed me, or how much fun Harmon has with me while your back's turned, I can't do whatever the hell it is you're asking me to do. You'll be wasting both our time if you don't let me walk out of here."

Langley smiled resignedly. "I can see it's going to take longer to persuade you than I thought. That's okay. I'm a patient woman. And when you finally do make the right choice, you'll see how sensible you've been."

FIVE

Carina had expected to spend the rest of the evening in her room and she'd been looking forward to using the time trying to figure out how to get out of here. But Langley Dirksen had other plans. After dinner was eaten, in silence—Reyes hadn't yet spoken—Langley announced they would be attending "Mech Battle."

Reyes punched the air. "Yes!" He paused and added, "I *can* go too, right?"

"You may," Langley replied graciously. "It will be good for you and our guest to get to know each other better."

Carina nearly dropped her glass. She darted a look at the young man, who seemed embarrassed by his mother's remark. Did Langley really imagine the two of them might strike up a romance? The idea was insane. Even if Reyes wasn't the son of her kidnapper, he was just a kid.

"You're joking, right?" she asked Langley. "And anyway, I don't want to go to your stupid event. I demand you release me. I haven't done anything wrong. I haven't committed any crimes and you have no right to hold me like this."

"Not committed any crimes?" Langley asked. "Well, maybe you aren't a criminal, but your situation might be better if you were. My dear, you were captured aboard a Sherrerr shuttle. You're worse than a criminal. You're an enemy prisoner." Her polite expression transformed to hostility. "You *have* no rights." Then the mask of politeness fell over her features again. "But let's not squabble. I'm not so foolish as to believe that compelling you to work for us is the best solution in the circumstances. Whatever we managed to force you to do, you would exert the minimum effort, and no doubt you would try to secretly sabotage your results.

"It would be to both our benefits if we can come to a mutually agreeable arrangement. I know you don't believe so at the moment, but it's true. As hard as it may be for you to accept, I don't want you to work under duress. And so, as an enticement, I would like you to see the kind of lifestyle you could live and the things you could have if you agree to use your abilities to help us." She looked again at Carina's worn, dirty clothes. "I take it you won't agree to change before we go?"

"No, I won't."

"Very well. We'll leave in five minutes or so. Reyes, please keep our guest entertained until then." Langley rose and left the room.

Carina picked up a gnawed rib and nibbled at the remnants of meat that clung to it, speculating what the kid might do. Harmon still hovered in the background, so Reyes would probably have to follow his mother's order. It looked like Langley ran the show and if Reyes didn't do as he was told the matriarch would soon hear about it.

Reyes looked about as uncomfortable as Carina had ever seen anyone look. After a few moments, he said, "She isn't as bad as she comes across, you know."

Carina put down her rib bone and gave a short laugh. "You mean your mom? That's some compliment. *Not as bad as she comes across.* I hope someone says that about me one day." She pushed back her chair and stood up, wiping her greasy hands on her pants. She glanced at the kid, who seemed to be chewing over her words. She'd been planning on ignoring the spoiled brat, but she reasoned that it wouldn't hurt to have a young, impressionable ally. "So, what's this Mech Battle we're going to? Mechs battling, I guess?"

Reyes's eyes lit up, either due to the mention of the event or Carina's willingness to speak to him. "It isn't exactly mechs. That would be boring. It's new inventions especially for fighting."

"You mean like weaponized armor?" Carina had heard of armor that was more like an exoskeleton and had weapons attached. Equipment like that had a place in some battles, but it wasn't generally used in the military. It was too bulky and it had marginally slower reaction times. A soldier in a mech suit was slower than a soldier in regular armor.

"Sometimes it's kind of like that," Reyes replied, "but you never know what it'll be until the competitors come into the pit. That's the fun of it. They can wear almost whatever they like. There are only a few rules. They can't use anything that might be dangerous to the audience, like explosives or projectiles. But that's about it."

Carina's interest was no longer feigned. She'd been in plenty of engagements. The idea of watching newly invented mechs fighting sounded interesting. "So who controls them?"

"I don't know to be honest. Men and women. That isn't important, is it? There are a few major sponsors of the battles. I guess they pay the fighters to compete."

"How dangerous is it?" Carina asked, imagining the fighters were probably ex-soldiers or mercs.

"Oh, pretty dangerous. People have died. It's rare that a fighter doesn't have to retire from the match due to injury."

Carina doubted the competitors were only paid a set fee. She'd encountered similar arrangements on other worlds. Usually, the fighters received a percentage of the house's take, and there was always gambling at such events. The fighters would be betting on themselves too. "How do they tell who's won?"

"That's easy. You know the winner when the first mech is incapacitated. As soon as a competitor can't fight back, the match is over."

"Should be interesting," Carina said, giving Reyes a conspiratorial wink. He grinned. It looked like she might have made a friend.

———

For her second journey by hover transport, Carina was allowed to sit up front. Her short conversation with Reyes had persuaded her to ditch her oppositional stance. Her defiance would only work against her. If Langley Dirksen believed she was on the verge of joining the Dirksens, she might become less vigilant.

A woman Carina hadn't seen before sat at the front of the vehicle, controlling it. Behind her sat Langley and her son. Harmon sat next to Carina in the back seat.

"I never heard of Dirksens living on this planet," Carina remarked. "I thought it was neutral territory."

"We were forced to move here after the Sherrerrs began to expand their range," Langley replied. "As far as I know, they aren't aware we've taken control of Ostillon, and that's how we'd like to keep it."

What had she meant by "taken control of Ostillon"? If the Dirksens' methods were like the Sherrerrs,' they'd probably enacted a military coup of the planet's government or governments, imposed harsh taxes on businesses and individuals, and recruiting local thugs into a militia, turning them against their own people and encouraging them to support themselves with protection money. She shuddered. There was no way she wanted to help the Dirksens, even to get back at the Sherrerrs who had allowed her mother's evil treatment.

However, she didn't mention her feelings to Langley. "What's your role in the Dirksen clan, if you don't mind me asking?"

"My, what a polite question," Langley replied. "I thought you could be nice if you tried. Well, I guess you might call me one of the inner circle. I'm responsible for many of our larger businesses, which is why I was very interested to hear about you." She turned in her seat to look Carina in the eyes. "Believe me, you could have received much worse treatment from some of my associates. Some would want revenge for the offenses we've suffered at the hands of the Sherrerrs in recent times. They would love the opportunity for someone to bear they brunt of their anger. Luckily for you, and I think for the rest of my clan too, you fell into my hands. Others might not understand how valuable you are to us unharmed and compliant. You would be wise to remember that if you aren't agreeable I won't be able to protect you from the rest of my clan forever."

Carina broke eye contact with the matriarch to look out the transport's window. Already she was under the threat of violence, torture, and whatever else the Dirksens had in store. So much for Langley's fine words.

The lights of the towers of the metropolis rose in the distance, a multicolored kaleidoscope. Hover transports moved across the city, shifting the pattern. "Has Ostillon always been this high tech? Or has it developed since the Dirksens' arrival?"

Langley had turned to face forward once more. "Ostillon has changed almost beyond recognition over the last few cycles. My clan generally hate to live in backward places without modern conveniences. Of course, some aspects of the older culture cling on. You'll see one example of it tonight. On our other stronghold worlds, the Mech Battle would never be allowed. It's far too uncivilized. But it's such a popular sport in Ostillon, it would have been counterproductive to outlaw it. Besides, it allows the population to vent some of the natural aggression they feel in response to our takeover."

By the time they arrived at the Mech Battle stadium, Carina's curiosity had risen further. If the contest was as riotous as Langley implied, she might have an opportunity to slip away. A crowd was a good place to hide. She was glad she hadn't changed into the fine clothes offered to her, which would have made her easier to spot.

They went through a private entrance in the back of the stadium directly to a small, empty box that overlooked a wide, dusty, very deep pit. The stadium was split into halves, with two tall walls separating the sides. Some of the audience was in the pit, though they were being rapidly evacuated, and the side shows set up at the edges were being dismantled. Though no fighting was yet taking place, the noise of the crowd was deafening. Twenty to thirty thousand people were present.

Harmon shut the door to the box and stood in front of it, his bulk almost covering its entire frame. The woman who had controlled the transport also remained in the box, sitting next to Carina. Langley had taken out an interface she was consulting, and Reyes sat at the front of the box, peering into the pit.

A compere spoke from somewhere Carina couldn't see, announcing that the first battle would commence in five minutes. Reyes asked his mother, shouting over the hubbub, "Who are you betting on tonight?"

"Spearcorps," she replied. "They did very well last time."

"Go Spearcorps," exclaimed Reyes, returning his gaze to the pit.

The ground shook, and what Carina had taken to be walls on each side of the stadium split down the center. The walls were massive gates, and through both strode the most amazing mech fighting machines she had ever seen.

Six

Parthenia was so tired she could barely stay upright. Darius had fallen asleep long ago as she carried him. He was resting against her back and she struggled to hold onto his relaxed body. He seemed ready to slip off at any moment.

It was so dark she could only just make out the shapes of the vegetation, yet she'd continued walking long after sunset, too frightened to stop and lie down to sleep. The narrow track they'd been following had disappeared in the darkness and she was going wherever she could pass between the trees. As dusk had fallen the noises of the forest had grown louder. *Things* were moving around her. Were they following her? Nothing had drawn close—yet. Were the night creatures only waiting for her to stop before they pounced? Her legs felt like they were on the verge of collapsing. She'd passed what she'd thought was the end of her strength hours ago. It was pure fear that kept her putting one foot in front of the other.

Thorns had torn her dress to rags. Whenever her clothing caught on one, she no longer stopped to remove it. She pulled herself free roughly, heedless of tears. She'd walked tens of kilometers, she guessed, farther than she'd ever walked. The forest had to be huge, unless she'd only walked in circles. She shook her head. She had to stop thinking about that and concentrate on reaching the end of the woods.

Why hadn't Carina Sent to her? She couldn't understand it. Had her sister decided to abandon her family? Parthenia knew that she and her siblings were a lot of bother. They weren't tough like Carina. They'd been coddled all their lives and didn't know how to do hardly anything for themselves. Perhaps Carina had decided she would be better off without them. It was true. She *would* be better off without them.

Parthenia had promised herself she wouldn't cry. Her arms were so tired from holding Darius's legs they trembled. Her back ached from bending over to prevent him from falling. Her leg muscles throbbed. She was also painfully hungry and thirsty. She'd wanted to be brave, but as she accepted that Carina might never come for them, tears spilled down her cheeks.

It seemed so unfair. She couldn't believe that after all their efforts to escape —from their dash through the corridors of the flagship *Nightfall* under fire, through the long chilly days aboard the shuttle, to being suddenly Transported to the middle of nowhere on a remote planet—everything would end for her and Darius on their first night by themselves. She wished they'd been able to stay with the others. She wouldn't have minded so much if she'd been with her family. But wishing wasn't going to change anything.

Parthenia had reached her limit. She was now walking so slowly she was barely moving. Whether she stopped or not, the night creatures could catch them if they wanted. She might as well stop, she guessed.

"Don't worry, Parthenia," said Darius sleepily. "Carina will come soon."

"I didn't know you were awake," Parthenia replied, comforted by the sound of her brother's voice close to her ear.

"Yes, I woke up. I want to get down now."

Parthenia bent her knees and Darius slipped off her back. The relief was wonderful. She stretched her arms.

"It's dark," said Darius. He moved closer and wrapped his arms around her.

"It's still night time," Parthenia replied. "Can you walk now? We should keep moving."

"Do we have some water yet?"

"No. But we've walked a long way. We must be nearly out of the forest now. If we carry on walking, we might find a house soon, and we can ask the people who live there for a drink." It was odd how trying to be positive for Darius's sake made her feel better. She thought she could manage to go a little farther now she was relieved of her brother's weight.

"Hmm..." The little boy looked around. "Okay." He took her hand and they set off again.

Darius's hand was cold. Parthenia was cold too, despite her physical exertion. That was another reason to keep going. If they stopped moving they might become dangerously chilled.

"What's that?" Darius asked. He was pointing off to his left.

Parthenia looked in the same direction but all she could see was the black shadows of trees. "I don't know what you're looking at. What can you see?"

"There's a light over there. Is it the house where we can get water?"

"A light! Where?"

"Right there," the little boy replied pedantically as if his sister were stupid.

"I can't..." Parthenia squatted down to her brother's level and followed the direction of his gaze. He was right. Through a gap in the vegetation a small blue light shined steadily in the distance. She hadn't been able to see it, but Darius was short enough to see the space. She gripped her brother's arms tightly. "It *is* a light. Good job, Darius. Good job. Let's go there, shall we?"

"Yes, let's get some water."

Traveling in the direction of the light proved hard, however. The trees were clumped together more tightly that way than any other, and they lost sight of the light several times as they went along. Trying to head toward the blue glow involved pushing past thick ferns and bushes, resulting in many scratches for both of them. At one point, they lost sight of the tiny light entirely and Parthenia almost gave up hope of ever finding it again. They were forced to double back a long way and try a different route. Eventually, though, the tree trunks and undergrowth thinned out and the blue spot grew nearer. As the wider landscape became more visible, Parthenia realized the beam was shining from the top of a tower and the base of the tower was somewhere below the level of the forest.

In his eagerness to reach the light and the water he desperately wanted, Darius let go of her hand and ran ahead.

"Darius," Parthenia called. "Stop! Wait for me." Her brother didn't answer. "Darius! Darius! Stop!"

"Wh—" Her brother gave a gasp and cried out.

"Darius!" Parthenia rushed forward. Somewhere in front of her, vegetation was being smashed by a falling body. It was as she'd feared. They'd reached a ridge and her brother had run right over the edge.

"Darius," she called down. All she could see was the dark shadows of trees.

"Parthenia! Help!"

"Where are you?" She stepped gingerly down the steep slope, holding a branch to prevent herself from sliding on the loose, dry leaves.

"I'm here!"

"Hold on. Don't move. I'm coming to get you." Parthenia eased down the incline, heading toward her brother's voice. "Keep talking so I can find you."

"I'm here, here, here!"

Despite the dire circumstances, Parthenia almost smiled. "That's good. Don't stop."

"Here I am. Here I am. Here I am." Darius echoed his own words several more times, his tone becoming more sing-song as he went on.

Parthenia finally saw her brother clinging to some tree roots. The spot he was at was particularly steep. She wasn't sure how to reach him, and if he let go of the roots to try to climb up to her he would probably slide away.

"You found me," he exclaimed.

"Yes, but don't move, okay? Don't let go."

"Okay."

"Are you all right? Have you hurt anything?"

"I bumped my leg. It hurts a bit."

"Okay. Just hold on. I'm going to try to get down to you. But don't let go until I say so."

Parthenia had an idea. If she went on all fours and crawled backward down the slope, she thought she could reach her brother and he could climb onto her. Then she could carry on moving slowly downward until they hopefully encountered an area that was less steep.

Her plan worked at first. She reached Darius, though the rough ground hurt her knees and hands. But as soon as her brother let go of the root he was holding and tried to climb onto her, he fell again. Parthenia shouted and tried to grab him, and then suddenly she was falling too. She slithered down the coarse surface, hitting bushes and vines, bouncing from tree trunks until finally, mercifully, all her motion ceased.

Dazed, it took Parthenia a moment to take in her surroundings. She was at the bottom of a muddy ditch and the slope she'd come down was dark and shadowy above her. For the first time that night, she could also see the wide, starry sky.

"Parthenia," Darius called. "Where are you?"

"Here," she replied. "Where are you?" To her amazement, Darius came walking along the bottom of the ditch toward her. He didn't seem to have been seriously harmed by his rapid descent.

"We fell," he said. "Are you hurt?"

Parthenia moved her arms and legs. She hadn't broken anything as far as she could tell, but when she tried to stand, she gave a small scream and fell over. She'd done something to her right ankle. "I think I did hurt myself, Darius. Can you help me?"

Her brother came closer and she put her arm over his shoulders. They were both coated in evil-smelling mud from the ditch. Parthenia hoped there was someone at the tower who would help them. Neither of them were in a position to go any farther tonight, and if they didn't get water or food soon, things would look very bad.

The smooth, black silhouette of the tower and its blue light were easy to spot against the stars but not so easy to reach. They walked—or rather, Parthenia hopped—along the ditch but there didn't seem to be any way out of it. They were forced to scale its slippery side. Parthenia pushed Darius up to the top of the edge, putting her weight on her good leg, so he could climb over onto the ground above. Then after several tries she managed to climb out too.

She stood on one leg, leaning on her brother's shoulder. Behind them, the forest overshadowed the sky. Parthenia could just make out black shapes flying above it. She shivered and turned in the other direction. The land was flatter though still quite wild. The tower was the only building she could see and it displayed the only artificial light for kilometers around. She wondered what purpose it served. They were very lucky Darius had seen it.

"Let's go ask the people for some water," Darius urged.

Parthenia partly walked, partly hopped beside him as they made their way through rough scrub to the base of the tower. The building was about as wide as a house but stood seven or eight stories tall. She couldn't see an entrance. Her heart sank, but then she realized she was being stupid. Propping herself up with one hand on the cold, polished stone of the tower wall, she hopped around it to the other side, Darius trailing.

There was the entrance. A metal door was flush with the wall, following its curve. A small light shined above the door but otherwise there was no other ornament save a security pad.

Her throat tight, Parthenia pressed the key on the pad. She feared there might be no answer, and yet she also feared who might answer if there was.

SEVEN

The mechs strode powerfully into the pit, their steps shaking the floor of the box where Carina sat. She'd never before seen anything even resembling the mechanical fighting machines that were about to do battle.

She could just make out their human operators ensconced in control centers in the mechs' chests. Thick metal walls protected the chambers, and the windows were narrow slits, allowing the operators limited real life visuals of their surroundings. Carina guessed the control centers held interface screens that relayed data from sensors as well as feedback from the mechs' systems. The windows were a last resort if the mechs' sensors were destroyed.

The machines stood roughly two stories tall. If it hadn't been for their massive size and power, they might almost have been caricatures of the kinds of mechs Carina knew. As a merc, she'd operated the exoskeletons aboard her band's ship, the *Duchess*. But their machines had been antiquated and mostly used for handling supplies. Though they were fitted with weapons, no one would have dared to fight in them. That had been one of the disadvantages of fighting for a commercial outfit: making do with outdated equipment.

Remembering her life as a merc, Carina looked forward to the day she never had to fight again. She would be happy if she could only reunite her little family and keep them safe. Yet these two metal monsters interested her. It was easy to see why the crowd was wild with anticipation: the battle would be spectacular. Even Langley was flushed with excitement. Her eyes were bright as she gazed at the mechs.

Langley's fingers quickly skimmed her interface, placing her bets. Carina wondered how much ill-gotten credit the Dirksen matriarch was frittering away. It was no wonder the clan had decided not to stamp out the Mech Battles. The contest was a gambler's dream. The chances of winning a bet were probably around fifty percent—it wouldn't make sense to stage battles where the opponents weren't evenly matched. Of course, the chances of losing were around fifty percent too, but that part of the equation was rarely considered.

Also, the outcome might not be clear until the final moment. Bets probably continued throughout the battle, odds rising and lowering according to the performance of each mech. Once more, Carina wondered who those barely visible faces inside the great mechanical beasts belonged to. It was possible a successful fighter could retire on his or her winnings from one battle. Though the arena only seated a few tens of thousands of people, the spectacle was no doubt being broadcast and the betting could be planet-wide.

The mechs were moving their various parts, apparently checking all their systems were working before the battle commenced. It was all for show, of course. No fighter in their right minds would enter the pit without performing extensive checks. No, the motions were all intended to bring the crowd to a frenzy and prompt them to lay out even more money. The preparations were having their desired effect too. The audience was so loud Carina could barely hear herself think. The stadium seemed to vibrate with the noise of shouting. And the battle hadn't even begun.

The mechs began to circle the pit.

Carina had been expecting Langley to check on her reaction to the event. Langley probably wanted her to appreciate the older woman's generosity in bringing her. But the matriarch was so intent on the battle, she ignored her. Langley's gaze only switched from her interface to the pit and back again.

Harmon wasn't equally entranced. As he stood at the back of the box in front of its exit, he stared at Carina, his hands folded in front of him, formidable. She scowled at the burly thug. He was definitely going to be the biggest obstacle to her escape. On her right sat the transport driver, looking bored.

A great metallic crash sounded from the pit. She had missed the beginning of the battle. The gigantic mechs were gripping each other with their enormous pincer-like grabbers. They grappled, their massive gears straining with the effort. Hisses and screeches and the noise of bending metal sounded through the stadium, and the crowd roared.

One mech was slowly overpowering the other, forcing it over to one side. Carina guessed that a way to win was to force the opponent to fall over. Then, gravity would confer a big advantage, allowing the still-standing mech to crush the other. A prone position might expose vulnerable areas too.

But in this case, the mech that seemed to be losing didn't fall. It managed to disengage and twisted away so fast its attacker nearly overbalanced. The mech's bending to one side had been a feint and it had nearly worked. But the attacking mech pulled back in time to remain upright.

"Oh," exclaimed Langley. Her fingers moved over her interface. Had she bet on the duped mech? When Carina peered more closely at the machines in the pit, she could make out SPEARCORPS across the faux "head" of the attacking mech. Out of curiosity, she spied out the name of its opponent: PYRECO. It was another name that was meaningless to her. The two were probably major conglomerates on the planet and perhaps the territory.

The Pyreco mech swung its pincer up at the Spearcorps mech's head and connected with such force it bent backward. The crowd gave a massive *Ohhhh!* Despite the whirring of gears and sounds of protesting metal the Spearcorps operator couldn't straighten the head. It wasn't serious damage, Carina guessed. A mech rarely used its head for fighting. But the effect would be to unbalance the machine. Now the Spearcorps mech was much more vulnerable to toppling over.

It responded by immediately grabbing the Pyreco mech in a fierce clinch. At close quarters, it was much more difficult to overbalance your opponent. Spearcorps drove Pyreco against the wall of the stadium. The audience in that section surged in a panic to get away from the gigantic machines, though the pit was beneath their feet.

By this time, Reyes was leaning over the edge of the box and yelling at the top of his voice. If he leaned much farther, he would be in danger of falling out.

A cataclysmic crash came from the pit. Pyreco was down. Spearcorps, its head bent weirdly backward, rained blows on its opponent. Pyreco tried repeatedly to rise, but each time Spearcorps was too fast and beat the mech down again. It was painful to watch the fallen mech's movements. Though it was just a machine and its operator wasn't in a lot of danger, its desperate efforts to escape were almost pitiful.

"Yes," exclaimed Langley, clutching her interface in sweaty palms. "Yes! Hit it. Hit it. Hit it."

"Go Spearcorps," roared Reyes, now on standing upright, his fists beating the air. "Spearcorps are the best!"

Pyreco didn't give up even though it was clearly beaten. Carina wondered if there was a cost to losing other than humiliation. The operator might have overextended themselves financially with their bets. Another explanation for Pyreco's tenacity was the battle was staged and the outcome preordained. If

Pyreco was being paid to take a dive, its defeat had to look convincing or the punters would suspect.

Spearcorps ceased hitting the prone mech. After a moment's checking that there really was no more life in its opponent, the mech raised its pincers to the sky. This time, the response from the crowd was so loud, Carina actually covered her ears. The stadium gates opened and Spearcorps strode triumphantly out. Pyreco was in no condition to leave so easily. Transports zoomed through the other gate and hovered around the fallen mech.

People in overalls jumped out onto the massive limbs and torso of the mechanical monster and walked over it, assessing the damage. It would take a while to remove the machine from the pit now it was immobile. Carina asked Langley's driver, "Do we leave soon?"

"Leave?" the woman replied. "That was only the first match. There's another four to go yet."

"Four more?" Carina said. "We'll be here all night."

"Exactly." The driver rolled her eyes and yawned, covering her mouth.

Although the Mech Battle had been somewhat interesting, Carina didn't relish the idea of sitting through another four. She looked at Harmon, who didn't seem to have taken his eyes off her the entire time. She sighed. It was going to be a long night.

———

The battles that followed weren't very much different from the first. Spearcorps fought in two of them. The winner of the first battle had to face newcomers until it lost. From what Carina could understand, if a mech won all five battles, it received an additional pay out. By the time the third engagement arrived, however, Spearcorps was too battered to put up much of a fight. Its unbalanced head proved its undoing when it was toppled within a minute of the battle's beginning.

Langley looked crestfallen at the result, but she wanted to stay and watch the remaining two battles nevertheless. Reyes quickly switched allegiance to the winning mech as soon as it looked like it was all over for Spearcorps.

To Carina's relief, the end of the fifth battle finally arrived. The mechanics entered on their transports to see to the removal of the losing mech. Carina expected that Langley would finally be ready to leave, but the Dirksen woman remained in her seat.

Reyes turned around and said, "Can't we go now, Mother? No one will notice."

"Don't be ridiculous," Langley snapped. "Of course they'll notice. When will you ever learn the importance of appearances in these matters?"

"What's happening?" Carina asked the driver. "What are we waiting for?"

"Urgh, just some stupid Ostillonian ritual," she replied. "It only takes a few minutes."

Carina watched with mild interest to see what the ritual entailed. The fallen mech was being dismantled on the field as it couldn't be repaired sufficiently to make its own way out. During the times she'd visited new worlds in her travels as a merc, she only ever spent brief episodes planetside. Her band, the Black Dogs, would do their job and leave as quickly as they'd arrived. So Carina had never been allowed time to learn about the worlds and their people. She'd heard of various religions over the years but she'd never gotten to know much about them.

When a young woman wearing ceremonial robes walked out to the center of the pit, Carina stood up for a better view. The woman squatted down and took some items out from a bag. First, she piled up sticks as if to make a fire, and then she took out a metal bowl. After pouring clear liquid into the bowl from a bottle, she grabbed a little soil from the ground and sprinkled it in.

Carina frowned, wondering what the woman was doing. Was she going to cook something? She looked again. Although she was watching from a great height, Carina could swear the woman was filing something made of metal so the particles also fell into the bowl.

Her heart seemed to stop. Could it be possible? It couldn't be. She had to be mistaken.

But then the priestess took a fragment of dry twig and also filed it over the bowl. She was adding sawdust to the liquid too. It was all Carina could do to remain upright and not allow Langley or Reyes to see her shock as the woman in the pit lit the fire.

She was making elixir. Right there in front of the entire crowd. Was it possible no one knew what she was doing? Was the woman herself aware?

After making the elixir, the woman lifted the bowl with tongs and held it up to the crowd. They murmured some kind of prayer Carina couldn't make out. Langley and Reyes said nothing. Then the woman tipped out the elixir onto the ground of the pit.

Mech Battle was over, and Carina was left with a mystery the likes of which she'd never known.

EIGHT

The man said he was a ranger. Parthenia wasn't exactly sure what a ranger did, but she assumed he worked in the land that lay around the tower. When the man had opened the tower door she'd taken a step back. He was so tall and his hair and beard were so black and shaggy, he looked for a moment like a big, black wild animal. Of course, it had only been the darkness and her exhaustion that made her think so. When he'd spoken, his voice had been gentle after his initial surprise.

He'd noticed her limping and offered to carry her up the stairs that wound around the tower's interior wall, apologizing for the lack of an elevator. "I'm alone out here. If I lost power, I'd be stuck," he'd explained.

Parthenia had declined his offer and made her way up the spiral staircase with Darius' help. Now, sitting in the round room the ranger had brought them to, she could finally relax. Or could she? It suddenly occurred to her that the man would want to know why she and Darius were by themselves in the middle of nowhere.

All the time they'd been wandering through the forest, she'd only thought about the danger they were in and wondered what had happened to Carina and the others, or what might happen if they didn't get to safety. She hadn't thought up a story to explain their presence here if they found someone they could ask for help.

Parthenia had no idea what the clan allegiance of the planet was. If Ostillon were under the hegemony of the Sherrerrs, there was no way she could let it be known she was a member of that family. If she did, their rescuer's first move would be to return her and Darius to their clan as soon as possible, regardless of anything she said. Although she was nearly an adult, Darius was still a child, but, more pertinently, the ranger would want to avoid upsetting the rulers of that world.

He wasn't pressing for answers just yet, thankfully. He was bringing them food. "I'll turn on the heating," he said. "You two look frozen." The drinks he'd placed in front of them steamed. When Darius made a grab for his, the ranger cautioned, "Not yet, little one. Let it cool down first."

"Oh, please," Darius said, his big brown eyes pleading. "Can I have some water?"

"Of course," the man replied. "I'll get you some right away. Just a moment." He went over to the small kitchen area and poured out a glass of water.

The circular room was multipurpose. Parthenia and Darius sat on a small sofa in the living area. The ranger had put down their food on a knee-high table in front of them. The rest of the room apart from the kitchenette was taken up with a range of equipment, most of which Parthenia didn't recognize. She guessed the ranger used it in his work.

While Darius was gulping down his water, the ranger went to a control panel near the staircase. "There," he said after pressing the screen. "It'll be toasty in here soon. You would like some water too, I guess?" he asked Parthenia.

"I would, please," she replied. She'd been thinking up and rejecting one story about their background after another. She had to make up something plausible and wished she had more time. If only she'd used the hours they'd been wandering in the forest more sensibly.

"Are you in pain?" the ranger asked, bringing her some water.

"I am," she replied, seizing the opportunity to delay his inevitable questions. "I hurt my ankle."

"Of course you did," said the man. "I was forgetting. I don't get many visitors out here. You two have taken me by surprise. Let me wash your leg then I can take a look."

Parthenia's legs and most of the rest of her were covered in mud. Darius also had a thick, brown, smelly coating. They were both disgusting, in fact.

The ranger filled a bowl with warm water and brought it over to the sofa along with a washcloth. He removed her mud-caked shoe. Her foot was grimy. As he washed away the dirt from her ankle the skin that emerged was puffy and purple. The ranger gently prodded it, causing her to wince. Now she could see her injury, it seemed to throb more painfully.

"Can you move your toes?" asked the ranger.

She tried. She managed to wiggle them all, though it hurt her to do it.

The ranger said, "How about your ankle? Can you move that?"

She gently lifted her foot upward. "Ow!"

"Okay. Don't try any more. I don't think it's broken. I have a treatment cell we can put your foot in overnight while you sleep. It'll detect any fractures and it'll speed up the healing process."

"Are you a splicer?" Darius asked. He was regarding the ranger over the rim of his mug of hot drink.

"No, or I don't think so," the man replied. "What's a splicer?"

Parthenia's stomach tightened. They were getting into dangerous territory. If Darius used words that weren't used in Ostillon, the man would know they were from offplanet.

"Someone who helps people when they're sick," Darius replied.

"You mean a medic," said the man.

"No," said Darius, "I mean a—"

"That's right," Parthenia interrupted and turned to Darius. "A medic. That's what you mean." She went on, "He's only six. He gets confused sometimes."

"No, I don't," Darius exclaimed indignantly. "I mean a—"

"Be quiet, Darius," Parthenia snapped.

"Darius," the ranger said. "That's a nice name."

Dammit. She cursed herself for making yet another stupid mistake. She should have thought up fake names for both of them. Her clan was searching everywhere for them. How many Dariuses traveling with Parthenias could there be? Yet she couldn't give the ranger a false name for herself now without Darius reacting and making it obvious she was lying. To avoid delaying the inevitable she said with a heavy heart, "I'm Parthenia."

"Another nice name," the ranger said.

He didn't show any signs of recognition, she noted with some relief. It was something to be grateful for, but she knew now the ranger knew their real names they had to leave as soon as they possibly could. They must also give no indication of where they were going. News of the missing Sherrerr children would probably arrive soon and then the ranger would be bound to remember them.

"I'm Jace," he said, still gently examining her ankle. "So, what are—"

"Ouch," Parthenia exclaimed, though Jace hadn't actually hurt her. She'd only wanted to stall him a little longer. What could she tell him about what they were doing here?

"Oh, I'm sorry," he said. He stood and wiped dirt from his hands with the wet cloth. "Your ankle's clean enough now anyway. Would you two like to wash off the rest of that mud?"

She readily agreed to delaying the moment she would have to spin her tale. She also welcomed the opportunity to prep Darius so he wouldn't give away that she was lying.

"The bathroom is on the next level," Jace said apologetically.

"That's okay," Parthenia said. "I can manage." With Darius' help, she hopped over to the stairway, which continued to wind around the wall of the room before disappearing into a hole in the ceiling. Jace led them up the stairs to the next floor. This room was his bedroom, and above the kitchenette on the floor below was a bathroom.

He found two clean shirts for them to wear and told them he would wash their dirty clothes, though Parthenia wasn't sure her dress was worth the effort. It was mostly rags.

The ranger descended the stairs and she went with Darius into the bathroom. As she helped her brother to wash off all the mud, she quietly explained to him that she might have to tell Jace some things that weren't true.

"But it's wrong to lie," Darius protested.

"It is, usually," she replied. "But sometimes we have to lie. Like if telling a lie stops someone from being hurt. Then it's okay."

"Is it?"

"Yes, it is. You know you can't tell anyone about being a mage, don't you? If someone asked you if you could Cast, you would say no. That's lying, right? This is similar. We can't tell Jace who we are or where we're from. If we do, we might end up being hurt. Or someone we love could be hurt. You wouldn't want that, would you?"

"No, I wouldn't," Darius replied emphatically.

"Then, if you hear me say something you know isn't true, you mustn't jump in and deny it, okay?"

"Okay."

Parthenia finished helping her brother dry himself and then put a shirt on him before sending him out to wait for her while she washed. She undressed and hopped into the shower. It was a very basic kind and it had no blower so you had to dry yourself with towels, but she didn't care. Washing away the disgusting mud was blissful, even though it made all her cuts and scrapes sting. She was bruised and scratched head to toe and when she washed her hair the rinse water ran brown.

She wondered what Mother would have made of her and her brother if she'd seen them as filthy and disheveled as the poorest village children. Then she cried, because she knew that her mother wouldn't have minded at all. It had been their father who would be driven to a rage by messy hair or a besmirched face. She missed Mother so much.

When she was clean and dry, she put on the shirt Jace had given her and hopped out of the bathroom. Darius had disappeared. Gripped by fear he was telling Jace their life histories she hopped in the direction of the stairs but in her haste she stumbled and fell. Then she noticed a stick propped against the bathroom wall that hadn't been there before. Thinking it was for her, she took it and used it to help her walk to the stairs.

"Darius," she called. "Are you down there?"

"He's eating," Jace replied. "Do you need some help coming down?"

"No, I'll be fine." Parthenia went carefully from step to step, the warm air of the living area wafting up to her welcomingly.

Darius watched as she came down. He didn't look troubled or guilty, so she guessed he hadn't said anything he shouldn't have. His cheeks were bulging with food.

"Feeling better?" Jace asked.

"Yes, lots," she replied. "Thank you for helping us. I don't know what we would have done if we hadn't found you."

"It's no problem. Though I have to say you're the first two young waifs who have ever walked out of the woods around here as far as I know."

"How did you know we came from the forest and not from the other direction?" Parthenia asked. This was it. She was going to have to tell Jace the story she'd made up while she was in the shower. She doubted it was very convincing but it was the best she had.

"I guessed that was where you got your scratches. Not many thorns in the scrub around here. You fell down the forest ridge into the ditch, right?"

"We did," she conceded. That part of her story was true. "I guess you must be wondering what we were doing there."

"I was, actually. The forest belongs to the Dirksens. It was lucky for you that you came here and found me before you were picked up by one of their gamekeepers. There are severe penalties for trespassing on Dirksen land. Or, worse still, you could have been mistaken for game and shot. How did you end up in there?"

The forest belonged to the Dirksens? So the Sherrerr rivals controlled Ostillon. Parthenia didn't know whether that was good or bad news for her and her mage siblings. "Well, we—"

Parthenia? Can you hear me?

Jace was looking at her expectantly.

Parthenia? It was Ferne. He was Sending, at just about the worst possible moment. She had to answer him.

"Is something wrong?" Jace asked.

Parthenia wailed and covered her face. She pretended to sob. It was the only thing she could think of to do that would give her space to reply. *I hear you. Are you okay? Is Oriana with you?*

We're all right. We only just managed to make some elixir. How are you and Darius?

We're okay but I don't know where we are. I can't speak right now.

Darius put an arm over her shoulders, consoling her, not knowing she was speaking to Ferne.

Okay. I'll Send again in an hour, Ferne said. Then he was gone.

er relief at hearing from her brother was so great she really did cry a little, which helped to maintain her subterfuge. She wiped her eyes. "Sorry. We had a terrible time today. I was explaining what we were doing in the forest, wasn't I? Well..."

Ferne was okay and so was Oriana. And they'd managed to make elixir. Parthenia felt a massive weight drop from her as she told Jace her story. With luck, she and Darius would be able to reunite with their siblings tonight. But what had happened to Carina? That was a mystery that remained to be solved.

NINE

Harmon woke Carina up by prodding her and stepping away as she came around. He was clearly trying to avoid being punched again. After the Mech Battle had ended and they returned to Langley's estate in the early hours of the morning, she spent couple of hours working toward her escape before finally falling, exhausted, into bed. She'd scraped away some of the mortar between the bricks in the wall, but it would take her several days to create a hole large enough for her to crawl through.

She had only slept a few hours before Harmon came in to wake her. Langley Dirksen was giving her no respite. She guessed the older woman didn't want to leave her to her own devices for too long, knowing she would be doing her utmost to leave. It was wise of Langley, but Carina was determined to get out soon nevertheless. The longer she remained here, the more agitated the Dirksen matriarch would become at her refusal to comply with her demands, and the temptation to force the issue would increase. Carina knew only too well what that might entail.

She also wanted to leave because she was worried about her siblings. She couldn't stop wondering where they were and what they were doing. They could be in dire danger and there wasn't anything she could do about it, or at least not while Langley Dirksen had her locked up. She also wanted to find out more about the ritual she'd witnessed the previous evening. What it meant she had no idea, but it had to mean something.

After a breakfast during which neither Langley nor Reyes appeared—*they* were apparently free to sleep in after their late night—Harmon told Carina she had the freedom of the first floor of the house, though she was never to leave his sight.

So, her shadow in tow, Carina spent an hour wandering through the mansion's rooms. She didn't bother hiding the fact she was trying to find escape routes and relished the look of frustrated anger her behavior provoked in Harmon. She guessed he expected her to be more cowed by his presence.

Each room she entered, she checked the windows, examined the ceilings, and looked for secret doors. Though she'd never been inside such a luxurious residence before, she'd read that secret doors and passages were often found in such places.

The mansion contained rooms that appeared to have been unused for years: lounges full of dusty furniture, playrooms stocked with piles of toys, a holo room with twenty seats for viewing vids, and an expansive bare room that seemed to be for large gatherings like parties or dances. Most of the rooms had a stale, neglected air. Carina also wandered into the staff area. When she went into the kitchen, the man and woman working there were alarmed by her presence. She quickly checked the place over. Here, she would find something she could use to create a naked flame, she was sure. And the pot on the windowsill that held a plant would provide the soil she needed. Noting there was no lock on the door, she left.

"What about outside?" she asked Harmon as they reached the end of the corridor that led to the entrance hall. "Can I go out into the grounds?"

"What do you think?" He cocked an eyebrow at her.

"There's only one way to find out." She strode toward the front doors. Harmon was quickly behind her. He grabbed her hair and yanked her back.

"Harmon," a voice admonished from the top of the double staircase. "Please don't treat our guest so roughly."

Langley Dirksen was wearing a loose gown of silky material, and her hair was down around her shoulders. She descended the staircase. "Good morning, Miss Whoever-You-Are." As she reached the bottom of the stairs, she said, "Really, I can't go on not knowing your name. Won't you tell me it? Just your first name, so that I have something I can call you."

"Oh, all right," Carina said. "I guess it won't hurt."

Langley smiled brightly at her small victory.

"You can call me... Prisoner," said Carina. Langley's expression fell. "Or maybe Captive? Detainee?" She put a finger to her lips and frowned. "I know! Just call me Caged One. That'll do. Or would you prefer Slave? It's up to you. I don't mind."

"That isn't funny," Langley Dirksen said. She looked as though she was about to stamp her foot. "Why can't you be reasonable? Believe me, you could have things a lot worse. I could give you over to others in my family. They're asking for you, you know. It's only because you happened to arrive within my jurisdiction that I've managed to hold on to you. But I can't protect you forever. If I don't show them some results soon they'll be demanding you. I won't have much choice but to give you to them and then you'll find the rest of my clan won't be as lenient with you as I have."

Carina didn't doubt that Langley was telling her the truth. The information didn't have its desired effect, however. She only resolved to work harder to escape as soon as she possibly could. "I don't even know what it is you expect me to do. I rescued some kid. So what? I was only doing my job. Nothing extraordinary about it. If you do hand me over to the rest of your evil family, they'll be just as disappointed in me as you are. So let me go."

Langley tutted. "So stubborn. I'm going to eat breakfast. Tonight I'm having a small dinner party. I want you to attend. Perhaps when you meet some of the people who would like you for themselves, you might change your mind. I really am your best option. I hope for your sake you realize that."

———

Langley insisted on Carina's presence while the older woman went about her daily business. Carina hated sitting around with nothing to do while Langley chatted with business colleagues over vidcalls or discussed the management of her estates. By the time evening arrived, she was simmering with barely controlled anger, partly fueled by plain boredom. Langley sent her up to her room to "get ready for the soiree."

It was the first time she'd been allowed to be alone in her room all day. A selection of fine dresses had been prepared for her. She took great pleasure in ripping them all to shreds and throwing them out into the hall. But taking out her frustration on the dresses did little to appease her feelings. She was furious at being forced to attend the coming social event like a performing animal, and she'd devised a plan that would result in her leaving at its earliest stages.

When Harmon witnessed her destruction of the dresses, he followed her into the suite, strode over, and stood in front of her, his fists clenched. He managed to restrain himself, however. He only pushed her down, marched out, and closed and locked the door.

She leapt up and ran into her bedroom. She had a short time before she would have to go down to the party. She closed the bedroom door and pulled the bed away from the wall. Taking up the base of the metal ornament she'd left there, she carried on scraping away at the mortar between the bricks. If she could escape into the next room, she might be able to go from there to the kitchen where she could create elixir.

As she worked, she thought of Langley's son, Reyes. The kid hadn't appeared all day. She guessed he usually avoided his mother's company. That's certainly what she would have done in his position. She doubted she would see him that evening either.

After ten minutes she heard the main door to the suite open. She jumped up and pushed her bed into position, throwing herself onto it just in time as Harmon opened her bedroom door. He frowned, seeming to sense she'd been doing something she shouldn't have. He looked around the room. When he couldn't locate any evidence of subversive behavior, he said, "Come with me."

She walked across to her guard. It was time for her to party. Her clothes were dirtier and smellier than ever. *Good,* she thought. Anything she could do to ruin Langley Dirksen's fun and reputation would be worth it.

When she arrived in the lounge where Langley was holding her gathering, several guests were already there, richly dressed and adorned with jewelry. Some of the women wore elaborate hairstyles that had probably taken hours for their hairdressers to craft. All the guests turned when Carina entered the room. Their eyes popped and silence fell like a death knell.

"Am I in the right place?" she announced loudly. "I was told there was a party here. I love parties." She marched to the nearest group, which consisted of a woman and two men standing together, drinks in hand. Their mouths gaped. "You don't mind, do you?" she asked the woman. Taking her drink from her hand, Carina drained it, wiped her mouth on her sleeve, and returned the empty glass. "Urgh. That tasted terrible. How could you drink it? What about yours?" She snatched a drink from one of the men and drank it down. "Not bad. Getting better." When she moved to take the other man's drink, he put his hand in front of it protectively and glared at Langley.

The matriarch was sitting with three women on a sofa and chairs. Her shock at Carina's behavior quickly turned to fury. She rose to her feet and said coldly to Harmon, "Take her away."

Harmon grabbed Carina's upper arm and tried to force her from the room but she dug her heels into the carpet and resisted. She wasn't going to miss out on the opportunity to get revenge by creating the biggest spectacle she could. "Oh surely the party isn't over yet. I'm having so much fun." She twisted from Harmon's grasp and dodged past him before running around the edge of the room. As she passed a table spread with food, she grabbed the tablecloth and dragged all the dishes onto the floor. "Whoops!"

Gasps came from the guests along with a few titters. Langley was crimson, Carina noted with great satisfaction. Then Harmon caught her.

Not making the same mistake twice, this time he picked her up and carried her over his shoulder. The man was just too large and strong for her to do much about it. But as she was carried from the room, she lifted her head and waved at the gawping party guests. "*So* nice to meet you all. Sorry I can't stay."

It was in that final glimpse that one of the partygoers caught Carina's eye. A woman who was sitting with Langley had an unusual hairstyle. Her hair was wound into a spiral above her head. It wasn't the style that caught Carina's attention so much as the fact that it looked familiar. She was sure she'd seen the woman somewhere before.

When they reached the stairs, Harmon climbed them still carrying her. He carried her down the hall to her suite where he threw her on the floor. He left and locked the door but a few minutes later he was back, a satisfied smirk on his face. "I want to thank you for your little performance. Mistress just gave me permission to teach you to behave better. I'm going to enjoy this."

Harmon moved closer, smiling as he reached for her.

"Not as much as I am," said Carina, punching toward his groin. Harmon caught her fist in his giant paw and twisted, causing her to spin around to avoid a broken wrist. He switched his grip to her forearm and dragged her to her feet. She flew at him, aiming a kick at his knee, but he chopped sideways, the edge of his hand whacking her ear and skull and sending her sprawling. Her ear hurt like a bitch and began to ring.

This time, she waited for him.

"What's wrong?" he taunted. "Not used to fighting with men?"

As he grabbed her arm and lifted his other hand to strike her, she drove an elbow into his thick neck. He dropped her like she was a stick on fire and coughed, nursing his throat. His eyes narrowed and his nostrils flared. Ferocity drove him toward her. She stood her ground, waiting for the last split second before he reached her, then stepped aside, ready to kick him down.

He had anticipated her move. Both his arms were stretched out and she couldn't avoid his grasp. He had her by the waist. In one smooth movement he scooped her up over his head and threw her down. When she was on the floor he proceeded to kick her over and over again, grunting with the effort. She curled into a ball and tried to protect herself as well as she could.

———

When Harmon had finished and gone away, she lay still for a while. She checked that none of her bones were broken and she still had all her teeth.

Then she got up and went into the bedroom. She figured she would be left alone for the night now, which meant she had many hours to work on removing bricks from the wall.

TEN

Pale, pre-dawn light was softening the night sky outside her bedroom window by the time Carina wiggled the final brick free. She placed it softly on the rug with all the others. The hole she'd made in the wall that adjoined the next room was narrow, but she estimated it was now just wide enough for her to squeeze through. The room beyond was dark and she hadn't heard any noises from it, not even the steady breathing of someone asleep. She hoped it was empty and the door leading from it wasn't locked.

She gently rubbed dust from her sore, bleeding fingers and bent down to the hole before putting her arms through up to her shoulders. This part of passing through the gap would be the most difficult, except perhaps when it came to her hips. Her head low between her arms, she wriggled forward, twisting her body and easing her shoulders into the narrow space. The edges of the bricks caught on her. She pushed harder with her legs, hoping she wouldn't get stuck. She would hate for Harmon to find her in such a humiliating position.

The hard corners bit into her shoulders. She couldn't move forward and neither could she move backward. She began to regret her impatience at trying to get through the hole. Maybe she should have removed another brick. But she couldn't afford the time it would have taken. If she was going to escape she had to do it now while the inhabitants of the estate were asleep.

Was Harmon asleep too? Or was he outside her door, wide awake? If he was out in the hall, he would be bound to see her escape from the next room. But he couldn't be. The man had to sleep.

If he was outside she couldn't help it. It was a chance she had to take. After her behavior at Langley's party, the woman was sure to hand her over to her even nastier cousins today. Perhaps Carina had gone too far the previous evening but her actions had given her the time she needed to break out of her room.

That was if she could break out of her room. She braced her knees against the carpet and pushed as hard as she could. The bricks scraped painfully against her shoulders, but the soreness was no worse than what she already felt due to Harmon's ministrations. The pressure built. She gasped. Her shoulders slipped through.

Now she only had to bring the rest of herself into the shadowy room next door. She crawled forward on her elbows until her hips reached the hole. Once more, she stuck against the sides. Pulling forward with her forearms and pushing with her toes, she dragged her hips through the gap, wincing as her hip bones ground against the hard surface.

She was in the next room. She lay on the floor for a moment, assessing her surroundings. The room was a bedroom like the one she'd just left. The door was in the same place too. She guessed she was in another suite similar to hers except in a mirrored layout.

She got to her feet and tiptoed to the door. After listening at it for a moment, she gently turned the handle and opened it a crack. The next room was dark too and seemed empty. She walked softly into it and over to the door that led to the hall.

Her pulse loud in the quiet of the sleeping house, she slowly turned the door handle, thankful that Langley wasn't as in love with modern conveniences as her brethren. If the door had been automatic, it might only have responded to those who had security clearance on the estate's system. A plain mechanical handle suited her fine. As she turned the knob as far as it would go, the door moved. It wasn't locked.

Now all she had to do was to get downstairs to the kitchen. If she could just have five or ten minutes to herself in there, it would be enough to make elixir and she could finally set about finding her family. She pulled the door toward her until the gap gave her a narrow view of the hall.

Damn. She could see a man's legs sprawling out. He had to be sitting down. She took a closer look. The legs didn't belong to Harmon. This man was smaller and wearing different clothes and shoes. She opened the door wider until she could see the rest of the guard. A light-haired man she hadn't seen before was sitting directly in front of her door. He was asleep. His chin was on his chest and she could even make out a thin trail of drool.

She estimated that about twenty meters of hall lay between her and the stairway. She only had to walk twenty meters without waking the guard to reach the stairs. But she had to walk right past him.

There was no time like the present. Dawn was rapidly approaching, and so might Harmon in order to take over from his sub. She opened the door and stepped into the hallway. The rugs in the Dirksen mansion were soft, thick, and perfect for muffling footsteps. Her heart in her throat, she took a step toward the guard and then another, keeping close to the wall.

He woke up.

She froze. The guard sat upright and stretched. He noticed the drool on his chin and wiped it off. He crossed his arms.

She was a statue, waiting for him to look in her direction. Or hear her breathing, or the sound of her heart thumping. How come he couldn't hear her heart? It was loud as a drum in her ears.

The guard adjusted his position some more and crossed and uncrossed his legs. After a few moments, his eyes closed. A few moments later his head dropped forward. Slowly, one arm slipped down his chest. It was followed by the other until both his arms were hanging down his sides and he was asleep again.

She crept past him, forcing herself to go slowly and quietly when all she wanted to do was run. Without looking back, she walked to the top of the stairs. A glance down the hallway told her the guard was still asleep. At the bottom of the stairs all was dark.

She had to hurry. The kitchen staff would arrive at their jobs soon to prepare a fancy breakfast for Langley and her son. She trod lightly down the stairs. Moving quickly through the dark, silent house, she headed toward the kitchen.

Ten minutes. That was all she needed. Maybe five. She could probably make the elixir in five minutes if she found all she needed immediately.

The kitchen door came into sight. She was nearly there. It wouldn't be locked. The door had no lock.

"'Morning." A figure stepped out from a dark room into the corridor in front of her, barring her way. He walked into the scarce light. It was Reyes. Langley's son stood between her and her freedom.

"Couldn't sleep?" Reyes asked. "I suffer from insomnia a bit myself. Pain in the ass, isn't it?"

She stared at the young man. He looked different somehow. Perhaps it was due to the half-light, but he looked older, and much more sinister.

"Where were you going?" Reyes asked. He glanced over his shoulder. "The kitchen? Can't wait for breakfast, huh? I guess you must be hungry after you missed the party last night. Mother told me what you did. I wish I'd been there to see it. It sounds hilarious. I would have loved to see all their faces. Pompous, puffed-up lot, they are."

She was calculating if she could close the distance between them and knock Reyes out before he had time to shout and raise the household. Probably not, but she didn't have any other option except to try.

"Don't let me get in your way," Reyes said. "If you want to eat, eat." He stepped back and waved an arm, motioning for her to pass him.

That was when she saw the gun. He'd been holding it casually behind his back.

When he saw her look at his weapon, he said, "Oh, don't worry about this. I'm not planning to hurt you."

She was confused. If he didn't want to stop her, why was he armed inside his own home? And why didn't he want to stop her? She walked toward the young man, not taking her eyes off him. If he was going to allow her free passage she wasn't about to refuse it, but there was clearly a catch somewhere that she wasn't getting.

Cautiously, she walked past him. He had to know she wasn't going to the kitchen because she was hungry. He might not know how she planned to escape from there, given that there were no exit doors, but he had to know that was her intention.

As she reached the kitchen door, he said, "You never told us your name. I'd like to know your name."

"You don't have any more right to that than you did to lock me up here," she replied. She opened the door.

"You're right," Reyes said. "You're absolutely right. I told Mother that. But she's used to getting her way. They all are. I'm not like them, you know. I hate them. They're my family and they've given me everything I could want, but I still hate them. I wish I could come with you. Here, take this." He reached into his pocket and pulled out folded plaspaper.

When she looked at him distrustingly, wondering if it was a ruse to make her approach him, Reyes said, "It's cash. People use it when they don't want their purchases to be traced. You'll need it."

She stepped over to him and took the money.

"Good luck," said Reyes.

She took a final look at him. The gangly youth had lost his sinister aspect. He now looked forlorn. His arms drooped at his sides and his weapon dangled from his hand. Had his Mother made him patrol the house that night to prevent her escape? Was he defying the matriarch by letting her go?

She went into the kitchen and closed the door. Reyes Dirksen wasn't her problem. She began to search for what she needed.

Eleven

Ferne arrived in the early hours of the morning, just as Parthenia had asked him to when he Sent to her for the second time. She'd been terrified that her brother would get his Transport Cast wrong and appear in the room below hers. That was where Jace was sleeping after insisting that she and Darius take his bed. It was the only bed in the place, and Parthenia guessed that the ranger was sleeping on the floor in his living room. While she'd waited for Ferne to arrive at the agreed time, she'd imagined him Transporting himself directly on top of Jace's prone figure, giving him the fright of his life and ruining everything.

She needn't have worried. Ferne appeared right next to the large bed where she and Darius had lain for the last few hours. Darius was sleeping heavily, entirely unaware that Parthenia had been in contact with his brother. She hadn't dared to trust the six year old with the good news. He'd been keeping their secrets fairly well for his age but she didn't want to rely on him.

Parthenia hadn't slept at all. Exhausted though she was, she'd forced herself to stay awake. If they were to be successful at leaving the ranger's tower, they had to do everything correctly. Jace seemed like a nice, kind man, but Parthenia didn't really know him. She didn't know how he might react to a boy suddenly appearing from nowhere. If he were to take the elixir Ferne was bringing they would all be stuck here and Oriana would be left alone.

Ferne's arrival out of thin air filled her with happiness. She climbed out of bed and hugged him. He'd brought elixir as he'd said he would. They would both need to drink it to Transport themselves and Darius back to Oriana. The steps would be a little complicated but they could manage it.

Parthenia released Ferne from her arms and whispered, "You look terrible." He did. He was filthy and his hair was full of bits of dead plants.

"Thanks," her brother replied. "Have you got any food?"

"Just a little," said Parthenia. She'd asked Jace if they could keep some food with them that night in case they were hungry. It was an odd request considering the amount they'd already eaten—especially Darius, who had stuffed his face—but the ranger had good-naturedly agreed. She held up the remains of her dress which she'd wrapped around the nuts and bread Jace had given them.

"Great," Ferne said. "So, how are we going to do this?"

"You take Darius with you. If we get separated, it's better he's with someone who can make elixir. I'll Locate Oriana, then Transport myself there. Have you brought something from her?"

Ferne handed Parthenia a few strands of hair. "Who takes the elixir with them?"

"Oh, I didn't think of that. Wait a minute." She went into the bathroom and brought out a cup. "I wish I had another bottle but this will have to do." Ferne poured elixir into it.

"You take the rest," Parthenia said. "Even if I can't Locate Oriana, I'll be able to Transport myself out of here."

"Okay," said Ferne. "We better wake Darius."

Noises of someone moving around came from the room below. Parthenia stared at Ferne. Had they woken up Jace with their talking? She thought they'd been quiet, but the ranger's lonely situation probably made him sensitive to the sound of other voices.

"Quick," Parthenia urged Ferne. "Don't bother waking him. Just take his shoes with you and go."

Ferne sipped elixir and ran to Darius' side. Parthenia winced at the noise of her brother's quick footsteps on the wooden floor. Jace would hear them for sure. Ferne grabbed his sleeping brother's hand and closed his eyes. A few seconds later, they were gone.

Parthenia sighed with relief. Darius was safe. Now it was her turn. She took a mouthful of elixir. Delving into the dark of her mind, she Cast Locate, focusing on the strands of hair she held, seeking out Oriana.

Her sister was far away. Right across the continent. Carina had Transported her pairs of siblings a great distance apart, due to the speed of the Sherrerr shuttle as it passed overhead. But all Parthenia had to do was Transport herself to Oriana. Ferne and Darius would be there already and most of their family would be reunited.

She opened her eyes to take another drink of elixir to Cast again—and found herself looking directly at Jace. He was standing on the stairs, his body halfway into the room and halfway below it. His bushy eyebrows were raised.

"What are you doing? Can't you sleep?"

Parthenia gulped down the elixir. She had no choice about it. She would have to Cast right in front of the ranger. If she didn't do it now she might never get another chance. She'd drained the last of the elixir Ferne had given her. If she didn't Transport out of that place, she would also face some very awkward questions about where Darius had gone.

She closed her eyes and tried to write the character within her mind.

"Parthenia?" Jace's heavy footsteps invaded her thinking. He was coming up the stairs. He was walking over to her. "Are you having a bad dream?"

Please stop talking to me. Parthenia fought to concentrate on the character and the Cast. If she didn't make it soon the effect of the elixir would wear off and she would be stuck here, a continent's distance from her sister and brothers.

She felt a hand on her shoulder. *No!* If the ranger didn't remove his hand she was in danger of Transporting him with her. And *that* would require a whole lot of explaining. Parthenia stepped backward, breaking contact with Jace. With a huge effort of concentration, she finished writing the character. Now to leave. She had to go to her family.

"Where's your brother gone?" Jace asked. Then louder and angrily, he said, "What's going on?"

A shiver of sensation passed over her and she opened her eyes. The Cast had worked. She was far from the tower and in a new place, which was in near darkness. The air was warm and moist and strange sounds were coming from all around her, as well as a strong smell of—

"Parthenia," Darius exclaimed. He barreled into her, almost knocking her from her feet. "I thought you'd never come. What took you so long?"

He was hugging her so tightly around her waist he was crushing her. She gently pulled his arms away, only for them to be replaced by those of Ferne and Oriana. Laughing, crying, Parthenia gave up. She stood in a huddle with her brothers and sister for a while, just being joyful they were together again.

When they had calmed down and stepped apart she asked, "Where are we? And what's that awful smell?"

Now she could focus on her surroundings, she found she was looking at rough, dirty walls made of wood.

"We're in a barn," said Oriana. "It was the only place we could find to hide. But everything we need to make elixir is in here. We even found an old bottle. But it took us hours and hours to get a fire started. And now it's gone out. I didn't want to make it bigger in case someone noticed, and I was worried I might burn the place down. The animals hated it too. I think they were frightened of it."

"Animals?" Parthenia asked.

"Yes," said Ferne. "Come out and meet them. That's what... well, they're responsible for what you can smell. They're big but they're quite friendly once they get to know you."

Darius took Parthenia's hand, and with Ferne and Oriana he led her out of the small enclosed space where she had arrived from her Transport. She hated to think what Jace would make of her disappearing before his eyes. Now not only did he know their names, he also knew what they could do. If he heard a report of missing children using their names and performing strange tricks he would have an interesting tale to tell.

She tried not to worry about it. They were on the other side of the country, far from the Dirksens' forest. If they were careful, they could stay out of danger long enough for Carina to find them. The whereabouts of her older sister was another thing Parthenia tried not to worry about.

They turned a corner into a wider space, and she halted in fear. Huge animals loomed in the semi-darkness. "You didn't say they were that big," she whispered fiercely at Ferne.

"Honestly," he replied, "they seem to be harmless. I quite like them."

The animals' bodies were as tall as she was, but their heads were half as high again at the end of their long necks. They were short haired except for longer hair that grew from the backs of their necks and hung down over their eyes. All the animals were tethered to a bar by straps that connected to a kind of cage of straps around their heads and faces.

They were eating some of the same dead plant bits that were tangled in Ferne's hair, and Parthenia noted that though the animals' teeth were large they weren't pointed like those of predators. Perhaps they weren't dangerous after all, but she was sure she wouldn't be going near one any time soon.

"I don't suppose you brought any more food?" Oriana asked hopefully. It was clearly wishful thinking on her sister's part. It was obvious Parthenia didn't have anything else with her except the ranger's shirt she was wearing. She'd even dropped the empty cup before she Transported.

"I'm sorry, Oriana," she said. "Haven't you or Ferne found anything to eat since we left the ship?"

"Here," said Ferne, "let's eat what we do have." He unwrapped the cloth parcel Parthenia had given him and handed Oriana some bread.

"Can I have some?" Darius asked.

"Let Oriana and Ferne have it all," said Parthenia. "We already ate, remember?"

"I remember," her little brother replied. "But I'm still hungry."

"Well, Ferne and Oriana are hungrier."

"Okay," said Darius. His young mind flitted to another subject. "It was a big surprise to wake up here. Did you say goodbye to Jace?"

"Hmm..." Parthenia said. "Yes, kind of."

"I'm glad we're all together again," Darius said, watching Oriana take another bite of bread. "But where's Carina?"

TWELVE

Carina had Transported herself to a spot outside the stadium where the Mech Battles were held. It was one of the few places she knew on Ostillon. As soon as she appeared, she checked all around her. The massive stadium stood to her right and spreading out between her and the town was the parking lot. A few hover vehicles dotted it, perhaps temporarily abandoned by owners too inebriated to find them in the crush at the end of the show. She also noticed for the first time the large workshops that jutted out from behind the stadium. She guessed that was where the giant mechs were built and repaired.

Then she recalled the odd ceremony she'd witnessed being held at the end of the Mech Battles. The origins and meaning of the ceremony were a mystery she would love to solve but she had other priorities.

Although she was exhausted from working through the night and ached all over due to Harmon's beatings, the earliness of the hour was counting in her favor. There was no sign of any movement nearby and she didn't think her sudden appearance had been observed.

She checked the bottle she'd taken from the estate kitchen and tucked inside her shirt. The hard, smooth shape felt comforting to the touch. It was full of elixir. She finally felt somewhat relieved and hopeful for the future. She'd escaped Langley Dirksen's estate and now she was free to find her mage siblings.

After following the stadium wall around, she hit the long road that led through the lot and into the metropolis. She set off down the road quickly. The sooner she reached the comparative anonymity of the city streets the better.

Somewhere on that large continent Parthenia, Darius, Ferne, and Oriana were probably struggling to survive. She had to find them before they did something that revealed their mage powers. Ma would have drilled it into them that they were never to reveal their abilities to strangers, but her sisters and brothers had virtually no experience of the outside world. She wouldn't have been surprised if one of them had already done something risky. If they were caught saving them would be a lot harder. Even if they were being very cautious, hunger, thirst, and exposure to the elements would tempt them to do things they shouldn't and there were always evil people waiting to take advantage of others.

At the thought of evil people, Castiel popped into her mind. She'd successfully avoided thinking about her other half-brother over the last few days, but now she wondered what had happened to him. As with Parthenia, Darius, Oriana, and Ferne, she had Transported Castiel and her other half-sister, Nahla, to the planet surface while the Sherrerr shuttle was being boarded. She'd Transported Castiel and Nahla first, in fact, glad to say goodbye to them.

She felt a twinge of guilt at sending Nahla down to the surface with Castiel. The little girl didn't seem to be naturally bad but she worshipped her older brother, and he enjoyed exerting his strong influence over her. Castiel was as malevolent and malicious as his father, Stefan Sherrerr. What concerned her even more was the fact that he had asserted strongly he could Cast. Like Nahla, no one thought he had inherited their mother's mage powers. But after reluctantly taking the pair of them with her when she escaped from the Sherrerrs, Castiel had boasted he could Cast if he were given elixir.

If he was right and by some quirk of nature his ability hadn't developed until he'd hit puberty, the prospect was terrifying. He'd watched his siblings' lessons on Casting. He probably knew all the characters and principles. All he would need was some practice. She didn't even want to think of what her oldest half-brother might do were he given the chance to act out his nastiest fantasies. What was worse, he hated her passionately and all his other siblings except Nahla. They were physical reminders of feelings of inadequacy he had experienced while growing up, unable to Cast as most of his brothers and sisters could. And if his ego and pride were anything approaching his father's, those feelings would be unbearable.

She hoped she had Transported him and his minion sister far from everyone else in her remaining family.

She was drawing close the thoroughfare that would lead her into the city. The sun was coming up, and the city was wakening along with it. Every so often a hover vehicle would pass along the road, usually high up and traveling very fast. The tall building complexes she had seen from the spaceport were in the distance. She was heading toward a low-rise part of town that seemed poorer and older. She guessed this was a part of the city the Dirksens hadn't gotten around to developing yet.

It was a good place for her to be. She would be able to pay for things using the plaspaper money Reyes had given to her. First on her list of things she needed were new clothes. The ones she was wearing were so dirty and stank so bad she disgusted even herself. More importantly, she had to get rid of anything that identified her. Langley Dirksen would have the streets combed for her as soon as the matriarch knew she was missing. She should cut her hair too, she mused.

The obvious thing for her to do would be to get as far from the neighborhood of the Dirksen estate as quickly as she could. Yet she didn't want to leave the place just yet. The metropolis was probably the capital of that region if not the entire continent, so it would be here she would have the easiest access to useful information, news reports, and so on. Also, the Dirksens might have already put up road blocks, guessing she would try to escape the city.

She reached the thoroughfare that formed a T with the road from the stadium. She stepped into it and turned left. A few pedestrians were already walking the streets. As they passed the men and women threw looks she guessed were not only due to her disheveled state. Her clothes, which had been provided by the Sherrerrs, were not what was usually worn here. She had to blend in with the local population but she wasn't sure how to go about it.

Hover transports were beginning to fill the roadway. Though it was only two lanes wide, the lanes were three tiers high. The highest tier was the fast lane and slower vehicles occupied the lane just above the ground. The vehicles pulled off into parking spots at the road's edge when they wanted to stop. In one of the spots was a stall selling handmade artwork. She glanced at the items idly as she passed by. The objects were beautiful: multicolored opalescent containers and simple decorative plaques.

Catching her looking at the display, the stallholder said, "See something you like? Special discount for my first customer of the day."

She smiled, barely deciphering the man's thick accent. She shook her head and walked on. But the encounter had sparked something. The elderly man running the stall reminded her of her grandmother. Nai Nai had collected pebbles in the wild lands around the slum settlement where Carina had grown up, polishing them to reveal their beautiful natural colors before offering them for sale. In truth, the stones were nearly worthless and the living Nai Nai had scraped had been meager, but it had been just about the only time Carina could remember being truly happy.

She turned around and went back to the stall. The short stallholder was gazing upward absently at the expensive vehicles flashing past in the fast lane overhead. When he noticed her return, he grinned and stood up so quickly he knocked over his stool. As he stooped to pick it up, he said, "Changed your mind? Something caught your eye? Which piece is it you're interested in. I can recommend—"

"Have you had breakfast?" she asked.

The stallholder's eyes grew so wide the whites showed all around. "Breakfast? I... why do you ask?"

"You remind me of someone. She's been dead a long time, but you would be doing me a favor if you ate breakfast with me."

"Oh, well," said the man. "I'm not going to turn down the offer of free food. Of course I'll eat breakfast with you."

"Thanks. Where can I buy it?"

The old man gave her directions to a shop down a nearby alley and in a few minutes she had returned with hot, filled buns and an opaque, smooth tea. The stallholder pulled out a second stool and after she sat down they ate.

She hardly knew the reason for her sudden impulse but she guessed it wouldn't hurt to speak to a local and learn something of how people lived on Ostillon. She might learn how to avoid sticking out and how she might be able to find her siblings.

"This person I remind you of," said the old man, "is it a grandparent?"

"Yes. My grandmother brought me up. She sold pretty things too. Pebbles, though. Not like what you have here. Did you make all these things yourself?"

"Me?" The stallholder laughed. "Oh no. I could never make anything like this. My son is the artist. He had an accident as a child and he can't walk."

"I'm sorry," said Carina. She guessed the man was too poor to pay a splicer to fix his son's legs, but it would have been rude to mention it. "Your son is very talented."

"Thank you. I'm proud of him. I can tell by your accent you aren't from around here. Are you visiting family in the city? Or perhaps looking for a job?"

The state of her clothes and the bruises Harmon had left on her face, told the old man she wasn't much better off than him. She decided to run with his impression of her—it wasn't that far from the truth after all, and she might learn something useful. "That's right. Do you know where I might find some work?"

"I guess you're looking for something off the books?" He winked at her.

"Yeah, I am. Do you have that kind of thing around here?" She knew exactly what the stallholder was alluding to. The situation was the same every-where she went. The clan-affiliated upper classes jealously guarded their wealth and privilege, the aspiring middle classes held a firm allegiance to the system and clung to the false hope that they might one day move upward, and the semi-illegal, shady underclass didn't—or chose not to—fit in. Sometimes these lower-class individuals' birth details had never been registered, they'd angered a clan member, or they'd committed a crime and were wanted by the authorities. Whatever the reason for their position, they lived outside the system.

"Of course," the stallholder replied. "Isn't that kind of thing to be found everywhere? There's an agency that hires casual workers for all kinds of legiti-mate and less-than legitimate work about half a klick down this road. Just tell them you lost your ID. They'll understand what you mean. They'll give you a uniform and pay cash at the end of the day."

A uniform would be a great disguise. She doubted the Dirksen thugs Langley sent out to find her would be looking for someone wearing a local uniform. "Thanks. That sounds like exactly what I need."

"Thank you for the breakfast. I hope our little chat has brought back some happy memories for you."

She smiled. "It has." The stallholder didn't only remind her of her dear, sweet, quick-tempered Nai Nai because of his age and situation: he was also just as kind and considerate. It was nice to feel looked after, rather than being the one who was looking out for everyone else.

Their breakfast was finished, and she had to get off the street and change her appearance soon before people came looking for her. She thanked the old man for his time and wished him good luck with his sales before leaving.

Thirteen

Carina ran a hand through her newly shorn hair. She'd told the barber to cut it short. She had something resembling her merc's military cut. It felt good.

Her head seemed lighter and she felt freer, though the sight of her battered face in the barber's mirror had been a bit of a shock. It was twelve hours or longer since Harmon had worked her over and the bruises were really beginning to bloom. She wasn't going to make much of an impression at the employment agency, but she had decided that a day or two's work was her best option. The Dirksens would be looking for her in places where people went to lie low: cheap hotels, derelict buildings, seedy parts of town. The clan's bully boys wouldn't be looking for ordinary people doing ordinary jobs, unless they were a lot smarter than typical. She also hoped to become more familiar with life on Ostillon. A better knowledge of the world might help her locate her siblings.

The agency receptionist took in her disheveled appearance in one withering glance. She hadn't been able to find anywhere open at that early hour that sold clothes. But she clearly didn't look too awful to work. The receptionist pointed toward a row of interfaces along the wall of the shabby office. "Input your details. The system will match you with what's available today."

"I don't have any ID. I lost it."

The receptionist frowned. "Where are you from?"

"Offplanet."

"Makes sense. I couldn't place your accent. Okay. Pick out a uniform that fits, put it on, and wait outside. Someone will be along to collect the day laborers soon."

She noticed the box beside the receptionist's desk that was full of old, worn overalls.

"You get paid when you return your uniform," said the receptionist. "Dirty is okay but if it's torn or damaged the repair cost comes out of your wages."

She had thought it a little weird for the agency to provide a uniform but now the policy made sense. It was hard to avoid damaging your clothes while working manually. The agency used the uniform rule as a ploy to keep back some of the workers' wages. Still, she was there mostly for camouflage, not for money. She still had the bills Reyes had given to her.

As she rooted through the box to find overalls that wouldn't look too ridiculous on her, she wondered if Reyes had gotten in trouble for letting her go. Was Langley's mansion fitted with security cameras? She guessed not or Reyes wouldn't have been so bold. For all his brave talk, he'd acted submissively while in his mother's company.

The only overalls that didn't come up too short on her lanky legs had a tear across one knee. "I'm taking these," she said to the receptionist and showed her the tear. "But look, they're already damaged."

The receptionist said, "Sure. Okay." From her manner, it was obvious she was going to deny ever seeing the tear when Carina returned later on that day.

She put on the overalls over her dirty clothes and went outside. Over the next hour, more people went into the agency and came out again wearing a uniform. They joined her and the group grew. No one spoke much, though nods passed between workers who knew each other. She didn't talk either, not wanting to alert the others to her offworld accent. When a young girl smiled at her, however, she returned the smile. The girl reminded her of Parthenia, though she was a little older. In fact, the girl was probably her own age, Carina realized wryly. It was only that she thought of herself as older.

After another half an hour or so, as her sleepless night began to really catch up with her, a large hover transport arrived. Before it had even drawn to a stop, the workers raced to crowd around its rear entrance. The doors opened, and the people at the front of the crowd tried to climb aboard. Two men stood there, however, and they pushed the over-eager laborers back, pressing the men and women's chests with the soles of their boots.

"We need thirteen today," one of the men said. There were many more than thirteen people hoping for work. There had to be twice that number.

The men began to point and count. As they numbered off, the people they'd chosen forced themselves through the ranks to the front and the men let them aboard. When she noticed one of the men's gazes drawing near, she lifted up onto her tiptoes to make herself seem taller. "Eleven," said the man, pointing at her.

The other laborers stepped aside resentfully as she passed through the crowd and climbed into the back of the transport.

"Hey, honey," called the young woman who had smiled at her. She was smiling again, this time at one of the men. "Don't forget me."

Carina didn't rate the woman's chances. She was the smallest and weakest of all of them. Yet to her surprise, the man called, "Thirteen" and waved her aboard.

A few nasty names floated in the young woman's wake as she stepped up and into the vehicle. She put her hand behind her back and made a gesture with her fingers that Carina guessed meant something obscene on Ostillon. The seat next to hers was free, and the woman sat down.

"Phew," she remarked. "I thought I wouldn't make it. You're new, right?"

"Yeah," said Carina, and turned away to gaze out the window as the transport pulled into the traffic in the middle lane.

"Hey," said the woman, "don't worry. I'm not going to give you away." She lowered her tone. "Everyone here has a secret. Jonas over there embezzled millions from his father's company. Adrienne killed a man. Kali is hiding out from his psycho wife."

"Shuttup, Asha," said a man sitting in front of them, who Carina assumed was Kali. Ignoring him, Asha went on, "So you see, we can't turn you in because we all have something to hide ourselves."

"Okay."

Asha waited for her to say more and when Carina remained silent, she said, "What's your name?"

"Tamira. You can call me Tammy."

"Good to meet you, Tammy," said Asha. "As you're new, I'll show you the ropes. First, your uniform: don't bother trying to avoid tearing it. It doesn't matter what it looks like when you hand it back, they're gonna dock you five percent. You could turn in a brand new set of overalls and they would still dock you five. So don't worry about it. Second: we get free lunch but we only get fifteen minutes to eat it. If you're late back, they'll dock you ten percent for every minute. So if you're ten minutes late, *you* owe *them*, see?"

"Okay, I get it. Thanks."

"I haven't finished. No restroom breaks except over lunch. So try not to drink too much or you'll be in pain before we knock off."

"All right."

Asha leaned closer and said in a lowered tone, "One more thing. If you do the boys a favor, you'll get work whenever you want it."

Carina had been continuing to look out the window while Asha was speaking, but at this latest comment she turned and stared at the other woman.

"What?" Asha asked defensively. "It takes ten minutes and if you're guaranteed work from it, what do you care? I'm just saying, when your bruises go down, you won't look too bad. I bet they'd go for you. Only remember I was the one who told you, okay? I get in first."

"Yeah, thanks. But I won't be competing with you on that."

Asha shrugged. "Just trying to be helpful."

"I know. I appreciate it." Though Asha's methods weren't for her, Carina didn't think less of the woman. In that kind of life people did whatever it took to get by.

When they arrived at the job site, she was surprised to discover it was one of the complex apartment blocks, newly built. One of the supervisors told the workers they were to remove all the construction debris, dust, and dirt, ready for the decoration crews who were arriving tomorrow. She had been expecting heavier work, but she guessed that machines took care of most of the buildings' construction. The Dirksens loved their high tech.

As soon as the workers disembarked from the transport, one of the supervisors took Asha by the arm and led her away into a room. The door closed and the other supervisor addressed the remaining crew.

"There's twenty-six floors, so you have to clean two each. At six o'clock we'll check every floor and if we find any dirt or trash no one gets paid. Got it?"

Sighs and groans came from the group but no one dared to openly protest the unfair rules. Instead, the men and women began to shout out the floors they would clean. She was too slow to catch on. In a few seconds the verbal claiming was over and the only floors left were twenty-three through twenty-six. Two of them would be Asha's—when she returned from doing the other supervisor a 'favor'—and the other two would be Carina's.

Thirteen cleaning machines stood in the bare, dusty lobby. The devices were old and battered. They were also large and heavy, she discovered when she tried to move one of the two that hadn't been claimed. It was then she discovered the elevators weren't working yet.

The door to the room where Asha had gone with the supervisor opened and she emerged with the man. She walked over to Carina, who was squatting next to her machine, trying to figure out how it worked. All the other workers were leaving to begin their jobs.

"Huh," Asha said, watching the departing men and women. "I bet they left us with the broken ones."

"Have you used these before?"

"Yeah. It's always the same machines for this job, though I shouldn't complain. This is one of the best kinds of work we can get. But only if the damn machines aren't broken." She pressed a button on the remaining machine. When nothing happened, she said, "Yep. Like I thought. What about yours?"

Carina pressed the same button. Her machine started up and gave out a low hum, but then it died. "Can't we just tell the bosses our machines don't work?"

"They'd only tell us to borrow someone else's, and how likely do you think that is? No. We have to try to fix them or we're stuck." She lifted up the cowling on her machine. "But these aren't complicated. It's just a loose wire or something."

Asha fiddled with her own and Carina's cleaning machines for a while and managed to get them both working. Then together they carried the machines up to the top floors, one at a time. They were far too heavy for one person to carry alone.

After demonstrating to Carina how her machine worked, Asha went downstairs to floor twenty-three. The morning was wearing on and Carina had to clean floors twenty-five and twenty-six before the day was out. She was still sore from Harmon's beating, her hands ached from spending the night removing the bricks from the wall, and she was groggy with tiredness.

If it had only been her who would suffer the repercussions of failing to do her job, she might have lain down and gone to sleep. But if she did that twelve other people would lose their day's wages, and they were the types who couldn't afford it. She pushed her cleaning machine to the farthest apartment on the floor and started it up. They were designed to work automatically, Asha had told her.

The apartment was full of odd bits and pieces left over from the construction work, which Carina had to take all the way downstairs to a dumpster. She began to carry out the trash and build a pile next to the stairwell, thinking she could push the lot down the stairs at the end of the day.

When she returned to her cleaning machine, instead of working methodically across the floor and up the walls of the room, it was spinning in a circle. The area it had worked was spotless but the rest of the place remained dirty. She cursed and tried to turn the machine off but it was spinning too fast. Whenever she reached in to press the button, it whirled out of her reach.

She swore again, loudly. She kicked the machine and sent it scooting over to the wall, which it rapidly climbed before continuing up and onto the ceiling where it began spinning again.

She uttered words only mercs used—and then only out of the hearing of their officers—as she jumped up to try to reach the machine's controls.

She heard laughing from the doorway. Asha was standing there, her arms folded. "I was wondering how you were getting on."

Carina ceased her efforts and rested her hands on her knees, panting. She laughed too. "Not very well."

"Don't worry. We'll get it down. I wanted to ask you something. As you're new in town, I thought maybe you don't have anywhere to stay. Would you like to sleep at my place tonight? I have a spare room."

Asha seemed nice and she was right—Carina didn't have anywhere to stay tonight. "Thanks." Although she couldn't ever tell Asha her true reason for being on Ostillon, perhaps her new acquaintance could give her some tips for finding people on that world. She could begin her search for her siblings.

Fourteen

Parthenia was awake before her brothers and sisters. She pushed down the smelly, hairy animal blanket they'd covered themselves with to help keep out the chill of the night and sat up. Darius had somehow worked himself fully under the remaining blanket and was lying cross ways. Oriana and Ferne were sleeping back to back, their heads resting on a thin pillow they'd made from the raggedy dress Parthenia had used to hold the food.

The barn had no windows, but pale daylight shone through cracks between the planks of the walls. On the other side of the wide space the animals were shifting about as if agitated. Parthenia wondered what was the matter with them.

Her joy at being reunited with Ferne and Oriana remained but she knew their situation was as dangerous as ever. Their Sherrerr relatives would be searching for them and the clan wouldn't give up that search for a long time—most likely as long the memory of the mage children lasted, down the generations. The children had unfortunately proven the power and value of their abilities when they blew up the Dirksens' shipyard.

As soon as the others woke, they would have to decide where to go and what to do next. Parthenia thought it might be best to find out where the capital city was and go there. It seemed to make sense that to find someone you went to the most important place in the country. What they would do when they got there, she didn't know, but she didn't have any better ideas. They might find it easier to live in a big city too, where there were jobs and lots of people to hide among.

Parthenia didn't know how they would travel to the city, or, now that she thought of it, where the capital was located. But maybe they could ask someone. More urgently, they needed to find food. Her belly was already grumbling in spite of the meal provided by Jace the previous evening. She wondered what the ranger had made of her and her little brother's disappearance. She hoped he hadn't told anyone, and particularly not the Dirksens, who she guessed were his employers.

Darius groaned and turned over, pulling the blanket off Oriana. He sat up, still under the blanket. Parthenia tugged it off of his head. He blinked and looked around, taking everything in like he was trying to figure out where he was. When he saw her he smiled. "When's breakfast?"

She was about to answer when her brother's words sparked a realization. That was why the animals were moving around so much. They were hungry. And that meant someone was on their way to feed them.

"Parthenia?" said Darius. "When's—"

"Shhh." She reached over him to shake Oriana's shoulder. "Wake up. We have to leave," she said as her sister's eyes opened. "Wake up Ferne."

Parthenia stood and helped Darius to his feet too. The only thing they had to take with them was the elixir. Where was it? She didn't know where Ferne had put the precious liquid. Ferne was sitting up and rubbing his eyes.

Just as she said, "Ferne—" the lock on the barn door rattled and a moment later the door swung open. The golden light of sunrise flooded in, silhouetting the figure who stood in the doorway. Oriana and Ferne jumped to their feet.

"What the...?" said the figure. It was a woman, though she was tall and broad. She continued more angrily, "What are you doing in my barn?" The woman stomped farther inside, swung the door closed, and dropped the latch. "Are you here to steal my horses?"

"No," Parthenia protested. "We aren't here to steal anything. We only needed somewhere to sleep. We're sorry. We haven't touched anything, honestly. We'll leave now."

"Oh no, you won't. You aren't going anywhere. You're trespassing and I'm going to call the authorities. But before I do that, I'm going to search you. I want to make sure you haven't stolen something." The woman's eyes narrowed as she scanned the children from head to toe. "Those aren't yours," she exclaimed, pointing at Parthenia's bracelets. Oriana was wearing one and Parthenia was wearing the other. "They're far too valuable for urchins like you. Hand them over."

"They belong to me," Parthenia protested. "They were a present from my father."

"Give them here. If you can prove they're yours, you can have them back."

Oriana pulled off her bracelet and placed it in the woman's outstretched hand. "Please don't call anyone. Please."

The woman frowned. "Why? Are you in trouble for something? Whatever it is you've done, you're runaways. That little boy is far too young to be away from his parents. You." She pointed at Parthenia. "Give me your bracelet." When Parthenia had done as she'd been asked, the woman slipped the bracelets inside her shirt. "And you." She was looking at Ferne. "Come here and turn out your pockets."

"No," shouted Parthenia. Ferne might have the elixir. She couldn't risk the woman taking it. They all stared at her. "Ferne. If you do have anything in your pockets, give it to me."

"Don't you dare," the woman said, striding across to Parthenia's brother. "Whatever you have, it's mine and I want it back."

Ferne reached into his pants pocket and took out a bottle. It held a small amount of elixir. Only enough for one Cast remained. As the woman moved to grab the bottle, Ferne tossed it to Parthenia. She caught it and unscrewed the lid. The woman was only one step away but Parthenia managed to swallow the last of the elixir before she snatched it.

"This is mine," the woman exclaimed, staring at the empty bottle. "You took it from the things I stored at the back of the barn. You *are* thieves."

"But it's only an old bottle," said Darius.

"How dare you," the woman blustered. She turned on the other children with narrow eyes. "What else have you taken?"

The children were watching Parthenia, however. She closed her eyes, hoping the woman would leave her alone long enough for her to Cast. She couldn't Transport all four of them but she could do something else.

"What's wrong with you?" she heard the woman ask. "Open your eyes! What are you doing?"

Parthenia struggled to concentrate and write the character she had in mind. She heard the sound of struggling.

"Mmmwharrrrr," exclaimed the woman. "Get off me!"

Parthenia was deep inside her mind, writing the strokes of the character one by one. She Cast. When she opened her eyes, the woman was on her back and Ferne and Oriana were on top of her, holding her down. Darius was sitting on her head.

Despite the seriousness of the situation, Parthenia giggled. "You can leave her alone now." When the three children stood up, the woman remained on the ground. She was limp and though her eyes were open they were glassy and unfocused.

"Did you Enthrall her?" Oriana asked.

"Yes. It was all I could think to do at the time. But I think it's going to work to our benefit. I have an idea." Parthenia walked over to the woman and looked down at her. "What's your name?"

"Marcia."

"Okay, get up, Marcia."

The woman slowly rose to her feet. Her arms hung limply and her mouth was open.

"Do you have a vehicle?" Parthenia asked.

"Yes."

"Good. I want you to take us all to the capital city."

Without a word, Marcia turned and walked out of the barn.

"Quickly," Parthenia said. "Put on your shoes." As soon as they could the four children followed the Enthralled woman.

"Don't you think we should go in her house to make some more elixir before we leave?" Ferne asked.

"No," Parthenia replied. "We don't know who else might be there. I don't want to risk it."

The strange procession marched down the path that led from the barn and across a field. Marcia was heading in the direction of the farmhouse. Parthenia hoped no one was watching from the windows. They had to be such an odd sight, anyone seeing them would be bound to come out and investigate.

"Do you know how far it is to the capital?" Oriana asked Parthenia.

"No, I don't have any idea."

"But what if your Enthrall wears off before we arrive?"

"Then I guess we'll just have to go the rest of the way by ourselves."

Ferne laughed. "Our new friend is going to be very confused when she comes out of it."

They had arrived at a shed that stood next to the farmhouse. Marcia opened both doors wide, revealing a shiny vehicle with a pointed nose. It rested directly on the ground and didn't appear to have any wheels. Parthenia wondered how it moved.

Marcia was walking into the shed. The door of the vehicle opened to her touch, and the children scrambled to catch up with her and take seats inside.

Enthrall was an unpredictable Cast. Its effect on the victim's mind varied according to their mental characteristics. Intelligent, strong-willed people could resist it to an extent, and the less intelligent who were easily persuaded could be so affected by Enthrall they lost touch with what was happening around them. Marcia seemed to be so heavily influenced there was a chance she might drive away and leave the children behind, not realizing they weren't with her.

Parthenia closed the driver's door for Marcia as she didn't seem about to. The woman started the vehicle. It rose up, causing the children to gasp. Marcia drove out and onto the small lane that ran in front of the farmhouse. She drove between the trees all the way down to a larger road and pulled out directly into it without looking for oncoming traffic. A truck blared at them and rose above and over them to avoid a collision.

It was going to be a hairy ride.

"Marcia," Parthenia said. "Don't drive dangerously. Don't drive in front of other vehicles."

"Maybe there's an automatic setting," Oriana suggested.

"Yes," said Parthenia. "Marcia. If your vehicle can travel automatically, input the capital city as the destination and stop driving."

Marcia tapped keys on a pad next to the seat. Her arms relaxed.

"Phew," said Ferne, also relaxing in his seat. "Hey," he said, "I forgot to ask. Why are we going to the capital?"

"I thought it might be somewhere we could find Carina," Parthenia replied. "I don't know what else to do."

"Will we find Carina soon?" Darius asked.

"I don't know," Parthenia replied. "I hope so."

The traffic on the highway was building up as more and more of the hover vehicles joined it from side roads. Parthenia wondered why, if the vehicles could fly, they didn't travel directly over land to their destinations, but she guessed that requiring them to follow roads like wheeled vehicles was for safety. Or maybe the Dirksens reserved the skies for their own vehicles.

She couldn't see anything resembling a city in the distance. From her seat next to Marcia, she had a good view of the vehicle's dash but nothing on it stated the distance to their destination. The capital could be hours or days away.

While they were traveling along, she prepped her brothers and sister with the story she'd made up to tell Jace. If they needed to explain themselves to strangers, they were to pretend they had gotten lost and they only needed directions to the nearest town or city, from where they would contact their parents. They were to say they were going home after visiting their relatives and that Parthenia was looking after them. She would pretend to be eighteen.

As soon as she could find out more information about the country, she would pick a distant town for them to name as their home. She told her sister and brothers they could to fill in more details to make the story sound plausible but they were not to deviate from the main parts. The children began to make up names for the relatives they had been visiting and fill in other small facts, enjoying themselves with imagining a normal family life and upbringing, until the story almost felt real.

If only it were real. Their fantasy life sounded much more pleasant than their current situation. She and Darius were still wearing the shirts Jace had lent to them. They didn't have anything else to wear. None of them had any food or water or money to buy any. As soon as Marcia was no longer Enthralled their problems would return.

Parthenia hoped they would reach the capital soon.

FIFTEEN

Asha's apartment was cramped but it contained the small, spare bedroom where she'd said Carina could sleep. What Asha hadn't mentioned was her live-in boyfriend. When they had arrived after their long day's work, he'd been lying on the sofa in the small living room. The boyfriend, who Asha introduced as Cavin, seemed to be extremely relaxed and cheerful. He was sprawled out as he played games on an interface.

"Hey, babe," he said to Asha after she'd shown Carina the spare room. "When are we gonna eat?"

"Soon, honey. Soon." Asha went into the tiny kitchen and Carina followed her. "You can take a shower while I cook," Asha said. "I'll clean up after dinner."

"Aren't you too tired to cook?" Carina asked. "How about I buy us some takeout? I saw we passed some restaurants on the way here." The little hole-in-the-wall eating joints Carina had seen were clearly off-network. Rather than taking net orders and sending out the food via drones, those kinds of places sold on the street, for cash.

Asha looked relieved. "Well, if you're offering..."

"Sure. If I give him the money maybe Cavin can go and buy us something. You two must know the best places."

"Oh." Asha peeked around Carina into the living room. "Cavin's... It's better not to do that. I'll go."

"No, in that case I'll go. You shower. I'll be back soon."

Cavin didn't acknowledge Carina as she returned through the lounge and left the apartment. She went down in the elevator to the ground floor, though the clanking of the ancient mechanism didn't inspire much trust. The streets in that area were too narrow for hover vehicles. Apartment blocks towered on both sides and skinny children played games with toys they'd made from trash.

Carina was immediately thrown back to her own childhood. She'd been a skinny kid playing with trash once too, though at the time she'd barely known life could be better. She didn't pity the kids too much. She'd been happy enough with very little except the love and care of her grandmother, for as long as the old woman had lived anyway.

Skirting the playing children, she walked down the dirty street and stopped at the first restaurant she saw. The place sold only one thing: a soup with noodles and meat. The origin of the meat wasn't specified. She bought three large containers covered with lids. The boy who was serving was so young he could easily have been one of the kids she had passed. After paying for the food, she returned to Asha's apartment.

Cavin hadn't changed position all the time she'd been gone and he was still playing on the interface. Asha came out of the shower dressed in a bathrobe. "Great, I love that soup. Thanks, Tammy. Put them down on the table. I'll get chopsticks and spoons."

Cavin finally moved, swinging his feet off the sofa and reaching for the nearest container. He peeled back the lid, took the chopsticks Asha handed him, and began to eat. Carina also dug into the steaming broth and noodles. The food was welcome after the puny, poor quality lunch they'd received at work. After the first mouthful, however, she lowered her chopsticks and stared into the bowl.

"Is something wrong?" Asha asked. "Don't you like it?"

"No," Carina replied. "Nothing's wrong. It tastes good." She resumed eating but the feeling that had made her pause persisted. The noodle soup tasted almost exactly like the one Nai Nai used to make. She wondered if she was imagining it. After her grandmother had died, Carina had never again come across the dishes the old woman had cooked. Yet the more she ate, the more certain she was that, halfway across the galactic sector from her childhood home, she was eating a dish she'd thought was a family recipe.

Asha was watching her. "Something is wrong, isn't it? Do you feel sick? We've never gotten ill from eating this before."

"It's okay. I'm fine. The food's great."

Cavin was eating at a fast rate. Anticipating the man would be back on the interface the moment he'd finished, Carina said, "I was wondering, would it be okay if I checked the news after dinner?"

"Sure," Asha replied. "Any particular reason? Not a lot goes on around here. Or at least not much that actually gets reported."

"No," said Carina. "No reason. Just want to catch up. You mean that news about the Dirksens doesn't get reported, right? I heard they only arrived a few years ago. What was it like?"

Asha made a noise of disgust. "It was awful and it's only gotten worse. The actual takeover was pretty bloodless. The Dirksens had done their research and found out exactly who held the power. After they arrived, they targeted only those people and took them out. Their families too. But the rest of us they left alone, just about. It all happened so fast, and our military was always weak. I guess no one ever thought anyone would be interested in our boring little planet. Turned out we were wrong. We hardly put up a fight. The Dirksens tried to sugar-coat it of course. They sent out propaganda telling us the planetary government was corrupt and that they were here to liberate us. They said we were backward and they would help us modernize. They gave us the hover drive technology, saying it was the first step in our "upgrade."

"But their tune soon changed. The Dirksens basically replaced everyone who had any money or influence in Ostillonian society with someone affiliated with their clan. If you weren't prepared to hand over a percentage of profits and kiss their asses they replaced you, one way or another. After news of disappearances, suicides, and accidental deaths started getting around, no one resisted any longer. Once you felt a Dirksen hand on your shoulder you gave them what they wanted, or accepted that your days were numbered."

"And what's it like now?" Carina asked, wondering how much of the mechanics of the takeover were Langley Dirksen's responsibility. The woman seemed to think her family's control of Ostillon was benevolent.

"They're slowly tearing everything apart," said Asha. "I mean, we didn't know how good we had it until the Dirksens started sticking their noses in wherever they thought they could turn a profit. You know the work we did today? Well, things didn't ever used to be that bad. There was always some kind of work if you wanted it. You didn't use to see people left behind. Now the supervisors are making ten people do the work of twenty and pocketing the extra wages. Everyone takes their cut all the way to the top and the Dirksens don't only ignore it, they positively encourage it. It's us poor saps at the bottom who lose out every time, and things are only set to get worse."

Cavin drained the dregs of broth from his container and put it down. He pushed the bowl away and reached for the interface.

"Er, could I check that?" Carina asked.

"Yeah, let Tammy use it for a minute, hon," said Asha.

Wordlessly, Cavin passed the screen over. He got up and went into the bathroom. Carina quickly set to work scanning the news for the region and the international news for the planet. There was no mention of four unidentifiable children being found. However, no reports mentioned strange, inexplicable activities or events either, she noted with relief. It looked like her mage siblings had managed to stay out of trouble so far.

While she had use of the interface, she looked up general information about Ostillon. The ritual at the Mech Battles still played on her mind. She was certain the fact that the person had created elixir was not a coincidence, but she also couldn't even guess what it meant. Mage history said their kind had lived in that galactic sector, dispersed and hidden, ever since it was first settled eons previously. The story she had learned from Nai Nai was that mages had been one of the first groups of colonizers, running from persecution on humanity's original home, a lost planet called Earth.

It made sense that something of their influence might remain in the cultures and religions of worlds they'd settled. Had Ostillon been one of those worlds? And if it had, was the fact significant? If mages had lived on the planet they appeared to have been long forgotten. No one seemed to know that elixir was being created in the ritual, so it had lost its meaning.

Cavin was getting restless. At his third cough, she returned the interface to him. "I'll take a shower now if that's okay," she said to Asha.

"Sure," Asha said. "Take your time. The hot water comes with the rent, though that's changing next month." She sighed and began to clear away the empty food containers. "Everything gets more and more expensive all the time."

Carina went into the bathroom and closed the door. She found it didn't have a lock but that didn't bother her. Both Cavin and Asha knew she was in there. She undressed. There was nowhere to put her clothes except on the basin so she piled them into it and stepped into the stall.

For the first time since Harmon's beating she could properly assess the damage. Bruises stood out on her back, upper arms, and thighs. It wasn't the first time she'd come off badly in a fight, and Stefan Sherrerr would have treated her worse, but this time she particularly hated the effects. More than ever, the injustice of what had happened angered her. The Dirksens and Sherrerrs were a menace across the sector. She wished she was in a position to fight them, but what could she realistically do? The most she could hope for would be to find her siblings and escape far from their influence, perhaps even to another sector.

As she pondered the rivalry between the clans, a memory popped into her mind. Ever since noticing the woman with the spiral hair design at Langley's party, she'd been wondering where she'd seen her before. Now she knew: it had been at the Sherrerr stronghold on Ithiya. She'd gone to see Calvaley to ask permission to visit Bryce in the men's quarters but the Sherrerr officer had been taking a holo call.

She hadn't seen the other caller's face but the hairstyle was so distinctive she was sure it was the same person. The last place she would have expected to see an acquaintance of the Sherrerrs was at a Dirksen gathering. It was no wonder it had taken her so long to make the connection. What did it mean? Was Langley's friend an informant? A Sherrerr spy? Had she interrupted a call where the woman was passing secret information to Calvaley?

As she washed soap out of her hair, she wondered if she should do anything about her revelation. It took her less than a second to come to a decision. No. What did she care if the Dirksens had a spy in their midst? She had nothing to gain from telling them and a whole lot to lose. Yet she feared what the fact might mean for Asha and other Ostillonians. Langley Dirksen had said the planet was a hidden bolthole for her clan. If someone the Dirksens trusted was feeding the Sherrerrs classified information, Ostillon wouldn't remain a secret for very long.

She had seen first hand the devastation of a planetwide attack. Asha might think things were bad now but they were probably going to get much worse.

A creak distracted her from her thoughts. The bathroom door was opening. At first, she expected that Asha wanted to ask or tell her something but the door only opened a short distance. A male hand and arm appeared, groping toward the basin where she had put her clothes. Cavin. Cavin was trying to steal her stuff.

She jumped out of the shower and slammed the door on his arm. Cavin shrieked. She opened and slammed the door twice more, and then threw it open. He fell to his knees, still screaming. Asha ran through from the kitchen.

"What did you do to him?" she shouted.

"Not as much as I'd like to do," said Carina, grabbing her clothes.

"She broke my arm," Cavin sobbed. "I think she broke it."

"Get out of my apartment," Asha said. "After everything I did for you, you go and attack my boyfriend."

"He was trying to steal from me," said Carina. "How else do you think this happened? Why would I hit him for no reason?" She began to get dressed.

"My arm," Cavin wept. "It hurts so bad."

"So what if he was trying to steal from you?" said Asha. "You didn't have to half kill him!"

Carina pulled on her top. "Do yourself a favor, Asha. Get rid of him. He's a bum and he's using you."

"No! Don't listen to her, Asha. I love you." Cavin cursed and tenderly touched his assaulted arm.

"Get out," Asha said to Carina. "Just leave, Tammy. And don't bother turning up for work tomorrow. I'll make sure you won't be hired."

"Don't worry," Carina said. "I'm not staying here another second." She marched to the door and went out.

Too angry to wait for the elevator, she took the stairs. As she ran down the steps two at a time, she wondered where she could spend the night. The Dirksens would still be searching for her intensively. She had to find somewhere they wouldn't think to look.

Sixteen

Several hours later, Carina was dead on her feet. She hadn't slept since the night of the Mech Battle, and even then it had only been for a few hours. She'd also been beaten, she'd worked through the small hours to escape from Langley's estate, and then she'd labored all day. She was on her last legs, yet she didn't seem able to find anywhere she considered safe to sleep.

As she'd wandered around the capital's downtown, Carina had taken the opportunity to buy new clothes. After pushing her old ones down a trash chute, she'd begun her search for a safe sleeping place.

Asha's apartment had been ideal. The Dirksens would never have found her there, in one of thousands of semi-legal residences. Now her options were limited. Without ID, the more expensive places were off limits. In time, she could solve that problem, but not quickly. Yet she feared staying at the cheapest hotels and hostels where ID wasn't required. They would be the first places the Dirksens would look.

Rounding the corner of a quiet street, she saw a heavily decorated building that rose from the ground in four tiers of decreasing size. Judging by the people wandering in and out of it, the structure seemed to be a public place. She walked down the street and through the wide, doorless entrance. The interior was as brightly decorated as the exterior, only while the walls outside were covered in patterns, inside the decorations were re-enactments of stories or events.

The building seemed to be a place of worship. Several people were kneeling facing a group of deities. One person had prostrated himself, his forehead pressed against the floor as he mumbled. None of the worshipers took any notice of her.

Again, she recalled the enigmatic ritual she'd witnessed after the Mech Battles. Was this place dedicated to the same religion? On the various worlds she'd visited as a merc, several faiths usually competed for the inhabitants' devotion. But at that moment, she was too tired to investigate further. She had to sleep.

On each side of the altar holding the statues of the deities, passages led deeper into the building. She took the right-hand one. Depictions of the religion's stories continued along its walls before it opened out into a space on the other side of the statues. This room held benches, presumably for lengthier sessions of worship. Other than the benches and a low, wide, cold brazier standing on the stone floor, the place was empty. She hoped it would remain so for a few hours at least, or that anyone who came in would leave her to worship in her own way. She stretched out on a narrow bench, lay her head in the crook of her arm, and was instantly asleep.

———

A gentle shake of her shoulder woke her. Despite the lightness of the touch, she still barely prevented herself from punching her awakener. Her fist stopped a whisker from the young priestess' face, and the woman drew back in alarm.

"Sorry," Carina said, sitting up. "I'm so sorry. You startled me." She didn't know how long she'd slept but she remained groggy with tiredness.

"I apologize for waking you," said the priestess. She wore a long cloak and a cowl so her features and figure were obscure, but she was so slight and her voice was so high and soft she seemed very young. "We have a morning ceremony. You're welcome to remain here but we need to use this bench."

"No, it's okay. I'll leave."

"You really don't have to leave," said the priestess. "Perhaps you would like something to eat after the ceremony?"

Now that she was fully awake, Carina gave some thought to the young woman's suggestion. Perhaps it wouldn't hurt to stick around in the place of worship for a while. She might be able to discover something about the ritual at the Mech Battles. "Thank you. I'll stay."

The priestess nodded. "You may stand in the corner over there." She left through a small door at the back of the room.

Carina stood up and stretched. Then she winced as her bruises reminded her of their existence. Music began to float through the open doorway—

twangs of stringed instruments and the regular beat of a drum. She went over to the corner and waited.

Figures wearing the same hoods and floor-length robes as the priestess entered the chamber in single file, each carrying a scroll of plaspaper. She spotted the young priestess, the shortest in the ranks. The twelve disciples took seats, one at each end of the benches. They began to chant in a foreign language, repeating what sounded like six or seven words over and over again. Then one of the priests stood and stepped solemnly to the brazier. He pressed a switch and flames sprang up. At the same time the whine of a fan came from above. When the fire was burning strongly, he unfurled his sheet of plaspaper and dropped it into the flames.

She glimpsed some writing on the sheet, then it was gone to ashes that were drawn upward to the fan. The priest returned to his bench. When he had sat down, the other devotee sitting on his bench did the same thing, though she thought the word he uttered was different from the first's. She was a little disappointed. She'd been hoping the disciples might make elixir on the brazier, but perhaps they didn't follow the religious practice she'd witnessed in the Mech Battle stadium.

The ceremony continued. Each disciple disposed of their sheet in the brazier's flames. As she was thinking wryly that it might be less effort to put the scrolls down a trash chute, she saw the writing on the paper clearly for the first time. She stood bolt upright. Then the sheet was gone and the fan above hungrily vacuumed up its ashes.

She'd seen a character. She hadn't been able to make out which one, but the sweeping strokes were so familiar she was sure she hadn't been mistaken.

Only one sheet remained unburned. It belonged to the young priestess. As the child approached the brazier, Carina craned to see what was written on it but the priestess was carrying the scroll close to her chest. She unfurled the sheet. The flames burned high as she held it out. The priestess spoke her word and dropped the paper into the fire.

Her heart sank. There was no character on the paper. It only displayed a random pattern of dots and numbers. She slumped against the wall. Had she imagined the character on the other scroll? Perhaps it was only because she'd just woken up and was still tired that she thought she'd seen something significant.

Someone had turned off the brazier and the priests and priestesses were filing out of the chamber. The young priestess was at the end of the line. Before she left the chamber, she gestured to Carina to wait.

She returned to a bench and sat down. After a few moments, the priestess reappeared carrying some food wrapped in a napkin.

"It isn't much," she said, "but you're very welcome to share with us."

"Thanks," Carina said. Thinking she might as well inquire about the religion anyway, she added, "Do you have a moment? I wanted to ask you something."

"What would you like to know?"

"I was at the Mech Battles the other night and I saw the ceremony at the end. Is that something your sect performs?"

"The Libation? Yes. We do that, though I've never had the privilege myself. It's a great honor and it will be many years before I am worthy, if I ever am."

"I was wondering what it meant."

"The Libation means many things. It gives thanks for the protection of the people, for one. You see, many years ago two great superpowers on Ostillon were at war. It was to put an end to the war that the Mech Battles were invented. Legend says that originally it was only two fighters representing each side, who fought with weapons. The mechs came later. A second reason for the Libation is to absolve the fighters' guilt if they killed their opponent. The Libation absorbs the sins of the competitors and washes them away when it is poured onto the soil."

"I see," said Carina. "But is there any significance to the ingredients used to create it? I thought I saw the priestess drop wood and soil into it." She didn't go into any more detail. She didn't want to give away how familiar she was with the creation of elixir.

"Oh yes, the ingredients are very significant. They... I can show you if you'd like me to when you finish eating."

Carina had been munching on the moist wafers the priestess had given her. She popped the last one into her mouth and said, "All finished."

Though the young girl's features were almost entirely obscured by her cowl, Carina thought she saw her smile. The priestess rose, and Carina followed her through a passage into the front of the building.

Daylight from the doorway now illuminated the room, washing out the colors of the friezes. The priestess led her to a section of the wall that displayed a pastoral scene. As she drew nearer, she realized the scene portrayed the five Elements. A stream ran through grass, representing Water. Lightning was striking a tree, and the first flickers of flame were outlining its branches. So there was both Wood and Fire. It was a natural landscape, so Earth was all around. Buried to its hilt in one spot next to the stream was a dagger or a sword, obviously made of Metal.

Beneath the scene was writing in a script she didn't recognize. "What does this say?" she asked, pointing.

"The language is very old," the priestess replied, "but it explains what sins belong to each material. Water represents lust. Wood is stubbornness. Metal is impatience..."

Carina was looking at the wall, but she was facing the entrance. As the priestess spoke, someone poked their head in briefly, withdrawing the second they saw her.

Not waiting to hear the rest of the priestess' explanation, Carina sped out of the building. The person who had looked in was running away. She set off in pursuit.

How Reyes had discovered where she was, she didn't know, but she was going to find out.

SEVENTEEN

Parthenia realized she hadn't heard any of the other children speak for a while. She checked over her shoulder. Darius was lying with his head on Ferne's lap and Ferne had his head on Oriana's shoulder. Oriana was slumped against the door. All three were deeply asleep. Parthenia sighed. She was tired too but she had to remain awake. Marcia could return to her normal self at any minute.

The woman had stared blankly ahead all the hours they'd been traveling, only slowly blinking every so often and shifting a little in her seat. Parthenia could hardly believe how long the Enthrall Cast had lasted. Yet despite their long journey they still didn't seem to be drawing near to the capital city.

The countryside was much greener than any place Parthenia had seen on Ithiya. They'd passed through farmland and alongside wide, lush estuaries before they'd reached the forest that currently lined the road. The place looked similar to the woods she and Darius had wandered through for hours and she wondered if it was in fact the same place, though she hadn't seen the ranger's tower.

Jace had seemed a nice man but she dreaded seeing him again. Not because he was so large and foreboding, but because she'd disappeared right before his eyes. She hoped he hadn't told anyone. She resolved to absolutely avoid Casting in front of anyone else again. Then she remembered that was exactly what she'd done around Marcia. Once more, she sighed.

She had allowed herself to be Enthralled more than once when the twins and Darius were learning the Cast. She recalled that coming out of it was like being in a dream and you slowly realized that you weren't in a dream at all—that everything around you was real. It wasn't like waking up from sleep. It was a strange sensation and quite unsettling.

Watching the farmer's profile, she wondered when she would wake up. It had to be soon, and then what would happen? She hoped Marcia didn't grab the vehicle's controls in her shock and surprise and cause them to crash. As they were traveling on automatic, she didn't think that was likely but she wished she could be sure.

When Marcia did come around, they would have to deal with her reaction and get away from her somehow. If only they would reach the city outskirts, then she could command Marcia to stop the vehicle and let them out. But the capital was nowhere to be seen, and if they left the vehicle while they were in a forested area, they would be in the same position she had been in with Darius when they arrived.

As she was about to turn away and refocus her attention on the road, Marcia closed her hanging jaw and smacked her lips.

Oh no! "Oriana," Parthenia hissed toward the back of the vehicle. "Ferne!" But the twins didn't wake.

Marcia's limp hands twitched.

Parthenia reached over her seat to prod her siblings to wakefulness. She didn't want to hasten Marcia's return to reality by speaking loudly. Parthenia could just reach Darius' leg. She poked him. He brushed at his leg but didn't properly wake up. She nudged her brother again.

"What?" he said sleepily.

"Wake up Ferne and Oriana. Quickly! Marcia's coming around."

The farmer began to blink rapidly. Her eyes regained their focus. Darius had sat up and he was shaking Ferne. Marcia lifted her hands onto her lap. A frown creased her forehead.

Parthenia had perhaps a few seconds remaining while the Enthrall Cast had some power. "Marcia," she snapped.

The woman's head turned toward her. Marcia's eyes grew wide.

"Stop the vehicle," Parthenia said sternly.

"Wh-what...? Why? What am I...?"

"Do as I say," Parthenia said. "Immediately."

Marcia shook her head in confusion but her hands took the controls. "How did I get here? I don't remember..." The hover vehicle rapidly slowed and sank toward the ground.

"Get ready to bail," Parthenia said to her siblings.

"Hold on," Marcia exclaimed. "You're the children who were in my barn. I remember now. You're a bunch of thieves." Her voice rose in volume as she spoke.

The vehicle was on the side of the busy highway. Ignoring Marcia's words, Parthenia went to open her door. It was locked.

"We can't get out," Oriana said.

"Open the doors, Marcia," Parthenia commanded.

"No way," the woman replied. "What am I doing here? How did you all come here with me? What did you do to me?"

"I said, open the doors," Parthenia repeated, hoping against hope that some tiny dreg of the Enthrall Cast might remain.

"I will not," Marcia said. "I'm taking you all to the authorities. I don't know what you did to me, but you're all criminals and I'm not letting you get away with it. Wait. I know what's happening! You want to steal my vehicle, don't you? And you want to kidnap me too." She moved her hands to the controls again.

Parthenia desperately tried to think of a way to stop her from turning them in. The only solution that occurred was almost ridiculous but she couldn't think of anything else. "Marcia, I'm telling you, if you don't let us out of this vehicle right now, I'll control you again. I can make you do whatever I want. How else do you think you came to be here? Open the doors now or I'll do it!" She tried to look angry and threatening though inside she was quaking with fear.

Marcia seemed about to refuse. Her lips twisted in anger. But then she relented. She gave the voice command and the locks popped. The children scrambled out.

"Quick, into the forest," Parthenia shouted, grabbing Darius' hand. She wanted to get everyone out of sight of the road and away from Marcia before the woman changed her mind. Holding onto her youngest brother, Parthenia slithered down the embankment at the road's edge and under a wire fence.

"She's comming someone," shouted Oriana as she tumbled down beside Parthenia. "I saw her."

"Run," yelled Parthenia. Gripping Darius' hand, she set off through the low plants and in amongst the trees. Then she slowed and turned, worried they might become separated if they didn't take care. Oriana wasn't far behind but Ferne was veering away. She called her brother's name. "This way," she shouted. "We have to stick together."

As soon as she saw her brother change direction, Parthenia plunged once more into the undergrowth. The plants weren't thorny like the ones in the first forest she and Darius had encountered on Ostillon, she noticed with relief.

Parthenia pushed deeper and deeper through the densely packed trees. She didn't have any idea where she was taking everyone but it was the best she could do for the moment. They had to avoid capture and if that meant getting lost again, that was how it had to be. Regularly checking that Oriana and Ferne were keeping up, Parthenia ran on, panting, for a short while.

"Ow," Darius exclaimed.

She had accidentally dragged him into a tree. "Sorry!" She slowed and stopped. "Are you okay?"

Darius rubbed his nose. "Yes, I'm all right."

They'd put considerable distance between themselves and the road. She thought it would be safe to stop for a moment and catch their breath. Ferne bent over, his hands on his knees. Oriana leaned against a tree. For several minutes, no one spoke. Then, after their breathing began to return to normal, Ferne said, "What's that? Can you hear it?"

Parthenia had to listen hard before she heard the noise too. It was a soft thumping sound. She'd mistaken it for her heartbeat at first but then she realized it was coming from somewhere not far from where they stood. The children stared at each other. What could be causing it? Darius opened his mouth to speak but Parthenia raised a finger, motioning him to silence. She beckoned Oriana and Ferne to come closer. She cupped a hand to her mouth to whisper to them but a second noise interrupted her. This time it was unmistakable—it was the sound of voices, and they were rapidly getting louder.

Oriana crouched down and Ferne and Parthenia quickly followed her lead. Parthenia pulled Darius down with her. Luckily, the undergrowth was tall enough to hide them. The children sat on their haunches beneath the leafy fronds, staring at each other through the plant stalks.

Parthenia still hadn't figured out what the soft thumping sound was. Like the voices, it was growing louder.

No one dared to speak. They could only hope the people wouldn't see them or come so close they tripped over them. Parthenia strained to hear what they were saying.

"So that's four for me and only three for you," a man said. "Shall we call it a day?"

"No, absolutely not," said a woman. "That isn't fair. If I go back with fewer kills than you, they'll never shut up about it. No. Let's stay out a while. I'm sure I can bag another."

"If you like," the man said, "though I don't fancy your chances."

"I know. We haven't seen much game at all today."

"That's true, but that isn't what I meant."

"Huh? What did you mean?"

"Isn't it obvious? I'm a much better shot than you."

"What? What are you talking about? You just got lucky."

Parthenia was looking in the direction of the approaching voices. The light was dim under the plants, but eventually she spotted movement. She gasped. Legs were coming toward them, but they weren't human legs. They belonged to the kind of animals she'd seen in Marcia's barn. Ferne and Oriana's eyes were round as they saw the legs too. The animals' steps were what was making the thumping sound. Even Darius noticed and pointed. Parthenia nodded at him and put a finger to her lips.

The most amazing thing about the approaching legs wasn't what they were, but what was missing from the scene. Along with the thuds of the walking animals, the voices were growing louder. But no people were visible. What could it mean? Were the people on the animals, sitting on their backs? Parthenia had never seen such a thing, not even on vids.

Her heart was racing. Two of those huge animals she'd seen in the barn were almost upon them but she didn't dare try to move out of their way. The slightest shift would bring her into contact with plant stalks—the plants would move and the people would know there was something in the undergrowth.

Another painful realization hit: the people on the animals were hunting. That was what they'd been talking about when they mentioned "kills." If she or one of her siblings changed position, the hunters might mistake them for game and shoot at them. She cringed and tensed. She was right in the path of one of the animals. It was going to step on her. She braced herself.

But the long legs shifted slightly to one side, narrowly avoiding her, as if the beast knew she was there. With much rustling of leaves, the two animals passed by, leaving everyone unscathed. Parthenia let out a long, silent exhale and watched the eight legs retreat out of sight.

When she could no longer hear the animals or the people, she cautiously poked her head out of the foliage. The forest looked the same as when they'd first hidden. Aside from the plant life and insects buzzing in shafts of afternoon sunlight through the trees, it was empty. Parthenia stood and helped Darius to his feet.

"Can we talk now?" he asked.

Ferne and Oriana also stood up.

"Yes," Parthenia replied. "But only quietly."

"Where should we go?" Ferne asked.

"I'm not sure," said Parthenia. "We definitely can't go back to the road. If anyone's looking for us we'll be very easy to spot there. I guess we'll just have to walk until we finally reach the city, or maybe a town."

"Which way is it, though?" Oriana asked. "What direction were we headed in when we left the vehicle?"

"Uhhh..." Parthenia didn't know. She'd entirely lost her sense of direction when they were running through the trees. Oriana and Ferne also looked confused, however, so she said, "I'm pretty sure it's this way." She took Darius' hand again and walked confidently ahead. She didn't want her siblings to know how lost they were. It would only make them worry. Perhaps she'd guessed correctly, she reasoned. Or maybe they would hit upon a village or town eventually.

Trying to be brave for the sake of her sister and brothers, Parthenia led the little party through the forest. She pushed her memory of her previous desperate walk with Darius to the back of her mind.

Eighteen

Carina caught up with Reyes at the end of the street. She launched herself at him and grabbed him around his thighs. They both hit the ground. Before Reyes could get up, she climbed onto his back and pinned him down. Passersby drew back in alarm and hastened away.

Reyes struggled to squirm out from under her for several moments before saying, "Okay, okay. I give up. Get off of me."

"Don't try to run," she said, releasing her pressure on his shoulders, "or I'll catch you again and I won't be so gentle next time." She moved off his back and stood up.

As he also rose to his feet, Reyes said, "I didn't think you were gentle this time."

"Then don't risk it."

"You really were a soldier, weren't you? Like Mother said. I didn't think a girl could hold me down."

She snorted derisively. "Plenty of female soldiers could beat your ass in a fight without trying. If I were you I wouldn't go around saying they couldn't."

Reyes rubbed his shoulder. "I don't know why you were chasing me anyway. I haven't hurt you. I let you escape, remember?"

"As soon as you saw me looking at you back there, you set off running. If you didn't have anything to hide, why run away? You weren't in that place by accident. You knew I was there and you came to check on me. How did you know that?" Pedestrians were still staring at the two as they passed by. "Wait. Let's get off this street."

She took Reyes' skinny upper arm and guided him along the sidewalk before pushing him down the first alley they arrived at. She walked along the narrow lane with him until they reached a spot between two towering apartment blocks that was empty of people. After halting, she pushed Reyes against a wall—not roughly but hard enough to reinforce that she was in charge.

"How did you know where to find me?" she reiterated.

"Honestly, it was just a coincidence. I often go to that temple. When I saw you there, I knew you would think I was spying on you, so I ran."

"No. You're lying."

"I'm not. Really."

She was tempted to force the truth out of the kid with the threat of—or actual—violence, but she'd experienced plenty of that kind of persuasion herself. She wanted to avoid dispensing it to others if she could. She tried a different tactic. "Okay. So if you go to that place all the time, what's the main picture on the left wall? What does it show?" She had been looking at the frieze only minutes before. Her question wasn't difficult for someone familiar with the building's interior.

Reyes looked panicked. "It, er, shows... It's a scene of... of—"

"Right," she said. "So we've established that you lied when you said it was a coincidence you were at that place. You don't always go there. Yet you knew where I was. But how?" She was directing the question at herself as much as at Reyes. Carina was fairly confident she hadn't been followed, and she had no identity or footprint in Ostillon's systems.

Reyes protested, "Like I said—"

"Oh, stop wasting my time," she snapped. She regarded the young man. He seemed about the same age as Parthenia. "Look. You're still young enough to not involve yourself with criminals and thugs, even if they are your family. You don't have to go along with everything they do just because you're related. You don't seem like a bad kid. Why don't you get out while you can? Go someplace else and start a new life. A clean life where you aren't hurting anyone. Only first tell me how you knew where I was."

Her words seemed to penetrate Reyes' conscience. He lost his guarded expression and looked down as if ashamed to meet her gaze. "It isn't as easy as you think, even if I did want to leave. But I can't anyway. It would break Mother's heart. I know she doesn't seem like a good person to you, but she isn't as bad as the others and she loves me. I'm all she has."

"Then take her with you."

"Huh. She'd never listen to me. Besides, she loves being a Dirksen. It's her whole life."

She gasped. While she'd been talking to Reyes, in the back of her mind she'd continued to try to figure out how he'd found her. The answer had just come. "I'm carrying a tracer, aren't I? Where is it? How did your mother get it into me?"

"Nnnno. That isn't true."

She grabbed Reyes' bony shoulders and pushed him into the wall. "Yes it is! There's no other way you could have found me. Have you been following me all this time?"

"I, er..." Reyes slumped and hung his head. He nodded. "I haven't been following you the whole time, but you are carrying a tracer. More than one, in fact. I'm sorry."

She swore. "Where are they?" She tried to remember everything that had happened at Langley's mansion. Had they injected tracers into her while she was asleep? No. She would have woken up. She was sleeping on a hair trigger these days. Had they drugged her? She was sure she would have noticed.

"They were in the food you ate at breakfast the morning after we went to see the Mech Battles," said Reyes. "The type mother used passes through the stomach and latches onto the inside of the small intestine. You ate several but you wouldn't have noticed anything."

Feeling nauseated, she pressed a hand to her stomach. She had to get the tracers out immediately. "So that's why neither of you came down to breakfast that morning. You couldn't eat the food."

Reyes nodded again. He looked up at her, a defeated expression in his eyes. "Would you be willing to come with me somewhere?"

"Where?" Carina asked. "And is this to do with getting these tracers out of me?"

"No. I honestly don't know how to do that. But you'll be safe with me. I just want to talk."

She wasn't sure if she could trust the young Dirksen. On the other hand, if he really was wavering in his allegiance to his mother's clan he could be very useful. She was willing to take a chance. "Okay."

Reyes continued down the alley and she walked with him.

The young man said, "Mother isn't as bad as you think, you know."

"You mentioned that already." She wanted to tell Reyes what his family's thugs had done to her brother. That might open Reyes' eyes about exactly what he was involved in. But sje couldn't say anything about Darius' experiences at the hands of the Dirksens without revealing more to Reyes than was safe. She hadn't yet admitted to anyone that she was the merc who had rescued Darius and she wasn't about to, despite the evidence of the vid. It didn't matter how different from the rest of the Dirksens Reyes thought he and his mother were. Yet she wanted to find out whatever she could about the clan. Perhaps she might learn something that would help her locate her siblings.

Reyes seemed to be looking for something as they walked along the alley. When they reached the end, they turned into another narrow lane and continued along it. The district was seedy. The residents were too poor even for clothes driers. Rows of wet garments hung across apartment balconies and the street didn't look like it had seen an autocleaner in a long time.

She was having second thoughts about going with Reyes. She needed to take out the tracers and she didn't know for sure what Reyes would tell her. He might not know anything useful.

Finally, after turning down several more alleyways and entering deeper and deeper into the poverty-stricken neighborhood, Reyes seemed to find what he was looking for. He stopped at a door that didn't seem any different from the others except that the wall next to it bore a pattern of scratches. The door had no security panel. Reyes tapped at it instead. When it opened a burly man not unlike Harmon stood there, his expression angry and sullen. But then he recognized Reyes and stepped backward, ducking his head.

"Wait a minute. If you think I'm going to follow you into some clandestine hideaway guarded by your mother's henchmen, you're mistaken."

"And if I wanted to recapture you, I could have done it at the temple," said Reyes. "I'm not forcing you to go in. You're free to leave now if you want."

She hesitated then said, "I do want to. I worked too hard to escape from your clan to risk this."

"Okay. Maybe we can go someplace else."

"No. I changed my mind. I've wasted too much time already. Goodbye, Reyes, and good luck living with thugs. I hope you don't turn into one of them." She began to walk away.

"Hold on," Reyes said, running after her. "What are you going to do about the tracers?"

She replied, still walking quickly, "Don't worry. I'll figure something out."

"Wait. I was going to say that maybe I can help you."

"Really? How?" She wasn't sure she believed him. After all, he'd already said he couldn't help her, or at least not with the tracers. When Reyes didn't reply immediately, she continued, "Forget about it. And stop following me or I'll force you to stop."

The young man halted. As she walked away from him, he called out, "I still don't know your name."

Nineteen

Carina had to find somewhere private to try to extract all the tracers. She wasn't looking forward to the task. When she'd Transported the Sherrerr tracers out of her brothers and sisters while they were escaping on the shuttle, she'd only been working on one per child and she'd known exactly where the devices were. Now, she didn't know how many Dirksen tracers were clinging to her guts, or their precise location. She would be using guesswork with her own body, and a delicate area of her body too. A damaged muscle would heal naturally in time, but she hated to think what she might do if she hurt her intestines.

Where to go? She continued deeper into the maze of streets. It was a warren of cheap apartment blocks served by small eateries and convenience stores. After stopping and checking behind her several times, she was finally convinced that neither Reyes nor anyone else was following her. Not that it mattered as long as she carried the Dirksen tracers.

Langley had tricked her into swallowing them in case she attempted to escape, of course. The Dirksen matriarch had been right on that score. Reyes hadn't mentioned what had happened at the estate since her escape. Did his mother know that he'd let her go? He also hadn't explained why he'd been checking up on her.

Or had she been set up? Had Langley Dirksen deliberately made it easy for her to get out of the mansion? Reyes had even been carrying cash to hand to her. It was all too convenient.

So many questions. And she had walked away from the only person who might answer them. Perhaps she'd done the wrong thing. Her friend, Bryce, had told her once that she was too distrustful. He'd said that not everyone was out to exploit mages for their own ends; that some people genuinely wanted to help.

He'd been right. The soldiers aboard the Sherrerr flagship had deliberately missed with their shots, allowing her and her family to escape. Perhaps Reyes really was a good guy, despite his family affiliations. Ah well. Now she would never know.

Then, as her hand touched the bills in her pocket, she realized she hadn't quite shut the door on Reyes Dirksen just yet.

She finally spotted what she was looking for: a small sign in a window high up in an apartment block. After counting the stories down to the ground, she walked through the security-free entrance. Only one elevator served the building and it was broken. She began to climb the stairs, counting each floor as she went up.

When she reached the story where the sign had been displayed, she tried to figure out which apartment it belonged to but she couldn't tell which it was. She couldn't remember in which direction the street lay and the hallway was windowless.

She went from door to door, pressing the panels until someone finally answered. It was a child, perhaps only seven or eight years old. She wondered if Ostillon was entirely staffed by children and if that explained why they were always hanging around. Didn't the planetary government provide schools? The little girl looked up at her expectantly.

"I want to speak to the person renting out a place on this floor."

The little girl only continued to gaze at her.

"I said, I—"

"That would be me," said a portly middle-aged man, waddling hurriedly toward the doorway. "Go back to your room," he said to the girl.

She moved away, but slowly, casting backward glances at Carina as she dragged her feet down the hall.

"So you'd like to rent my apartment?" the man asked eagerly.

"I'd like to *see* the apartment," said Carina. She didn't want the landlord to know she was desperate for a place. She only had a limited amount of money and no means of getting any more right now. She asked, "But if I like it, do you take cash?"

"My dear," the man replied. "I only take cash."

It turned out the apartment for rent was directly next door. The landlord keyed a code into the panel and the lock clicked open. The place was almost exactly as Carina had expected it to be—awful. It hadn't been cleaned in a long while. The windows were so grimy they were almost opaque and the bathroom and tiny kitchen were covered in stains.

"The place cleans up beautifully," the man said. "I would do it myself only I have a bad back. And with my grandchild to look after, I simply don't have the time. I was going to—"

"How much for a week?" she interrupted.

When the man named the figure, she didn't know if it was expensive or cheap according to the local rates, but she guessed he was probably trying to rip her off. He would be able to tell from her accent that she wasn't an Ostillonian.

"Are you joking?" she spluttered. "You think you'll get away with charging that much for a place like this?"

"Oh, wait," said the man. "What am I thinking? That's the rent for my other apartment that has twice as many rooms." He dropped his figure by a third.

She said, "That's still far too much."

The man shaved off a small percentage of the proposed rent. She was tired of haggling and she needed to remove the tracers as soon as possible. "All right, I'll take it—"

"Excellent."

"If you include an interface."

"An interface? You don't have one?"

"Mine was stolen and I haven't ordered another yet. I need something to bridge the gap."

The man frowned disbelievingly but said, "Well, that's easy enough. You can have one of my old ones, though I'll want it back at the end of your tenancy."

"Agreed," said Carina.

"And you pay me your week's rent up front. Now."

She reached into her pocket to pull out the cash. When her hand touched the bills Reyes had given her she stopped and took out the money she'd earned for her day's labor instead. It wasn't enough. She added some notes from Reyes' money to the pile and handed it to her landlord.

He counted the bills carefully and slipped them into the money belt he wore. "What's your name?" he asked.

"Tamira."

"Tamira what?"

"I'll tell you if I stay longer than a week."

"Ha," the man said. "If you say so. I'll send my granddaughter over with the interface later. Water and power aren't included in your rent, by the way." He told her the door code and left.

Adding the point about the utilities after the deal was struck was a typical trick, but she dismissed it. She hoped she wouldn't be in the place for longer than a few days. She couldn't contact her siblings through Casting, but she hoped she could find them through more conventional means, perhaps utilizing the planetary network.

She had an urgent task to complete first. She was about to take a sip of elixir and set to work when her door chimed. When she went to open it she found the little girl standing there wearing a solemn expression and holding an interface.

"Thanks," she said as the girl handed the device over.

She didn't reply but only skipped slowly back to her grandfather's apartment and went inside.

Carina carried the interface into the bedroom and put it down. Searching for information that might lead to the whereabouts of her sisters and brothers would have to wait just a little while.

She sat down on the bare, dirty floor and gently rubbed her stomach. She wasn't sure exactly where her small intestines were. Transporting objects you couldn't see was tricky. Transporting objects out of your body when you only had a rough idea of their location was plain stupid. But what choice did she have? Until she was free of the tiny electronic bugs, the Dirksens could swoop in at any moment and pick her up.

As soon as she'd removed the tracers, she would have to take them somewhere else and dump them or destroy them. When the Dirksens came for her they would go to the devices' last known location, and she didn't want that to be her newly rented apartment.

She took a sip of elixir, placed a hand on her stomach, and closed her eyes.

Twenty

A wind was rising, setting the trees into motion. The noises of the forest increased, rustling, creaking, and murmuring. The insects had retreated since the temperature dropped and the breeze arose. Parthenia hoped rain wasn't on its way. She and Darius were still wearing nothing except the shirts Jace had given them and Oriana and Ferne weren't much better clothed.

At least they were heading toward the capital city, or so she hoped. She'd spotted shuttlecraft traveling overhead and because they always went in a particular direction she'd concluded they were on their way to or from a spaceport. She'd taken her pick of the two possible directions in which the spaceport might lie and for the last half an hour or so they'd been walking toward—or away from—the place. Her chances of being correct were only fifty-fifty, but they were the best odds they were going to get.

Ferne was carrying Darius. Not because her youngest brother was tired, but just for fun. Parthenia was grateful to Ferne for entertaining the little boy and taking his mind off the thirst, hunger, and fatigue they all felt. Ferne was pretending to be one of the animals from Marcia's barn and Darius was pretending to be a hunter. He was holding an imaginary weapon and firing behind while telling Ferne to go faster.

"What are you shooting at now, Darius?" Oriana asked. Previously the boy's targets had been various monsters of his imagination. This time, however, he replied, "Father's guards are chasing us. But it's okay. I'm killing all of them."

Oriana caught Parthenia's eye, her eyebrows raised. Parthenia returned the look. Poor Darius. It would take them all a long time to get over their terrifying escape from Father's family. She was still struggling with the role she'd played in his death. She didn't think she would ever come to terms with it.

"You get 'em, Darius," said Ferne.

Her little brother screwed up one eye to take aim and fired his finger at the invisible guards.

A loud thunk resounded, and a thick cylinder of wing-tipped metal appeared in the tree trunk next to Ferne's head.

The children froze.

Someone was firing at them.

"Run," Parthenia shouted. The children sped away through the trees. She wanted to tell Ferne to give Darius to her. Her little brother was heavy for a twelve-year-old to carry. But she didn't dare stop long enough to make the switch.

Another loud thunk sounded. "Hurry," she called. She hoped they wouldn't get split up, but putting distance between themselves and the hunters was the priority.

Why were they being shot at? Did the hunters really want to kill children? A third wooden thunk resounded and Oriana squealed. The bolt had nearly hit her.

Now, above the sound of the wind, Parthenia could hear the thump of the feet of the animals the hunters rode, getting closer. How the large beasts maneuvered between the trees, Parthenia didn't understand, but they managed it. The thought gave her an idea.

Over to one side was a dense grouping of trees. Ordinarily she would have avoided such a place, but in this case it was ideal. "Over there," she panted to her siblings. They changed direction and ran for the trees.

A fourth bolt whistled past her ear. She bit back the shout of fear that rose to her lips. The trees were giving the children some cover. She didn't want to give the hunters a clear indication of their whereabouts.

Oriana was the fastest runner of them all. She'd reached the thick trunks of the dense clump of trees. In a moment, she'd slipped between them and disappeared. Parthenia reached them next. She hopped behind a tree and watched. Ferne was lagging far behind, struggling with Darius' weight, but finally he ran up with his little brother clinging to his back.

Just as he reached her, Ferne cried out and fell forward. Darius tumbled off of him. One of the hunter's bolts was sticking out from the back of Ferne's thigh.

"Ferne," she screamed. She couldn't help herself. Her brother raised his head, his face twisted with pain.

A burst of sound and movement a short distance away distracted Parthenia from her brother. The hunters on their animals were speeding closer. Then the animals slowed, making a strange, high-pitched sound. One of the hunters cursed. "It's kids," he said. "What are they doing here?"

Parthenia helped Ferne to his feet. "Run, Darius," she said. "Run into the trees. Find Oriana."

The woman exclaimed, "You shot one of them!"

"No, I didn't," the man protested. "That was you."

"Can you walk?" Parthenia asked Ferne.

He was white and shaking but he nodded. She wrapped his arm over her shoulder and half-helping, half-carrying her brother, she took him out of sight of the hunters. As soon as they'd made it a short way through the narrow spaces between the trunks, she lowered her brother to the ground. Blood was running down his leg and he looked ready to pass out. If the hunters followed them and caught up with them, there wasn't anything she could do about it. She only hoped Oriana and Darius might get away.

But while she sat with her injured brother on the forest floor, no sounds of pursuit followed them. Parthenia guessed the hunters might get into trouble for accidentally shooting children, even if they were trespassing.

"Ferne," Parthenia said. "I'm so sorry. That must hurt really badly. I'm going to do whatever I can to help."

Her brother only nodded, his lips tightly compressed.

But what could she do? If she had elixir, she could Transport the bolt out of Ferne's leg and then Cast Heal on the wound. But she had no elixir nor a way of making any. The children were alone and friendless.

For the thousandth time, she wondered what had happened to Carina. If only she were there she would know what to do. Parthenia felt she'd made one mistake after another.

"Ferne," Oriana exclaimed as she came through the trees, holding onto Darius' hand. She fell to her knees at her brother's side and burst into tears. "Ferne, don't die. Please don't die. We're nearly there. We can make you better."

"What?" Parthenia asked. "We're nearly where?"

"We're at the city," Darius said. "Oriana and I found it. Come and look, Parthenia. We can take Ferne to a splicer and make him better. Come on, I'll show you." He grabbed her hand and tried to pull her to her feet.

Leaving Ferne with Oriana, she got up and went with Darius. Not more than a minute away, the trees faded out entirely. She found herself looking at a wire fence. Beyond the fence stood a landing bay, and beyond that were the low buildings of a spaceport. Farther away the city stood, its buildings rising higher in the distance.

They'd made it to their destination, but Darius wasn't right in all he'd said. They would never get Ferne to a splicer from their current location. She would have to fix her brother's leg somehow before they could go on.

Twenty-One

As Carina sat at the edge of the bedroom in her rented apartment, she recalled removing the Sherrerr tracers from her siblings when they were escaping on the shuttle. That had been so much easier. For one thing, she'd seen the tracer that the Dirksens had cut out of Darius, so she knew the size and appearance of the devices. And she'd known almost precisely where to find them in her siblings' bodies.

By contrast, removing the Dirksen tracers from her intestines was going to be like hunting in the dark with a double-edged knife. One false step and she could cause herself some serious harm.

She swallowed. The truth was, she was almost certainly going to inflict some damage. She doubted the best mage in the galaxy could Cast with the accuracy required to lift out the tiny tracers without affecting the surrounding tissue, even without operating blindfolded. No, there was no point in kidding herself—this was going to hurt.

She took out the bottle of elixir she'd carried with her all the way from Langley's mansion. She'd hoarded the liquid, saving it for emergencies just like this. She unscrewed the cap. Then she paused.

She couldn't figure out why the Dirksens hadn't picked her up yet. Should she have given Reyes a chance to explain? No. That would have been too risky. The information he held might have been useful yet she felt she'd made the best choice in the circumstances. It was time to get as far away from the Dirksens and the Sherrerrs as she could—after she found her brothers and sisters.

She realized she was going over her decision as a way of putting off something she dreaded to do. She refocused and mentally reached out, feeling for the tracers. Now she knew they were there, it wasn't too hard to sense the devices in the depths of her gut. Their material was different from the rest of her flesh, but she couldn't tell how many there were. The tracers were all bunched together.

It wouldn't be a good idea to try to Transport all of them out of her at once. She was fearful of accidentally pinching out a large piece of her intestine at the same time. Although she could Cast Heal and fix the injury, she might not be able to do that if she was in too much pain or had passed out.

She breathed in and out, deeply and slowly, and centered her mind on the tiny devices embedded in her intestines. She wrote the Transport character and sent out the Cast. She winced as she mentally gripped a tracer and lifted it out and away, placing it on the floor beside her. She opened an eye to look at the thing. It was a tiny metal bead—a red-stained, silver fleck on the grimy floor.

One.

She couldn't feel any ill effects yet. No pain or even discomfort. She took another sip of elixir. It was time to remove number two.

———

She wasn't sure if she'd removed seven or eight tracers. She'd lost count, and the devices were too small to see clearly in their little bloody pile beside her. She was in pain and she was feeling faint, though she wasn't sure if the faintness was due to the repeated Casting or the damage she'd caused. The more tracers she'd removed, the harder it had become to locate the devices. She thought she could sense one final tracer but she wasn't sure. Her foggy mind and her aching stomach were strong distractions.

She took another sip of elixir and pressed on. She had to get all the tracers out. The Dirksens only needed one in order to find her. She forced her tired mind to concentrate and reached inside herself. Was there something still there? It was so hard to tell. The site where the tracers had burrowed was damaged and bleeding. She would have to Cast Heal soon.

But only when she'd removed the final tracer from her system. She only had enough elixir to Cast twice more. She had to save Heal until last. She strained her senses and mentally probed her gut. She felt something—some kind of anomaly. Was it a tracer? Perhaps her damaged tissue was confusing her. No matter. She would Transport a small piece out and then immediately Heal herself.

As she Cast Transport, a sharp pain pierced her insides. She gasped and opened her eyes. Something was wrong. She'd gone too far. Pain radiated from her gut. She had to Cast Heal. She swallowed the last of her elixir and closed her eyes. She tried to center herself and write the character, but she was in too much pain. She was slipping away. Everything went black.

Twenty-Two

Carina awoke to a familiar sensation. She could feel the faint vibration of a starship's engine. For a moment, groggy with pain and too much Casting, she thought she was back aboard the Dirksen ship. She opened her eyes, expecting to see the shaven-headed officer watching her, waiting for her to slip up during his subtle interrogation. Instead, she saw a young man's profile. Reyes was sitting at a starship's flight controls. A low ceiling was above her and she was pressed against a wall. She was lying in the reclined seat of a small shuttlecraft.

She sat bolt upright. Pain from her stomach lanced through her and she cried out.

Reyes turned and looked down. "Stay still." He placed a hand on her shoulder, gently restraining her. "I'm taking you to a doctor."

She didn't have the strength to resist. She was so tired and she'd definitely done something to her gut. If she had some elixir left she could fix herself but she remembered she'd drunk the last of it. As she gave up struggling, Reyes lifted his hand.

"I'm glad you've come around," he said. "I was worried about you. We'll be at the hospital in another minute."

"You tracked me through those tracers."

"Of course."

"Damn."

"It was lucky for you I did. I don't know what's wrong with you but you were out cold when I found you."

"Huh. An old guy let you in, right?"

"A little girl, actually. She said her pops was sleeping."

Carina guessed the old man hadn't taken long to spend her week's rent money on his favorite addiction. There wasn't a lot else to look forward to in districts like that, she knew too well. "You carried me out all by yourself?"

"Hey, I'm stronger than I look. ... And you came around a little and helped. Maybe you don't remember. I only had to get you to the roof where I'd landed my star racer."

"Why did you come for me? I thought you were going to leave me alone."

"You did? I never said that."

"It was kind of implied, I thought. After the whole kidnapping thing." Her wooziness wasn't dissipating. If anything, it was getting worse. She wasn't sure if she was going to pass out again or throw up. The latter alternative won. Her vomit was brown and granular. "Sorry."

Reyes glanced down at her production, now slowly spreading over the shiny floor of the tiny shuttlecraft. "Don't worry about it. I'm sure glad I decided to come and get you though."

"How come you turned up just then? Did you know I was sick?"

"Yeah. The tracers don't only signal their position. They transmit the subject's health status along with a few other things."

"Pretty clever. You Dirksens love your high tech."

"Don't call me a Dirksen, please. Just call me Reyes. I don't like to think of myself as one of them anymore. I decided I'm going to divorce myself from my clan, just as soon as I exploit the benefits of being a member one more time." He gave a wry smile. Returning his attention to the controls, he said, "We're here. There should be medics to meet us. I comm'd ahead."

The shuttlecraft rapidly lost altitude, increasing her nausea. The engine cut out and half of the roof of the vehicle lifted. It was raining outside. She was instantly soaked. Two medics were suddenly checking her over. The next moment, she was being lifted out and onto a gurney. The medics raced with her across the rooftop, through open double doors, and into an elevator.

Reyes stepped in as the elevator doors closed. He stood over her, resting his hand on the gurney rail. One of the medics was cutting open her clothes.

"I only just bought these," she protested. Everyone was overreacting. She'd been injured plenty of times while working as a merc. If she only had a mouthful of elixir she could fix her problems herself.

A medic was running a scanner across her stomach. The woman showed the other medic the results.

"Did you eat something sharp?" the female medic asked.

"No, someone fed me something noxious." She glared at Reyes, who looked away.

The medics didn't say anything else. Did they know Reyes was a Dirksen? Would the hospital check Ostillon's databases for her genetic profile? What would the staff do when they couldn't find her on the planetary system?

She couldn't stay here to be treated. It was too risky. But as she tried to sit up she gasped with pain.

"Lie down," admonished the female medic, pushing her shoulders to the gurney. "Where do you think you're going?"

"Away from here," Carina exclaimed, struggling with her.

"Please stay still," said Reyes. "I'm really only trying to help you. No one here is going to hurt you or even ask you who you are. You don't have to worry."

In her current state of health, she didn't have much choice but to give in. She wouldn't be able to fight off three people and escape. She wasn't sure she could even stay upright.

As the elevator reached its floor and the doors opened, she passed out again.

———

When she came around for the second time the pain in her stomach was gone. She was in a hospital bed and Reyes was sitting beside her reading an interface, not yet aware she was awake.

Though she felt a lot better, her wooziness hadn't entirely gone away. She guessed it was an after-effect of the drugs she'd been given while her insides were being fixed. Relief washed through her. While she'd tried to pretend to herself that the damage she'd inflicted while removing the tracers was no big deal, deep down she'd actually been quite scared. She hoped she wouldn't ever have to attempt such a thing again.

Now she was better and the tracers were gone she could begin searching for her siblings right away. They'd been on their own for days. She hated to think what might have happened to them.

She pushed back her covers and sat up half way but the movement made her head spin. She slumped down.

"Whoa," said Reyes. "Take it easy." He pulled the covers over her.

She noticed she was wearing a hospital gown. "Where are my clothes?" She wouldn't have gotten far dressed as she was. What had she been thinking?

"The medics cut your clothes off you, remember?" said Reyes. "Your money is in the drawer next to your bed. I can get you some more clothes.

I'll order them for you now. What do you want?" He took up his interface again.

"Wait. What are you doing?"

"Huh? I'm buying you some clothes. Didn't you hear? Don't worry. The anesthetic will wear off soon."

"I mean, what are you doing here, now, with me?"

"What do you think I'm doing? I'm looking after you. The surgeon said your operation went well. Said you're as good as new now."

"Thanks, but..."

"But what?"

"I don't get it. What's all this about?"

Reyes said, "I told you already. I'm leaving my mother's clan. What you were saying was right. They *are* a bunch of thugs. I never really saw it before because I was brought up in the middle of it. I believed Mother when she explained that we Dirksens were helping to develop and modernize other societies to their benefit. It just took me a while to realize it was all garbage. Excuses.

"It's hard when it's your close family who's doing evil things. That was what I wanted to talk to you about before, only you didn't give me a chance. Then I saw what you'd done to yourself trying to remove the tracers. That made up my mind. I'm never going back home. I still love my mother but I can't accept what she does and I don't want to be a part of it.

"I haven't told her about my decision yet," Reyes went on. "I'll let her figure it out for herself. Until she does, I can make use of my status. But only to do good things. Like helping you. No one here will ask who you are or what happened to you. There won't be any record of your treatment on the hospital records. And..." he smiled slyly, lifting his interface, "I can order whatever I want until my account is closed."

"Yeah," Carina said, "and your mother will be able to find out exactly what you ordered and where it was delivered."

Reyes' face fell. "I didn't think of that."

"If you do plan on doing a disappearing act, you'll need to be a lot more careful. It isn't easy to stay hidden. Not easy at all."

"I guess that's true."

The young man looked troubled and she felt a little sorry for him. It was a bold, brave, and perhaps foolish step he was taking. She didn't think he was mature or experienced enough to understand all the implications. Yet he was doing the right thing. Overall, she was glad her previous goading seemed to have tipped him into a decision he'd been brooding about for a while.

"What do you plan to do?" she asked, wondering if he had a plan at all.

"I'm not sure."

He didn't.

"Maybe I can get a job," Reyes continued. "I have my star racer. I can sleep in that."

"You don't think your mother might have put a tracer on it?"

"I don't think so but you're right, it's a possibility. I should have it scanned. It was my present for my sixteenth birthday. I don't think it's registered. No Dirksen registers anything."

"Of course not," she said. "Why would they? That might force them to operate within the law, which would be ridiculous."

Reyes' wry smile returned. "I like your sense of humor. How are you feeling now?"

In truth, she was still feeling the effects of the anesthetic, but she felt much better than she had before. "I'm okay. I think I'll be able to leave soon."

"Don't do that," said Reyes. "Rest a while longer. The surgeon said you should wait until tomorrow to go home."

"That isn't going to work for me. I have some things I have to do urgently."

"Please, stay here for a couple more hours. Allow some time for the drugs to wear off. Maybe I can help you do whatever it is that's so urgent."

"Well..." She considered. Could she trust him? Reyes had saved her when she was in a dangerous position. Bryce had always said she too distrustful. She wondered what had happened to her friend. She hoped he'd made it back to his family.

She looked into Reyes' eyes. He gazed back openly, unblinking.

"Maybe you can help me."

Twenty-Three

"I can't do it," Oriana sobbed. "I just can't do it."

"It's okay," Parthenia replied, taking her sister's hands in her own. Oriana's palms were red and raw from trying to start a fire. "I'll think of something else."

"The wood's too wet," Oriana said. "In the barn it was bone dry, and even then it took me ages to make it smolder. Here, outside, it's too damp. I'm sure that's the problem."

"I guess you're right," Parthenia replied. "It was a miracle you started a fire at all the first time you tried. I wouldn't have known how to do it."

"I saw it in a vid," said Oriana. "Ferne showed me." She burst into sobs again.

Ferne was lying to one side under a tree. He was on his front, the bolt the hunters had shot him with still sticking out of the back of his thigh. He was awake but in so much pain he'd hardly spoken over the last few hours.

"Just pull it out," he said between clenched teeth. "I can't stand having that thing stuck in me. Please, pull it out. We can tie something around my leg and then we can go into the city."

Parthenia had been trying to avoid that solution to their problem. As it was, Ferne's wound currently only bled when he moved. She was worried that if they pulled the bolt out they might not be able to stop the bleeding and her brother might bleed to death. She didn't want to tell him that, though. If only they had some elixir. Just a couple of mouthfuls was all it would take. But they couldn't start a fire.

Oriana was holding her poor, sore hands under her armpits. Parthenia put an arm around her sister's shoulders. Her own hands were hurting too from trying to help.

Darius was where he'd been for hours, sitting at the wire fence watching shuttles take off and land at the spaceport.

Parthenia was trying to be strong but she felt like crying. No matter how hard she tried she couldn't figure a way out of their situation. If she could make it into the city, it might be easier for her to make some elixir. The process was so simple and the ingredients so mundane, it shouldn't be too hard. But she didn't want to leave Ferne, even if Oriana stayed with him. What if the hunters came looking for them? She didn't know what might happen while she was gone.

She'd been parted from the twins once already. She didn't want to leave them on their own again. The responsibility weighed on her heavily. At some point during the trials of that day, she had given up hope of Carina finding and helping them. For whatever reason, her older sister clearly wasn't going to turn up. They were on their own. Yet Parthenia had learned she wasn't up to the task that had befallen her. She'd made so many bad decisions.

Dusk had fallen and was turning to night. The lights from the spaceport meant they weren't in darkness, but Parthenia remembered with a shudder the sounds of night creatures in the forest where she and Darius had first been lost. Also, though no one had complained, she knew everyone was extremely thirsty and hungry.

Perhaps it was time for her to face the truth about what she had to do. As she made her decision, Darius turned away from the fence, stood up, and walked over to her. He wrapped his arms around her neck and hugged her. Her little brother didn't say a word. She knew he had sensed her mood and was trying to offer some comfort.

"It's no good," Parthenia announced. "I'm going to have to leave you and find someone I can ask for help."

"No," Ferne muttered. "I keep telling you. Pull the damned thing out. I'll be fine. I would do it myself if I could reach it."

"We can't," Oriana said. "Parthenia's right. It wouldn't be safe. We aren't splicers. We don't know what we're doing. It isn't like Casting. You could die."

"Dying would be better than going back to living how we were," Ferne said.

He'd spoken the thought that was on all their minds. If anyone discovered who they were or what they could do, the best they could look forward to was a life of captivity. But while their lives with Father and Mother had been luxurious, they couldn't expect the same treatment at the hands of the Dirksens.

Parthenia wondered what the clan might do to her if they figured out she was responsible for many of their business deals going awry.

But what else could she do? Feeling like a failure, she said, "I'm the oldest and I'm making this decision. We can't stay here trying to make fire forever. At least this way we have a chance. It doesn't automatically follow that whoever we ask for help is going to do something bad to us. Maybe they'll be kind and not ask any questions. When Darius and I were lost we found someone who helped us."

"I agree with Parthenia," Oriana said. "You can't stay as you are, Ferne. You need help. If we have to take a risk to find someone to help you that's what we have to do."

Ferne closed his eyes in pain and turned his head away.

"Okay," Parthenia said. "Let's go over our story one more time. We don't know the name of any places here, so we'll make one up. We'll say we're from Riverfield. There has to be somewhere called Riverfield. Then the rest of the story is the same as we said before."

All the children except Ferne rehearsed their cover story. Parthenia wasn't sure it sounded authentic but it was the best she could come up with. It would have to do. When they'd repeated all the details a few times, she said, "Right. I want you all to stay here. I'm going to try to find someone."

"Where will you go?" Darius asked.

"I'm going into the spaceport. It's the closest place that has people in it. Now, none of you must move from this spot while I'm gone. Especially you, Darius. No matter what happens, you mustn't leave Oriana. Do you understand?"

"I want to go with you," said Darius.

"No, you can't." If something bad happened she didn't want Darius with her.

"What if you don't come back?" Oriana asked, her eyes glistening in the darkness.

Parthenia didn't know what to reply. As she struggled to think, a shuttle passed overhead, momentarily lighting up her sister and brothers with its beams. She ran to hug and kiss them, just in case. "I will come back."

———

The spaceport was full of passengers. Parthenia had walked around the perimeter fence until it met the road that led to the facility. She went through the transparent doors as they parted and entered the busy hall. After the quiet of the forest the noise of announcements and crowds of chattering people were almost painful. Everyone seemed to be in a hurry. Who should she approach? She didn't want to speak to anyone in authority in case they asked her awkward questions.

She decided to target people who were on their way out of the spaceport because they wouldn't be in a hurry to catch their flight. Yet after glancing at her odd clothes—she had never felt so aware she was still wearing Jace's shirt up until that moment—everyone she went up to ignored her and went on their way.

"Please…" she said, trying to catch the attention of a mother with two children. "Please, can you help me?"

But the mother only pretended not to hear her and hurried her children along. Parthenia tried to approach another passenger but the result was the same. She'd never felt so alone and helpless as she stood by herself in the shifting crowds. What a change it was from the last time she'd been in a spaceport, with Father and Mother. Father had been so haughty and arrogant, arguing with the official about having to walk through the public departures hall.

She had to make someone stop and listen to her request. Ferne and the others were counting on her. A young couple were walking slowly over to the exit, arm in arm. They seemed to have kind faces.

"Excuse me," she said, planting herself in the couple's path so they couldn't avoid her. "My brother's had an accident. I need some help."

The couple had been entirely focused on each other. At her interruption, they looked surprised and then embarrassed. "I'm very sorry," said the woman, side-stepping her.

She grabbed her arm. "How can you be so uncaring? My brother's seriously hurt. Why won't you help?"

"Hey," the man shouted. "Let go of her." He tore her hand away. "Come on, honey," he said to the woman. "She probably wants money for drugs."

"No, I don't," she shouted, at her wit's end. If she didn't get some help soon, Ferne might die. She was worried her siblings might give up on her and try to pull the bolt out of his leg. "You have to help me! Someone has to help."

A guard she hadn't noticed before began to march toward her. She tensed. She didn't want that kind of attention. After a moment's indecision, she turned and ran… directly into another guard who had been approaching her from behind.

"Got you," the guard said as she grabbed her arm and twisted it behind her back.

Parthenia cried out at the sudden pain. She struggled but the guard only twisted her arm more tightly. She gasped. "Let me go! I haven't done anything."

"I don't believe that for a minute," said the guard. "But we'll soon find out. Come on. Let's go." By this time the other guard had also reached her. The two of them manhandled her across the spaceport hall. Suddenly, all the passengers to whom she'd been invisible only a moment before stopped and stared.

"I'm only here because I need help for my brother," she protested. "He's been hurt. He was shot in the forest. I had to leave him there with my other brother and sister."

"Shot? In the forest?" the male guard asked.

"Save your lies," said the female guard. "They won't do you any good."

"Why would I lie about something like that? I'm not asking for money. I'm asking for help. Please. You have to believe me."

The male guard was grave. "If your brother really is lying injured in the forest, there isn't anything we can do. That's Dirksen land. Whatever goes on in there is up to them."

"No! You have to help him. If you can't help him, let me go! Let me go back to him." She twisted and fought, trying to bite the guards' hands, trying anything to make them release her, but she couldn't break free.

The two guards hauled her, struggling and kicking, into a security room. She was beside herself with fear and rage. The guards pushed her into a corner, left the room, and locked the door.

Twenty-Four

As Reyes checked the Dirksens' comm records, Carina was having grave misgivings. Why had she told him she was looking for her brothers and sisters? If she hadn't been groggy from the anesthetic at the hospital she doubted she would have taken the risk. On the other hand, without his help she might never be able to locate Parthenia and the others. What chance did she really have of locating four children in an entire continent, or perhaps a whole planet?

Reyes had arranged new clothes for her after she insisted on leaving the hospital. They still hadn't quite left, however. They were sitting in Reyes' star racer on the roof of the building and he'd been going through the recorded comms for ages. She had passed some time looking out over the city while the sun came up and she'd passed some more examining Reyes' vehicle. It was tiny, holding only two people, yet he'd assured her it was interplanetary.

"Maybe this was a bad idea," she said as she finally lost patience waiting for him. "If there was any mention of my siblings on those files I'm sure you would have found it by now."

"Not necessarily," Reyes replied. "These are personal files and they aren't searchable. I have to go through them individually."

"Personal files? You mean that Dirksens have access to other clan members' personal comms?"

"Of course not."

"Then how come you can read them?"

"I figured out a way into the intra-clan comm system a few months ago. It was what I read there that partly fueled my decision to leave. Some of my family are depraved. It's sickening. Mother is about the best of all of them. Ah, wait. What's this?" His fingers swiped down the screen. "Huh. That's odd, and interesting."

"What?" She looked over his shoulder.

"It's an audio file that was deleted only a few minutes after it was made."

"That could be anything. And it's gone now anyway."

"Not from my records, it hasn't. Let's see..." He continued to work at the interface for a few moments. "Got it. I'll play it back."

"But you said it was deleted."

"When I discovered that deleting conversations and messages was somewhat of a habit in my clan I set up a system to automatically copy all comms. It's the deleted files that are the juiciest. I only have room to store the information for a few weeks before I have to clear it out but this comm was only made yesterday evening. Let's hear it."

The first voice they heard was a young woman's. It was tremulous. "Father?"

"Hello, Kiva. Where are you? Is everything all right?"

"No, it isn't. I think I... I..."

"What's wrong? Are you still out hunting? We wondered what had happened to you. Come home now. It's late."

"Father, I think I might have accidentally shot a child. I don't know what to do. Should I call for a medic?"

"A child? Don't be ridiculous. How could you have done that? You must be mistaken."

"I don't think I am. It was twilight and I couldn't see very well, only their moving shapes. There were four of them. They were running away. I shot at them, thinking they were game. Oh, Father. I hit one of them. I know I did. Pol saw it too. One of them fell down."

Carina's heart froze.

"I'm telling you you're mistaken," the man said sternly. "What would children have been doing in our hunting grounds? No Dirksen child has been shot. I would have heard about it."

"I don't think they were Dirksen children," the woman said. "I think—"

"Then it doesn't matter, does it? Come home immediately, Kiva, and never mention this again."

The comm ended. Carina's hand was over her mouth as she stared at the interface.

Reyes said, "I'm sorry. That might be them, right? It makes sense. If they're from offplanet, they wouldn't know it's dangerous to enter woods unless they know who owns them. I seriously doubt any Ostillonian child would have been wandering through a Dirksen hunting forest."

She struggled to reply. She could see visions of Darius lying dead on a forest floor. "Do you know where the comm originated?"

"Yes," Reyes replied. "I have the exact coordinates. It's a hunting lodge on the outskirts of the forest by the spaceport. Strap in and I'll take you there."

Reyes' star racer, as he called it, was a high-class spacecraft. She could barely feel or hear the engine as Reyes started it, and the ship's motion was as smooth as silk as they flew up and away from the hospital roof. She guessed the star racer's drive included the hover technology the Dirksens had brought to the planet.

As soon as they were high above the city Reyes accelerated. The force pushed her back into her seat.

"How long will it take to get there?" she asked.

"Not long. Ten or fifteen minutes," he replied, checking the controls.

"This place is close by then?"

"No. It's on the other side of the city. But up here we can fly direct and the star racer is fast."

She was twisting her hands in her lap, trying to ignore the image in her mind of Darius dying. "So your relatives go hunting?"

"It's a popular sport. They have forests all over the planet and hold competitions using ancient weaponry." He glanced at her. "Sorry."

"Do you go to them... These competitions?"

Reyes shook his head. "Not my kind of thing. Plus there's the fact that Mother's always there trying to partner me up with some girl or another."

"What, other Dirksens? Do you marry your cousins?"

"Only distant ones. Don't you?"

"No. I don't think so anyway." In fact, she had no idea how mages met and married. Nai Nai had never told her and during the brief time she'd spent with Ma the subject had never come up. She didn't know how her parents had gotten to know each other.

"That's another reason I want to leave the clan," Reyes said. "Mother's obsessed with making a good match for me, as she puts it. Like I shouldn't have any say in the matter."

"You're a bit young to be getting married."

"That's another objection of mine."

"Do we have far to go now?" Perhaps they wouldn't find anything at the hunting lodge. Perhaps the woman, Kiva, had been mistaken. Or if she hadn't, perhaps the children weren't Carina's siblings.

"Nearly there."

They continued the rest of the short journey in silence, Carina telling herself it probably wasn't one of her siblings who had been shot. Even if that had happened to any of them they would have Cast Heal.

The star racer slipped smoothly and quickly out of the sky. Its nose was tipped downward and the screen displayed a green expanse with a small clearing that was growing rapidly larger. At the center of the clearing a wooden building stood. The bare ground surrounding the lodge was empty.

"Wait," she said. "Is there any point in landing here? If that woman did shoot a child in the forest, she probably didn't do it right here. This is just where she was when she comm'd. And she won't be here now. She would have gone home like her father told her to."

"You're right," Reyes replied. "No one will be here at this time of day but it's the only clear space for kilometers around. If your sisters and brothers are nearby, they might have headed here."

He brought the star racer down on the lot outside the hunting lodge and opened the hatch. The air that flooded in was fresh, cool, and scented with tree oils. Carina climbed out and scanned the surrounding trees but the space below their canopies was dark and silent.

"Hey," she yelled. "Is anyone there? Are you hurt? We can help you."

No reply came.

She didn't want to give away the names of her siblings. She'd been hoping that if they heard her they would recognize her voice, but her brothers and sisters might not reply to someone yelling *Hey*. She cupped her hands around her mouth. "Parthenia," she called. "Parthenia! Can you hear me?"

Her voice echoed through the trees but received no answer. Reyes strode to the edge of the clearing. "Parthenia," he yelled. "Parthenia!"

They waited in silence as the sun crept over the tree tops and lit up the roof of the hunting lodge. They called again, but it soon became clear that if her siblings were in the forest they weren't within earshot.

"I don't know what to do," she said, her voice thick. She could tough out almost any situation, but the idea of one of her siblings lying injured somewhere was crippling her.

"I'm not sure either," Reyes said. "We can fly across the forest to look for them but the canopy makes it hard to see anything. Oh, wait. Maybe there is a way."

Twenty-Five

"Yes," Reyes exclaimed. "I do have a scanner." He was at the controls of his star racer. "I wasn't sure. I've never needed to use one."

"Can it tell humans from other living things?" asked Carina. "This place must be full of animals."

"Hmm... No, it can't. Good point."

"And it would take us forever to scan this place anyway. It must cover hundreds of square kilometers."

"It does." Reyes paused. "I'm sorry. I want to help. I feel responsible."

"Well, you didn't shoot anyone. Or did you?"

"No! I've never even fired a weapon. I hate the idea of hunting, and Mother always insisted that I work in the business side of the family, not the military. But these people are still my clan, and I don't think you would be split up from your siblings if we hadn't captured you."

"I can't deny that," Carina replied. "But I'm not giving up yet. I'm going to continue looking until I find them." She climbed out of the star racer into the lot once more. Her gaze searched the trees that brooded over the place. *If I were lost in a forest, where would I go?*

Reyes joined her. "Have you had an idea?"

"Just wondering how I might try to find my way out of here if I were on foot."

"It would be hard if you didn't know the place well. As soon as you're in the trees you can't see very far ahead, and all there is to follow are bridle paths and animal tracks."

"What about streams?" Carina asked. "They might have followed a stream, thinking it could lead them to a river and people."

"I don't recall any streams. Wait a minute and I'll check."

She wondered how Reyes remembered being in the forest when he'd said he didn't like hunting.

He returned from the star racer. "No. No streams. The land's pretty dry around here."

As they stood and thought a shuttle passed overhead. She looked up. "Where's that going?"

"How would I know?"

"You seem to know a lot of things. What I mean is, is it heading to the spaceport?"

"No. It's heading away from it."

"So shuttles fly over the forest when they take off from the spaceport?"

"Yes. Some do. Why?"

"Because if you were lost in a forest, a shuttle might be the only sign of civilization you could see. Come on. I have an idea."

———

"But that's about the only place I can't fly," Reyes protested.

They were nearing the spaceport and Carina had announced her idea of scanning along the forest edge. It was a long shot but it was somewhere to begin their search. She would head in the same direction as a shuttle was flying if she were lost. "Why not? I thought the Dirksens could do anything." She needed him to do as she wanted. It would take hours to search the area on foot.

"Because it's incredibly dangerous," said Reyes. "I'd be flying right across shuttle flight paths."

"I think as long as you keep low it shouldn't be a problem. The shuttles must have to clear the trees by a wide margin as a safety precaution. If you fly just above the canopy, nothing will even come close to colliding with us."

"But then I might hit a tree instead."

"Really? I didn't think you were that bad a pilot."

"I'm not a..." he exclaimed. "Huh. Very clever. Okay. I'll try. But don't blame me if the military arrives to escort us away."

"I'll take that chance."

He turned the star racer and headed in the opposite direction to the flight of the shuttle they'd seen minutes earlier. She was hoping her siblings had traveled toward the spaceport and not away from it. The departing shuttles were flying in different directions, which would mean her sisters and brothers could be anywhere if they'd followed one.

In truth, she didn't hold out much hope for her idea but it was the best one she had. If her siblings weren't near the spaceport, they would just have to search every square meter of the forest. And she would ask Reyes to continue searching the news and comms for any sign of them. They would have to turn up somewhere. She only hoped that when they did it wasn't because they'd revealed their abilities to the world.

They were approaching the spaceport, and at the same time a shuttle was approaching them, rising at a steep angle. She turned on the star racer's scanner, which registered heat from living bodies. She could already see the moving forms of animals beneath them, otherwise invisible beneath the canopy, but she couldn't see anything that appeared even vaguely human.

Reyes tutted.

"What's wrong?"

In answer, he spoke a voice command: "On speaker."

"Star racer pilot," said a voice, "your craft is not registered. Who are you? Please reverse your heading immediately."

"Spaceport Traffic Control?" Carina asked.

"Yeah," said Reyes. "Speaker off." He slipped his headset off his head and let it rest on his shoulders. "They're gonna get real mad at me real soon. What can you see?" He glanced at the scanner display.

"Lots of animals. No people."

"We're nearly at the spaceport. I'll start at the northern end and fly south."

The star racer turned again as another shuttle passed overhead, closer this time. She was certain that if the shuttle's pilot had a warning klaxon, he would have blasted it.

They reached the northern boundary of the forest, which was a highway that also ran along the edge of the spaceport. She peered even more keenly at the scanner. "Go as slow as you can. We're so near the ground I can barely register what I'm seeing before we're a long way past it."

What she could see were the shadowy shapes of trees dotted with the moving green forms of warm objects. Some were only sparks on the image: birds. Others were long, four-legged animals with even longer tails. Other figures were more human-shaped but they were moving rapidly through the trees in a non-human manner.

They were about halfway down the line of the fence when she saw them: three green shapes quite close together. They didn't look very much like people but they also didn't look like anything else she'd seen. "Wait. I might have something. Can you circle back?"

"Are you sure it's worth it?" Reyes asked. "I don't think Traffic Control is going to tolerate me here much longer."

"Just circle back," she snapped.

"Okay, okay."

She felt the star racer turn. When they arrived at the spot where she'd seen the strange forms on the scanner, Reyes hovered above it. Two of the forms had changed position. They were moving, heading away from the third figure, which she now recognized as a person lying down.

"Land here," she commanded.

"I can't. There isn't room."

"There has to be. This thing is tiny."

"There's no space. The trees are growing right up to the fence."

She cursed. She was sure the forms she could see were people. If they were her siblings, she didn't know why there were only three of them. But the story of one of them being shot tied in with the person lying on the ground, and if the two figures running away were her other siblings, it would make sense for them to leave at the approach of an unknown spacecraft.

"Open the back hatch," she told Reyes.

"What? While we're in flight? You're crazy."

"Open the hatch and I'll jump into the canopy."

"No. You'll kill yourself. Let me find somewhere to land then we'll walk back to this spot. There's probably a clearing nearby."

"Just do what I say. Don't worry. I've done this loads of times before." She had never done it before but she didn't want to waste time. They might never find their way to the spot, or find the two children who were running.

"If you're sure," Reyes said. He gave the command and the hatch opened. "Make sure you jump well away from the ship. The exhaust is hot."

Now she could see the tree canopy below, she wasn't so sure about her plan anymore. So, before she had more time to think about it, she took three fast steps over to the open hatch and leapt out.

A heartbeat later, she hit leaves and branches, breaking them and falling through until she collided with a thick branch, which knocked the wind out of her. She wrapped her arms and legs around the branch but the force of her fall carried her around it to the other side. She found herself clinging on upside down and struggling to breathe. Her ribs seared with pain every breath she took. She'd broken at least one rib and probably more as far as she could tell.

But she was alive. She wriggled along the branch toward the trunk, each movement agony. By the time she reached her goal she could breath again. She tried to inhaled deeply but stopped and gasped at the feeling of knives piercing her lungs.

She tried again. "Parthenia," she yelled. "Oriana! Don't run. It's me."

She climbed onto the tree trunk and half-scrambled, half-fell down the tree, stopping only once to call out to her siblings again. She hit the forest floor, covered in bleeding gashes and her chest a mess of pain. "Parthenia," she repeated, though she couldn't muster much volume.

The forest was silent. Had she been wrong? Were the figures she'd seen not her siblings after all? Her eyes filled with tears. Then she heard the noise of something running—something human, and perhaps more than one of them.

A little boy burst from the trees. *Darius!*

"Carina," he shouted joyfully. "I knew you'd come. I knew it." He barreled into her, causing her to cry out in pain.

Oriana was close behind him but she wasn't so happy to see her. She looked distraught. "Do you have some elixir?" she blurted. "Please, give it to me. Ferne is dying."

Twenty-Six

Ferne was lying on his back beneath a tree near the fence. He was deathly pale and the forest floor all around him was stained reddish-brown. His eyes were closed.

"I didn't want to do it," Oriana protested, almost hysterical. "I didn't want to do it, but when Parthenia didn't come back he made me. He said it was the only way he could come with us. He said either pull it out or leave him here."

Carina guessed her sister was referring to whatever it was Ferne had been shot with.

"So I did it," Oriana went on. "It was hard, and I really hurt him. Then when I finally got it out, blood started pouring out of his leg. I couldn't stop it."

Carina turned her unconscious brother over. The wound was on the back of his thigh and still seeping blood. She pushed the heel of her hand deep into it. Still, Ferne didn't stir. She guessed he didn't have long to live. If she had elixir, she might save him, but she'd drunk all of hers when she removed the tracers. They had to make some more, fast. But how?

"You couldn't make elixir?" she asked. "What are you missing? What do you need?"

"We only need fire," Darius replied. His recent joy at being reunited with her had entirely dissipated.

"Did you look for firestones?"

"What are they?" asked Oriana.

"You don't know?" Ma clearly hadn't told them. Or rather Stephan Sherrerr had made sure she didn't. "Never mind. Oriana, come here and do what I'm doing. Press down as hard as you can. I have to look for a firestone." She removed her hand as soon as her sister was ready to take her place.

She set off on her search. It wasn't likely there would be firestones or any other kinds of stone lying on the surface of the forest floor, but it was the only way she might save Ferne. Darius was following her.

"Go back to Oriana and Ferne. Wait with them."

"I want to stay with you. Please, Carina."

"No, I'm sorry. You'll only slow me down."

He turned and sloped back the way he'd come. She returned her attention to the forest floor. It was littered with dry leaves that overlay dark brown mold. The leaf mold had to be centuries old. It was moist and spongy.

She was concentrating so intensely as she searched she didn't notice Reyes until he called. She looked up to see him some distance away. "Did you find them?" he shouted.

She sprinted toward him, yelling, "Do you have anything that can start a fire?"

"A fire? No, of course not. Why do you want to start a fire? Did you find your brothers and sisters?"

She reached him. "I found them. But I have to make a fire. Don't you have anything at all? Please, think. Is there something on your star racer? Where did you land it?"

"Sorry, I would help you if I could but I don't have anything like that."

She grabbed the front of his jacket with both hands. "Where's the star racer?"

When Reyes turned to point, she set off immediately, not waiting to hear what he had to say. There had to be something inside the spacecraft she could use to make a spark and light some tinder. Perhaps she could short a circuit.

As she neared the star racer, she found her problem had been solved. The forest was burning. The heat from the landing spacecraft had ignited the dry leaf litter. It wasn't a big fire yet but it grew fiercer as she approached it. The flames were being blown toward her. She could see the rear of the vehicle through them.

She grabbed a fallen branch and ran over to a patch of burning forest floor. The end of the dry tree limb soon kindled. On her way back to the children, carrying the torch over her head, she passed Reyes as he caught up to her. "I'd get your spacecraft out of here fast if I were you."

She would have to get the children out of the forest quickly too. Just as soon as she Healed Ferne.

As the color began to return to Ferne's face, Carina put her head down and listened at her brother's chest. His heart was beating strongly. For a moment, she couldn't move. Tears of relief welled up and spilled from her eyes onto him. She'd Healed him just in time.

"Is he going to be all right?" Oriana asked anxiously.

She couldn't speak. She nodded. Oriana threw herself over both of them. Carina gasped as the agony of her broken ribs tore through her.

Hearing her sister's reaction, Oriana quickly moved off. "Are you hurt? I'm so sorry."

Carina grimaced. She took a sip of the hot elixir and set about Healing herself. As soon as she'd finished, the acrid scent of smoke filled her nostrils. The forest fire was getting closer, but Ferne remained unconscious. She would have to carry him.

"We have to go," she said to Oriana and Darius. She grabbed Ferne under his armpits and put him over her shoulder before rising slowly to her feet. But she was forgetting someone. "Where's Parthenia?" Oriana had said something about their sister not coming back.

"She went to get help," said Darius. "But that was last night."

A shadow settled over her as she wondered what had happened to her oldest sister. "Don't worry. We'll look for her. But we have to get out of the forest first. A fire is heading this way." Smoke was already making the sky hazy and wreathing between the trees. She was sure the air had grown warmer too.

Carrying Ferne, who was as limp as a rag doll, she led Oriana and Darius into the trees. She didn't get far before she realized she was walking toward the fire, not away from it. The ash in the air was growing thick and she could hear the roar of the flames. The conflagration had spread quickly. She doubled back toward the fence, thinking they could walk along it to reach the highway that lay to the north. As they walked, however, a tree a short distance in front of them began to smolder.

She cursed and turned. They would have to go the other way. But the smoke in the place they'd only just left was growing thick.

Darius' hand slipped into hers and gripped it tightly. He looked up, his eyes wide and scared. Oriana coughed and pulled her shirt up and over her mouth and nose.

It was no good. The only way to avoid the fire was to climb over the fence. Carina looked up at the top of it, which was twice her own height. She might make it there carrying Ferne, but she didn't know how she would climb over and hold onto her brother at the same time. She might easily drop him and a fall from that height could kill him.

"We're going to have to climb our way out of this," she said. "But you two are great climbers, right?"

"Yes," Darius said. "I'm a good climber."

"You go first. Oriana, you climb under Darius. And both of you be careful when you're climbing down."

"But what about all the shuttles on the other side?" Oriana asked. "Won't it be dangerous out on the landing ground? Won't we get arrested?"

Neither of Oriana's points had escaped her attention but she couldn't do anything about them right now. They would have to face those problems after they'd avoided becoming forest barbecue.

Darius hadn't waited to be told twice. He was already halfway up the fence.

"We'll figure that out later," she replied. "You go up now. I don't want Darius to be on his own."

Oriana began climbing. The air was beginning to choke Carina and she was coated in sweat. She adjusted Ferne so he was sitting firmly pushed up against her neck. Grabbing the links of the fence, she started to climb.

It wasn't easy but she thought she could do it, though she still hadn't figured out how she would climb over the top. Darius was already over and heading down the other side. Oriana was nearly there too.

When Carina reached the top she paused. Her toes were pushed into gaps in the wires and one hand gripped the fence while the other held onto Ferne's side to prevent him from slipping off. She needed two hands free to climb over, which would mean letting go of Ferne. She continued to hesitate, not knowing what to do.

Then Reyes arrived.

His star racer was lowering out of the sky, a safe distance from Darius and Oriana but at the edge of the spaceport's landing ground. He was really going to annoy Air Traffic Control. He landed and the hatch opened.

Oriana was looking scared. She didn't know who Reyes was.

"It's okay," Carina called down. "He's a friend."

"Wait there," Reyes shouted, running toward her. "I'll help." He worked his way up the links of wire. "Can you pass him to me?"

"Yes, but please be careful. Don't let go of him."

"Of course I won't."

With great care, she transferred Ferne over to Reyes, who balanced the boy's limp form on his shoulder. As Reyes began to descend the fence, Carina climbed over, catching a glimpse of tree tops on fire. She sped down the wires to catch up to Reyes and shadow him, ready to catch Ferne if he started to fall.

They reached the ground together just as a tree bordering the fence burst into flames. Military vehicles were speeding toward them across the shuttle landing field.

"Quick, everyone into the star racer," Reyes shouted.

"We can't all fit in that," Oriana said.

"We're going to have to," said Carina. Reyes was already at his vehicle, still carrying Ferne. She took Darius' hand. "Come on."

They piled into the tiny space. Reyes had lain Ferne on the passenger seat and taken the pilot's seat.

"I'm closing the hatch," he said. "Breathe in."

Carina, Oriana, and Darius squeezed into whatever spare space they could find. The hatch of the star racer closed against Carina's back, pushing her down. The spacecraft lifted and everyone was crushed together further by the acceleration force as Reyes flew away from the spaceport.

Three out of four of her mage siblings were safe—for now. But what had happened to Parthenia?

Twenty-Seven

Parthenia had spent the night in the security room. The guards hadn't even given her a cot to sleep on and so she'd been forced to curl up on the cold floor, napping fitfully over the long hours she'd been left alone. Aside from a couple of restroom visits, she hadn't been allowed out and no one would tell her what was going to happen to her or listen when she tried to tell them her brother needed help.

She couldn't stop thinking about Ferne, Oriana, and Darius, alone in the forest overnight. She'd told them she would be back but she'd failed to keep her promise. They needed her but she didn't know how to return to them. She was out of her mind with worry, to the extent that she barely considered how much danger she was in herself.

The female guard had brought her breakfast then left her alone, once again refusing to hear her pleas. Parthenia guessed something would happen to her soon. The guards had taken her into custody late the previous evening. Their boss had probably gone home by then but now it was morning he or she would be back at work and ready to deal with the stray girl who had been annoying the passengers.

Parthenia was mentally rehearsing her cover story when the door to the small room opened and the female guard came inside. Someone else entered behind her—an older man wearing a civilian suit, not a uniform. His hair was white with age, which was odd. Having your genes spliced so your hair never changed color no matter how old you grew was a standard treatment. Even the servants at Parthenia's family estate on Ithiya had undergone the procedure.

The older man also wore a small, neat mustache—another anomaly. Parthenia knew few men who hadn't arranged for the permanent removal of their facial hair not long after puberty, for convenience's sake.

The man sat down and put a finger to his mouth as he regarded her. "Would you mind telling me your name?"

"Penny. Penny Sharp."

"And where are you from, Penny?"

"I'm from Riverfield." Her next words fell out of her mouth in a rush. "I was traveling with my family but we got lost. My brother's hurt and he needs help. I've told your guard many times but she won't listen to me."

The man turned to the guard. "Check her again. I want to be sure."

The guard was carrying an ID scanner. She leaned over Parthenia. "Open up."

She had been subjected to the same test twice before during the previous evening. She opened her lips. The result would be the same, and it meant she was in trouble.

The guard put a probe into Parthenia's mouth and wiped it along the inside of her cheek. The machine bleeped. The guard turned the display screen toward the man.

"Well, Penny Sharp," he said, "according to this you don't exist. Now, ordinarily I wouldn't be very surprised to come across an unregistered vagrant hanging around the spaceport. But you aren't a regular member of the invisible fringe, are you? There's no such place as Riverfield on all of Ostillon, and the fact that you lied about your origins tells me you have something to hide. What is it? Are you working with smugglers?"

"Am I working with smugglers?" Parthenia asked, her worries temporarily forgotten in her amazement at the man's question. "If I were a member of a smuggling gang, do you think I would go around drawing attention to myself by dressing like this and asking people for help?"

Even the guard looked embarrassed by her superior's question.

The older man colored and coughed before muttering, "You could have been acting as a diversion. Anyway, what you were doing is irrelevant. As an unregistered individual we have a duty to hand you over to the appropriate authorities. It's clear that you aren't Ostillonian, therefore I'm going to send you to the Illegal Migrant Holding Facility." He stood up. "Someone will be along to collect you soon." He went out.

The female guard tutted. "If you'd been more polite and asked nicely, he might have let you go." She also left, and the lock click closed.

Parthenia's head sunk onto her arms. Why had she been rude to the spaceport official? Now she would never get back to Ferne and the others.

———

The Illegal Migrant Holding Facility was full to the brim. She was put in a cell with at least ten other girls and women. They all stared at her when she arrived. And after the cell door was locked and the guard walked away, no one spoke to her.

"Excuse me," she said to the person nearest to her—a girl about her own age who had bouncy blonde curls, "what happens here? Do we ever get to leave?"

"There's a few ways out," the girl replied, looking Parthenia up and down. "Proving your identity, bribing the warden, or sleeping with the guards. Those are the main ones anyway."

At Parthenia's shocked expression the girl laughed. "I was kidding for the last one."

"Yeah," another woman chipped in. "You have to sleep with the guards just to eat."

"That's why Laury's so fat," said a third.

The golden-haired girl turned and glared at the speaker.

Parthenia asked, "And what happens if you don't do any of those things?"

"It's off to the asteroid mines with you," Laury replied.

"What? Forced labor? Can they do that?" Parthenia realized what a fool she sounded as the words left her mouth. Her own clan had done the same, if not worse.

"If you don't exist," said Laury, "they can do what they like."

Parthenia's low mood sunk even further. How could she help her brothers and sister if she was stuck on a mine somewhere? She might never see them again. What would become of them all by themselves? And what would happen to Ferne if he didn't get medical help?

She eased through the crowded cell, stepping over women who were sitting or lying on the floor, until she reached the little window. It looked out onto a square yard where a few of the inmates were wandering aimlessly. Shuttles from the spaceport were crossing the small patch of sky. Parthenia felt like crying but she didn't want to show her emotion in front of all these strange women.

She rested her elbows on the ledge of the high window. Ever since escaping from the Sherrerrs, everything had gone from bad to worse and Parthenia had no idea how to turn things around. Fate seemed to be pushing her down a road that ended in nothing but loneliness and despair and there wasn't anything she could do about it.

Was she going to live out the rest of her life slaving away on an asteroid, never seeing her family again or finding out what had happened to them? The only saving grace in her situation was that things couldn't get any worse.

As she aimlessly watched the sad figures of inmates meandering around the exercise yard, the murmur of voices in the cell behind her grew louder. She heard snatches of comments like, "Here he is again," and, "I wonder who he's looking for."

Mildly curious about what the women were talking about, she turned around. A young man was moving down the corridor that linked the cells, accompanied by a guard. He looked so different from the last time she'd seen him, she almost didn't recognize him. When she did, she nearly froze. She had just enough presence of mind to turn away.

Her back facing the visitor, her heart raced as she stared sightlessly out of the window, hoping beyond hope he would pass by without noticing her.

But her brother wasn't so unobservant as to not recognize his sister, even from behind.

"Parthenia," Castiel said. "How nice to see you again."

Twenty-Eight

"Where are you taking us?" Carina asked Reyes, her neck painfully scrunched up. Before he could answer, she also said, "Darius, could you scoot under Ferne's seat? I can see some room there."

Her little brother did as she'd asked him, shuffling along on his bottom to the space under the reclined passenger seat, where he fitted comfortably.

"That's better," Oriana breathed, moving into the place Darius had occupied, which allowed Carina to change position and straighten up.

"Back to the hospital, of course," Reyes replied. "Your brother needs a medic."

"No," Carina said. "He's fine."

Reyes gave her a quizzical look over his shoulder but at that moment, Ferne stirred and his eyes opened. The first thing he saw was her. Before she had a chance to warn him, Ferne blurted her name and tried to sit up.

"I feel terrible," he said as he gave up his attempt and lay back down. "What happened?" He reached for his leg. "Did you—"

"Ferne," Oriana hissed. "Shuttup."

He finally noticed Reyes. His lips clamped closed and he gave Carina an apologetic look.

Reyes said, "Were you the one who was shot? Are you hurt?"

"I..." Ferne began.

"He wasn't shot," said Oriana. "Or, he was nearly shot. He was just exhausted because we'd been walking through the forest for so long."

It was a terrible excuse to explain Ferne's unconsciousness, but Carina didn't blame her sister. She couldn't think of a credible explanation herself. And Oriana had thought it through: if Reyes found out that Ferne had been shot he would want to know why he didn't have an injury, and that would require a whole lot more explaining.

"Okay," Reyes said. "I understand there are things you don't want me to know, *Carina* and family. But don't forget I helped save your lives back there. You don't have to treat me like an enemy."

"Reyes," said Carina, "you're right. I'm sorry. Thank you for helping me find my sister and brothers. I couldn't have done it without you." Then she said, "Ferne, if you're feeling better, can you raise your seat? We can hardly move in here."

After some more shuffling around the star racer was still cramped but more comfortable. They couldn't stay in it forever, though. More to the point, they had to find Parthenia. "Reyes, can you turn back to the spaceport? I think my other sister might be there. She left to go and get help but she didn't come back."

"Return to the spaceport?" Reyes asked, incredulous. "I was lucky I wasn't arrested. If this spacecraft was registered Mother would be pulling a lot of strings for me right now."

"I thought Dirksens could do whatever they wanted," Carina said.

"He's a Dirksen?" Oriana exclaimed, her voice laced with disgust. She tried to ease away from Reyes' seat but there was no room.

"He says he's leaving his clan," said Carina.

"I am leaving them," Reyes said. "I would have thought what I just did would prove that to you."

"I do appreciate it. But we can manage by ourselves from here. So if you wouldn't mind landing and letting us out?"

"You said you think your other sister might be at the spaceport? Let me see what I can find out."

"You can check official comms as well as your clan's?"

"Official comms are easier." Reyes set the star racer to automatic flight and began to search again on his interface. This time, he found the information within a few minutes. "A young woman was detained at the spaceport on suspicion of smuggling. She was transferred to the Illegal Migrant Holding Facility around an hour ago."

"That has to be her," Carina said. "Can we get her out? You can use your influence, can't you?"

"Not so keen to get rid of me any longer?" Reyes asked sarcastically. "I don't know. Maybe. Mother's comms have been building up for hours. She's going crazy but I don't think she suspects what I plan to do yet. She probably thinks I'm rebelling a little but I'll come home soon. So if we turn up at the facility I'll still be a Dirksen to be feared, rather than one to be reported. I guess it's worth a try."

"Thank you," said Carina.

"I hope you'll accept I'm on your side if I manage to do this," Reyes said as he input a new destination to the star racer's navigation.

She sighed but didn't say anything. The problem was, she and her siblings didn't belong to a side. She only wanted to gather them together so she could protect them and decide what they were going to do next. She didn't know what vision Reyes had of his involvement with them once they'd found Parthenia, but she had no intention of having anything else to do with him. He already knew her name and was probably wondering about Ferne's mysterious unconsciousness and how that fitted in with the comm that stated a child had been shot. It was far too much dangerous information.

They landed outside a dark, one-story building. Black, unmarked hover vehicles were parked outside, and the whole place exuded a depressive air. Carina hoped that if Parthenia had been taken here, they could get her out as soon as possible.

A guard was leaning nonchalantly against the wall in the lobby when they went inside, but he quickly stood to attention when he spotted them. She wasn't sure if it was because he recognized Reyes or because they were strangers.

Reyes walked up to a woman in uniform who was sitting behind a transparent screen. She glared at him. "Yes?"

"I'm Reyes Dirksen."

The woman's expression softened a little but not much. "Can I help you, sir?"

"I'm looking for a young girl. She was brought in this morning from the spaceport."

"Do you have a name?"

Reyes looked over his shoulder at Carina, but she didn't know what to tell him. She doubted Parthenia would have told anyone her real name, especially her surname, but she didn't know what name she would have given.

"Penny Sharp," Oriana called out.

The woman checked her list. She looked up, frowning. "We did have a Penny Sharp here this morning but she was taken away."

"What?" Carina said, stepping forward. "Where did she go? Who took her?"

"Well, I'm surprised you don't know. She was checked out by a Dirksen."

TWENTY-NINE

erne, Oriana, and Darius waited outside Reyes' star racer while he combed through the Dirksens' personal comms once more, this time trying to discover which of his relatives had removed Parthenia from the Illegal Migrant Holding Center. Carina sat next to him, watching over his shoulder in case he missed something.

The back hatch of Reyes' vehicle was up, allowing in the noises of the busy street. Hover vehicles hissed passed, and every so often a large, unmarked, multi-passenger van stopped to unload or pick up detainees at the center. Carina would glance at these scruffy, unkempt individuals just to check that, by some miracle, her sister hadn't been returned. She was clinging to the hope that whatever Dirksen had taken Parthenia hadn't known about the girl's powers, and that she'd been removed for some other reason.

But Parthenia didn't appear, and though Reyes searched for hours he couldn't find anything that alluded to Carina's sister.

"It's odd," he said. "We do use people from the center for various things, but there's nothing in the official record about someone being picked up today and no mention of it in any personal comms."

"What do you think that means?" Carina asked. "Could the receptionist have been lying?"

Reyes shook his head. "She wouldn't dare, even if she had a reason to lie, which she didn't as far as I know. It's very strange."

Outside the star racer, Darius suddenly burst into tears. He wailed, his face pressed into his hands. Carina jumped out and went to him. "What's wrong?" she asked, putting an arm around his shoulders.

"I'm hungry," he sobbed.

"Oh, I'm so sorry," said Carina. Her concern about Parthenia had made her forget that her other siblings had spent the night and probably the previous day in the forest without anything to eat. And Ferne had spent a lot of that time severely injured.

She stuck her head inside Reyes' vehicle. "I have to buy some food. Do you know where I can go? Is there somewhere nearby?"

Looking up from his interface screen, Reyes replied, "I can do better than that. You're all going to need somewhere to sleep as well as food and clothes and everything else. If you squeeze inside once more, I can take you somewhere."

"Er..."

"What's wrong?"

"I don't know if that's a good idea. Maybe it's better that we part ways now. You need to continue with breaking away from your family." She didn't want Reyes to know where she and her siblings were staying and she didn't want him to get to know them well. She might be able to hide her abilities from him but she wasn't confident her sister or brothers could.

"You're never going to get your other sister back without my help," Reyes said, his expression grave. "I can assure you. The fact that I can't find any mention of her probably means the security surrounding her is very high level. You'll never breach it alone. I can't force you to stick with me for a while longer, but you would be stupid if you didn't."

She hated it but what he was saying was true. She called to Darius and the others to climb inside Reyes' tiny vehicle.

―――――

The apartment he showed them wasn't much better than the one Carina had rented from the old man, but it was sparsely furnished. There were two bedrooms.

"Great," said Ferne. "One for boys and one for girls."

"I'll sleep on the sofa, thanks," said Reyes.

Carina stared at him. "You're planning on staying here too?"

"Why not? It makes sense, doesn't it? That way I can help you more easily. And I don't have anywhere else to go."

"Uh, okay."

Reyes had paid their landlord from his own money, so Carina felt it would be ungrateful and churlish to refuse him, yet she remained deeply uncomfortable about the Dirksen man's proximity to her siblings.

Ferne had declared which room belonged to the boys, and he and Darius were already bouncing on the bed, Darius' ravenous hunger of less than an hour ago apparently entirely forgotten.

"Come and eat," Carina called to the boys. She opened the bag of takeout food Reyes had bought on their way over and began to take off the lids. "Ferne, check in the kitchen for bowls and cutlery," she said to her brother as he pulled out a chair at the rickety table.

Darius didn't wait on niceties. He reached for piece of meat poking out from a dish. "Wash your hands," she admonished.

"Yes," Oriana said. "Come on, Darius."

As Carina was laying the table, she could hear Oriana speaking in a hushed tone to Darius in the bathroom.

"I know," the little boy exclaimed.

Carina winced internally. Her sister had undoubtedly been reminding their brother not to allude to anything to do with Casting while Reyes was around.

There were only four seats at the table, so Reyes took his food to the sofa to eat. Carina sat down and waited while her brothers and sister filled their bowls. For the first time since she'd found them in the forest, she could stop what she was doing and simply appreciate the fact that most of her family were reunited. She resolved to do her damnedest to prevent them from being separated again.

When everyone was eating, she also spooned some food into her bowl. The cereal was white grains and the main dish was meat in a sauce. She ate a mouthful, but as she was chewing, she stopped and put down her spoon.

"Don't you like it?" Ferne asked, his mouth full. "I think it's great." Before he swallowed he piled another spoonful of grains and sauce into his mouth.

She had stopped because she had the same sense of deja vu she'd experienced at Asha's apartment. The flavor of the food was familiar. The last time she'd eaten it, however, she'd been living with Nai Nai. Like the noodle soup, the dish they were eating had been another of her grandmother's specialties.

"It is good," she said. She continued to eat. If Reyes hadn't been present, she could have told Ferne and the others about her discovery, but she hesitated to mention anything personal around a Dirksen, no matter how strongly he professed that he no longer wanted to be a part of his clan.

After everyone had eaten, she insisted that the three children go and lie down. Though they were excited to be reunited with her and anxious to find Parthenia, they could hardly have slept the previous night. Also, though she didn't know what had happened after she'd Transported them from the Sherrerr shuttle, she doubted it was anything good. They would need time to recoup their energy.

As she'd predicted, Oriana, Ferne, and Darius quickly fell asleep. She closed the blinds in the bedrooms and went out into the lounge, where Reyes was searching for information on Parthenia once more.

She sat down beside him. "Still nothing?"

The young man's long, fine hair hung over his face as he leaned forward. "Nope." He sighed, leaned back against the sofa, and brushed his hair out of his eyes. "There isn't a single reference I can see. I'm sorry. I'll continue to look after I've had a rest."

"Thanks. I do appreciate what you're doing for my family."

"Consider it my way of trying to put things right. When I think of all the things my clan have done over the years.... And I'm probably not even aware of half of it. It was only a couple of years ago I began to realize what Mother and other Dirksens were doing was wrong. Up until then I accepted that was how life was. I thought we deserved everything we had and that if people didn't have anything it was because they'd hadn't worked hard enough. The sheer evilness of what we were doing went over my head."

"Well, it's good you realized it finally. It's a shame the rest of your family haven't arrived at the same insight."

"Yeah." Reyes frowned. "You know, I've been putting something off that I really ought to do."

"What's that?"

"I should read Mother's comms. I won't reply. I want to make use of my status as long as I can to help you, so I'm not going to declare anything to her. But I have to face up to what I'm doing."

He leaned forward again and lifted his screen. Even from her position she could see he had tens if not hundreds of messages waiting from his mother. Reyes began to open and scan them, spending no more than a few seconds on each. She could imagine what they said—variations on *Where are you?* and *When are you coming home?*

But then Reyes opened a message that seemed to occupy a lot of his attention. He read it top to bottom, then his fingers flicked as he quickly opened the next message, and then the next. He let the interface fall to his lap.

"Is everything okay?" she asked, wondering what Langley Dirksen had said to her son that could be so devastating.

Reyes turned to her. "My mother has her—your sister. I'd swear it."

THIRTY

The estate Castiel had brought Parthenia to reminded her of her home on Ithiya, only it was far larger. The house was at least three times as big and the grounds stretched so far she couldn't see the boundaries.

Castiel had wanted to walk in the grounds while they waited for someone. He hadn't said who. Nahla trailed behind Parthenia and their brother. The little girl hadn't spoken a word since Parthenia had arrived. A man called Harmon walked even farther behind the group. He was large, with broad shoulders and a thick, muscly neck.

Parthenia guessed he was there to prevent her from running away. Yet in fact his presence wasn't required. She wouldn't have dared to run from Castiel —not after he'd demonstrated that he could now Cast.

He'd used Nahla as a subject for his demonstration. In a room inside the mansion, he had sipped elixir he must have made himself, and he'd Cast Transport on their sister. Parthenia had thought he would do something simple like move her from one side of the room to the other, but instead he'd lifted her up to the ceiling.

Poor Nahla had hung there, plainly terrified but uncomplaining. It had been Parthenia who had begged Castiel to put their sister down, and safely, knowing he could release Nahla and let her fall. In the end, he had lowered the little girl rather than dropped her—until she was a meter above the floor, when he did allow her to drop.

He had smiled with satisfaction at the cry of pain she gave when she hit the floor.

Later, as they walked across the lawn, he said, "I know how sentimental I must sound, but I'm glad to see you again, Parthenia."

"Really?" she replied. "I can't say I feel the same."

"Oh, now that's unkind. Did you hear that, Nahla? Parthenia doesn't like us. She isn't happy to be reunited with her own flesh and blood."

"I don't know why you say *us* like that. I am pleased to see Nahla, or maybe *relieved* is a better word. Relieved that you haven't seriously hurt her, yet. Though that demonstration in the house just now tells me you're perfectly capable of it. Probably looking forward to it, in fact."

His expression darkened. "If anything bad happens to Nahla, it will be entirely justified, I'm sure."

She made a noise of disgust. "You sound just like Father."

"I certainly hope so. He was a great man, and he was in the prime of his life when he was cut down by our evil bitch of a mother—with *your* help." He turned to face her, malevolence simmering in his eyes. His voice was soft, which made his words all the more terrifying. "And believe me, I haven't forgotten it."

"Huh. Full of bravado after the fact, aren't you? I don't recall you doing anything to help him at the time."

He drew himself up and clenched his fists. Between his teeth he said, "That was because I wasn't sure if I could Cast at the time. Now I know I can, I won't allow anyone to do anything I don't want them to." His rage abated and he walked on. "Besides, I wanted to get away from our clan. We never received the respect we deserved from them. After everything we did—turning around their failing businesses, increasing their power and influence—we were still treated little better than slaves. They should have been bowing down to us, asking for our help and giving us rich rewards instead of locking us away and only bringing us out whenever they needed their performing monkeys."

Parthenia inwardly smiled at his words. Once more he was using "us" incorrectly. He had personally done nothing whatsoever to help the Sherrerrs and he'd enjoyed favor and numerous privileges that hadn't been allowed to his mage siblings. Also, it had been their father who had treated the mages like slaves—the very man Castiel had just been praising. From what she could understand, the other Sherrerrs were either disinterested or uncaring about how Stefan Sherrerr used his children, providing the clan could benefit from her and the others' abilities.

However, she was careful to show no sign of her wry amusement. She had already angered him once and gotten away with it but she might not be so lucky again. It was a lesson she'd learned well at the hands of their father.

"*There* you are," said a voice.

She turned to see a middle-aged woman standing in the mansion at a set of open double doors. She was richly dressed. Smiling warmly, the woman stepped out of the doorway and walked toward them over the neatly clipped grass.

"I wondered where you'd gone," the woman said as she drew nearer. "Castiel, please introduce me to our guest."

"Naturally." Smiling sardonically, he said, "I'd like you to meet my sister, Parthenia. Parthenia, this is our host, Langley Dirksen."

"I'm very pleased to meet you, Parthenia."

She didn't reply. While she knew she would never get away with being rude to Castiel, she was willing to test the boundaries with this new person who was clearly colluding with him.

As she saw her reaction, Langley Dirksen grimaced. "My, that look is familiar," she remarked to Castiel. "I can see the resemblance to her sister."

"Yes, she does look a bit like Carina, doesn't she? Though Carina isn't a Sherrerr like the rest of us. Parthenia and I only share a mother with her. We had different fathers."

Parthenia wondered what else Castiel had told the Dirksen woman. She had a feeling it was probably everything, including all he knew about Casting. He might even have exaggerated his explanation of mage powers. He had always been prone to boasting. She was also curious about what her brother was doing on a Dirksen estate and, more importantly, what he intended to do with her. It was unlikely to be anything pleasant.

"So is this the one your father used to take to business meetings?" Langley asked.

"Parthenia did do some of that, yes, though I also performed several key roles."

Parthenia could hardly believe his last remark, which was utterly false. Before she could say anything, however, he flashed her a warning look.

"And it was Carina who extracted your youngest brother from our custody."

"That's right. Though we didn't know anything about her at the time."

"Hmmm...." Langley glanced at Parthenia. "Would you mind taking a stroll with me?" she asked Castiel. "Your sisters can wait here with Harmon."

"By all means," Castiel said. The pair walked off across the lawn, away from the huge house.

Turning to her large guard, Parthenia said, "Can we go inside? I want to sit down."

Harmon considered for a moment before giving a short nod. She went through the double doors into a lounge. Nahla traipsed along behind her.

While both the girls sat on sumptuous sofas, Harmon stood with his back to the doorway, blocking most of the light.

As they waited for Castiel and Langley to return, Parthenia wondered what the Dirksen woman's words had meant. She seemed to know Carina somehow and she didn't particularly like her. Parthenia was certain the feeling had been mutual. On the one hand, she was relieved to hear her sister was alive and well, but on the other she was dismayed to discover Carina had been captured by the Dirksens. She wondered how it had happened. Her sister was so smart and resourceful she would never have fallen into Dirksen hands easily.

Where was Carina now? Was she somewhere in the mansion? Or had she managed to escape? Langley Dirksen's words hadn't made it clear. Parthenia resolved to find out and help her sister if she could. If Carina was being held captive that explained why she hadn't come to find her mage siblings. She hadn't been able to Cast Locate using one of her bracelets.

My bracelets! She gasped. The farmer called Marcia had taken them when she'd found Parthenia and the others in the barn, and they'd forgotten to take them back before they'd fled into the forest. Now Oriana had no way of finding where she was, and she had none of her siblings' belongings to use to Locate them either. They might never find each other again.

Her throat tightened and her eyes filled with tears as she was reminded of poor wounded Ferne, and Oriana and Darius, who might still be waiting for her in the forest, though they'd probably realized by now she wasn't coming back. What would they do without her?

Harmon stepped aside to allow Castiel to enter the lounge from the garden. Parthenia rubbed her eyes to rid them of tears but Castiel noticed the gesture.

"Are you upset, dear sister?" he asked. "Don't worry. You don't have anything to fear. Our lives are going to be so much better than the exploitation we suffered at the hands of the Sherrerrs. Langley has made it clear how highly she values our skills, and she appreciates that we will truly commit to the Dirksen cause."

"I think you mean *your* life with the Dirksens," Parthenia retorted. "You don't have any right to tell me what I can and can't do."

"I may not have the right, but I have the means," Castiel said. He took out his bottle of elixir. "As long as I have this and you don't, I can do what I like."

"As long as you have that and I don't, I'm useless to you. So that's an empty threat." Parthenia didn't go on, guessing she was skirting the limits of what he would tolerate from her.

"You'll soon find out whether my threats are empty. What do you have that belongs to Carina? Hand it over. I'm going to find that bitch and bring her here."

"I don't have anything."

"Don't lie. She must have given you something before she Transported you off the shuttle. She knew you would need something to Locate her. Of course, she didn't give anything to Nahla and me because she never wanted to see us again."

He was close to the truth of what had actually happened, but she kept her lips sealed. It was clear from what he said that Carina was free, which was some consolation. Even if Parthenia had one of her sister's belongings, she would never willingly hand it over. She would never betray Carina.

"Hmpf." Castiel dropped into a seat and folded his arms over his chest. "It doesn't matter. She'll find out where you are eventually and she'll try to rescue you. We can grab her then, and we'll get the rest of them."

With a sinking heart, she realized he was correct. No matter how hard she tried to avoid helping him capture their older sister, she couldn't prevent herself from being bait.

THIRTY-ONE

Carina was uncomfortable with the idea of leaving Oriana, Ferne, and Darius alone while she went to rescue Parthenia but she didn't have any choice. It was far too risky to take them with her. Reyes, however, would be coming along. Although she knew her sister was probably somewhere in Langley Dirksen's mansion, she didn't know exactly where. The place had to have a hundred rooms. She needed Reyes to find out her sister's exact location and guide her there.

Langley's comms to her son hadn't explicitly stated that she was holding Parthenia captive. The implication of the woman's words was clear, however. She'd said things like: *Come home soon, darling. I have exciting news. It doesn't matter that the Sherrerr girl left us. Someone else is here who possesses the same abilities.* Carina could only conclude that, somehow, the Dirksen matriarch had discovered Parthenia's abilities—perhaps the young girl had been observed Casting—and Langley had wasted no time in removing her sister from the Illegal Migrant Holding Center and taking her to the Dirksen estate.

Reyes had never mentioned Carina's 'abilities,' though he had to know his mother's reasons for holding her captive. And when he'd picked them up from the burning forest he'd been curious about Ferne's unconscious state, knowing that one of the children had supposedly been shot. Yet Reyes hadn't followed up with any questions about their powers. She guessed he didn't want to broach a sensitive subject. It followed that he hadn't mentioned anything when showing her his mother's comms. He let her draw the same conclusion from them as he had.

"Are you sure you can get Parthenia?" Darius asked as she prepared to leave.

"I'm going to try my hardest, but I can't promise anything. If I can't bring her back tonight I won't stop trying until I can."

"But you won't let them catch you, will you?"

"Of course not."

"Because I'll be really sad if I don't see you again."

"I'd be sad about that too." She squatted down to look her youngest brother in his eyes. "You must do whatever Oriana and Ferne tell you, no questions asked, okay?"

"Okay." Darius looked down. "I just wish we could all be together again."

"We will be, hopefully after tonight." She kissed and hugged him and Oriana and Ferne, then turned to Reyes. "I'm all set. Are you ready?"

"I don't have anything to prepare. I'm waiting on you."

She had prepared. While she'd kept Reyes distracted in the living room, Ferne and Oriana had made more elixir in the kitchen. She was bringing a full bottle with her. She was very reluctant to use it within Reyes' sight, but if she needed to Cast while he was around in order to get Parthenia out, so be it.

They left the apartment and went to his star racer. The plan was that he would land in his mother's estate grounds, far from the house. She would exit the vehicle, then Reyes would continue on to the mansion, returning home as if he hadn't been missing for two days. After he'd endured his mother's predicted ire, he would discover where Parthenia was being held. Next, he would meet Carina at one of the rear entrances to the home after everyone had retired for the night.

According to Reyes, the final part of the plan entailed her, Parthenia, and himself then leaving his home together. But for her, this was the part where her own plan deviated. As soon as she was in sight of her sister, she would Transport them both out of the house and far away. Though she appreciated what Reyes had done to help them, she didn't think she would ever feel safe with him around. Nai Nai's lesson remained ingrained in her mind, despite her friend Bryce demonstrating that not everyone was out to use mages for their own ends.

The minute she reunited Parthenia with her mage siblings, Reyes Dirksen would be on his own.

The metropolis was bright with artificial light, outshining the starlight. Reyes had input his mother's estate as the destination and his star racer made its own way while he leaned back in his seat, resting the ankle of one leg on the knee of the other. He seemed unusually pensive.

"I guess it's got to be hard for you to go home tonight," said Carina.

"Yeah." Reyes picked at his nails. "I'm not looking forward to pretending I'm back for good, or that I don't have a problem with what my family does." He bit off a hangnail. "Or lying to Mother, if I'm honest. You know, she isn't really a—"

"Bad person. Yeah. I know."

"You sound like you don't."

"Reyes, I know she's your mom and it's hard for you to see her behavior objectively, but just think about what her and the rest of your clan have done. You know a lot more about that than me, but I know Langley Dirksen kept me captive and she tricked me into eating tracers that nearly killed me to remove. Are those the actions of a good person?"

"But if you'd only agreed to what she was proposing she wouldn't have done either of those things," Reyes said. "She really wanted to work with you, not against you. And she couldn't afford to let you go. What if you'd gone back to work for the Sherrerrs? It would have been stupid of her to allow that to happen. The Sherrerrs are evil. If they take control of the entire sector, everyone will suffer for it."

She sat up in her seat. She could hardly believe what she was hearing. Did the kid really have no idea of the suffering of people on Ostillon, like Asha? "First of all," she said, "I thought you didn't want to be a Dirksen any longer. Why are you defending them? And secondly, I've seen what Sherrerrs *and* Dirksens do to the people they control and they're equally bad. People on both sides try to justify their evil acts by saying they're necessary to achieve peace and prosperity. But that's all their arguments are: attempts at justification. I don't know who's worse—the people who don't care they're cruel or the people who behave cruelly and pretend to themselves they have some kind of higher purpose."

Reyes didn't answer.

She went on, "Your mother might think she would treat me well if I agreed to do what she said, but it wouldn't last. As soon as I said no to something she wanted she would try to force me to obey her. She would stop seeing me as a human being. I would become an impediment to her plans and all her fine words would fly out the window, as I soon found out after a day at your place."

"I really don't think—"

"You really have no idea what you're talking about," she snapped. She was tempted to tell him about all that had happened to Ma. That might convince him of the truth of what she was saying. But the last thing she wanted to do was give Reyes Dirksen any more information about herself or mages, especially considering that she hopefully wouldn't see him again after tonight. Instead, she said, "If you start out a relationship in a bad way, like by coercing someone or lying to them, things won't ever change, they'll only get worse. You can't do something bad and tell yourself that in the future you'll behave better. It isn't going to happen. What you did at the start sets the pattern. So please, don't try to assure me that the woman who kidnapped me and whose guard beat me up has my best interests at heart. It's insulting."

A corner of his lips lifted. "Well, that told me, I guess."

They'd left the city and were flying over dark countryside. She could make out faint lights in the distance, which she assumed were shining from the windows of the Dirksen mansion.

"Just another couple of minutes," said Reyes. "I'm going to set down just inside the estate walls. You'll have an hour's walk to the house. Is that okay?"

"If that's the safest way to do it, that's absolutely fine."

"It'll be a while before Mother goes to bed, so we have plenty of time. Only make sure to watch out for guards. They patrol the grounds sometimes, but not much. Dirksens don't expect to be attacked on a home planet, so the guards are only checking for vagrants and burglars."

"I am a kind of burglar, only I'll be stealing my own family's treasure."

Thirty-Two

The Dirksen mansion was silent as Carina approached it after her long walk. The dark windows were blank eyes. She wondered which window it was she'd looked out of during her captivity. A shudder ran through her as she recalled her time there. Her experience had been nothing like what Ma had endured for years, but she was in no doubt that, had she stayed, her life would have been similar eventually.

She was armed with nothing except elixir. She hoped it would be all she needed to slip inside the place and Transport herself and Parthenia out. Once her sister was free and her mage siblings were reunited, she could begin to think about how she would get everyone offplanet. She hadn't forgotten about the Sherrerr spy at Langley's party and what her presence probably meant.

Several pairs of double doors ran along the first floor at the rear of the mansion. She was pleased to see that, as arranged, Reyes had left one of them slightly ajar. Her heart was thumping as she opened the door wider. She peeked through into a quiet, dark room. It seemed empty. She slipped inside.

Reyes was waiting. He stepped out of the shadow of a corner and beckoned her. She tiptoed across the room, avoiding the large chaise longue that stood in her way.

"She's in the suite you slept in," Reyes whispered as soon as she was close enough to hear him.

So Langley was trying out her soft coercion on Parthenia too. It was better than throwing her in the cellar immediately. She hoped the Dirksen matriarch hadn't already fed her sister their tiny tracers.

She followed Reyes out of the lounge into the downstairs corridor. "You should wait here," she said to him quietly. "I can remember where the suite is." As soon as she laid eyes on Parthenia, she would Transport them both out of the place. She wanted Reyes out of the way so he wouldn't witness her Casting. Also, Reyes would probably be more of a hindrance than a help if she had to deal with Harmon.

Reyes shook his head. "I want to help."

It wasn't the time or place to argue about it. She went in front of him and walked softly down the corridor to the stairs. Her hand on her bottle of elixir, she began to climb the steps, placing each foot gently on the treads. Reyes was directly behind her. She listened intently, hoping to hear the sleep-breathing of Harmon or another guard. Surprising an unconscious guard was the best break she could hope for. She heard nothing.

As she approached the top of the stairs, she unscrewed the lid on the elixir bottle. She didn't want to Cast in front of Reyes but she also knew that if Harmon was on guard duty she would never defeat him without some extra help. She sipped and swallowed a mouthful of elixir as her head rose above the level of the second floor.

Harmon was standing, silent and bulky, in front of the suite door. Unlike the man who had been guarding her the night she escaped, he hadn't brought along a chair to nap the night away.

She turned to Reyes and gestured to him with a flat hand. *Wait.* She closed her eyes and Cast her first—but hopefully not her last—Transport of the evening. She sent out the Cast and opened her eyes. To her great satisfaction, Harmon flew upward. His head struck the ceiling with a crack, but before he fell down the Cast also caught him and dropped him quietly to the floor. He landed with barely a bump and lay sprawled out and motionless.

Harmon was out cold, but she didn't know for how long. The man's skull was probably extremely thick. She ran lightly along the hall to the suite door, leaving Reyes to do whatever he wanted. She tried the door but it was locked, of course. With plenty of elixir on her, that wasn't a problem. In a few moments, the Unlock Cast had done its work. A quick glance at Harmon told her he remained dead to the world. She went inside the room. Her plan had nearly succeeded. Her heart lifted.

The lounge of the suite was exactly as she remembered. It was empty, so Parthenia had to be in the bedroom, asleep. No problem. She could Transport her sister without waking her up. Swallowing another mouthful of elixir, she opened the bedroom door.

She was surprised to see the bed was empty. Had Reyes misunderstood and directed her to the wrong suite? A muffled whimper drew her attention.

She swung around and nearly froze in shock. In a white nightgown in a far corner of the bedroom, Parthenia stood. She was gagged. Even more of a surprise was the person standing by her side: Castiel. Carina reacted instinctively. Castiel's presence didn't matter. Now she could see Parthenia she could Transport her. She closed her eyes. With a great effort of concentration, she Cast.

Almost immediately, a shockwave hit her, knocking her from her feet. The wave was so intense, so reeking of evil, she was momentarily dazed. She was on the floor. Parthenia was staring at her, eyes wide and panicky above her gag. Then she figured out what had happened. As she'd Cast Transport, someone else had Cast Repulse, throwing the force of her Cast back at her.

Parthenia wouldn't have sent the defensive Cast, which meant only one thing.

Castiel was smiling triumphantly. "You have no idea of the satisfaction that gave me, Carina. I have finally demonstrated my natural superiority over you. All our brothers and sisters thought you were so wonderful and powerful and wise, just because you'd learned true Casting, not the watered-down version Mother taught. But I knew *I* was the one who truly deserved their respect and awe, not you. Now my gift has finally arrived and my chance has come to receive my due, from you and all the others. The things I'll do, Carina, the victories I'll achieve with me leading all of you."

She was barely listening to Castiel as she went over her options. Of all the obstacles she'd imagined she might face in rescuing her sister, this one had never entered her mind. She couldn't Transport Parthenia while their brother was here to stop her. Though the power of his Repulse had surprised her, she thought she could probably defeat him at Casting. However, she was entirely unprepared. She would need time to think up a strategy and tactics.

A sound came from the other room. She saw with relief that Reyes had come into the suite. Maybe he could pin Castiel down or otherwise distract him and she could retrieve Parthenia. She rose to her feet. "Reyes, quick, come here. Grab that boy."

"Oh, no," Reyes said, advancing. "It isn't him I'll be grabbing." He lunged at her. She stepped aside just in time, and his momentum carried him past her. What was he doing?

Then she saw it all. Right from the beginning, the entire escapade had been an elaborate trap set by Langley and her son. They'd allowed her to escape and since then they'd been stringing her along, hoping to find out more about Casting and her connections with other mages.

Reyes lunged for a second time. She kicked out at him, catching him in his stomach. That stopped him, momentarily. He bent over, coughing.

She had to act fast. Harmon would be returning to consciousness any minute and Castiel could Cast at her. She would be entering into a battle she could not win. If she remained here, both she and Parthenia would be trapped. She only had one choice, though it broke her heart to do it. She tipped the elixir bottle into her mouth and swallowed. "I'm sorry," she said to Parthenia. "But don't give up hope. I'm coming back."

With that, she Cast Transport and was gone.

THIRTY-THREE

Carina appeared in the street outside the temple. Luckily, it was the middle of the night so no one was around. She hoped the twins had done exactly as she'd asked and Transported themselves and Darius to the same place not long after she and Reyes had left.

The Dirksen kid had betrayed her after all. Just when she'd begun to trust him. For a while, she'd believed he might be different from the rest of his clan. But he'd only been pretending so that he could be around her and learn about Casting. He and his mother had probably wanted to see if she knew other mages—maybe they were hoping she was in contact with Darius. The Dirksens had known about his existence for a long time. She was glad she'd taken the precaution of telling her siblings to leave the apartment. Reyes had probably arranged for his people to go there and kidnap her sister and brothers as soon as she was gone.

And Castiel.... Her brother's reappearance had been even more of a surprise. His Casting ability was a serious concern, especially the nature of his Casts. The Repulse she had experienced had felt *wrong*. And the fact that his ability had shown itself so late in his development was odd too. What it meant, she didn't know. Not for the first time she rued the fact that she'd been so young when Nai Nai died and that Ma had been so sick and with so little time to live while she had known her. As a result, her knowledge of mage lore was sparse.

She walked through the quiet courtyard in front of the temple and passed across the doorless threshold. The temple had been the only place she could think of to send her siblings where they would be safe, and then it would only be for a little while. Dirksen thugs would search everywhere Reyes could think of that she might go. She would have to take her siblings somewhere else soon.

The ancient frieze on the wall of the temple's antechamber seemed to greet her. What had the priestess been telling her about the painting when Reyes had stuck his head in the door? It had been something about how each Element in the scene represented a sin. She couldn't remember which material represented which sin, but the priestess' explanation had seemed very strange. It was nothing like her understanding of what they meant, based on the knowledge Nai Nai had passed down.

Yet in the morning ritual, she had seen a priest burn a character. The other acolytes may have been burning characters too. She hadn't been paying attention. However, the final scroll to be burned had displayed only dots and figures. The religion of the temple seemed to be tied up with magehood but she didn't understand how.

She also didn't have time to figure it out. Quickly, she went down a passage to one side of the central statues of deities and emerged in the larger, rear room where she'd spent a night sleeping on a bench. The room was empty. Where were Oriana and Ferne and Darius?

Her stomach clenched. Had her siblings Transported here or not? Were they still in the apartment or, more likely, in the custody of the Dirksen clan by now? As she stood hesitating about what to do, the young priestess who had helped her the last time she was here came out of the door at the rear of the chamber.

"I believe you're looking for some children?" she asked.

"Yes, I am."

"They're waiting for you in here. Please come through." The hooded figure returned through the door.

She hesitated again. Was this another trap? Had the Dirksens arrived here before her?

Darius popped out. "Carina!" He called behind him, "She's here, everyone!" before running over to her and grabbing her hand. Then he stopped. "Where's Parthenia?"

"I'm sorry, Darius. I couldn't get her."

The little boy's features fell.

She continued, "But I'm going to go back." Just as soon as she'd figured out how to free her sister.

His face brightened. "You'll get her. I know you will. Come on. Everyone's waiting for you."

He pulled her through the doorway into a small, dingy room lit by nothing but an old lamp and a small fire burning in a grate. The priestess was nowhere to be seen. Oriana and Ferne were here, however, sitting down facing her as she came through the door. Someone else was here too. A man sat opposite the twins, his back toward her. Her hand gripped Darius' tighter. Who had infiltrated her family this time?

The man stood up and turned. At first she didn't recognize him. Then she took a closer look and nearly fell over. It was Bryce.

"Carina." He strode over and enveloped her in a hug.

Through her surprise, she hugged him back, but then she pulled away. "What are you doing here? I thought you'd gone back to Ithiya."

"Why would you think that?"

"You have to run your family's business."

He frowned. "Yeah, I remember that's what you thought I was going to do the last time we were separated. You were wrong then—what made you think you'd be right this time around? Carina, don't you get it? I want to be with *you.*"

Ferne put his hand over his mouth and snickered. Oriana elbowed him in the side. Bryce glanced at the twins over his shoulder then returned his gaze to Carina, mildly embarrassed but not really caring. Before she could think of a suitable reply to his declaration, he went on, "Wait. Where's Parthenia? The kids said you'd gone to rescue her from the Dirksens."

"I couldn't," she replied, entirely forgetting her surprise at Bryce's appearance as she recalled the scared eyes of her sister. "Everything's worse than I thought. Castiel has her."

"Castiel?" exclaimed Ferne and Oriana in unison.

She told them Castiel had skillfully inserted himself into Langley Dirksen's household. "He must have decided to ally himself with the Dirksens. Then he set about trying to find us so we can be his acolytes. I have to try again to get Parthenia out, and soon. They might move her somewhere else and I don't trust Castiel not to do something awful to her."

She knew that if her oldest brother was anything like his father, there were no depths he wouldn't sink to, though she didn't want to go into details in front of the children.

"Why is Castiel helping the Dirksens?" Oriana asked. "He's a Sherrerr. It doesn't make any sense."

"He probably has some deluded idea about lording it over them. Idiot. As if any of the Dirksens are going to allow some kid to boss them around. He'll receive a wake-up call soon enough. But I plan on us being long gone before that happens. I just need to get Parthenia first."

"Well I'm here to help you," Bryce said.

She studied her friend. Though they'd only been apart for a short time, he seemed to have changed. His beard was thicker and he'd filled out a little. That was why she hadn't recognized him immediately. "I don't understand. How did you find us? Is it just a coincidence you were here when the children arrived?"

"No coincidence. When you Transported me to the planet—alone...." He glared at her. "I appeared in this city. I nearly frightened the life out of a tramp. He ran off shouting something about ghosts. You ran out of elixir, didn't you? That was why you sent me here by myself."

"Yeah, I'd used it all up. I only had enough left for one person."

"So whoever was boarding the shuttle—you decided you were going to face them alone? Don't do that to me in the future, okay? I would have stayed with you if I'd known the situation but you didn't give me a choice."

"Okay." Having Bryce with her when she'd been captured by the Dirksens would have complicated matters tenfold, but her friend did have a point.

"When I realized you hadn't Transported yourself too," he continued, "I thought I would try to find you and your brothers and sisters. From then onward I've been wandering the city, visiting places where people might go to lie low. A couple of days ago I came here. It was the only place where someone who fitted your description had been seen. The priestess said you'd been interested in the pictures out in the front, so I guessed you might return. Since then I've been back two or three times a day, hoping you would show."

"Bryce was just leaving when we Transported to the courtyard," Oriana said. "We made him jump."

"You certainly did," he said.

She smiled. She was relieved that Bryce was okay, though she was also somewhat alarmed by his feelings for her.

The priestess returned to the chamber. "Will you be spending the night here?" she asked. "We have a small room for the homeless, though it only holds two beds. However, you're all welcome to stay."

"Yes, we are," Darius said. "I'm tired."

"No," said Carina. "Thank you, but we're leaving now."

"Why?" Oriana asked.

"Yes, why can't we stay?" asked Ferne. "I'm tired too."

"It isn't safe for us. Other people might guess we're here. People who want to hurt us. We'll have to find somewhere else to sleep tonight." She paused. "But..." She didn't know when she would return to the temple, if ever. She might never have the chance to find out what link the religion had with magehood. "Before we go," she said, "could you tell me more about your religion? Or do you have anything I could read about it?"

THIRTY-FOUR

After finding a hotel to stay at, Carina opened the room's interface to find the religion's database while the children settled down to sleep. The holy book of the religion was too old and fragile to be handled, but each page had been copied onto a database that was free to anyone to read. The priestess had given her the name of the site before they left. Bryce sat down beside her as she studied the pages.

The pictures of the holy book were in the same style as the friezes that decorated the temple, only much better quality and in greater detail. She hadn't seen much art in her life, but the images in the religious text looked well-painted to her. Though the figures were tiny, their facial expressions were naturalistic and nuanced, and the landscapes and buildings represented looked realistic, though they were unfamiliar and archaic.

"I wonder why they put all this stuff in a book?" Bryce asked. "Why not create it on an interface? A file wouldn't suffer the same wear and tear."

"I guess they thought a book would last longer."

"They thought a book would last longer? From what I can tell, the thing's falling apart."

"Yes, but the priestess said the book was thousands of years old. Do you know of any files that old? I don't."

"True enough. What does it say?"

The text was legible but the language was indecipherable. "Oh, look. There's a translation." She opened the relevant page.

In the beginning, the People came, arrived from the stars that gave them birth. They traveled in celestial vessels filled with every food they might desire in an unending supply, provided to give them nourishment throughout their long voyage.

First to set foot on the Given Planet was Lomeq. She brought with her two sons: Sear and Sorn. Sear and Sorn brought with them their wives, Lani and Pirlu. Sear and Lani brought with them five children...

"Do we have to read this?" Bryce asked. "It's just a long list of names."

"You don't have to read anything. Go to bed if you like. But you're right. I don't think I'm going to learn much here."

"What are you looking for anyway? I didn't know you were interested in religion."

"I'm not." Carina explained what had prompted her to investigate the religious beliefs on Ostillon.

"You think it might have something to do with mages? I would have thought you would know all about them, considering you are one."

In the time she and Bryce had spent on the shuttle after escaping from the Sherrerrs, Carina hadn't told him much about her past. She'd been careful to keep the conversation about him or other, neutral, topics. But she guessed he had proven his loyalty and trustworthiness enough for her to tell him about mage lore.

"I only know what my grandmother told me," she explained, "and she died when I was young so I don't remember everything very well. Mage history, how to Cast, everything in fact, all we know about being a mage is passed on orally. Nothing is ever written down, and we don't have family photographs or anything else that might link us to other mages. It's the only way we can remain safe."

"So you don't know any other mages apart from your family?"

"That's right. I didn't even know them until I happened to rescue Darius from the Dirksens. And then I didn't find out he was my brother until Stefan Sherrerr found me and reunited me with Ma."

"Wow, that must have been a lonely life."

"Yeah." She paused, thinking that Bryce was one of the few people she'd met who had some idea of what she'd been through. "Anyway, if there is something in this religion that has to do with mages, I want to find out more if I can."

"Okay. What else does it say?" He swiped to the next page.

The initial chapter of the holy book went into a lot of detail about the first settlers on the planet. It also explained that the world was a paradise provided for the colonists by their deities. The information was quite interesting, but it wasn't until the second chapter Carina saw anything that seemed significant.

In the second year, the People tilled the fields, grew crops, and harvested them. The People hunted in the woods and brought home meat. They birthed more children and their numbers swelled. All was good and the People lived in peace and prosperity.

But then they discovered their new world was blighted. An alien race had arrived before them and stolen their rightful home. These others were not People. They had disguised themselves to resemble People so they could walk among them and befriend them.

Yet these others tricked the People, doing things that People could not. The aliens could disappear in the wink of an eye and reappear in another place altogether. They could move objects without touching them. They could bend the People to do their bidding.

The alien race was evil and the People knew they would never be safe until the aliens were expelled from the world.

Her hand went to her mouth.

Bryce said what was on her mind. "The aliens sound like mages."

———

By the time Carina finished reading the holy book, it was so late it was nearly morning. She closed the interface and went to bed. She had time to sleep for a couple of hours before the children woke up. Then she had to make a plan on how to rescue Parthenia.

Bryce was squeezed into a narrow space between Darius and the wall on one of the two beds, with Ferne sleeping at the other edge of the bed, on the verge of falling off. Darius was lying on his back between them, arms outstretched, looking like a sea creature she had seen once on a forgotten planet. The animal had been flat and its five limbs splayed out.

With only Oriana to share a bed with, she had more room than poor Bryce or Ferne, yet though she was exhausted, she didn't fall asleep right away. The stories from the ancient book replayed in her mind, though she saw them from the perspective of the mages.

What had happened during the time in which the book was set had become clear to her when she'd read between the lines. Thousands of years ago, mages had settled on Ostillon. The planet might have been one of the first they'd fled to after leaving Earth. Then, some time later, another group of settlers had arrived. The new colonists might have already been following a religion that told them the planet was their rightful home, or the religion might have sprung up as divine justification for the persecution of mages.

It was plain that the newcomers had felt threatened by the mages' powers.

Her ancestors might have become lax about hiding what they could do since leaving Earth possibly many generations before. Whatever the reason, the new settlers hadn't wanted to share their world with these people who had strange abilities. They deemed the practices of mages immoral and probably made them illegal. The Elements that were so important to mages became representative of sins, and the Characters had to be destroyed—perhaps a metaphor for what the colonists wanted to do to the mages.

The ritual at the end of the Mech Battles performance suddenly made sense. The priestess had said that pouring the elixir into the sand was to cleanse the participants of their sins. At some point, the newcomers had justified pouring away stocks of elixir by saying they were purifying the mages of evil.

The only reminder that mages had once lived on Ostillon were their inaccurate representation in stories in a holy book and a few traditional dishes in the local cuisine.

Though in her time the planet was a nowhere place at the edge of the galactic sector, at one point in its history it must have been one of the first to have been settled from Earth. Her heart skipped a beat. Did that mean Earth was comparatively nearby?

"Can't sleep?" Bryce whispered from across the room.

She lifted herself onto her elbow. "No. You neither?"

"Uh uh. I know it's asking a lot, but I need more than a hands-breadth of space to relax in."

She chuckled. "Sorry about Darius. Push him out of the way if you like. I don't think he'll wake up."

"It's okay. I just realized... I never told you how happy I was to find you again."

"Bryce, I'm happy you found me too." She really meant it. For the first time in her life, she thought she'd met a non-mage she could completely trust.

THIRTY-FIVE

Parthenia had cried herself to sleep, and the following morning when Harmon woke her and told her she had to go down to breakfast, she refused. The large man bristled but seemed to think twice about his response. He said nothing and left the suite. Another guard arrived to take his place. Harmon had been watching her all night, presumably to catch Carina if she repeated her rescue attempt.

A few minutes later, Langley Dirksen arrived and sent the replacement guard out. She was dressed in loose fitting, light pajamas covered by a robe made of a similarly fine, expensive material. She was only lightly made up. Perhaps it was due to the dim light through the window blinds or the woman's age and luxurious clothes, but Parthenia was briefly reminded of her mother. Another bout of sobbing threatened and it was as much as she could do to control herself.

Langley seemed to sense her vulnerable state. The woman's expression was soft with sympathy as she stood in the bedroom doorway. "Do you mind if I come in?"

Determined not to open her mouth lest she begin to cry, Parthenia didn't reply.

Langley came in anyway. She sat next to her on the side of her bed. "My dear, you look exhausted. I imagine that you hardly slept. There's no need for you to come down to breakfast if you don't feel like it. I can ask one of the maids to bring something up to you. How does that sound?"

Finally, Parthenia trusted herself to speak. "I'm not hungry."

"Is that so? I'm surprised. Your sister had quite the appetite."

At the mention of Carina's name, Parthenia's lower lip turned out and she had to swallow. She'd seen Carina for only a moment—less than a minute—for the first time since she'd arrived on Ostillon. After waiting and hoping for so long her sister would find and help her and her siblings, Carina had finally appeared, but then she'd left again. She'd left her in the hands of Castiel and the Dirksens. She was trying hard not to feel abandoned but she wasn't succeeding.

Langley reached out and placed a hand on top of hers. She snatched her hand away and thrust it under the coverlet.

"Parthenia... May I call you that? I understand how you feel and I know I would feel the same in your circumstances. You've had a very difficult time recently. Your brother has told me all about it. You must have been terrified to find yourself alone on a strange planet with no one to turn to. I can't imagine what you must have been forced to do to survive. You must be very brave and resourceful. I doubt I could have done the same. I have so much admiration for you."

Langley was gazing in her eyes, a soft, compassionate expression on her face. She continued, "You see, you and I are quite alike, aren't we? We were both raised within the comfort and privilege of a powerful clan. We wanted for nothing, and—if your parents were as indulgent as mine—we could have whatever we asked for. To live a life like that and then suddenly find yourself in an entirely different environment where you had absolutely nothing and were in fear for your life, what a challenge that must have been, and yet you met it." Tilting her head, Langley paused, allowing her words to linger.

She was right, Parthenia realized. She'd had a terrible time when she had walked with Darius through the forest. She'd had to seek help from the ranger, and do so many other things including going for help when Ferne had been shot. All the time she'd worried that she was making bad decisions, but actually she'd done as well as could have been expected. Perhaps she'd been too hard on herself. But what did any of that matter? She wanted to make sure that Carina had helped Ferne and her siblings. "I want to leave," she blurted.

"But why?" Langley asked. "Don't you like it here? This is a beautiful room in a beautiful house. We have wonderful grounds for you to wander in. You can have whatever you want. You only need to ask for it. Isn't this the life you're used to?"

"I want to be with my family. It doesn't matter that this is the kind of life I used to lead. Maybe I wasn't happy then. Have you considered that?" Despite her words, Parthenia recognized the truth of what Langley was saying. Her time on Ostillon since Carina had Transported her down here had been awful.

A small part of her did yearn for the indulgent life she was accustomed to, even though she'd known that Mother was unhappy and no one except Father had much freedom. At least she'd never suffered a moment's physical discomfort. At least she'd been safe.

"Your brother has told me about your lives on Ithiya, and, to be honest, it doesn't sound that bad. None of us can have everything we want. That would be selfish and unreasonable. We must accept that sometimes sacrifices and compromises are necessary. That's the correct, mature attitude to have in life. Don't you agree?"

Parthenia *did* agree, but she didn't want to say so. Agreeing with Langley Dirksen felt wrong. Of course it was wrong. The woman was holding her against her will. Parthenia was muddled. "You shouldn't listen to Castiel. He's a bad person. He scared and hurt Nahla and last night he gagged me and forced me to stay beside him when Carina came to rescue me."

"Ah, your sister," said Langley. "Another troubled young lady. She also didn't understand the advantages of using her powers for good. But you were talking about Castiel, weren't you? I agree, his behavior is excessive at times. I shall speak to him about it. Of course, he had to prevent your sister from taking you from us and returning you to hardship and a difficult life, but he must learn to be more kind and reasonable. Perhaps you can help me to persuade him."

Once more, she was at a loss. Castiel certainly did need to learn to behave better, but she didn't feel she was the person who should teach him. That wasn't her responsibility. Or was it? She was his older sister after all. And Mother had loved Castiel the same as she'd loved all her children. Perhaps she'd seen good in him that wasn't apparent to anyone else. Maybe Mother would have liked her to show Castiel some compassion.

"I... Er..."

Langley smiled. She pressed her hand where it lay beneath the covers. The woman's touch felt warm and comforting. She suddenly missed her mother very, very much.

"Don't worry, dear," said Langley. "You're still upset from everything you've been through since you arrived. It's entirely understandable that you need to recover and think things through before making any decisions. Take all the time you want. You're at a very important crossroads in your life. One way lies a wonderful life doing good and helping people while enjoying the best every world has to offer, the other way lies uncertainty, never knowing where your next meal will come from, and fear of discovery preventing you from helping others." Langley stood up and tightened the ties on her robe. "Would you like something to eat? Breakfast is still warm."

She looked down. This time, guilt bothered her while she refused to reply. For a powerful member of a powerful clan, Langley Dirksen didn't seem as bad as she would have imagined.

Langley left, and she gave vent to her feelings again, burying her face in her pillow. Even when she'd been trapped in the security room at the spaceport or in the cell at the holding center, she had never felt so alone. At those times, she'd been focused on returning to her siblings and desperately worried about them. Now she guessed Carina was with them. That had to be how her older sister had discovered where she was. It meant that Darius, Oriana, Ferne, and Carina were all together and Parthenia was the one who was apart from them.

Carina had come for her just as she'd said she would. Her sister had kept true to her word, and yet... The awful feeling that had pervaded her the previous night returned. Carina had left her. She'd left, even though she knew she was trapped and Castiel was holding her hostage.

Why had Carina gone away? She could do anything. She was an amazing fighter and she could Cast expertly, while Castiel was new to the skill. He should have been easy for Carina to defeat. Yet after only a brief try, she had abandoned her to the Dirksens. She'd said she would come back but would she? And when?

Thirty-Six

Carina, Bryce, and the children crowded around a table at a diner. It was a small, cheap, grubby place, but she had still checked the establishment took cash before they sat down. Bryce had money from some casual labor he'd picked up to survive while searching for them. The man behind the counter nodded in reply without removing his gaze from an erotic holo playing on a lower counter, barely out of view. She asked him to turn down the volume a little so the children wouldn't hear.

Oriana, Ferne, and Darius squabbled over who would be first to order from the interface at the table until she made them stop. She told them she would order the worst-tasting breakfast on the menu if they didn't behave.

She rolled her eyes at Bryce, reflecting that, for children who had been brought up by a cruel monster, they sometimes showed little sign of it. She guessed that Ma must have shielded them from Stefan's nastiness much of the time.

Bryce was wearing an amused expression.

"What?" Carina asked. "Is something funny?"

"You're pretty young to be a mom."

"Huh. I didn't get a lot of choice about it."

"Well, you're doing a great job, especially considering it was thrust upon you."

She glanced at the twins and Darius, who had begun to argue again—this time about what the others were ordering—though more quietly. They seemed distracted enough to not be listening.

"Honestly, though it's hard," she said, "I couldn't be happier. I didn't have anyone I could be open with about being a mage until I met this little gang. It's isolating to be always keeping back a part of yourself from everyone you know. For a long while, I thought I was used to it. But then when I met Darius and I discovered there was perhaps an entire family of mages I could meet, I was so excited.... I realized I'd been sad, deep down, for a long time." She drew breath, a feeling of panic rising in her. Although she knew its cause—her words to Bryce were probably the most frank she'd ever been about her feelings to anyone, ever—that didn't dampen her visceral reaction.

"Anyway," she went on, quickly steering away from dwelling on her emotions, "now I only need to get Parthenia back. Then we can all be together. I just haven't figured out how yet."

Perhaps sensing her discomfort, he also focused on the new topic. "What happened when you went to the Dirksen estate?"

She filled him in, finishing with, "Part of the problem is that in any plan I think up, Castiel is an unknown. If we end up Casting directly at each other, it's hard to be sure I can defeat him. I got some sense of his power last night and at the time I thought I would probably be stronger than him if it were put to the test, but I wouldn't like to bet on it."

"What if you had the others helping you?"

She shook her head emphatically. "I'm not taking them with me. It's too risky."

An ancient servitor trundled up to the table, its shelves bearing breakfast dishes. She lifted the plates out and slid them across to the children, who had already forgotten what they ordered. Three dishes were passed back due to their being apparently unfit for human consumption. Bryce picked up some kind of toasted vegetable, nibbled on it, and announced it was the most delicious thing he'd ever tasted.

"Wait," Ferne said, "I remember I ordered that."

"It's mine now," Bryce retorted. "You said you didn't want it."

"But I changed my mind."

"Oh, okay. Here you go then." Bryce pushed the plate back.

She grinned. "How come you're so good at this?"

"I'm the eldest of a similar brood."

"Well, don't do any more of that. I'm hungry, and from the look of it there aren't going to be any leftovers."

As everyone ate, she tried to think up a plan for extracting Parthenia from the Dirksen estate. If it had only been non-mages she was facing, she didn't think she would have had too many problems. Casting gave her an edge in most situations. But going up against another mage brought up the possibility of an entirely different set of scenarios. Castiel's time spent witnessing Ma's lessons on Casting with his siblings probably meant he knew just about everything she could do. He would be able to think up defenses and counterattacks to defeat her.

Darius was fidgeting vigorously in his seat.

"Is something wrong?" she asked.

"I need to go to the bathroom."

She slid across the bench and stood up to let him out. As she sat down again, Darius said, "I know how we can get Parthenia back."

"Really?" Carina said, wondering if her little brother could read her thoughts. "How?"

"We fly in on Reyes' star racer and grab her. Then we fly away again."

"That's a good idea, Darius, but we can't borrow Reyes' star racer. He isn't our friend anymore."

"Oh, good," Darius said. "I never liked him. I didn't like the feeling he gave me."

"You didn't? Why didn't you tell me?"

"I don't know. You didn't ask."

"Uh.... Next time you get that feeling about someone, Darius, let me know, okay?"

"Okay." The little boy skipped off to the restroom at the back of the diner.

"What was that about?" Bryce asked.

"Darius is a special kind of mage, I think. Ma suspected it too. He picks up on people's emotions very strongly."

"So he knew there was something off about the Dirksen guy?"

"Yeah, I think he did. I wish I'd thought to ask him."

"Shame he didn't tell you."

"It probably wouldn't have made a lot of difference. I would have gone to get Parthenia anyway, thinking I could easily Transport us both out of there, no matter what trap the Dirksen woman had laid for me. I didn't know Castiel was waiting."

"I was wondering," Bryce said, "if Castiel can Cast, why didn't he just put you in a locked room the minute he saw you?"

"Because I had elixir with me and I would have Cast my way out again. He needed to get the elixir off me first. Besides, I think he's playing a longer game. He wants all of us, not only me and Parthenia. Then he can play at being the head of a mage family, just like his dad. Maybe he's hoping I'll bring everyone along next time."

Darius returned and she moved again to let him back into his seat.

"Did you figure out how we're going to get Parthenia?" he asked.

"Not yet."

"I wish we had a star racer. Then it would be easy."

She didn't think that rescuing their sister was going to be easy at all, star racer or not. But Darius' suggestion had given her an idea. Maybe she'd been focusing too heavily on Castiel's mage power and not enough on what he couldn't do. Her brother had no military experience, and Langley and the other Dirksens wouldn't suspect she might try to extract her sister with brute force. An armed attack would take them by surprise. But how could she buy weapons?

"What's wrong?" Darius asked.

"I thought I had an idea but I realized it won't work. It would cost a lot of money that we don't have."

"We could work for it," said Bryce. "Or maybe I could ask my parents for some."

"Both of those would take too long. We have to get Parthenia out soon. If we wait weeks or months they might move her somewhere else, even offplanet. My plan would require a lot of cash and we would need it fast, like in the next few days."

Her eyes widened and she sat up straight.

"You thought of an idea," Darius exclaimed. He clapped his hands. "Yay! We're going to get Parthenia."

THIRTY-SEVEN

The Mech Battle company secretary didn't take Carina seriously. The woman looked her up and down before saying, "Sorry, we're all booked up for the next few months. Come back later."

"I'm an ex-merc," Carina said. "I've used mechs before."

"Sorry, that wouldn't make us any less booked up even if I believed you."

"Please. Give me a chance. I would put on a really good show."

"Look, I'm trying to do you a favor. Find another way to earn a fast buck, okay? Because if you go in that pit, you aren't coming out alive."

As she spoke a door behind her slid open and a heavily muscled, very hairy man walked out into the lobby.

"Mech fighting is for people like this great lunk," the secretary said. "It isn't for young women."

The man grinned at being called a 'lunk.' "Another idiot kid who wants to fight?" he asked the secretary, not making eye contact with Carina.

"Yeah," she replied. "You finished for the day?"

"Yep. Off to get this scar taken out." He showed the woman a broad, angry, fresh scar running from his shoulder down his back. "I like to leave them a while to impress the girls, but this one's a pain in the ass. Restricts movement in my arm."

"Call that a scar?" Carina asked. "That's nothing. Take a look at these." She turned and lifted her top over her back. During her time as a merc she'd gotten into plenty of scrapes where the cheap armor provided by the company hadn't been adequate protection. Shipboard medical facilities didn't cover scar removal and Carina never wanted to go to splicers planetside. She guessed that mage abilities were in her genetic code and she didn't want anyone getting their hands on hers if she could help it.

From the silence behind her, she guessed that the secretary and the lunk were suitably impressed. She lowered her top and turned to face them. "What do you say?" she asked.

The woman glanced at the Mech Battle fighter, whose eyebrows were raised. She pointed toward an old cargo mech standing in the corner of the room. "If you can operate that, I'll put your name down. Don't get your hopes up too much though. The boss has the final say."

Carina went over to the ancient machine. It was even older than the outdated models she'd worked with during her time on her company's ship, *Duchess*. Stepping backward and upward into the mech's center, she sought out the feet and hand controls. The front shield lowered automatically, also giving her access to the eye-tracking controls. She was locked in and ready to go.

She walked the mech forward. Its response time was slow, each leg moving as much as a quarter second after she activated it. She hoped the models they used for fighting weren't similarly sluggish.

Odd mechanical parts were piled in the middle of the floor. She was supposed to demonstrate she could pick them up and manipulate them, but she needed to do something much showier and more memorable if she were to be picked to fight.

She walked the mech past the pile and approached the secretary's desk, the hiss, clunk, hiss, clunk of the mech's legs loud in her ears. The secretary looked alarmed. "No, no, no," she exclaimed. "Go back there. Move those things around."

Carina continued on her original track. The secretary jumped up and backed against the wall. But it wasn't her she wanted.

The lunk was standing behind the desk, his hands on his hips, smiling broadly. Carina guessed he must be impressed. She was about to impress him further. She reached forward with the mech's pincers. At the last second, the man realized what she was about to do and he tried to jump out of the way. He was too late.

She grabbed him around his biceps. She held him firmly enough that he wouldn't slip but delicately enough not to hurt him. When she had a good grip on his biceps, she used the mech's second set of pincers to grab his thighs.

"Whoaaaaa," the lunk exclaimed, chuckling. "Take it easy, girl."

She lifted him up, then turned him horizontal so he was parallel with the ceiling.

"Oh my stars," the secretary wailed. "Put him down!"

Carina spun the man around once. As he was roaring with laughter, she spun him around a second time. Then she lowered him to his previous position. As soon as she'd released him, he doubled over, slapping the desk and laughing too hard to speak. Carina walked the mech back to the wall and climbed out of it.

The secretary had been crouching while all this had been going on. She stood and straightened her clothes. "Well, that was quite the demonstration," she said as she returned to her desk. "You didn't need to go quite that far. I would have put your name down anyway." She opened her interface. "What is it?"

"Tamira... Lan."

"Can I see your ID?"

"Oh. I don't have any."

"Ah," said the secretary. "That could be a problem."

"Give her a chance," said the lunk. "You know half the IDs you see in here are fake. The boss will love her."

"Hmm... Okay, Tamira—"

"Call me Tammy."

"Tammy. The owner will be here at five, a couple of hours before the show starts. If you come back then, perhaps he'll give you a shot."

"Tonight?" Carina asked.

"No. Definitely not tonight. But he might find you something within the next few days."

Her disappointment must have shown.

"It's the best I can do," said the secretary. "Take it or leave it."

Without a large sum of money, her plan to attack the Dirksen estate military-style would never work. She needed a hover vessel, weapons, and ammunition at the very least. Ideally, she would like smoke grenades and other accessories that would make the rescue attempt easier. Winning a Mech Battle was the only way she knew that she could obtain the necessary funds quickly.

She hoped a few days wouldn't make too much of a difference to Parthenia, and that Langley wouldn't move her sister someplace else. Then it occurred to her that the waiting time would allow her and Bryce to earn more money, which they could then bet on her winning her fight.

Of course, there was the small detail of her winning to consider. That wasn't guaranteed at all. She'd never actually fought in any mech, let alone the monsters used for the Mech Battles. But what the secretary offered was better than any alternative she knew. "I'll take it. I'll be back later."

Bryce was waiting for her outside. "They turned you down, right?"

"What? Of course not. They were practically begging me to fight, and tonight. I had to put them off for a few days. We need to earn some money and make some arrangements."

They walked down the long road through the lot that led into the city. The last time she had walked this road she hadn't thought she would ever be back, and least of all that she would be fighting in a Mech Battle.

"They turned you down at first, though," Bryce said, "didn't they?"

"Yeah. I had to show off a bit to persuade them."

"I thought so. Where to next?"

"Wait a minute." She took out a flask of elixir, sipped a little, and then Sent to Oriana. After checking the children were okay in their hotel room, she said, "We have to see about those arrangements."

THIRTY-EIGHT

Langley Dirksen had given Parthenia an exquisite dress to wear to the soiree. Somehow the woman had known exactly the most flattering colors, style, and fitting. Though Parthenia felt embarrassed to admit it as she gazed at herself in a mirror, she had never looked so beautiful. Mixed in with her embarrassment was a large portion of guilt.

She shouldn't have agreed to meet Langley Dirksen's relations, friends, and business associates at the informal party. She felt sure that Carina wouldn't have agreed to it in her position. Yet Parthenia had feared what might happen if she said no. When Langley had asked her, she had noticed the woman's expression turn rigid as she waited for an answer, then relax when she had reluctantly said yes.

She'd only acquiesced because she was worried what Castiel might do to her if she didn't, or—even worse—what he might do to Nahla. Her brother had already caught on that she was frightened he would hurt her little sister and, like his father before him, he wouldn't be slow to exploit the fact. Castiel had been watching from the corner of the room when Langley Dirksen had made her request and he'd smiled when Parthenia nodded.

A familiar feeling of suffocation was sinking over her. Though it was only her second day in the mansion, she was beginning to feel very much at home. So many things contributed to the sensation: luxurious surroundings, servants, expensive, perfectly cooked meals and polite, well-mannered behavior expected at all times. Most influential of all to her, however, was Castiel's presence. Like a brooding malevolence, he seemed to be around her wherever she went, watching and judging, ready to pounce when she stepped out of line. Just like their father.

She hated how she was so used to the environment that it felt comfortable. She didn't know how she could ever break out of it. She didn't dare to try. Perhaps she didn't want to try. If she failed in her attempt she might lose all hope.

Don't give up hope, Carina had said. But she hadn't said when she would be back, or how she would help her escape. A constant guard meant that Carina couldn't Transport in and Transport out with her. And the Dirksen estate was probably heavily defended. What chance did Carina stand against the might of the Dirksens? She was only one person and their siblings were too young to be of much help.

On the other hand, Carina had managed to escape from the Sherrerrs, Parthenia had to admit. If her sister could do that, maybe she could defeat the Dirksens too. She would try not to give up hope.

In the meantime, she would go along with whatever Langley Dirksen wanted. It would keep Castiel happy and hopefully prevent him from hurting Nahla as a coercion tactic. It shouldn't be too hard. All her life, Parthenia had been wearing pretty dresses and smiling nicely to keep everyone happy. Another short period of the same wouldn't hurt.

———

When she arrived at the party downstairs, Langley Dirksen's guests all turned to look at her. They seemed apprehensive, almost afraid of what she might do or say. She could feel herself blush in response to all the attention. She hovered in the doorway, tempted to turn around and go back to her suite.

"Come in, dear," Langley called from across the room. She was sitting with a group of women who all wore fantastical hairstyles. Langley rose and swept across the room to take her arm. "You look *stunning*," she whispered in her ear as she guided her through the groups of partygoers, who were returning to their conversations now she had made her entrance.

She experienced the same guilty thrill she'd felt when she'd looked at herself in the mirror in her bedroom. Her feelings were in turmoil. Her younger mage sisters and brothers were struggling to survive, even if Carina had found them as she hoped. Yet here she was, wearing beautiful clothes and going to parties. It wasn't what she'd chosen, yet she hadn't refused to participate either.

She caught sight of a pair of dark eyes through the crowd and inwardly flinched. Castiel was here, watching her. He was wearing a suit and looking much older than his years. He gave her a wink and turned away to speak to someone in his group. It was as though he knew exactly how she felt and the knowledge of her discomfort and inner conflict pleased him. She wondered if Castiel was like Darius: able to pick up on the emotions of those around him, no matter how hard they tried to hide them.

The women in Langley's group were gazing at her as Langley brought her over. Like Langley, they all had a slightly greedy look, though none displayed even an ounce of extra fat. They had all probably been at a splicer's today, having their bodies refined to perfection for the party.

"Everyone," said Langley, "this is Parthenia, the very special young woman I was telling you about."

"Lovely to meet you, Parthenia," said a woman whose hair rose up from her head in a perfect spiral. "Effy, move along, dear," she said to another woman sitting on the sofa. "Make room for Parthenia."

Effy shifted across the sofa, creating space for one more person. Parthenia sank down, a sudden desire to escape overwhelming her. She wanted to sink right into the furniture and away from these predatory women. The spiral-haired woman handed her a bowl containing iced treats. The bowl itself was also icy, refrigerated by the table it had been sitting on.

"Try one," the woman said. "They're delicious." She was staring at her intensely, almost angrily, though Parthenia couldn't figure out why. It was the first time they'd met. She took a treat and ate it, grateful that it melted and slipped down her throat easily. Her mouth was as dry as a bone.

"I have very big plans in store for Parthenia," Langley said. "Very big. We're going to work closely together, aren't we, my dear? I imagine she'll become like a daughter to me."

Parthenia coughed.

"How exciting," Effy said. "Parthenia, I heard you only just arrived on Ostillon. What do you think of the place so far?"

"Oh, it seems nice." It was all she could think to say. Most of her time on Ostillon had been spent running and hiding. It wasn't like she'd taken a tour of the place.

"I love it here," Effy enthused, continuing as if she hadn't heard what Parthenia had said. "It's so quaint! So many ancient customs are still alive. Like hunting. Have any of you been hunting?" she asked the group generally.

The spiral-haired woman rolled her eyes. "We've all been hunting, as you know perfectly well. Personally, I didn't care for it. Riding those animals— what are they called? Horses, I believe—it left me unable to even walk. I had to have deep muscle therapy from my splicer to feel normal again."

"Mmm... Deep muscle therapy from your splicer," said a dark-haired woman who hadn't spoken before. "Now that's something I wouldn't say no to."

"Er, excuse me," Langley said. "We have a young lady present, don't forget."

"Oh don't be silly," the dark-haired woman said, "I'm sure she knows a thing or two about what I mean."

Parthenia sank deeper into her seat.

"Mother," a voice said.

She looked up to see a lanky young man standing to one side of the group of women. Her chest tightened as she recognized him. He'd been in her suite the previous night when Carina had tried to rescue her.

"Reyes," Langley said, "I'm so glad you've come down to join us this time."

"As Parthenia's here, I thought I should," Reyes replied. "She'll get bored talking to all you old folk."

This brought cries of outrage from the women. "Huh, *old*," Effy huffed.

"He's just teasing you," said Langley. "But he has a point. Reyes, why don't you take Parthenia for a walk? It's getting stuffy in here and, yes, we old folk are very boring."

Reyes held out his hand to Parthenia and she felt obliged to take it. He helped her up then led her to the open double doors at the back of the room.

Outside, the air was cool and refreshing. She had been riddled with tension but she felt some of it slip away, despite the fact that Langley's son had tried to grab Carina before she escaped.

"You were upstairs in my room last night," Parthenia said. "My sister seemed to know you."

"Yeah, I spent some time with Carina over the last few days. She's a cool person but she's misguided."

"How is she misguided?"

"She only sees the bad in everything. Mother tried to persuade her to help the Dirksen cause but she wouldn't. I tried to point out that what we're doing is for the good over the long term. But Carina was too short-sighted to see it."

"Are the Dirksens doing things for the good?" She'd never really understood what it was that the Sherrerrs did. All she'd known about were the meetings Father had taken her to, when he'd given her detailed instructions on what he wanted her to do. Beyond that, Sherrerr business was a mystery to her.

"Absolutely. We've made enormous improvements to Ostillon since arriving here. It was a backward place before. Really primitive. But now it's thriving." He turned to her. "That's the kind of thing you'd be helping us do if you worked with us."

THIRTY-NINE

Carina had been working for the labor agency for three days and she still hadn't seen Asha. No one could tell her why the woman hadn't turned up for work. At first, she hadn't been too worried. She wanted to work until the boss at the Mech Battle company arranged a fight for her so she could earn money to bet on herself. But she also had good reasons for wanting to reconnect with Asha.

She had expected to meet a cool reception at the agency because Asha had told her she would pull strings so Carina couldn't work there. But the agency receptionist barely seemed to remember her.

At the end of her third day of work, Carina decided that if she couldn't see Asha there, she would just have to go to her apartment, even if that did mean facing the vile Cavin. She had only been to Asha's home once. It was deep within the warren of cheap, rundown blocks in the heart of the city. She lost her way several times before finally finding the street too narrow for hover vehicles. After she passed the noodle soup shop with its child server, she knew she was in the right place.

She pressed the security panel next to Asha's door three or four times and was on the verge of leaving when the door opened a crack.

"Tammy?"

"Asha, I... What happened to you?"

Though Asha was looking out through a narrow space, it was easy to see her face was purple with bruises.

"Oh, I had an accident."

Carina's heart sank. "Let me guess. Your face had an accidental encounter with Cavin's fist. Where is he? Is he here?"

"He's here, but he's asleep."

"Let me in. I want to speak with him."

"No, I don't want that. I can figure this out by myself."

"You know what?" said Carina. "You're right. I'd love nothing more than to come in there and bash Cavin's brains out for you, but I know that wouldn't do any good. You *do* need to figure this out by yourself. But I really want to speak to him. I need him for something."

"Oh, okay. I guess you can come in then."

Inside Asha's apartment everything was in disarray. It looked as if a major fight had taken place, or maybe the mess had only resulted from Asha trying to escape her no-good boyfriend. Asha hadn't been in to work because she was too beat up or perhaps because Cavin had decided to prevent her. If the latter were the case, as soon as they ran out of money the ban on Asha working would be lifted. The idea of Cavin himself working was likely unthinkable to either of them. Carina had known many similar couples and families in the slum settlement where she'd grown up.

Cavin looked like part of the general mess. He was lying on the sofa, one leg and one arm hanging down, snoring. It was an unusual time of day for a nap. She wondered if he was drugged up. If he was that would make him difficult to talk to, but on the other hand, it would mean she'd come to the right person.

She pulled the sofa out from the wall. Cavin didn't stir. She went around the back and lifted up the sofa, tipping him onto the floor. She could have just pulled him off but she didn't want to get her hands dirty.

"Arghhh," he exclaimed, waking up. "Asha, what the hell are you.... Oh, it's you."

Carina was standing behind the sofa. "I need weapons and a fast hover vehicle. Something like a star racer but a little bigger."

He wiped drool from his mouth. "Yeah, okay. So what does that have to do with me?"

"You know someone who can get them for me."

"Huh. No, I don't," Cavin replied, sitting up and rubbing his messy hair.

"Then you know someone who knows someone."

"What if I do? Why should I help you? My arm still hurts, you know."

"Because I'll pay you a—small—percentage of the cost."

He looked as though his ears had pricked up. But then he said, "Pay me with what? You don't have that kind of money or you wouldn't have been working with Asha."

"I think she might," Asha said. She'd been standing in the corner watching the interaction between Carina and her boyfriend. She walked over to him and handed him their interface. Carina could see the screen, which displayed a Mech Battle advertisement. To her dismay, she saw herself being touted as a new challenger for the fight taking place tomorrow night.

When the boss had agreed to let her take part, he'd made her stand with legs apart and pressing her fists to her hips while he took photographs. She had thought they were just publicity images to be displayed in the stadium, not across the planetary networks. She'd been stupid, she now realized. The only saving grace was that the manager had given her a mask to wear for *a sense of mystery*. Her stage name would be Dark Avenger and she would be fighting on behalf of Pyreco.

Although her face wasn't visible in the advertisement anyone who knew her would guess it was her—anyone including Castiel, Langley, and Reyes. And the latter two had a love of the Mech Battles. They were bound to see her, and then they would know exactly where she would be tomorrow night. But there was nothing she could do about it. She had to go ahead with her plan or she would never be able to rescue Parthenia.

Cavin was looking from the screen to her and back again. "You're right, Asha. It is her. And look at the odds!"

Betting on the fight had already started. As an unknown newcomer, the bookies were offering odds of twenty to one for her to win her first battle and a hundred to one if she won the tournament.

Cavin said, "So this is where you're planning on getting your money? Ha! You and every other idiot before you. You'll be lucky if you come out of it intact."

"That isn't your call. I only need you to put me in touch with someone who has the stuff I want. Look, I'll pay you even if I don't make a deal, okay?"

Asha's boyfriend fingered his stubble. "All right. But you pay me up front."

"No. After the fight. I'm betting everything I have on myself."

"No way. You'll lose and then you won't have anything."

"I'm not going to lose."

"Of course you are. What do you know about fighting?"

"More than you think. Did you say your arm still hurt?"

Cavin rubbed the aforementioned arm. He waved dismissively and sat down. "Okay. Come back later tonight. Give me three hours to set something up. I'll try, but I'm not promising anything. And these people are gonna say no anyway. Then I'll be in trouble for wasting their time. So you better come through with the cash."

"She will, hon," said Asha. "I can get her some work. She'll pay you back." She gave Carina a tiny apologetic smile.

Carina sighed.

When Carina returned to Asha and Cavin's apartment later that night, Cavin directed her to another spot where she was to meet the people who could supply her with what she needed. After some bickering over how much and when she should pay Cavin for his service, she set out again. It was already late, and she was grateful that Bryce was around to look after the twins and Darius while she was gone.

Cavin had told her to go to the rooftop of a derelict apartment block a couple of streets away and wait there. When she arrived at the building, she saw that although signs were posted stating the place was condemned and dangerous to enter, squatters had moved in. The low beams of portable lamps and flickers of firelight shone from the windows, occasionally dimming as figures passed across the sources of light.

Carina wasn't afraid of people who lived like this, mostly due to the fact that she had once been in a similar situation herself, but she wished she had a weapon of some kind. If anyone threatened her, flashing a weapon would quickly dissuade them from further action. She didn't want to waste time fighting. It might make her late for her appointment. But she had no weapon, only a flask of elixir.

She passed through the doorless entrance. The elevators were not only not working, they were absent. The open doors revealed dark, gaping shafts. She went to the stairs and began to climb. On her way up, she sidestepped piles of trash and jumped over prone bodies that she hoped were only sleeping. She was reminded of the new block she and Asha had helped to clean before the decorators arrived. This place was quite the contrast.

When she reached the top, she found the fire door to the roof was swinging off one broken hinge. She tugged at it until it fully broke away, then laid it flat on the rooftop. If she needed to leave the impending meeting fast, she didn't want to be struggling to get past the remains of a door.

The rooftop was empty. No exact time had been set for the meeting, so Carina was forced to wait and hope the dealers in illegal arms would actually turn up. She was entirely unknown to them and had no ready cash, so their main incentive would probably be curiosity.

She went to the edge and gazed down to the ground about twenty-five stories below. If her prospective associates decided to drop her off the roof, she doubted she would be able to Cast Transport before she hit the ground. And if she did manage it, would her velocity continue with her to the new location? She didn't know and she didn't want to find out.

The city was quietening down, though the spaceport in the distance remained busy with the fast-moving lights of shuttles taking off and landing. As she watched the brilliantly colored spots, she realized that one—no, two— were heading in her direction. She watched them for several moments to make sure she was correct, and then ran over to the stairwell entrance and stood behind it to avoid being baked in the heat of the shuttles landing.

Sounds of engine noise grew louder while she waited. The noise grew so loud she had to cover her ears, and then the engines cut out. When she heard the shuttle doors opening, she stepped from her refuge, slowly and cautiously. Spooking the kind of people she was meeting was never wise.

Only one person seemed to be in charge, she was relieved to see. The woman sauntered forward in front of her subordinates: two males and a female. All wore floor-length coats made of some kind of animal skin. Its patterning was intricate and beautiful, though it would have looked better on the animals. The boss and her lackeys were also heavily jeweled. They wore tight gem-studded collars of a subtly glowing metal and hand ornaments that could double as knuckledusters.

Cavin did indeed know people who knew people. Carina swallowed, aware of how comparatively unimpressive she looked.

The boss seemed to think so too, from the way she was looking her up and down, the expression on her face souring. Cavin had probably been forced to talk Carina up as a prospective business associate before the black market weapons trader would agree to meet her. Now the woman was experiencing a considerable letdown.

Deciding it would be better not to give her time to conclude she had nothing to gain from the meeting, Carina opened the bargaining process without preamble. She stated her laundry list of proposed purchases, which included as many weapons and explosive devices as she and Bryce could carry as well as a vehicle that would seat six. "I'd prefer space-ready, but a fast hover vehicle would do if that's all you can manage."

The boss hadn't spoken a word while she talked. Silence fell, and after a moment the woman looked over her shoulder at the others and gave a slight shake of her head. She turned to leave.

"I can pay a lot," Carina blurted. She fingered the flask of elixir in her pocket.

The woman faced her again. "That's what I was waiting to hear. How much?"

When Carina named a figure, the woman laughed. Then she stopped and said, "You are joking, right?"

"I can go higher. What would you say is a fair price?"

"Four times what you said. That might be a good place to start for the weapons. It'll be more for the vehicle. And I want half up front."

The deal was impossible for her to fulfill. Winning the tournament and the bets she placed on herself would only give her half of what the woman wanted. "I'm not sure. I have to figure out if I'll have enough."

"I'll take less if you pay it all now."

That would have been an incredibly stupid thing to do. If Carina gave over any money she would be certain to never see the woman again. She seemed to think she was an idiot.

"I need time to think about it."

"One minute."

"I'm going to take a drink," said Carina, knowing that pulling something out of her pocket suddenly might elicit an undesirable, deadly response from the lackeys. As she'd predicted, everyone tensed up.

"Wait," said the boss. She beckoned one of her subordinates and nodded toward her. The man walked up to Carina and patted her over. He quickly found the elixir flask and pulled it out. He opened it, sniffed the contents, and wrinkled his nose.

"Just some weird tea," he said to his boss, pushing the flask into her hands before returning to his side of the divide.

Not hearing any further objections, she swallowed a mouthful of elixir. She returned the flask to her pocket, and then rubbed her forehead as if thinking. While her hand covered her face, she closed her eyes. It was a struggle to Cast Enthrall while under pressure, knowing that all her plans and hopes rode on her Cast succeeding, but eventually she managed it.

She wasn't home free, however. She had only Enthralled the boss. She might have managed to affect more of those present but that would have diluted the Cast so it wasn't as long lasting. She needed the boss to be Enthralled for long enough to make the arrangements. Then she would be unlikely to back out, even if she couldn't remember why she had agreed to the deal.

"I can't pay it all now," Carina said, "or even part of it. In fact, I can only pay you half of what you want when I receive the goods, but I can..." She needed something that sounded at least a little convincing to the others or they would think their boss had gone mad. "I can work for you. Afterward."

The man who had searched her started sniggering.

"Okay," the woman said.

The man abruptly stopped laughing and stared at his boss. He then stared at his colleagues, who also seemed to not quite believe what they'd just heard. The man looked as though he wanted to say something, but he kept quiet.

"Thanks," Carina said. "I appreciate it." She explained where and when she wanted the weapons and vehicle, which would be after she'd won the tournament. If she won the tournament. If she didn't, she would have to lie very low indeed, assuming Castiel didn't kidnap her.

FORTY-ONE

"Come on," said Reyes. "You'll love it. I promise." He pushed the visor into Parthenia's hands.

She looked up into the young man's happy, eager face. Reyes had barely left her alone over the last few days, but Parthenia hadn't really minded. His nearly constant company meant that Castiel had little opportunity to be alone with her, and she was grateful for that, even if Reyes' attention was overwhelming at times.

"What do we have to do?" she asked. "I don't think I understand."

"Come outside and put on the visor. The game will make more sense to you then."

Parthenia stepped through the open doors that led to the lawn. It was a beautiful day, and not for the first time, she felt a little guilty about enjoying the luxury of beautiful surroundings and fine living while her siblings were probably scraping by somewhere. Although 'enjoying' was perhaps too strong a word to describe her feelings about her captivity. She was confused and conflicted. Langley and Reyes constantly talked to her about all the good she could do with her powers, but they had also accepted Castiel into their midst. He was cruel and vicious, and Parthenia couldn't understand why they tolerated him.

"Put it on," Reyes urged.

She pushed the band down over her head and lowered the visor. The pleasant gardens were transformed into an industrial scene. She was inside an old, abandoned factory. Machines towered over her and high above a defective fan spun, its clunk-clunk-clunk echoing.

"There are code words for weapons," Reyes said. "You just have to think of them and they'll appear. You can think of shields too, but you have to bend down to the ground and raise them up or they won't appear. To see the list, think the word 'menu'."

"Oh, I understand now. Ferne and Oriana were asking for a system like this for ages, but Father would never allow it. So it's a kind of battle?"

"That's right. It's more fun with more people, but we can still have a good game with only two of us. We can go wherever we want on the estate. The game will expand into new areas. Do you get it now? Do you want to play?"

She wasn't very keen on the idea. She didn't much like games that involved fighting. She preferred games that tested your wits. But agreeing to play with Reyes would mean a few more hours that Castiel wouldn't bother her. "Okay. I'll need a little time to figure out what everything means."

"Sure. Let's walk down to the grove. We won't be disturbed there and it'll give you a while to read the menu."

As they walked away from the house Reyes took her hand, which felt a bit weird, but she didn't protest. She was disoriented by walking in the new setting and trying to read the list that hovered before her in mid-air. The game modified her sense of touch as well as sight and hearing. Although she knew she was walking on grass, her feet felt as though they were hitting hard, bare metal. Even her sense of smell was affected, she realized. The warm, fresh, clean air she'd been breathing a moment ago seemed to have been replaced by a dusty, acrid atmosphere.

She was beginning to find the list of weapons bewildering. Before she'd read half of it she'd forgotten what was at the top. And she didn't know what many of the words meant. "What's a lightknife?"

"It's an energy beam about as long as your forearm," Reyes replied. "Great for close fighting. If someone has you in a clinch, think *lightknife* and slip it between their ribs. It's high-powered, though, so you run out of energy if you use it for more than a few seconds. That's one for emergencies."

The idea of slipping anything between someone's ribs sounded horrific, even if it was only make-believe. She was beginning to regret her decision. She glanced at Reyes, wondering how he would take it if she backed out, and jumped as she caught sight of him. In the game, he was wearing heavy armor topped by a helmet shaped like a bird of prey.

He turned and said, "What do you think? Cool, huh?"

"Am I wearing something like that?"

"You're wearing the default costume. I customized mine myself. Switch to overview and you'll see."

She thought 'overview' and immediately saw the factory from a high viewpoint. Two figures were walking through it. One was Reyes, with his bird-like helmet, and the other was a woman wearing less heavy or stylized armor. She hardly recognized herself. Instead, she was reminded of Carina. Her heart felt heavy at the memory of her sister. She'd said she would come back but that had been days ago.

"Nearly there," Reyes said.

The game represented the trees of the grove on the Dirksen estate as pillars that rose from the factory floor to the vaulted ceiling. Where the ground was uneven, the game had made the floor broken and pitted. They reached the pillars and walked in among them.

"Are you ready?" Reyes asked.

"Not really. I know some of the words, but I don't understand exactly what we're supposed to be doing."

"That's easy. We fight each other."

"That's all we have to do?"

"Basically. If you die, you lose. Then we start again. Shall we make it the best out of five? We can use the pillars as cover."

What had given Reyes the idea she would like the game, she had no clue. She had a feeling it was going to be over very quickly, after she'd been killed five times. "Hmm... Okay."

"We can start from opposite ends of the grove and work our way in. What do you say?"

"All right then. I'll wait here. You go to the other side."

"Okay." Reyes set off through the pillars.

She thought 'arm rocket' and the weapon appeared on her wrist while its specs rose in her vision. Was it the right choice? She didn't know, but it was one of the few names she could understand.

While she was trying to decide if she should pick something else, Reyes reappeared from between the pillars. She raised her arm rocket to fire at him, but he lifted his hands. "Don't shoot," he said, laughing.

When he'd returned to her side, he continued, "You don't much like this game, do you?"

"No, not really."

He lifted his helmet and reached out to remove hers too. Suddenly, she was back in the grounds of the Dirksen estate. The air smelled fresh and earthy under the trees and the dappled sunlight was warm.

Reyes Dirksen was smiling down at her. "Sorry. I should have been more considerate. I thought you might like to fight. All my friends love it. But you aren't like that, are you?"

"I guess not." She wanted to tell him more. She wanted to tell him how she'd been brought up to be ladylike, and that her father had despised the idea of any of his children doing anything as rough and uncouth as fighting. But revealing even that much about her past felt wrong.

"Shall we take a walk through the trees then, as we're here?" Reyes asked. Without waiting for an answer, he took Parthenia's hand and set off.

As she'd already denied him the chance to play his game she thought it would be churlish to protest, so she went with him, dangling her visor in her other hand.

"This is my favorite part of the estate," said Reyes. "When I was younger, if I wanted to hide from my mother I would come here. I would sometimes spend hours up a tree watching the servants searching for me."

She smiled. Though his mother was holding her captive, she couldn't help herself from empathizing with him. Their upbringings had been similar. Belonging to a powerful clan brought privilege and comfort—extravagance, in fact—but it had its downsides.

"It's so hot," Reyes said. "Let's stop here in the shade for a moment."

She wondered at this proposal. The day wasn't particularly hot. Reyes led her under overhanging boughs to the hushed, shaded interior around a tree's thick trunk.

"I wanted to tell you, Parthenia," said Reyes. "I'm so glad you came into my life. I like you a lot."

She stiffened. How should she respond? If she rejected him outright, what might he or his mother do? "Well, I like you too," she said. She was about to qualify her statement, but Reyes was too fast. He swooped in for a kiss. She swerved out of the way.

"What's wrong?" Reyes exclaimed. "You just said you liked me."

"Not like that."

"Why? Why not?" His fists were clenched and his face was turning red with anger.

She didn't know what to say. Whatever she said—*because your mother is holding me against my will and you think that's okay* was what sprang to mind —would only anger him further.

She pushed through the branches and out into the grove.

"Don't run away from me," Reyes shouted. "Come back here."

She ran through the grove, dodging trees, heading toward the mansion. It felt strange to be heading to her prison as a place of refuge. But what else could she do? She was trapped. When would Carina come?

Forty-Two

Carina lifted the giant main pincers of her mech and lowered them, testing them to their fullest extent. In response, a light appeared in her head-up display. Check. She tested the secondary pincers. Check. She turned in a circle, testing the maneuverability of the legs. Heavy thunks resounded and her visual displayed 360 degrees of the rear part of the stadium, where the mechs and their tech teams waited for the battle to start.

From her position, she couldn't see her opponent but she could hear him or her going through the same checks. It was as she'd thought when she'd seen her first Mech Battle: the operators put the machines through thorough checks before entering the arena. The moves they went through in front of the crowd before engaging in the fight were only for show.

This gave her an idea. If she acted on it she would never be allowed to participate in another battle but that didn't matter. She only needed to win this one. The black market arms dealer would be waiting for her after the show, ready with the weapons and everything else she needed, provided she had her prize money and winnings. Bryce had bet everything they'd earned over the previous days.

"Tammy," the mech manager's voice sounded over Carina's comm. "All set? Everything okay?"

"Yeah, everything's working fine."

"I can see that. I'm asking about you."

"Oh, er... I'm good. Looking forward to it."

The man—who went by his old stage name of The Stomper—had been nervous about giving her a chance, but excitement had overtaken his nerves as the betting on the battle mounted up. His ploy of selling her as a mysterious young newcomer had worked. Her masked image had been displayed on all the entertainment channels, and the manager had even scored an interview on a late-night show, where he'd made up a bunch of nonsense to intrigue the audience. She had caught a glimpse of the show before she'd turned it off in disgust. He'd told the interviewer it was a grudge match: that her family had once worked for Spearcorps, who were sponsoring the opposing team, but they'd all been laid off and were now on the streets.

"Man," The Stomper had said, "the Dark Avenger really hates Spearcorps. It makes her mad just to hear the name."

The audience most likely knew it was all untrue but they didn't care. Believing in the fantasy was fun and a distraction from the slow crippling of their autonomy and freedom by the Dirksens.

The resulting increased interest had worked in her favor. The stadium was sold out.

"Great," said The Stomper. "Try to last as long as you can out there. Give them a good show. If the fight's over in a couple of minutes we'll get complaints."

She rolled her eyes. "Thanks for the vote of confidence."

"I'm just saying…"

Ignoring him, she rechecked the mech's weapons. They were limited due to the safety factor. If a mech hurt an audience member, the company would receive more than complaints.

Each of her main pincers converted to massive hammers, and huge spikes could spring out from the mech's knees. Short-range grapples fired from the machine's midriff in case she wanted to hold the other mech at close quarters and her pincers were gone. She figured in that scenario she could hit it with her —the mech's—head. Her secondary pincers doubled as drills.

She had to give The Stomper some credit: the mech she was fighting in was one of the least beat up he had to choose from. Though the fact only emphasized his lack of faith in her.

An ear-piercing jangle sounded. One minute to go. The noise of the crowd permeated even through her solid surroundings. Somewhere out there, Castiel was probably waiting. Would he try to Transport her out from her mech the minute he saw her? It would be a difficult Cast, even for an experienced mage. She would barely be visible through the narrow slits in the control center, and Castiel would have to Cast at some distance.

Nevertheless, the possibility was her greatest danger, so with great misgiving she'd asked Bryce to bring the twins and Darius along to the battle.

Without their help, she would never be able to Repulse Castiel's Casts. She would be too busy fighting. Her siblings would have their work cut out for them tonight, and they would need to remain hidden from Castiel, though he would know they were here somewhere.

"You're on in ten," The Stomper said. "Good luck, Tammy."

"Thanks."

She gripped the controls and focused. She had only one goal: win five fights. She had to trust her siblings to do their work or she would find herself back on the Dirksen estate and Parthenia would remain captive.

The gigantic doors in front of her split down the middle and swung inward. A roar went up. Her display blinked and darkened in response to the brilliant lights shining from the pit. Across the stadium, she could see another set of doors opening and her opponent standing in shadow, light reflecting softly from dull metal.

The other mech took a step, beginning its walk into the stadium.

She waited.

"Go in now," said The Stomper.

She didn't reply.

"Move, Tammy."

The other mech was inside the pit and was beginning its performance of pretending to check its systems.

"Tammy," The Stomper yelled. "What the hell are you waiting for? Get in there!"

Watching the mech, she waited a little longer. The noise of the crowd was rapidly fading, degenerating to confused babbles.

The Stomper shouted, "If you don't move now, so help me I'll—"

She ran through the doors. "Ran" was a strong word to describe the lumbering gait of the giant mech from a standing start, but she pushed the machine to its extreme speed. She only had one chance and she had to get it right.

The other mech didn't even notice her coming. She slammed into it, knocking it off its feet and into the doors, which had only just closed. The mech bounced against the wall, splintering the rock-hard surface, and slid to the ground.

The crowd went crazy.

Disregarding the ear-splitting howls and whoops, she let her momentum carry her over to the prone mech. The Stomper was bellowing something but she ignored him too. After raising her pincers and simultaneously turning them into hammers, she brought them down with maximum force on the hip junctions of the opposing mech. They were perhaps the toughest parts but she had the perfect shot. If she damaged them, the mech wouldn't be able to move and the fight would be over.

But her opponent wasn't going to give up easily. Projectiles on thick metal ropes shot out and pierced her mech's midriff. The pointed end of one protruded into her cab. A damage report appeared in her display. She sent her secondary pincers to sever the ropes while she struck again at her opponent's hips. Her plan seemed to be working. The mech was trying to stand but its legs were moving oddly.

The secondary pincers couldn't cut the ropes. They couldn't even make a dent. It didn't matter. She brought her hammers down for a third time. The shock of the impact jolted her. She also registered a blow to her legs. The other mech was attacking her with its pincers.

She was convinced the third impact on the mech's hips had done the job. She backed up to move out of reach. She needed her mech to last her through four more battles. The ropes that attached her to the other mech held fast, however, and she found herself dragging it across the floor of the pit. Her mech's systems complained about the additional weight. Another blow struck her legs.

She didn't know what to do. She had no way to cut the ropes but if she didn't move out of range of the other mech hers would soon suffer a lot of damage. Why hadn't they called the fight? Her opponent was incapacitated. She'd clearly won.

She backed up some more. This time, the tension on the ropes tore them from their mooring on the opposing mech. The sudden release caused her to overbalance. Her machine tumbled down.

The horn sounded. The fight was finally called.

Four more to go.

FORTY-THREE

Parthenia hated the noise of the crowd and she wasn't remotely interested in Mech Battles. Two giant machines fighting each other wasn't a spectacle she relished. A sharp, pulsing headache was irritating her but other than that, she was utterly bored.

Castiel seemed to be finding something about her amusing. Every time he snuck a sidelong glance at her, he smirked. Her brother's enjoyment of her misery wasn't a new phenomenon by any means, but Parthenia suspected there was something else underlying his amusement. She refused to gratify him further by asking what he found funny, however, so she resigned herself to remaining in the dark.

He probably had a nasty plan to execute later on. She only hoped it wasn't going to be aimed at poor Nahla, who had suffered from his spite several times over the past few days. Castiel insisted on using her as a subject on which to practice his Casting skills. He Enthralled her to do stupid, embarrassing, and even dangerous things. When he'd made her walk around the entire estate naked, so that every servant, guard, and gardener saw her, even Langley had been appalled and asked him to stop.

This had resulted in a stand-off of a kind. Langley saw herself as the head of the household with the final say on everything that happened beneath her roof. It wasn't an unreasonable claim, or at least to everyone except Castiel. Langley had gently admonished him and suggested that, if he had to use a living person for his experiments, to choose one of the servants and not his own sister.

Castiel had been furious, though she suspected she was the only one who truly understood the depths of his anger. He'd mastered himself—that time. He'd stalked away, not responding to Langley at all. But Parthenia wondered what would happen the next time the two clashed. Langley Dirksen seemed to think that Casting was similar to performing magic tricks. She didn't understand what an immoral mage could do. She had no idea, for example, of the Split Cast that had killed Father.

Parthenia wondered if she should warn Langley but she doubted the woman would listen. She would only think she was trying to undermine Castiel in the hope that she might Cast and escape. And Reyes hadn't spoken to her since she'd rejected him in the grove, which was a good thing. He'd shown his true colors when he was angry that she wouldn't kiss him. Parthenia realized he'd been manipulating her all along. It would be extremely convenient for the Dirksens to have a mage in the family.

From the corner of her eye, she noticed Castiel sip from a bottle. He was Casting, and as far as she knew it was for the third or fourth time this evening, but why? She scanned the stadium. She couldn't see anything her brother might want to influence. Unless he was only trying to affect the outcome of the battle. That was possible. Langley was betting furiously.

A roar went up so loud Parthenia winced and covered her ears. Her head felt like it was going to burst. She wished she could have just a sip of elixir to Cast Heal on herself but Castiel would never allow it. He would think she wanted it to Transport herself far away, which of course she would.

The battle below was over. The winning mech was leaving the pit and techs were entering from the other side to remove the loser. The crowd was quietening as people began to leave their seats and move around during the interval.

"Well, well, well," Castiel said, "our half-sister's quite the fighter, isn't she?"

Through the pounding of her head, Parthenia took a moment to register what her brother had said. Even then, she didn't guess right away what he was referring to. "What do you mean?"

"Carina, you idiot," Castiel sneered. "How dumb are you? I can't believe you haven't noticed her image displayed all over the stadium. She just won that battle."

Her mouth fell open as she gazed up at the figure of a woman wearing a mask flashing on the display board. It *was* Carina. How had she missed it?

"Of course," Castiel continued, "she's a pretty good mage too, though not as good as me. When she's under my control I'll be sure to make use of all her talents."

Parthenia shot a look at her brother. Did his statement mean what it seemed to imply? Castiel's expression was neutral and far-gazing, lost in dreams of power and control. Parthenia imagined what would be the outcome if her brother tried to force himself on Carina. If he were lucky, he might leave the encounter intact. She sniggered.

Castiel heard. He spun to face her. "What's so funny?" he demanded. "You think you can get away with laughing at me? I'll... I'll...."

Langley placed a hand gently on his shoulder. She was sitting behind him. "It wouldn't be wise to do anything rash in front of all these people, Castiel. Please consider the Dirksen reputation."

He shrugged her off and scowled. After a moment, he leaned close to Parthenia and spoke into her ear. "That bitch might think she has a hold over me, but I'm only tolerating her until I find my feet. I'm going to rule the Dirksen clan, and after I've crushed the Sherrerrs into dust, I'm going to rule this entire sector. People complain about the two clans, but they don't know the meaning of suffering. They won't know what's hit them when I'm in charge. They'll look back on these days like they were paradise. So you better watch out, Parthenia. You better not laugh at me again. I won't forget it. I'll make you pay, and there won't be anyone who can stop me."

Castiel's words chilled her. Though she knew what her brother was capable of, hearing him state his intentions out loud was horrifying. And he could do it, she realized. He could do everything he wanted to because he was a mage.

The second battle was about to start. The doors the mechs entered through were opening. Castiel took a swig of elixir. She gasped. *That* was what he was doing! He was trying to Transport Carina out of her mech. Castiel closed his eyes. She wanted to do something, but what? If she knocked him to distract him, he would only ask Harmon to take her outside. She would have lost her chance. She had to do something effective and long-lasting.

As she dithered Castiel must have made his Cast, for he opened his eyes and muttered something that she couldn't hear over the noise of the crowd. The mechs below had entered into battle. He stood up and searched the stadium with his gaze, then he turned and spoke to Langley.

Her eyebrows lifted in response to his comment. She beckoned Harmon and told him the news, and he in turn spoke into his comm.

Though she loathed speaking to Castiel, Parthenia had a feeling that whatever it was he'd realized, it was pertinent information. She shouted over the crowd, "What is it Castiel? Has Carina left?"

"Ha! No. You guessed I was trying to Transport her? Well, you'll be delighted to hear our dear siblings are here somewhere. They've stupidly revealed themselves by attempting to Repulse my Casts. I thought I noticed something odd going on earlier. Now I'm convinced of it. So it looks as though

I have all my little birds in one trap. Very convenient." He gave her a ghoulish smile.

She turned from him in disgust. She hated the thought of being related to him. More than that, she hated how powerless she felt. She couldn't bear the thought of all her sisters and brothers being under his control, and his plans for the future sounded monstrous. But what could she do? She was just one person and she couldn't even fight.

Below her, the mechs were battling hard. Carina seemed to be winning but Parthenia found it hard to tell. She wondered why her sister had decided to take part. It was very strange, especially since it had led to Castiel discovering her. And now it looked like the Dirksen thugs were roaming the crowds looking for their siblings too.

If Castiel succeeded in capturing their remaining family they would be back to a life of servitude—possibly a worse one than they'd endured under Father. Their Mother had been there to protect them to an extent, but Castiel had no one to moderate his behavior.

Parthenia watched Carina fight, wishing she was as strong and brave as her sister. Castiel sipped from his elixir again and closed his eyes. He was entirely unafraid of her, she realized. He was comfortably certain she would sit next to him passively and do nothing to stop him.

A mighty crash resounded below as the mechs collided. Then another crash sounded, though this one was more like thunder and it came from outside the stadium. After a short, confused pause, the crowd returned to their shouts and chanting.

Parthenia's heart was racing. The scenario of the future that was playing out in her mind terrified her. She couldn't let it happen. She just couldn't. Even if she didn't manage to save herself, she had to do something to save her brothers and sisters. She had to make a gesture, no matter how insignificant.

A deafening boom sounded and echoed through the stadium. Again, the noise hadn't come from the mechs. The crowd grew quieter as they tried to understand what was happening. Castiel was also puzzled. He peered around, his bottle of elixir in his hand.

She took her chance. She grabbed it. Castiel registered a moment of shock before trying to snatch it back. He was too late. She threw the bottle down so hard it smashed. The elixir soaked into the floor. Castiel looked up at her, white with rage.

She didn't care. She'd made her gesture. Now what else could she do?

FORTY-FOUR

The third battle of the evening was turning out to be Carina's hardest yet. It wasn't surprising. Her mech had taken considerable damage. The techs had done their best to patch up the machine over the interval but nearly half the display wasn't lit and neither of her secondary pincers were working. Also, the first mech she'd faced had pummeled one of her legs so much it didn't function properly and was slowing her down.

For close-quarters fighting, that didn't matter too much—it wasn't like she could run away from her opponent—but Carina needed as much of her mech as possible to be working if she were to survive to the final round.

One thing to be thankful for was that her mage siblings were doing a good job of deflecting Castiel's Casts. Though she could hardly see any of the crowd, Carina knew her brother had to be here. She hoped her brothers and sister would be able to keep up their efforts all night, and that Langley's thugs wouldn't find them. Bryce had assured her they would be hard to discover in the packed stadium, but that didn't stop her from worrying.

A pincer gripped her mech's head. *Damn.* She'd allowed herself to become distracted. Carina turned on the spot, twisting out of the grip, though the scraping and rending noises this caused were painful to her ears. Her remaining systems were still intact so the damage was probably surface-only.

When fighting, it paid to vary your technique. Her current opponent would have watched her previous battles in order to attempt to predict what she might do. Carina had already used up her one chance at surprising the opposition by foregoing custom and launching straight into an attack—a move

The Stomper had severely admonished her for. He'd said she'd nearly forfeited the match, except the officials couldn't find anything in the rule book to say she couldn't do that.

In her second battle, she'd bypassed obvious moves once again. She hadn't even attempted to hit her opponent. Instead, she'd run straight into him, chest to chest, grappled him, and drilled into his knees with her transformed secondary pincers. That had been what had ruined the pincers, though it had won her the fight.

This time, she needed something new. While she was thinking, she smashed into her opponent. At the same time, a crash sounded outside that hadn't come from the collision. She was puzzled. She'd thought she'd heard loud noises in her previous fight—and they had to be exceptionally loud for her to hear them over everything else. She'd thought a massive thunderstorm was on its way, but the latest sound hadn't been thunder.

A bang exploded above her. Carina felt the shockwave in her bones. Her head-up display flashed and disappeared. Her mech had received a colossal blow to the head. The system might reboot and kick in again but for now she was working blind.

In one way, it was frustrating. In another, it was liberating. She had learned the ropes of hand-to-hand fighting long ago. With her computer system out, her mech was just an extension of her.

She peered through the slit and spotted the looming shadow of her opponent, who was gearing up for another strike. She spun away on her good leg, turned 360 degrees, and flailed both her main pincers into her opponent's side. The other mech had missed her entirely when she moved and was raising itself again.

The concussion vibrated through her cabin, but she hadn't managed to hit hard enough to knock down her opponent. She would have to resort to a tactic she'd been hoping to save for the final battle. It was a desperate measure that would result in more damage to her mech but she couldn't think of anything else.

She activated the circular saw in her mech's head. At least, she hoped she activated it because her display wasn't telling her. Then she heard a satisfying buzz over the screams of the crowd. The onlookers clearly knew what she intended and loved the spectacle.

Carina drove into her opponent. She wouldn't be able to get a good swing at him this way, but she hoped to saw into his mech and mess up his systems so badly he couldn't operate. The opposing mech controller had two options: try to get away or also activate his saw.

The noise of buzzing and grinding redoubled. Her opponent had chosen the latter option, which was bad news but hopefully worse news for the other mech. She had a few seconds' head start. Now it was just a waiting game. She tried to pummel him as well, despite the constraints of the confined space.

A whistling sound pierced the air, quickly followed by the roar of an explosion. The excited screams of the crowd turned to shrieks of horror. Carina leaned forward to see out of the narrow view hole but all that was visible was the blank metal of the other mech. What was going on? That last thing she'd heard had sounded like—

"We're under attack! We're being attacked!"

It was the other mech operator shouting at her.

Of course! That was the source of the other explosions: the Sherrerrs had launched their takeover of Ostillon. A crackling fizz filled the stadium and light flared into her cabin. Wails and shouts were coming from the crowd. She could imagine the panic and rush to leave. She hoped Bryce and the kids weren't hurt and Bryce could get them all out safely. But what should she do?

Her saw was still operating and her opponent was yelling for her to turn it off. She tried but the saw didn't respond. "I can't," she called out. "My system's down. Nothing's working."

The other mech moved away. Without the counterpressure, her mech began to fall. She hit the ground face down and dangled in her safety straps. The saw in her mech's head continued to grind away.

She couldn't see a thing. All her viewing slits were coated in the dust her saw was throwing up in showers. The sounds from outside were a jumble of panicked voices punctuated by the bombardment of the Sherrerr forces. The techs who were responsible for her machine would be running for their lives. She was on her own.

She unfastened her straps one by one, gradually lowering herself to the front of her chamber, which was now the floor. She crawled up the side to the door and punched the exit button. Predictably, the door remained closed. It would run on the same system as the rest of the mech. If she'd been trapped in there after a fight, the techs would have their own way of opening it. Now, she didn't know how she was going to get out.

Carina began to search around in the near darkness. There had to be a manual release mechanism somewhere. The Stomper hadn't bothered to show her what to do in an emergency, but it didn't make any sense to leave the operator with no way of getting out by themselves.

Her fingers probed the bumpy surfaces. As she searched, the realization hit that her entire plan had fallen apart. She wouldn't win her prize or her bets, and the arms dealer wouldn't be waiting for her with the stuff she needed.

Parthenia would remain trapped on the Dirksen estate—only now she would be moved somewhere else, perhaps to another planet as the Dirksens fled Ostillon.

Dammit. Her heart ached for her sister. She couldn't bear the thought of her being held captive by Castiel, a clone of his father. With an entire galactic sector to search, how would she ever find her?

FORTY-FIVE

The stadium was in utter chaos. Parthenia had guessed her father's clan was attacking Ostillon. She was trying to fight against the flow of the crowd, but it was hopeless. Then she noticed the seating was nearly empty. Everyone was crowding into the aisles. She edged along a row and began climbing over the seats.

She had to reach Carina. Her sister's mech was down and disabled, and she was sure she hadn't seen her sister emerge from it. As she reached for a seat, her hand twinged with pain. She rubbed her knuckles, smiled, and continued on.

All around her the people surged and pushed, heading in the opposite direction. Another hissing, crackling projectile arrived, impacting close by the stadium. Whoever was attacking, they were intent on destroying the city. She had to help Carina out and get her away. The stadium had already received a glancing blow, destroying part of an outer wall. It was only a matter of time before the place would be razed to rubble.

Parthenia wished she could shout to her sister to reassure her that someone was coming but she would never be heard over the noise. There was also the chance that one of Langley's guards might notice her and recapture her. She hoped they would be fleeing the stadium too or helping Langley and Reyes to safety. Perhaps they were carrying Castiel out with them. She smiled again.

She'd reached the lowest tier of seating, at the very edge of the pit. Now she was here, however, she couldn't see any way down. The drop was too deep to jump. If she had elixir she could Transport in, but she had none. She ran around the edge. It was deserted except for jumbles of coats and other belongings left behind by the fleeing spectators.

There had to be a way into the pit. Why couldn't she find it? She noticed a dark, empty exit between the seats. Seeing no other option, she ran through and down the stairs at the end of the passage. The noises from outside grew fainter as she descended, following each turn of the stairs and ignoring the doors at each landing. The air became cool and moist. She was definitely heading into the depths of the stadium.

Finally, the stairs came to an end. She pushed open a set of double doors. She had reached the pit. Up close, the two mechs looked even more enormous than they had from above. The center of the standing one was open, its operator gone. The prone mech—Carina's—was still working. The saw in its head was gouging a deep trough in the sand and throwing up a cloud of dust.

She ran over to Carina's mech. She could barely make head or tail of the thing but she guessed Carina had to be somewhere in its center. The dust was choking her. She lifted her shirt over her nose and squinted to keep it out of her eyes. When she arrived at the belly of the mech, she banged on its side. "Carina! Can you hear me?" Her fist striking the metal made no sound, or at least nothing she could hear over the whine of the saw, the still-noisy crowd, and the regular explosions of air-to-ground fire.

"Carina," she shouted at the top of her voice before subsiding into a fit of coughing. Surely there had to be a way to see inside the mech? She wiped dust from her face and stepped closer to the spinning saw. A ridge ran up the side of the machine where a bank of dust had built up.

She pulled her sleeve over her hand and wiped the ridge clean. It was the edge of a narrow slit. She peered through it but she could only see darkness. She put her mouth to the slit. "Carina! Are you in there?"

Then she turned her head and placed her ear against the gap. Did she hear an answer? She thought so. She moved her head to call inside again, but she saw a pair of eyes looking out at her.

"Carina," she cried in happiness. Four fingers poked through the slit. Parthenia grabbed them. "How can I get you out?" she shouted.

Her sister's reply was faint. "I don't know. Can you see anything? Like a manual override?"

She couldn't even see the exit to the machine, let alone the mechanism to open it. She asked her sister where she should be looking. When she'd finally found the spot and cleared away the dust to search the area, she still couldn't find anything to open the hatch. She returned to the slit to tell Carina the bad news.

As she was walking around the giant machine, part of the stadium exploded. Debris began to rain down. Her ears were ringing. She put her arms over her head for protection and continued to return to Carina. She called to her sister through the gap. The four fingers reappeared and she grasped them. "I couldn't find it," she yelled, though her voice sounded faint. "I don't know how to get you out."

If Carina replied, she didn't hear her. She held on to her sister's fingers and sank down to the ground. She wanted so much to help her but she didn't know what else to do. She couldn't get inside the machine or move it. The stadium was being steadily demolished and Carina was trapped. How could she save her sister?

As she held Carina's fingers, she rubbed away the tears that were mixing with dust on her face. She had finally stood up for herself when she'd gotten away from Castiel. But it wasn't enough. It didn't matter how brave she was if she couldn't help the people she loved.

———

Parthenia had resigned herself to staying with Carina no matter what happened. She couldn't leave her sister here to die trapped inside an ugly mechanical monster. When they'd been together on *Nightfall*, it would have been much easier for Carina to escape if she'd been alone, but she'd risked her life to take all her family with her—even Castiel, though he didn't appreciate it. She could never abandon her now.

Another explosion resounded. As she looked up to see what part of the stadium had been hit, she saw figures running out to her from one of the entrances to the pit. She cringed. So Langley had left behind some guards to find her. Parthenia had thought they must have all left.

But then she noticed through the dust and gloom that three of the figures were shorter than they should be. One of them was very short. Her heart nearly burst with joy.

"Darius," she yelled. She leapt up and ran to the little boy, scooping him into her arms. Oriana and Ferne grabbed her, jumping up and down with happiness.

"Wait," Darius said, struggling. "I have to get Carina out."

"Can you?" she asked as she put him down. "Have you got some elixir?"

The fourth figure walked up. She was shocked to see Carina's friend, Bryce.

"We've got some left, but not a lot," he said, handing a bottle to Darius. "Do your work, kid."

Clutching the bottle in his little hand, Darius ran over to the mech. He reached up to Carina's fingers. In another moment, their sister was out of the machine and standing next to him. As the two embraced, Parthenia burst into tears again. "I can't believe it. We finally did it. We're finally together again." As she spoke, however, she realized that wasn't exactly true.

"Come on," Carina shouted as she began to run.

Everyone sprinted with her to one of the sets of massive mech entrance doors. One of the doors remained ajar, and they slipped through it to the backstage area. The noise of the bombing faded somewhat. Carina led them through the workshop areas and offices until they emerged from the building into the parking lot.

The vehicles that remained were wrecked and in places the ground was cratered.

"We need to Transport somewhere," said Carina, "but I don't know where we'll be safe from the Sherrerr attack."

They jogged across the lot while they thought about what they should do.

"You should thank Darius," Bryce said to Parthenia. "All the time you were in the pit Dirksen guards were spotting you and coming in to get you. Darius Transported them away."

"His Casts are so powerful," Oriana broke in. "He's been moving them to the other side of the planet so they couldn't quickly return in a hover vehicle."

"He must have Transported about thirty of them," Ferne exclaimed.

"I was worried that Castiel would Cast you out of there when the bombardment started," Bryce said.

She laughed. "Well, he wouldn't have been able to for a while. I knocked him out!"

"You did what?" Bryce asked.

"I broke his elixir bottle, and then I punched him. Like this." She made a fist and swung forcefully into the air. "I really hurt my hand, but I don't care. It was fantastic. His eyes rolled back and he keeled over. He was out cold. And then, when I looked around, the bodyguard, Harmon, was gone, and everyone was distracted by the bombing, so I jumped over the edge of the box and into the crowd below."

"But what about when Castiel comes around?" Oriana asked. "Won't he be able to Locate you? He must have something you were in contact with."

"I don't think so. I made a point of washing everything I wore or used every night and I was careful to always clean out my hairbrush. He might think he has something he can use, but he doesn't."

"I know," said Carina, spinning around. "We should go to the forest. The Sherrerrs won't bother attacking that. They'll target inhabited areas and tactical sites."

"But wait," Parthenia said. "We're forgetting Nahla. We have to get her, Carina. We can't leave her there with that monster."

"You mean go back to Langley Dirksen's estate?" Carina looked troubled. "I feel sorry for Nahla too, but do you really think she wants to leave Castiel? She seems to adore him."

"Not any more. Not since he learned to Cast. He's been behaving terribly toward her. It reminds me of how Father used to treat Mother. I'm sure she hates him now. She's just too frightened to show it. We have to help her. Even if she isn't a mage she's still one of us."

"Parthenia," Carina said sadly. "I hear you. But it's too dangerous for any of us to go there. We would have to search to find her and someone would be sure to spot us."

"Not if we know exactly where she is," said Parthenia. She pulled out a handkerchief. "It's hers. She was using it the other day when she had a cold."

"Oh, er..." Carina wrinkled her nose and took the handkerchief, pinching it between her thumb and forefinger. "Okay. That could work. Let's Transport to the forest first."

FORTY-SIX

Carina appeared in a dark room. All she could hear was the sound of someone breathing, deeply and regularly, as if asleep. As her eyes became accustomed to the darkness, she realized with relief she was in the right place. She also realized that Castiel was an idiot. No one else was here except little Nahla, fast asleep in bed. Her brother hadn't imagined anyone would bother to take her from him. He probably thought everyone else held her in the same low regard as he did.

Langley's mansion didn't seem to have been attacked by the Sherrerrs yet, which was odd. If her suspicion that the woman she'd spotted was one of their spies, the Sherrerrs definitely knew exactly where the estate was and that a high-ranking Dirksen lived here. Well, it wasn't a puzzle she needed to figure out. She hoped to leave the Sherrerr/Dirksen struggle for power behind as soon as she could.

The elixir was down to its last dregs. After she Transported Nahla and herself out they would only have a little left. They would have to find a way to make some more, which might be challenging in a burnt forest. Never mind. Saving the little girl was absolutely worth it.

In two steps, she was beside her bed. Kneeling down, she took Nahla's hand where it lay on the blanket, then swallowed some elixir. She Cast.

They appeared in the forest. Nahla's eyes opened and she sat bolt upright in surprise.

"Yay! Carina's back," Darius yelled. "She got Nahla."

The children ran over to their sister and started making a fuss of her. They began to explain to the shocked girl where she was and what had happened.

"Wait," Carina said. "We have to check Nahla and Parthenia for tracers. Darius, here's the last of the elixir. I'm pretty sure you'll be able to sense them if they're there. Do you want to do it?"

Her brother took the bottle and set to work. After checking both his sisters for the devices he declared confidently that he'd found them. In a matter of moments, he had also removed them without causing any harm. Ferne set off to scatter the tracers over a wide area before the family moved on.

Relieved they were finally free of the Dirksens, Carina walked over to Bryce where he was leaning against the burned remains of a tree. He hugged her and wrapped his arms around her waist. She rested her head on his chest. She was exhausted. Three mech fights had tired her out and the emotional turmoil of the night's events had also drained her.

"It's strange how things turn out, isn't it?" Bryce said. "This wasn't the plan, but you ended up getting Parthenia back anyway, and now you have another member of the family with you."

"Yeah, I hope Parthenia's right about Nahla no longer having any loyalty to Castiel. If she has, she could easily betray us."

"I don't think she will. She's just a little girl."

"Darius is just a little boy, yet he saved me and Parthenia tonight, according to what you say."

"He did. He was amazing."

Carina watched her youngest brother chatting with Nahla, his head of thick, tousled hair bobbing around and his arms making expansive gestures. So much mage power in such a little body. She wondered what he would be capable of when he grew up.

"So, what now?" Bryce asked.

"We have to find a way to go offplanet. If the Sherrerrs' attack is successful and they find Castiel they'll be looking for us too. I want to get everyone as far from both the clans as I can." She was about to tell Bryce about her desire to find Earth when Parthenia walked up to them.

"Thank you for rescuing Nahla. You won't regret it. She's so happy to be away from him."

"I'm glad she's away from him too," Carina said. "I hope she recovers from his maltreatment."

"I think she will," said Parthenia. "We're all better since leaving the Sherrerrs, even though things have been so hard. But I wanted to ask you, what are we going to do now?"

"I was wondering the same," said Bryce.

"Because we have to do something to stop Castiel," Parthenia continued.

Carina made a noise of disgust. "Is he really any of our business any longer? Let the Dirksens have him, or the Sherrerrs, or whoever else wants him."

"But no one else can stop him but us," Parthenia protested. "You should have heard what he was telling me tonight. He plans on taking over the Dirksens and then the Sherrerrs and then whoever else might stand in his way until the entire sector is under his control. Can you imagine how things would be if a mage like Castiel were in charge?"

Carina wanted to disagree with her sister. She wanted nothing more to do with Castiel. But she knew exactly what Parthenia meant and she knew her sister was right. A heaviness settled over her heart as she realized her work wasn't over. She couldn't take her sisters and brothers and escape to somewhere safe. She would have to find a way to defeat the son of an evil father.

"Okay," she said. "I get it. We have to do something, but I don't know what. The truth is, I don't know what I'm dealing with in Castiel. I don't know why his mage abilities developed so late, the same as I don't know why Darius picks up on everyone's emotions and can throw thirty grown men and women halfway around a planet without breaking a sweat."

"But I thought you knew all about mages," Parthenia said.

"Not at all. My grandmother died when I was quite young. Though she might have told me a lot I must have forgotten half of it. I don't even know how Ma and Dad managed to meet when mages are so isolated and secretive."

"Oh, I know that," exclaimed Parthenia. "Mother told me she'd been married before and that she'd met her first husband at a festival...somewhere. I can't remember right now but it'll come back to me if I think about it. She swore me to secrecy, of course, so Father wouldn't find out what I knew."

"Really?" said Carina. It was a lead if only a small one.

"Weren't you saying there was some information about mages in that religion's holy book?" Bryce asked.

"Yes," Carina said uncertainly, "though I had to read between the lines."

"Well, that's a start, isn't it?"

"I guess so."

Parthenia returned to the group of children, who were laughing and chatting as if they hadn't a care in the world. It was hard to believe what they'd each endured recently. If the boys and girls had been at home or in a park, no one could have guessed the trials they had been subjected to over the previous days.

Yet they were under the stars in the remains of a forest fire, the sky flashing and booms pulsing from the Sherrerr bombardment in the distance. They had no food or water or anywhere to sleep, and they had a challenging time ahead, striving to prevent their malevolent brother from achieving his bid for ultimate power.

Carina hoped with all her heart that, whatever happened, her little family would come out the other side unscathed.

WILDFIRE & STEEL

ONE

Ostillon was at war. The Sherrerrs were attacking the Dirksens' base planet, and Carina and her siblings were running out of places to hide.

For days they had traveled from refuge to refuge, fearing the collapse of their latest home from bombardment, or that Castiel was on their tail. They had not seen their evil brother, however, and for the moment the bombing had stopped.

"We have to try to find some food, Bryce," said Carina. "The kids haven't eaten since yesterday."

"I know. Let's go now while it's quiet."

They had discovered a basement in an abandoned house the previous day, and with practised ease Carina's siblings had made the place as comfortable as possible. Parthenia and the twins, Oriana and Ferne, had dragged rugs down from the upper floors, and Nahla had made it her job to furnish the place with cushions.

The mage children and their non-mage sister, Nahla, were keeping themselves occupied with quiet games. The youngest sibling, Darius, had found a pack of playing cards and was arranging them face upward in rows. To avoid discovery by their brother, they had to remain inconspicuous. But children's games would not put food in their bellies.

Carina asked her oldest sister, Parthenia, to watch the younger children. Parthenia agreed. She was always quick to help in whatever way she could. Carina and Bryce climbed the stairs from the basement and emerged in the kitchen. The pantry and cupboards had been the first places they had searched when they arrived, but the food storage spaces were predictably empty.

The war had thrown Ostillon into chaos. All the regular systems of food distribution had broken down, and people had to take whatever they could find. Carina had not figured out what she would do when the day came that she couldn't feed her siblings.

After checking the street was deserted, Carina and Bryce passed the front door, which had jammed open due to its warped frame. They ran to the end of the street on the shadowed side where the rays of the rising sun hadn't reached. While they searched for food someone would eventually see them, but it was important that no one guessed where they'd come from. The last thing she wanted was someone snooping in their hideout while she was gone. It was the best she could do to protect those she had to leave behind.

They headed out of the residential area and toward the nearest commercial district. They had to travel on foot. Carina could have unlocked a vehicle with a Cast, but no working autocars were to be found. Anyone with the ability to leave the city had driven away days ago.

She spotted the bombed-out bakery from halfway down the street. The building's ruins were still smoldering from the most recent attack, but looters had already infiltrated the place. She could see shadows of figures moving inside the broken remains. If she and Bryce didn't enter it soon there wouldn't be anything left to scavenge.

She nudged him with her elbow and pointed.

"I see it."

They crossed the road and sped up their pace. Carina hoped no one would give them any trouble. Usually, if plenty of goods remained, there was no fighting. Everyone took as much as they could carry and quickly departed. But if most of the goods had been taken people grew belligerent and things got physical. She wasn't bothered by the prospect of fighting the Ostillonian citizens, who were not trained military, but she didn't want to hurt anyone.

As they arrived at the demolished bakery, she spied an older couple coming down the street from the other direction. More hungry people hoping for something to fill their bellies. A smoking rafter had crashed down and was bisecting the doorway. She quickly ducked below it and went inside the shop.

"Be careful," Bryce said as he followed her. "I don't like the look of that ceiling."

Little of the ceiling remained. The passage of the air strike was clearly marked from the roof two floors above, and the clear morning sky lit the bakery's interior.

"Never mind that," Carina replied. "We need to hurry."

The store at the front was already empty. Others had arrived before them to take whatever baked goods had remained on the shelves. The place stank of smoke and burned wood and the air was hazy. Carina walked through to the back of the building.

"Out of my way," a burly man warned, meeting her from the opposite direction. He was carrying a sack of flour over his shoulder.

"Carina," said Bryce in a warning voice.

She stepped backward to give him room to pass. "Don't worry, I'm not going to do anything," she said to Bryce. She guessed more sacks of ingredients were stored in the back. If it came down to it, she would do everything in her power so that her family didn't starve, including fighting, but things weren't so bad that she'd been forced to challenge someone else for their food, yet.

When the man had passed her by, Carina stepped into the backroom of the bakery. The Sherrerrs' attack hadn't penetrated here and the power in the city had been off for days, so the place was dark.

She could hear scuffling, and she paused a moment so her eyes could adjust to the low light. A few seconds later she saw the source of the noise: two figures were grappling over something. One of the figures was gripping a small sack to her chest and the other, also a woman, was trying to pry it from her fingers. Carina guessed the sack contained salt or a similar precious substance.

Bryce had gone past, his hands outstretched to feel his way in the dark. "Here! Here's something. Carina, come and help me lift it."

"Let go," one of the fighting women exclaimed. "I saw it first. It's mine."

"You might have *seen* it first," her opponent replied, "but I *took* it first. Go and look for some more yourself if you want it that bad." She released her hold on the bag to grab the other woman's hair, wrenching her head down. Screeching, the assaulted woman punched the other in the face. The bag dropped to the ground, spilling its contents. Both women wailed with dismay, dropped to their knees, and began to fight over who would scoop the spilled material back into the bag.

Carina quickly strode past the scene and joined Bryce, who was twisting the neck of a large sack in his hands, preparing to pick it up.

"Are you sure you can carry it?" she asked, eyeing the size of the bag.

"I'm going to try."

Bryce's frame had been coltish when Carina first met him, probably due to the disease he'd been suffering from, but since he'd been cured he'd put on muscle. She guessed he was now stronger than her so she let him take the lead. But as he heaved the sack upward she helped by gripping the sides and lifting.

"Let's go," Bryce panted. He marched toward the front of the bakery, his back bent under the weight of the flour.

She hoped they would make it back to their latest hideout. She would take a turn in carrying the sack. And if they couldn't manage it, they could always tip some of the flour out somewhere hidden and return for it later. Pleased with their find, she followed Bryce into the front of the bakery.

The older couple she'd seen in the street a few minutes previously was now barring the store exit. The man and woman were dressed in clothes that had once been fine but were now grimy and torn. The pair stood in intimidating silence, their intent clear from their glares.

Bryce had halted, his knuckles white from the strain of holding the heavy sack.

"Hand it over," said the man. "Then you can go." His arms were folded over his chest in an attempt to look intimidating.

Carina felt a trace of pity for the couple. Though Ostillon had only been at war for a short time the residents were already showing signs of starvation. Formerly well-off, these two were clearly unused to surviving in difficult circumstances.

"There's plenty more back there," she said, gesturing behind her. "We don't have to fight over this."

"I don't believe you," said the older woman. "How do we know you haven't taken the last one? This is the first place we've found that hasn't already been ransacked floor to roof."

Bryce dropped the sack. "Here, take it. We can get another one."

"No," said Carina. "They can get their own." She walked up to the couple. "Move out of our way. We aren't a charity. Stop wasting our time. I told you there's more inside. Go and look for yourselves."

When the man and woman still didn't budge, she grabbed one of their shoulders each and pulled the pair forward, out of the doorway. The woman stumbled.

"Hey," the man exclaimed, raising a fist, "how dare you—"

Carina deflected his blow and punched his jaw. She hit him hard enough to make him stagger but not black out.

Wisely, the man heeded the warning. Rather than fight back, he went to his wife's side and hurled insults at Carina.

She helped Bryce as he lifted the sack onto his back. They stepped out into the street.

"Why did you have to hit him?" asked Bryce. "They were old, and there was plenty to go around."

"That wasn't the point. If those two are going to survive, they need to learn to pick their fights. We're obviously younger and stronger than them. If they aren't careful they'll die quicker than by starvation. Things on Ostillon are going to get a lot worse before they get better. I hope I taught them a lesson."

"So what you're saying is," Bryce said with a wry smile, "you manhandled that woman and punched that guy for their own good?"

"Something like that."

They were walking briskly and looking around them. Now they'd finally found something to eat, they had to make it across the city to their latest refuge without losing their precious find to another looter.

As always, Carina was carrying a metal canister of elixir, but she could only use the liquid to Cast as a last resort. Castiel was undoubtedly scouring the war-torn planet for his mage siblings. He would be on the watch for news of strange, inexplicable occurrences, like things moving without being touched or people disappearing into thin air.

The problem of what to do about her Dark Mage sibling had plagued Carina ever since she'd agreed with Parthenia that she had to do *something*. All she'd accomplished so far was to keep her family out of his clutches. That, and provide them with food and a safe place to sleep. She would have to be content with the fact they had survived another day.

The puzzle of how to deal with Castiel would have to wait a while.

Two

"What is it?" Darius asked, jumping up onto his toes and bouncing when Carina and Bryce carried the sack between them downstairs into the basement. "What did you find?"

"Some kind of flour," Carina replied, dropping her end of the heavy sack. Her back was sore and her hands were aching and raw from gripping the rough material. Every day she and Bryce had to walk farther to find food. Looters were steadily cleaning out the city. She wondered if the time had come to relocate somewhere else on Ostillon.

"Is that all?" Darius asked. He'd opened the sack, revealing the grainy white powder. He looked up at Carina, his big brown eyes plaintive.

"What do you mean, is that all?" asked Bryce. "We can make some delicious fried cakes from this stuff."

"Except we don't have any oil or fat," Oriana said.

"Baked cakes, then," Bryce replied.

Oriana pouted and rested her chin on her hand. She was sitting next to her twin on a broken-down sofa that had been dumped in the basement of the abandoned, partially demolished house.

Parthenia was playing a card game with Nahla on the dusty rug. She put down her cards, stood up, and walked to the sack. "This looks great. Very fresh. Thanks, Carina and Bryce, for finding it for us. I guess it's still pretty dangerous out there." She looked pointedly at Oriana, who muttered, "Thanks, Carina and Bryce."

Darius murmured something unintelligible and returned to the cards.

"I'll make us something to eat," Parthenia said. "You two sit down and rest."

Carina could have hugged her sister. Of her four mage siblings, Parthenia was the only one who wasn't showing the effects of their luxurious, privileged upbringing. Though initially Darius, Oriana, and Ferne had risen to the challenges of a harder life, the novelty had clearly worn off. Parthenia was the only one who hadn't complained even once.

Carina struggled to pity the others. They might have fallen from the highest to the lowest tier of society, but they were leading the same life she had lived for six years after Nai Nai had died. Hunger, cold, and danger were daily obstacles to be faced. She hated to admit it, but she was disappointed in them.

"I'm going to rinse off," said Bryce. Flour from the sack had coated his neck and hair.

"Let's start a fire," Carina said to Parthenia.

"There's no need. I can do it myself."

"I know you can. I only want to help." Carina dragged the sack of flour across the basement floor to the cooking area.

In one corner of the basement at the back of the house, a window opened high on the wall. Parthenia had made a small hearth from closely stacked stones on the concrete floor. Carina was pleased to see that a stack of wood had appeared nearby. Parthenia must have sent the children to gather it while she and Bryce had been gone. Now the power in the city was out, fire was their only source of warmth and heat for cooking. And of course, naked flames were essential for making elixir.

The wood was very dry and looked like it came from an item of furniture. Dry wood was essential to avoid creating smoke that would choke them in the small room and, worse, alert others to their presence.

Parthenia scooped out a couple of cups of flour into a bowl and stirred in water until the flour clumped into crumbs. Then she clenched the crumbs together to make a ball and began to knead it.

"You look like you know what you're doing," said Carina.

"I would watch our chef in the kitchen sometimes, when Father wasn't home. Cooking looked like fun. I didn't think I would ever have the chance to do it, though. Father would have had a fit if I'd told him I wanted to do something as demeaning as create dishes for others."

Carina picked up a frying pan they had taken from another abandoned home days previously and brushed the dust from it. Oriana was correct in saying they had no fat for frying, but perhaps if they were careful the flour cakes wouldn't stick. She piled pieces of wood in the hearth and then balanced an iron grid on stones so that it sat over the sticks.

Bryce returned, his hair wet. He invited Nahla and Darius to play cards and sat down with them.

"It's a shame there's no Cast for cooking," Parthenia said. She pulled a piece of dough from her ball and began to flatten it into a disc.

Carina said, "I used to think that too when I had no home. I can understand that it isn't possible to create food from nothing, but why we can't transform raw ingredients into cooked, I don't know. If there is a Cast for that, Nai Nai never let on. She always cooked everything from scratch. Maybe cooking is too complex. Casting seems to only cover simple actions, like Locate, Send, Transport...and Fire."

She lifted her elixir canister and took a sip of the liquid. The Fire Cast was one of the first Nai Nai had taught her. She concentrated for a moment and wrote the character in her mind. When she opened her eyes, the wood in the hearth was already smoking. A moment later a flame licked up and quickly the rest of the sticks caught alight.

Parthenia put the frying pan on the iron grid and after the pan had warmed, she put a circle of uncooked dough into it.

Her expression was closed and somber. Carina wondered what she was thinking. Parthenia had spent so much of her life hiding her true feelings out of fear of angering her father, neutral features were a habit.

Carina put a hand on her sister's shoulder. "Thanks for all your help. We couldn't do this without you."

The response Carina received was unexpected.

"Do what, exactly?" Parthenia said tightly as she broke off a second piece of dough and began to roll it between the palms of her hands.

"You know what I mean. You've helped us to stay safe and survive."

"Oh, thanks." Parthenia's tone was hard and her eyes had turned stony. She picked up a stick to push under the flat flour cake in the frying pan to flip it.

"Parthenia, what's wrong?"

Her sister glanced over her shoulder at Bryce, Nahla, and Darius, playing cards on the rug, and Oriana and Ferne, who were dozing on the sofa. She said softly, "When are we going to do something about Castiel? We have to find him. We have to stop him."

Carina sat back on her haunches. "So that's what's been bothering you? You know we can't Locate Castiel. Unless we have something personal of his, we can't do it. He could be anywhere on Ostillon, or he might even have left the planet."

"But he's probably still at Langley's estate. We could look there. Carina, you've seen what he's doing. We can't let him continue."

Carina was only too aware of what Castiel had been doing. Though they hadn't caught sight of their brother, twice they had seen evidence of his activities. Sherrerr forces had managed to break through the Dirksen defenses and land at the spaceport, but the troops running from the landing craft had burst into flames. They had also seen airborne Sherrerr shuttles Split into two pieces and their occupants plummet to their deaths. Unable to find Castiel, Carina and her siblings hadn't been able to Repulse his Casts. They had been forced to watch the scenes helplessly, in dismay.

Castiel had been active in defending Ostillon from the Sherrerr attack, and Carina guessed that he'd only begun to explore the range of devastation he could inflict on the Dirksens' enemies.

"I know," Carina answered her sister. "I know we should do something. I just don't know how to stop him. We can't go to Langley's estate, assuming he's still living there. We would be captured the minute we came anywhere near the place. It's too risky. And I don't have any other ideas."

In truth, she had not put serious effort into catching Castiel. She doubted she could manage it alone, yet she feared for the lives and freedom of her siblings if they helped her. The war between the Sherrerrs and the Dirksens wasn't her fault or her problem. Why should she risk her family by trying to put an end to Castiel's attacks?

Another worry niggled at her: what would she do with Castiel if she succeeded in capturing him? Could she kill her half-brother in cold blood, cruel and evil as he was? She'd already killed enough people to last her a lifetime. And if she couldn't kill Castiel, what then? How could she keep him confined for the rest of his life?

"Oh no," Parthenia exclaimed. Smoke was oozing from the cooking flour cake. She tried to push the cake out of the pan with the stick, but it was stuck.

"Dammit," Carina said. She grabbed the pan but the handle was hot. Wincing, she pulled down her sleeve and tried again. This time she removed the frying pan from the grid and put it on the floor.

"Is the food ready yet?" Darius called out.

Parthenia leaned forward to poke the burnt cake with her stick, trying to remove it from the pan. But as she did so the bowl of dough on her lap fell off and landed upside down. She gave a groan and lifted the bowl. The dough was dirty and ruined.

"It's okay," said Carina. "We can make some more."

Parthenia rose to her feet to scoop more flour out of the sack.

An explosion roared above. The basement shuddered. Parthenia was thrown to the floor.

Nahla and Darius were screaming, but Carina couldn't hear a thing. Bryce stared upward, his mouth hanging open. She followed his gaze. A crack was splitting the ceiling apart. Grainy dust rained down into her eyes.

"Get under the sofa," she yelled at the kids. Her voice sounded distant and faint.

Parthenia was trying to stand. Carina launched herself at her sister, forcing her down. She covered Parthenia with her body. Bryce dove over Darius and Nahla.

Something heavy and solid crashed into the back of her head, and she knew no more.

THREE

arina could smell grass. It seemed so long since she had smelled that green scent. She inhaled deeply, savoring the aroma. Warm air was bathing her. She heard insects chirping.

She opened her eyes. She was on her back, and above her a pale blue sky stretched wide. Tall stalks of wild grass surrounded her, motionless in the still air. A scratching sound was coming from her right-hand side. Carina turned her head. Only a few centimeters from her nose, a long-legged insect crouched on a grass blade and rubbed its serrated limbs together.

Someone grabbed her shirt and tugged at her, turning her over. Agony flared up from her thigh. She yelled out in pain. She was back in the basement. Dust was choking her, her ears rang, and above her the sky was aflame.

Bryce's face appeared in her view. "Carina, are you okay?" She could barely hear him but she could read his lips. How long had she been out? It felt like only a few seconds. He was lifting chunks of rubble away from her.

"I'm okay," she replied. She tried to move, but excruciating pain lanced from her leg again. "I think my leg's broken."

She felt movement below her. She remembered she was lying on Parthenia. Her sister was trying to get up.

"Find the elixir, Bryce. Bring it to me." He disappeared from her view. She tried to move off her sister but the slightest motion sent nauseating waves of pain. "Darius! Nahla!" She gasped. "Where are you?" She couldn't see anything except the remains of the basement ceiling. Jagged edges lined the break.

Through the gap she saw red and orange clouds, reflecting fire. A smoky haze blew across the sky.

Parthenia twisted and Carina cried out as her leg jerked. The broken ends of her bones ground against each other. "Please, stay still," she said to her sister. Perhaps Parthenia answered but Carina didn't hear.

Bryce was back and she felt faint with relief. He was holding the familiar canister. He unscrewed the lid and put a hand behind her head, lifting her to take a sip. She swallowed the elixir and shut her eyes. The pain made it hard to concentrate. She had to focus.

She imagined herself pushing the pain from her leg down into a box, closing the lid, and locking it. A sense of calm arrived. She wrote Heal and Cast the character out, willing it downward to her broken bone.

She exhaled, long and slow. Gingerly, she reached her mind out to her leg. The pain was gone.

She found her hearing was also returning. She could hear a hum growing louder, filling her ears. It wasn't a hum. It was a roar. The roar of flames. Had the Sherrerrs bombed the city with incendiary explosives? Or had the clan attempted another landing, and Castiel had Cast Fire on the city?

Parthenia moved beneath her again. Carina shifted off her sister and took the elixir canister from Bryce. Parthenia crawled out from rubble and plaster dust.

"Are you all right?" Carina asked her.

Parthenia nodded.

The remains of the basement lay around them. The sack of flour had been exploded by a block of masonry. The sofa was in pieces. The window had shattered.

"Where are the others?" Carina asked Bryce.

"They're okay. They're outside already. I took them upstairs and came back for you. We have to get out of this area. Now."

"But we need to bring the elixir," said Parthenia.

"It's all gone," Bryce replied. "The container was crushed. We only have what's left in the canister."

"It's okay," said Carina. "We can make more."

They stepped over the rubble-strewn floor to the staircase and climbed stairs choked with debris from the destroyed house. At the top of the stairs the rest of the children were grouped in a huddle anxiously waiting. Their clothes and exposed skin were blackened with smoke.

"Where to now?" Bryce asked when they reached the top.

Carina didn't know. Burning buildings surrounded them. As her gaze lit upon one it collapsed, sending sparks shooting into the sky and red-hot bricks scattering across the street. She scanned three hundred and sixty degrees. Every avenue seemed to be blocked. A man flew from a doorway, on fire, screaming. She grabbed the two younger children's heads and buried their faces in her stomach. The man hurtled down the road as if trying to escape the flames consuming him.

"We have to Transport," she said. "If we try to walk out of here..." She didn't need to say more.

"But where can we go?" Oriana wailed. "We don't know anywhere that's safe anymore."

"Nowhere is safe for certain," said Parthenia. "But we can get away from the city. We can go somewhere unpopulated that won't be of interest to the Sherrerrs." She held Darius' shoulders and turned him around. "Do you remember the forest we were in when we first came to Ostillon? Do you think you can Transport us all there?"

The little boy's face was pale and his eyes were wide with fear, but he nodded.

"Are you sure it's safe, Parthenia?" Carina asked. "How far away is this place?"

"I don't know exactly. It's on this continent. I think Darius can do it."

"Not all of us at once, though" said Carina. "It's too risky. Two at a time, in case something goes wrong. And let's swap personal things so we can find each other again if we're separated."

They hastily emptied pockets and found small items to share around. Darius had a pair of dice that he split between Parthenia and Oriana. Nahla gave Carina a hair ribbon. Bryce had nothing except a ring. He pulled it from his finger and pushed it into Carina's open hand, folding her fingers over it. In ten or fifteen seconds they were done.

The buildings around were going up like torches. The air was growing unbearably hot and Carina was struggling to breathe. She handed Darius the canister.

"Who goes first?" he asked.

"Bryce, Ferne, and Nahla together."

"No," said Oriana. "I want to stay with Ferne."

"I want Bryce to be with Nahla," said Carina.

"I can do it," Darius said. "Nahla is only little, like me."

Oriana pouted, but she hugged her twin goodbye.

"Transport those three first," Carina told Darius, "then Oriana and Parthenia, and then you and me."

She had a lot of faith in her little brother's mage power, but fear he would fail clutched at her. He was young and he was frightened, which would make it more difficult for him to Cast.

"Do I Transport everyone to outside the ranger's tower?" he asked Parthenia.

"No, that's too dangerous," she answered. "He might still be there. He could see us appear from nowhere. Aim for somewhere half a kilometer away, out in the wild country beyond the tower. But not in the forest."

"Okay." Darius sipped elixir and closed his eyes. In another couple of seconds, Bryce, Ferne, and Nahla were gone.

"Hurry up and Transport me," Oriana said. "I don't want to lose Ferne."

A crack split the air, and with a rumbling crash a wall collapsed a few meters behind them. Burning masonry tumbled toward them.

"Watch out," Carina cried. Grabbing Darius' arm she dragged him away. Parthenia and Oriana crowded close. The roaring of the flames was growing louder.

"Please hurry, Darius," Oriana begged.

He lifted the canister again and took another sip. How much elixir was left? Carina didn't know. She hoped none of the liquid had slopped out when she'd pulled Darius away from the collapsing wall.

Parthenia and Oriana disappeared.

"Is there enough left for both of us?" she asked.

Darius shook the canister. "I think so."

"Okay. When you're ready."

Her little brother tipped up the canister and swallowed the remains of the elixir. He closed his eyes. Concentration creased his brow.

"Just don't put me in mud."

A small smile lit Darius' face, and she gripped his hand.

They Transported.

FOUR

Castiel watched the shuttle's display in silence. The Dirksen pilot was flying them closer to the Sherrerr flagship, *Nightfall*. True to her name, the massive vessel was dark against the stars, carrying no external lighting.

The ship had hung in the Floria planetary system for days, like a brooding overlord, while the Sherrerrs launched their deadly attacks on Ostillon's military installations, manufacturing and transportation hubs, and major cities. For days, no Dirksen military spacecraft had broken through the ship's defenses. Many had been destroyed in the attempt.

As Castiel watched, more Dirksen military vessels were harrying *Nightfall* in an effort to distract her crew from the small, unarmed shuttle.

Dirksen reinforcements were on their way to the Floria system, but if nothing turned the tide in the battle for Ostillon by the time they arrived the planet would be smoking ash and rubble.

Castiel recalled a Sherrerr attack on another Dirksen planet, Cestrarth, a military stronghold. His half-sister, Carina, had destroyed an ocean side military base there. In that attack the Sherrerrs had wanted to preserve as much of the planet's infrastructure as they could, and they'd succeeded. The capture of Cestrarth had yielded valuable equipment and intel, and the planet was now a Sherrerr stronghold.

His father's clan clearly had no intention of treating Ostillon in the same manner. Their attack had been relentless and devastating. Did the Sherrerrs know the world harbored the mages who had escaped them? The moment

Carina had taken the mages from *Nightfall* the Sherrerrs had lost key, highly effective resources. If the clan thought retrieval of them would be impossible, it made sense to attempt to destroy the mages instead.

Mages made excellent weapons, as the Sherrerrs aboard *Nightfall* were about to discover.

"Are you within range to do your thing yet?" Reyes Dirksen asked. "I don't think we can get much closer without attracting their attention."

"Don't speak to me," said Castiel. "I have to concentrate." Ignoring Langley Dirksen's son sitting next to him, he filled a beaker with elixir. He'd been watching the battle, noting the position of *Nightfall's* weapons when they fired. He regretted he hadn't asked his father for a tour of the ship during the weeks he'd lived aboard it. If he'd known where the fuel tanks were situated he could have Cast Fire into them, the same as his brothers and sisters had when they destroyed the Dirksen shipyard.

Langley Dirksen had warned him that capturing the ship was preferable to destroying it. Such a vessel would be a valuable asset for the Dirksens. Nonetheless, Castiel itched to make a spectacular end to *Nightfall.* That would make the clan take notice of him. His standing among them would rise to heady heights. As it was, his contribution to Ostillon's defense had been all but ignored, it seemed. He knew he could do so much more and rise so much higher, if only they would let him.

Another of his problems lay in the fact that more than half of his long-distance Casts failed. He hadn't had the same practice as his siblings, and though he'd watched many of the lessons their mother had taught, the information she'd passed on had been patchy and unreliable. Carina had demonstrated what a properly trained mage could do.

"I really think you should do something now," urged Reyes.

"And I said, be quiet!" Castiel snapped. He hated Langley's son. Langley had insisted that Reyes must be his constant companion, as if he were a child who needed a chaperone. Yet Reyes was only three years older than himself. Langley was attempting to control and keep tabs on him, but she was overstepping the mark.

Langley Dirksen was one of several problems Castiel intended to solve when he had the opportunity, when he had helped to rid Ostillon of the Sherrerrs' presence and showed the Dirksens that a new force had appeared in their midst.

He lifted the beaker to his lips and swallowed its contents in several large gulps. He'd practised the Cast he intended to make many times with success, but he'd never attempted it on such a scale before. He could not use Split again. Though his strength and skill grew stronger every day, he could not tear such an immense vessel as *Nightfall* in two. Also, despite his annoyance, he had heeded Langley's exhortation to avoid damaging the ship if he could.

What he intended would not be spectacular, but it would be effective. The remaining Dirksen fleet would be able to move in and complete *Nightfall's* defeat.

Castiel closed his eyes, centered his consciousness, and dove deep into his mind, just as his mother had taught his siblings. In his mind's eye, he wrote the character, Break. Next, he copied it several times. Finally, he propelled the characters at the Sherrerr flagship, aiming them according to his memory of *Nightfall's* weapons. Break was a simple Cast that required little strength but sending the characters across the void exhausted him.

"Have you done it yet?" Reyes's voice intruded.

"Dammit," Castiel yelled, leaping to his feet. His flailing arm knocked over the jug of elixir and it clattered on the floor, the liquid spilling out in a flood. He leaned his face into Reyes's and said softly, "If you speak to me again while I'm Casting, I'll rip you apart."

Reyes' eyes became hooded and his expression sullen. If Castiel's warning scared him, he didn't show it. Castiel threw himself into his seat and rubbed his temple. He muttered, "It's done."

The shuttle pilot had diplomatically ignored the altercation. He said, "The Sherrerr ship has stopped firing."

Castiel returned his attention to the display. What the pilot had said wasn't strictly true. One of *Nightfall's* pulse weapons continued to operate, but his Cast had taken out most of its offensive capabilities. Relief and delight mingled in his chest. His Casting ability was improving. He doubted Carina could have done any better.

The Dirksen ships were not slow to take advantage of *Nightfall's* weakness. They were drawing closer to the ship and concentrating their fire on the remaining weapons.

"You did it," said Reyes, though his tone was not celebratory.

Was Reyes jealous? Castiel didn't particularly care. If Langley Dirksen's son envied his ability, the fact meant nothing to him. Except for one thing: though the Dirksens as a group might relish the fact that they had a mage working for them, the Dirksens as individuals might be less happy about the situation. Castiel imagined that politics and power struggles within the clan could yet impede his progress.

His sudden appearance and rise to prominence could arouse suspicion and envy among its members. With the exception of Langley, the Dirksens might deeply distrust anyone who carried the name Sherrerr, no matter how many times Castiel demonstrated his loyalty.

Then there was the natural resentment that mage abilities excited in people. Castiel was all too aware of this. He had felt the same way himself for many years. He guessed some of the Dirksens would like nothing better than to put an end to this upstart intruder, even at the clan's expense. He was certain that this was how Reyes felt, and especially so. Langley Dirksen's son had once been the focus of his mother's attention, but now that attention was directed at Castiel.

"They're boarding her," the pilot exclaimed.

Castiel couldn't see any Dirksen ships next to *Nightfall* on the shuttle's display. He had removed his comm in order to concentrate on Casting, so he slid the device into his ear. One of the Dirksen vessels had indeed successfully gained entry to *Nightfall*. The boarders would be fighting the ship's crew in the passageways, trying to gain control of the ship.

"Retreating to a safe distance," said the pilot.

"Why?" Castiel asked.

"I'm guessing the Sherrerrs might not want us to have their ship," said Reyes.

"You got it," the pilot said.

Acceleration forced Castiel forward as the shuttle swept away from *Nightfall*. Dirksen ships were taking out the weapon that his Cast had failed to break. Other Sherrerr ships continued to try to defend the flagship, but the Dirksens were successfully fending them off.

The battle for Ostillon was turning, and Castiel's contribution to the fight had been instrumental, the key success. No Dirksen could deny it.

In return, he would demand recognition. He wanted a seat at the Dirksen war council. His own dwelling and compensation were to be expected, but what he wanted and needed was control. Without power within the clan his position could become precarious.

As the shuttle sped from the scene of the battle, Castiel closely watched the result of his work unfold. A second Dirksen ship gained access to *Nightfall*. The ship's final working weapon ceased firing. A shuttle departed from the second boarding Dirksen ship, possibly transporting Sherrerr captives to Ostillon.

Nightfall hung in silence in the glittering black, Dirksen vessels surrounding it. Brilliant streaks of pulse fire cut across space as the remaining Sherrerr ships fought to save their captain.

He wished he knew a Cast that would allow him to see inside things. He greatly desired to watch the close combat of the Sherrerr and Dirksen forces in *Nightfall*. He wanted to see the exchanges of fire, the hand-to-hand combat, and the blood. He wanted to hear the screams. But that was all denied to him.

Was there such a See Cast? He didn't know if it didn't exist or if Mother had kept it secret.

He recalled that brat, Darius, claiming he had invented a new Cast once. If it was true, the first thing he would do when he captured his brother would be to force him to create more Casts. Was Darius on Ostillon? Castiel hoped so. He hoped that, along with his other siblings, Darius had not been able to escape. Things were soon to become more stable, and then Castiel would be able to initiate a thorough search for his brothers and sisters.

As long as they were free they would be a threat. He needed to have them under his control, as well as benefit from their power.

Castiel heard a third Dirksen ship had latched onto *Nightfall*. The flagship was truly defeated.

The pilot cursed, breaking Castiel's train of thought. He looked up at the display. *Nightfall's* dark hull was rent with radiant light. She was blasting apart.

"Are we safe?" Reyes asked.

"Still working on it," came the pilot's stiff reply.

Rather than allow their flagship to fall into Dirksen hands, the Sherrerr command had given the order to self-destruct. As Castiel watched, *Nightfall's* hulking form dissolved into a snowstorm of speeding, flashing debris.

It was the beginning of the end of the Sherrerrs, and the commencement of Castiel's journey to power.

FIVE

"When we settle down somewhere," said Parthenia as she scraped fine wood shavings from a stick with a knife, "the first thing I'm going to do is brew enough elixir to fill a water tank."

Carina smiled. She was squatting next to her sister, waiting for her to finish adding elixir ingredients to the metal canister. It was good to hear Parthenia talk about the future lives they would lead and not harp on about catching Castiel. Perhaps she'd given up on the idea.

A gust of cold wind blew, cutting through Carina's clothing and raising goosebumps on her skin.

"Hurry up, Parthenia," Oriana said. "It's freezing here and I'm starving. Even if we manage to catch anything it's going to take ages to cook it."

Darius had done exactly as Parthenia had asked him and Transported them to the wild lands on the other side of the continent, near where he and his sister had first arrived on Ostillon. His effort had used up the last of their elixir.

It was a bleak wilderness. Aside from the tall tower in the distance where, according to Parthenia, a ranger called Jace lived, the area was empty of human habitations. The reason was obvious: the land was poorly drained and swampy. On higher ground beyond the tower a dark, dense forest grew.

They were safe for the moment, that was clear. But the downside of uninhabited regions was that they contained little to support human life. There was no fresh, clean water, nothing to eat, and nowhere to shelter. If they hadn't had the ability to Cast, they wouldn't have lasted longer than a few days. As it was, survival was still difficult.

After long searching, Carina had managed to find a firestone. Bryce had discovered an old bird's nest that would serve for tinder in a thicket, and the children had gathered whatever dry wood they could find. The water had come from one of the many pools in the area. Though it wasn't clear, let alone clean, boiling the water would make it safe to drink. They also had Carina's canister in which to brew the elixir. When Parthenia had added all the ingredients, Carina would make a fire.

But she remained worried about their long-term prospects. They had been hiding from Dirksen patrols and Sherrerr attacks for nearly a week, struggling to find enough to eat and to stay warm and dry. She felt they had been circling the edge of a drain, managing to avoid being sucked down for now, but how much longer could they keep it up?

"It's ready," Parthenia said, putting down Carina's knife.

"Good job," said Carina. "Okay, everyone. Gather around. I want you to watch me."

"But we've watched you do that before," said Nahla.

"I know. And as soon as we have plenty of materials and time, I'm going to make you all practice until you can do this yourselves. You never know, one day you might not have me around."

Darius grabbed Carina around her neck. "You're always going to be around."

"I hope so," she said. "But you're going to watch me carefully anyway, right?"

Darius replied, "Uh huh," and sat on his haunches, staring so intently at the little pile of tinder Carina almost laughed.

"Oh, hurry up," said Oriana. "I'm so hungry."

Carina struck the knife against the firestone, causing sparks to fly onto the tinder. Before long smoke began to ooze from the dry material. She teased a glow by blowing steadily into its center. When a flame licked up, she put the tinder into the little pile of sticks and knelt on the ground so she could blow into the pile. She added thicker sticks when more flames sprang up. Soon, the metal canister was sitting at the edge of a small fire, its contents simmering.

"Are you sure there are things we can eat in there?" Ferne asked Parthenia as they waited for the elixir to be ready. He was referring to the forest at the top of the ridge about half a kilometer away.

"There are *things*," his sister replied. "I'm guessing we can eat them."

"Providing we can catch them," Oriana said, her hand absent-mindedly resting on her stomach.

"This should help," said Carina. The elixir had simmered long enough. She lifted the hot canister away from the embers so the liquid could cool.

With sufficient time, she guessed she might be able to make a trap to catch a forest-dwelling animal, but she'd had an idea that might be quicker and less reliant on woodcraft.

"Bryce," she said, "I'd feel better if you stayed here with the younger children. Do you mind? You could make us a shelter to sleep in tonight while I'm gone."

He looked at the forest and then the sun, which was entering the lower quarter of the sky. "Are you sure you're going to be okay in there by yourself?"

"If Parthenia and Darius spent hours walking through it alone without incident, maybe that means nothing dangerous lives there. But I wasn't planning on going by myself. I wanted to take Ferne with me."

"Cool," said Ferne. "I'd love to come."

"Can I come too?" Oriana asked.

"No," replied Carina. "I only need one of you in case I catch something heavy." She wanted to encourage her sister to be more independent and less clingy with her brother. For all Carina knew, the two could be separated at some point. Oriana was old enough to survive alone, if she didn't pine for Ferne.

"Okay," said Bryce. "I already found a dryish spot about four hundred meters that way." He pointed in the opposite direction to the forest. "When you come back, look for us over there."

"We will," said Carina as she pulled her shirt sleeve over her hand again to pick up the canister and screw on the lid. The elixir would cool some more on the way to the forest.

"Be careful climbing that ridge," said Parthenia. "It's slippery."

"Come on," Carina said to Ferne, who happily jumped up and joined her side as she began to walk toward the forest.

"What are we going to do after we catch Castiel?" Ferne asked when they'd been walking for a few minutes.

"What do you mean? Are you asking what we're going to do with him or where we'll go next?"

"Both, I guess."

"Honestly, Ferne, I'm not happy about taking you all with me to help capture Castiel. I know I agreed with Parthenia that he's too dangerous to be left to his own devices, but I'm having second thoughts about involving you guys too. The Sherrerrs and the Dirksens won't stop at anything to get him back, or to capture any of you. I've been wondering if I should take you all away and try to put as much distance between ourselves and Castiel, and the entire galactic sector as possible."

"Maybe we should kill him," Ferne said quietly. He was looking away from Carina as he spoke.

"I don't know if I could do that." And if anyone was going to do it, it had to be her. She couldn't expect any of Castiel's siblings to murder their brother, no matter what he'd done. Their mother had already killed their father. That was enough trauma for a lifetime.

———

A ditch sat at the bottom of the ridge where the forest grew. They slid down the bank into the lower area and Carina found herself up to her knees in mud. This stuff was slimy and evil-smelling too. Ferne, being lighter, hadn't sunk in so deeply. He helped her free her legs from the clinging suction. They crossed the ditch and began to climb the bank.

The canister of elixir had cooled until it was only warm. Carina slipped the container into her shirt so she had both hands free to scale the steep slope.

Ferne climbed beside her. At one point, his grip on a tree root slipped and he slithered down a short distance. She waited for him to return to her level.

"I used to think it would be nice not to have to live in our big house with Father," Ferne said as he toiled upward, panting. "I wanted to go to school like other kids and play outside in parks and in the streets."

"You might still be able to do that, one day."

He reached her and they continued to climb together. The top of the ridge and the outskirts of the forest lay a few meters higher.

"I know this must sound funny," said Ferne, "but sometimes I almost wish I was back in our house in Ithiya."

"I think it's natural to feel like that. Your life was a lot easier then. Living out in the real world is hard." She guessed he also missed his mother, though he didn't say it. Wishing Ma was alive again would mean wishing the woman continued to remember her life of enslavement and torture, the murder of the man she loved, and everything else she'd endured. She'd suffered enough and had been glad to let go. Ma was better off where she'd gone, wherever that was, though Carina missed her too.

She reached upward, grabbed clumps of grass, and pulled herself up onto the level surface. She turned around and held out a hand to help her brother up. Then they walked quickly into the trees. Behind them, the sun was already lowering to the horizon. It was a good time of day to be catching animals. The ones who were around during the daytime would be going to their sleeping spots and the nocturnal beasts would be waking up and moving around.

But they had a long evening ahead of them. Assuming they could catch something, they still had to carry their catch down the ridge, cross the odorous ditch, climb out of it, and then find the rest of their party in the darkness. Casting Transport would be a temptation but they couldn't waste precious elixir on doing things they could do themselves.

She searched for animal tracks in the failing light. If she could find a well-used trail, it would make her task easier. She didn't find one before the evening grew too dark to see well, but they did walk into an area of open ground among the trees. She looked for a branch low on a tree, and said to Ferne, "This one's good. Let's climb up."

"You're planning on catching a bird?" he asked.

"I'm planning on catching whatever happens by."

"Oh, I get it."

They climbed about four meters up into the tree and stopped at a branch that overlooked the open ground and would bear their weight. Now it was only a matter of waiting and watching.

Carina had heard that an animal's sense of smell was stronger than a human's, and she worried that any wild creature that came near would detect their scent and be frightened away. She needed the animal to stick around long enough for her to Cast. She hoped the stench from the mud in the ditch would cover their scent.

Ferne shifted close to her, causing the leaves in the tree to rustle. She put her arm around her brother and they benefited from their mutual warmth as they waited. Night fell and the air grew colder. Forest noises started up in the stillness—distant nocturnal bird calls, shuffling and scraping in the under-growth, and the calls of frogs—but Carina saw nothing she could Cast upon.

She became stiff and her muscles ached. She knew Ferne must feel worse than her after the soft life he'd led, yet he remained stoic.

Finally, their patience was rewarded. Ferne must have heard the noise first, for she felt him stiffen a moment before she also registered the sound of an animal walking close by. She held her breath and hoped the beast would enter the open patch of ground. In anticipation, and to avoid spooking the creature by her movement, she removed the lid from her canister and lifted the container to her lips, all the while never taking her eyes from the gap in the tree's leaves where she could see the forest floor, barely visible in the darkness.

A four-legged animal stepped daintily into the spot. Its limbs were slim and delicate. An elegant neck rose from its body and led up to a head that tapered to a fine nose. Small horns sprouted next to each of the creature's ears. The animal was so beautiful, she hesitated to take the next step, but she had a family to feed.

She drank a mouthful of elixir and closed her eyes, keeping the image and location of the animal clear in her mind. She Cast Enthrall. When she opened her eyes, the creature had disappeared. Had her Cast missed?

Ferne began to climb down the tree.

"Where are you going?" she asked.

"You got it. It moved away but then it stopped. I can see it from here."

She also dropped to the branch below and then the next until she reached the ground. Ferne was already with the creature. It was standing still, alive but motionless. If she had been able to communicate with it she could have instructed the animal to do whatever she wanted now it was Enthralled. But she didn't want to do that.

She quickly pushed the animal down onto its side and then knelt on its neck. "You probably want to look away," she said to Ferne. As her brother turned around, she grabbed the animal's head and twisted it hard, breaking the creature's neck.

Dinner was arranged. But what kind of life would the following days bring? How long could they survive as they had been, hunters and hunted? She decided she needed to talk with her siblings tonight. They could not continue to live on Ostillon.

Six

Carina licked her fingers and then wiped them on her pants, noticing how grubby the material looked even in the poor light from the campfire.

The animal she'd killed in the forest had filled everyone's bellies, according to the looks of satisfaction on Bryce and her siblings' faces. It was the first time since the Sherrerrs had launched their attack they had all had plenty to eat.

"This is a good shelter you built while Ferne and I were gone," she said. With help from the children, Bryce had slung a long, straight branch between two small trees and then piled many more branches against it before covering the lean-to with dead plant material. The open side of the construction faced the fire and the ground beneath it was piled with more dead grass and ferns.

"It is, isn't it?" said Parthenia. "If you can find more animals for us to eat, we can live here for days. Now that we have elixir a fire won't be a problem. We only have to remember to keep our supply topped up so we don't run out again."

Darius and Nahla were already asleep, curled up like family pets next to the fire. Everyone else was looking sleepy too, but it seemed to Carina this was a good time to tell the others her decision.

She took a breath, knowing that Parthenia wasn't going to like what she was about to hear. "Actually, I was thinking it was time we moved on."

"You mean we should go back to the capital?" Parthenia asked. "I guess so. We aren't likely to find Castiel around here. But—"

"No, I mean we should leave Ostillon. I think I need to face up to the fact that it's too dangerous for you all here with Castiel around. I need to take you somewhere safe. Then maybe I'll return to deal with him."

"But we don't have time for that," Parthenia said. "We have to stop him now. He plans on taking over the Dirksen clan. When he's in control of everything he'll be untouchable, and who knows what horrible, evil things he'll do? Imagine if Father had ever run the Sherrerrs. He would have treated everyone the same way he treated Mother. It would have been hell."

"I understand what you're saying. But is any of that our fault? The Sherrerrs turned a blind eye to how your father treated Ma, and the Dirksens worked hard to get their own mage. Well, now they have one. They'll reap what they sowed."

"I'm not talking about the Sherrerrs and Dirksens, I'm talking about the ordinary people. If Castiel gets any real power, they'll suffer terribly."

"She's right," said Bryce. "With Castiel running the show, it's going to be a bloodbath."

Carina thought back to her childhood and the cruelty she'd endured at the hands of the 'ordinary people'. She thought about the number of times she'd been beaten and tortured by non-mages. She had spent most of her short life viewing regular folk as a threat, yet she also hadn't forgotten the help she'd received from Bryce and from the military on the *Nightfall* when she'd escaped with her family.

Her shoulders sagged and she nodded. "You're right. I have to prevent Castiel from doing his worst. But not here or now. You are all my responsibility, and we're barely surviving day to day. When I know you're safe I'll find Castiel and try to stop him."

"Do we get any say in this?" Parthenia asked.

"We'll go outsystem," said Carina, ignoring her sister. "We'll find somewhere quiet and off the trade routes. When you're settled I'll hunt for Castiel and remove him from the scene." She remained unsure of exactly what the latter entailed, but she would cross that bridge when she came to it.

"How can we leave Ostillon?" asked Ferne, chewing on a bone. "We don't have a ship."

"No," Carina replied, "but maybe we can get one, especially now that everything's in disarray due to the war."

"Can you fly it too?" Bryce asked.

"I should be able to figure it out. I flew the Sherrerr shuttle, remember?"

Oriana said, "But where can we go? How do we know what planets are safe?"

"I'll figure that out too. The first thing we need to do is find ourselves some transportation."

"You sure have a lot of figuring out to do," said Bryce.

———

Later on, Carina and Bryce were lying face to face inside the lean-to. Everyone else was asleep and Carina was heading in the same direction. Bryce had his back to the fire and she faced him. Darius lay behind her and the rest of the children occupied the remaining space.

"Are you sure about leaving Ostillon?" Bryce asked softly.

She forced open her closing eyelids. "I'm sure. I know we need to do something about Castiel, but we're too weak right now. When I was a merc I learned the hard way what happens when your enemy outclasses you. Our company owner put us in hard-to-win situations more than once. That woman has blood on her hands. I'm not going to make the same mistake with my family. I hate Castiel and fear what he might do, but going in weak and unprepared isn't going to work. We could all end up dead."

"Okay, I hear you."

They looked into each other's eyes for a few moments without speaking. She recalled the first time she'd met Bryce. It had been months previously, when she'd been at the end of her hope of finding another mage. Bryce had followed her home while she was in a drunken haze.

They'd kissed. In all the time they'd spent together since then they'd never been so close again. He'd helped her aboard the Sherrerr flagship, nearly at the cost of his own life, and he'd searched for her on Ostillon for days. He'd said he wanted to be with her. But could a relationship between a mage and non-mage ever work out? Would Bryce be able to resist the desire to control her for his own gain?

She didn't know. She couldn't deny that he had proven his loyalty and trustworthiness several times over, but how long would that last? She feared becoming closer to him, knowing that her feelings would make her vulnerable.

"Good night," she whispered.

"Good night."

After Bryce fell asleep, Carina also began to drift off.

She was on a plain of tall grasses and wildflowers. A young, strong sun was scorching her exposed skin. The buzzing of insects filled her ears. She knew she'd been in that place before but she couldn't remember when. Distant voices sounded behind her, and when she turned around she saw some people approaching, wading through the grass as if walking through a shallow sea.

She didn't think she could have imagined a more dissimilar group. One was very old and swathed in robes, barely hobbling along and using a stick for support. Another was tall and broad with a beard that reached to his middle. A third wasn't much more than a child, about Parthenia's age.

As she was watching the group, the oldest lifted her head and looked directly at her. She raised a hand in greeting, and for some reason Carina felt compelled to return the salute.

But before she could lift her hand, something drew her back to Ostillon.

She opened her eyes and immediately knew what had wakened her.

Footsteps.

They were drawing closer. The walker was doing his or her best to be silent, but the ground was littered with plant matter. From her position next to Bryce, she could see only the night sky. She lifted her head to peer over her sleeping companion. The fire had died down but the embers glowed, making it difficult to see much, but she could make out a tall, black figure ten or twelve meters away from their camp, moving slowly toward them.

She had prepared for exactly such an event. Darius was sleeping against her back. She had told him what he had to do. She only hoped that grogginess from being woken from a deep sleep wouldn't affect his Casts.

She reached behind her, groped for her brother's shoulder, and sharply shook it.

"Darius, wake up," she muttered. With relief she felt her brother stir. "Someone's coming. Remember what I said? Do it now."

Despite his young age, Darius quickly and silently responded to her request. Carina was proud of how fast her little brother had learned to react quickly in dangerous situations. Proud but also sad. She hoped he would be able to live a more normal childhood one day.

He was moving, feeling for the elixir canister she'd given him. Carina fixed her eyes on the approaching dark stranger. Who was he? Was he the ranger Parthenia had mentioned? She guessed the man must have spotted the glow of their fire. She'd thought they weren't in sight of his tower.

Was there nowhere on Ostillon where they could safely hide?

No. They had to escape the planet, providing this stranger didn't catch them first.

Suddenly, Bryce was gone. Darius had made his first Cast. Bryce, Nahla, and Oriana would have an abrupt awakening after their Transport. No one now lay between her and the stranger.

The shadowy figure was at the fire. She heard Ferne or Parthenia stir, probably awoken by the abrupt disappearance of their sleeping companions. Then their movements turned to silence as Darius Transported them from the place.

The strange, large man stepped forward. He was standing above Carina, looking down into her open eyes. He was black-haired and his face was wreathed in a thick, black beard.

Hurry up, Darius!

"No! Wait," the man exclaimed.

He disappeared along with the fire, the swampy wood, and the darkness.

SEVEN

The shuttle that had carried Castiel and Reyes from the battle was landing at the spaceport, and Castiel's excitement was mounting at the thought of the reception he was about to receive. Would Sable Dirksen herself be waiting to congratulate him? Or perhaps he would be conveyed to her residence for a private audience. After all, it might be too much to expect the head of the Dirksen clan to travel out to meet him, in spite of the significant service he had performed in striking a monumental blow against the Sherrerrs.

The pilot gave the signal that it was safe to disembark. Castiel immediately rose from his seat and almost collided with Reyes.

"I should be first onto the ramp, don't you think?" Castiel asked.

"Why? What difference does it make?"

Castiel only gave him a knowing smirk in response. Langley's son had to be brimming with jealousy over his achievements. It was no surprise, but Reyes couldn't hope to live up to his abilities. He had better accept it for his own peace of mind. Not that Castiel cared.

After pushing Reyes aside, Castiel strode the short distance to the shuttle's ramp. It was dark outside though dawn was approaching. The lights at the capital's domestic spaceport were not shining, no doubt as a safety measure. He peered into the darkness, seeking in vain the figures he expected to see. He'd thought Langley would be there at the very least to express her praise for his success.

But look as hard as he could, he could see nothing except the dark shape of a hover vehicle near the end of the ramp.

Reyes took his turn to push him out of the way before walking toward the vehicle. "What were you expecting? A welcoming committee?" he sneered. "They don't care who you are. You're only a tool to them."

Castiel hesitated, shocked at the unexpectedly lackluster response to his achievement. He had destroyed the Sherrerr flagship, for stars' sake. Or, rather, the Sherrerrs had destroyed it themselves, but he had incapacitated the vessel and turned the tide of the battle. He could hardly believe that no one had been sent out to congratulate him.

Ire simmering in his breast, he stomped after Reyes. Langley's son was likely to leave without him if he wasn't quick. He climbed into the hover vehicle and then sat in furious silence as they were whisked from the spaceport.

From the corner of his eye he could see the amused look on Reyes' face. An urge to punch the expression away rose up. What would Langley do if he hit her son? What *could* she do? He had plenty of elixir. He would be able to inflict a lot of damage on her and other Dirksens before he ran out.

But what then? He didn't have enough elixir to kill them all, and he didn't want to. The clan was useful to him. Their networks of people, supplies, and military power spanned the regions under their control in the galactic sector. It would take him years to build a similar infrastructure. It made more sense to use the one that was already available.

Castiel purposely relaxed his clenched fists, recalling that his father had rarely reacted in haste. He should follow his parent's example. The Dirksens were clearly too stupid to grasp his true worth. Demonstrating their error to them would take time. He had to be patient, and he had to concentrate his efforts on giving them explicit examples of his power. He had to impress them and, perhaps even more importantly, he had to intimidate them. Fear brought respect.

Father had controlled his family through fear. If it hadn't been for that bitch Carina, he would have raised the family's status to the top of the Sherrerr clan. Castiel wanted to follow his father's lead and succeed where he had failed, albeit in a rival clan.

When they arrived at Langley's mansion, the woman was waiting at the door, dressed in a shimmering gown. Castiel climbed out of their vehicle and walked to the entrance. Langley embraced Reyes first, Castiel was not slow to note. Then she hugged him, but he didn't move his arms from his sides and remained stiff-backed.

Langley's jubilant expression faltered and she looked a little afraid, presumably as she realized what she'd done wrong. "Come in, come in. I took the liberty of arranging a victory celebration. I hope you don't mind. You must be tired. Would you like to freshen up and change before joining us?"

Somewhat mollified, Castiel replied, "No, it's fine. I can go straight in." So the Dirksens had organized a reception for him after all. Perhaps he would not need to provide them with a potent demonstration of his abilities.

Reyes asked to be excused from attending the party, saying he was tired and would go to bed. Castiel guessed he hated the prospect of seeing someone else steal the limelight.

Reyes left them in the hall and Castiel went with Langley to her entertaining room. As he stepped through the open double doors, he scanned the space to see who was present to offer their congratulations. Dark displeasure settled over him again. Only seven or eight people were here, and he had met them all previously at Langley's soirees. They were minor figures in the Dirksen clan.

The head of the military division would probably be too busy to make the event, but where was Sable Dirksen? Didn't she realize what he'd done for her?

Langley was watching him nervously. "Why don't you come in and sit down? You must be exhausted. What would you like to drink?"

"You're right," said Castiel. "I am exhausted. I changed my mind. I think I'll retire for the evening." Without another glance at the assembled inconsequential Dirksens and hangers-on, he spun around and left the room.

He strode to the staircase and climbed the steps two at a time. When he reached his room, he unlocked the door and marched inside, slamming the door closed. He carefully locked it. He had insisted on a new lock and that he held the only key. As the only mage the Dirksens had, he couldn't be too careful.

He paced up and down, fuming. Who the hell did they think they were? Did they really imagine that he would put up with their neglect and slights?

He halted, realizing he mustn't allow their rudeness and stupidity to get to him. He didn't want to do anything rash and jeopardize his current position, unfairly low though it was. He sat down on his bed and pulled off his shoes as he considered his next step.

He returned to his earlier plan of giving a clear, intimidating demonstration of what he could do. There had to be something that would make the Dirksens sit up and take notice of him. They had to understand he wasn't some insignificant foot soldier who could perform convenient tricks.

He picked up his interface and logged into the news network. He scanned the information. It was sparse. The news of the defeat of the *Nightfall* had only just begun to filter through to the media.

He was curious about the fallout from the flagship's destruction, wondering how he could exploit the event. The Dirksen ships and crews that had been boarding the Sherrerr flagship had all been destroyed, but the remainder of the Sherrerr fleet had withdrawn from the field of battle. It looked like Ostillon was saved, for the time being.

Anger rose up in his belly again. *He* had saved Ostillon, and the Dirksens had rewarded him with a lukewarm party with nobodies.

The news updated and the new information caught his attention. Several prisoners had been taken from the Sherrerr ship before it self-destructed. Who might they be? Father had introduced him to several of the higher-ranking officers. They had clearly been uninterested in him at the time and only condescending to his father, but that didn't matter. This could be the opportunity he was looking for.

He didn't know what the Dirksen interrogation methods were, but he was confident he could Cast something that would be more effective. Spectacularly effective, in fact.

When Sable Dirksen saw what he could do, she was guaranteed to show him the respect he deserved.

Eight

Dawn was arriving at the spaceport. Darius had Transported Carina and the others to another remembered spot on Ostillon: outside the spaceport fence. It was the place where Ferne had almost died from a Dirksen crossbow bolt.

Reyes Dirksen's star racer had sparked a fire in the forested area, but the undergrowth was beginning to grow back. Rain had fallen recently. The early morning air was chilly and humid and the new, young forest vegetation was sodden.

Carina crouched at the fence, surveying the take-off and landing zones and the hangars. Descending through the clouds high above was a shuttle coming in to land. The place had been taken over by Dirksen military, no doubt due to their own spaceport's destruction. The presence of military vessels was a big impediment. Stealing a military craft would be way more difficult than sneaking onto a civilian vessel and ejecting the pilot.

The problem with Casting was the lag. A round fired from a gun was immensely faster than the operation of a Cast. Even slipping a knife under someone's ribs was quicker. That was the reason Stefan Sherrerr had been able to control his mage wife and children. It also meant the ability to Cast wasn't a sure-fire guarantee they could steal a ship.

After her inadequate amount of sleep, Carina eyes and head were sore with tiredness. In the remains of the forest behind her, the children waited. Unable to lie down due to the wet ground, they were complaining about being cold and exhausted. But she didn't want to waste time resting before they made their attempt to leave Ostillon. They were back in dangerous territory, where Sherrerrs could launch another attack or Castiel might find them.

The incident at their campsite in the uninhabited wild lands had made their danger even clearer. If someone could find them there in the wilderness, nowhere on Ostillon was safe. They had to leave at the earliest opportunity.

A hand on her shoulder jolted Carina from her ruminations. Bryce was beside her, his features drawn with tiredness. She guessed she looked the same. Trying to survive the last few days had taken its toll on everyone.

"What do you think?" Bryce asked, nodding at the shuttle that was lowering to the ground a couple hundred meters away.

"No, not that one. An incoming vessel is likely to be low on fuel. What we want is one about to take off, carrying enough fuel to take us a reasonable distance. Then we have to hope there's another system within shuttle range. I don't remember noticing one on the map when we were on our way here after escaping the *Nightfall*. Then we have to pray we aren't shot to pieces trying to navigate through a battlefield." She gave Bryce a tight smile.

"But if we try to steal a shuttle that's about to depart, won't troops be on their way over to it?"

"Yeah, probably." Her lips drew to a line. "This isn't going to be easy." She stood up, her leg muscles stiff with squatting for too long in the damp weeds, and walked over to her brothers and sisters. They were huddled in a group under the blackened limbs of a dead tree. Darius was writing numbers in the dirt with a stick, and the others were sitting on their haunches, listless, pale, and sleepy-eyed. Only Parthenia was active, replenishing their small supply of elixir over a smoky fire.

That was another reason they had to act quickly. It was only a matter of time until someone at the spaceport became curious about the line of smoke reaching up into the sky, now clearly visible in the growing light of the approaching sun.

"Listen, everyone," Carina said. "I need your help. I need ideas on how we can work together to steal a ship and get off this planet. We have to cross the open space of the landing and take-off zone, get aboard a ship, and fly it out of here. And we have to do all of that without being shot. I've run a few scenarios through my head, like Casting Fire on a building to create a distraction or Transporting troops a safe distance away, but everything seems too risky. I don't know if a fire will distract everyone, and even if we managed to Transport every soldier out of that place, more could arrive in shuttles from the battle any minute."

"Instead of Transporting the soldiers away," said Ferne, "could we Transport their weapons to us? Then we can fight them."

Carina smiled. "You think we can take on *all* the troops?"

"We can try."

Parthenia suddenly rose to her feet. "Whatever you all decide to do, you can count me out. I'm staying here. You can take all the elixir. I'll make some more for myself when you're gone."

"What?!" Carina exclaimed. "No! No way, Parthenia. You have to come with us. If you stay here alone you'll die. Or, even worse, Castiel will catch you."

"I won't leave this planet while he's still a danger," said Parthenia. "I just won't do it, and you can't make me. You've decided for all of us, without even a discussion about it. Who made you the leader? I don't have to do whatever you say just because you're the oldest."

"I'm not trying to boss you around. I'm trying to save your life, you idiot." As soon as she'd spoken, Carina regretted her words. She shouldn't have been so blunt, but she was running on a couple of hours' sleep and she was worried out of her mind about how she was going to protect everyone.

But the damage was done. Parthenia strode away into the darkness.

"Dammit." Carina walked after her sister. "I'm sorry, Parthenia. I shouldn't have said that. Please, come back. Don't go off by yourself. It's dangerous around here."

"Leave me alone," Parthenia yelled. "Go and steal your spaceship. If I have to stay here and stop Castiel by myself that's what I'll do."

"No." Carina had caught up to her. She grabbed her arm. Parthenia halted and faced her.

Carina said, "I can't let you do something so stupid. If you take on Castiel alone he'll catch you and keep you captive. He'll torture you until you do whatever he says. Do you want to end up like Ma?"

"Then help me. Don't run away. We'll never be this close to him again. If we leave now we'll lose our best chance."

Carina tried to think of a way to make her sister understand how wrong she was. Parthenia still saw Castiel not as a highly dangerous mage but as her brother and so her responsibility. She was only fifteen and had no perspective on the situation. Carina was three years plus a lifetime of hardship older.

She made another attempt to make her sister see reason. "Look. I promise I won't give up on trying to stop Castiel. I'll come back. I only—"

"That's what you said before." Parthenia's eyes were hard, glittering in the rays of the rising sun.

"What? When?"

"When Castiel was holding me at Langley Dirksen's mansion. You tried to rescue me, but then when things got tough you left. You said you would come back, but you didn't. I had to get away from him myself."

Carina was momentarily lost for words. What Parthenia was saying was true. Faced with the surprise Repulse Casts from Castiel, she had been forced to leave her sister in his clutches. She'd intended to return with a military-style assault, but then the Sherrerrs had begun their attack.

She grabbed her sister's shoulders. "But I hadn't abandoned you. You saw me fighting in that mech battle, right? I was trying to win enough money to buy weapons. I was coming back for you. I just didn't get a chance. I would never have left you with Castiel, Parthenia. Not while I had breath in my body. Please believe me."

Parthenia's defiant expression wavered. She broke eye contact. "It doesn't matter now. I'm staying here. Take the others somewhere safe and then come back and help me deal with Castiel, if that's what you really want. You can use the elixir canister to Locate me when you return. I've touched it often enough."

Carina was about to speak, but then she changed her mind. She could tell her sister had passed the point where she could be reasoned with. It was no surprise. They were all at the end of their tether. But that meant more than anything that they had to get away, and soon, before fatigue and stress caused one of them to make a fatal error.

"Okay," said Carina. "If your mind's made up."

"It is."

Carina gave her sister a brief hug before turning and walking back to the group.

Not for a second would she entertain the idea of leaving Parthenia behind on Ostillon.

NINE

"Where's Parthenia?" Darius asked as soon as Carina returned from speaking with her sister.

Her little brother had drawn numbers all over the damp dirt under the dead tree, and he'd managed to transfer plenty of dirt onto his face too. His voice trembled. The little boy was on edge, only just holding himself together. Guiltily, Carina recalled his sensitivity to the emotions of people around him. They were all suffering their individual fears and worries, but Darius was suffering his and everyone else's too. No wonder he seemed to spend every spare moment obsessively writing numbers. He was probably trying to distract himself from the extreme feelings that resonated inside him.

"She's gone for a walk," Carina replied.

"But she is coming with us, right?" asked Oriana.

"Yes, she is."

"Phew," Ferne said. "Thank the stars for that. I'd hate to leave her behind."

At the spaceport a military shuttle was taking off, carrying troops to Dirksen ships defending the planet. They needed to leave too, and soon.

"We aren't leaving Parthenia behind," said Carina. "I'm going to go and get her. Give me the elixir, Oriana."

The girl reflexively lifted the canister, but then she paused. "Why? What are you planning to do with it?"

Glances passed between the siblings. The possible reasons Carina would need elixir to bring their sister back were very few.

"Just give it to me," Carina snapped, and held out her hand.

Oriana moved the canister close to her chest. "If you're planning what I think you're planning, I don't think you should do that."

Carina reached out and snatched the container from her sister's grasp. "I didn't ask your opinion." She marched into the forest again, pacing quickly to return to Parthenia before she lost her under the trees.

When she spotted her sister's figure moving among the blackened tree trunks, she called her name, adding, "Wait a second."

Carina was gratified to see Parthenia pause, and she sped up her pace.

"What do you want?" asked Parthenia. "Did you change your mind? Are you staying to help me with Castiel after all?"

"I just want to give you something," Carina replied, stalling for time.

"What?" Parthenia's features scrunched into a squint as she peered at Carina, noticing she was holding something behind her back.

Carina was close enough. Even if Parthenia ran, she wouldn't have time to run out of sight. Carina removed the canister lid and sipped elixir.

"What are you doing?" Parthenia asked. Then realization dawned. "No! How could you? How could you do that to me?" She backed away. She turned and began to run.

Carina Cast, and her sister's footsteps slowed to an amble.

"Parthenia, come here."

Carina's sister reversed her direction and returned. The guilt Carina had felt when she remembered Darius' ultra-sensitivity to others' emotions was nothing compared to the remorse and shame that swept through her now. When Parthenia drew close enough to see her eyes in the weak morning light it was clear that, inside, she was fighting Carina's instruction with all the will she could muster. Sadly for her, no one possessed the mental strength to defy a fresh Enthrall Cast. However, the fury and fire in Parthenia's gaze indicated that Carina would have to watch her carefully.

"Let's go back to the others," said Carina.

Her siblings had obviously been discussing what she might be doing while she was away. They watched in silence as Carina and Parthenia walked up.

"Oh, Carina," Oriana breathed, watching Parthenia's slow, dragging steps. "What have you done?"

Darius threw down his stick, hugged himself, and began rocking as if he was in terrible pain.

"I've done what I had to do," Carina replied.

There was an unwritten rule among mages that you never Cast Enthrall on another mage against their will. Practising on each other while learning the

Cast was fine, but it could only be with the other person's consent. Taking away another person's control of themselves was only acceptable if the mage was in danger and you were trying to save them from harm. A mage would have to be doing something truly terrible to justify another mage Casting Enthrall against them for any other reason. Parthenia had only wanted to exercise her free will.

"Has anyone had any ideas on how we can steal a shuttle?" Carina asked, keeping an eye on Parthenia.

"But, Carina...." said Ferne, his tone soft and distraught.

"I said has anyone had any ideas on how we can steal a shuttle?" she repeated forcefully. "I'm guessing we have enough elixir for about ten Casts. That should do it, but which ones should we use? Bryce? Do you have a plan?" She felt about to fall apart. Shame and guilt over breaching her sister's trust were killing her. Would Parthenia ever forgive her for what she'd done? Perhaps not, but Carina was also certain she would Enthrall her sister again in a heartbeat. If Parthenia hated her for the rest of her life that was okay. At least this way she might live.

Darius murmured something too quietly for Carina to catch. "What did you say?" she asked, touching his shoulder. Darius flinched and looked up at her suspiciously.

Had she lost his love too? She bit her lip. "Darius, if you've thought of a way we can get out of here, please, tell me."

"I can Cloak us," he replied. "Or, I think I can. But we have to stay close together."

Of course. After everything that had happened since the Dirksen patrol ship had boarded the stolen Sherrerr shuttle, she had forgotten the Cast her brother seemed to have invented.

"So no one else will see us cross the spaceport?" she asked. "We won't be seen entering the ship?"

"I don't think so. I don't know for sure. I only ever did it on myself before, except when we were running away from Father's clan." Darius winced like pain was wracking him.

"Okay, let's try it." And the sooner the better. If Parthenia was especially strong willed—and Carina was guessing she was—the Enthrall Cast wouldn't last long. She would be forced to use more elixir to Cast again, and again, until she had gotten her sister so far from Ostillon she wouldn't be able to return.

———

Bryce, Ferne, Oriana, and Darius were on the other side of the fence, waiting.

"Parthenia, climb the fence," Carina repeated. At her first command, her sister's limbs had moved but then they had frozen. The Cast and Parthenia's willpower were battling within her. Carina could hardly believe the Cast was losing influence so quickly. Her sister's inner strength was powerful, and she was clearly also raging inside.

"Climb the fence!" Carina yelled.

Parthenia jerked forward like an automaton. She raised her hands and gripped the wires, her features twisting.

Darius pressed his hands against his face and turned away.

Parthenia began to climb. Carina kept pace with her. "Oriana, make sure you have the elixir ready to hand to me as soon as I reach you." She fixed her gaze on Parthenia, fearing to see her other sister's reaction to the instruction.

Barely able to restrain her impatience, Carina watched Parthenia climb over the top of the fence. As she climbed down the other side, Carina followed her, hoping Parthenia would remain under the control of the Enthrall Cast all the way onto the shuttle.

Carina jumped the last couple of meters of fence.

"Are you ready, Darius?" she asked.

"I don't know." He moved his hands away from his face. Tears had mixed with the dirt, creating wet grime that lined the depressions of his eyes and lips.

"What do you mean you don't know?" She glanced toward the spaceport. If they were going to act, they had to be quick.

"I can't think. It hurts too much."

"You're hurt?" Then she understood. "You mean it hurts inside?"

Darius gave two quick nods.

She knelt on the wet ground and hugged her little brother. "I'm sorry. I'm so sorry we're all hurting you. But can you please try? I'll hold you if it helps."

"Okay." Darius' voice was quiet. "I'll try."

"Oriana," Carina said.

Her sister handed her the elixir and she held the canister's open mouth to Darius' lips. The boy took two large swallows before closing his eyes. She held him as she imagined Ma would have done, gently and comfortingly. The poor kid. He'd been through too much, and now the fate of all of them rested on his shoulders. But she had no choice except to ask this of him if he and his siblings were to be safe.

"It's done," Darius whispered.

"It is?" Nothing seemed any different. She wasn't sure what she'd been expecting but she'd been expecting *something*. "Are you sure we're Cloaked? Is there a way we can tell?"

"When I played hide-and-go-seek I could always see myself. I only knew it was working when no one could see me."

Great. Darius appeared to have invented a Cast that threw a barrier of invisibility over objects, rather than making the things themselves invisible. "Okay, everyone. It's time to go."

Parthenia's eyes blazed.

"You too, sis," said Carina. "Sorry, but this is how it has to be." She gripped the elixir canister tightly as they set off across the shuttle landing area. "Bryce, can you watch for any vessels coming in to land?"

"Oh, don't worry. I already thought of that," he replied, his gaze turned upward.

If Darius' Cast had worked and they were not visible, an incoming shuttle could land right on top of them. The Cloak Cast had made the Sherrerr shuttle they had used to escape undetectable to scanning equipment.

They were fast-walking in a huddle. Carina had maneuvered Parthenia so she was in the middle and she stuck close to her side.

In the distance a line of troops appeared and began a slow jog across the landing ground. Everyone except Parthenia drew a collective breath. If the Cast hadn't worked and they could see the soldiers, that had to mean the soldiers would see them. But none of the men or women reacted. There was an audible sigh as they understood they were Cloaked.

She checked the direction the troops were traveling and followed the line with her gaze. She found herself looking at a military shuttle that had seen better days. But despite the vessel's decrepit appearance, it was definitely where the soldiers were headed. Engineers were swapping out fuel rods.

"That's our flight over there." She grabbed Parthenia's upper arm. "Run, everyone, but stick together so you don't move outside Darius' Cast. If we don't want a big fight we have to reach that ship before its passengers."

The mage family broke into a run. She could feel Parthenia's resistance in her bicep. The muscle was cramping in her grip. She could also hear a low groaning or growling sound. She looked around, trying to see where the noise was coming from. Then she realized it originated in her sister. Parthenia was trying to speak.

Just another few minutes. Please.

She doubted any guards would have been posted at the vessel, but she guessed there might be personnel inside. The pilot would be there for sure, waiting to ferry the approaching detachment of troops to the battle.

She checked the speed of the soldiers who were running toward the shuttle. She estimated her little group would arrive first, but not by much. They would have to close the doors fast, but what to do with the pilot? They couldn't take him or her along.

A sudden alteration in the running soldiers' attitude caught her attention. They were staring directly at them! No. Not all of them. Only Ferne, who was in the front. He must have run too far ahead.

"Ferne, slow up," she called.

Her brother eased his pace, but the damage had been done. "Hey! What the hell do you...? Huh? Where'd he go?" The troop leader turned to his subordinates as if to confirm he hadn't been seeing things. The men and women looked just as confused as him.

The pause allowed Carina and her family to reach the shuttle first with time to spare. She ran up the ramp without braking, forcing Parthenia onward. Inside, two privates were lounging on the seats. They froze in surprise, mouths and eyes wide. She must have run outside Darius' cloak.

The other mages and Bryce burst into the cabin. She saw everyone except Darius. She would have to trust he remained Cloaked.

Thanking the stars they only had two Dirksen soldiers to fight, she went for one, leaving the other to Bryce. She grabbed the shocked woman's weapon from her grasp, hauled her to her feet, and forced the muzzle into her back. Pushing the woman in front of her, Carina compelled her to leave the shuttle. Bryce's target followed soon after. When the two soldiers set foot off the ramp, she told them to run or feel the heat of the shuttle's engines as she took off.

As she returned to the cabin, the pilot conveniently appeared.

"Please do the honors," Carina said to Bryce as she pushed past the pilot to reach the flight controls. "Darius, Cloak the ship, as soon as you can."

Her gaze roved the displays and interfaces. Thankfully, the old-style, basic vessel had the equivalent old-style basic controls.

"Pilot's gone," Bryce yelled. She closed the doors. Now she only had to—

"Parthenia, no!" someone shouted. Carina recognized Ferne's voice.

The sound of fighting was coming from behind her. *Dammit.* Parthenia was already shaking off the Enthrall Cast. Carina jumped up and ran into the cabin.

Bryce was trying to hold on to Parthenia but she was fighting like a wild thing trying to grab the manual override for the doors. Carina couldn't risk her sister trying to escape while they were taking off. She ran up to Parthenia and punched her in the jaw. Her sister's eyes rolled back and she fell limp into Bryce's arms.

The dull sound of rounds being fired into the hull was coming from outside. Assuming Darius had Cloaked the shuttle, the soldiers were firing blind at the place they had last seen it.

If she had wanted to send an unmistakable message to Castiel about the location of his mage brothers and sisters she could not have done a better job.

She ran back to the pilot's seat and started up the vessel's engines. The only safe option left was to leave Ostillon. She flew the shuttle into the morning sky.

Ten

I t had taken an escalating series of threats the following day, culminating in the ultimatum that Castiel would abandon the Dirksens entirely and set out on his own, before by late evening Langley finally agreed to forward his request for an audience with Sable Dirksen. Reyes' bug-eyed mother had let down her facade and displayed real anger and rancor for the first time. He guessed she wasn't as important in the clan as she liked to make out, and that she'd intended to use him to raise herself, claiming credit for all he did.

The assent from the head of the Dirksens arrived. Confident that Sable Dirksen was clearly curious to meet him, Castiel was soon on his way to an unknown destination. Langley's servants did not transport him. He had waited to be picked up, and when the hover car arrived, it was unmarked.

He gazed out the window of the vehicle, trying to track where he was going. The driver had lifted the car a couple hundred meters above ground level, and they were traveling fast. Castiel lost all sense of where he was. The driver hadn't spoken a word to him yet, and Castiel doubted very much that she would tell him where they were going.

The long journey should have been tiring, especially considering he hadn't slept since defeating the *Nightfall*, but he found he was alert with anticipation. He congratulated himself on making exactly the correct move. Who did Langley Dirksen think she was, denying him his right to shine? Who was she to make herself his 'manager'?

He looked down at his clothes. Though Langley had supplied him with new suits, he worried that his appearance wasn't fine enough for the company he expected to meet soon. Father had—quite rightly—always been particular about such things. The problem couldn't be remedied. His clothes would have to do. He planned on impressing the leading Dirksens in other ways.

A mountain range in the distance was looming closer and seemed to be the place the driver was heading toward. He peered ahead at the white peaks reflecting the moonlight. Sable Dirksen certainly seemed to prefer living in remote places. It was no surprise the Sherrerrs hadn't discovered her base and destroyed it.

A realization hit, and his stomach muscles tightened. The privilege of access to the head of the clan carried a heavy price. As soon as he knew her secret location, his life would be forever under threat. If he did not live up to whatever expectation Sable Dirksen had of him, she might decide his existence was a risk she wasn't prepared to take.

He recalled that the Dirksens had cut Darius' tracer out of him when they held him captive. The clan could be brutal in their methods. Castiel felt for his elixir bottle and took a little comfort in its heavy reassurance on the seat next to him. It was true the Dirksens could be vicious, but then so could he.

The speeding hover vessel approached the mountains at an incredible pace. Soon they were swooping through a narrow pass. A face of a slope was rapidly approaching, dead ahead, but the driver wasn't turning the vehicle. Was she having some kind of seizure?

"Hey!" he shouted. But it was too late. He threw up his arms. They were going to fly right into solid rock and be smashed to pieces on the mountainside.

But instead of hitting the slope, the vehicle passed through it and they emerged inside a brightly lit natural cavern. Disbelieving what had happened, he looked over his shoulder and saw a rock wall. The slope must have been some kind of hologram. The driver braked heavily, throwing him forward. Then they were rapidly lowering to the cave floor.

The driver still did not speak a single word. The soft hum of the engine ceased and the door next to Castiel opened. As he stepped out he saw three similar hover vehicles and a fast-looking, immaculate shuttle also docked in the cavern. Ahead of him, two doors pulled apart. The message was clear.

He set off toward the open doorway, his finger hooked through the handle of the elixir canister, trepidation creeping up on him. But he had made his bid and he had won. Now he had to see it through to its conclusion.

"Please come this way," said a man.

From his clothes, the man seemed to be a servant. Castiel didn't deign to speak to him but followed him through rough-hewn passageways. The floor was worn smooth and though the walls were rough, in some places they were shiny, as if people had rubbed against them for centuries. Along the corners of the passage long, carved decorations ran where the walls met the ceiling. Most of the carvings were of animals he did not recognize.

He had the impression the place had been inhabited for hundreds or thousands of years, but he didn't think it was Dirksens who had lived here. According to what Langley had told him, the clan had only inhabited the planet in substantial numbers for a few years.

They arrived at a set of doors that stood twice as high as Castiel. The servant said something into a panel, and the doors split apart.

This was it. He was about to meet the person who wielded the ultimate power in the Dirksen clan. He breathed in deeply and stepped through the opening. A single, large stone chair stood directly ahead of him on the far side of the vast chamber. But the chair was empty. Puzzled, he looked around the hall.

"I'm over here," said a voice.

His eyes widened when he saw the voice's owner. A young woman who looked not much older than himself sat in a luxuriously padded armchair at the end of the room. Her hair was short and dark, and she was wearing expensive pajamas under a robe. The chair faced a fire of burning logs, at which the young woman was toasting her bare feet.

"It's warmer here," she said. "This place is so fucking cold."

When he hesitated, Sable Dirksen went on. "Well, are you going to speak to me or not? Or did I get up out of my warm, comfortable bed in the middle of the night for nothing?"

He jerked into action, closed his gaping mouth, and walked with what he hoped was a confident swagger to stand in front of the clan leader. Should he bow? Kneel? He hadn't thought this part through.

"My name's Castiel."

"Castiel *Sherrerr*. I know. Langley told me about you. So the old spider has finally given up her prize. You are a prize, right?"

Despite her young years, Sable Dirksen's stare was disarming.

"I can do things that others can't," he said. Noting Sable's condescending smirk, he added, more strongly, "I am a mage. I helped to defeat the *Nightfall*. I broke its weapons so that it could be boarded." He paused, uncomfortably aware he was falling over himself trying to convince her of his worth. Things weren't going how he'd imagined. He'd imagined performing an impressive feat that would amaze Sable Dirksen, not trying to explain himself like a naughty schoolboy.

"Would you like me to demonstrate?" His nervousness subsided sufficiently for him to remember his original purpose. "I heard some prisoners were taken from the *Nightfall* before it self-destructed. I could interrogate them. Persuade them to tell you everything they know."

Sable's smirk turned into a smile. "You like that kind of thing, do you? I have to admit, when I saw you for the first time just now, I was disappointed. After talking you down for so long to suit her own ends, Langley went to the opposite extreme and talked you up. I guess she wanted me to remember this big favor she was doing me. Yet you don't look like much."

Bitch. How dare she? He fought to keep his expression under control. However, if Sable cared what he thought of her words, she didn't show it.

"But maybe there's more to you than meets the eye," she continued. She raised the back of her hand to her mouth and yawned. "Okay, let's see what you can do." Sliding her bare feet into slippers, she rose from the armchair and walked across the chamber toward an open door in the corner.

Feeling like a lap dog, he followed her. When he had taken over the Dirksen clan, Sable would pay for her words. Walking behind her, he became aware of the movement of her buttocks underneath the rich silken material of her robe. He recalled his father's domination of his mother. Yes, he would pay Sable Dirksen back, in many ways.

She led him down a set of stairs. The surface of the walls was smooth, as if cut by machine. He guessed this part of the mountain castle was a Dirksen add-on. They came to a sealed, steel door that slid open as Sable arrived at it. If there was a security mechanism he could not see it. The door somehow recognized authorized persons.

They stepped into the narrow corridor beyond, where the chill of the cold stone that Sable had mentioned became even more noticeable. More steel doors were set at regular intervals along the passageway. No guards were in place. He scanned the ceiling. All he could discern that was out of the ordinary was a row of black dots. Perhaps they were cameras, or weapons.

"Here we are," Sable announced. Once more, the door opened as she drew near to it. Behind it stood a transparent wall, and in the cell beyond a woman lay curled on the bare, stone floor. She was nearly naked, and what rags remained on her were blood-stained. Her flesh bore the marks of torture. She was shaking with cold and when she saw them looking in, she shrank into the cell corner. She appeared to sob, though no sound came through the transparent wall.

Despite her state, the woman looked familiar. He couldn't remember where he'd seen her on the *Nightfall*. Had she been one of the troops, perhaps? Or was she higher ranking? Father hadn't allowed him to walk around the ship very much. He tried to place the woman in his memory.

"Whoops," Sable said. "Wrong one." She backed out of the doorway and gestured for him to leave too, but he had finally recognized the woman's terrified face.

"I know her," he blurted. The prisoner had not been on the *Nightfall* at all, hence his confusion. "She was at one of Langley's parties." He recalled the woman's hair styled into a spiral above her head. That, and the fact that she'd been beautifully dressed the previous time he had encountered her, had added to his confusion.

"Hmm, well spotted," said Sable, adding, "She's a nasty little spy. *Langley's* spy, as you noticed. It'll be a long time before she'll live down her association with the person who revealed our presence on Ostillon to the Sherrerrs."

The cell door closed.

"I'm sure that one has more to tell us," said Sable, "but then I'll take great pleasure in dispatching her. If there's one thing I can't stand, it's disloyalty." She paused and glanced at him before moving to the neighboring door. As it opened, Sable's gaze fell upon him again. Once more, those hard, dark eyes pierced him.

If she hated traitors so much, what did she think of *him*? He was a Sherrerr, yet here he was on the Dirksens' side, offering to help them. Would she ever grow to trust him? But then, he didn't want her trust. He wanted her power.

He looked through the transparent wall of the second cell. This time he immediately recognized the prisoner. *Tremoille.* The Dirksens had gotten themselves a Sherrerr admiral.

Though she was as bloody as the former captive, Tremoille didn't display anywhere near the same terror or submission. Recognition dawned in her eyes as she saw Castiel, but otherwise her features betrayed no emotion.

"You know who you have here, right?" Castiel asked Sable.

"We don't know her name, only her position. Unless she stole someone else's uniform. I'm certain an admiral has a lot to tell us, otherwise I would have had her executed by now. But she's a tough old witch and hasn't revealed a thing."

"She's called Tremoille."

"Thanks. That may be useful to know. Is that all you can do, though? I'd heard you've had some success with affecting spacecraft. I was expecting something more impressive."

He snorted dismissively. "I spent some time aboard the *Nightfall* and I recognize her, that's all." His gaze roved Tremoille's body. The woman had withstood significant abuse. Though he wasn't familiar with the Sherrerrs' military arm, he guessed she had probably been well-trained to withstand interrogation. Employing the regular methods for extracting sensitive information would not produce results. It was the perfect opportunity to demonstrate what he could do as a mage.

He stared into Tremoille's eyes as he considered his tactics. What might his father have done in similar circumstances? The answer came, but his method required more than one captive.

"I heard that you had captured a few prisoners from the *Nightfall*," he said.

"We have three," Sable replied. "But this one will do for your demonstration."

"I need two, together."

Sable frowned. "In the same cell?"

"No. One of them has to be able to see her."

"Ah, I think I understand your intention. As it happens, this prisoner has a neighbor." Sable went to the door of the next cell and did something at a panel. Tremoille's cell wall became transparent, revealing a second prisoner from the *Nightfall*. Castiel was interested to see the Dirksens had also captured Calvaley, another high-ranking Sherrerr officer. Calvaley registered his recognition of Castiel with the lifting of his upper lip in disgust.

"Good," said Castiel. "He'll do nicely. He must be able to hear as well as see what's going on."

"Done," said Sable, still at the panel. "And they can both hear us now too."

"Right." His moment had arrived. He was about to Cast, but then he realized he'd been concentrating on the persuasion part of the interrogation, not on what information Sable wanted him to extract. "What is it that you want to know?"

"Well, since your family has so kindly destroyed one of our main shipyards, it would be nice if we could return the favor."

Sherrerr shipyard locations would definitely be something Tremoille and Calvaley would know. "Did you hear that?" Castiel asked them. "You know what I and my siblings can do. Tell us the shipyard locations, or you'll regret it."

Tremoille spat blood and said, "Fuck off you little c—"

"Shame your sister didn't do the same to you as she did to your father," said Calvaley. "He got what he deserved in the end."

Castiel's hands curled into fists. "My father was worth more than all the rest of the Sherrerrs put together!" It was actually his mother, not Carina, who had killed Father, but he was not about to inform Calvaley of that.

Sable raised a hand to her mouth to cover a smile. Castiel breathed out heavily. "Tell us the shipyard coordinates." He waited. "Last chance."

When neither of the Sherrerr officers answered, Castiel was actually pleased. This was going to be enjoyable. He unstoppered his elixir bottle and took a swig. Then he closed his eyes to concentrate. He'd practised the Cast on animals on Langley's estate, with varying results. But the animals had always died eventually, and that was all that mattered.

Castiel wrote the character and sent it out, deciding at the last minute to send it at Tremoille. Calvaley had insulted his father's memory, but Tremoille had called him a nasty word. He wasn't going to stand for that, especially not with Sable Dirksen as a witness. He had to show her he wouldn't allow anyone to disrespect him.

Tremoille shrieked and clasped her back. She began to wriggle around, as if trying to escape something. But there was no escaping the Split Cast. Calvaley was on his feet and shouting, banging his cell wall with his fists. His words were drowned out by Tremoille's howls of agony.

Castiel was gratified to note Sable's amazement at what was happening. He had finally gotten her full attention. Calvaley was pounding and kicking the wall in fury while Tremoille writhed. A pool of her blood was widening around her. Then, all too soon, it was over.

Calvaley turned his face from the contorted, mangled figure.

"Keep the lights on and their shared wall transparent," Castiel said with as much authority as he could muster. "Let him see her for the rest of the night. Then in the morning we can ask him for the coordinates again."

Sable pulled her gaze from Tremoille's remains. "Come out here." She closed Tremoille's cell door.

"That was dumb," she said. "I didn't know you were going to kill her. Now we're one Sherrerr prisoner down, and a useful one at that. You should have told me what you were going to do."

When he opened his mouth to reply, she held up a hand to silence him. "But I have to admit, you have some interesting skills. Maybe we can find a use for you."

He cursed inwardly. *Enthrall.* He should have tried the Enthrall Cast. What a stupid mistake. He might have been able to force them to answer questions without hurting them. He'd been trying too hard to impress Sable.

"There's plenty more I can do," he said. "That's only a small part of it. Let me try again."

"No. I want to think about it before I let you loose on my prisoners again. That's enough for now." Sable yawned. "I'm going back to bed. Come with me."

They left the prisoner cells and returned to the older part of the castle. Sable took him up another flight of stairs. At the top, the servant who had met him at the entrance was waiting.

"Find him a room," She told the servant. Then, without saying another word, she walked away down the corridor.

In this part of the mountain castle, carpet ran along the floor, softening footsteps and reducing the chill. He followed the servant, but he glanced repeatedly over his shoulder to see what Sable was doing.

She stopped at a room at the far end of the corridor. Four men stood outside it. At first, he thought they were guards, but during one long glance backward, he saw Sable look each man up and down before poking one in the chest. Her choice followed her into her room.

That night, his thoughts were diverted from his killing of Tremoille to what he'd seen Sable do. He wondered if one day he would be joining her in her room.

ELEVEN

According to the data Carina was seeing from the shuttle's scanners, Dirksen and Sherrerr ships had clearly slogged it out hard for control of Ostillon. As well as the traces of heavy and prolonged pulse fire, it looked like something big had exploded. The interplanetary space was a mess.

She set a trajectory that would take them in the opposite direction from the fast-moving cloud of flotsam.

Cloak was a useful Cast. The shuttle's scanners could receive data yet other ships' scanners were apparently not picking up their presence. Otherwise the ships in the vicinity would be giving them five seconds to explain themselves.

How long would the Cloak last? Carina was about to leave the controls to go and ask Darius when she heard someone run up behind her. Before she could turn to see who it was, she was slapped across the back of her head. She spun around and caught Parthenia's arm as she was about to land another blow.

Carina stood up, maintaining her grip on her sister's arm. They locked gazes. Carina released Parthenia. Her sister hit her again, slapping her forcefully across the face. Carina bore the attack as Parthenia continued to rain blows on her head and face. She didn't defend herself.

Parthenia's fist split Carina's gum across her tooth and hot blood oozed into her mouth. Her ear rang from Parthenia hitting it. Then her sister landed a blow on the bridge of her nose. Blood burst out and ran down her face. The pain brought tears to her eyes.

Eventually Bryce realized what was happening and ran into the cabin. He grabbed Parthenia's shoulders and pulled her away. She didn't resist.

"What the hell do you think you're doing?"

Parthenia didn't take her eyes off Carina. She took a step closer. Bryce inserted his arm between them to prevent her from resuming her attack.

"Don't ever speak to me again," Parthenia hissed. She turned and stalked out of the cabin.

"Stars, you're a mess," said Bryce. "I'll find something to help you clean up. Are you okay?"

"I'm fine."

Carina sat down and put her head in her hands. Blood dripped from her nose onto the console. "I don't blame her. It's no more than I deserve."

"No more than you deserve? She should be on her knees thanking you for saving her life. She would have died on Ostillon by herself."

"I know, but what I did was wrong. She's old enough to decide for herself what risks she wants to take. I just couldn't bear to lose her. Not after what happened to Ma. I was being selfish. Now she'll hate me forever, justifiably."

"At least she'll be alive," said Bryce. "I can understand she would be angry, but she's overreacting. She has to know you did it for her own good."

Carina pressed her sleeve against her nose to stem the flow of blood. "You don't understand. Casting Enthrall on another mage goes against everything we stand for. It's a Cast you're only really supposed to use in self-defense. It's entirely against our code to use it to gain advantage over someone, especially another mage. Double-especially your own family. I guess Ma made that clear to them at some point. What I did was far worse than abandoning Parthenia to her fate. I wouldn't be surprised if the rest of them hated me now as well."

"I'm sure they don't, and that Parthenia will come around eventually. If they hate you for saving their sister from Castiel, they're a bunch of idiots."

Carina smiled and then regretted it as her cut gum sent out a sliver of pain. Her nose hurt like a bitch too. "They're only kids, Bryce, and they were protected from the harsh realities of life as they were growing up. When you consider that, they've all done amazingly well over the last few weeks. I'm proud of them."

"If you say so. I'll try to find a cloth and some water."

She hoped the shuttle was stocked with water and other emergency supplies. As it was a military vessel, she would have been surprised if it wasn't, but it was a possibility. The ship was so old it had probably been brought out of storage for the battle. She hoped it contained what they would need to sustain them during their trip to their next destination, wherever that might be.

She checked the fuel level and was gratified to see it was registering one hundred percent. Next, she checked the shuttle's range. Her heart sank. The little vessel would not take them far. She brought up the local region's star map and drew a sphere at the boundary of the farthest the shuttle would take them without refueling.

"Bryce asked me to help you," said Nahla, standing at the cabin doorway. She was holding a piece of cloth and a water ration.

Carina had hardly spoken to the little girl since rescuing her from Langley Dirksen's mansion. Little Nahla had been constantly quiet and submissive, meekly going along with whatever they did. Carina hadn't even asked her if she was pleased she had taken her away from Castiel.

"Thanks," Carina said.

Nahla moved closer and dampened the cloth with water from the container before carefully dabbing at the drying blood on Carina's face. She touched Carina's nose, which made her suck in a breath and wince. Nahla drew away in fear.

"It's okay," said Carina. "It just hurts a bit." As Nahla resumed her gentle cleaning, she asked, "What's Bryce doing?"

"He's talking to Parthenia."

It was nice of him but Carina doubted it would do any good. She knew that in Parthenia's position she would have reacted just the same, if not worse.

"Are you glad you aren't with Castiel anymore?" she asked, hoping that at least one of her half-siblings didn't despise her.

"Yes, I am. I thought he was a nice brother, but he was mean to me. I didn't want to stay with him anymore."

"That's good to hear, Nahla. Thank you."

The little girl blushed and looked down, unused to receiving approval.

Stefan Sherrerr had screwed up his offspring in so many different ways.

———

"Not another freezing trip," Oriana whined.

Their shuttle had departed the Floria system, and Carina was explaining their destination options. Only two star systems with inhabited planets were within range and to reach either of them would entail a reenactment of their flight from the *Nightfall*, when they had endured life support set at the minimum level for survival to eke out the fuel.

"We don't have a lot of choice about it," Carina snapped. Her nose continued to throb. She wondered if it was broken.

Parthenia hated her, and now she realized she'd persuaded her family to leave Ostillon only to face the prospect of a dangerous journey and an uncertain arrival. "So, which is it to be? The ship's data banks don't carry much information on either system. Both have only one habitable planet, and they're both backwater places, which is good."

"Huh," said Bryce. "You mean like Ostillon?"

"Right," Carina sighed. "Like I thought Ostillon was. So I guess we have no idea what the hell we're going to find."

"I vote we go to whichever is closest in that case," Ferne said.

"There's only three or four days' difference in traveling time," said Carina. "The one that's farthest away seems a slightly better bet. Its name is Pirine. The nearer one is mostly rock. That's called Goania. The inhabitants might have to ration water."

"But do these worlds belong to the Sherrerrs or the Dirksens?" asked Parthenia. "Isn't that the most important question we should be asking?"

"The ship's database is way outdated," Carina replied. "According to that, both systems are neutral, which really means they're disputed, as we know. But what difference does it make? Both clans are after us. Maybe I should try to take you out of this galactic sector entirely. Now the Sherrerrs and the Dirksens know about mages, it may be the only way you'll ever be safe."

"I'm not doing that," Parthenia said. "As soon as I can, I'm returning to Ostillon to find Castiel. And if he's left the planet I'm going to search for him. I'm not going to rest until I make sure he'll never hurt anyone again."

"I haven't given up on doing that either," Carina said. "Just not with you guys in tow."

Parthenia refused to acknowledge her words.

"I vote we go to the closest planet," Oriana said. "The rocky one. The less time we spend freezing in space the better."

"But we need water for Casting," said Carina. "If it's in short supply, that could make things difficult for us."

"Then as soon as we've refueled," Oriana said, "we leave for Pirine."

"Pirine isn't anywhere near Goania," said Carina. "That's why I wanted to talk to you about it now. We're hanging in space outside the Floria system. Once we make a decision we can't change our minds. Do you know how much it costs to fuel even a little, ancient ship like this? After we arrive at the new place, assuming we aren't detected and manage to hide the shuttle, it will take us months to work and save enough money for another journey. Whatever we decide now has to be the right choice."

Carina was beginning to rethink her decision to open the question of their destination to her brothers and sisters. She'd wanted to include them in the planning more because she was feeling bad over what she'd done to Parthenia.

She was also wondering if she'd done the right thing in escaping Ostillon. News of their escape must have gotten back to Castiel, and ships would be searching for the fine trace of a single, small shuttle fleeing the system.

Bryce had been silent for the discussion but he finally spoke. "In my opinion, you're over thinking it. We don't know enough to make an informed decision and we have no way of finding out any more information. Pirine could be a secret Sherrerr military base and Goania could be a Dirksen prison planet for all we know. Just pick one and we'll go there. We'll have to take whatever comes to us no matter what."

"So, Goania?" Carina asked.

"I guess so."

"Yes, Goania," Oriana said.

Ferne nodded.

Darius said, "I want to go wherever you think is best, Carina."

"I don't mind," said Nahla.

"I vote we return to Ostillon," said Parthenia.

"I'm sorry, but that isn't an option," Carina said. "Looks like Goania it is. I'll set the coordinates. Can you all please scour the ship for whatever you can find to help us get through the next four weeks?"

"Four weeks?!" Oriana was aghast. "That's twice as long as it took us to get to Ostillon."

"We could always go to Pirine," Carina said. "That would take us four and a half weeks."

"Ugh, I hope we find something different from ration bars to eat."

Carina doubted the shuttle had been stocked with anything else. She only hoped the rations weren't as old as the vessel itself. Leaving the others to figure out how they were going to survive the journey, she returned to the pilot's controls to input Goania's coordinates and pare down every energy consuming system on the ship to its minimum sustainable level.

They were in for a tough journey, but perhaps arriving at Goania would prove the beginning of a brighter future.

———

The bare interior of the military shuttle didn't make for the best sleeping quarters, though the vessel contained emergency gear and the children had sufficient imagination to make tolerable beds from it in the narrow aisles between seats. Carina set the quiet and active shifts. It helped to have a routine and well-defined 'days' and 'nights' to keep them from descending into apathy and depression. In the quiet shift, Carina and Bryce slept next to each other for warmth and the girls and boys similarly huddled up.

There wasn't much to do except sleep. They didn't have the ingredients to make elixir and the supply that they had was precious. They needed to save it so Darius could Cloak the ship again when they landed on Goania. After that, they might need all the Casts they could muster to remain safe.

Carina grew to enjoy settling into Bryce's arms to sleep. The physical closeness of him was her only comfort. She was wracked with self-doubt over what she was doing and fear for the lives of her siblings. Parthenia still wasn't talking to her, though the rest of her siblings didn't appear to also hate her guts. Nonetheless if that was what it took to keep them alive she would bear it.

One quiet shift, soon after she dozed off, Carina found herself on the grassy plain once more. She immediately recognized the place. She knew she'd been here many times. She also knew she was dreaming. How come she didn't recall these dreams when she awoke?

The plain was empty and all she could hear was the wind in the grass. Feeling eyes on her back, she spun around. There they were. In the distance, the familiar figures were toiling in her direction. Again, she saw the extremely old woman swathed in robes, the almost-giant of a man with a long beard, and the childlike figure.

They seemed far away, however. The last time she'd seen them they had been closer, so close the old woman had been able to look her in the eyes.

Where was she? And why did she keep returning to this place regularly when she slept? She set off walking through the grass toward the people in the distance. Perhaps if she could meet them she could ask them for an explanation. She walked quickly, wading through the thigh-high grass. She didn't know how long she would remain asleep. Time seemed to pass differently in the dream world.

But though she strode as fast as she could, she didn't draw any nearer to the group. If anything, she appeared to be moving away from them. Forcing her way through the high grass was hard. She halted while she caught her breath. Her gaze remained on the walking people, and as she watched she frowned. Though she was still and they were walking toward her, they were actually growing more distant.

What was happening? The uniform, grassy plain seemed to be growing wider as she watched. She would have to run if she wanted to draw close to them, run faster than the expansion of the plain.

"We're going the wrong way!"

Someone was shouting in her ear. Someone she knew.

Darius. What was he doing on the plain?

She woke up. Her covering had fallen off and the chill cabin air was invading her bones. Darius was hovering next to her, the same as he had been in her dream, though he was shadowy in the dim cabin, not brightly lit by a hot sun as he'd been a moment previously.

"We're going the wrong way," Darius repeated. "I didn't understand."

Bryce began to wake.

Carina sat up. "Not so loud. Everyone's trying to sleep."

"We have to turn around," said Darius.

"We can't turn around. We…Come with me." She took a cover and wrapped it around herself before going into the pilot's cabin, bringing Darius along.

"Did you have a bad dream?" she asked after closing the door.

"No, I didn't. I had a nice dream. I'm sorry, Carina. It's all my fault. I didn't understand, and I kept forgetting. And then when we were talking about where to go next, I didn't want to say anything because I wanted to do whatever you decided. But now they're telling me I made a mistake."

"They're telling you? Who are telling you?"

"The people in the *dream*," Darius explained, as if Carina was a little simple-minded.

"What people? Wait."

Darius was shaking with cold.

"Come here." She wrapped her arms around him so the blanket covered them both. "What have you been dreaming about?"

Though Darius didn't seem to have had a nightmare, he'd clearly dreamt something that had gotten him worked up and confused.

"I can't remember very well, but I'm in a new place. Outside in a field. There are people there talking to me. One of them's an old lady. She talks to me a lot, but I can't remember most of what she says. Only that we need to go to the planet with the numbers. I remembered that when we were deciding where to go, but I didn't want to say anything. I thought it was just a dream. Then tonight she was cross with me. She said we're going the wrong way and we have to turn around."

"Okay, I get it," said Carina. Darius was worried and stressed and it was affecting his sleep. It wasn't surprising, given everything that had happened. His anxiety was playing out in his dreams. She hugged her brother tightly. "I hear what you're saying, sweetheart, but it's too late for us to turn around now. We have to go to Goania because we don't have enough fuel to get us anywhere else. But it's going to be okay, Darius."

"No!" Her brother struggled free from her arms and faced her. "We have to go to the planet with the numbers."

"What do you mean? That doesn't make any sense."

"The woman said we must go to the planet that has the numbers."

Numbers? Darius had been drawing numbers obsessively for weeks. Carina decided to humor him. "What numbers? Do you want to show me?" She opened the pilot's interface and brought up the keyboard. "Type them here."

Darius tapped three sets of numbers onto the screen. Her chest tightened. She hadn't taken much notice of her brother's scrawlings, but seeing the numbers on an interface made her realize immediately they looked like galactic coordinates. What was more, the coordinates looked familiar. Her heart sinking, she looked up Pirine's coordinates. They were the same.

Noticing her expression, or perhaps absorbing her feeling, Darius' chin trembled. "I was right, wasn't I? The planet with the numbers is the one we were supposed to be going to. And I didn't tell you."

"It's okay. It's okay." She hugged her brother again while she thought things over. "Darius, who told you where we were supposed to go?" A tingling of familiarity was teasing her mind. She'd been dreaming too when Darius had woken her up. For a moment she'd thought he was part of her dream.

"The old lady," Darius replied. "But there were other people there too. I'm not sure how many."

"The old lady?" The thought of an older woman also rang a bell in Carina's mind.

The cabin door opened. Bryce was standing there, a blanket over his shoulders and his hair ruffed up. "Is everything all right?"

"Yeah, we're okay," said Carina. "You can go back to sleep."

"But we have to turn around," Darius almost yelled. His little body stiffened in Carina's arms.

"I told you, we can't. Maybe after we arrive at Goania we can refuel after a few weeks and then go to Pirine."

"Why would we want to go to Pirine?" asked Bryce. He stepped into the cabin and closed the door.

"Someone in Darius' dreams is telling him to go there. He even knew the coordinates." Carina nodded at the interface screen.

Bryce peered at the numbers. "Holy shit. That's weird."

"You're telling me. And the weirdest thing is, I think I might have been having a similar dream."

"Well, that's...." Bryce paused. He touched the cabin wall. "Hey, have we stopped?"

"Huh?" Then she noticed it too. The slight vibration of a spaceship in motion was absent. The shuttle's engine had stopped. She wiped Pirine's coordinates from the interface and brought up the operations display.

The engine was offline. But why? They had enough fuel for another two weeks' travel. Had something gone wrong somewhere? Carina ran a diagnostic.

Everything was fine, except.... She groaned. The fuel level read one hundred percent. It was impossible considering the distance they'd traveled. The gauge was faulty. The shuttle must have been carrying far less fuel than she'd thought when they set out. They hadn't had enough fuel to get them anywhere.

"What's wrong?" asked Bryce.

The Dirksens had only been using the shuttle to transport troops to and from the planet surface. They hadn't required the vessel to travel long distances. As long as the fuel was topped up, it didn't matter that they didn't know exactly how much the vessel was carrying. The mechanics were probably waiting until after the battle to fix the fault.

"Carina," Bryce said, "why have we stopped?"

"We're out of fuel."

"What? How come?"

Shit. Shit. Shit. "This ship's a piece of junk, that's how come."

She brought up their position. The display said exactly what she knew it would. They were halfway to Goania, in deep space, and far from any trade routes.

There was a click and the display flashed, *Main fuel supply exhausted. Emergency backup supply activated. Minimal life support only.* They were already running on minimal life support.

Carina did the only thing possible in the situation. It was better to be picked up than to die in the loneliness of space, even if their rescuer was a Sherrerr or a Dirksen. The chances anyone would come within range to notice the signal were slim, but it was their only hope.

She activated the distress beacon.

Twelve

Castiel woke to a chilly atmosphere in his room in the Dirksens' mountain castle. He had fallen asleep quickly after leaving Sable Dirksen, tired after the previous day's events. He didn't know how long he'd slept. The room had no windows and contained nothing to tell him the time.

He turned on the light. The room's walls were rough hewn from the pale gray mountain stone. A smaller version of the fireplace Castiel had seen in the great hall occupied the central spot on the wall opposite the bed, its grate bare. In a corner stood a wash-basin, also roughly cut from the mountain's stone. A spigot overhung the basin. In another corner sat a clothes chest. A mirror hung on the wall. And that was it. Castiel concluded that Sable Dirksen rarely hosted guests, and that when she did she took little care to spoil them with luxury.

He rose from his bed, dressed himself, and took his bottle of elixir out from underneath the covers where it had lain all night. The bottle was warmed by his body heat and he found it reassuring to hold. He would have to arrange the making of a plentiful supply soon. He had taught one of Langley's servants the method and he would do the same in his new habitation.

Castiel suddenly halted on his way to the door. Should he tell Sable about his need for elixir? It seemed unavoidable. Anyone with half a brain would notice he always took a sip of the liquid before he Cast. How much more about being a mage should he tell her, however? Whatever he told her could give her control over him, and that was the last thing he wanted. He wasn't prepared to become another clan lackey, a tool to do their bidding. If the Dirksens wanted to make use of his services, they would have to show him the respect he deserved.

He shivered. The castle really was cold, as Sable had complained. He was surprised that the Dirksens, with their love of high-tech, had failed at adequately heating the place.

He opened the door and nearly walked into the guard who was standing directly outside. For a few moments Castiel feared the man would try to prevent him from leaving, but the guard only offered to take him to Sable.

She was sitting where he'd first seen her, next to a fire in the great hall. She was alone again, but this time she was dressed. Sable Dirksen's dark tunic flared out at the shoulders and overhung narrow pants. She looked far more like the head of the Dirksen clan this morning than she had last night, though she still seemed ridiculously young for the position. Castiel judged it unwise to voice his impressions.

Another armchair had been added opposite Sable's as well as a small table on which breakfast dishes stood. Castiel sat down at the armchair without being invited, determined to maintain an attitude of confidence and control.

"Good morning," he said as he helped himself to breakfast.

Sable's dark-eyed gaze flicked at him. "How did you sleep?"

"Well, thank you." He was amusedly reminded of the conversational style of his father and mother. So much had passed unsaid between them. "Though my room was cold."

"Ah, yes. We've never been able to heat this older section of the castle adequately. The stone seems to suck all warmth out of the air no matter what heating devices we install. I keep a fire lit here all the time."

Castiel continued to eat while he considered how best to approach the subject of his desired role in the Dirksen clan.

"I'm curious to learn more about the ability you demonstrated last night," said Sable. "How did you kill that Sherrerr admiral?"

"It's just something I can do. Among many other things."

"Like what?"

Castiel put down his plate. "I'd rather talk about your plans for me."

"It's hard to make any plans unless I know how I can use you."

"If you tell me more about what the Dirksens intend to accomplish, I could explain how I can help."

"We intend many things. Apart from killing people in a rather horrible way, what else do you have to offer?"

Castiel pursed his lips and stared at Sable. They were already at stalemate and they'd barely been talking for one minute.

But then the Dirksen clan leader raised a finger to her ear and leaned slightly forward as if listening. "Send him in," she said, adding, to Castiel, "You can stay."

This permission-giving irked him. He felt his status was above being told when he could remain or leave, but he resigned himself to bearing the insult for the time being.

A shaven-headed officer in a Dirksen uniform entered the hall. He took in Castiel's presence with a brief glance as he strode to stand in front of Sable and saluted. "I am honored to formally convey the news that our forces have successfully repulsed the Sherrerr attack, ma'am. Shortly after the *Nightfall* self-destructed, the rest of the Sherrerr fleet departed. A thorough check of the system has discovered no enemy ships."

"Thank you, Commander Kee. That is good news." Sable paused, then added. "Commander, I would like to introduce you to Castiel Sherrerr."

The man quickly suppressed his look of surprise and delivered a curt nod to Castiel.

"He's been on Ostillon for some time, staying at Langley Dirksen's residence. I believe I'm correct in saying he has renounced his affiliation with his clan?" Sable looked toward Castiel for confirmation.

"Yes, of course," Castiel blurted.

"Perhaps you're wondering if he's connected to the young merc in the Sherrerr shuttle you picked up?" Sable asked the commander. "The answer is yes. From what I understand, the two are related. He gave me a demonstration of his strange power last night when I asked him to interrogate a prisoner. He killed her."

"*Killed*, ma'am?" Kee's eyebrows lifted.

"The commander is one of our top interrogators," Sable explained to Castiel. "It seems he also disapproves of your methods."

"That was...hasty of me, I admit," Castiel said. "But I have other things I can try, if you'll give me a second chance."

"Uh..." said Commander Kee, clearly dying to object but unable to break protocol and speak without first being addressed. "Permission to—"

"Don't worry, Commander. I won't be letting him loose on any more of our precious prisoners just yet. Not until I have a much better understanding of what he does. While you're here, why don't you go and see what you can find out from the remaining ones? When they hear their friends have departed and they're alone without a hope of rescue they might feel more inclined to divulge something."

"Yes, ma'am."

Kee saluted and left, striding toward the exit that led to the lower level.

"Castiel," said Sable, "I feel like we've gotten off on the wrong foot. Why don't we try again? Would you like me to show you around my abode? It's quite an unusual residence, isn't it?"

"I-I'd like that," replied Castiel, somewhat taken aback by her sudden change of attitude.

"Come with me. We'll start at the peak." Sable rose and led Castiel across the hall to a small elevator. "I had to have this put in when I arrived," she said as the doors opened. "The castle floors rise to the very top of the mountain, but all there was to move between them was stairs. Can you believe it?"

They stepped inside the elevator and the doors closed.

"So what I was thinking was correct," said Castiel. "The Dirksens didn't build this place."

"That's right. We squeezed the secret of its existence inadvertently from an Ostillonian official. I forget who it was. He thought the information might buy him some clemency. He was wrong. I found the castle perfect for my needs, however, so I moved in. I've added some sections since then."

Castiel surveyed Sable from the corners of his eyes. He knew the Dirksens had taken over the planet several years previously. How old had their leader been then? She had to be older than she looked.

They rode the elevator to the top floor, and the doors opened to reveal a small, round room encircled by narrow, arched windows without glass. They stepped out and Castiel immediately walked to a window. A keen wind blew through it. The view was magnificent. They were at the very top of the mountain and he could see for miles all around.

"It's certainly something, right?" Sable said. "I come up here sometimes to think."

"But doesn't this place give away the fact that there's something inside the mountain? Aren't you worried someone looking at the mountain range could spot it?"

"It isn't visible from the outside, the same as the entrance you flew in through."

"That's amazing. I don't think the Sherrerrs have that tech yet."

Sable gave a small chuckle. "We don't have that tech either. It's how the place was when we arrived. We needed precise directions from the Ostillonian to find it. He said the few locals who know about it don't talk of it because they think the place is cursed. I have to say, considering the problems we have with heating it, sometimes I'm inclined to agree."

They spent a few minutes gazing at the view before descending to the level below. As the morning progressed, Castiel saw most of the castle. Several of the rooms rose stories high. These were the coldest parts of the castle and they were entirely bare, as if Sable never used them. She also showed him many rooms and suites for sleeping and living, and the usual service areas. While they were walking the corridors they passed servants and people in rich clothes. Though Sable nodded greetings at the latter, she did not introduce Castiel to them. He guessed they were high-ranking Dirksens.

He was impressed by the size and intricacy of the place, as well as mildly curious about who had constructed it. One thing he noticed was that all of the residential areas contained spigots, even though the restrooms were plentiful. In all, however, he found himself becoming bored. He imagined there were more exciting and influential things he could be doing if Sable would allow him.

As they walked, she asked him about his experiences at Langley Dirksen's estate. He guessed that she was mining him for information on Langley's behavior regarding him. Though she didn't give much away, Castiel understood that Langley had misled Sable about how long he'd stayed at her mansion and what he'd done. He didn't hesitate to set Sable right. He felt no loyalty to Langley whatsoever. She had stymied his attempts to rise in the Dirksen hierarchy.

When they returned to the great hall, Commander Kee was awaiting them.

"Commander," said Sable, "did you find out anything useful?"

"Not yet, ma'am," he replied. "I hope you don't mind, but I took the liberty of removing the remains of the dead prisoner. I'm afraid to say the death has probably set back my work for several weeks." His face was rigid as he steadfastly refused to look at Castiel.

"I'm sorry to hear it," said Sable, "but it can't be helped. Please continue to work with the officers this afternoon. In the meantime, would you join us for lunch?"

"I would be delighted, ma'am."

"Castiel, please take a seat while I make the arrangements. Kee, come with me." Sable left with the commander.

Castiel sat down, wondering if the Dirksen leader had taken Kee into her room at night. As he watched her leave, he again hoped to be one of the chosen. He was young, but he was already growing a beard. Perhaps in time Sable would come to respect and desire him.

———

He spent the next half hour watching servants prepare for a formal lunch. They brought in straight-backed chairs and a table, and spread the table with a cloth before setting out the dining wear. Castiel wasn't impressed by the finery, if that was Sable's intention. His upbringing had made him used to such things. He grew bored. He was tempted to Transport something out of a servant's hands just to make them jump. But he decided against the idea. He didn't want to waste elixir until he had a stable supply.

Finally, when the servants had brought in the food and drinks, Sable and Commander Kee returned. Sable invited Castiel to join them.

A servant filled his glass with wine, to his great pleasure. The Dirksen leader was treating him like an adult. He lifted the glass and took a large gulp of the alcohol. It didn't taste as good as he'd thought it would, but he enjoyed the pleasant, hot feeling as the liquid slid down his throat into his stomach.

When the servants had uncovered all the dishes, they withdrew.

Castiel took another large swallow of wine. An unfamiliar wooziness began to invade his mind. Over the brim of his glass, he noticed Kee watching him. Was he drinking too much? Castiel set down his glass.

"Please help yourself," Sable said to Castiel. "I hope you don't mind no servants waiting on us. I hate having people hovering around me as I eat."

"I don't mind," Castiel said. "Though I'm used to servants."

"I guess you must be," said Kee, "as one of the most important members of the Sherrerrs."

"Oh, I wasn't...." Castiel paused, uncertain as to what would be most beneficial for him to tell them regarding his position in the Sherrerr hierarchy. From things his father had said, he'd guessed that his family hadn't been as important as Father would have liked. But that had changed on the *Nightfall*, when Carina and the others had blown up the Dirksen shipyard. "I mean, yes, that's right."

"Your clan must be feeling your loss acutely, I imagine," Sable said.

"Yes, they must be," said Castiel. "Acutely. They don't have any mages on their side anymore, you see."

Was that a flicker of a glance between Sable and Kee? Castiel wasn't sure, but it didn't matter. They might think they'd won a tidbit of information, but he was feeling suddenly generous.

He took a spoonful of food from a dish and piled it on his plate. The wine and the cold of the castle were making him hungry. Sable and Kee also ate and drank a little wine.

"We guessed the Sherrerrs had some kind of special advantage over us," Sable said. "We've known it for years. The problem was figuring out what it was. I'm glad you're here to enlighten us."

"I'm not only here to enlighten you, I'm here to help you. The *Nightfall* is only one example of what I can do. There's plenty more I have to offer...for the right price," Castiel said, his confidence swelling. Now they were finally having the conversation he'd wanted all along.

"Why don't you begin by telling us all about mages?" said Kee. "I don't know anything about them."

"Mages?" Castiel said. "Where do I start? Let me think for a moment." He drank some more wine. He felt dizzy and relaxed. "Well, it's an ability that runs in families. My mother was a mage—"

"Was?" Kee interjected.

"Yes. Both of my parents are dead. Anyway, I inherited my ability from her."

"Fascinating," said Kee, resting his chin on steepled fingertips. "Tell me more."

Castiel, gratified to have Sable and Kee's full attention, told them everything he remembered from eavesdropping on his mother's lessons. He told them about all the Casts he knew, and elixir, and the Characters, and even the snippets about Seasons and other stuff he'd gleaned, though those parts hadn't made much sense to him.

Sable and Kee listened quietly as he spoke, only interrupting to ask for clarification or more details. Castiel's sense of self-importance grew and he began to embellish his descriptions with stories of services he'd performed for the Sherrerrs. In truth, it had been Parthenia who had performed most of the feats he described, but if his abilities had developed earlier *he* would have done them so that didn't matter.

Feeling hungry, he wound down and began to eat his food, which had grown cold on his plate.

"Thank you," said Kee. "That was very enlightening. Just one more thing. You have sisters and brothers who are mages too, if I'm not mistaken?"

Castiel's mouth was full so he only nodded. He'd deliberately left out any mention of Carina and the others. He hadn't wanted Sable or Kee to get the idea that any of his siblings were more valuable to them than himself.

"Langley told me you have at least three sisters," said Sable. "and we're aware of a much younger boy who I presume is your brother."

Castiel swallowed. "I have another brother too. But you don't need them. They can't do as much as I can."

"I believe I've met one of your sisters myself," said Kee. "But even if your siblings' abilities aren't as great as yours they're a danger to us nevertheless. Do you know what's happened to them? Are they still on Ostillon?"

"I've been searching for signs of them, but I haven't turned up anything yet."

"What sort of signs?" asked Kee.

"Reports of extraordinary events, like fires starting for no reason, or people appearing out of thin air. But the war eclipsed all the news reports. I haven't noticed anything I thought worth pursuing. Though I doubt they've left the planet. No domestic ships have departed Ostillon since the Sherrerr attack began, right? I was waiting for the war to end so I could comb the planet for them. They can't hide forever."

Kee frowned. "I heard something strange only yesterday, not long after the *Nightfall* was destroyed. A company sergeant said the shuttle transport his soldiers were to board disappeared. They were going to be court martialed, but when the officials checked the camera footage, the vessel did seem to disappear. Could your siblings have had something to do with that?"

"An entire shuttle?" Castiel thought about it. He guessed it was possible that Carina might have been able to Transport an entire space vessel. But then the soldiers would have seen the shuttle move. Then he remembered their flight from the *Nightfall*, after Mother had killed Father. Darius had babbled something about how he'd 'done it.' *Damn.* Had Darius made his special Cast again? "It might be possible."

Kee cursed. "I bet they've returned to the Sherrerrs."

"No," Castiel said. "They would never do that. If they have left Ostillon, they've only run away. We won't be seeing them again." He was annoyed. He'd hoped to use his siblings for his own ends, but in some ways he was better off without them. Now the Dirksens only had one mage at their disposal, he had more control.

"I wouldn't be too sure of that," said Sable. "If these people aren't here and working with us, they're a liability. I'm not going to be happy as long as I know these mages are roaming the galaxy. Kee, I want you to find them. Find out which vessel went missing. Scan the outer system and the heliopause. None of the Sherrerr ships will leave a trace like a shuttle's. Hopefully, whatever Castiel's brother did it won't last forever and you'll be able to detect something. Follow the trace. They'll be at the end of it."

"If you send a ship after them I should be on it," said Castiel. "They're mages. You'll need my help to capture them."

"You think they could defeat a destroyer with these Casts you told us about?" Kee asked.

"No, but..." It was unlikely that even Carina could repel a large military craft, and Castiel was reluctant to give the impression that any one of his siblings' powers was stronger than his own.

"I think we can manage," said Sable with a condescending smile. "Please get on it now, Kee."

"Yes, ma'am." The commander stood and left the hall.

If the Dirksens did find Castiel's siblings, he would have to be very careful. He would have to ensure his brothers and sisters remained under *his* control and not the Dirksens'. He also had to watch out they didn't try to usurp his new position in the clan.

Castiel was about to take another sip of wine, but his stomach felt bad. His wooziness had increased, and a horrible feeling was creeping over him. He put down his fork. He didn't feel at all well, and he couldn't remember exactly what he'd told Sable and Kee. The details were hazy, but he suspected he might have told them more than was wise.

All of a sudden, saliva flooded his mouth. He only just had time to turn his head and lean over before he vomited. A sour mix of wine and half-digested food poured out of him in great gushes, splattering on the stone floor and splashing onto his legs.

Hot shame and tears welled up, but there was nothing he could do to stop the humiliating event. His experiences at Sable Dirksen's headquarters were definitely not turning out so well after all.

Thirteen

The news that the shuttle was out of fuel and they were adrift went down about as well as Carina expected.

Oriana wailed, "Noooo!"

Parthenia gave Carina a sour look that said, *So you thought you were saving me?*

Ferne was silent and stoic. Nahla didn't seem to know how was best to react.

Darius said, "I'm sorry I didn't tell you, Carina."

"You don't have anything to be sorry for."

"Sorry you didn't tell her what?" Oriana asked. "Does that mean we could have avoided this?"

"It's nothing," said Carina. "Just a dream Darius was having. He thinks we should have gone to Pirine."

"Well, should we?" asked Oriana. "What kind of dream?"

"Look, we're here now. There's no point in talking about what ifs. Our distress signal will be picked up eventually and someone will come along and save us. We have plenty of rations and water. We only have to be patient and wait."

Carina was trying to be more upbeat than she felt. She'd deliberately left out the fact that they were in the middle of nowhere, in sparsely trafficked space where cargo transporters and other inter-system craft rarely traveled. Telling her family more than they needed to know served no purpose and would only make them more afraid.

"So we can look forward to even more weeks of this?" asked Oriana. "I'm not sure I can stand it."

"You're going to have to stand it," Carina snapped.

"Yes," said Ferne. "Stop whining, Oriana. I'm sick of your constant complaints."

Oriana's face fell at this rare rebuke from her twin. She stood up and stalked away. As there were very few places for her to stalk to, realistically, she faced the bulkhead with her arms folded.

Ferne rolled his eyes but didn't otherwise react. In the end it was little Nahla who went to attend to Oriana's sulk. She put a hand on her sister's back and also faced the wall, perhaps to offer some companionship. Oriana didn't react but tolerated the little girl's presence.

"Okay," Carina said. "Let's make a start by figuring out how few ration bars we can eat a day and still survive. We haven't been keeping count because we thought we had plenty to last us. But we should think about how many we need to not feel too hungry."

"We should make a cleaning schedule too," said Bryce. "We haven't been cleaning up after ourselves and it shows. This place is disgusting."

"You're right," Carina said. "Great idea." Bryce's suggestion made her feel a bit less alone in her responsibility to save all their lives.

"Aww, I hate cleaning," said Darius.

"How would you know?" Parthenia asked. "You've never cleaned anything in your life. None of us has, really. We always had servants to do that kind of thing."

Carina tensed. Was Parthenia going to start complaining too?

But her sister continued, "So now's a good time to start. I'll put together a rota."

Carina thanked her, but Parthenia pretended she hadn't heard.

The meeting broke up. Carina was wondering if she should talk to Oriana when an alarm sounded in the pilot's cabin. She groaned. What had gone wrong now? Giving Bryce a worried look, she went to find out.

The scanners indicated a ship was approaching. She couldn't believe it. How was it possible that another vessel had heard their distress signal so quickly? She was about to shout out the joyful news when a realization hit. The ship had not hailed them, and it was almost impossible their signal had been picked up so quickly.

What was far more likely was the ship had been on their tail, and now the shuttle had stopped the pursuers had caught up.

Just when she was thinking they were in a bad way, things had gotten even worse.

"What is it?" Bryce asked as he entered the cabin.

"Enemy ship. I'm guessing it's the Dirksens'."

"Are you sure? Maybe it's come to rescue us."

"Not likely. Not so soon. And I can't think of a better explanation for a ship suddenly appearing the minute we stop. Can you?"

"No. So, what do we do?"

Carina was already running through the possible courses of action. They had enough elixir for a few Casts. They would have no choice about being boarded. The little shuttle carried no weaponry. The question was, what could they do after that to avoid being taken back to Ostillon?

Could they take over an entire ship? It would be hard, probably impossible, but they had to try.

Carina checked the scan readings on the approaching ship. The fact the vessel wasn't hailing them confirmed her conclusion this was no rescue. She only hoped Castiel hadn't ordered the Dirksens to blow his siblings to pieces.

But the vessel was a destroyer and already within range to fire. If Castiel had wanted them dead they would be atomized by now. No. He wanted the mages alive and under his control.

"I hope Castiel isn't aboard," said Carina, "or we're screwed. If he isn't, we stand a chance. We can use the remaining elixir to Cast the best we can and take command of the ship."

"You want to try to take command of an entire destroyer?" asked Bryce, watching the display.

"Do you have any better ideas? We can't get away from it, and the only alternative to taking it over is to trigger its self-destruct. If we did that we would be right back where we started: adrift with scant hope of rescue."

"I guess you're right."

"Okay, take over the ship is what we do. It'll reach us in a couple of minutes. I have to tell the others what's happening and make a plan."

But as she stepped past Bryce to leave the cabin, he said, "Carina, wait. Look."

She swung around to look again at the display, and her eyes popped. Another ship was approaching. *Two* ships? Carina checked and double-checked the readings, wondering if the faulty fuel gauge wasn't the only problem with the shuttle's instruments. But as far as she could tell the information was accurate.

"What's happening?" Ferne asked, poking his head around the cabin door.

"Uh, I have no idea," Carina replied.

Then the first ship fired on the newcomer.

"What the hell?" Bryce exclaimed.

A beat later the pulse hit. The second ship appeared to survive the blast.

"Are they fighting over us?" asked Bryce. "Is the other one a Sherrerr ship?"

It was the only explanation, but the answer brought more questions. It was conceivable the Dirksens had tracked them to their current position by following their trace. Darius' Cloak Cast would have dissipated eventually. But how had the Sherrerrs found them? Or had they been following the Dirksens' destroyer?

The Dirksen ship fired again, and again the pulse impacted the Sherrerr vessel at close quarters. Somehow, the vessel withstood the second blow, and once more it didn't return fire. Carina watched the battle curiously, more worried about what would happen afterward than which side won. The mages' fate was equally dicey whatever the outcome.

She couldn't understand why the Sherrerr ship wasn't returning fire. Its captain didn't seem to be trying to engage in a parley.

Then the readings went crazy. A split second later, something hit the shuttle. The force of the impact threw her against the bulkhead. Her back collided with a strut, and the next few minutes were confused chaos as the vessel tumbled over and over. She was flung around the pilot's cabin, colliding with Bryce. She put her head down and tucked herself into a ball to minimize the damage to her body.

Finally, the tumbling slowed enough for her to grab the back of the pilot's seat and steady herself. Bryce was out cold, bobbing next to the ceiling. Blood welled from a cut on his head, forming a thick pool of red that dispersed in globules. The a-grav was out.

"Bryce." She pushed against the shuttle console with her feet to reach him. He moaned and his eyes opened. He was coming around. "Bryce, can you hear me? Are you okay?"

His gaze focused on her. "I'm all right, I think. Head hurts."

Letting go of his shirt, she propelled herself into the main cabin of the slowly spinning vessel. The children were scared and crying. There were several bumps and grazes, but no one seemed to have suffered a serious injury. The piles of makeshift bedding had served as buffers between them and the hard shell of the cabin interior.

"What's going on?" Ferne asked. "Is someone attacking us?"

"I don't know," Carina replied. "I don't think so." If either of the battling ships had wanted to destroy the shuttle they could have done so easily and no one would have had time to register what had happened.

"Carina," Bryce called.

She gripped the handlebars that lined the bulkhead and pulled herself into the pilot's cabin. Bryce was hanging over the controls, droplets of blood suspended in a cloud around his head.

"It's gone. The destroyer that arrived first. It's been blown to bits."

"So that's what happened," said Carina. "The Sherrerr ship finally fired back. The debris hit us."

A warning flashed on the console display and at the same time yet another alarm began to wail. She cursed. The shuttle was leaking atmosphere.

"As if we don't have enough problems." She swept the interface with her fingers, bringing up the site of the leak. The shuttle should auto repair, but she wanted to check that it was. "Shit." The vessel hadn't been alerting them to a leak, but *leaks*. The impact of the exploded ship's debris had riddled them full of holes. It was a miracle no one had been hit.

She hoped the Sherrerr ship intended to pick them up quickly. They were losing air so fast, if it didn't they were dead.

She devoted the shuttle's remaining power to atmosphere generation to try to match the loss, or they would all be unconscious in minutes. Meanwhile, she briefed the others on what to do if they were boarded. She hadn't given up on her idea of taking over the enemy ship.

A comm arrived. "Unidentified shuttle prepare to be boarded."

It was odd the other ship hadn't identified itself. She would have expected a Sherrerr vessel to state its affiliation.

"Are you ready, everyone?" she asked.

Darius was going to lead their defense, Enthralling whoever came through the hatch. Then they would have an indefinite amount of time to 'persuade' the Enthralled to give up their weapons and take them to their ship's bridge.

It wouldn't be easy, but they really might be able to do it.

Carina floated on one side of the hatch, waiting. Bryce waited on the other side. The children clung to the backs of seats, doing their best to hide. Darius peaked around his seat, looking nervous.

The hatch lock released and the portal opened.

Carina gave Darius a nod. He nodded back and swallowed elixir before shutting his eyes. People emerged through the shuttle entrance.

Now, Darius.

Her brother cried out and jerked backward, as if impacted by an unseen force.

Carina reeled in shock. What was going on? Who had Repulsed Darius' Cast? Had Castiel returned to the Sherrerrs?

Bryce barreled into the side of one of the boarders, sending the man careening into the others. Carina also pushed off the wall and dove into the melee. She tried to wrest a weapon from its owner's grip. She was battling the assailants, spinning in zero-g.

Suddenly, she found herself looking at the stock of a pulse rifle. A curse formed on her lips but she didn't have time to utter it before she was knocked out.

FOURTEEN

Castiel stood in the bright Ostillonian sunlight, hot and angry. Standing on the balcony of a building in the capital, he took a swig of elixir. He concentrated on writing the Transport character, then sent out the Cast toward the roof of a collapsed house. The roof lifted, shedding dust and fragments of plaster, drifted out into the street, and fell to the road with a crash.

Bystanders who had been near the spot where the shattered roof had landed hastily scattered, looking up at him in fear.

He didn't care what the people thought of him. They shouldn't have been standing so near the damaged building. He wished he could Cast some kind of pain or misfortune at them.

Sable had set him the task of helping to clear destroyed and unsafe buildings. When she'd made her request, she'd been extremely flattering, telling him how invaluable his services would be and how much recognition and gratitude he would receive. He'd thought she'd meant recognition and gratitude from the high-ranking Dirksens. Now he understood that in fact she'd meant the people of Ostillon.

What did he care what the lowly folk of that planet thought of him? If he cared anything at all about their feelings, he would have preferred to have their fear and respect, not their gratitude.

It hadn't taken him long to realize it had all been a trick. Sable had side-lined him just as smoothly as Langley had, if not more so. At least Langley had arranged for him to have a hand in defeating the Sherrerr attack. Sable seemed intent on making him some kind of glorified janitor or handyman.

It was ridiculous, and he was determined to do something about it. If approaching the head of the clan hadn't worked to elevate his status, he would have to take more drastic measures.

Only he hadn't decided exactly what just yet.

Castiel left the balcony and climbed the stairs to the roof, where a hover vehicle awaited him. He had a few more tasks to complete today. Though he was loath to do them, he thought he might as well and spend the time figuring out his next steps. It never hurt to practice Casting.

He climbed into the vehicle, and the driver lifted them up over the city. It was indeed a devastated place. Parts of the metropolis had been entirely razed by the Sherrerr attack. In other places great craters opened like wounds, surrounded by charred remains of buildings. The amount of work required to restore the once-thriving capital would be enormous. But it was not his problem.

Castiel recalled the conversation he'd had with Sable in the great hall of her mountain castle yesterday evening. He'd tried every well-mannered tactic he could think of to persuade the woman to expand her use of his abilities, but she'd managed to rebuff each point.

We're devoting our efforts to recuperation and planning at the moment, Sable had said. *When the time is right, I'll introduce you to the rest of the council. I'm sure they will suggest other roles you can play. We need to understand better what you can do and figure out how to fit you into our advancement and expansion. Have some patience, Castiel. Your moment to shine will come.*

It had all sounded reassuring, but Sable had been careful to never mention exactly *when* his moment would come. He wasn't dumb. He was being put off, perhaps indefinitely. Did she fear his powers? He guessed so. Most people did.

The hover vehicle alighted in a street. The place looked like it had been a poor, derelict area even before it had suffered the Sherrerr bombardment. His task was to demolish an apartment block that had received a direct hit. Half of the building was torn away and the other half was leaning at a dangerous angle.

Castiel looked up at the broken rooms, their contents revealed to the world. Clothes hung from the torn floors. Wall decorations fluttered in the breeze. On the second floor, a corpse sat in a bathtub, a look of surprise on its rotting face.

"Ugh, disgusting."

His driver didn't answer.

There was a knock on his window. A little girl was standing there, her face and clothes filthy and her hair a tangle of knots.

"Have you come to rescue my grandpa?" the girl asked, though her voice was muffled by the glass.

Castiel looked down at her rags and then up at her face once more before turning his head away pointedly. The little girl rubbed her eyes and wandered to the rear of the vehicle.

"Please move farther down the street," he instructed the driver.

"The exhaust may burn the child."

"And?"

The driver opened his door and climbed out.

"My grandpa's stuck in there," said the girl, pointing at the precarious apartment block. "Can you get him out, please?"

The driver shooed her away. He returned to his seat and moved the vehicle another ten meters along the street.

"If the man's been in that building all this time, he must be dead by now," Castiel said, half to himself. He wasn't a law enforcement officer or a splicer. If Sable had wanted to have people rescued, she should have sent someone else.

He swigged his elixir, wrote the Break character, and delivered the Cast to the building remains. The structure rumbled and shook. The little girl stared at it and screamed. Bricks and concrete began to shatter and fall, and just in time the girl sped out of the way.

Castiel watched the slow, sliding collapse of walls, rooms, and apartments. Clouds of dust rose, obscuring the demolished site. As the dust began to settle, he looked with pleasure on the pile of rubble that now blocked the street. Only hover vehicles would be able to traverse it. The girl was nowhere to be seen.

Perhaps he should have done a better job. He could Transport some of the rubble away and create a gap. But he would not. If Sable wouldn't bend to persuasion, perhaps he could show enough apparent incompetence to be assigned to different duties. Even doing nothing would be better than his current work.

He'd been cooperative, but maybe the time for cooperation was over. Sable had seen what he was capable of when he killed Tremoille. She should be more careful about how she treated him, especially if she refused to allow him to rise in the clan. Someone who has nothing, has nothing to lose.

That was the answer. No more playing nice. He would return to the mountain castle and lay it on the line for Sable. Either she would give him a position worthy of his abilities or he would use them against her.

"Take me back to the headquarters," Castiel told the driver.

"I thought we had more assignments, sir."

"Don't talk back. Do as you're told."

Immediately, the vehicle lifted from the dusty street. When they were high above the capital, the driver turned and flew them in the direction of the mountains.

———

As the vehicle landed inside the mountain castle, Castiel opened the door and stepped out, intent on confronting Sable. She might be the head of the Dirksen clan, but she was still only one woman, and a young one at that. She was an ordinary human being, while *he* was a mage. She would listen to him or she would suffer for it.

He strode into the great hall. The stone chair was empty as always, but so was Sable's usual seat by the fire, where she would conduct her business via interface or in person. And the fire was out, as if she hadn't been there all day.

A servant who had been cleaning the hall when Castiel entered, hurried toward an exit.

"Hey, you," Castiel shouted. "Where is Madam Dirksen?"

"I don't know, sir. The mistress left this morning, not long after yourself."

He cursed. He didn't know how to contact her. She hadn't shown him enough respect to tell him. Her disregard really was unbearable.

While he hesitated, wondering what to do, his interface chirruped. He'd received a message. He pulled out the device and read it. The message was from Sable. How had she found out where he was so soon?

I see you've returned early, Castiel Sherrerr.

I wanted to speak to you this evening, but something urgent has called me away. I've been thinking about your brothers and sisters. There's still no message from the Torpille, *the ship that went after the shuttle they stole. I can only assume the worst, that somehow they destroyed their pursuer.*

Your siblings must be captured and punished for their crime. I'm also concerned about what they might do while at liberty. Perhaps they will gather a force of mages and attack us. I want to prevent this possibility.

I have sent another ship to try to discover what happened to the Torpille. *If the ship is lost, I hope to find out where your siblings went.*

Perhaps I should have taken your advice and allowed you to go with the ship. S.D.

Castiel's anger and frustration drained away. This was more like it. Sable Dirksen was finally recognizing his worth in the clan. He would insist on going along on any further expeditions to discover his siblings' whereabouts. He would be there when they were captured.

With Carina and the others under his control, he would create an entire wing of a new Dirksen force. A mage division. Like it or not, his brothers and sisters would help him cut a swathe through the Sherrerr-controlled areas of the galactic sector. They would be unstoppable. Then, when the time was right, he would make his move and assume control of the Dirksen clan.

He had a vision of four women standing outside his bedroom. All of them beautiful. All for his use. One of the women was Sable Dirksen. He saw himself walk up and down the line, surveying each woman from head to toe. Perhaps, if she was lucky, one night he would choose the former leader of the Dirksen clan.

But that was for the future. Sable's message had calmed him somewhat. He was glad he'd heard from her rather than seen her in person. His anger might have made him hasty and he could have said things he later regretted.

He must remember that though he was a mage, he was alone. He had no guards to command, nowhere secure to sleep. His room had a lock, but that didn't mean he was safe. Someone could still break in and steal his elixir while he slept, leaving him powerless.

He must not let ambition and impatience be his downfall. Father had waited years to play a bigger role in Sherrerr affairs. He must exercise the same restraint.

Yet the days' frustrations had left him tired. He decided to go to his room and rest while he awaited Sable's return. He left the hall and climbed the cold stone stairs to the corridor that led to his room. When he arrived he was surprised to see the door stood a little ajar. Someone was inside. Was someone searching his things?

But when he stepped in, he found the intruder was only the servant who had been assigned to him. The young woman was preparing his fire.

"Oh, I'm sorry, sir. I wasn't expecting you back so early. I'll finish as quickly as I can and leave you alone."

The good news about Sable's change of attitude had left him feeling generous. "Don't worry. Take your time." He lay down on his bed and put his hands behind his head. From under half-closed eyes, he watched the young woman pile wood into the grate and light it.

He had become accustomed to the servant over the weeks she'd performed her duties. He could almost say he liked her. She was always extremely respectful. He didn't think she'd even once looked him in the eye, and she rarely addressed him unless he spoke to her directly.

She was also—he hadn't failed to notice—very pretty.

He watched her languidly, imagining her as one of the women he would line up outside his door. What if he chose her over Sable? Ha! That would make the ex-clan leader spit.

"All done, sir," said the servant, straightening up.

Smoke was rising from the wood and circling lazily up the chimney.

"I hope it warms your room nicely," the young woman continued, keeping her gaze firmly downward. "This place is always so chilly."

The sentences were probably the most the servant had spoken to him at one encounter. He was surprised, and intrigued. She seemed to have a purpose to her loquaciousness, but he couldn't figure out what it was.

"It is cold in this castle," he agreed, sitting up.

The servant lifted her head and looked him directly in the eyes. "Is there anything else I can do for you, sir?"

His throat tightened. Did she mean what he thought she meant? Were his fantasies about to become reality? He almost said, *Like what*? but quickly realized what a fool he would sound. Instead, he tried to see how far he could take this potential opportunity. "Actually, there is."

The servant approached his bed, her gaze locked onto his. There could be no mistaking her intent. When she reached him, she bent down to take off her shoes.

He almost couldn't believe it. It was finally happening. He'd imagined a different kind of scenario, where he would take what he wanted whether the girl agreed to let him or not. So this was strange. But good. Good enough. She had to find him irresistible.

She sat on the edge of his bed and began to unfasten her blouse.

Fifteen

When Carina woke the first thing she noticed was the familiar vibration of a ship's engine. The boarders must have carried her onto their vessel. She was lying on a padded surface rather than the hard floor of a cell, and she didn't seem to be restrained. *Good*. The Sherrerrs who had captured them were clearly idiots.

She opened her eyes to slits. The room was white and brightly lit. She could hear someone moving around, but she couldn't see the person due to the angle of her head. Her eyes faced the corner of the ceiling. She didn't want to move or her captors would know she was awake. If they thought she remained unconscious they might say something significant.

In the end, it was Darius' voice she heard.

"Ow! Don't do that! No!"

She was up in an instant, launching herself in the direction of her brother's voice. Darius was lying on his front on a bed, and someone was leaning over him and touching his hair. She leapt onto the man's back and grabbed his forehead and chin before wrenching his head around, trying to break his neck.

"Whaaaaa! Argh!" The man stumbled backward, sending her crashing into the wall. He stumbled forward. She clung onto his back, feeling for his eyes. Together, they fell into some equipment. The metal implements scattered over the floor. The man fell down and rolled onto his back, trying to dislodge her.

"Help!" he shouted. "Someone help me!"

She had raked her nails over his face but failed to damage his eyes. She switched tactics and gripped his neck, digging hard into his arteries. Moments later he relaxed under her grip. She crawled out from underneath his large, heavy body.

One down, how many more to go? With disappointment she saw he was unarmed. She stood up. There was a movement in the doorway. She turned, but before she could see what had caused it she felt the familiar and dreaded burst of a stun hitting her in the side.

The next time she woke, she felt tight restraints around her wrists and ankles. Those Sherrerr troops were getting smarter. But when she opened her eyes, she was surprised to see Bryce looking down at her.

"You're back with us?" He touched her hair affectionately. "Don't worry. You're safe. We're all safe."

"Huh?" She lifted her head. She was in the same place. Now she had time to have a good look at it, she realized it was a medical bay. Darius lay in the next bed along from hers, asleep.

"They put me here to talk to you as soon as you woke up," said Bryce. "So you wouldn't go on another rampage. You already made yourself one enemy in that splicer you attacked."

"I don't give a shit about a Sherrerr splicer."

"He isn't a Sherrerr. He's a mage."

"He's a *what*?" In order to see Darius better, she had lifted her head. It hit her pillow with a thump. "What the hell are you talking about?"

"That guy you tried to kill? He's a mage. They all call him a Healer, though. He was cleaning dried blood out of Darius' hair when you woke up and launched a full-scale assault." Bryce seemed to find what he was saying very funny.

"I.... Oh." Her mind was spinning. "Mages picked us up? How? Who are they? Bryce, what's going on?" She wondered if she'd been stunned in the head and was in a waking dream, or going mad.

"I don't know what's going on any more than you do. Apart from what I've told you. They've said they'll explain everything soon. They also said they aren't going to hurt us. They're here to help."

———

Carina sat opposite the man she'd attacked, feeling slightly abashed about what she'd done. But the scratches she'd gouged on his face were gone and she guessed he must have Healed any further damage she'd done. From the look he was giving her, however, his opinion of her would take longer to heal.

They were seated in a meeting room aboard the mages' ship, the *Haihu*.

Only she and her oldest sister had been invited to the meeting. Bryce, as a non-mage, had been excluded, and her brothers and sisters were deemed too young to attend. Parthenia was making her hatred clear, as usual. She was sitting several seats away at the round table.

In all, four other mages were present, including an older woman, a young man, and a young woman. The Healer was a large, black-haired man. She caught her breath. She recognized him. He was one of the people she'd seen in her recurring dream. Parthenia was also looking at him curiously.

"Shall we get the introductions over with?" the older, white-haired woman asked. "I'm Eira, your captain. This is Ren, our navigator...." The young man nodded. "And Ione, our weapons officer." The redhead smiled. "I believe you've already met our Healer, Justin."

Justin did not smile.

"I'm Carina, and this is my sister, Parthenia."

"Thank you," Eira said. Her gaze lingered a long moment on Carina and her sister before she continued, "Some explanations are in order, from both sides. I'm hoping we can clear everything up today, or if not, over the course of our journey to Pirine. As you are both mages, I'm sure I don't need to explain the importance of never divulging to anyone what you are about to hear. It is for your siblings' safety as well as the safety of all mages that we keep our secrets close to our hearts. We can only know what is essential to us at each stage of our lives. If, stars forbid, one day you are forced to give up your knowledge, you will be less likely to imperil the future of our clan."

"I know," said Carina.

Parthenia echoed, "I understand."

"*You* are here, my dear," Eira said to Carina, "because you are close to the age where you could choose your match. You've been summoned to a Matching." Responding to Carina and Parthenia's puzzled looks, the captain went on, addressing Carina again, "You have been dreaming of coming to Pirine, haven't you?"

"I think I've been having dreams, yes. But they faded quickly when I woke up. I didn't know what they were about. I didn't know I was being called to go somewhere."

Eira sighed and traded glances with Justin. "Our Spirit Mage is very old and weak. Her Casting is not powerful any longer. We've heard similar reports from the young mages who have already arrived. To explain, every five galactic years, young men and women mages are Summoned by a Spirit Mage to a Matching. The event takes place over several months, and the young mages can get to know each other and perhaps choose a life partner. That is what your dreams have been about, Carina. I'm guessing you have no living relatives apart from your younger sisters and brothers?"

"That's right."

Eira looked pained. She continued, "If you had an older mage in your life, he or she would have explained what the dreams meant."

"Right...," said Carina, "but Darius has been having the dreams too, I think. He's only six."

"He has been Summoned too," said Eira, "though for a different reason. Your brother is a Spirit Mage. Only one or two are born per generation. As I said, our current Spirit Mage who performs the Summons Cast is ancient. She has been Summoning your brother to take over from her. She must train him quickly before she dies.

"She has a stronger connection with your brother than other mages," said Eira. "That was how she knew he was coming, and how she also knew his path had been diverted. We set out to retrieve him. It was a dangerous expedition. We were forced to destroy the ship pursuing you, and that act will attract unwanted attention. But it was vital that we found your brother. Without a Spirit Mage our clan will die out."

"I've never heard of a Summon Cast," Parthenia interjected.

"That's because you can't do it," Justin replied. "Only Spirit Mages can."

"Excuse me," said Parthenia, "but you look like someone I met once. Do you have a brother on Ostillon?"

"Ah, so it was you who wandered up to Jace's tower by the forest."

"It was my brother and I. So Jace was a mage all along? And I worked so hard to get away from him. If only I'd known, he could have helped us."

"He would have helped you however he could," said Justin, "and gladly. But by the time he realized what you were, you'd slipped away."

"I Cast Transport right in front of him."

"It was quite a shock, from what he says."

"That's the problem with all the secrecy, right?" said Ren. "We could be the friend of another mage all our lives and never know it."

"You met a mage on Ostillon?" Carina asked her sister.

Parthenia's expression turned sour and she replied without looking at Carina. "He was the ranger who helped me and Darius when we found our way out of the forest." She turned to Justin. "He's a good man. He saved us when we couldn't go any farther. The next time you see him, please thank him for me."

"You can thank him yourself," said Justin. "He'll be on Pirine soon, if he hasn't already arrived."

"He's coming to the Matching too? I thought it was just for young people."

Justin laughed, a deep-bellied chuckle. "He's only thirty-five. I'll tell him you said that. But Jace is coming to the Matching because—"

"Justin," Eira said sharply.

"Sorry," said the Healer, suddenly serious. "I was forgetting. Jace will be at the Matching too, Parthenia. He would have arrived earlier, but he was having problems leaving Ostillon due to the war."

"Is the war over now?" Carina asked.

"Yes, the Dirksens managed to repel the Sherrerr attack," said Eira.

"Probably with my other brother's help."

"What? A mage is helping the Dirksens?"

"It's a long story."

"We have a lot to discuss."

"You have another brother?" asked Ione. "You have a big family."

"He's my half-sibling, like Parthenia and all the others."

"So you two have different parents?" Eira said. "I'm surprised. You look so alike, it's obvious you're sisters. Do you mind telling me, do you share a mother?"

"We did," Carina replied. "Her name was Faye."

Eira's features clouded. "I feared it was so. I saw the resemblance right away but I hoped I was mistaken. She's dead, then?"

"She died a few months ago," said Carina.

"And Kris?"

"He passed on many years ago, before Parthenia was born."

Justin leaned forward and spread his arms on the table. "There are many sad tales to be told here, but let's save them for later. They're in the past now. You said you have another brother who you think is helping the Dirksens?"

"Ma had six children after me," said Carina. "Parthenia is the eldest. The second child is a boy called Castiel. My mother thought he wasn't a mage, but then around the time she died he developed mage powers. Unfortunately, he'd watched the lessons she had given the other children so he knew what he had to do in order to Cast."

"You say 'unfortunately?'" said Eira. "I'm guessing his behavior is not what you would expect from a mage."

"No, it isn't," said Parthenia. "Castiel is cruel and he lusts for power and control. He has to be stopped. I wanted to try to stop him, but Carina forced me to leave Ostillon." The venomous look she shot Carina left the room in an embarrassed silence.

"That seems to be yet another subject we can explore more deeply later," said Justin. "Are you in agreement over the nature of this young man?"

"There's no doubt about it," she replied. "I'm not sure why he is as he is.

Perhaps he takes after his father, or perhaps growing up without mage ability in a family of mages has warped him, but Castiel is evil."

Eira's somber expression deepened.

"I'm so glad you found us," said Parthenia. "Maybe we can work together to defeat my brother?"

"We certainly need to address that question," said Eira. "I'm not sure what the answer is."

"I'm worried that Castiel and the Dirksens may follow us," said Carina. "I think the ship you attacked when you found us belonged to that clan."

"It did," Justin said. "We had a rather terse exchange of comms. The ship's captain stated you were escaped prisoners of war. We declined to believe them." He smiled grimly.

"But when the Dirksens don't hear anything from their ship they'll send out another to find out what happened to it. Then they'll pick up your trace and follow it the same as they followed ours."

"No, they won't," said Eira. "Don't worry, Ren has Cast Obscure on our trail and will continue to do so. It's extremely unlikely they would discover our path, and if they do, they would also need to search all of Pirine to find us."

Carina wasn't entirely reassured by Eira's words, but she bowed to the older woman's long experience. She also had more questions she was urged to ask. "Can you tell me more about my mother and father? I grew up without them. My Nai Nai brought me up. I only met my mother again not long before she died."

"I would love to," Eira replied. "I propose that we bring the meeting to a close first, however. I think we've touched on all the important topics for today. Thank you for what you've told us. Remember, do not tell anyone else anything we've discussed here. Your non-mage friend and your brothers and sisters will naturally make some guesses about what's happening, but it's really best for everyone that they know as little as possible for certain."

Carina imagined it would be hard to not tell Bryce why they were going to Pirine, how the mages had found them, or answer any other mysteries that had been cleared up for her. But he probably wouldn't press her for answers. He understood the need for secrecy.

The fact that she was supposed to attend this 'Matching' troubled her more. She wasn't of a mind to match to anyone.

People were leaving the meeting room. Justin had risen from his seat and was walking past Carina when he halted and she felt a heavy hand on her shoulder. When she looked up, he held out his other hand. Somewhat bewildered, she grasped it and they shook.

"There are not many who have made me cry for help," he said, a twinkle in the depths of his deep-set eyes.

"I'm sorry. I hope I didn't hurt you."

"Nothing a little Casting couldn't fix." He released his grip and walked out.

———

Carina was pleased to see her brothers and sisters put on weight and lose their worry lines as the days passed while the *Haihu* took them to Pirine. Bryce also relaxed and cheered up considerably as the journey wore on. As she had predicted, he didn't push her for information.

Eira spent some time reminiscing with her about her mother and father. It turned out that she'd gotten to know them at a Matching long ago, when Carina's parents had met. Eira told her what she recalled, mainly about how much in love her parents had seemed. That was one reason Eira remembered them so well.

She listened hungrily as Eira spoke of her mother. She wanted to overlay her final memories of the poor woman, ravaged with disease and long years of cruelty, with mental images of her as a young, happy, innocent person in the first flush of love.

When Eira told her about her father, she built memories of a man she had all but forgotten. She wished so much that mage lore didn't prohibit keeping images of loved ones. She could barely remember Ba's face.

She didn't tell Darius anything about what lay ahead of him on Pirine, partly because she didn't have much of an idea what Eira's mention of 'training' actually meant. The captain had said she couldn't tell her any more. The prospect worried her. Darius was only six years old. He might be a Spirit Mage but he was still only a little boy, much too young to have the responsibility of the future of mages on his shoulders.

Finally, the day came when they arrived at Pirine's star system. Eira announced the fact when she came into the small mess one morning.

Oriana clapped her hands. "Wonderful! I can finally have a proper bath. And real food...though the ship's food is also nice," she added, remembering her manners.

"We're all looking forward to real food," said Eira kindly. "But I'm afraid a bath won't be possible where we're going. I'll explain to you what happens next. We have to hide the *Haihu* at the edge of the system, then we take a shuttle in."

"How come we don't go straight to Pirine?" Ferne asked. "I thought it was a mage planet."

"There are no mage planets, Ferne," said Eira. "Not any longer. Whenever mages settled a new planet, non-mages would come along and drive them out, until finally they had to hide within non-mage populations. Pirine is no exception, though the people there are more tolerant and less suspicious of outsiders than most. We must keep our abilities secret on Pirine the same as everywhere. However, at the place we're going, everyone is a mage. It's a temporary encampment. After we arrive there, I must ask you not to question anyone about where they're from, or even ask their names if they do not volunteer them."

"How long will we be staying?" asked Darius.

"That isn't clear yet," Eira replied. "We'll be transferring to the shuttle in about an hour. Make sure you're ready."

The *Haihu*'s shuttle was a small silver oblong that barely fit everyone. Carina was quiet as they sped through the system toward the distant sun. So much had happened in the previous weeks. They had been in so much danger, but they had all survived relatively unscathed. Bryce, who was sitting next to her, took her hand. She smiled, but then an idea struck her. Would the mages at the encampment accept Bryce and Nahla?

Darius was sitting on Parthenia's lap because there weren't enough seats for everyone. He piped up, rather proudly, "Eira, do you want me to Cloak the ship?"

"What's that?" asked Justin.

Carina explained about Darius' special Cast, and Eira said, "Yes, we would like that very much indeed. The Pirine authorities aren't tight on security but there's no point in taking risks we can avoid."

Two hours later, the shuttle touched down. It was a relief to leave the cramped ship. When Carina walked out the exit ramp, she was greeted by a familiar sight. They had landed in the middle of a grassy plain stretching out in all directions.

She had never been to Pirine in her life, but she realized she'd visited the planet many times in her dreams.

"Please move forward," said Eira from behind. "You're blocking the exit. We must hide the shuttle as soon as we can."

Carina walked out into the hot, dry atmosphere. It was around midday, and the air was exactly as she'd dreamed it: full of the scent of wildflowers and the sound of insects.

"But where are we going to sleep?" asked Oriana.

"Over there," said Justin, pointing behind the shuttle.

Carina turned and saw a collection of tents in the distance.

"Ugh," said Oriana, "we're going to sleep in those?!"

"Oh shut up," said Ferne. "It'll be great."

They headed out toward the campsite, along a lightly worn path through the tall grass. A sound from behind made Carina turn, and she was just in time to see the shuttle disappearing beneath a shelter disguised as a pile of boulders.

Before they had crossed half the distance, another familiar sight appeared. A very old woman hobbled from out of the shadow of a tent. It was the woman from Carina's dreams, who she now remembered clear as day, right down to the woman's piercing stare. Though she was almost bent double, she moved at a surprising speed as she closed the distance between them.

She suddenly paused and lifted one hand to shade her eyes while the other remained on her stick. "Darius," she called, her voice thin and feeble. "Darius! I can see you. Come here, my sweet boy."

Darius turned questioning eyes to Carina. She didn't know what to say. The old woman, who she guessed was the Spirit Mage, clearly recognized Darius. "Should I go, Carina?"

"I guess so."

Her brother walked faster than the group so he was soon farther ahead. He met with the Spirit Mage about half a minute before the rest of them caught up to him. The mage had one bony arm across Darius' shoulders and was leaning her ancient face close to his youthful one. Her expression seemed to convey joy, but Carina also thought she saw a horrible glint of avarice in the old woman's eyes.

Darius looked fearful.

SIXTEEN

Winter had arrived quickly at the mountain castle, and the rooms had grown even colder. As Castiel's servant, who he'd learned was called Vera, left his bed, he told her to maintain a constant fire for him. The innuendo of his request wasn't lost on him, and he smirked as she dressed.

When his servant went out and closed the door, however, his smile faded. The wonder and pleasure he'd experienced when she'd offered herself so readily a few weeks ago had quickly palled. He'd discovered that fruit so easily acquired held no sweetness.

At the same time, his desire for Sable Dirksen had escalated. While Vera was in his bed, Castiel imagined she was Sable. He even used the clan leader's name, and he acted out the degradations and perversions he planned to use on her when she became his. When that might happen was still uncertain, but he believed he edged closer toward the goal every day.

Castiel threw back the covers and climbed out of bed. Despite the heating system the Dirksens had installed and the crackling fire in the grate, he shivered. The clammy chill never went away in the mountain castle abode. He pulled on his pants and put on a shirt, and then the thick, padded jacket he'd ordered to be made. His clothes felt tight. He guessed he'd done some growing. His arms and chest certainly seemed more muscular.

He faced the mirror and checked out his appearance. His beard nearly covered most of his jaw and his face had lost some of its roundness. He imagined he must look similar to his father when he was young. All the more fitting that he should achieve Father's ambition. What a pity he would not be around to witness it. He would have liked to make the old man proud.

It was nearly time for dinner. Castiel left his room to go downstairs to the great hall. He didn't care about punctuality, but these days dinnertime was about the only time of the day when he could reliably speak to Sable. Most days she was gone from the castle, though she never told him where she went.

He walked down the steps, remembering that horrible period when Sable had set him to helping with the restoration of the capital. How demeaning that had been. He should have refused her request, or made his protest earlier. His most recent task of trying to extract information from the Sherrerr spy who had given away intel about Ostillon had been far more enjoyable.

He hadn't managed to find out anything useful, he had to admit, but he had had fun trying.

When he strutted into the hall, he was surprised by the sight of a guest for dinner. Commander Kee had joined them. Castiel hadn't seen the man since his first day at the castle, when he'd made the unfortunate error of killing Tremoille. He wondered what had happened to Calvaley. He hadn't heard anything about the old man.

"Commander Kee," said Castiel in a statesman-like manner as he arrived at the dining table, "you're with us again. Do you have something important to report?"

Kee gave him a sardonic look, and Castiel noticed the man failed to stand up and salute him.

"Now then, Castiel," said a voice. Sable stood in the doorway. "Don't tempt the commander into giving away secrets." She entered the hall, looking magnificent. She was wearing a floor-length, high-necked gown made of a rich, thick, black fabric. Castiel had expected a woman of her wealth and status to wear expensive jewelry, like the kind his father had given his mother, but as always Sable wore none. Somehow the absence of decoration made her appear more impressive.

Kee pushed back his chair, stood, and saluted as she approached the table. Castiel scowled and pulled out a chair, deliberately scraping the legs across the stone floor. He threw himself into his seat. How dare Sable imply he was not allowed to hear Dirksen secrets. How much longer would he be treated as an outsider? Sable and Kee ignored his petulance and sat down.

"Thank you for joining us, Commander," said Sable. "I know you must be tired after your flight."

"It's always a pleasure to attend you, ma'am."

"I read over your report just now, but I'd also like to hear it in your own words. That was why I requested your presence tonight."

"Ah...." Kee's gaze flicked to Castiel.

"You can speak freely in front of Castiel. This business concerns him."

Castiel perked up. "I'm all ears." He took a sip of wine. Over his weeks at Sable's castle, he'd become more accustomed to the drink and could now tolerate three or four glasses before becoming unsteady. He'd been careful not to repeat the shameful event of his first taste of alcohol.

"In that case," said Kee, "as I wrote, ma'am, we confirmed the debris we found was from the *Torpille*, the destroyer we sent in pursuit of the mage children. We were unable to establish the cause of the ship's destruction. We found no impact site. It was as if the ship exploded from within."

"They probably Cast Fire into the ship's fuel tanks," said Castiel with a tone that he hoped made him appear knowledgeable. "That was how Carina and the others destroyed your shipyard. They knew where the tanks were, you see."

"I thought you said it was *you* who destroyed our shipyard?" said Sable.

"Oh, er." Castiel felt blood heating his cheeks. "That was what I meant."

"Continue, Kee."

"I'm not convinced it was the mage children who destroyed the *Torpille*. It might have been another ship. We found the shuttle, adrift but empty, without any bodies inside. That made little sense to me. The only explanation accounting for all the evidence was the *Torpille* picked up the mages but then was destroyed by an unknown force. Would the mage children commit an act of self-destruction? It seemed unlikely.

"So we searched. That was the cause of our delay, ma'am. We were combing the territory for any signs of a trace from a third ship. Luckily for us the area is rarely frequented. We finally picked up some patchy signs a week's travel from the site of the *Torpille's* destruction. They led in the direction of a planetary system with a single inhabited planet called Pirine."

"I looked up Pirine when I saw your report," said Sable. "The planet doesn't seem to have any significance. I don't understand why a ship from there would travel out to the shuttle to collect the children. Perhaps Castiel can shed some light? Do you remember hearing anyone in your family refer to that planet?"

Castiel trawled his memory. "No, I don't. I think it's unlikely anyone did. We never used to talk about other planets. Father didn't place much emphasis on galactic topography in our education."

"Could the ship have been a Sherrerr vessel?" Sable asked Kee.

"Impossible to say yet, ma'am."

"Pirine has never demonstrated sufficient potential for either us or the Sherrerrs to take control of it. The economy is almost entirely agrarian due to the scarcity of natural resources. The only explanation for what you observed that makes sense to me is that a portion of the Sherrerr fleet fled there after their failed attempt to take Ostillon. Did you find any evidence that might support that scenario, Kee?"

"We didn't approach the planet closely, but from what we could tell the evidence of space traffic seemed normal for a planet of Pirine's low economic and political importance. But the trace we were following disappeared at the system's edge. Consequently, we weren't able to ascertain where the ship landed, if in fact it ended up on Pirine itself."

"Disappearing traces," said Sable. "That sounds like mage work. You mean these people could be hiding out on an uninhabited planet or moon somewhere in the system?"

"A moon would be the only possibility. The other planets are high-gravity or gaseous giants, unfit for human life."

"Hmmm. Well, it seems we have narrowed down the possibilities considerably. Thank you for your excellent work, Kee. Now we have to act. What do you think we should do, Castiel?"

Jerked from reverie, Castiel splashed wine on himself. He put down his glass and picked up a napkin. As he dabbed at himself, disconcerted, he replied, "We should travel to Pirine and find my brothers and sisters. As you said, Sable, as long as they aren't working for us they're a liability. We can't allow the Sherrerrs to have them."

"They would be even less of a liability if we killed them," said Sable. "What do you think about that?"

"Killed them?" The idea appealed. He'd always imagined himself controlling his siblings in the same way as Father had. As well as all the things he could do with their help, it would be payback for years of living as a second-class member of his own family.

Yet Sable had a point. With no other mages around, his own abilities would become rarer and more precious. He would have no competition, no one to make him look lesser.

The thought of ending the lives of the siblings he'd grown up with gave him a strange sensation. Was this how guilt felt? Never mind. He would soon get over it. "It might be difficult to kill them due to their abilities, especially my half-sister, Carina. She trained as a merc. But though they can Cast, they're still human and can be killed the same ways."

Kee had been watching Castiel as he spoke. At this last sentence he turned his head away in disgust. Sable's expression remained enigmatic. Castiel recalled her statement the first time he'd met her, that she couldn't stand disloyalty. Had he said the wrong thing? It couldn't be helped. If his siblings' deaths were necessary for his elevation to power, so be it. He wouldn't shed a tear for any of them, least of all Carina.

"Very well," said Sable. "What's clear is that we must prepare a small fleet to fly to Pirine. I want to find these mages before they become a threat. If we can't put them to work for us, we'll put them out of action, permanently. How long will it take for you to equip a cruiser?"

"The repairs on the *Elsinore* are nearly complete, ma'am," said Kee. "I would only need another two days to make her ready."

"Good. We can work out the details later. Castiel, are you excited to finally have something to get your teeth into?"

"Me? You mean I'm going too?"

"Of course. Who better to defeat mages than another mage?"

"Great!" Castiel exclaimed. Then he reasserted his composure. "That's excellent news. I'll look forward to it."

———

Despite his intention to restrain himself, Castiel drank too much that evening. He was overjoyed that Sable was finally including him in an important, noteworthy task. While she and Kee chatted about what troops to assign to finding and capturing or killing his siblings, Castiel ran through many scenarios in his mind, each involving a moment of supreme triumph.

He would either decisively Repulse his brothers and sisters' Casts, resulting in their capture, or he would order soldiers to shoot them. Or perhaps he would trick them into a trap and lock them up, depriving them of their elixir so they were weak and helpless.

The last scenario triggered a realization: he hadn't brought his elixir with him to the dining table. Not long after he'd arrived at the castle, he'd told Sable he needed something more convenient and portable than his glass bottle in which to carry the liquid essential to Casting. She'd suggested he commission an Ostillonian craftsman to create something. Castiel had found a metalworker who had made him an ornate canister inscribed with his initials. Usually, he went everywhere with it, but tonight he didn't have it with him.

The warmth the alcohol had given him drained away in a moment and was replaced by a chill. Castiel felt naked, and Sable and Kee, who were chatting animatedly about ship-to-ground weapons, seemed suddenly dark and distant. Without his elixir, he was nothing and nobody. Sable could kick him out of the castle and tell one of her servants to break his back on a rock, and there would be nothing he could do about it.

"Are you feeling unwell?" Sable asked, noticing the change in him.

"Maybe ma'am should ask someone to bring a bucket," Kee quipped.

Castiel swallowed. "I'm all right. I'm just tired. I think I'll go to bed now."

"Good night, then," said Sable, immediately returning her attention to Kee.

Castiel stood up, the backs of his knees pushing away his chair. He wavered and grabbed the tabletop for support. Kee rolled his eyes. Castiel walked off unsteadily. He had to get to his elixir. He'd left it in his room. He only needed to feel the reassuring touch of the cold metal canister. He vowed never to be without it again.

He took the elevator even though his room was on the next floor. It was faster and he didn't trust himself on the steps. To fall down would be the height of embarrassment. When the elevator doors opened, he leaned on one edge for support as he stepped out into the corridor.

As soon as he reached his room Castiel went straight to the bedside drawer where he kept the canister. He pulled it open and blinked for a few moments as he took in what he saw. Horror struck him. The drawer was empty! He pulled out the one below it and the third one. Then he pulled out all the drawers and scrabbled around the empty frame. He pulled the furniture away from the wall and threw it across the room. Where could his elixir be? He was certain he'd put the canister in its usual place before Vera had come to pay him her daily visit.

Castiel searched his room, stripping the covers from his bed, tossing the pillows onto the floor. He peered underneath the bed, and then dragged it away from the wall. He remembered the clothing chest in the corner of the room. Of course! He must have put the elixir in there by accident. But when he lifted the lid and hauled out all the clothes, the canister wasn't inside. Where could it be?

He grabbed his hair in frustration. He had to find the precious liquid. Everything depended on it. If it wasn't in his room it had to be because someone had stolen it. Perhaps Vera was the thief. The stupid girl was infatuated with him. She'd taken it in order to have something of his. Or perhaps another servant had taken it, imagining they could sell the canister for a good price.

That had to be the answer. One of the servants had taken it. He would have to find out who it was and demand that Sable fire them—after punishing them heavily.

He marched out of his room, anger driving away the effects of his excessive drinking. He ran down the stairs and rushed into the great hall. "One of your servants has stolen my elixir," he blurted.

Kee was standing and pushing in his chair. Sable was draining her glass. Both turned to Castiel, their eyes widening at his outburst.

"I demand that all the servants' quarters are searched until it's found. And the thief must be punished severely."

"Your elixir?" asked Kee. "Do you mean this?" He picked up Castiel's canister from the tabletop.

It had been there all along! He must have put it down somewhere he couldn't see it and, in his drunken state, he'd assumed he'd forgotten it.

He wished he could undo his outburst. He wished he could wind time back by one minute. But he couldn't.

"Yes," he said quietly, "that's it."

Kee maintained a sardonic gaze on Castiel as he crossed the hall. The commander held the canister out at arm's length, waiting for Castiel to take it from him. When the container changed hands, Castiel returned to the staircase, feeling Sable and Kee watching him the entire way. They were silent, but after he'd climbed a few steps and was out of their sight, Sable's laughter peeled out and was quickly joined by Kee's loud, deep chuckles.

Castiel opened the door to his room and surveyed the mess he'd created. He was furious. He hated Sable and Kee for laughing at his mistake. He hated that he'd done something so stupid.

One thing was clear: he wasn't going to sleep in the disarray caused by his frantic search. He went to his interface and called the servants' quarters, demanding that Vera come up to his room instantly and tidy it up.

He flung himself onto his bed. He would take out his anger on the girl. A minute later there was a knock at the door and it opened. The servant panting outside wasn't Vera but another young girl.

Castiel sat up in surprise. "Where's Vera?"

"I don't know, sir," the girl replied, catching her breath. "I was told I am to be your room servant from now on. My name is—"

"I don't give a shit what your name is. I want to know what...." Did he really want to know what had happened to Vera? Not at all. Or at least, not if this girl could meet his needs in the same way. She was certainly as pretty as Vera had been.

"I want you to tidy up this mess," he said, "but that isn't all. Come over here."

The girl took quick steps across the room until she was only a few feet from his side.

"Take off your clothes."

To Castiel's surprise, the girl complied with his instructions without a moment's hesitation. His eyes widened. It was so easy! Vera hadn't been a fluke.

It was much easier than he'd been led to believe in stories he'd read and dramas he'd watched. But maybe it wasn't so remarkable. After all, he was an important member of the Dirksen household. Of course the girl would do whatever he wanted. Perhaps what was happening was normal in rich and powerful clans.

Come to think of it, he remembered seeing his father caressing the female servants in the mansion on Ithiya.

So this *was* normal. If only he'd realized earlier, he could have had so much more fun.

The girl was naked.

"Well, what are you waiting for?" Castiel barked. "Get on the bed." His former anger over his embarrassing mistake returned. He would work it out of his system on this girl. She would soon perform her service in as much discomfort and pain as he could inflict, and afterward he would watch as she tidied up his room.

He used the servant roughly, yet though she didn't enjoy it, she didn't seem to mind too much. He wondered if she'd been beaten frequently at home and so she'd become insensitive to pain.

When he was finished, he pushed her away. "Get dressed—no, wait. Pick up in here before putting your clothes on. Then you can leave."

"Yes, sir." The girl climbed off the bed and Castiel let his gaze linger on her welts and developing bruises. He had exhausted himself. He could have performed more interesting feats by Casting, but it would not have been as satisfying or cathartic. Expending his strength was much better. His drunkenness had worn off too and he felt the beginnings of a headache. When the girl was gone, he would Heal himself before he slept.

His eyelids drooping, he watched the servant as she folded the clothes scattered about the floor and carefully laid them inside the chest in the corner. Was she smiling to herself? It seemed she was. His eyelids lifted and he pulled himself back from the brink of sleep.

Why was the girl smiling? Was she a masochist? Had she enjoyed all that he'd done to her? He felt cheated. What he'd done was for his pleasure, not hers. If she liked it, that took away most of the point of the exercise.

He thought back to Vera. She also hadn't seemed to particularly mind what he did to her, no matter how brutal he'd been. It was a strange coincidence that the two servants had reacted in the same way.

It was too much of a coincidence. He wasn't as experienced as he hoped to become, but even he knew that most women didn't like being ill-treated. He'd seen his mother shrink from his father's approach often enough.

So, why— He sat bolt upright. "You." He pointed at her, though he couldn't possibly mean anyone else. "Why are you here?"

"I'm your room servant, sir."

He was out of bed in an instant and by her side. He grabbed a fistful of the girl's hair and wrenched it, twisting her neck and bending her head almost to the floor. "Why are you really here?"

"Owww, please, sir! Please, let go!" She fell to her knees.

"Ha, you don't like it so much now, do you? Not now there's no point to it? Not now you aren't exciting me." Castiel had a vision of throwing the girl down and stomping on her face until she told him the answer. But Sable Dirksen had probably threatened even worse punishments.

Sable was no mage, however. She couldn't stop him from finding out the truth, though he already knew it. He just wanted to hear it from the girl's lips.

"Stay there." In three strides he was across the room and taking his elixir canister from the drawer. He sipped the liquid, closed his eyes, and Cast Enthrall. He opened his eyes. The girl's stare was blank when he returned to her.

"You, why were you sent here?"

"I am your room—"

He kicked her. "What was the other reason you were sent here?"

"I am to allow you to use me, sir."

"And why is that?" Castiel's hands were clenching into fists.

"So that I may become pregnant, sir. If I give birth to a live child sired by you, my family will be richly rewarded."

He let out a roar and punched the girl in the face.

"And Vera? She is pregnant? That's why you replaced her?"

"Yes, sir."

Castiel knocked the girl down. She lay where she fell, blood oozing from her nose. He began to kick her, over and over.

Sable Dirksen had been tricking him the whole time. After he'd told her that magehood was passed on from parent to child, she'd hatched a plan to force him to sire children for her. More mages who would be entirely under her control.

Damn her! Damn Sable Dirksen and all her schemes. He would not forget her treachery and deceit. Not for a very long time.

SEVENTEEN

When Carina and her siblings had arrived at the Matching, they carried little more with them than the clothes on their backs. Not long after they walked into the camp, however, with Eira, Justin, and the rest of the crew of the *Haihu*, they had food, somewhere to sleep, and the warmest welcome Carina had ever known.

It had taken her days to become accustomed to the idea that she no longer had to hide what she was from strangers, because everyone she met was the same as her. She had never known a time when she had not been forced to keep her abilities secret, with the threat of torture, slavery, or death hanging over her. The new sense of freedom was dizzying, and her brothers and sisters seemed to feel the same. After a childhood spent living under the domination of their father in a household full of pain, and long months of hiding and running, they could finally relax and be themselves.

The boys and girls had become more childlike, playing endlessly in the long grass of the prairie. Even Parthenia had joined in their games of tag or hide-and-go-seek. Over the days they had grown fatter and the color returned to their faces.

While the children played, Carina had spent time wandering around the camp. She discovered that there was no formal structure to the Matching. Over the course of months, young mages would arrive, spend as much time at the camp as they wanted, and then leave at a time of their choosing. Some left with partners they had met, others had the locations of new friends memorized in order to arrange later meetings. A few left without either of these things, but it seemed not unhappily. Perhaps they would return for the next Matching, or perhaps they were content to remain single.

The young mages passed their days meeting and talking with others, over meals or drinks. Some had brought musical instruments and gave performances, others sang, recited poetry, or put on plays. Some taught skills like cooking and crafting.

Carina's memory of her dreams became stronger now she was actually at the place she'd dreamed about, and the camp retained a dreamlike quality. She almost could not believe it was real. Was it because it felt too good to be true, and if she truly believed in it, the place might suddenly vanish in a puff of smoke?

As if to keep her anchored in the more familiar, harsh world outside the Matching, two aspects of the camp marred her experience. The first was that she did not fit in. The young mages she met had clearly been raised in loving families and if they had experienced hardship it was only of the economic kind. The second problem Carina had with the camp was how Darius' days were spent.

While his brothers and sisters played, he spent most of his time with the Spirit Mage. When he returned to their tent after a long day of training with the old woman, he was often too tired to play and he would fall asleep soon after dinner.

Darius said he was helping the Spirit Mage, whose name was Magda, with her Summoning, and she had begun to teach him some things only Spirit Mages could do. Carina's unease about the situation increased but she wasn't sure what to do about it. One thing that particularly saddened her was that Darius was asleep in the evenings when the Spirit Mage told her stories, though she guessed Darius would eventually know all the stories himself.

It turned out that one of Magda's roles was to function as the repository for the oral history of the clan. Every night, a couple of hours after sunset, someone would build a large fire at the center of the encampment, and the Spirit Mage would sit beside it and tell a story from the mages' ancient past. She told a different story every night, and would often say she knew more stories than she could tell at one Matching.

Though Carina disliked the way the old woman had monopolized Darius, she would often attend these story tellings. Parthenia would come to listen to the stories too, but Carina knew better than to attempt to sit with her sister. When she'd tried, Parthenia had gotten up and walked away, drawing the curious stares of others. So instead, Carina usually found a space at the edge of the crowd far from the fire and sat on a blanket spread over the damp, flattened grass. She would cover her shoulders with another blanket, and listen.

One evening the Spirit Mage told a very old story from the time the mages departed their home planet, Earth. Carina's attention increased in focus when she understood what the subject was to be. She had never given up her dream of returning to Earth one day.

"At that time, most of Earth's population was living in a country called Antarctica," said Magda, "which spanned the southern pole. The equatorial regions were desert wastelands, too hot for human survival, and the land masses in between were tropical wildernesses, disease-ridden, and the sites of frequent hurricanes, tornadoes, and floods. Some communities survived in the high mountains, and the mage clan was one of these.

"Earth had not always been in this state, with so few areas suitable for human habitation. Humanity had lived and thrived all over the globe for hundreds of thousands of years. But successive decades of poor management of the planet had driven its systems to extremes that were not compatible with human life in most areas.

"The planetary government's proposed solution to this crisis was to approach the mage clan and insist they use their special abilities to fix the damage and return Earth to its previous, livable state. No amount of explanation would convince the government this was a task that was entirely beyond mages. Or perhaps the government did not want to hear. Perhaps all it needed was a scapegoat, for its next step was to announce to the world's media that the mage clan had refused to aid humankind, that it was waiting for non-mages to die out. Then mages would make Earth into a paradise only they could enjoy.

"The government employed technology that put words into the mouths of the Mage Council on vids and holos. Try as they might to deny the lies, the mages were not believed. Perhaps the rest of the population wanted to believe the deceit, which made them easy to convince. By that time, mages had long been feared and hated. Rumors abounded of what kind of people they were and how they lived in their secret mountain castles, most of which were untrue. The mages were so divorced from regular human life, they rarely attempted to correct what was said about them.

"Due to the government's propaganda as it sought to deflect the blame for its failings, resentment against mages grew ever stronger. The clan came to the decision that remaining on Earth was simply too dangerous. If they did not leave, one day their mountain abodes would be attacked and they would be murdered or enslaved. The engine that permitted interstellar travel had been invented, and the mages determined they would be among the first to abandon Earth for the stars.

"It took them longer than two Earth years to construct their colony ship, but eventually the day came when they were to board the vessel and depart their home forever. A few of the clan did not want to leave. Many sad goodbyes were said, and then the thousands began to Transport to the launch site.

"Though the construction of the ship had taken place in great secrecy, word had gotten out to the general populace that the mages were departing Earth. The first mages Transporting into the site found a scene of bloody murder and destruction. People who had hated mages all their lives also did not want them to leave. They demanded the clan remain on Earth and help the rest of humankind. They said it was their duty and responsibility.

"So these non-mages had tried to prevent the ship from leaving by killing those who guarded it. They were also trying to sabotage the engines when the colonists arrived. A battle ensued, and though the mages Transported many of those who were trying to prevent them from leaving, for the first time they were forced to kill in order to protect themselves. They won the battle, and they knew their time on Earth was done.

"Thus it was, with sorrow and shame our ancestors departed their home, never to return."

The Spirit Mage fell silent. The story was over. After the mage had taken a drink and a few moments to gather her thoughts, she would begin another. The evening was growing late, and possibly the next story she told would be the last tonight.

Parts of this story of leaving Earth were new to Carina. Ma had told her that mages had left due to persecution, but she hadn't given her the details about the state of the planet. Carina wondered if her ambition to return to Earth was foolish. She might go to a massive effort to arrive at the home planet only to find a barren wilderness.

As she was contemplating this idea, a figure approached out of the darkness. The man was tall and broad and at first she thought it was Justin who had come to listen, but then she saw the man's beard was shorter.

She peered over at him and was surprised to see him sit down next to Parthenia. The two talked quietly while the Spirit Mage began her next story. She guessed the newcomer was Justin's brother, the ranger at the tower on Ostillon.

She did not listen to the new story. Disappointment tormented her. The Spirit Mage's tale seemed to have sucked away her hopes for a future of safety and happiness, far from this galactic sector. She realized she had been listening to Magda's stories so avidly because she'd been hoping to hear information that would give clues to Earth's location. But the latest story had driven home the fact that her clan had been intent on getting as far from Earth as they could, not returning there. In the story that had been passed down no galactic coordinates were mentioned.

Yet there was the Map, which Carina had drawn thousands of times over as a child and which she still recalled every time she meditated. Someone in the distant past of mages had wanted Earth's location to be remembered, perhaps long after its galactic coordinates had become obsolete and meaningless.

She pondered the problem, withdrawing into herself, until before she knew it the Spirit Mage's final story was over and the crowd was breaking up to go to bed. She stood and shook out her legs to ease their stiffness. Parthenia and the ranger remained seated together and talking. Carina walked over to the pair.

The ranger noticed her approaching and rose to his feet, holding out his hand. "Carina, my name is Jace. It's nice to meet you again."

Parthenia turned her face away.

Carina shook the ranger's hand, somewhat perplexed. "Again? Have we already met?"

"Yes, though only briefly, before you and your brothers and sisters disappeared."

"Huh?" She wondered what he meant. Then the penny dropped and her eyes widened. "Of course. How stupid of me. That was you at the forest on Ostillon."

"It was. I was walking alone after dark, laying low and waiting for the hostilities between the Sherrerrs and Dirksens to blow over so I could leave the planet and come here, when I spotted a fire in among the trees. I made my way over, wondering who could be there, so far from civilization. I saw your shelter and went over for a closer look.

"Imagine my surprise when the sleepers in the shelter began to disappear before my eyes. It didn't take me long to realize you were mages Transporting yourselves away, afraid of discovery. And then I also guessed you must have something to do with the mage children I had helped weeks previously, one of whom I've finally found again." He smiled at Parthenia, but she continued to hold her face averted.

Jace frowned in confusion.

"It's okay," said Carina. "It isn't you Parthenia is mad at, it's me." She took a breath and let it out in a sigh, ashamed of what she was about to admit. "I cast Enthrall on her to force her to leave Ostillon."

"You...?" asked Jace, eyes widening. "That was...." He paused, too polite to state his opinion.

"A terrible thing to do," said Carina. "I know, and I hated to do it, but I didn't want Parthenia to die." Her guilt and unhappiness regarding her relationship with her sister overcame her and words flooded from her mouth without hindrance.

"She means so much to me. Her help was invaluable when we escaped the

Sherrerrs. I could never have done it without her, and after that she kept our brothers and sister safe in dangerous, difficult circumstances. She's quick-thinking, resourceful, and smart, and I love her. I couldn't leave her on Ostillon, even if it meant taking away her free will. I'm sorry for it, but I don't regret it. I would do the same again because I can't bear to lose her, not after losing Ma."

Carina hadn't been aware what she was going to say before she said it. Yet she'd meant it all and was glad she'd had the opportunity to tell her sister how she felt.

Parthenia's head remained turned away, but Carina sensed a small change in her, as if her sister had been affected by what she'd said.

"I think I understand what happened," said Jace. "You faced a hard choice."

"I didn't have a good option to pick."

"But I don't know that staying on Ostillon was as dangerous as you think," said Jace. "As long as you avoided the populated areas you should have been fairly safe. I myself only had to wait until regular space travel was allowed again before I could leave."

"Oh, don't you know about our brother, Castiel?" asked Parthenia.

"No, I haven't heard that name. I only just arrived."

"That's a long story," said Carina, "and a discussion we need to have with Magda, Justin, and anyone else who's in charge here. But the short version is, I believe our brother may be a Dark Mage, and he's helping the Dirksens."

"A Dark Mage?" asked Jace. "That is bad news. So that was why you didn't want to leave your sister on Ostillon? It makes more sense now. Dark Mages are difficult to defeat, even for many mages working together. You could not have accomplished that alone, Parthenia."

"But we must try," she said. "We can't allow Castiel to do whatever he wants. He's cruel and vicious. He'll cause untold suffering."

"You mean like the untold suffering non-mages have caused us over millenia?" asked Carina. "Honestly, the more I think about it, the less certain I am we should do anything about Castiel. Hearing the Spirit Mage's story has made me consider changing my mind. Think about it, Parthenia. The Sherrerrs knew what your father was doing, and they didn't do anything to stop him. They *chose* not to do anything, because you were all useful to them. Why should we help humankind when they've never helped us? We haven't done anything to deserve the persecution we've suffered. I know I said I would go back to Ostillon to tackle Castiel, but now I'm not so sure."

"How can you say that?" Parthenia exclaimed. "Castiel deserves to be punished for everything he's done. He must be locked away and prevented from harming anyone. And we're the only ones who can defeat him."

"I don't know about that either. Your father did a good job of controlling his mage wife and offspring. Maybe Castiel isn't as invincible as you think. Maybe the Dirksens already have him under their control. Even now he could be suffering torture to force him to do their bidding. I'm sorry, Parthenia. I'm not sure this is our fight."

Jace said, "One thing is certain, this subject needs further discussion, but not tonight. Let me speak with my brother and the Spirit Mage. What to do about a Dark Mage in our midst is a decision that will impact us all."

EIGHTEEN

As the Dirksen fleet prepared to set out for Pirine, Castiel was careful not to let Sable know he was aware of her plans to trick him into siring children. When the new girl came to his room, he Enthralled her and made her believe she had slept with him, and he remembered to rough her up a little to make the lie seem convincing. Sable Dirksen might have gotten one child out of him but she would not get any more.

Castiel's mind had ranged across the various ways he might get his revenge on Sable Dirksen. He'd imagined killing her in a range of painful ways. He'd imagined imprisoning her and forcing her to bear his children, who *he* would then control. He'd imagined subjecting her to endless torture. But in the end he'd dismissed them all. For the time being, he was only one mage. The power he wielded was not sufficient to defeat all the Dirksens who would defend their leader.

Yet the incident with the servant girl had strengthened his resolve to do *something*. It was clear that Sable was only tolerating him, using him for her own ends. She had no intention of allowing him into the inner circle of influential, powerful Dirksens. He was not a significant figure, he was only a tool.

One thing she hadn't considered, however, was the fact that mages had to be trained. When he'd explained to her that the ability was passed from parent to child, he'd skated over his mother's role in teaching the children. At the time, he'd been downplaying the fact because he'd wanted to make himself appear more impressive, but the omission had worked in his favor in a different way.

Sable Dirksen could breed as many mage offspring as she liked, but they would be useless to her without proper training. Now he came to think of it, he wasn't sure he could train anyone else to be a mage even if he wanted to. He'd realized long ago his mother had been a poor teacher deliberately. He would do no better than her and probably worse. He also had an inkling he would lose his talent over time if he didn't practice other things, but he wasn't clear on what they were.

So he had two problems: Sable Dirksen intended on dispensing with him in one way or another eventually, and he needed proper training if he was not to lose his powers. The answer to both of these problems was a single person: Carina. Of all his siblings, she was the only one who had been properly trained. Carina really knew what she was talking about, and she could teach him to be more powerful, so powerful he could foil Sable's plans to use him for her own ends.

And if he caught Carina, he would have his brothers and sisters too. That would make six mages. With a force as strong as that he wouldn't need Sherrerrs or Dirksens. He could build an empire large and powerful enough to take on and defeat both clans.

That was what he had to do. Finding and capturing his siblings had to be his top priority. Luckily for him, Sable's plans were dovetailing into his own.

The day after he had Enthralled the servant girl and discovered Sable's scheme, Castiel descended the stairs to the great hall in a positive mood. Tiredness stalked him after his long night of worry, but he mentally brushed aside the small discomfort. For the first time since arriving at the mountain castle, he finally felt like he knew exactly where he stood and what he needed to do.

"You seem cheerful this morning," Sable commented as he sat down at the dining table. Kee was also here. Had he spent the previous night with Sable? For once, Castiel experienced no twinge of jealousy. He no longer wanted the small thing that remained for Sable to offer him. He would not sully himself with an intimate relationship with the snake.

"I am cheerful," Castiel replied. "My latest servant is a very pretty, willing young woman. I appreciate you finding her for me after the previous one left so suddenly." He could not resist playing along with Sable's plan in order to see her reaction.

If Commander Kee was aware of Sable's scheme, he gave no sign of it after hearing Castiel's response. The man ignored him as he always did unless speaking directly to him.

Sable was a master of subterfuge as she, too, didn't do anything other than smile indulgently at his comment. *Bitch!* She wouldn't be smiling for much longer.

———

The day finally came when the fleet was ready, and Castiel and Sable went together to the shuttle that would fly them up to the battlecruiser, *Elsinore*. No one knew what they would encounter at Pirine. Perhaps the population of that world was aware of mages and would rise up to defend them. Perhaps the Dirksens would have a long search on their hands to find Carina and the rest of his siblings. Whatever they might encounter, Sable and Kee had tried to prepare for all eventualities.

All Castiel had to take care of for the trip was his elixir supply. When he'd been aboard the *Nightfall*, his father had brought along a tank of the stuff. Mindful of the fact that he might be involved in a protracted battle, Castiel had made similar preparations. Yet he had insisted on bringing along a supply of ingredients too. The thought of the impending journey had made him painfully aware that without elixir, he was helpless. He didn't even know how to fire a weapon.

Elsinore was a very different ship from *Nightfall*. The passageways were narrower and the bridge held only Kee, as commander of the vessel, the pilot, navigator, and comms and weapons officers. No signs stated the function of each room or section. The crew were expected to know. When Castiel had wandered onto the bridge unwittingly, Kee and the other officers glared at him in silence until he left.

A low-ranking crew member had shown Castiel to his cabin after he disembarked the shuttle. The room was a far cry from the suite his family had been assigned on the *Nightfall*. It was small and contained no private bathroom. He would be forced to use the communal restroom facilities for that section. As if that wasn't bad enough, his bed was one of two, and the crew member who had shown him the place told him not to stow his luggage on the other bunk because someone else would be using it.

Who his bunk mate might be, Castiel had no idea, but whoever it was, it was unconscionable that he had to share at all. But he didn't know what he could do about it. Like it or not, he needed these people for the moment. All he could do was bide his time and plot his revenge for the many insults that had been piled upon him.

Worse still, there wasn't enough space to accommodate the tank of elixir he'd brought along. The container would have to be stowed in the galley, along with ingredients for cooking. It was outrageous. The taste of elixir was disgusting so it was unlikely the liquid would end up in a stew, but nevertheless the fact that it wasn't near to hand made Castiel extremely uncomfortable.

After accidentally walking onto the bridge, he had returned to his room.

Or, rather, he tried to return. He had already lost his bearings in the passageways of the large ship. Everywhere seemed to look the same, though he guessed there were subtle differences and clues that were unknown to him.

His wanderings resulted in giving him an informal tour of the *Elsinore*. From the mess to the briefing room, he got to know the ship pretty well. He even happened upon Sable's quarters when he spotted her leaving a room. He caught a glimpse of the interior, which was substantially larger and more luxurious than his own.

He wondered who would be lining up outside the room the next quiet shift, and whether the Dirksen leader would manage to work her way through the entire crew before they reached Pirine.

When he finally found his cabin again, he was irked to see someone lying in the top bunk. He'd left a bag on the bed to claim it, and the person had moved the bag to the bottom bunk.

He was even more irked when the man turned on his side to see who had come in. Reyes Dirksen's hateful visage confronted him. He would be forced to spend weeks cooped up with one of the most loathsome people on Ostillon.

Reyes didn't look surprised to see him. He only smirked and lay down again. So Reyes had been given the information about his bunk mate while Castiel had been kept in the dark. Had Sable Dirksen deliberately put them together to make it easier for Reyes to spy on him?

Castiel sat on the lower bunk, weighing his options. Reyes' move to secure the top bunk was obviously a ploy to signal his dominance. Castiel couldn't allow the step to go unchallenged, but he was unsure of what to do. Hate him as he might, Reyes was older, taller, and stronger. He couldn't physically remove him from the bunk.

Also, much as Castiel hated to admit it, Reyes was pretty smart. He doubted he could trick him into giving up the superior sleeping place.

All he had as an advantage was Casting. That was going to be the only thing he could use to force Reyes out of his bed and show him who was boss. He went through a mental list of the Casts he knew: Transport, Locate, Enthrall, Rise, Fire, Heal, Clear, Break, Lock, Repulse, Send and Open were the ones he had practised often. And there was Split too, but he didn't think the Dirksens would take kindly to him using Split on Reyes, satisfying though it might be. They would soon put an end to his affiliation with them through ending his life, mage or not.

No, he needed to do something effective but that didn't cause long-term damage. He made his choice, sipped elixir, and began to Cast.

He opened his eyes and waited for Reyes' response. It wasn't long coming.

"Hey," resounded an angry shout from above. "Put me down!"

Castiel watched with amusement as Reyes floated out from his bunk and across the narrow ceiling. He was twisting and writhing, ineffectively fighting the Cast.

"I said, put me down," Reyes reiterated furiously.

"Are you sure about that?" Castiel asked. He glanced at the floor and back up toward Reyes. "Looks like a nasty drop to me. But if you insist...."

Reyes, realizing what would happen if Castiel did as he'd asked, said, "Put me back on my bunk, I mean, you moron."

"Those are brave words for someone floating helplessly in my grasp. I'd like an apology."

Reyes only glared at him. Then he cast a look at the floor, as if judging how much he would be hurt by falling the distance. "Go on, drop me. I promise I'll hurt you more than it'll hurt me."

Castiel sat up. He'd had enough of Reyes. He'd had enough of all the Dirksens. If they thought they were going to walk all over him they had another think coming. He would start with Langley Dirksen's son. "Believe me, I can hurt you even more than you can imagine. Did you hear what I did to the Sherrerr admiral? I tore her in two. She died screaming in agony."

He watched Reyes' expression as he registered this fact. He had heard, Castiel could tell. His bravado had begun to weaken.

"And don't think I won't do it," said Castiel. "Just because I can't do it now, it doesn't mean I won't do it at some later date, when I have the power and influence to put a stop to anyone who might want to avenge your life. So you better watch out, Reyes Dirksen. You piss me off, and I won't ever forget it."

Castiel released him, and he hit the floor hard. Reyes yelled in pain and anger, but Castiel's threat had taken effect. Reyes didn't retaliate, and when Castiel climbed up to the top bunk, he didn't respond.

The Dirksen youth sat on the floor for a moment before getting up and slamming out of the cabin. There was blood on the bare metal. He smiled. He must have broken the idiot's nose. Good. He hoped it would serve as a warning to him and to all the other Dirksens. They might treat him like nothing but a tool to be used, but he would remember it. He would note who showed him favor and who disrespected him, and when the time came they would pay.

Nineteen

Darius had returned to the tent after another long day spent with the Spirit Mage. Dinner had already been eaten, but Carina had saved some for him. While the others went out to the natural spring at the camp's center to wash away the dirt and dust accumulated during the day, she sat with her sleepy brother, encouraging him to eat more before he went to bed.

He did force down a few more mouthfuls before his eyelids drooped and his head nodded. Bryce picked up the little boy and carried him to his sleeping spot at the edge of the large tent.

"He can't go on like this," she said after Bryce returned to her side. They sat outside the open tent flap, watching the evening bustle of the camp. She wasn't worried about Darius overhearing her. He would be dead to the world until morning, when he would rise and wearily set out for the Spirit Mage's tent again.

"It does seem excessive work for a young kid," Bryce said. "Have you spoken to Justin or Eira about it?"

"I haven't seen Eira for days. I think she leaves every so often to ferry in new arrivals as a way of avoiding attracting too much attention. I did speak to Justin, but he only said that learning from the Spirit Mage was Darius' destiny. No other Spirit Mage has appeared in decades, and it's vital that Magda passes on as much knowledge as she can to Darius before she dies. But he's just a little boy."

She understood the older mage's perspective: without a Spirit Mage there could be no Matching, and with no Matching the mages and their culture would eventually die out. Yet it seemed wrong to place all that responsibility on the shoulders of a six year old.

"I don't know what to say," said Bryce. "It's mage business."

She rubbed her temples. She didn't know what to do for the best. After spending so many years cut off from her mage kindred, she knew little more than Bryce did.

"How have the other mages been treating you and Nahla?" she asked. In her preoccupation with Darius and the novelty of living among hundreds of mages, she'd forgotten that her friend's experience would be very different from her own.

"I'm not sure they know we aren't mages. I haven't told anyone, and Nahla has no reason to either. For once, mage reluctance to tell anyone anything is working out for us."

She smiled. "But, considering this is a Matching, have you been approached?" She raised her eyebrows in mock curiosity.

"*Maaaybe.* How about you?"

"Ugh, I have far too much going on to think about things like that. What do you think about spending your life with a mage?"

"I think the ones I know already are enough trouble."

She laughed, but then she grew somber. There was one mage who was more than enough trouble for everyone: Castiel. All the mages that, as far as Carina could tell, were 'in charge' knew about her half-brother, but no one had mentioned what should be done about him. Would the responsibility fall to her? And if it did, should she do anything? The more time she spent at the Matching, the more distant the problem of a Dark Mage had become. She wouldn't need much persuasion to abandon the difficult, dangerous task of putting a stop to his activities.

———

The next day, Carina was walking through the camp and she happened to pass by the Spirit Mage's tent. She was debating whether to go inside and ask to speak to the old woman about Darius, and perhaps about Castiel too when, to her surprise, Magda poked her head through the open flap.

"Carina, please come in for a moment," she said before withdrawing into the tent.

Reluctantly, Carina lifted the flap and went inside. It was the first time she'd seen the interior of Magda's tent. The floor was spread with rugs, and utensils, lamps, and ornaments hung from the struts. Two full bags made of thick, embroidered cloth sat in one corner. The Spirit Mage also had a decorative decanter full of elixir and a couple of beakers.

"Darius isn't here?" Carina asked.

"I sent him home early. The child was tired. Perhaps I have been pushing him too hard."

"Perhaps you have," said Carina, trying but failing to keep an accusatory tone out of her voice.

"You care about him very much, don't you?"

"Of course I do. He's my brother."

"And he's also the only Spirit Mage who has come forward. I know I'm asking a lot of him, Carina, but I have little time left in which to teach him."

The old woman appeared suddenly frail and ancient, and Carina felt a pang of pity. Yet her sympathies remained with her brother.

"Sit down, dear."

Carina didn't sit. She remained standing, stooped under the tent's low roof. "What do you want to talk to me about?"

Magda, who was cross-legged on the floor, reached up and took Carina's hand in her own. "I feel your presence whenever you walk past my tent. You are full of pain. You are radiating hurt. I think you bear the most suffering of anyone in this camp. I'm surprised Darius can tolerate being around you for long. I want to help you, if I can."

Magda's words surprised Carina. She'd never imagined her presence might bring her brother discomfort. The knowledge hardened her bitterness. "I don't think there's anything you can do to help me, unless you can change the past."

"No one can do that, but sometimes it helps to explore it, accept it, and move on."

"You think I should accept everything that's happened?" Carina remained stubbornly standing. "How's that going to help me?"

"Please, sit. I want to tell you about Faye and Kris."

The mention of her parents' names broke through Carina's defenses. Her resolve not to open herself up to this woman quavered. She lowered herself to her knees. "What do you want to tell me about them?"

"Or perhaps it would be better if I showed your parents to you?"

"Showed them to me? How?" Mages could not keep images or recordings of each other. Everyone knew that.

"Spirit Mages do not only remember stories. One thing I have been teaching your brother is how to memorize what he sees. When he is older and I am dead, he will be able to pass on these images. It's the only way we have of keeping a record of our kind. Carina, I was at the Matching where your parents met. I remember them. Would you like to see them?"

Was there anything in the galaxy Carina wanted more than to see her parents again? Perhaps, but not many things. She would give a lot to see them as they had been when they were young and before harm had come to them. "Yes, I would."

"Good. Close your eyes. I will Send my memories to you. It may take some time, so please have patience."

Carina did as the woman asked. Outside, the carefree sounds of the camp continued. She could hear people talking and laughing. In the distance, musical instruments played and people sang along. Someone had started a fire and she could hear it crackling. Faint smells of food cooking invaded the tent.

But she saw only darkness, until she saw them.

The setting was the same. She could see the camp and the people, almost identical to the present, but the scene must have been from more than twenty years previously.

Ma and Ba were walking through the long grass at the edge of the camp, just talking, but the look of love that passed between them was so strong it was almost palpable. Ma looked exactly how Carina remembered her as a child, but more distinct and real. Her face was fresh and plump, not thin and sallow as it had been after years of torture from Stefan Sherrerr. Ba was a young, strong man, maybe not as handsome or strong-looking as some, but his expression was honest and kind.

It was too much. Instead of bringing her joy, the sight opened deep wounds inside Carina—wounds that had festered under scars she had forced herself to grow. The image of her parents so young and innocent, so full of love and happiness, so unaware of the horrors that lay in their future, caused her almost unbearable agony.

Her eyes snapped open. "Stop! Stop it!" She leapt up, knocking her head against a hanging cooking pot, and ran out of the tent. Momentarily blinded by the strong sunlight and confused by her emotional state, she paused. Then she set off through the camp, hardly knowing where she was going.

What had Magda been thinking? She was either an idiot or a sadist. Carina couldn't understand why the old woman would subject her to something so painful. She had made everything worse, not better.

She strode on, unheeding of the glances of the young mages, until she found she had somehow made her way back to her own tent. She stumbled inside. The place was dark and quiet. Only Bryce was there, stretched out and snoozing. Carina's entrance woke him.

"Hey," he said, "what's—"

"Where's Darius? Magda said she sent him back because he looked tired."

"He's gone to play in the prairie. I guess he missed his brothers and sisters more than sleep."

When she realized Bryce was alone in the tent and the children were not around, she turned and fastened the entrance.

"What are you doing?"

She had gone over to Bryce. He sat up. Welcoming the news they would be alone for a while, she kissed him hard on the mouth. For a moment Bryce was too shocked to respond, but then he kissed her back and pulled her close.

She remembered the first night they'd met, on Ithiya. Bryce had kissed her then. She hadn't forgotten what a good kisser he was. As they held each other tightly, her pain began to lose its edge. She needed to push it all away, push the hurt back down where it belonged.

But then Bryce stopped kissing her. He looked into her surprised eyes, and then disengaged himself from their embrace. He gripped her arms, holding her distant from him. "Carina, what is this? What's going on?"

"What? Nothing's going on. Let's do it." She leaned in to kiss him again, but Bryce moved his head backward.

He gave her a strange look. "Has something happened? Something's wrong, isn't it? This isn't like you."

She could feel her cheeks turning scarlet. "I don't know what you're talking about." She tried to kiss him again but he turned away.

"Carina, I—"

"For stars' sake! Do I have to put in a request?"

Bryce was shaking his head. "Something's rattled you. I can tell. Is this what you used to do with your merc buddies to get over your feelings when you were upset?" His tone was challenging.

She moved away from him, blinking away tears, shame tingling every fiber of her being. "How dare you.... If you don't want me, that's fine. Only I got a different impression."

"I'm sorry. That didn't come out how I meant it."

But she was already leaving. She couldn't bear the embarrassment. How would she look Bryce in the eye now?

"Please don't go. It's just that it wouldn't be right for our first time, not like this. Not because you're hurting. I don't want it to be—"

She didn't hear any more. She was outside the tent and walking away. She left the camp by the quickest route and marched onto the prairie. She continued walking, long kilometers, into the evening and the night.

She didn't return until the pale gray pre-dawn light suffused the sky. The camp was quiet and everyone was asleep.

TWENTY

Castiel hated traveling aboard a starship. He hated the claustrophobic conditions and the inconvenience. He also hated all his traveling companions: Commander Kee and his crew, the troops on board, Sable Dirksen, another clan member called Barrett, and most of all Reyes. Castiel figured that Sable had made them bunk mates so Reyes could spy on him. Though he'd put Reyes in his place by ousting him from the top bunk, Castiel was at a loss about what else he could do against the smug upstart.

His position remained uncertain and shaky. Sable could use him, but he was not indispensable. To improve his position, he needed people he could directly control. Until then, he didn't want to risk the disfavor of the Dirksens. Providing he did their bidding they would tolerate him as an ally, perhaps. As soon as he stepped out of line his days would be numbered.

Since the incident when he had dropped Reyes on his face, the two roommates hadn't spoken a word to each other, which was exactly how he liked it. However, it was clear that Reyes was well liked by everyone aboard the vessel. He had plenty of social interactions, while no one spoke a word more than was necessary to Castiel.

Mealtimes were the worst. Sable sat with Kee, Barrett, Reyes, and a couple of high-ranking officers. *He* was not invited to sit at the same table, and Sable had given him an icy stare the first time he'd tried. When he sat at the tables for the rest of the crew, no one sat with him.

As the weeks had worn on, his anger at this unsubtle ostracization had grown.

The final straw came when he returned to his cabin at the beginning of the quiet shift to find that Reyes had once more occupied the top bunk. He could hardly believe the older boy's audacity and stupidity. Didn't he know he was about to end up face down on the floor again, only thrown, not dropped this time?

"What the hell do you think you're doing?" he exclaimed. "Get down from there. That's my bed and you know it."

Reyes leaned over the edge of the bunk and glared at him. "Make me."

"All right, I will. You asked for it."

Castiel took out his elixir bottle. He wondered how hard he could throw Reyes without any retribution from Sable. Then fury seized him. He was sick and tired of everyone's treatment of him. He would throw Reyes from the ceiling to the floor and perhaps bounce him around the cabin with some Transport Casts. Maybe he would stop short of actually killing him.

He didn't care what Sable said or did. He had enough elixir to inflict some serious damage on someone before anyone could stop him, come what may.

Reyes was watching him. Castiel took a swig from his canister without breaking eye contact with the Dirksen brat. When the liquid hit his tongue, he spat it out in surprise. The taste was wrong. It wasn't elixir. He took another sip. The liquid was plain water. He stared at the canister. How had they managed to switch the contents? He kept it by his side all the time.

Reyes was laughing. "I wish you could see your face. It's quite the picture." His laugh faded and his expression grew malevolent. "Not so cocky now, huh?"

Fear began to creep up on Castiel. Without his elixir, he felt naked and very vulnerable. He turned to leave, but there came the sound of movement behind him. A heavy weight landed on his back. Reyes had jumped onto him. His face hit the door. He heard the crunch of his nose breaking. Agony stabbed at him and hot blood gushed out.

He yelled. Reyes' impact had forced him to the deck. Two hands grabbed his hair and lifted his head before slamming it into the floor, again and again. Reyes was yelling at him.

"You're nothing but a traitor, Castiel Sherrerr, betraying your own kind. Your sister isn't even a Sherrerr but she refused to help us. *She* had some honor. You're nothing but a slime ball. A turd. A faithless, disloyal, two-faced toad."

Finally, the banging of his head on the floor stopped. Reyes climbed off his back. Castiel heard him stand, then Reyes' boot thudded into his side and pain erupted again. Reyes kicked him three or four more times. He moved away and the door opened.

"You'll be given your potion when *we* want you to use it," said Reyes. "And if you use it on one of us again, we'll kill you."

The door closed.

Castiel lay still. The blood from his nose had formed a lukewarm, sticky pool around his face. He had never hurt so much in his life. His head throbbed. It felt like Reyes was still banging it on the floor. His side ached where Reyes' boot had landed. He fought the urge to vomit. He fought the urge to cry even more. He would not shed tears like a baby. He was a man, and he would behave like one. That was what Father would have wanted.

In time, he found the strength to sit up, though he didn't move from the floor. He sat in his blood and brooded on his pain and hurt. He would never forget this moment. He had tried to help the Dirksens. All he'd desired had been to progress to his rightful place at the head of the clan. If they'd allowed him that, they all could have benefited. But instead the clan had chosen to use him, like he was nothing. They wanted what he had to offer, but they refused to give anything back, not even the recognition he was owed.

So be it. He had played along and so he would continue, for exactly as long as it suited him. Then they would all pay, and pay dearly.

———

As if Reyes' attack had been a trigger, Castiel noticed a deepening in the coldness he experienced from everyone aboard the ship. He was not confined to his cabin, as he'd suspected might happen, but no one spoke a word to him. No one looked at him. If he didn't move aside in the passageways, the crew would walk right into him. It was like he was invisible, a ghost who didn't know he was dead yet.

The supply of elixir he'd brought aboard the ship had, predictably, disappeared from the galley. When he asked the cook where it was, the man had looked through him as though he wasn't there. He guessed the liquid would reappear when they arrived at Pirine, but he wasn't even sure of that.

As he drifted about the ship while the seemingly endless journey dragged on, Castiel wondered why, if he was no longer considered an ally but only someone to be used, the Dirksens hadn't put him in the brig. When the answer to this puzzle hit him, his cheeks turned fiery red with anger and shame. The reason the Dirksens hadn't locked him up wasn't due to fear of retribution, but the exact opposite: they didn't fear him at all. They hadn't confined him because they couldn't be bothered.

This new understanding hit hard, and it was as much as Castiel could do to not take a knife and murder Sable Dirksen. The attention she'd shown him, scant as it was, had all been a sham. She'd only been playing with him, drawing as much information from him as she could. Now that she had what she wanted, all pretense was gone.

Fanciful ideas of revenge Castiel had formed previously devolved into a simmering black hatred, not only of the Dirksens, but of everyone else who had disrespected him over the years. He hated all of humanity, in fact. The only person who had ever treated him as he deserved was Father, and he was dead.

Castiel decided he would never show mercy to any human being.

Then the announcement came. The *Elsinore* had arrived at Pirine.

Twenty-One

Carina's experience of the Matching had turned from pleasure to bitter unhappiness. Her friendship with Bryce was ruined, Parthenia still hated her, and the Spirit Mage seemed intent on overwhelming Darius with knowledge.

The old woman seemed to cause her nothing but heartache. Though Darius' admiration and almost hero-worship of her had been over the top and unwarranted, Carina had been touched by it. The news that her presence caused her beloved brother pain had come as a shock, and she didn't know how to deal with it.

The only saving graces of her family's current situation were that Oriana and Ferne were finally, truly happy, and that Nahla was coming out of her shell. Her little personality was blossoming and it warmed Carina's heart to see it. The girl had spent so long in Castiel's shadow and following around at his heels, Carina had feared she would never get over it. But the kindness of Oriana and Ferne along with the young mages at the camp had paid off. Nahla no longer spoke in whispers or hung back from joining in activities.

If only Carina could similarly blossom. Though she was younger than many of the women and men at the Matching, she felt older and battle-worn, and she didn't know if she would ever be fixed.

Various young men had approached her over the weeks in subtle but unmistakable ways. Carina had equally subtly rejected their advances. She was in no mood for love, and she had alienated the one person she might have considered in that way, through her clumsy proposition.

What was it Bryce had asked her during that shameful moment? Something about resorting to doing that with her fellow mercs when something upset her. She hadn't thought about it, but maybe he had a point.

Having nothing better to do one evening, Carina decided to listen to another of the Spirit Mage's stories. Darius and Nahla were already asleep and Oriana and Ferne agreed to look after them. Carina walked through the camp in the heavy twilight toward the large, central fire where the Spirit Mage told her tales.

The woman was sitting on the far side of the fire so she could only hear her story, which had already begun. She sat cross-legged, rested an elbow on one knee and her chin on her palm, closed her eyes, and began to listen.

The Dark Mage had been working in secret—

Her ears pricked up. This was the first story of a Dark Mage the Spirit Mage had told as far as she knew. She listened more intently, hoping to hear something useful.

When the story was over, despite the late hour, Carina decided to speak to the Spirit Mage before she returned to her tent. She had, if she was honest, all but given up on the idea of returning to Ostillon to try to find her mage half-brother and prevent him from exercising his powers for evil. But the Spirit Mage's story had forced her to reconsider. Perhaps mages did have a duty to protect the rest of humankind from the evil possibilities of Casting.

Carina caught up to the old woman. "I'd like to talk about what you said tonight, if you don't mind."

"I don't mind at all. Did you enjoy the story?"

"I don't know if 'enjoy' is the right word to describe how I felt about it. Did you hear that I have a half-brother who I believe is a Dark Mage?"

"I did. The mage council has decided to wait to see what eventuates before making a decision about what we should do."

"The mage council?"

"Ah," said Magda, putting her hand to her mouth. "I shouldn't have let that slip. I apologize. I'm getting old. Please don't ask me any more about what I said."

It wasn't hard to guess the facts behind the old woman's slip up. Justin, Jace, the *Haihu's* captain, and other, older mages Carina had seen were clearly members of some organization involved in overseeing the activities of mages. Like most things in mage life, the council was secret.

But one thing was clear: the mage council was not going to tackle Castiel, or at least not until he did something truly dreadful. If anyone was going to take away his ability to commit evil acts, it was down to his family.

"I'm sorry that showing you the images of your parents upset you the other day," the old woman continued. "That wasn't my intention."

"It's okay," Carina replied. "I understand now that you were trying to help. You couldn't have known the effect it would have. I didn't know it myself. And though it did make me unhappy at the time, I'm glad I have those memories now."

The Spirit Mage reached out to Carina's forearm and gripped it tightly. "I try to help, you see, but I don't always succeed. I was only given the gift of feeling what others feel, but not the wisdom of how to make them feel better. It's been the labor of my life to learn that, but I was a poor student."

Though Carina was no Spirit Mage, she sensed the woman's deep sorrow and for the first time saw things from her perspective. The woman had an unenviable responsibility. She carried thousands of years of mage lore in her mind and it was her duty to pass that on as fully and faithfully as she could. If she failed it would mean the loss of their history and everything that made them who they were. Carina had only seen her as someone who was taking Darius away and overloading his young mind. She had seen the toll it was taking on him. He was constantly fatigued and low spirited.

But the Spirit Mage was trying to save their clan before it was too late, and Darius was her only means of doing so.

"I'm glad you don't hate me for what I did," said the mage. "Though I don't think that after this Matching we will part as friends."

"Huh? Why not?" Carina had a sudden sense of foreboding.

"Please come inside so we can talk."

They were at the old woman's tent. She lifted the flap to invite Carina to enter first and then followed her. The interior was dark, only the light from the dying campfire creating a glow through the wall. The woman lit a lamp and invited her to sit down.

As she had done when she'd shown Carina her memory of her parents, the Spirit Mage sat opposite her and took Carina's hands in her own.

"I wish you were older, and one of Darius' parents. But you are the closest person he has to a parent now. Carina, there's no easy way to say this. I know how much Darius means to you."

Carina's stomach tightened. What was the woman going to say?

"When the Matching is over, Darius must come with me."

Carina snatched her hands away. "No way. Absolutely not. He's far too young. He needs to be with the family he has left. He needs to be with me."

The Spirit Mage's eyes were sad. "I guessed that would be how you would feel. Nevertheless...."

"Nevertheless nothing! You're right. I am the closest thing Darius has to a parent. I have the final say over what he does and where he goes. And I don't give permission for you to take him anywhere. He's six years old, for stars' sake. He's much too young to leave his family." Despite her words, Carina was deeply conflicted. Keeping Darius by her side meant he would be subjected to her emotional pain.

"He is very young," said the mage. "But he will be well cared for. Carina, please listen to me. This is unavoidable. Jace, Justin, and all the others agree. The work I've done with Darius so far is only the beginning of what I must teach him. If I were only to see him at Matchings, it would take decades to impart everything he must learn. And I have so little time left. He has to live with me so he can study every day. The future of our kind depends on it."

"I don't care. He's just a little boy. It's too much to ask of him. It isn't fair."

"I agree. It isn't fair. And yet that's the situation we find ourselves in. Such is the lot of mages. We sacrifice so much in order to keep our heritage continuing."

"Then maybe it's time to give up."

The Spirit Mage had been looking downward, but at this she raised her head. "You mean give up being mages?"

"Maybe we should. Maybe it's the only sensible thing to do. Ma told me once it was only because someone stumbled on the secret of our abilities millenia ago that we realized we weren't the same as other people. If we give up, we'll go back to being like everyone else. No running, no hiding, no persecution, torture, and rape. Did you hear what my mother went through?"

"No, I didn't, but I know. It's written on your heart."

Carina's eyes stung. "And my father—murdered. All because they wanted to use their powers to help people. Now you're telling me you have to rip a little boy away from his family so he can help to keep magehood alive. Why? What's the point? We don't use our abilities to improve humankind, we only use them to help ourselves, in secret. We live our lives in fear. Maybe it's time to call it a day, right now."

She stood up, crouching under the low ceiling. "You're right. I am the person who is responsible for Darius, and I say no. He isn't going anywhere with you. He's coming with us. In fact, I don't even know why we're here. I'm not interested in Matching with anyone and all my brothers and sisters are too young. We'll be leaving in the morning."

She left the tent without looking back. She was furious. How dare the old witch think she could just take Darius away for her own ends? He wasn't a sack of flour to be carted around, passed to whoever wanted him.

When she arrived at her tent, everyone was asleep. In the dim light, Carina surveyed the low, black humps that represented everyone she cared about. No one was going to take any of them away from her, and she would kill anyone who tried. She had already lost three of the most important people in her life and endured years of isolation and loneliness. She wasn't going to lose anyone else.

She tiptoed between the sleeping forms to reach her spot and slipped under her blanket. She was settling down, her mind still whirling from the conversation with the Spirit Mage, when someone gently grasped her foot. It was Bryce, who slept along from her.

"Everything okay?" he whispered.

She was too choked up to answer. She silently shook her head, though she doubted Bryce could see the gesture. A moment later she heard him leave his spot and crawl over. He lay down opposite her. She couldn't see much more of him than the glint of his eyes in the darkness.

His proximity brought back the vivid memory of her failed seduction and her face became hot. She was glad he couldn't see her.

"What's up?" he murmured.

"The mages want Darius to leave us and go with the Spirit Mage when the Matching is over."

"You're kidding!"

"I wish I was."

"You aren't going to let them take him, right?"

"Of course not. But that means we have to leave tomorrow, early."

"Okay, that's what we'll do. I'm not sure how far the closest city is, but we can make it there."

"What if they try to stop us?" She didn't know how the mage council would react, and, stupidly, in her anger she'd announced her intention. There would be no slipping away quietly while no one was looking. She didn't relish the idea of fighting off a thousand mages in order to leave, even with Darius' exceptional ability on their side.

"I don't think they will," Bryce replied. "They'll probably only try to argue you out of it, but I doubt they'll try to stop you physically. Mages seem to be gentle, non-confrontational people."

"I wouldn't be too sure about that. I wouldn't have survived long as a merc by being gentle and non-confrontational."

"Good point."

A pause stretched out.

"Bryce...I'm sorry—"

He kissed her. "It's okay."

———

The following day, the news they were going to leave the Matching didn't go down well among Carina's brothers and sisters, with one exception.

After Carina made the announcement, Parthenia said, "So we're finally going back to Ostillon to deal with Castiel?"

"I think so," said Carina. Maybe she'd been wrong all along. If the Matching had taught her anything, it was that her family should stick together and take care of their own, whether that meant a small boy's welfare or preventing his elder brother from committing terrible acts.

"Great! At last."

"But don't I have to stay with the Spirit Mage?" asked Darius.

"No, not any longer," Carina replied. "You've spent enough time with her already." As she spoke knots of anxiety formed in her stomach. Was she doing the right thing? She just didn't know. Nothing seemed right, but if one thing was for sure, her family was not going to be split up again.

Oriana and Ferne looked glum but didn't say anything. Nahla began to pack their few belongings.

"How are we going to leave?" Darius asked.

It was a good point. They had arrived via the *Haihu's* shuttle. Even if the mages agreed to their leaving, Carina doubted they would give them a ride to the nearest spaceport. She didn't know how the other people at the camp had traveled here, or where the nearest city was. Perhaps leaving the Matching wouldn't be so easy after all.

The tent flap was open, and the morning sunlight was suddenly cut off as a large figure appeared in the entrance. It was Jace.

The children stopped their packing, but the newcomer's expression registered that he understood what was happening. "The Spirit Mage Sent to me when I woke up. She told me you might be leaving. I see that you are."

His tone was neutral. Carina couldn't guess what he thought of her decision or if he would try to stop them. She sized him up. Though he was far larger than her, she might be able to take him if he didn't know how to fight.

"That's right," she replied. "I'm not prepared to let Darius go with the Spirit Mage."

"I understand...Is it okay if I come in so we can talk?"

"I guess so," Carina said warily. "But I'm warning you, if you try to stop us you'll regret it."

Jace halted as he entered the tent, stooping low, and looked Carina in the eyes. "It seems you haven't learned much about mages in your time here." He sat down and continued, "Have you considered that you could also live on the Spirit Mage's world and see Darius whenever you wanted to?"

"I-I..." Carina felt suddenly foolish. "No, I hadn't considered that. But he's too young to be trained in this way. The fate of all mages is too heavy a burden to place on the shoulders of a young child. Besides, we have other work to do. We must find our Dark Mage brother and stop him from hurting anyone."

"So, you don't want Darius to live with an old lady in safety on a backwater planet, but you're happy to take him into conflict with a Dark Mage?"

The way Jace put it made Carina think again, but she quickly came to the same decision. "I know how it sounds, but I will keep Darius safe, and the rest of the younger children too. You have to understand that we're a family. We have our own path to follow. And though you say the Spirit Mage lives on a safe, backwater planet, that's exactly what Ostillon was before the Dirksens decided to make it their base. The same with my home planet—safe, boring, and dirt poor. But that didn't stop Regians from paying us a visit and starting a massacre. Nowhere in this galactic sector is safe with a Dark Mage running loose. Castiel is our brother and it's up to us to neutralize him. Then we can leave the Sherrerrs and the Dirksens to continue their feud while we search for Earth."

She took a breath. There, she'd said it, crazy as it sounded.

Jace's eyebrows rose. "You have it all figured out, don't you?" His words sounded mocking but his intonation was serious. "If that's your wish, no one here will stop you."

"You won't?" She found it hard to believe he would give in so easily. "But the Spirit Mage was telling me it's vital Darius is trained by her. She seemed to think the future of mage lore depended on it."

"She may well be correct. On the other hand, perhaps another Spirit Mage will appear. Maybe someone older than Darius, who has been lost or delayed. Who knows what may happen? But I am convinced your intention is sincere and you are capable of protecting those in your charge. It is clear you would give your life before you allowed them to come to harm. In any case, you have always been free to leave whenever you wanted. It would go against everything we stand for to keep you here by force."

Relief washed over Carina. She wouldn't have to fight Jace. He was a good man and she would have regretted it.

"Do you have a plan for reaching the city?" he asked.

"Not exactly. I thought we would have to walk there."

"You aren't well equipped for that. I will wait outside while you finish packing, then I'll take you to your transportation."

It didn't take them long to pack. They had the clothes they'd been wearing when they'd arrived, plus a few donated belongings. Nahla had been given a doll made from dried grass that she treated as the most precious thing she'd ever owned. Her attachment to the toy was odd considering all the valuable things she must have been given in her former life.

When they were ready, they stepped out into the sunlight. A pile of full cloth bags had appeared beside their tent.

"Who do they belong to?" asked Oriana.

"They're all of yours," Jace replied. "Word has gotten around that you're leaving. People know you have nothing so they wanted to help you out."

Carina's throat felt thick and her eyes stung. "Even though we're taking away the next Spirit Mage?"

"Even so," said Jace.

Her surprise and gratitude almost made her change her mind about leaving. But she was convinced she was doing the right thing. She spotted the edges of weapon butts poking out of a bulky bag. "Are those guns?"

"The city isn't well policed," replied Jace. "Those are for your protection, but I wouldn't go flashing them around if I were you. There's no sense in inviting trouble."

"I understand," said Carina. "Please give everyone our thanks."

"I will, but they don't need it. They're only doing the same for you as they would for any fellow mage. That's one reason we have survived for so long, I believe. We always help each other. Are you ready?"

"Yes. Let's go." Carina told the others to take a bag and picked up the weapons bag herself. The heavy weight of steel was comforting and familiar. She felt a whole lot safer when armed.

"Oh, we have lots of elixir," said Darius, opening a bag.

"Good," said Carina. "Come on, everyone. The morning's passing and we have a long journey ahead."

Jace led them through the camp, past the central fire pit, now black and faintly smoking, and into a section where Carina had never been. The young mages were rising, preparing their breakfasts, and talking. The scene was one she had seen many times but now she realized she might be seeing it for the last time, a pang of sadness hit her. Would she ever see her people gathered in such numbers again? She doubted it. A mage's life was a lonely one. All the more reason to keep her family close together.

"Do you think you'll ever be back?" asked Bryce, as if he'd read her thoughts.

"I don't think so."

"But what if you're Summoned again?"

"Oh, I wouldn't go. What would be the point?"

And with those words, Carina realized that at some point over the previous few days, she had found herself already Matched. Bryce held her gaze as they came to their mutual understanding, and then he nodded, satisfied.

At the edge of the campsite stood Justin, the *Haihu's* captain, Eira, and the ship's hands, Ren and Ione.

"Are we taking the shuttle?" Carina asked.

"No," replied Jace. "My brother and the ship's crew are here to help Transport you all. We'll go to a location a few kilometers from the city and then you can make your way in quietly. We try to attract as little attention as possible."

"We? You're coming too?"

"Of course. I will stay with you until I'm sure you're safe."

"Thank you."

"It's no problem. Are you all ready?"

As soon as it was clear they were all prepared to depart the camp, Justin and the other mages Transported them.

Twenty-Two

Kee was taking a landing party to Pirine's largest city, Ulcawell. Castiel was to accompany the group and, worse still, Reyes was to be his 'minder'. He was enjoying brandishing a weapon.

Kee addressed the team in the *Elsinore's* shuttle bay. He had assembled eight soldiers and four regular crew as well as Castiel and Reyes. Barrett Dirksen was also coming along. Castiel had not figured out the man's role in the Dirksen clan. Slim, dark-skinned, and black-haired, he dressed plainly but expensively, as Sable did, though Castiel could not see an actual family resemblance. But his status was clear from Kee's deference to him.

"There's no point in trying to hide who we are," said Kee to the party. "A battlecruiser in orbit is kind of hard to disguise, and as soon as we arrive at Ulcawell spaceport we'll be met with plenty of questions. But I'm sure I don't need to remind you that you are not to give away the true reason for our presence on Pirine. If anyone asks what we're doing here, the answer you must give is that we're paying a diplomatic visit as a gesture of friendship from the Dirksen Federation."

So that's Barrett Dirksen's role, thought Castiel. The man was to play the diplomat while Kee got on with the real task of locating Carina and their brothers and sisters.

"Remember," Kee continued, "your role is to mingle with the local population. Ask about new arrivals on Pirine. A group of five children and a young woman looking after them. This is a quiet place with a small population.

Someone might have noticed them. Also ask about reports of odd happenings, things that cannot ordinarily happen."

"Permission to speak, sir," said a soldier.

"Yes, corporal?"

"Could you give us a few examples?"

Kee turned to Castiel. "What do you suggest?"

Castiel was about to refuse to answer, but Reyes was one step ahead of him. He knocked the butt of a weapon into Castiel's shoulder and said, "Tell him."

A quiet fury had been simmering in Castiel for days, threatening to boil over, but he managed to keep a lid on it. "You might hear reports of people acting strangely, as if not under their own control, doors unlocking themselves, things moved by unseen hands. That kind of thing. Mages can also Transport themselves from place to place, so you might hear of people suddenly disappearing or appearing. But we're usually very careful never to do that anywhere that it might be noticed."

Except when trying to escape. The moment he was allowed to get his hands on some elixir, that was Castiel's plan. He would Cast Transport and put as much distance between himself and Kee, Reyes, and the rest of the landing party as he could. Pirine might be the middle of nowhere in terms of significance in the galactic sector, but he would rather be stranded here than spend another minute under the control of the Dirksens.

His experience of the last few days had taught him that all his plans had come to nothing. He had become a slave to the clan, to be treated the same as his father had treated his mother and his mage siblings.

Yet he had not resigned himself to a sense of inevitability about his fate. He had only given up on relying on others to assign him the power that was fitting to his abilities. Now he knew that if he was to rise to prominence he would have to do it alone.

Only first he had to escape.

His plan carried a certain level of risk. Reyes had delighted in telling him that Sable had given permission to shoot him the moment his actions became suspicious, such as if a Cast took too long to work. But it was a risk he was willing to take.

His situation was not the same as Mother's. He would not be abandoning anyone by Transporting himself away, or splitting up a family. He had no one he loved who would be tortured as punishment for his transgression. The Dirksens had less control over him than they thought, and if the right opportunity arrived, they were about to learn that fact.

The landing party was walking up the ramp to enter the shuttle.

"You too," Reyes said to Castiel, pushing him again with his weapon.

"Enjoying yourself?" asked Castiel as he stepped onto the ramp.

"As a matter of fact, I am," said Reyes, grinning. "It's a pain in the ass to have to hang around with a loser like you. I might as well get what I can out of it."

"Don't think I'll forget this, Reyes Dirksen."

"Oh, I'm sure you won't forget it. You'll just never be able to do anything about it."

They walked into the shuttle's interior. Reyes made Castiel sit down in a seat at the back of the vessel. The rest of the party took their seats too, and Kee went into the pilot's cabin. The shuttle doors didn't close, and after a few minutes, Castiel and everyone else was looking around, wondering what was causing the delay.

Footsteps sounded on the shuttle's ramp, and Sable Dirksen entered. Despite his hatred of the head of the Dirksen clan, he was forced to admit she looked sublime. She was wearing a calf-length dress heavily brocaded in threads made from precious metals. Iridescent gemstones studded the fabric, and the choker around her neck seemed to be made from the shell of a rare mollusk. He remembered his father giving his mother a hair comb made from the same, extremely expensive material, and flying into a rage when she wasn't delighted with her gift.

"Don't look at her," Reyes hissed. "You aren't fit to kiss her feet."

Castiel saw the look in his guard's eyes and recognized his own lust and covetousness toward Sable Dirksen. He smirked. The chances of Reyes Dirksen possessing her were probably little better than his own.

Sable passed them by without a glance and disappeared into the pilot's cabin. The shuttle doors closed and the vessel took off.

So Sable had decided she would also form part of the 'diplomatic mission' to Pirine. Perhaps she wanted to be on hand if and when his mage siblings were captured. He doubted that would actually happen. There was no guarantee they had ever come to Pirine, and if they had, Carina was smart enough to keep them all hidden.

Sable could not remain on Pirine forever. Eventually she would have to concede defeat and depart.

These combined realizations made his heart sink. If no sign of mages could be found on the planet, it was unlikely he would be called upon to Cast. He would never be allowed access to elixir, and he would never have the opportunity to escape.

He would remain a prisoner indefinitely. Perhaps Sable would never require him to Cast. Perhaps she would take him back to Ostillon and lock him away in a cell deep under the mountain castle, along with Calvaley. If he were in Sable's position, that is probably what he would do.

She had spoken of mages as threats and liabilities, and, after all, at the end of the day he would always be a Sherrerr.

"Thinking about what you're going to do to find your sister?" asked Reyes, leaning uncomfortably into Castiel's shoulder.

He didn't deign to answer.

"I would, if I were you," said Reyes. "If I were you," he repeated, "I would make myself as useful as possible. Otherwise we might see no reason for keeping you alive."

Castiel stared doggedly ahead at the seatback in front of him. Would the Dirksens actually execute him? He hadn't considered that. The notion that someone would or could put an end to his life was too detestable to contemplate. Yet now Reyes had brought up the possibility, he could not exclude it.

His resolve to escape the Dirksens at the earliest opportunity became even more urgent. Remaining under their control was a constant threat to his liberty and his life.

The shuttle was touching down in Ulcawell Spaceport, and Sable and Kee emerged from the pilot's cabin. Kee began to address the troops and members of the *Elsinore's* crew. Sable walked directly to the back of the cabin, where Reyes and Castiel sat.

She was holding something in her hand. When Castiel recognized it, dismay coursed through him.

"Reyes, put these on his wrist and your own."

Reyes took the handcuffs and did as he'd been instructed, closing one band around his left wrist and one around Castiel's right.

Sable gave Reyes a metal fob that Castiel assumed was the unlocking device. "You're both to accompany Kee. Do whatever he says. And if Castiel tries to escape, shoot to kill, remember?"

"Yes, ma'am."

"I would rather have the filthy little traitor dead than working against us." Sable shot Castiel a glance filled with disgust before leaving them.

"Not going far now, huh?" asked Reyes, lifting his left arm.

Castiel's right arm was dragged upward by the cuffs. Their appearance had certainly made things more difficult. If he managed to Cast Transport without being shot, Reyes would be coming along.

Twenty-Three

I f it weren't for the city she could see in the distance, Carina would have thought she hadn't moved. They were surrounded by the high, tough grass of the prairie. Except she could hear something else.

"Oh no," Parthenia blurted. "It's those horrible animals."

Carina turned to see what her sister was talking about. Several meters away thirty or forty large, four-legged animals were enclosed by a fence. A dwelling stood next to the fence along with a barn. The door opened and a middle-aged woman came out.

"Are you talking about my horses, young lady?" asked the woman. "They aren't horrible."

Parthenia flushed and looked at her feet.

"You better get used to them," said Jace, smiling. "They're your transportation."

"Huh?" Carina asked. "How can they take us into the city?"

"We have to sit on their backs," said Ferne. "There were horses on Ostillon too. Didn't you ever see any? The first night we spent there, we slept in a barn that held horses. I think they're nice."

"Do we have to use them?" asked Parthenia.

Jace replied, "There are no roads hereabouts. That's what helps to keep this place unnoticed. It's the safest route into the city for all of you. We can't risk people popping up out of nowhere all the time."

Carina sized up the creatures. She could see how it might be possible to sit on their backs, though it didn't look like it would be very comfortable.

"So, will the little ones sit with the grown ups?" the woman asked Jace.

"Yes, that would be best."

"Okay, can you give me a hand to saddle them up?"

Jace left them to help the woman.

"I'm not sure about this," said Parthenia.

She addressed her comment to Carina. It was the first time she'd spoken normally to her sister since Carina had Enthralled her.

"It'll be all right," Carina replied. "I'm sure Jace wouldn't have brought us here otherwise."

They stood and watched the woman catch and then attach some kind of harness to the animals and then put a seat on their backs.

As she led the first horse over, the woman said, "You don't have anything to be frightened of. I picked the quietest, gentlest ones. They're a bit slow, but they won't bolt or try to throw you off. This is Rainbow. Who wants her?"

"I do," said Oriana. Her face was bright with excitement.

"Step up here then," the woman said, gesturing to a box next to the fence.

When Oriana was in place, the woman led the horse over to her and explained how to climb onto it. Soon, Oriana was sitting on the back of the beast looking like she'd just received the best birthday present ever. The woman taught her how to hold the straps that controlled the creature's head and told it which way to go. She also told her how gentle kicks would encourage it to go faster.

"But you'll only be walking into town," the woman concluded. "The horses will follow Jace's naturally. You won't need to do much."

While Carina had been watching Oriana, Jace had mounted one of the horses and walked it over.

"Jump up onto the step, Darius," he said. "You can ride in front of me."

A shadow of distrust passed over Carina's heart. Was Jace about to disappear with the precious new Spirit Mage? She caught Jace watching her expression. He gave a slight shake of his head as if rankled.

Darius leapt onto the steps and allowed Jace to lift him onto the horse. He was beaming with pleasure the same as Oriana.

Soon, they were all seated aboard the animals, their provisions slung over their shoulders. Jace thanked the woman and said goodbye. Carina noticed that he hadn't once spoken her name. He kicked his horse and rode to the front, heading out along a track worn through the grass. Carina's animal didn't need any direction from her. It followed Jace's without her guidance or urging.

Parthenia looked scared and was holding on tightly, but Carina guessed she would be fine in time. The motion of the horse as it walked was soothing.

"Do horses live on many planets in this region?" Ferne asked Jace.

"Only five planets as far as I'm aware. I've heard that mages brought them on their colony ship when leaving Earth."

"I can't imagine these creatures living on a starship," said Carina.

"Perhaps they brought them in Deep Sleep," Jace replied.

Deep Sleep was used to travel long distances that took months or years, such as when traveling out of the galactic sector. She had never been on a ship with that kind of equipment.

"Do you think that's how the mages first came to this region?" she asked.

"It's certainly possible. Sadly, we'll never know. That first ship must have rotted to dust thousands of years ago."

Carina got the sudden urge to talk more with the man. He would soon be leaving them and she might never see him again. He probably knew more than most mages about their origins and that first journey.

She gave her horse an experimental kick. The animal responded by moving a little faster. By trial and error, she finally found herself riding next to Jace. He glanced across at her with a quizzical but not displeased look.

"Is it correct that mages were the first colonists of Ostillon?"

"That's generally thought to be the case, but how did you know?"

She told him about the religious scripture she'd read on the planet, which seemed to tell the story from the viewpoint of the second wave of colonists, who were regular humans.

"Hmm.... Mage lore relates that story a little differently, but that seems to be basically what happened. The mages tried to get along with the newcomers, but the new arrivals were too frightened of mage powers. It was the same story as what happened on Earth: the mages were persecuted and driven into hiding. There's actually a place in the mountains not far from the capital that was their final refuge. Then it was decided the best course of action would be to split up and scatter to the stars to live in secret and only meet at certain gatherings like the Matching."

"You mean there are other gatherings?"

"You know I can't tell you any more, Carina."

"Okay, I understand. Sorry for asking. But...."

Jace rolled his eyes.

"Do you know the Ostillonians burn Characters as a ritual?"

"I do. They also burn the Map."

"Ah, of course." She recalled the moment in the temple when she'd seen a paper thrown into the ritual flames. "The paper covered in dots."

"That's right. It's the Map, and it has numbers too."

She sat upright in her saddle and swiveled to face him. "You're kidding! They must be coordinates."

"If they are, they're wrong."

"How do you know?"

"Because people have traveled to them. They lead to empty space."

"What people?"

"Mages who lived a long time before you or I. You aren't the first person to try to find their way back, you know. Earth is lost, Carina. You should forget about it."

"Do you think the entire system was blown apart?"

"I think they would have found the remains of it if that were the case, but according to the stories there was nothing. Either Earth never existed and our origin story is a myth, or the coordinates are wrong."

The conversation was such a revelation, Carina rode on in silence for a while as she digested the information. "I think the coordinates must be wrong. They were written so long ago, we no longer use the same system for mapping the galaxy."

"Whatever the answer is, it means we can never go back. It would be impossible to find an unknown planet without correct coordinates. The galaxy is too vast to search."

"But we know they came to Ostillon or a nearby planet first. That's a start."

"We know nothing of the kind. It's all guesses. And, anyway, if you did manage to find Earth, what are you imagining you'll find there? Mages left the place for a reason. What makes you think it's livable or we'll be welcomed back?"

She didn't have good answers to the questions. "I guess I would just like to see where my ancestors came from. And maybe I hope that things might have changed there in the intervening time. Wouldn't it be wonderful if we had a home where we could live without fear of torture and slavery?"

"Mages had that on Ostillon, and look what happened. It's the nature of humans to fear anyone different from themselves and to persecute them. Human nature will never change."

"I used to think that too, but Bryce taught me differently."

Jace's expression twisted as if he were uncomfortable. "There's an exception to every rule."

As they rode, the city drew nearer, and soon they reached the end of a street of cheap, one-story houses and shacks that petered out into the prairie.

"This is where we part ways," Jace announced. He halted his horse and immediately the rest of the animals followed suit, except for Oriana's, which turned its head as if wanting to go home.

"Whoa, there," Jace called at the animal, causing it to stop and shuffle restlessly on the dirt track. "Don't try to get down yourselves," he said to the younger riders. "Wait for me to help you."

Carina watched him dismount and then did the same herself as he lifted Darius down. Soon, everyone was off their horses and waiting while Jace tied a line between the animals to lead them home.

When he was finally done, he strode to Carina and enveloped her in an unexpected hug. Though she wasn't a small woman, she felt crushed in the large man's embrace. He released her and thrust a packet into her hands. "It's the local currency," he explained. "Earned by honest means."

"But I can't accept—"

"We're mages. We help each other. One day you'll have the opportunity to help someone else. Now, that money should pay for a few night's lodging and food. Simple, low-paid work shouldn't be too hard to find. Good luck, Carina, and the rest of you. I hope our paths cross again someday."

Before she had the opportunity to answer, Jace had swung himself up onto his large horse and walked it away. They watched as the train of animals slowly departed.

"It looks like that's it. Let's find somewhere to stay."

Twenty-Four

Castiel peered at the feed from the spy drone, amazed by what he saw. He was sitting in a room at the hotel suite the local government had assigned to the Dirksen delegation, watching a scene that was opening entirely new avenues of discovery about the world of mages.

Reyes was restless as he sat beside him, joined to Castiel's wrist by handcuffs. Castiel smiled. After nearly a week on Pirine, Reyes seemed to have entirely lost his smug delight at being his guard. The knowledge brought him a modicum of pleasure. It was one of his few sources of happiness in his current situation.

Reyes had been ruthless and exacting in his performance of his duties. The only time he would take off the handcuffs was when Castiel needed to use the bathroom, and then he fastened the other cuff to a pipe before going outside to wait.

Within a couple of days the metal bands had begun to chafe both their wrists. Reyes pulled down his sleeve to act as a buffer—doing nothing to help Castiel, naturally—but it was clear the cuff continued to irritate him.

After all, as long as Castiel was fastened to Reyes, Reyes was fastened to him. Reyes might have the freedom to dictate where they went and what they did, to an extent, but he was equally inconvenienced and restricted. He took out his frustration on Castiel through insults and taunts, though the mean words did not seem to make him feel any better.

Castiel had found he could bear it all if he clung on to the notion that Reyes was suffering almost as much as himself.

Then the news had arrived that the landing party might have found the mages, and the possibility had thrown a new light on everything.

Only, they hadn't apparently found *Castiel's* mages, but *some* mages. Rather a lot of them.

Commander Kee got the credit for the discovery. When he and the rest of the landing party had put out feelers, asking about strangers from outsystem who had arrived recently, specifically a young woman with five children, the answers that came back were entirely unexpected.

No one remembered seeing that particular group, but the local gossip was full of news that a gathering of 'wilderfolk' was going on, out on the prairie, and that people had been arriving for weeks in one way or another. No one minded nor did anything about it except to speculate what they were doing. The land was public, and the wilderfolk did no harm. They were expected to leave the place undamaged as they always did.

Anyone else might have ignored the information as irrelevant. Castiel certainly thought so the first time he heard it. What could possibly be interesting or useful about a group of vagrants setting up camp, probably in order to abuse brain-destroying drugs and perform weird rituals? But Kee did not seem to dismiss any information until he knew it to be worthless.

The commander had inquired more about this group and sent out soldiers dressed in civilian clothes to try to enter the camp. The attempt only brought more questions. There was no road to the campsite. The wilderfolk seemed to have walked for a day or more through long prairie grass to reach it, though there were no tracks.

So Kee had sent in the spy drones, and that was when everything had been blown out of the water.

Castiel never tired of watching the feed from the tiny drones, which looked like flies. He had never seen so many mages all in one place at once. He had never even imagined so many existed. Mother had always avoided talking about anything to do with mages unless Father forced her. Consequently, Castiel's knowledge of them was sparse.

He had formed the impression that Casting was something done rarely and for special purposes, yet the images from the encampment showed people starting fires, Transporting objects or themselves, Rising water from a spring, and performing other Casts as if it were the most ordinary behavior.

"Your sister led us to a nest of mages," Reyes sneered. "You should be proud."

"Bullshit," Castiel replied. "We don't even know if she's on Pirine, let alone at that campsite. No reports have come in about her."

"She's here. I'd bet money on it. It's only a matter of time until she turns up."

"I doubt it. If she's on Pirine, where is she?" Castiel nodded toward the screen that displayed the drone feed. "We've seen hours of recordings now and no one's spotted her."

"Unless you have, and you're lying."

"Why would I lie? Why would I want to protect her?"

"Yeah, you're right. I was forgetting what a sniveling little squealer you are. You wouldn't piss on your family if it was on fire."

Castiel couldn't think of a suitable comeback, so he only said, "You know what Carina looks like, and the rest of them too. If any of my siblings were there you would have seen them by now."

Kee came into the room. Sable was with him. Castiel hadn't seen her for days, while she and Barrett had been attending meetings with the Pirinian governments. Sable's garb had reverted to its usual expensive simplicity.

Kee turned off the drone feed and addressed the room.

"We have received permission from the Pirinians to round up the mages and deport them. What we're actually going to do is surround the encampment overnight and move in at dawn, killing as many as we can. Realistically, taking into account these people's special abilities, we can't expect to wipe them all out, but we should be able to make a serious dent in their numbers and make them think twice about ever interfering in Dirksen business. The rest of the company is on its way down from the *Elsinore* as I speak."

Killing as many as we can? It was to be a massacre. The deliberate, controlled mass murder of unarmed people who had committed no crimes and had no clan affiliation. Castiel had thought Kee was somewhat soft-hearted. That was what his interrogation techniques had seemed to indicate. It appeared that impression had been incorrect.

Reyes shifted in his seat beside Castiel. When he looked at the older boy, Reyes had turned pale. Was he shocked? Even Castiel himself was surprised by the viciousness of Kee's plan. The commander certainly didn't pull his punches. Or was the idea Sable's? She wasn't the head of the clan for nothing.

Kee went on to explain the finer points of the operation, which was to take place at sunrise tomorrow. Castiel wondered what he and Reyes were supposed to be doing while all this bloodshed went on, but Kee did not say.

The commander was in the middle of stating the importance of separating the mages from their elixir at all costs, when Sable raised a hand to her ear and frowned. She had heard some news. Her features brightened with uncharacteristic glee.

She placed a hand on Kee's arm, signaling him to stop. She whispered in his ear, and then swiftly strode out.

Kee's dark eyes focused on Castiel, and he gave a small smile. "You're in luck, Castiel Sherrerr. We've found Carina and the rest of your sisters and brothers. I think it's time you had a family reunion."

TWENTY-FIVE

Carina and her family stepped from the prairie onto the dust road. Their priority was to find somewhere they could sleep tonight. Carina planned on leaving Parthenia in charge while she and Bryce went out to look for work.

The wages for the low-level jobs they might expect to find would be small, and they had five children to feed as well as themselves. That would place a considerable delay on Carina's plan to return to Ostillon and face up to Castiel. It would take a long time to save enough for passage to the planet, yet there wasn't anything she could do about it. Protecting her siblings came first.

The suburb the mages had entered was old and unkempt. Carina found this a little odd. Usually, newer buildings were found at the edge of metropolises. That was where expansion took place. On the other hand, Pirine was not a rich, quickly developing place.

Until she could afford to buy an interface, they would have to rely on face-to-face encounters to find lodging and work. Carina's fingers closed around the local currency Jace had given her, which was tucked into her pocket. All they needed was a room and bathroom. A kitchen would be good too. Cooking at home was usually cheaper than buying street food.

"Should we knock at someone's door and ask if they know anyone who has a place to rent?" Parthenia asked.

"Let's walk a few more streets into the city," said Carina.

They passed along the wide roads, lined with trees and one-story houses. It was not the kind of neighborhood where she would expect to find rental places. The area was somewhere that families lived, children growing up and playing in the large yards.

As they walked, Carina remembered a similar search on Ostillon, trying to find work and a place to stay. She also recalled Reyes Dirksen and his convoluted plan to return her to his mother's clutches. At the time, his assertions that he'd planned on leaving the Dirksens had seemed convincing. Perhaps he'd been genuinely considering the idea. But loyalty to his family had won out in the end.

"I'm tired," Oriana announced. "I want to sit down. Riding on that horse hurt my bottom."

"Oriana," said Ferne, exasperation edging his tone, "stop complaining. We're all tired."

"I'm only saying," his sister replied, indignant.

"We could ask at one of these houses if they know somewhere we can stay," said Parthenia.

Carina didn't hold out much hope but it wouldn't hurt to try. They had walked a few hundred meters into the city.

"Okay," she said. "I'll ask. You all wait here."

While the children clustered on the sidewalk she strode to the nearest house and looked into the security panel. If anyone was home their house system would notify them they had a visitor. She waited.

A minute later, the door opened. A short, old woman stood in the doorway and removed buds from her ears. "Yes?"

"Sorry for disturbing you. We're looking for somewhere to stay." She glanced at her siblings and saw them through an outsider's eyes: dusty, disheveled, and needy looking. How different from the rich, privileged children she had first met. They had descended to a level of society very familiar to her. "I was wondering if you might be able to point us in the direction of a place to rent?"

The old woman's gaze took in Carina, Bryce, and the boys and girls in one brief look. "You won't find anything like that around here. You need to go into the city center."

"Okay, thanks." Carina turned and stepped down from the porch.

As she returned to her waiting family, she shook her head, but then the old woman called out, "Hey, wait a minute. Come back."

When Carina reached the porch again, the woman said, "How much are you willing to pay? I have a spare room. It isn't much, but you could put a couple of mattresses on the floor."

Carina had no idea how much to offer. She named a sum that seemed fair for a week's rent. When the woman's eyes widened and she quickly accepted,

Carina realized she'd suggested too much. "Could I see the room first?" If it was tiny or awful, she would back out of the deal.

The old woman introduced herself as Bridget and invited Carina into the house. "I'm Tamira," Carina said. "Most people call me Tammy." She doubted that Castiel would have made his way to Pirine to look for them, but the precaution wouldn't hurt. She would tell the children to make up fake names as well. She hoped Darius would remember to use them.

The room was not tiny or awful. It was large and clean, though Bridget had used it as a storeroom. "I can move that stuff out in a jiffy. What do you think?"

Carina thought that as somewhere they could stay for the next week while they got on their feet, the room would do fine. She told Bridget she would take it. "But we don't have any mattresses. Will it bother you if we sleep on the floor?"

"Makes no difference to me. You can swing from the ceiling for all I care."

As Carina walked through the house again on her way to tell her family the good news, she saw that Bridget's furniture was old and threadbare, and the place had not been decorated for many years. She felt less bad about over-estimating her offer for the rent. The woman could clearly use the money.

"Are you wilderfolk?" Bridget asked before Carina stepped through the front door.

"Wilderfolk?"

Bridget looked down, embarrassed. "I'm sorry. I don't mean to pry."

"It's okay, but I don't know what you're talking about."

"Are you from the group camping out on the prairie right now?"

"We...." Carina didn't see any reason to lie, and she couldn't think up a credible background story at such short notice. "Yes, we are. Is that what people call us?"

"We do. I hope you don't think that's rude."

"No, it's fine." Carina's curiosity was piqued. "What do people say about us?"

"Only that you all seem to meet up every few years, here on Pirine or some-where nearby. You gather and live in a camp for a few months, and then you go. No one knows why for sure, though I've heard some rumors. Not that I believe them, of course. People love to gossip and think the worst of everyone, don't they? I'm sure you're all fine folk, just going about your business. Nothing wrong with that."

It would have been impossible for the Pirinians not to notice several hundred people gathering for months, but Carina hadn't considered how the

Matching might be perceived by outsiders. Should she Send to Jace to tell him what she'd learned?

But she couldn't if she wanted to. She didn't have anything of his to Locate him. The money he'd given her would be imprinted with the trace of many hands. Anyway, she decided, Jace and the rest of the mage council were probably aware of the mages' image as 'wilderfolk.' It seemed harmless enough.

"I'll go and tell my family to come in."

Oriana was delighted with the news that she didn't have to walk any farther. She and the rest of Carina's family followed her into Bridget's home. The old woman was already moving things out of her spare room. Carina and Bryce offered to help her, while the children opened the bags the young mages had given them and began to take out blankets and other donated possessions.

Soon, the room was empty of Bridget's stored boxes, which she had crammed into spare corners of her home. From what Carina could tell, Bridget seemed to live alone. She guessed the old woman might have been tempted by the idea of some company as well as the rent money.

Carina watched her brothers and sisters as they unpacked and made themselves at home, gabbling noisily and bantering with each other. Company was certainly something Carina could provide, in spades.

Then she noticed Oriana wasn't helping. She sat in a corner, her arms folded and her lips in a pout.

Ferne asked, "What is wrong with you, Oriana? Why won't you help?"

"I don't like this place. I want to go back out on the prairie. I don't want to live in a house. I liked our tent and living with all the mages. It isn't fair."

Carina rolled her eyes. Oriana was turning into a real pain in the ass. Something would have to be done about that, but if the girl's spoilt entitlement was the worst Carina had to face, she would be happy to settle for it.

Twenty-Six

Bridget had been kind enough to cook them dinner, so Carina and Bryce didn't have to leave the house to buy food. The old woman wouldn't even accept the money Carina offered her. In fact, she'd seemed embarrassed that she wanted to pay, and she had wondered if she'd violated a cultural expectation, perhaps insulting Bridget with her offer. It was always hard to navigate the social norms when visiting a new planet.

They were too many to fit around Bridget's small table, so they ate in their room, sitting cross-legged on the cloths the other mages had given them. The children had also discovered light, metallic bowls, plates, and cutlery among the offerings. The generosity of the young mages at the Matching gave Carina a twinge of regret. Had she done the right thing to leave, taking Darius with her? Would the current gathering be the last in the history of mages? She rubbed her forehead to ease the headache she'd had for hours.

"What's wrong?" Bryce asked before popping a spoonful of Bridget's delicious stew into his mouth.

"Just wondering if we should be doing this."

"No, we shouldn't," Oriana said. "But it isn't too late to change our minds. We could Transport back to the camp right now if we wanted to. We all know where it is."

"Don't be stupid," said Ferne. "What would Bridget think if she came in to find an empty room when no one has gone out of the door?"

"Well we don't have to leave like that," Oriana retorted. "We could leave in the morning. Go somewhere quiet where no one can see us."

"No," said Parthenia. "We have to return to Ostillon. We have to find Castiel and stop him from helping the Dirksens."

"Maybe I should go back to Magda, Carina," Darius said, concern written in his big, brown eyes.

"We aren't going anywhere," said Carina, recalling guiltily that she had not allowed her brother the opportunity to say goodbye to his teacher and mentor.

Her headache was pounding and the split in her family's opinions was making it worse. If anything was clear, it was that they had to stay together and have a common purpose. Their time at the Matching had only served to divide everyone. "We have a plan and we're sticking to it."

"*You* have a plan, more like," said Oriana.

Ferne poked her in the ribs, and she shoved him in the chest with the heel of her hand.

"Stop it!" Carina snapped.

"Come on, kids," said Bryce. "Knock it off. Things aren't going to be easy for the next few months. We need to make a special effort to be nice and get along."

Ferne and Oriana looked daggers at each other, but they stopped fighting. However, Oriana pushed her spoon into her bowl and put the bowl down. "I've had enough." She stood up and walked to a corner of the room, where she began to make herself a bed on the floor.

"Don't worry," Bryce said softly to Carina. "She'll come around."

Oriana overheard and narrowed her eyes at him. She viciously plumped up a cushion and threw it down.

The small spat left everyone out of sorts. The rest of their dinner was eaten in silence except for the scraping of spoons. Ferne finished Oriana's stew, and when everyone had eaten, Parthenia offered to take the utensils to the kitchen to wash. Nahla went with her.

The sight of the little girl trotting alongside her older sister, her arms full of dirty bowls, warmed Carina's heart. She was so glad she'd extracted Nahla from her brother's clutches. How odd it was that the sibling who had once had the closest relationship with Castiel had turned out to be the least trouble.

While Parthenia and Nahla were filling Bridget's kitchen washer, the old woman came into the bedroom. "Is everything all right? Will you be turning in for the night soon?"

"Yes," Carina answered. "It's been a long day." And she and Bryce would have a long day tomorrow, looking for work. She would have to talk to Parthenia about how she would keep the children occupied. Maybe she could help them practice their Casting, providing Bridget wasn't around.

"I hope you sleep well," Bridget said. "It won't be very comfortable, lying on the floor. I wish I had something I could lend you, but I don't have anything."

"Don't worry about it, please," said Carina. "We're used to it."

Bridget left them and a few minutes later Parthenia and Nahla were back with their clean utensils. Everyone prepared to go to sleep.

Realistically, the children would have to find ways to contribute to the household budget if the family was to ever leave Pirine. Carina recalled the years she'd spent helping Nai Nai gather and polish beautiful stones to sell. It hadn't been an easy life but at the time she hadn't known any different so it hadn't seemed so bad.

The same could not be said for her sisters and brothers. But they would manage. Even Oriana would get over herself eventually. No matter how hard things got, at least they would have each other.

Oriana had already lain down, her back to everyone. Carina helped the others to fix up their beds. In truth, the hard floor wouldn't be as comfortable as the compressed prairie grass under their tent at the Matching, but they would be okay. Everything would be okay.

———

Carina was sound asleep, her head on Bryce's shoulder, when light and noises wakened her. She opened her eyes and found herself looking into a muzzle. She drew in a sharp breath and stiffened. For a moment, she thought she was having a nightmare, but no, she was awake, and what was happening was very, very real.

"Don't move," said the soldier at the other end of the weapon.

Assuming the order didn't apply to her eyes, Carina's gaze roved the room. Another soldier stood next to the first, pointing a weapon in the direction of Bryce's head. From the tenseness of his muscles, she guessed he was already awake.

She squinted toward the door and was entirely unsurprised to see Castiel standing there. What did surprise her was that Reyes was with him, and that the two were handcuffed to each other. This fact threw her into confusion. Was Reyes guarding Castiel, or vice versa, and why?

"Get up," said a voice to her left. Another soldier had spoken, presumably to Parthenia or Darius. Both of them had been lying on that side of her when they'd all gone to sleep.

She heard movement and the sound of quiet sobs. *Darius. Fuck.*

"I hope you're happy, taking a six year old prisoner," she said to Castiel.

The soldier knocked her forehead with the muzzle. "Shut up."

She had been expecting some kind of gloating retort or at the very least a smirk from Castiel, but she got nothing. The Dark Mage looked gloomy. Reyes' expression was even gloomier.

What was going on?

"Your turn," her guard said.

She slowly rose to her feet, taking in the room with her improved vantage point. Bryce stood up beside her, ordered to by his guard. Parthenia and Darius also had a guard each, and so did Nahla and Ferne. That made six soldiers in total. The Dirksens were clearly taking no chances.

The men and women were armed but not wearing armor, Carina noted, trying to figure out how the hell she could help her family escape. She needed to do something, and soon. Once they were all locked away somewhere it would be much harder to regain their freedom.

The soldiers had already found the weapons Jace had given them. The bag was open and next to the door, its contents plain to see. The elixir supplies were out of reach, and even if she managed to reach them, there was the eternal problem of the lag. She would be dead before she could Cast.

Darius' guard was searching him, roughly patting down the little boy as if he were an arch criminal who would pull a knife on them at any moment. Satisfied that Darius wasn't about to murder anyone, the soldier moved to her while Parthenia's guard covered her and her brother.

The soldier's hands were thorough as he felt her body, but she wasn't carrying anything useful on her person. She'd mistakenly thought they were relatively safe in Bridget's home. The old woman must have betrayed them. Her embarrassment when Carina had offered to pay for their food suddenly made more sense. Bridget must have made the call by then.

Had the local authorities issued an alert about a 'wilderfolk' family coming in from the prairie? Maybe they'd offered a reward. The old woman seemed poor enough to be easily bribed.

It was Bryce's turn to be searched.

"I'm sorry, Carina," said Reyes.

Castiel stared at him.

"Sorry?" she asked. "Sorry for what? For imprisoning children? For subjecting us all to a life of captivity and slavery? Or maybe for something else? I'd love to hear which of the hundreds of thousands of crimes your clan has perpetrated that you're sorry for."

"I thought it was all necessary, for the greater good, you know?' Reyes could not meet her gaze. "I had no idea what my clan was capable of. I've been naive. I understand that now."

She shook her head in disgust. "Please, spare me." Then she added, "If you feel so bad, why not let us go? There's still time. Order these soldiers to release us."

"I can't do that. They aren't operating under my orders. I'm only here as an observer."

"The Dirksens plan to kill all the mages," said Castiel, sneering. "That's what's eating him up. Even *I* think it's excessive, and I guess that's saying something."

"They...what?" asked Parthenia. Her mouth hung open and her cheeks lost their color.

"It's nearly dawn, so they'll be starting soon," said Castiel. "Out at that camp on the prairie. You must know it. That's why you're here, right? Sable Dirksen and Kee found out all about it yesterday. They plan to send a clear message to mages to never use their powers against them."

"But why?" asked Parthenia, horror in her voice. "Why would they think mages would harm them? Mages only ever do good."

"I beg to differ," said Castiel, smirking.

"This is your fault," yelled Parthenia. "You've made the Dirksens feel threatened by all you've done. If any one of those mages die you'll have blood on your hands."

"Make her be quiet," Castiel said to the soldiers, but they ignored him. "Anyway," he continued, "let's not forget who started this. It was you who did all that Casting for Father, helping him with all those business deals. That was what first alerted the Dirksens to our existence. They've feared our powers since then."

"That was because he made me!" Parthenia exclaimed.

Carina was struggling to absorb the news that the mages at the Matching were about to be attacked. All the young women and men, Justin, Jace, Magda —they could all die. Of course, as soon as they realized what was happening, they would be able to Transport themselves away, but there was bound to be a lot of bloodshed.

She was also confused about Castiel's place among the Dirksens. He seemed to have no status, if their soldiers didn't follow his orders.

"What are you doing?" she asked him. "Why are you here?"

"I'm to make sure none of you Casts. Not that I really give a shit. Not anymore."

So Castiel was in Reyes' custody. And Reyes was undergoing a moment of remorse. Carina wondered if she could exploit the situation somehow. Maybe there was a chance they could escape.

Then it hit her. Where was Oriana?

The revelation came as such a shock she swung around to check that her sister really was missing.

"Keep still," her guard barked, and swiped the side of her head with the muzzle of his gun.

The crack dazed her.

"Hey, leave her alone," shouted Bryce. His guard thrust his weapon into his chest.

Blood trickled down her face.

Where had Oriana gone?

Twenty-Seven

Oriana listened to the sound of everyone's breathing. One by one, most of her sisters and brothers had fallen asleep, and so had Bryce. Only Carina had remained awake. Now, finally, Oriana heard her eldest sister's breaths become deep and regular like the others'.

She would wait another five minutes or so and then she would leave. While she waited, Oriana remembered the nights she had snuck out of her room, when she'd lived on Ithiya and Mother and Father had been alive. Those secret nocturnal excursions around the mansion and into the garden had been the only times she'd felt truly alone. No servants had been watching her, surreptitiously or not. Father had not been silently judging her with his cold eyes. Mother had not been regarding her with pain and sorrow in every look.

In those brief times she had wandered Father's estate in the dead of night, when the entire household slept, Oriana had felt free. It had been an illusion. None of them had been free, not even Father. He had been a slave to his pride, arrogance, and ambition.

Was what she planned to do due to pride or arrogance? No. She only wanted to be free. She wanted to choose her own life. She had been through enough hard times. She deserved to make her own decisions on how she lived.

Oriana slowly sat up and pushed down her blanket. Ferne was sound asleep, dribbling like he always did, the starlight through the window lighting up his face. Everyone else was shadowy lumps in the darkness.

She had already thought out her list of what she needed to take. Clothes, elixir, her brush and toothbrush, and a couple of blankets. That would be all she would need. She had packed a bag while she'd been getting ready for bed. No one had even noticed what she was doing.

A sense of self-satisfaction warmed her. She had made careful preparations. She wasn't a silly little girl, running away for no reason. She had made a decision maturely, and now she was going to act on it.

Oriana stood up, picking up her filled bag from the floor. She picked up her shoes in her other hand. She would put them on when she was outside the house so the noise of her footsteps wouldn't wake anyone up.

As she took a last look at her family and Bryce, something tugged at her heart, causing a sharp pain. Would she see her brothers and sisters again? She didn't know, but she hoped so.

Don't be silly, she told herself. *Of course you'll see them again. They'll all attend the Matching eventually. You can see them there.*

Feeling a little better, Oriana tiptoed across the room with its sleeping figures around the edges, eased open the door, and stepped out. She closed the door, leaving it slightly ajar to avoid making any noise. The hall was very dark, but she could see light through a window in the door. Hoping the woman who owned the house didn't set her security system to monitor internal movement, Oriana walked along the hall, opened the front door, and slipped out.

She guessed it had to be the early hours of the morning. Lights were on in the distant city center, but the only lights she could see by were the handful of dim streetlights that lined the road.

She shivered. The coldness and dampness of the night was already invading her bones. She looked up and down the street. Would anyone see her if she Transported right here and now? Probably not, but there was no sense in taking chances. She needed to go somewhere she could not be observed.

She walked along the sidewalk, heading back toward the prairie. She imagined how nice it would be to live among the young mages again, carefree and happy. At the campsite she didn't have to hide what she was or live in constant fear of discovery and capture.

Someone would take pity on her and accept her into their family, she was sure. Perhaps that nice ranger, Jace, from Ostillon. On the other hand, that wasn't such a good idea. Castiel was on Ostillon, and he was the one member of her family she did not want to meet again.

It didn't really matter who she ended up with. All the mages were nice and kind. She would find someone. She wouldn't have to live the lifetime of hardship Carina seemed intent upon.

Oriana scanned the road from side to side, trying to find somewhere not overlooked. In a few minutes' time she would be back at the prairie and her new life would begin.

TWENTY-EIGHT

arina saw Castiel watching her, amusement in his eyes. *He knew!* He knew Oriana was missing and he hadn't said anything.

Reyes had to know too. He'd met all her brothers and sisters. The only person he hadn't met was Bryce, who had appeared later.

Both Castiel and Reyes had not let on to the soldiers that the party they were taking prisoner had one extra person: Bryce, and that one of them was missing. And because there were enough guards for one per prisoner, they hadn't suspected anything.

"Carina," said Darius, "where did Oriana go?"

"Huh?" said one of the soldiers. "Who are you talking about?"

Shit!

Carina stared at her young brother, willing him to be silent. He looked back, confused, and then opened his mouth to speak again.

No, Darius! No!

Then he was gone. Vanished into thin air. Parthenia had disappeared too.

"What the fuck?" a soldier yelled. "How do they do that?"

"Never mind that," shouted another. "We have to stop them. Grab the rest."

Darius and Parthenia had been Transported. Oriana must have done it. She had to be watching them from somewhere. The only possible place was the window. Carina forced herself not to look at it.

Her guard lunged at her, trying to grab her arm. She shoved him to one side. Oriana would be preparing to Transport the others. If a soldier was holding onto one of the mages, he might Transport with them.

"Fight," Carina cried. "Push them away from you!"

She heard the hiss of a pulse round and the thump of a body hitting the floor. Her guard reached for her again. She kicked his knee and heard a crunch. The man screamed. She spun around. Ferne was down! His bastard guard had fired at him.

But then Ferne was gone, and so was Nahla.

Only herself and Bryce were left. Carina's guard was rolling and groaning on the floor, but Bryce was locked in a struggle with his.

Castiel and Reyes stood in the doorway and did nothing.

From outside came the sound of someone shouting, "What's going on in there?"

Carina ran at the soldier holding on to Bryce.

She was within a step of him when she Transported.

———

Carina was in darkness, momentum carrying her forward. She crashed into Bryce and the soldier, and all three of them fell to the ground, hitting grass. They had to be somewhere in the yards around Bridget's house, but as she tussled with the guard who had grabbed Bryce she realized they were out on the prairie. A stiff wind was blowing, causing the tents to flap.

"Let go of him," Carina shouted, standing up to get a better look at Bryce and his assailant. The guard's weapon was trapped under him, and he was rolling around too much to punch him in the jaw. So she did the next best thing. She kicked one of his legs open and drove her heel into the man's groin as hard as she could.

That persuaded him to give up. While the guard rolled on the ground in silent agony, Bryce shook himself and stood up.

"Remind me to never piss you off."

Carina relieved the guard of his weapon, and then straightened up and turned full circle. "I don't believe it."

Oriana had Transported them all back to the mages' camp. The camp that was about to be attacked. Darius, Parthenia, Ferne, and Nahla were all here too.

She scanned the horizon beyond the tents full of sleeping mages. A rosy patch told her dawn was about to break.

Oriana suddenly appeared, Transporting herself in. "I'm sorry, I'm so sorry," she sobbed. "I'm sorry I ran away. I wanted to come back here. I didn't want to spend my life scraping to get by, always on the move. But then I realized I would miss you all too much. I went back to the house, and I saw soldiers, and—"

"You're sorry?" said Bryce. "You just saved all our lives."

"Not yet," said Carina. The sensible thing would be to leave right away, to Transport the hell out of the massacre waiting to happen. But there was no way she could abandon her kindred to such a terrible fate. "We have to wake everyone up."

"What?" Oriana asked. "Why?"

"The Dirksens are about to attack," said Ferne.

Oriana's eyes grew wide, and her brothers and sisters seemed frozen by the enormity of the evil about to befall the young mages.

Carina ran to the nearest tent, ripped open the flap, and yelled, "Wake up! You're being attacked. You have to Transport away from the camp! Come on, hurry," she said to Bryce and her siblings. "Help me."

This galvanized them into action, and they began to run to other tents.

"I'll go and tell Magda," said Darius.

"No, you won't," Carina replied. "You're staying here with me." She was not about to lose her brother to the Spirit Mage again.

And then she realized what she'd done. The camp was about to come under fire, and she had just sent her brothers and sisters away from her, where she could not protect them. They would all become separated. How would they find each other again?

"Wait!" she shouted. "Come back!" But Parthenia and the others didn't hear her. The noise in the camp was growing louder as the young mages woke up and asked each other what was going on. Bryce had also disappeared.

Damn!

Jace. She needed to speak to him. Or Justin. Someone who was in charge.

The mages she had woken were not Transporting. They were standing around and chatting.

"You have to get out of here," she yelled at a group. "The camp is about to be attacked."

"Aren't you the one who left?" one of them asked. "The new Spirit Mage's sister?"

"Yes. And I've come back to warn you, you must leave. Dirksen soldiers are about to attack and kill everyone."

"But how do you know?"

"It would take too long to explain. You must believe me."

A scream echoed across from somewhere out at the edge of the camp, borne along on the strong breeze.

"It's begun. Now do you believe me?"

The mages' expressions grew frightened. One of them nodded and returned to her tent.

"Grab whatever you can, quickly. Take all the elixir you can carry, and Transport as far from here as possible. Hide out somewhere until it's safe to leave Pirine. But before you Transport, Send to someone else in the camp and tell them to do the same."

Carina grabbed Darius' hand. "Do you know where Jace and Justin's tent is?"

"No. Only the Spirit Mage's."

"Ugh, then the Spirit Mage's it'll have to be."

Screams and shouts were sounding from another direction. The soldiers were closing in. Mages were already dying. She had to try to save as many as she could, but she couldn't do it alone. By the time everyone received a warning the soldiers would be halfway through the camp.

In fact, now she thought about it, the Spirit Mage was exactly the person she needed to see.

When they burst into the old woman's tent, she was sound asleep despite the increasing mayhem going on around her. She grabbed Magda's shoulder and roughly shook it.

"Be gentle, Carina," said Darius. "She's very old."

"I know, but..." She bit her lip. Without the Spirit Mage's help, hundreds of people would die.

The rheumy eyes opened and blinked blearily. "What...? Carina, my dear. You came back."

A scream of protest, suddenly cut off, came through the walls of the tent.

"What was that?" Magda asked.

Carina said, "Can you Send to everyone in the camp? You Summoned them all, right? Can you Send to them? It's very important."

"Yes, I...." She sat up, pushing down the blankets that covered her. "What's happening?"

"The Dirksens are attacking, and they plan on killing every mage they find."

Magda's mouth gaped. She looked at Darius.

"It's true," he said.

"Bring me my elixir," said Magda.

Darius had already grabbed it. He handed the Spirit Mage the canister and she removed the lid. "Do it with me, Darius. I'll need your help. You know how." After he nodded his agreement, she added, "Drink half of it. You'll need it."

Between them, Magda and Darius drank the entire canister of elixir. Then they held hands and closed their eyes.

All around, the sounds of fear, dismay, and confusion were rising, bubbling up like water in the spring at the center of the encampment. But Carina could hear another sound: a muted, rustling roar. She couldn't figure out what it was.

Magda and Darius unclasped their hands. As Magda opened her eyes, her skin increased in pallor. She looked exhausted.

"I've done my best," she said. "I cannot do any more right now."

Darius also looked tired.

Then Carina suddenly recognized the sound that had been puzzling her. It was fire. The Dirksens had set the camp on fire.

Rather than go from tent to tent, they were trying to drive out all the mages into the open, where the soldiers could pick them off, like hunters shooting game. She felt as though she were about to vomit.

"Can we go and find Parthenia and the others now?" Darius asked.

"We can." Then a thought struck her. "Darius, can you Send to them, even though you don't have anything of theirs? The same as you did just now to the mages in the camp?"

His little face brightened. "Yes, I can!" But then his features darkened again. "But not to Bryce or Nahla."

"It's okay, we can find them. Tell the others to come here, to the Spirit Mage's tent."

While waiting for Darius to Cast, she said to Magda, "You should leave. It isn't safe anywhere in the camp now. The soldiers will be here soon." *Or the fire will reach you.*

"No," the Spirit Mage replied. "My place is here. Until everyone has gone. My role is to save magehood for the future and I will do that to my last breath."

"But you're the repository of our history. If you die, our history dies with you."

"Our history did not seem so important to you yesterday," said Magda, her eyes twinkling. "You have a lot to learn, Carina. If I run out on my people, there's no point in me remembering anything."

She did not have time to argue with the old woman. She knew what she was doing. "Did you Send to the others?" she asked Darius.

"I did."

"Right. Let's go."

"Wait," said Magda. "Take some elixir with you, or you won't be able to Transport yourselves out."

Carina grabbed canisters for herself and Darius, and ran out of the tent.

The sky was red. The hues were from the rising sun and the burning encampment. Smoke and flames were billowing upward in the far reaches of the camp, but the breeze was blowing the fire closer every second.

Somewhere out there were Ferne, Parthenia, and Oriana, hopefully now heading toward the Spirit Mage's tent. She would have to find Bryce and Nahla. How, she didn't know yet. On the plus side, mages were Transporting away from the site. She could see them leave their tents, clutching bags, and then disappearing. She could also see shadowy moving forms inside tents, back-lit by the glow of flames, vanish from sight.

"Darius," she said, "I'm going to Transport you to the...." Where could she send her brother that would be safe?

"But I want to stay with you."

She was forced to acquiesce, as she could not think of a place on Pirine where Darius could wait for her in safety. "Okay. But stick to me like glue. Don't leave my side."

Darius gripped her hand, and they set off. As soon as she found Bryce and Nahla, they would return to Magda's tent to rendezvous with the others, and then they would all leave together. She didn't think there was anything else she could do to help the stricken mages. Though she carried the guard's weapon, she could not fight off tens, perhaps hundreds, of soldiers by herself.

Holding Darius' hand tightly, she ran along an avenue of tents. She shouted to the remaining mages to leave immediately, driving home Magda and Darius' message. She and Darius were running toward the flames, but she couldn't help it. The soldiers had set fire to the camp on all sides. Danger lay in every direction.

Where was Bryce? Where was Nahla?

Someone was heading toward them. She recognized her sister. "Parthenia!" she shouted. Her sister had Nahla with her! If there had been time, Carina would have kissed her. "Don't stop," she said. "Go to Magda's and wait for us. If you see any soldiers or the fire comes near, Transport to the trail we followed on the horses. About halfway along."

Parthenia nodded and Carina's two sisters ran past her.

Her heart lightening a fraction, she ran on. The campsite was beginning to look deserted. She hoped the majority of the mages had gotten away. The Dirksens would scour the planet for them, of course, but if the young men and women were careful, they stood a good chance of not being captured.

Carina and Darius were nearing the flames. She didn't dare to move any closer, yet there was no sign of Bryce. She guessed he must have gone to another area. If she didn't find him soon, the entire place would be ablaze.

Worse still, the roaring of the flames made it impossible to hear pulse rounds being fired. She had no idea if troops were approaching.

"*Jace!*" Darius screamed. He was staring off to one side, his hand like a vise on Carina's.

When she saw what her brother was looking at, her heart froze. A pillar of fire was stumbling between the tents. Was it Jace? She could not tell if it was him or his brother. The mage must have stayed behind after Magda's warning, to ensure the young mages Transported. The flames had overtaken him.

And that wasn't all. A soldier was emerging behind him in heat-resistant armor. His head covered in a specialized helmet and carrying an oxygen mix tank on his back, the soldier took aim at Jace, preparing to finish him off. But Carina's weapon was already at her shoulder and spitting pulse rounds at the man. She didn't release her trigger until he was down.

Darius was fumbling with the lid of his elixir, tears streaming down his face.

"There isn't anything you can do," she said. She didn't know a Cast that would extinguish flames, and even if she did, Jace was already too burned to survive.

"Yes, there is!" Darius shouted. "Please help me, Carina."

Still doubtful, she unscrewed Darius' canister and held it to his lips. The small boy swallowed a mouthful of elixir.

Too late. It was too late.

She could not bear to imagine the agony Jace was in. Perhaps it would have been kinder to allow the soldier to shoot him. Perhaps it would be kinder to do it herself.

She couldn't watch. If Darius put out the flames, what would they do then?

"I did it," Darius announced.

The man was on the ground. The flames had gone out. By some miracle, her brother had invented a new Cast to douse fire. Should she have let him? "Stay behind me. And don't look, okay?"

Jace was still alive. His burned body moved slowly on charred grass as they approached him. What had she done? He was dying. He deserved a quicker death.

Darius peeked from behind her and gasped at what he saw. Nevertheless, he said, "I can Heal him."

"I told you not to look. And, no you can't. You can't Heal a fatal condition. I think I'm going to have to...." She fingered the trigger of her weapon. How would she explain to Darius what she had to do?

"You cannot Heal him, Darius," Magda said, "but I can." The old woman had Transported here, somehow knowing what had happened.

She knelt down next to Jace and gently touched his burned skin. She opened her flask and drank elixir before she began to Cast.

Carina didn't know if Magda would be successful, but she also had no time to find out. She had to find Bryce and get out of here.

"Come with me," she said to Darius.

"But what about—"

"Don't argue."

Her little brother in tow, she fled the grisly scene. They hadn't gone more than twenty paces, however, before she saw figures approaching through the flames. Soldiers. They were walking steadily forward, scanning from side to side.

She halted. They hadn't yet seen her or Darius. There were about ten of them. The minute she shot at them they would shoot back, endangering her brother. Should she try to get out of sight or Cast Transport? Any movement was bound to catch the soldiers' attention.

In the end, the decision was made for her. Darius had spotted the troops too. He gave a shriek, ripped his hand from hers, and sprinted back toward Magda and Jace.

She had no choice except to follow him. A pulse round grazed her shoulder. They'd been spotted. She began to run a haphazard zigzag, desperately trying to avoid the soldiers' fire. Darius was running in a dead straight line. It was only a matter of time....

He had reached Magda and Jace, but the scene was not at all what she had expected. Magda was lying on her side, one arm flailed outward. Jace remained on his back, but all his burned skin had disappeared. He was Healed. He was alive.

Darius threw himself onto Magda. From the old woman's staring eyes, Carina realized she was dead. The Spirit Mage had brought Jace back to life at the sacrifice of her own.

A pulse round hit Carina square on her back. Unbearable agony spread from the wound. Her legs collapsed under her, and she found herself falling forward. This was no stunning blow. The soldiers' weapons were set to kill. This was the end.

Distantly, she could hear Darius crying out, howling in pain and grief. "I will save you, Carina. I will Heal you."

As her life ebbed away, she whispered, "No. No, don't, Darius."

Not like that. Not like Magda had done.

TWENTY-NINE

Carina opened her eyes and saw a smoky sky, red with the reflected flames of a fire. The air was filled with the fire's roar and the tang of burning. She remembered she was on Ostillon, in the basement of a house, and the Sherrerrs were bombarding the city. She had to get everyone out, but her leg was broken.

No, that wasn't right. That had happened weeks ago. Where was she now? Suddenly, the memory of Pirine, the Matching, and everything that had happened flooded back.

"No," she shouted, trying to sit up. "No, Darius. Don't do it!"

"She's alive!" exclaimed Parthenia. "Let's go."

A firm hand grasped Carina's wrist. "No," she repeated. "Stop him. Someone stop him." Darius had been trying to Heal her like Magda had Healed Jace. Only the Spirit Mage had died in the attempt. Darius could not give his life for hers. She wouldn't let him.

"Stay still," said Parthenia.

The grip on her wrist tightened. She felt herself Transported. The noise and smell of the fire was gone, and the sky was the pale pink of a natural dawn. She was lying on prairie grass. Her back ached where the pulse round had hit, but she was alive. She was alive, and her little brother had died to Heal her. She could not bear it. How could she go on living?

She turned onto her side, too anguished even to cry.

"Hey," someone said. She recognized Bryce's voice. She felt his hand on her shoulder. So he was okay. He'd escaped from the encampment with them. She was relieved, but she could not feel a flicker of happiness. She would never be happy again.

"Carina," said Bryce. "It's all right. We're all going to be okay."

She closed her eyes, pressed her lips together, and shook her head. They were not.... The understanding that Parthenia and Bryce were acting far too calmly for the situation finally pierced her fears. She sat up.

They were out on the prairie, entirely alone, the sea of tall grass stretching out around them. Parthenia had brought them to the place Carina had suggested, along the horse trail into the city. A small body lay nearby, but she couldn't bring herself to look at it. A terrible dread rose up in her when she tried.

Bryce was sitting next to her, his face and clothes blackened and smelling of smoke.

"Is...." She paused and swallowed. "Is Darius alive?"

"Of course he is," Bryce replied. "Is that what's bothering you? He's out of it, but he seems to be okay."

"Oh, thank the stars." Tears of relief poured from her eyes. She crawled over to her little brother. Like Bryce and everyone else, he bore the marks of the fire, but he was otherwise unharmed and he was breathing normally.

How in the world...? She could not figure it out. "What happened? I only remember being shot."

"I don't know what happened to you," said Bryce. "Oriana and Ferne found me and told me we were all meeting at the Spirit Mage's tent. When we arrived there, Parthenia and Nahla were waiting, but there was no sign of the mage or you two. We hung around, figuring you would turn up eventually. I think Ferne was about to Send to you. He was going to let you know we were all ready to go and only needed you to come back, when you and Darius appeared. Darius immediately passed out, and you looked to be half dead. But then you came around. Parthenia decided it was time to get out of there, and here we are."

Carina could only guess at most of it, though there was no doubt in her mind that Darius had saved her life. And apparently at great cost to himself, though not enough to kill him. Perhaps the Healing Cast had been too much for the old woman, but Darius, being younger, had survived it. He must have Transported her and himself to the Spirit Mage's tent before collapsing.

But what she could not figure out was why the soldiers had not shot her brother. They had been coming up behind her, and Darius had been right there, clearly a mage and a target to be taken out. Yet they had not shot him. Perhaps they had not been able to bring themselves to kill a little boy.

Perhaps there remained a smidgen of humanity at the heart of the most evil people.

She thought of Castiel. Though he'd known Oriana had gone missing, he had said nothing to the soldiers who had come to Bridget's house to take his family captive. She also thought of Reyes, who seemed to have finally comprehended the evilness of his clan.

She gasped. What had happened to Jace? He'd been alive when the troops had been approaching. Had they shot him or spared him like they had Darius?

"Looking for me, Carina?" said a deep voice behind her.

She swiveled around. The large man was sitting on the grass, entirely unburned and very much alive.

"I forgot," said Bryce. "Darius brought Jace with him too. I was kind of focused on you at the time."

They were all here: all her brothers and sisters, Bryce, and even Jace. But how many of the young mages had died in the Dirksens' attack?

"Do you know if most of the mages managed to get away?" she asked Jace.

The burly man's expression was sad as he replied, "Not all, but most, thanks to the help of your family." He paused. "It's strange how things turn out sometimes. I didn't want you to leave and take Darius from us, yet if you hadn't left, you wouldn't have found out about what the Dirksens planned to do. You wouldn't have warned us, and many more people would have been lost. So that is something to be thankful for."

"I'm sorry that Magda died," said Carina.

"So am I. Perhaps more than you will ever know. She was everything to us. She was our history, our culture, our future. She had barely begun to pass on all she knew to Darius. Now, I do not know what will happen. How can we continue when we've lost so much?"

Her heart ached with remorse and sadness. She had been so wrong about Magda. She had misinterpreted the Spirit Mage's deep need to safeguard mage lore as a desire to monopolize Darius. She realized how blind she had been, and now there was nothing she could do about it.

"Do not blame yourself for what has happened," said Jace, reading her expression. "The Dirksens are responsible for Magda's fate, not you."

"What should happen to Darius?"

"Though he is a powerful mage, Darius is very young, and he doesn't know anywhere near enough to take over as our clan's Spirit Mage. Everything has changed. A new era in magehood has begun, and I don't know what will happen to us. Perhaps it is the beginning of our end."

"Or perhaps it's the beginning of something new. Maybe we can find a different way of living where we no longer need to skulk and hide."

Jace looked downward and didn't answer.

"It's kind of empty and lonely out here," said Oriana. "Are we going to leave soon? Where are we going now?"

It was a big question, both for their immediate future and their long-term plans. The first thing they had to do was to go somewhere far from the Dirksens' soldiers. But then what?

"Maybe we should head into the city," Parthenia said. "But what about returning to Ostillon eventually? Castiel might go back there."

"Castiel?" said Carina. "I don't think we need to worry about him anymore. I'm pretty sure he isn't a danger to anyone. His plan to gain power and privilege has backfired spectacularly."

"Maybe that guy, Reyes, will take care of him," said Ferne.

"They certainly didn't seem to be best buddies," Bryce remarked.

"Are we going?" Ferne asked, standing up.

He was right to hurry them. The morning was wearing on. Dirksen soldiers would be scouring the prairie, hoping to find stray mages.

Carina sighed. "Let's go where we always go: somewhere safe, out of sight, where we won't attract too much attention. Then we'll have to see what we can do to leave Pirine without any Dirksens or Sherrerrs on our tail."

"And then what?" asked Oriana.

"I'm not sure." But in fact, she was. She had always been sure, deep down. She took a breath and said, "Maybe we should try to find Earth."

Jace gave a shake of his head. "You're chasing a dream, Carina."

"Do you have a better idea?"

"I have to admit I don't."

"Then a dream is better than nothing."

Carina's story continues in...

STAR MAGE SAGA BOOKS 4 - 6